HERZOG

THE VIKING CRITICAL LIBRARY

MALCOLM COWLEY, GENERAL EDITOR

WINESBURG, OHIO
by Sherwood Anderson
EDITED BY JOHN H. FERRES

DEATH OF A SALESMAN
by Arthur Miller
EDITED BY GERALD WEALES

A PORTRAIT OF THE ARTIST
AS A YOUNG MAN
by James Joyce
EDITED BY CHESTER G. ANDERSON

SONS AND LOVERS
by D. H. Lawrence
EDITED BY JULIAN MOYNAHAN

DUBLINERS
by James Joyce
EDITED BY ROBERT SCHOLES AND A. WALTON LITZ

THE POWER AND THE GLORY
by Graham Greene
EDITED BY R.W.B. LEWIS AND PETER J. CONN

THE CRUCIBLE
by Arthur Miller
EDITED BY GERALD WEALES

THE GRAPES OF WRATH
by John Steinbeck
EDITED BY PETER LISCA

ONE FLEW OVER
THE CUCKOO'S NEST
by Ken Kesey
EDITED BY JOHN C. PRATT

SAUL BELLOW

HERZOG

TEXT AND CRITICISM

EDITED BY IRVING HOWE

THE VIKING PRESS · NEW YORK

First published in 1976
by The Viking Press, Inc.
625 Madison Avenue,
New York, N.Y. 10022

Published simultaneously in Canada
by The Macmillan Company of Canada

LIBRARY OF CONGRESS CATALOGING IN PUBLICATION DATA
Bellow, Saul.
  Herzog.
  (The Viking critical library)
  Bibliography: p.
  I. Howe, Irving.   II. Title.
PZ3.B41937Hh7   [PS3503.E4488]   813'.5'2   75-42290
ISBN 0-670-36913-6
0-670-01810-4 pbk.

Printed in U.S.A.

CONTENTS

INTRODUCTION

When *Herzog* first appeared in 1964, the book received an extraordinary amount of public attention, both from literary critics and ordinary readers. Saul Bellow had by then been recognized as one of the two or three most distinguished living American novelists. *Herzog* became a best seller and won the National Book Award for fiction in 1965; more important, it turned out to be a novel that provoked people into hot debates, a novel which many readers felt they could identify with in some intensely personal way. I remember reading it during the summer of 1964 while on vacation. The publisher had sent bound proofsheets, and my wife and I sat on a beach tearing off each sheet as we read it, handing it to the other and waiting impatiently for the next one. We weren't quite sure as yet whether we liked the book, but we could hardly doubt that it was reaching us in some strong and direct way, pressing on nerves of deep feeling.

Nor was it hard to understand why *Herzog* should have evoked such intense responses. The book dealt with the mess in which an intelligent and gifted man finds himself during his middle years, and if there has been one dominant pattern in the life of educated Americans in the twentieth century it has been that all too many of them land in complicated personal messes during their middle years. No one chose to see himself simply as Moses Herzog—he was too evidently a loser, a sad sack, a *schlemiel*. But few readers were courageous or foolhardy enough to deny that some part of their intimate life, charged with confusions and yearnings, had been touched by Bellow's novel.

It wasn't just the fact of portraying a middle-age crisis which made people react so strongly to *Herzog*. That, after all, was a familiar enough subject in American fiction; every year scores of novels come out which rehearse this subject, and recently it has become popular in the movies too. What was distinctive about *Herzog* was that Bellow, even while having his "hero" taste fully the bitter dregs of defeat and humiliation, even while showing him in the worst indignities of collapsed morale, still seemed to be speaking for a possible recovery. What was exciting about the book was that Bellow had the courage—rather obliquely—to turn back to such old-fashioned ideas as personal responsibility, the exertion of the will in order to keep oneself from sinking. He brushed aside impatiently that literary pessimism which had become at least as much a cliché as the optimism of earlier decades. He refused to believe that we must forever remain victims of the disasters we contrive for ourselves, or inherit from others. Such ideas, ironically juggled by Moses Herzog (he is hardly the man to face anything directly), worked their way through the novel. And to some readers, this was bracing.

Precisely the same element of the book caused other critics and readers to dislike it. They felt that Bellow was going soft, maybe a little "bourgeois." They felt he was yielding to middle-class complacencies and sentimentalisms, denying the heritage of desperation which our anarchic century has imposed upon us. They felt Bellow was being taken in by his own character, showing himself insufficiently aware or critical of Moses Herzog's pomposities and self-indulgences.

Like a number of Bellow's other books, *Herzog* soon became an occasion for cultural debate, and while in a way this may be unfair to any novel, since there's always a risk that the book itself will be buried beneath the issues it stirs up, still it is also evidence that the book lives with the passions and troubles of a given moment.

There were other reasons for being drawn to *Herzog*. Though a comic novel, with some wildly hilarious sections, the basic intent behind it was a deep moral seriousness, a wish to recall men to their obligations, their duties, their possibilities in this world. If one laughed at or with Moses Herzog, if one found some of his shenanigans pitiable to the point of absurdity, one also knew that his plight was common enough in our time and that something very important was at stake in his survival—the possibility of combining intellectual consciousness with moral will.

Meanwhile, the book was a wonderful performance. Surrounding the central figure, himself no mean performer, is a gang of heart-wringers, "potato-lovers," con men, classy bitches, adorable darlings, and high-culture phonies. In Bellow's world everything becomes heightened, intensified, colored. The reality of our lives is there, of course, but it is a reality magnified to high performance. His characters talk—God, how they talk! They howl, they scream, they complain, they weep; they exercise every privilege and abuse every privilege which speech allows humanity. Language springs, leaps, tumbles. Bellow understands that the novelist has an obligation first and foremost to make his world interesting, to charm and overwhelm. Madeleine, Herzog's estranged wife, and her lover, Valentine Gersbach, are detestable; they are, as students used to say a few years ago, real phonies; but they are utterly alive. One waits for Gersbach's reappearance as one waits for the elder Karamazov in *The Brothers Karamazov*—sometimes it seems as if vitality is its own justification.

There are plenty of other questions, problems, issues which this novel raises for us, and some of them are discussed in the critical essays that follow the text of the novel and others in "Topics for Discussion and Papers" (which I have tried to keep simple and unpretentious, so that students using it need suffer a minimum of pain—perhaps none at all!).

I have begun the section of essays with a few of Bellow's own, since whenever he puts his mind to it he can turn out a brilliant piece of expository prose. These essays illuminate Bellow's work from within. Next comes a group of reviews that appeared shortly after the publication of *Herzog*, immediate favorable and unfavorable responses. And finally there are a few general essays on Bellow's work as a whole that throw light on his abiding themes and styles. Probably the amount of criticism in this volume is smaller than in other volumes in this series, but that is unavoidable since Bellow is a living writer, *Herzog* only a little more than a decade old, and there's not yet a large quantity of first-rate criticism from which to choose. But I think you'll find enough.

A last word: The editor of this book (and in this respect he is certain that he also speaks for the author of *Herzog*) believes that the primary aim of reading literature is pleasure, the kind of pleasure that comes from a quickening of consciousness, a growth of awareness. The main thing therefore is to read *Herzog* itself—and the rest matters only if or insofar as it helps you reach and enjoy the book.

June 1975   I.H.

CHRONOLOGY

1915   Born on June 10 in Lachine, a suburb of Montreal, Canada, of parents who had immigrated from St. Petersburg, Russia, in 1913.

1924   The Bellow family moves to Chicago, which becomes their permanent home.

1933   Graduates from Tuley High School (on Chicago's Northwest Side). Enrolls at the University of Chicago.

1935   Transfers to Northwestern University.

1937   Graduates from Northwestern with honors in sociology and anthropology.
        Does graduate work in anthropology at the University of Wisconsin in Madison. Leaves before the end of the year, realizing he wants to become a writer.

1938   Returns to Chicago. Works on the WPA Writers' Project.

1939   Supports himself for a number of years with teaching, odd jobs, work on the Index (*Syntopicon*) of the *Great Books* series (published by the Encyclopaedia Britannica, in collaboration with the University of Chicago)—and leads a bohemian life.

1941   "Two Morning Monologues," first published story.

1942   "The Mexican General."

1943   At work on *Dangling Man.*
        "Notes of a Dangling Man," an early version of sections of the novel (see Bibliography).

1944   *Dangling Man*, first novel, is published.

1946–1948   Teaches at the University of Minnesota in Minneapolis.

1947   *The Victim.*

1948   Awarded a Guggenheim fellowship.

1948–1950   Writes and lives in Paris and travels in Europe. Begins work on *The Adventures of Augie March*, and over the next few years early versions of a number of sections of the novel appear in various magazines (see Bibliography).

1949   "Sermon by Doctor Pep."

1950   Returns home to the United States and, for most of the next decade, lives in New York City and Dutchess County, New York. Teaches evening courses at New York University, Washington Square (later on the faculty of other colleges and universities). Reviews books, writes articles. Continues work on his novels, writes stories.

1951   "Looking for Mr. Green"; "By the Rock Wall"; "Address by Gooley MacDowell to the Hasbeens Club of Chicago."

1952   Creative Writing Fellow, Princeton University.

1953   *The Adventures of Augie March.* Awarded the National Book Award for Fiction.

Translates, from the Yiddish, Isaac Bashevis Singer's story "Gimpel the Fool."

1955   "A Father-to-Be."

1956   "The Gonzaga Manuscripts"; *Seize the Day* (first published in magazine, then in book form; see Bibliography).

1958   "Leaving the Yellow House."

1958–1960   Receives two-year Ford Foundation grant.

At work on *Henderson the Rain King*; early versions of two sections of the novel appear in magazines (see Bibliography).

1959   *Henderson the Rain King.*

1960–1962   Co-edits, with Keith Botsford and Aaron Asher, the periodical *The Noble Savage.*

1961–1964   Works, for the next three years, on *Herzog.* A number of sections of the novel, in early versions, appear in various magazines (see Bibliography).

1962   "Scenes from Humanitis," an early version of the play *The Last Analysis*

1963   Edits *Great Jewish Short Stories* and writes introduction to the collection.

Returns to Chicago in the fall.

1963–present   (1975) Professor, Committee on Social Thought, at the University of Chicago.

1964   *Herzog.* Bellow receives, for the second time, the National Book Award for Fiction.

The Last Analysis is produced in October, for a short run, on Broadway, directed by Joseph Anthony (producer, Stevens Productions), at the David Belasco Theatre.

Awarded the International Literary Prize (for *Herzog*).

1965   Writes three one-act plays: "Out from Under"; "Orange Soufflé"; "A Wen."

"Orange Soufflé" and "A Wen" are staged in April off-off

Broadway by Nancy Walker, for a private showing at the Loft.

1966   The three one-act plays are staged in May in London by the Traverse Company, directed by Charles Marowitz, at the Jeanette Cochrane Theatre, moving in June to the Fortune Theatre. Arthur Storch directs the plays in July at the Festival of Two Worlds in Spoleto, Italy, and presents them in October, under the title *Under the Weather*, for a short run (producer Theodore R. Brauer), at the Cort Theatre on Broadway.

1967   "The Old System."
        In June, Bellow covers the Six-Day War in Israel for *Newsday*, then published by Bill Moyers.

1968   "Mosby's Memoirs (story); *Mosby's Memoirs and Other Stories*.
        Receives the Jewish Heritage Award from B'nai B'rith.
        Receives the Croix de Chevalier des Arts et Lettres from the French government.
        Begins work on *Mr. Sammler's Planet*.

1969   Early version of *Mr. Sammler's Planet* appears, in two parts, in magazine form (see Bibliography).

1970   *Mr. Sammler's Planet*. Awarded, for the third time, the National Book Award for Fiction. Untitled work in progress.

1970–1974   At work on two novels.

1974   "Humboldt's Gift," excerpt from a novel in progress, appears in magazine form (see Bibliography).
        "Zetland: By a Character Witness," excerpt from another (so far untitled) novel in progress, appears in a collection (see Bibliography).
        The Portable Bellow.

1975   *Humboldt's Gift*.

I

HERZOG: THE TEXT

I F I am out of my mind, it's all right with me, thought Moses Herzog.

Some people thought he was cracked and for a time he himself had doubted that he was all there. But now, though he still behaved oddly, he felt confident, cheerful, clairvoyant, and strong. He had fallen under a spell and was writing letters to everyone under the sun. He was so stirred by these letters that from the end of June he moved from place to place with a valise full of papers. He had carried this valise from New York to Martha's Vineyard, but returned from the Vineyard immediately; two days later he flew to Chicago, and from Chicago he went to a village in western Massachusetts. Hidden in the country, he wrote endlessly, fanatically, to the newspapers, to people in public life, to friends and relatives and at last to the dead, his own obscure dead, and finally the famous dead.

It was the peak of summer in the Berkshires. Herzog was alone in the big old house. Normally particular about food, he now ate Silvercup bread from the paper package, beans from the can, and American cheese. Now and then he picked raspberries in the overgrown garden, lifting up the thorny canes with absent-minded caution. As for sleep, he slept on a mattress without sheets —it was his abandoned marriage bed—or in the hammock, covered by his coat. Tall bearded grass and locust and maple seedlings surrounded him in the yard. When he opened his eyes in the night, the stars were near like spiritual bodies. Fires, of course; gases—minerals, heat, atoms, but eloquent at five in the morning to a man lying in a hammock, wrapped in his overcoat.

When some new thought gripped his heart he went to the kitchen, his headquarters, to write it down. The white paint was scaling from the brick walls and Herzog sometimes wiped mouse droppings from the table with his sleeve, calmly wondering why field mice should have such a passion for wax and paraffin. They made holes in paraffin-sealed preserves; they gnawed birthday candles down to the wicks. A rat chewed into a package of bread, leaving the shape of its body in the layers of slices. Herzog ate the other half of the loaf spread with jam. He could share with rats too.

All the while, one corner of his mind remained open to the external world. He heard the crows in the morning. Their harsh call was delicious. He heard the thrushes at dusk. At night there was a barn owl. When he walked in the garden, excited by a mental letter, he saw roses winding about the rain spout; or mulberries—birds gorging in the mulberry tree. The days were hot, the evenings flushed and dusty. He looked keenly at everything but he felt half blind.

His friend, his former friend, Valentine, and his wife, his ex-wife Madeleine, had spread the rumor that his sanity had collapsed. Was it true?

He was taking a turn around the empty house and saw the shadow of his face in a gray, webby window. He looked weirdly tranquil. A radiant line went from mid-forehead over his straight nose and full, silent lips.

Late in spring Herzog had been overcome by the need to explain, to have it out, to justify, to put in perspective, to clarify, to make amends.

At that time he had been giving adult-education lectures in a New York night school. He was clear enough in April but by the end of May he began to ramble. It became apparent to his students that they would never learn much about The Roots of Romanticism but that they would see and hear odd things. One after another, the academic formalities dropped away. Professor Herzog had the unconscious frankness of a man deeply preoccupied. And toward the end of the term there were long pauses in his lectures. He would stop, muttering "Excuse me," reaching inside his coat for his pen. The table creaking, he wrote on scraps of paper with a great pressure of eagerness in his hand; he was absorbed, his eyes darkly circled. His white face showed everything—everything. He was reasoning, arguing, he was suffering, he had thought of a brilliant alternative—he was wide-open, he was narrow; his eyes, his mouth made everything silently clear—longing, bigotry, bitter anger. One could see it all. The class waited three minutes, five minutes, utterly silent.

At first there was no pattern to the notes he made. They were fragments—nonsense syllables, exclamations, twisted proverbs and quotations or, in the Yiddish of his long-dead mother, *Trepverter* —retorts that came too late, when you were already on your way down the stairs.

He wrote, for instance, *Death—die—live again—die again—live.*

No person, no death.

And, *On the knees of your soul? Might as well be useful. Scrub the floor.*

Next, *Answer a fool according to his folly lest he be wise in his own conceit.*

Answer not a fool according to his folly, lest thou be like unto him.

Choose one.

He noted also, *I see by Walter Winchell that J. S. Bach put on black gloves to compose a requiem mass.*

Herzog scarcely knew what to think of this scrawling. He yielded to the excitement that inspired it and suspected at times that it might be a symptom of disintegration. That did not frighten him. Lying on the sofa of the kitchenette apartment he had rented on 17th Street, he sometimes imagined he was an industry that manufactured personal history, and saw himself from birth to death. He conceded on a piece of paper,

I cannot justify.

Considering his entire life, he realized that he had mismanaged everything—everything. His life was, as the phrase goes, ruined. But since it had not been much to begin with, there was not much to grieve about. Thinking, on the malodorous sofa, of the centuries, the nineteenth, the sixteenth, the eighteenth, he turned up, from the last, a saying that he liked:

Grief, Sir, is a species of idleness.

He went on taking stock, lying face down on the sofa. Was he a clever man or an idiot? Well, he could not at this time claim to be clever. He might once have had the makings of a clever character, but he had chosen to be dreamy instead, and the sharpies cleaned him out. What more? He was losing his hair. He read the ads of the Thomas Scalp Specialists, with the exaggerated skepticism of a man whose craving to believe was deep, desperate. Scalp Experts! So . . . he was a formerly handsome man. His face revealed what a

3

beating he had taken. But he had asked to be beaten too, and had lent his attackers strength. That brought him to consider his character. What sort of character was it? Well, in the modern vocabulary, it was narcissistic; it was masochistic; it was anachronistic. His clinical picture was depressive—not the severest type; not a manic depressive. There were worse cripples around. If you believed, as everyone nowadays apparently did, that man was the sick animal, then was he even spectacularly sick, exceptionally blind, extraordinarily degraded? No. Was he intelligent? His intellect would have been more effective if he had had an aggressive paranoid character, eager for power. He was jealous but not exceptionally competitive, not a true paranoiac. And what about his learning?—He was obliged to admit, now, that he was not much of a professor, either. Oh, he was earnest, he had a certain large, immature sincerity, but he might never succeed in becoming systematic. He had made a brilliant start in his Ph.D. thesis—*The State of Nature in 17th and 18th Century English and French Political Philosophy*. He had to his credit also several articles and a book, *Romanticism and Christianity*. But the rest of his ambitious projects had dried up, one after another. On the strength of his early successes he had never had difficulty in finding jobs and obtaining research grants. The Narragansett Corporation had paid him fifteen thousand dollars over a number of years to continue his studies in Romanticism. The results lay in the closet, in an old valise—eight hundred pages of chaotic argument which had never found its focus. It was painful to think of it.

On the floor beside him were pieces of paper, and he occasionally leaned down to write.

He now set down, *Not that long disease, my life, but that long convalescence, my life. The liberal-bourgeois revision, the illusion of improvement, the poison of hope.*

He thought awhile of Mithridates, whose system learned to thrive on poison. He cheated his assassins, who made the mistake of using small doses, and was pickled, not destroyed.

Tutto fa brodo.

Resuming his self-examination, he admitted that he had been a bad husband—twice. Daisy, his first wife, he had treated miserably. Madeleine, his second, had tried to do *him* in. To his son and his daughter he was a loving but bad father. To his own parents he

4

had been an ungrateful child. To his country, an indifferent citizen. To his brothers and his sister, affectionate but remote. With his friends, an egotist. With love, lazy. With brightness, dull. With power, passive. With his own soul, evasive.

Satisfied with his own severity, positively enjoying the hardness and factual rigor of his judgment, he lay on his sofa, his arms rising behind him, his legs extended without aim.

But how charming we remain, notwithstanding.

Papa, poor man, could charm birds from the trees, crocodiles from mud. Madeleine, too, had great charm, and beauty of person also, and a brilliant mind. Valentine Gersbach, her lover, was a charming man, too, though in a heavier, brutal style. He had a thick chin, flaming copper hair that literally gushed from his head (no Thomas Scalp Specialists for him), and he walked on a wooden leg, gracefully bending and straightening like a gondolier. Herzog himself had no small amount of charm. But his sexual powers had been damaged by Madeleine. And without the ability to attract women, how was he to recover? It was in this respect that he felt most like a convalescent.

The paltriness of these sexual struggles.

With Madeleine, several years ago, Herzog had made a fresh start in life. He had won her away from the Church—when they met, she had just been converted. With twenty thousand dollars inherited from his charming father, to please his new wife, he quit an academic position which was perfectly respectable and bought a big old house in Ludeyville, Massachusetts. In the peaceful Berkshires where he had friends (the Valentine Gersbachs) it should be easy to write his second volume on the social ideas of the Romantics.

Herzog did not leave academic life because he was doing badly. On the contrary, his reputation was good. His thesis had been influential and was translated into French and German. His early book, not much noticed when it was published, was now on many reading lists, and the younger generation of historians accepted it as a model of the new sort of history, "history that interests *us*"—personal, *engagée*—and looks at the past with an intense need for contemporary relevance. As long as Moses was married to Daisy, he had led the perfectly ordinary life of an assistant professor, respected and stable. His first work showed by objective research

5

what Christianity was to Romanticism. In the second he was becoming tougher, more assertive, more ambitious. There was a great deal of ruggedness, actually, in his character. He had a strong will and a talent for polemics, a taste for the philosophy of history. In marrying Madeleine and resigning from the university (because she thought he should), digging in at Ludeyville, he showed a taste and talent also for danger and extremism, for heterodoxy, for ordeals, a fatal attraction to the "City of Destruction." What he planned was a history which really took into account the revolutions and mass convulsions of the twentieth century, accepting, with de Tocqueville, the universal and durable development of the equality of conditions, the progress of democracy.

But he couldn't deceive himself about this work. He was beginning seriously to distrust it. His ambitions received a sharp check. Hegel was giving him a great deal of trouble. Ten years earlier he had been certain he understood his ideas on consensus and civility, but something had gone wrong. He was distressed, impatient, angry. At the same time, he and his wife were behaving very peculiarly. She was dissatisfied. At first, she hadn't wanted him to be an ordinary professor, but she changed her mind after a year in the country. Madeleine considered herself too young, too intelligent, too vital, too sociable to be buried in the remote Berkshires. She decided to finish her graduate studies in Slavonic languages. Herzog wrote to Chicago about jobs. He had to find a position for Valentine Gersbach, too. Valentine was a radio announcer, a disk-jockey in Pittsfield. You couldn't leave people like Valentine and Phoebe stuck in this mournful countryside, alone, Madeleine said. Chicago was chosen because Herzog had grown up there, and was well-connected. So he taught courses in the Downtown College and Gersbach became educational director of an FM station in the Loop. The house near Ludeyville was closed up—twenty thousand dollars' worth of house, with books and English bone china and new appliances abandoned to the spiders, the moles, and the field mice—Papa's hard-earned money!

The Herzogs moved to the Midwest. But after about a year of this new Chicago life, Madeleine decided that she and Moses couldn't make it after all—she wanted a divorce. He had to give it, what could he do? And the divorce was painful. He was in love with Madeleine; he couldn't bear to leave his little daughter.

But Madeleine refused to be married to him, and people's wishes have to be respected. Slavery is dead.

The strain of the second divorce was too much for Herzog. He felt he was going to pieces—breaking up—and Dr. Edvig, the Chicago psychiatrist who treated both Herzogs, agreed that perhaps it was best for Moses to leave town. He came to an understanding with the dean of the Downtown College that he might come back when he was feeling better, and on money borrowed from his brother Shura he went to Europe. Not everyone threatened with a crackup can manage to go to Europe for relief. Most people have to keep on working; they report daily, they still ride the subway. Or else they drink, they go to the movies and sit there suffering. Herzog ought to have been grateful. Unless you are utterly exploded, there is always something to be grateful for. In fact, he was grateful.

He was not exactly idle in Europe, either. He made a cultural tour for the Narragansett Corporation, lecturing in Copenhagen, Warsaw, Cracow, Berlin, Belgrade, Istanbul, and Jerusalem. But in March when he came to Chicago again his condition was worse than it had been in November. He told his dean that it would probably be better for him to stay in New York. He did not see Madeleine during his visit. His behavior was so strange and to her mind so menacing, that she warned him through Gersbach not to come near the house on Harper Avenue. The police had a picture of him and would arrest him if he was seen in the block.

It was now becoming clear to Herzog, himself incapable of making plans, how well Madeleine had prepared to get rid of him. Six weeks before sending him away, she had had him lease a house near the Midway at two hundred dollars a month. When they moved in, he built shelves, cleared the garden, and repaired the garage door; he put up the storm windows. Only a week before she demanded a divorce, she had his things cleaned and pressed, but on the day he left the house, she flung them all into a carton which she then dumped down the cellar stairs. She needed more closet space. And other things happened, sad, comical, or cruel, depending on one's point of view. Until the very last day, the tone of Herzog's relations with Madeleine was quite serious—that is, ideas, personalities, issues were respected and discussed. When she

7

broke the news to him, for instance, she expressed herself with dignity, in that lovely, masterful style of hers. She had thought it over from every angle, she said, and she had to accept defeat. They could not make the grade together. She was prepared to shoulder some of the blame. Of course, Herzog was not entirely unprepared for this. But he had really thought matters were improving.

All this happened on a bright, keen fall day. He had been in the back yard putting in the storm windows. The first frost had already caught the tomatoes. The grass was dense and soft, with the peculiar beauty it gains when the cold days come and the gossamers lie on it in the morning; the dew is thick and lasting. The tomato vines had blackened and the red globes had burst.

He had seen Madeleine at the back window upstairs, putting June down for her nap, and later he heard the bath being run. Now she was calling from the kitchen door. A gust from the lake made the framed glass tremble in Herzog's arms. He propped it carefully against the porch and took off his canvas gloves but not his beret, as though he sensed that he would immediately go on a trip.

Madeleine hated her father violently, but it was not irrelevant that the old man was a famous impresario—sometimes called the American Stanislavsky. She had prepared the event with a certain theatrical genius of her own. She wore black stockings, high heels, a lavender dress with Indian brocade from Central America. She had on her opal earrings, her bracelets, and she was perfumed; her hair was combed with a new, clean part and her large eyelids shone with a bluish cosmetic. Her eyes were blue but the depth of the color was curiously affected by the variable tinge of the whites. Her nose, which descended in a straight elegant line from her brows, worked slightly when she was peculiarly stirred. To Herzog even this tic was precious. There was a flavor of subjugation in his love for Madeleine. Since she was domineering, and since he loved her, he had to accept the flavor that was given. In this confrontation in the untidy parlor, two kinds of egotism were present, and Herzog from his sofa in New York now contemplated them—hers in triumph (she had prepared a great moment, she was about to do what she longed most to do, strike a blow) and his egotism in abeyance, all converted into passivity. What he was about to suffer, he

8

deserved; he had sinned long and hard; he had earned it. This was it.

In the window on glass shelves there stood an ornamental collection of small glass bottles, Venetian and Swedish. They came with the house. The sun now caught them. They were pierced with the light. Herzog saw the waves, the threads of color, the spectral intersecting bars, and especially a great blot of flaming white on the center of the wall above Madeleine. She was saying, "We can't live together any more."

Her speech continued for several minutes. Her sentences were well formed. This speech had been rehearsed and it seemed also that he had been waiting for the performance to begin.

Theirs was not a marriage that could last. Madeleine had never loved him. She was telling him that. "It's painful to have to say I never loved you. I never will love you, either," she said. "So there's no point in going on."

Herzog said, "I do love you, Madeleine."

Step by step, Madeleine rose in distinction, in brilliance, in insight. Her color grew very rich, and her brows, and that Byzantine nose of hers, rose, moved; her blue eyes gained by the flush that kept deepening, rising from her chest and her throat. She was in an ecstasy of consciousness. It occurred to Herzog that she had beaten him so badly, her pride was so fully satisfied, that there was an overflow of strength into her intelligence. He realized that he was witnessing one of the very greatest moments of her life.

"You should hold on to that feeling," she said. "I believe it's true. You do love me. But I think you also understand what a humiliation it is to me to admit defeat in this marriage. I've put all I had into it. I'm crushed by this."

Crushed? She had never looked more glorious. There was an element of theater in those looks, but much more of passion.

And Herzog, a solid figure of a man, if pale and suffering, lying on his sofa in the lengthening evening of a New York spring, in the background the trembling energy of the city, a sense and flavor of river water, a stripe of beautifying and dramatic filth contributed by New Jersey to the sunset, Herzog in the coop of his privacy and still strong in body (his health was really a sort of miracle; he had done his best to be sick) pictured what might have

9

happened if instead of listening so intensely and thoughtfully he had hit Madeleine in the face. What if he had knocked her down, clutched her hair, dragged her screaming and fighting around the room, flogged her until her buttocks bled. What if he had! He should have torn her clothes, ripped off her necklace, brought his fists down on her head. He rejected this mental violence, sighing. He was afraid he was really given in secret to this sort of brutality. But suppose even that he had told *her* to leave the house. After all, it was *his* house. If she couldn't live with him, why didn't she leave? The scandal? There was no need to be driven away by a little scandal. It would have been painful, grotesque, but a scandal was after all a sort of service to the community. Only it had never entered Herzog's mind, in that parlor of flashing bottles, to stand his ground. He still thought perhaps that he could win by the appeal of passivity, of personality, win on the ground of being, after all, Moses—Moses Elkanah Herzog—a good man, and Madeleine's particular benefactor. He had done everything for her—everything!

"Have you discussed this decision with Doctor Edvig?" he said. "What does he think?"

"What difference could his opinion make to me? He can't tell me what to do. He can only help me understand. . . . I went to a lawyer," she said.

"Which lawyer?"

"Well, Sandor Himmelstein. Because he is a buddy of yours. He says you can stay with him until you make your new arrangements."

The conversation was over, and Herzog returned to the storm windows in the shadow and green damp of the back yard—to his obscure system of idiosyncrasies. A person of irregular tendencies, he practiced the art of circling among random facts to swoop down on the essentials. He often expected to take the essentials by surprise, by an amusing stratagem. But nothing of the sort happened as he maneuvered the rattling glass, standing among the frost-scorched drooping tomato vines tied to their stakes with strips of rag. The plant scent was strong. He continued with the windows because he couldn't allow himself to feel crippled. He dreaded the depths of feeling he would eventually have to face, when he could no longer call upon his eccentricities for relief.

In his posture of collapse on the sofa, arms abandoned over

his head and legs stretched away, lying with no more style than a chimpanzee, his eyes with greater than normal radiance watched his own work in the garden with detachment, as if he were looking through the front end of a telescope at a tiny clear image.

That suffering joker.

Two points therefore: He knew his scribbling, his letter-writing, was ridiculous. It was involuntary. His eccentricities had him in their power.

There is someone inside me. I am in his grip. When I speak of him I feel him in my head, pounding for order. He will ruin me.

It has been reported, he wrote, *that several teams of Russian Cosmonauts have been lost; disintegrated, we must assume. One was heard calling "SOS—world SOS." Soviet confirmation has been withheld.*

Dear Mama, As to why I haven't visited your grave in so long . . .

Dear Wanda, Dear Zinka, Dear Libbie, Dear Ramona, Dear Sono, I need help in the worst way. I am afraid of falling apart. Dear Edvig, the fact is that madness also has been denied me. I don't know why I should write to you at all. Dear Mr. President, Internal Revenue regulations will turn us into a nation of bookkeepers. The life of every citizen is becoming a business. This, it seems to me, is one of the worst interpretations of the meaning of human life history has ever seen. Man's life is not a business.

And how shall I sign this? thought Moses. Indignant citizen? Indignation is so wearing that one should reserve it for the main injustice.

Dear Daisy, he wrote to his first wife, *I know it's my turn to visit Marco in camp on Parents' Day but this year I'm afraid my presence might disturb him. I have been writing to him, and keeping up with his activities. It is unfortunately true, however, that he blames me for the breakup with Madeleine and feels I have deserted also his little half-sister. He is too young to understand the difference between the two divorces.* Here Herzog asked himself whether it would be appropriate to discuss the matter further with Daisy and, picturing to himself her handsome and angry face as she read his as yet unwritten letter, he decided against this. He continued, *I think it would be best for Marco not to see me. I have been sick—under the doctor's care.* He noted with distaste his own trick of appealing for sympathy. A personality had its own ways. A mind might observe them without approval. Herzog did not care for his own personality, and at the moment there was apparently nothing he could do about its impulses. *Rebuilding my health and strength gradually*—as a person of sound positive principles, modern and liberal, news of his progress (if true) should please her. As the victim of those impulses she must be looking in the paper for his obituary.

The strength of Herzog's constitution worked obstinately against his hypochondria. Early in June, when the general revival of life troubles many people, the new roses, even in shop windows, reminding them of their own failures, of sterility and death, Herzog went to have a medical checkup. He paid a visit to an elderly refugee, Dr. Emmerich, on the West Side, facing Central Park. A frowzy doorman with an odor of old age about him, wearing a cap from a Balkan campaign half a century gone, let him into the crumbling vault of the lobby. Herzog undressed in the examining room—a troubled, dire green; the dark walls seemed swollen with the disease of old buildings in New York. He was not a big man but he was sturdily built, his muscles developed by the hard work he had done in the country. He was vain of his muscles, the breadth and strength of his hands, the smoothness of his skin, but he saw through this too, and he feared being caught in the part of the aging, conceited handsome man. Old fool, he called himself, glancing away from the small mirror, the graying hair, the wrinkles of amusement and bitterness. Through the slats of the blind he looked instead at the brown rocks of the park, speckled with mica, and at the optimistic leaping green of June. It would tire soon, as leaves broadened and New York deposited its soot on the summer. It was, however, especially beautiful now, vivid in all particulars—the twigs, the small darts and subtly swelling shapes of green. Beauty is not a human invention. Dr. Emmerich, stooped but energetic, examined him, sounded his chest and back, flashed the light in his eyes, took his blood, felt his prostate gland, wired him for the electrocardiograph.

"Well, you are a healthy man—not twenty-one, but strong."

Herzog heard this with satisfaction, of course, but still he was faintly unhappy about it. He had been hoping for some definite sickness which would send him to a hospital for a while. He would not have to look after himself. His brothers, who had given up on him, more or less, would rally to him then and his sister Helen might come to take care of him. The family would meet his expenses and pay for Marco and June. That was out, now. Apart from the little infection he had caught in Poland, his health was sound, and even that infection, now cured, had been nonspecific. It might have been due to his mental state, to depression and fatigue, not to Wanda. For one horrible day he had thought it was gonorrhea. He must write to Wanda, he thought as he pulled his shirttails forward, buttoned his sleeves. *Chère Wanda,* he began, *Bonnes nouvelles. T'en seras contente.* It was another of his shady love affairs in French. For what other reason had he ground away at his Frazer and Squair in high school, and read Rousseau and de Maistre in college? His achievements were not only scholarly but sexual. And were those achievements? It was his pride that must be satisfied. His flesh got what was left over.

"Then what is the matter with you?" said Dr. Emmerich. An old man, hair grizzled like his own, face narrow and witty, looked up into his eyes. Herzog believed he understood his message. The doctor was telling him that in this decaying office he examined the truly weak, the desperately sick, stricken women, dying men. Then what did Herzog want with him? "You seem very excited," Emmerich said.

"Yes, that's it. I am excited."

"Do you want Miltown? Snakeroot? Do you have insomnia?"

"Not seriously," said Herzog. "My thoughts are shooting out all over the place."

"Do you want me to recommend a psychiatrist?"

"No, I've had all the psychiatry I can use."

"Then what about a holiday? Take a young lady to the country, the seashore. Do you still have the place in Massachusetts?"

"If I want to reopen it."

"Does your friend still live up there? The radio announcer. What is the name of the big fellow with red hair, with the wooden leg?"

"Valentine Gersbach is his name. No, he moved to Chicago when I—when we did."

"He's a very amusing man."

I 3

"Yes. Very."

"I heard of your divorce—who told me? I am sorry about it."

Looking for happiness—ought to be prepared for bad results.

Emmerich put on his Ben Franklin eyeglasses and wrote a few words on the file card. "The child is with Madeleine in Chicago, I suppose," said the doctor.

"Yes—"

Herzog tried to get Emmerich to reveal his opinion of Madeleine. She had been his patient, too. But Emmerich would say nothing. Of course not; a doctor must not discuss his patients. Still, an opinion might be construed out of the glances he gave Moses.

"She's a violent, hysterical woman," he told Emmerich. He saw from the old man's lips that he was about to answer; but then Emmerich decided to say nothing, and Moses, who had an odd habit of completing people's sentences for them, made a mental note about his own perplexing personality.

A strange heart. I myself can't account for it.

He now saw that he had come to Emmerich to accuse Madeleine, or simply to talk about her with someone who knew her and could take a realistic view of her.

"But you must have other women," said Emmerich. "Isn't there somebody? Do you have to eat dinner alone tonight?"

Herzog had Ramona. She was a lovely woman, but with her too there were problems, of course—there were bound to be problems. Ramona was a businesswoman, she owned a flower shop on Lexington Avenue. She was not young—probably in her thirties; she wouldn't tell Moses her exact age—but she was extremely attractive, slightly foreign, well-educated. When she inherited the business she was getting her M.A. at Columbia in art history. In fact, she was enrolled in Herzog's evening course. In principle, he opposed affairs with students, even with students like Ramona Donsell, who were obviously made for them.

Doing all the things a wild man does, he noted, *while remaining all the while an earnest person. In frightful earnest.*

Of course it was just this earnestness that attracted Ramona. Ideas excited her. She loved to talk. She was an excellent cook, too, and knew how to prepare shrimp Arnaud, which she served with Pouilly Fuissé. Herzog had supper with her several nights a week. In the cab passing from the drab lecture hall to Ramona's large West Side apartment, she had said she wanted him to feel how her heart was beating. He reached for her wrist, to take her pulse, but she said, "We are not young children, Professor," and put his hand elsewhere.

Within a few days Ramona was saying that this was no ordinary affair. She recognized, she said, that Moses was in a peculiar state, but there was something about him so dear, so loving, so healthy, and basically so steady—as if, having survived so many horrors, he had been purged of neurotic nonsense—that perhaps it had been simply a question of the right woman, all along. Her interest in him quickly became serious, and he consequently began to worry about her, to brood. He said to her a few days after his visit to Emmerich that the doctor had advised him to take a holiday. Ramona then said, "Of course you need a holiday. Why don't you go to Montauk? I have a house there, and I could come out weekends. Perhaps we could stay together all of July."

"I didn't know you owned a house," said Herzog.

"It was up for sale a few years ago, and it was really too big for me, alone, but I had just divorced Harold, and I needed a diversion."

She showed him colored slides of the cottage. With his eye to the viewer, he said, "It's very pretty. All those flowers." But he felt heavy-hearted—dreadful.

"One can have a marvelous time there. And you really ought to get some cheerful summer clothes. Why do you wear such drab things? You still have a youthful figure."

"I lost weight last winter, in Poland and Italy."

"Nonsense—why talk like that! You know you're a good-looking man. And you even take pride in being one. In Argentina they'd call you *macho*—masculine. You like to come on meek and tame, and cover up the devil that's in you. Why put that little devil down? Why not make friends with him—well, why not?"

Instead of answering, he wrote mentally, *Dear Ramona—Very dear Ramona. I like you very much—dear to me, a true friend. It might even go farther. But why is it that I, a lecturer, can't bear to be lectured? I think your wisdom gets me. Because you have the complete wisdom. Perhaps to excess. I do not like to refuse correction. I have a lot to be corrected about. Almost everything. And*

I know good luck when I see it. . . . This was the literal truth, every word of it. He did like Ramona.

She came from Buenos Aires. Her background was international —Spanish, French, Russian, Polish, and Jewish. She had gone to school in Switzerland and still spoke with a slight accent, full of charm. She was short but had a full, substantial figure, a good round seat, firm breasts (all these things mattered to Herzog; he might think himself a moralist but the shape of a woman's breasts mattered greatly). Ramona was unsure of her chin but had confidence in her lovely throat, and so she held her head fairly high. She walked with quick efficiency, rapping her heels in energetic Castilian style. Herzog was intoxicated by this clatter. She entered a room provocatively, swaggering slightly, one hand touching her thigh, as though she carried a knife in her garter belt. It seemed to be the fashion in Madrid, and it delighted Ramona to come on playfully in the role of a tough Spanish broad—*una navaja en la liga;* she taught him the expression. He thought often of that imaginary knife when he watched her in her underthings, which were extravagant and black, a strapless contrivance called the Merry Widow that drew in the waist and trailed red ribbons below. Her thighs were short, but deep and white. The skin darkened where it was compressed by the elastic garment. And silky tags hung down, and garter buckles. Her eyes were brown, sensitive and shrewd, erotic and calculating. She knew what she was up to. The warm odor, the downy arms, the fine bust and excellent white teeth and slightly bowed legs—they all worked. Moses, suffering, suffered in style. His luck never entirely deserted him. Perhaps he was luckier than he knew. Ramona tried to tell him so. "That bitch did you a favor," she said. "You'll be far better off."

Moses! he wrote, *winning as he weeps, weeping as he wins. Evidently can't believe in victories.*

Hitch your agony to a star.

But at the silent moment at which he faced Ramona he wrote, incapable of replying except by mental letter, *You are a great comfort to me. We are dealing with elements more or less stable, more or less controllable, more or less mad. It's true. I have a wild spirit in me though I look meek and mild. You think that sexual pleasure is all this spirit wants, and since we are giving him that sexual pleasure, then why shouldn't everything be well?*

Then he realized suddenly that Ramona had made herself into a sort of sexual professional (or priestess). He was used to dealing with vile amateurs lately. *I didn't know that I could make out with a true sack artist.*

But is that the secret goal of my vague pilgrimage? Do I see myself to be after long blundering an unrecognized son of Sodom and Dionysus—an Orphic type? (Ramona enjoyed speaking of Orphic types.) A petit-bourgeois Dionysian?

He noted: *Foo to all those categories!*

"Perhaps I will buy some summer clothes," he answered Ramona.

I do like fine apparel, he went on. *I used to rub my patent-leather shoes with butter, in early childhood. I overheard my Russian mother calling me "Krasavitz." And when I became a gloomy young student, with a soft handsome face, wasting my time in arrogant looks, I thought a great deal about trousers and shirts. It was only later, as an academic, that I became dowdy. I bought a gaudy vest in the Burlington Arcade last winter, and a pair of Swiss boots of the type I see now the Village fairies have adopted. Heartsore? Yes,* he further wrote, *and dressed-up, too. But my vanity will no longer give me much mileage and to tell you the truth I'm not even greatly impressed with my own tortured heart. It begins to seem another waste of time.*

Soberly deliberating, Herzog decided it would be better not to accept Ramona's offer. She was thirty-seven or thirty-eight years of age, he shrewdly reckoned, and this meant that she was looking for a husband. This, in itself, was not wicked, or even funny. Simple and general human conditions prevailed among the most seemingly sophisticated. Ramona had not learned those erotic monkeyshines in a manual, but in adventure, in confusion, and at times probably with a sinking heart, in brutal and often alien embraces. So now she must yearn for stability. She wanted to give her heart once and for all, and level with a good man, become Herzog's wife and quit being an easy lay. She often had a sober look. Her eyes touched him deeply.

Never idle, his mind's eye saw Montauk—white beaches, flashing light, glossy breakers, horseshoe crabs perishing in their armor, sea robins and blowfish. Herzog longed to lie down in his bathing trunks, and warm his troubled belly on the sand. But how could he? To accept too many favors from Ramona was dangerous. He might have to pay with his freedom. Of course he didn't need that freedom now; he needed a rest. Still, after resting, he might want his freedom again. He wasn't sure of that, either. But it was a possibility.

A holiday will give me more strength to bring to my neurotic life.

Still, Herzog considered, he did look terrible, caved-in; he was losing more hair, and this rapid deterioration he considered to be a surrender to Madeleine and Gersbach, her lover, and to all his enemies. He had more enemies and hatreds than anyone could easily guess from his thoughtful expression.

The night-school term was coming to an end, and Herzog convinced himself that his wisest move was to get away from Ramona too. He decided to go to the Vineyard, but, thinking it a bad thing to be entirely alone, he sent a night letter to a woman in Vineyard Haven, an old friend (they had once considered having an affair but this had never materialized and they were instead tenderly considerate of each other). In the wire he explained the situation and his friend Libbie Vane (Libbie Vane-Erikson-Sissler; she had just married for the third time and the house in the Haven belonged to her husband, an industrial chemist) telephoned him promptly, and very emotionally and sincerely invited him to come and stay as long as he liked.

"Rent me a room near the beach," Herzog requested.

"Come and stay with us."

"No, no. I can't do that. Why, you've just gotten married."

"Oh, Moses—please, don't be so romantic. Sissler and I have been living together three years."

"Still, it is a honeymoon, isn't it?"

"Oh, stop this nonsense. I'll be hurt if you don't stay here. We have six bedrooms. You come right out, I've heard what a rough time you've been having."

In the end—it was inevitable—he accepted. He felt, however, that he was acting badly. By wiring, he had practically forced her to invite him. He had helped Libbie greatly about ten years before, and he would have been more pleased with himself if he had not made her pay off. He knew better than to ask for help. He was

making a bore of himself—doing the weak thing, the corrup
thing.

But at least, he thought, I don't have to make matters worse.
I won't bore Libbie with my troubles, or spend the week crying on
her bosom. I'll take them out to dinner, her and her new husband. You have to fight for your life. That's the chief condition on
which you hold it. Then why be halfhearted? Ramona is right.
Get some light clothes. You can borrow more dough from brother
Shura—he likes that, and he knows you'll repay. That's living by
the approbative principle—you pay your debts.

Therefore, he went shopping for clothes. He examined the ads
in *The New Yorker* and *Esquire*. These now showed older men
with lined faces as well as young executives and athletes. Then,
after shaving more closely than usual and brushing his hair (could
he bear to see himself in the brilliant triple mirrors of a clothing
store?), he took the bus uptown. Starting at 59th Street, he worked
his way down Madison Avenue into the forties and back toward
the Plaza on Fifth. Then the gray clouds opened before the piercing sun. The windows glittered and Herzog looked into them,
shamefaced and excited. The new styles seemed to him reckless
and gaudy—madras coats, shorts with melting bursts of Kandinsky
colors, in which middle-aged or paunchy old men would be ludicrous. Better puritan restraint than the exhibition of pitiful puck-
ered knees and varicose veins, pelican bellies and the indecency
of haggard faces under sporty caps. Undoubtedly Valentine Gersbach, who had beat him out with Madeleine, surmounting the handicap of a wooden leg, could wear those handsome brilliant candy
stripes. Valentine was a dandy. He had a thick face and heavy jaws;
Moses thought he somewhat resembled Putzi Hanfstaengl, Hitler's
own pianist. But Gersbach had a pair of extraordinary eyes for a
red-haired man, brown, deep, hot eyes, full of life. The lashes, too,
were vital, ruddy-dark, long and childlike. And that hair was bear-
ishly thick. Valentine, furthermore, was exquisitely confident of his
appearance. You could see it. He knew he was a terribly handsome man. He expected women—all women—to be mad about him.
And many were, weren't they? Including the second Mrs. Herzog.

"Wear that? Me?" said Herzog to the salesman in a Fifth Avenue shop. But he bought a coat of crimson and white stripes. Then he said over his shoulder to the salesman that in the Old Country his family had worn black gabardines down to the ground.

From a youthful case of acne, the salesman had a rough skin. His face was red as a carnation, and he had a meat-flavored breath, a dog's breath. He was a trifle rude to Moses, for when he asked his waist size and Moses answered, "Thirty-four," the salesman said, "Don't boast." That had slipped out, and Moses was too gentlemanly to hold it against him. His heart worked somewhat with the painful satisfaction of restraint. Eyes lowered, he trod the gray carpet to the fitting room, and there, disrobing and working the new pants up over his shoes, he wrote the fellow a note. *Dear Mack. Dealing with poor jerks every day. Male pride. Effrontery. Conceit. Yourself obliged to be agreeable and winsome. Hard job if you happen to be a grudging, angry fellow. The candor of people in New York! Bless you, you are not nice. But in a false situation, as we all are. Must manage some civility. A true situation might well prove unendurable to us all. From civility I now have some pain in my belly. As for gabardines, I realize there are plenty of beards and gabardines just around the corner, in the diamond district. O Lord!* he concluded, *forgive all these trespasses. Lead me not into Penn Station.*

Dressed in Italian pants, furled at the bottom, and a blazer with slender lapels, red and white, he avoided full exposure in the triple, lighted mirror. His body seemed unaffected by his troubles, survived all blasts. It was his face that was devastated, especially about the eyes, so that it made him pale to see himself.

Preoccupied, the salesman among silent clothes racks did not hear Herzog's footfalls. He was brooding. Slow business. Another small recession. Only Moses was spending today. Money he intended to borrow from his money-making brother. Shura was not tight-fisted. Nor was brother Willie, for that matter. But Moses found it easier to take it from Shura, also something of a sinner, than from Willie, who was more respectable.

"The back fit all right?" Herzog turned.

"Like tailor-made," the salesman said.

He couldn't have cared less. It was perfectly plain. I can't get his interest, Herzog recognized. Then I'll do without, and screw him, too. I'll decide for myself. It's my move. Thus strengthened, he stepped between the mirrors, looking only at the coat. It was satisfactory.

"Wrap it up," he said. "I'll take the pants, too, but I want them today. Now."

"Can't do it. The tailor's busy."

"Today, or it's no dice," said Herzog. "I have to leave town."

Two can play this hard-nosed game.

"I'll see if I can get a rush on it," the salesman said.

He went, and Herzog undid the chased buttons. They had used the head of some Roman emperor to adorn the jacket of a pleasure-seeker, he noted. Alone, he put his tongue out at himself and then withdrew from the triple mirror. He remembered how much pleasure it gave Madeleine to try on clothes in shops and how much heart and pride there was in her when she looked at herself, touching, adjusting, her face glowing but severe, too, with the great blue eyes, the vivid bangs, the medallion profile. The satisfaction she took in herself was positively plural—imperial. And she had told Moses during one of their crises that she had had a new look at herself nude before the bathroom mirror. "Still young," she said, taking inventory, "young, beautiful, full of life. Why should I waste it all on you."

Why, God forbid! Herzog looked for something to write a note with, having left paper and pencil in the dressing room. He jotted on the back of the salesman's pad, *A bitch in time breeds contempt.*

Looking through piles of beachwear, now silently laughing at himself as if his heart were swimming upward, Herzog bought a pair of trunks for the Vineyard, and then a rack of old-fashioned straw hats caught his attention and he decided to have one of those too.

And was he getting all these things, he asked, because old Emmerich had prescribed a rest? Or was he preparing for new shenanigans—did he anticipate another entanglement at the Vineyard? With whom? How should he know with whom? Women were plentiful everywhere.

At home, he tried on his purchases. The bathing trunks were a little tight. But the oval straw hat pleased him, floating on the hair which still grew thickly at the sides. In it he looked like his father's cousin Elias Herzog, the flour salesman who had covered the northern Indiana territory for General Mills back in the twenties. Elias with his earnest Americanized clean-shaven face ate hard-boiled eggs and drank prohibition beer—home-brewed Polish piva. He gave the eggs a neat rap on the rail of the porch and peeled them scrupulously. He wore colorful sleeve garters and a skimmer like this one, set on this same head of hair shared also by *his* father, Rabbi Sandor-Alexander Herzog, who wore a beautiful beard as well, a radiant, broad-strung beard that hid the outline of his chin and also the velvet collar of his frock coat. Herzog's mother had had a weakness for Jews with handsome beards. In her family, too, all the elders had beards that were thick and rich, full of religion. She wanted Moses to become a rabbi and he seemed to himself gruesomely unlike a rabbi now in the trunks and straw hat, his face charged with heavy sadness, foolish utter longing of which a religious life might have purged him. That mouth!—heavy with desire and irreconcilable anger, the straight nose sometimes grim, the dark eyes! And his figure!—the long veins winding in the arms and filling in the hanging hands, an ancient system, of greater antiquity than the Jews themselves. The flat-topped hat, a crust of straw, had a red and white band, matching the coat. He removed the tissue paper from the sleeves and put it on, swelling out the stripes. Bare-legged, he looked like a Hindu.

Consider the lilies of the field, he remembered, *they toil not, neither do they spin, yet' Solomon in all his glory was not arrayed . . .*

He had been eight years old, in the children's ward of the Royal Victoria Hospital, Montreal, when he learned those words. A Christian lady came once a week and had him read aloud from the Bible. He read, *Give and it shall be given unto you: good measure, pressed down and shaken together and running over shall men give unto your bosom.*

From the hospital roof hung icicles like the teeth of fish, clear drops burning at their tips. Beside his bed, the goyische lady sat in her long skirts and button shoes. The hatpin projected from the back of her head like a trolley rod. A paste odor came from her clothing. And then she had him read, *Suffer the little children to come unto me.* She seemed to him a good woman. Her face, however, was strained and grim.

"Where do you live, little boy?"

"On Napoleon Street."

Where the Jews live.

"What does your father do?"

My father is a bootlegger. He has a still in Point-St. Charles. The spotters are after him. He has no money.

Only of course Moses would never have told her any of this. Even at five he would have known better. His mother had instructed him. "You must never say."

There was a certain wisdom in it, he thought, as if by staggering he could recover his balance, or by admitting a bit of madness come to his senses. And he enjoyed a joke on himself. Now, for instance, he had packed the summer clothes he couldn't afford and was making his getaway from Ramona. He knew how things would turn out if he went to Montauk with her. She would lead him like a tame bear in Easthampton, from cocktail party to cocktail party. He could imagine that—Ramona laughing, talking, her shoulders bare in one of her peasant blouses (they were marvelous, feminine shoulders, he had to admit that), her hair in black curls, her face, her mouth painted; he could smell the perfume. In the depths of a man's being there was something that responded with a quack to such perfume. Quack! A sexual reflex that had nothing to do with age or subtlety, wisdom, experience, history, *Wissenschaft, Bildung, Wahrheit*. In sickness or health there came the old quack-quack at the fragrance of perfumed, feminine skin. Yes, Ramona would lead him in his new pants and striped jacket, sipping a martini. . . . Martinis were poison to Herzog and he couldn't bear small talk. And so he would suck in his belly and stand on aching feet— he, the captive professor, she the mature, successful, laughing, sexual woman. Quack, quack!

His bag was packed, and he locked the windows and pulled the shades. He knew the apartment would smell mustier than ever when he came back from his bachelor holiday. Two marriages, two children, and he was setting off for a week of *carefree* rest. It was painful to his instincts, his Jewish family feelings, that his children should be growing up without him. But what could he do about that? To the sea! To the sea!—What sea? It was the bay— between East Chop and West Chop it wasn't sea; the water was quiet.

He went out, fighting his sadness over this solitary life. His chest expanded, and he caught his breath. "For Christ's sake, don't cry, you idiot! Live or die, but don't poison everything."

Why this door should need a police lock he didn't know. Crime was on the increase, but he had nothing worth stealing. Only some excited kid might think he had, and lie in wait, hopped-up, to hit him on the head. Herzog led the metal foot of the lock into its slot in the floor and turned the key. He then checked to be sure he hadn't forgotten his glasses. No, they were in his breast pocket. He had his pens, notebook, checkbook, a piece of kitchen towel he had torn off for his handkerchief, and the plastic container of Furadantin tablets. The tablets were for the infection he had caught in Poland. He was cured of it now, but he took an occasional pill just to be on the safe side. That was a frightening moment in Cracow, in the hotel room, when the symptom appeared. He thought, The clap—at last! After all these years. At my time of life! His heart sank.

He went to a British doctor, who scolded him sharply. "What have you been up to? Are you married?"

"No."

"Well, it isn't a clap. Pull up your trousers. You'll want a shot of penicillin, I suppose. All Americans do. Well, I shan't give it. Take this sulfa. No booze, mind you. Drink tea."

They are unforgiving about sexual offenses. The fellow was angry, biting, a snotty Limey doctor. And I so vulnerable, heavy with guilt.

I should have known that a woman like Wanda would not infect me with gonorrhea. She is *sincere,* loyal, devout toward the body, the flesh. She has the religion of civilized people, which is pleasure, creative and polymorphous pleasure. Her skin is subtle, white, silken, animate.

Dear Wanda, wrote Herzog. But she knew no English and he changed to French. *Chère Princesse, Je me souviens assez souvent . . . Je pense à la Marszalkowska, au brouillard.* Every third-, fourth-, tenth-rate man of the world knew how to woo a woman in French, and so did Herzog. Though he was not the type. The feelings he wanted to express were genuine. She had been extremely kind to him when he was ill, troubled, and what made her kindness even more significant was the radiant, buxom Polish beauty of the woman. She had weighty golden-reddish hair and a slightly tilted nose but with very fine lines, the tip amazingly delicate and shapely for such a fleshy person. Her color was white, but a healthy, strong white. She was dressed, like most women in Warsaw, in black stockings and long slender Italian shoes, but her fur coat was worn to the hide.

In my grief did I know what I was doing? noted Herzog on a separate page, as he waited for the elevator. *Providence,* he added, *takes care of the faithful. I sensed that I would meet such a person. I have had terrific luck.* "Luck" was many times underscored.

Herzog had seen her husband. He was a poor, reproachful-looking man, with heart disease. The sole fault Herzog had found with Wanda was that she insisted he meet Zygmunt. Moses had not yet grasped what this meant. Wanda rejected the suggestion of a divorce. She was perfectly satisfied with her marriage. She said it was all any marriage could be.

Ici tout est gâché.

Une dizaine de jours à Varsovie—pas longtemps. If you could call those foggy winter intervals days. The sun was shut up in a cold bottle. The soul shut up inside me. Enormous felt curtains kept the drafts out of the hotel lobby. The wooden tables were stained, warped, tea-scalded.

Her skin was white and remained white through every change of emotion. Her greenish eyes seemed let into her Polish face (nature, the seamstress). A full, soft-bosomed woman, she was too heavy for the stylish tapering Italian shoes she wore. Standing without the heels, in her black hose, her figure was very solid indeed. He missed her. When he took her hand, she said, "Ah, ne toushay pas. C'est dangeray." But she didn't mean it at all. (How he doted on his memories! What a funny sensual bird he was! Queer for recollections, perhaps? But why use harsh words. He was what he was.)

Still, he had been continually aware of drab Poland, in all directions freezing, drab, and ruddy gray, the stones still smelling of wartime murders. He thought he scented blood. He went many times to visit the ruins of the ghetto. Wanda was his guide.

He shook his head. But what could *he* do? He pressed the

elevator button again, this time with the corner of his Gladstone bag. He heard the sound of smooth motion in the shaft—greased tracks, power, efficient black machinery.

Guéri de cette petite maladie. He ought not to have mentioned it to Wanda, for she was simply shocked and hurt. *Pas grave du tout,* he wrote. He had made her cry.

The elevator stopped and he ended, *J'embrasse ces petites mains, amie.*

How do you say blond little cushioned knuckles in French?

I N the cab through hot streets where brick and brownstone buildings were crowded, Herzog held the strap and his large eyes were fixed on the sights of New York. The square shapes were vivid, not inert, they gave him a sense of fateful motion, almost of intimacy. Somehow he felt himself part of it all—in the rooms, in the stores, cellars—and at the same time he sensed the danger of these multiple excitements. But he'd be all right. He was overstimulated. He had to calm down these over-strained galloping nerves, put out this murky fire inside. He yearned for the Atlantic—the sand, the brine flavor, the therapy of cold water. He knew he would think better, clearer thoughts after bathing in the sea. His mother had believed in the good effects of bathing. But she had died so young. *He* could not allow himself to die yet. The children needed him. His duty was to live. To be sane, and to live, and to look after the kids. This was why he was running from the city now, overheated, eyes smarting. He was getting away from all burdens, practical questions, away also from Ramona. There were times when you wanted to creep into hiding, like an animal. Although he didn't know what lay ahead except the confining train which would impose rest on him (you can't run in a train) through Connecticut, Rhode Island, and Massachusetts, as far as Woods Hole, his reasoning was sound. Seashores are good for madmen—provided they're not too mad. He was all ready. The glad rags were in the bag under his feet, and the straw hat with the red and white band? It was on his head.

But all at once, the seat of the cab heating in the sun, he was aware that his angry spirit had stolen forward again, and that he was about to write letters. *Dear Smithers,* he began. *The other day at lunch*—those bureaucratic lunches which are a horror to me; my hindquarters become paralyzed, my blood fills up with adrenalin; my heart! I try to look right and proper but my face turns dead with boredom, my fantasy spills soup and gravy on everybody, and I want to scream out or faint away—*we were asked to suggest topics for new lecture courses and I said what about a series on marriage. I might as well have said "Currants" or "Gooseber-*

ries." Smithers is extremely happy with his lot. Birth is very chancy. Who knows what may happen? But his lot was to be Smithers and that was tremendous luck. He looks like Thomas E. Dewey. The same gap between the front teeth, the neat mustache. *Look, Smithers, I do have a good idea for a new course. You organization men have to depend on the likes of me. The people who come to evening classes are only ostensibly after culture. Their great need, their hunger, is for good sense, clarity, truth—even an atom of it. People are dying—it is no metaphor—for lack of something real to carry home when day is done. See how willing they are to accept the wildest nonsense.* O Smithers, my whiskered brother! what a responsibility we bear, in this fat country of ours! Think what America could mean to the world. Then see what it is. What a breed it might have produced. But look at us—at you, at me. Read the paper, if you can bear to.

But the cab had passed 30th Street and there was a cigar store on the corner which Herzog had entered a year ago to buy a carton of Virginia Rounds for his mother-in-law, Tennie, who lived a block away. He remembered going into the phone booth to tell her he was coming up. It was dark in there, and the patterned tin lining was worn black in places. *Dear Tennie, Perhaps we'll have a talk when I get back from the seashore. The message you sent through Lawyer Simkin that you didn't understand why I no longer came to see you is, to say the least, hard to figure. I know your life has been tough. You have no husband.* Tennie and Pontritter were divorced. The old impresario lived on 57th Street, where he ran a school for actors, and Tennie had her own two rooms on 31st, which looked like a stage set and were filled with mementos of her ex-husband's triumphs. All the posters were dominated by his name,

PONTRITTER
DIRECTS EUGENE O'NEILL, CHEKHOV

Though no longer man and wife, they had a relationship still. Pontritter took Tennie riding in his Thunderbird. They attended openings, went to dinner together. She was a slender woman of fifty-five, somewhat taller than Pon. But he was burly, masterful, there was a certain peevish power and intelligence in his dark face.

He liked Spanish costumes, and when Herzog last saw him he was wearing white duck trousers of bull-fighter's cut and alpargatas. Powerful, isolated threads of coarse white grew from his tanned scalp. Madeleine had inherited his eyes.

No husband. No daughter, Herzog wrote. But he began again, *Dear Tennie, I went to see Simkin about a certain matter, and he said to me, "Your mother-in-law's feelings are hurt."*

Simkin, sitting in his office, occupied a grand Sykes chair, beneath enormous rows of law books. A man is born to be orphaned, and to leave orphans after him, but a chair like that chair, if he can afford it, is a great comfort. Simkin was not so much sitting as lying in this seat. With his large thick back and small thighs, his head shaggy and aggressive and his hands folded small and timid on his belly, he spoke to Herzog in a diffident, almost meek tone. He called him "Professor" but not mockingly. Though Simkin was a clever lawyer, very rich, he respected Herzog. He had a weakness for confused high-minded people, for people with moral impulses like Moses. Hopeless! Very likely he looked at Moses and saw a grieving childish man, trying to keep his dignity. He noted the book on Herzog's knee, for Herzog typically carried a book to read on the subway or in the bus. What was it that day, Simmel on religion? Teilhard de Chardin? Whitehead? It's been years since I was really able to concentrate. Anyway, there was Simkin, short but also burly, eyes wreathed with twisting hairs, looking at him. In conversation his voice was very small, meek, almost faint, but when he answered his secretary's signal and switched on the intercom, it suddenly expanded. He said loudly and sternly, "Yah?"

"Mr. Dienstag on the phone."

"Who? That schmuck? I'm waiting for that affidavit. Tell him plaintiff will kick his ass if he can't produce it. He better get it this afternoon, that ludicrous shmegeggy!" Amplified, his tones were oceanic. Then he switched off, and said with resumed meekness to Moses, "Vei, vei! I get so tired of these divorces. What a situation! It gets more corrupt. Ten years ago I thought I could still keep up with it all. I felt I was worldly enough for it—realistic, cynical. But I was wrong. It's too much. This shnook of a chiropodist—what a hellcat *he* married. First she said she didn't want children, then she did, didn't, did. Finally, she threw her diaphragm in his face.

2 9

Went to the bank. Took thirty grand of joint money from the vault. Said he tried to push her in front of a car. Fought with his mother about a ring, furs, a chicken, God knows. And then the husband found letters to her from another fellow." Simkin rubbed his cunning, imposing head with small hands. Then he showed his small regular teeth, iron-hard, as though about to smile, but this was a reflective preliminary. He gave a compassionate sigh. "You know, Professor, Tennie's hurt by your silence."

"I suppose so. But I can't bring myself to go there yet."

"Sweet woman. And what a family of hellers! I'm just passing the message on, because she asked me."

"Yes."

"Very decent, Tennie . . ."

"I know. She knitted me a scarf. It took a year. I got it in the mail about a month ago. I should acknowledge it."

"Yes, why don't you. She's no enemy."

Simkin liked him; Herzog didn't doubt that. But as a practical realist a man like Simkin had to perform exercises, and a certain amount of malice kept him in condition. A fellow like Moses Herzog, a little soft-headed or impractical but ambitious mentally, somewhat arrogant, too, a pampered, futile fellow whose wife had just been taken away from him under very funny circumstances (far funnier than the case of the chiropodist, which made Simkin bring his little hands together with a small cry of mock horror)— this Moses was irresistible to a man like Simkin who loved to pity and to poke fun at the same time. He was a Reality-Instructor. Many such. I bring them out. Himmelstein is another, but cruel. It's the cruelty that gets me, not the realism. Of course Simkin knew all about Madeleine's affair with Valentine Gersbach, and what he didn't know his friends Pontritter and Tennie would tell him.

Tennie had led a bohemian life for thirty-five years, following her husband as if she had married a grocer not a theatrical genius, and she remained a kindly, elder-sister sort of woman, with long legs. But the legs went bad, and her dyed hair turned stiff and quill-like. She wore butterfly-shaped eyeglasses, and "abstract" jewelry.

What if I did come to see you? asked Herzog. *Then I'd sit in your parlor being nice, while bursting with the wrongs your daughter did me. The same wrongs you have accepted from Pontritter, and forgiven him.* She prepares the old man's income-tax returns for him. Keeps all his records, washes his socks. Last time, I saw his socks drying on the radiator in her bathroom. And she had been telling me how happy she was now that she was divorced—free to go her own way and develop her own personality. *I'm sorry for you, Tennie.*

But that beautiful masterful daughter of yours came to your apartment with Valentine, didn't she, and sent you with your little granddaughter to the zoo while they made love in your bed. He with the gushing red hair, and she with the blue eyes, beneath. What am I supposed to do now—come and sit and talk about plays and restaurants? Tennie would tell him about that Greek place on Tenth Avenue. She already had told him half a dozen times. "A friend" (Pontritter himself, of course) "took me to dinner at the Marathon. It was really so different. You know, the Greek people cook ground meat and rice in grape leaves, with very interesting spices. Anybody who feels like it can dance solo. The Greek people are very uninhibited. You should see those fat men take off their shoes and dance in front of the whole crowd." Tennie spoke with a girlish sweetness and affection to him, obscurely fond of him. Her teeth were like the awkward second teeth of a seven-year-old child.

Oh, yes, thought Herzog. Her condition is worse than mine. Divorced at fifty-five, still showing off her legs, unaware they now are gaunt. And diabetic. And the menopause. And abused by her daughter. If in self-defense, Tennie has a bit of wickedness, hypocrisy, and cunning of her own, how can you blame her? Of course she gave us, or lent—it was sometimes a loan and sometimes a wedding present—that hand-wrought Mexican silver cutlery, and she wants it back. That's why she sent word through Simkin about her hurt feelings. She doesn't want to lose her silver. It's not exactly cynical, either. She wants to be friends, and she wants the silver too. It's her treasure. *It's in the vault, in Pittsfield. Too heavy to lug to Chicago. I'll return it, of course. By and by.* I never could hang on to valuables—silver, gold. With me, money is not a medium. I am money's medium. It passes through me—taxes, insurance, mortgage, child support, rent, legal fees. All this dignified blundering costs plenty. If I married Ramona, it would be easier, perhaps.

The cab was held up by trucks in the garment district. The

electric machines thundered in the lofts and the whole street quivered. It sounded as though cloth were being torn, not sewn. The street was plunged, drowned in these waves of thunder. Through it a Negro pushed a wagon of ladies' coats. He had a beautiful beard and blew a gilt toy trumpet. You couldn't hear him.

Then the traffic opened and the cab rattled in low gear and jerked into second. "For Christ sake, let's make time," the driver said. They made a sweeping turn into Park Avenue and Herzog clutched the broken window handle. It wouldn't open. But if it opened dust would pour in. They were demolishing and raising buildings. The Avenue was filled with concrete-mixing trucks, smells of wet sand and powdery gray cement. Crashing, stamping pile-driving below, and, higher, structural steel, interminably and hungrily going up into the cooler, more delicate blue. Orange beams hung from the cranes like straws. But down in the street where the buses were spurting the poisonous exhaust of cheap fuel, and the cars were crammed together, it was stifling, grinding, the racket of machinery and the desperately purposeful crowds—horrible! He had to get out to the seashore where he could breathe. He ought to have booked a flight. But he had had enough of planes last winter, especially on the Polish airline. The machines were old. He took off from Warsaw airport in the front seat of a two-engine LOT plane, bracing his feet on the bulkhead before him and holding his hat. There were no seat belts. The wings were dented, the cowls scorched. There were mail pouches and crates sliding behind. They flew through angry spinning snow clouds over white Polish forests, fields, pits, factories, rivers dogging their banks, in, out, in, and a terrain of white and brown diagrams.

Anyway, a holiday should begin with a train ride, as it had when he was a kid in Montreal. The whole family took the streetcar to the Grand Trunk Station with a basket (frail, splintering wood) of pears, overripe, a bargain bought by Jonah Herzog at the Rachel Street Market, the fruit spotty, ready for wasps, just about to decay, but marvelously fragrant. And inside the train on the worn green bristle of the seats, Father Herzog sat peeling the fruit with his Russian pearl-handled knife. He peeled and twirled and cut with European efficiency. Meanwhile, the locomotive cried and the iron-studded cars began to move. Sun and girders divided the soot geometrically. By the factory walls the grimy weeds grew. A smell of malt came from the breweries.

The train crossed the St. Lawrence. Moses pressed the pedal and through the stained funnel of the toilet he saw the river frothing. Then he stood at the window. The water shone and curved on great slabs of rock, spinning into foam at the Lachine Rapids, where it sucked and rumbled. On the other shore was Caughnawaga, where the Indians lived in shacks raised on stilts. Then came the burnt summer fields. The windows were open. The echo of the train came back from the straw like a voice through a beard. The engine sowed cinders and soot over the fiery flowers and the hairy knobs of weed.

But that was forty years behind him. Now the train was ribbed for speed, a segmented tube of brilliant steel. There were no pears, no Willie, no Shura, no Helen, no Mother. Leaving the cab, he thought how his mother would moisten her handkerchief at her mouth and rub his face clean. He had no business to recall this, he knew, and turned toward Grand Central in his straw hat. He was of the mature generation now, and life was his to do something with, if he could. But he had not forgotten the odor of his mother's saliva on the handkerchief that summer morning in the squat hollow Canadian station, the black iron and the sublime brass. All children have cheeks and all mothers spittle to wipe them tenderly. These things either matter or they do not matter. It depends upon the universe, what it is. These acute memories are probably symptoms of disorder. To him, perpetual thought of death was a sin. Drive your cart and your plow over the bones of the dead.

In the crowds of Grand Central Station, Herzog in spite of all his efforts to do what was best could not remain rational. He felt it all slipping away from him in the subterranean roar of engines, voices, and feet and in the galleries with lights like drops of fat in yellow broth and the strong suffocating fragrance of underground New York. His collar grew wet and the sweat ran from his armpits down his ribs as he bought the ticket, and then he picked up a copy of the *Times,* and was about to get a bar of Cadbury's Caramello, but he denied himself that, thinking of the money he had spent on new clothes which would not fit if he ate carbohydrates. It would give the victory to the other side to let himself grow fat, jowly, sullen, with broad hips and a belly, and breathing hard. Ramona wouldn't like it either, and what Ramona liked mattered considerably. He seriously considered marrying her, notwithstanding that he seemed, just now, to be buying a ticket to escape from her. But this was in her best interests, too, if he was so confused—both visionary and muddy as he felt now, feverish, damaged, angry, quarrelsome, and shaky. He was going to phone her shop, but in his change there was only one nickel left, no dimes. He would have to break a bill, and he didn't want candy or gum. Then he thought of wiring her and saw that he would seem weak if he sent a telegram.

On the sultry platform of Grand Central he opened the bulky *Times* with its cut shreds at the edges, having set the valise on his feet. The hushed electric trucks were rushing by with mail bags, and he stared at the news with a peculiar effort. It was a hostile broth of black print *MoonraceberlinKhrushchwarncommitteegalacticXrayPhouma*. He saw twenty paces away the white soft face and independent look of a woman in a shining black straw hat which held her head in depth and eyes that even in the signal-dotted obscurity reached him with a force she could never be aware of. Those eyes might be blue, perhaps green, even gray—he would never know. But they were bitch eyes, that was certain. They expressed a sort of female arrogance which had an immediate sexual power over him; he experienced it again that very moment—a round face, the clear gaze of pale bitch eyes, a pair of proud legs.

I must write to Aunt Zelda, he suddenly decided. They mustn't think they can get away with it—make such a fool of me, put me on. He folded the thick paper and hurried into the train. The bitch-eyed girl was on the other track, and good riddance. He went into a New Haven car, and the russet door closed behind him on pneumatic hinges, stiff and hissing. The air inside was chill, air-conditioned. He was the first passenger and had his choice of seats.

He sat in a cramped position, pressing the valise to his chest, his traveling-desk, and writing rapidly in the spiral notebook. *Dear Zelda, Of course you have to be loyal to your niece. I am just an outsider. You and Herman said I was one of the family. If I was patsy enough to be affected (at my age) by this sort of "heart-felt" family garbage, why I deserve what I got. I was flattered by Herman's affection, because of his former underworld acquaintances. I was overcome with happy pride at being found "regular." It meant my muddled intellectual life, as a poor soldier of culture, hadn't ruined my human sympathies. What if I had written a book on the Romantics? A politician in the Cook County Democratic organization who knew the Syndicate, the Juice men, the Policy kings, Cosa Nostra, and all the hoods, still found me good company, heimisch, and took me along to the races, the hockey games.* But Herman is even more marginal to the Syndicate than poor Herzog to the practical world and both are at home in a pleasant heimisch environment and love the Russian bath and tea and smoked fish and herrings afterward. With restless women conspiring at home.

As long as I was Mady's good husband, I was a delightful person. Suddenly, because Madeleine decided that she wanted out—suddenly, I was a mad dog. The police were warned about me and there was talk of committing me to an institution. I know that my friend and Mady's lawyer, Sandor Himmelstein, called Dr. Edvig to ask whether I was crazy enough to be put in Manteno or Elgin. You took Madeleine's word as to my mental condition and so did others.

But you knew what she was up to—knew why she left Ludeyville for Chicago, why I had to find a job there for Valentine Gersbach, knew that I went house-hunting for the Gersbachs and arranged the private school for little Ephraim Gersbach. It must be very deep and primitive, the feeling people—women—have against a deceived husband, and I know now that you helped your niece by having Herman take me away to the hockey game.

Herzog was not angry at Herman—he didn't believe he was part of the conspiracy. *The Blackhawks against the Maple-Leafs.* Uncle Herman, mild, decent, clever, neat, in black loafers and beltless slacks, his high fedora standing up at the front like a fire helmet, his shirt with a tiny gargoyle on the breast pocket. In the rink the players mixed like hornets—swift, padded, yellow, black, red, rushing, slashing, whirling over the ice. Above the rink the tobacco smoke lay like a cloud of flash powder, explosive. Over the p.a. system the management begged the spectators not to throw pennies to catch the blades of the skates. Herzog with circled eyes tried to relax in Herman's company. He even won a bet and took him to Fritzel's for cheesecake. All the big names of Chicago were there. And what must Uncle Herman have been thinking? Suppose that he also knew that Madeleine and Gersbach were together? In spite of the air-conditioned chill of the New Haven car, Herzog felt the sweat break out on his face.

Last March when I came back from Europe, a case of nerves, and arrived in Chicago to see what could be done, if anything, to restore a little order, I was really in a goofy state. Partly it may have been the weather, and the time changes. It was spring in Italy. Palm trees in Turkey. In Galilee, the red anemones among stones. But in Chicago I ran into a blizzard in March. I was met by Gersbach, still my dearest friend as recently as that, looking at me with compassion. He wore a storm coat, black galoshes, a Kelly-green scarf, and had Junie in his arms. He hugged me. June kissed me on the face. We went to the waiting room and I unpacked the toys and little dresses I had bought, and a Florentine wallet for Valentine and Polish amber beads for Phoebe Gersbach. As it was past Junie's bedtime and the snowfall was getting heavy, Gersbach took me to the Surf Motel. He said he couldn't book me at the Windermere, closer to the house, a ten-minute walk. By morning a ten-inch snow had fallen. The lake was heaving and lit by white snow to a near horizon of storming gray. I phoned Madeleine but she hung up on me; Gersbach, but he was out of his office; Dr. Edvig, but he couldn't give me an appointment till next day. His own family, his sister, his stepmother, Herzog avoided. He went to see Aunt Zelda.

There were no cabs that day. He rode the buses, freezing when he changed in his covert-cloth coat and thin-soled loafers. The Umschands lived in a new suburb, to hell and gone, beyond Palos Park, on the fringe of the Forest Preserves. The blizzard had stopped by the time he got there, but the wind was cutting, and lumps of snow fell from twigs. Frost sealed the shop windows. At the package store, Herzog, not much of a drinker, picked up a bottle of Guckenheimer's 86 proof. It was early in the day, but his blood was cold. Thus he spoke to Aunt Zelda with a whisky breath.

"I'll heat the coffee up. You must be solid ice," she said.

In the suburban kitchen of enamel and copper, the white molded female forms bulged from all sides. The refrigerator, as if it had a heart, and the range with gentian flames under the pot. Zelda had made up her face and wore gold slacks and plastic-heeled slippers —transparent. They sat down. Looking through the glass-topped table, Herzog could see that her hands were pressed between her knees. When he began to talk, she lowered her eyes. She had a blond complexion, but her eyelids were darker, warmer, more brown, discolored but with a thick blue line drawn on each by a cosmetic pencil. Her downcast look, Moses at first took as agreement or sympathy; but he realized how wrong he was when he observed her nose. It was full of mistrust. By the way it moved he realized that she rejected everything he was saying. But he knew he was immoderate—worse than that, temporarily deranged. He tried to get a grip on himself. Half buttoned, red-eyed, unshaved, he looked disgraceful. Indecent. He was telling Zelda his side of the case. "I know she's turned you against me—poisoned your mind, Zelda."

"No, she respects you. She fell out of love with you, that's all. Women fall out of love."

"Love? Madeleine loved me? You know that's just middle-class bunk."

"She was crazy about you. I know she adored you once, Moses."

"No, no! Don't work on me like that. You know it isn't true. She's sick. She's a diseased woman—I took care of her."

"I'll admit you did," said Zelda. "What's true is true. But what disease . . ."

"Ah!" said Herzog harshly. "So you love the truth!"

He saw Madeleine's influence in this; she was forever talking about the truth. She could not bear lying. Nothing could throw Madeleine into a rage so quickly as a lie. And now she had Zelda on the same standard—Zelda, with dyed hair as dry as excelsior and the purplish lines on her lids, these caterpillar forms—Oh! thought Herzog in the train, the things women apply to their own flesh. And we must go along, must look, listen, heed, breathe in. And now Zelda, her face a little lined, her soft, powerful nostrils dilated with suspicion, and fascinated at his state (there was reality in Herzog now, not seen when he was affable), was giving him the business about truth.

"Haven't I always leveled with you?" she said. "I am not just another suburban hausfrau."

"You mean because Herman says he knows Luigi Boscolla, the hoodlum?"

"Don't pretend you can't understand me. . . ."

Herzog did not want to offend her. It suddenly was plain what made her talk like this. Madeleine had convinced Zelda that she too was exceptional. Everyone close to Madeleine, everyone drawn into the drama of her life became exceptional, deeply gifted, brilliant. It had happened also to him. By his dismissal from Madeleine's life, sent back into the darkness, he became again a spectator. But he saw Aunt Zelda was inspired by a new sense of herself. Herzog envied her even this closeness to Madeleine.

"Well, I know you aren't like the other wives out here. . . ."

Your kitchen is different, your Italian lamps, your carpets, your French provincial furniture, your Westinghouse, your mink, your country club, your cerebral palsy canisters are all different.

I am sure you were sincere. Not insincere. True insincerity is hard to find.

"Madeleine and I have always been more like sisters," said Zelda. "I'd love her no matter how she acted. But I'm glad to say she's been terrific, a serious person."

"Junk!"

"Just as serious as you are."

"Returning a husband like a cake dish or a bath towel to Field's."

"It didn't work out. You have your faults too. I'm sure you won't deny that."

"How could I?"

"Overbearing, gloomy. You brood a lot."

"That's true enough."

"Very demanding. Have to have your own way. She says you wore her out, asking for help, support."

"It's all correct. And more. I'm hasty, irascible, spoiled. And what else?"

"You've been reckless about women."

"Since Madeleine threw me out, maybe. Trying to get back my self-respect."

"No, while you still were married." Zelda's mouth tightened.

Herzog felt himself redden. A thick, hot, sick pressure filled his chest. His heart felt ill and his forehead instantly wet.

He muttered, "She made it tough for me, too. Sexually."

"Well, being older . . . But that's bygones," said Zelda. "Your big mistake was to bury yourself in the country so you could finish that project of yours—that study of whatchamajig. You never did wind it up, did you?"

"No," Herzog said.

"Then what was *that* all about."

Herzog tried to explain what it was about—that his study was supposed to have ended with a new angle on the modern condition, showing how life could be lived by renewing universal connections; overturning the last of the Romantic errors about the uniqueness of the Self; revising the old Western, Faustian ideology; investigating the social meaning of Nothingness. And more. But he checked himself, for she did not understand, and this offended her, especially as she believed she was no common hausfrau. She said, "It sounds very grand. Of course it must be important. But that's not the point. You were a fool to bury yourself and her, a young woman, in the Berkshires, with nobody to talk to."

"Except Valentine Gersbach, and Phoebe."

"That's right. That was bad. Especially winters. You should have had more sense. That house made a prisoner of her. It must have been just dreary, washing and cooking, and to have to hush the baby, or you'd raise hell, she said. You couldn't think when June was crying, and you'd rush from your room hollering."

"Yes, I was stupid—a blockhead. But that was one of the problems I was working on, you see, that people can be free now but the freedom doesn't have any content. It's like a howling emptiness. Madeleine shared my interests, I thought—she's a studious person."

"She says you were a dictator, a regular tyrant. You bullied her."

I do seem to be a broken-down monarch of some kind, he was thinking, like my old man, the princely immigrant and ineffectual bootlegger. And life was very bad in Ludeyville—terrible, I admit. But then didn't we buy the house because she wanted to, and move out when she wanted to? And didn't I make all the arrangements, even for the Gersbachs—so we could all leave the Berkshires together?

"What else did she complain of?" said Herzog.

Zelda considered him for a moment as though to see whether he was strong enough to take it, and said, "You were selfish."

Ah, that! He understood. The ejaculatio praecox! His look became stormy, his heart began to pound, and he said, "There was some trouble for a while. But not in the last two years. And hardly ever with other women." These were humiliating explanations. Zelda did not have to believe them, and that made him the pleader, and put him at a frightful disadvantage. He couldn't invite her upstairs for a demonstration, or produce affidavits from Wanda or Zinka. (Recalling, in the still standing train, the thwarted and angry eagerness of these attempted explanations, he had to laugh. Nothing but a wan smile passed over his face.) What crooks they were—Madeleine, Zelda . . . others. Some women didn't care how badly they damaged you. A girl, in Zelda's view, had a right to expect from her husband nightly erotic gratification, safety, money, insurance, furs, jewelry, cleaning women, drapes, dresses, hats, night clubs, country clubs, automobiles, theater!

"No man can satisfy a woman who doesn't want him," said Herzog.

"Well, isn't that your answer?"

Moses started to speak but he felt that he was going to make another foolish outcry. His face paled again and he kept his mouth shut. He was in terrible pain. It was so bad that he was far past claiming credit for his power to suffer as he had at times done. He sat silent, and heard the clothes dryer below whirling.

"Moses," said Zelda, "I want to make sure of one thing."

"What—"

"*Our* relationship." He was no longer looking at her darkened, painted lids but into her eyes, bright and brown. Her nostrils tensed softly. She showed him her sympathetic face. "We still are friends," she said.

"Well . . ." said Moses. "I'm fond of Herman. Of you."

"I *am* your friend. And I'm a truthful person."

He saw himself in the train window, hearing his own words clearly. "I think you're on the level."

"You believe me, don't you."

"I want to, naturally."

"You should. I've got your interests at heart, too. I keep an eye on little June."

"I'm grateful for that."

"But Madeleine is a good mother. And you don't have to worry. She doesn't run around with men. They phone her all the time, chasing after her. Well—she is a beauty, and a very rare type, too, because she is so brilliant. Down there in Hyde Park—as soon as everybody knew about the divorce, you'd be surprised who all started to call her."

"Good friends of mine, you mean."

"If she was just a fly-by-night, she could have her choice of men. But you know how serious she is. Anyhow, people like Moses Herzog don't grow on bushes, either. With your brains and charm, you won't be easy to replace. Anyhow, she's always at home. She's rethinking everything—her whole life. And there is nobody else. You know you can believe me."

Of course if you considered me dangerous it was your duty to lie. And I know I looked bad, my face swelled up, eyes red and wild. Female deceit, though, is a deep subject. Thrills of guile. Sexual complicity, conspiracy. Getting in on it. I watched you bully Herman to get a second car, and I know how you can bitch! You thought I might kill Mady and Valentine. But when I found out, why didn't I go to the pawnshop and buy a gun? Simpler yet, my father left a revolver in his desk. It's still there. But I'm no criminal, don't have it in me; frightful to myself, instead. Anyway, Zelda, I see you had tremendous pleasure, double excitement, lying from an overflowing heart.

All at once the train left the platform and entered the tunnel. Temporarily in darkness, Herzog held his pen. Smoothly the trickling walls passed. In dusty niches bulbs burned. Without religion. Then came a long incline and the train rose from underground and rode in sudden light on the embankment above the slums, upper Park Avenue. In the east Nineties an open hydrant gushed and kids in clinging drawers leaped screaming. Now came Spanish Harlem, heavy, dark, and hot, and Queens far off to the right, a thick document of brick, veiled in atmospheric dirt.

Herzog wrote, *Will never understand what women want. What*

do they want? They eat green salad and drink human blood.
Over Long Island Sound the air grew clearer. It gradually became very pure. The water was level and easy, soft blue, the grass brilliant, spattered with wildflowers—plenty of myrtle among these rocks, and wild strawberries blossoming.

I now know the whole funny, nasty, perverted truth about Madeleine. Much to think about. He now had ended.

But at the same high rate of speed, Herzog streaked off on another course, writing to an old friend in Chicago, Lucas Asphalter, a zoologist at the university. *What's gotten into you? I often read "human-interest" paragraphs but I never expect them to be about my friends. You can imagine how it shook me to see your name in the* Post. *Have you gone crazy? I know you adored that monkey of yours, and I'm sorry he's dead. But you should have known better than to try to revive him by mouth-to-mouth respiration. Especially as Rocco died of TB and must have been jumping with bugs.* Asphalter was queerly attached to his animals. Herzog suspected that he tended to humanize them. That macaque monkey of his, Rocco, was not an amusing creature, but obstinate and cranky, with a poor color, like a glum old Jewish uncle. But of course if he was slowly dying of consumption, he couldn't have looked very optimistic. Asphalter, so cheerful himself and indifferent to practical interests, something of a marginal academic type, without his Ph.D., taught comparative anatomy. With thick crepe-soled shoes, he wore a stained smock; he was bereaved of hair, of his youth, too, poor Luke. The sudden loss of his hair had left him with only one lock at the front, and made his handsome eyes, his arched brows prominent, his nostrils darker, hairier. *I hope he hasn't swallowed Rocco's bacilli. There's a new, deadlier strain at large, they say, and tuberculosis is coming back.* Asphalter was a bachelor at forty-five. His father had owned a flophouse on Madison Street. In his youth, Moses had been there often, visiting. And although for an interval of ten or fifteen years he and Asphalter had not been close friends, they had found, suddenly, a great deal in common. In fact it had been from Asphalter that Herzog learned what Madeleine was up to, and the part Gersbach had been playing in his life.

"Hate to tell you this, Mose," said Asphalter, in his office, "but you're mixed up with some awful nuts."

This was two days after the March blizzard. You wouldn't have known it had been raging winter that same week. The casement window was open on the Quadrangle. All the grimy cottonwoods had sprung to life, released red catkins from their sheaths. These dangled everywhere, perfuming the gray courtyard with its shut-in light. Rocco with sick eyes sat on his own straw chair, his look lusterless, his coat the color of stewed onions.

"I can't stand to see you knock yourself out," Asphalter said. "I'd better tell you—we have a lab assistant here who sits with your little girl, and she's been telling me about your wife."

"What about her?"

"And Valentine Gersbach. He's always there, on Harper Avenue."

"Sure. I know. He's the only reliable person on the scene. I trust him. He's been an awfully good friend."

"Yes, I know—I know, I know," said Asphalter. His pale round face was freckled, and his eyes large, fluid, dark, and, for Moses's sake, bitter in their dreaminess. "I certainly know. Valentine's quite an addition to the social life of Hyde Park, what's left of it. How did we ever get along without him. He's so genial—he's so noisy, with those Scotch and Japanese imitations, and that gravel voice. He drowns all conversation out. Full of life! Oh, yes, he's full of it! And because you brought him here, everybody thinks he's your special pal. He says so himself. Only . . ."

"Only what?"

Tense and quiet, Asphalter asked, "Don't you know?" He became very pale.

"What should I know?"

"I took it for granted because your intelligence is so high—way off the continuum—that you knew something or suspected."

Something frightful was about to descend on him. Herzog nerved himself for it.

"Madeleine, you mean? I understand, of course, that by and by, because she's still a young woman, she must . . . she will."

"No, no," said Asphalter. "Not by and by." He blurted it out. "All the while."

"Who!" said Herzog. All his blood rose, and just as quickly and massively left his brain. "You mean Gersbach?"

"That's right." Asphalter now had no control whatever over the nerves of his face; it had gone soft with the pain he felt. His mouth looked chapped, with black lines.

Herzog began to shout, "You can't talk like that! You can't say that!" He stared at Lucas, outraged. A dim, sick, faint feeling came over him. His body seemed to shrink, abruptly drained, hollow, numbed. He almost lost consciousness.

"Open your collar," said Asphalter. "My God, you aren't fainting, are you?" He began to force Herzog's head down. "Between the knees," he said.

"Let up," said Moses, but his head was hot and damp and he sat doubled over while Asphalter gave him first aid.

All the while, the large brown monkey, with arms folded over his chest, and red, dry eyes, was looking on, silently disseminating his grimness. Death, thought Herzog. The real thing. The animal was dying.

"You better?" Asphalter said.

"Just open a window. These zoology buildings stink."

"The window is open. Here, drink some water." He handed Moses a paper cup. "Take one of these. Take this first, and then the green and white. Prozine. I can't get the cotton out of the bottle. *My* hands are shaking."

Herzog refused the pills. "Luke . . . Is this really true, about Madeleine and Gersbach?" he said.

Intensely nervous, pale, warm, looking at him with his dark eyes, his mottled face, Asphalter said, "Christ! you don't think I'd invent such a thing. I probably haven't been tactful. I thought you must have had a pretty good idea. . . . But it's absolutely true." Asphalter in his soiled lab coat put it to him with a complicated helpless gesture—I lay it all before you, was what it said. His breathing was labored. "You didn't know *anything?*"

"No."

"But doesn't it make sense? Doesn't it add up now?"

Herzog rested his weight on the desk, knitting his fingers tightly. He stared at the dangling catkins, reddish and violet. Not to burst, not to die—to stay alive, was all he could hope for. "Who told you?" he said.

44

"Geraldine."

"Who?"

"Gerry—Geraldine Portnoy. I thought you knew her. Mady's sitter. She's down in the anatomy lab."

"What . . ."

"Human anatomy, in the Med School, around the corner. I go out with her. In fact, you know her, she was in one of your classes. Do you want to talk to her?"

"No," said Herzog violently.

"Well, she's written you a letter. She gave it to me and said she'd leave it up to me, whether I should hand it over or not."

"I can't read it now."

"Take it," said Asphalter. "You may want to read it later."

Herzog stuffed the envelope into his pocket.

He was wondering, as he sat in the plush seat of the train, holding his valise desk, and leaving New York State at seventy m.p.h., why he hadn't cried in Asphalter's office. He could burst into tears easily enough, and he was not inhibited with Asphalter, they were such old friends, so similar in their lives—their backgrounds, their habits, temperaments. But when Asphalter raised the lid, revealed the truth, something bad was released in his office overlooking the Quadrangle; like an odor, hot and raw; or a queer human fact, almost palpable. Tears were not relevant. The cause was too perverse, altogether too odd for all concerned. And then, too, Gersbach was a frequent weeper of distinguished emotional power. The hot tear was often in his magnanimous ruddy-brown eye. Only a few days earlier, when Herzog landed at O'Hare and hugged his little daughter, Gersbach had been there, a powerful, burly figure with tears of compassion in his eyes. So evidently, thought Moses, he's fucked up weeping for me, too. At moments I dislike having a face, a nose, lips, because he has them.

Yes, the shadow of death was on Rocco, then.

"Damn unpleasant," said Asphalter. He smoked a bit and put out his cigarette. The tray was filled with long butts—he used up two or three packs a day. "Let's have some drinks. Let's all have dinner tonight. I'm taking Geraldine to the Beachcomber, near-north. You can size her up for yourself."

Now Herzog had to consider some strange facts about Asphalter. It's possible that I influenced him, my emotionalism transmitted

45

itself to him. He had taken that brooding, hairy Rocco into his heart. How else could you account for such agitation—lifting Rocco in his arms and forcing his lips open, breathing mouth to mouth. I suspect Luke may be in a very bad way. I must try to think about him as he is—strangeness and all.

You'd better take the tuberculin test. I had no idea that you . . . Herzog broke off. A dining-car steward rang the chimes for lunch, but Herzog had no time to eat. He was about to begin another letter.

Dear Professor Byzhkovski, I thank you for your courtesy in Warsaw. Owing to the state of my health, our meeting must have been unsatisfactory to you. I sat in his apartment making paper hats and boats out of the *Trybuna Ludu* while he tried to get a conversation going. The professor—that tall powerful man in a sandy-tweed shooting costume of knickers and Norfolk jacket—must have been astonished. I'm convinced he has a kind nature. His blue eyes are the good sort. A fat but shapely face, thoughtful and manly. I kept folding the paper hats—I must have been thinking of the children. Mme. Byzhkovski asked me did I want jam in my tea, bending over hospitably. The furniture was richly polished, old, of a vanished Central European epoch—but then this present epoch is vanishing, too, and perhaps faster than all the others. *I hope you will forgive me. I have now had an opportunity to read your study of the American Occupation of West Germany. Many of the facts are disagreeable.* But I was never consulted by President Truman, nor by Mr. McCloy. *I must confess I haven't examined the German question as closely as I should. None of the governments are truthful, in my opinion. There is also an East German question not even touched upon in your monograph.*

I wandered in Hamburg into the red-light district. That is, I was told that I should see it. Some of the whores, in black lace underthings, wore German military boots and rapped at you with riding crops on the windowpanes. Broads with red complexions, calling and grinning. A cold, joyless day.

Dear Sir, wrote Herzog. *You have been very patient with the Bowery bums who enter your church, pass out drunk, defecate in the pews, break bottles on the gravestones, and commit more nuisances. I would suggest that as you can see Wall Street from your church door you might prepare a pamphlet to explain that the*

Bowery gives additional significance to it. Skid Row is the contrast-
ing institution, therefore necessary. Remind them of Lazarus and
Dives. Because of Lazarus, Dives gets an extra kick, a bonus, from
his luxuries. No, I don't believe Dives is having such a hot time,
either. And if he wants to free himself, the doom of Skid Row
awaits him. If there were a beautiful poverty, a moral poverty in
America, that would be subversive. Therefore it has to be ugly.
Therefore the bums are working for Wall Street—confessors of the
name. But the Reverend Beasley, where does he get his dough?
We have thought too little on this.

He then wrote, *Credit Department, Marshall Field & Co. I am*
no longer responsible for the debts of Madeleine P. Herzog. As of
March 10, we ceased to be husband and wife. So don't send me
any more bills—I was knocked over by the last—more than four
hundred dollars. For purchases made after the separation. Of
course I should have written sooner—to what is called the credit
nerve-center—Is there such a thing? Where can you find it?—but
I temporarily lost my bearings.

Dear Professor Hoyle, I don't think I understand just how the
Gold-Pore Theory works. How the heavier metals—iron, nickel—
get to the center of the earth, I think I see. But what about the con-
centration of lighter metals? Also, in your explanation of the for-
mation of smaller planets, including our tragic earth, *you speak of*
adhesive materials that bind the agglomerates of precipitated
matter. . . .

The wheels of the cars stormed underneath. Woods and pastures
ran up and receded, the rails of sidings sheathed in rust, the
dipping racing wires, and on the right the blue of the Sound,
deeper, stronger than before. Then the enameled shells of the com-
muters' cars, and the heaped bodies of junk cars, the shapes of old
New England mills with narrow, austere windows; villages, con-
vents; tugboats moving in the swelling fabric-like water; and then
plantations of pine, the needles on the ground of a life-giving russet
color. So, thought Herzog, acknowledging that his imagination of
the universe was elementary, the novae bursting and the worlds
coming into being, the invisible magnetic spokes by means of which
bodies kept one another in orbit. Astronomers made it all sound as
though the gases were shaken up inside a flask. Then after many
billions of years, light-years, this childlike but far from innocent

creature, a straw hat on his head, and a heart in his breast, part pure, part wicked, who would try to form his own shaky picture of this magnificent web.

Dear Dr. Bhave, he began again, *I read of your work in the* Observer *and at the time thought I'd like to join your movement. I've always wanted very much to lead a moral, useful, and active life. I never knew where to begin. One can't become Utopian. It only makes it harder to discover where your duty really lies. Persuading the owners of large estates to give up some land to impoverished peasants, however* . . . These dark men going on foot through India. In his vision Herzog saw their shining eyes, and the light of spirit within them. You must start with injustices that are obvious to everybody, not with big historical perspectives. *Recently, I saw* Pather Panchali. *I assume you know it, since the subject is rural India. Two things affected me greatly—the old crone scooping the mush with her fingers and later going into the weeds to die; and the death of the young girl in the rains.* Herzog, almost alone in the Fifth Avenue Playhouse, cried with the child's mother when the hysterical death music started. Some musician with a native brass horn, imitating sobs, playing a death noise. It was raining also in New York, as in rural India. His heart was aching. He too had a daughter, and his mother too had been a poor woman. He had slept on sheets made of flour sacks. The best type for the purpose was Ceresota.

What he had vaguely in mind was to offer his house and property in Ludeyville to the Bhave movement. But what could Bhave do with it? Send Hindus to the Berkshires? It wouldn't be fair to them. Anyway, there was a mortgage. A gift should be made in what they call "fee simple," and for that I'd have to raise another eight thousand bucks, and the Internal Revenue wouldn't give me a deduction on it. Foreign charities probably don't count. Bhave would be doing him a favor. That house was one of his biggest mistakes. It was bought in a dream of happiness, an old ruin of a place but with enormous possibilities—great old trees, formal gardens he could restore in his spare time. The place had been deserted for years. Duck hunters and lovers would break in and use it; and when Herzog posted the property the lovers and the hunters played jokes on him. Someone came in the night and left a used sanitary napkin in a covered dish on his desk, where he kept bundles of notes for his Romantic studies. That was his reception by the natives. A momentary light of self-humor passed over his face as the train flashed through meadows and sunny pines. Suppose I accepted the challenge. I could be Moses, the old Jew-man of Ludeyville, with a white beard, cutting the grass under the washline with my antique reel-mower. Eating woodchucks.

He wrote to his cousin Asher, in Beersheba, *I mentioned an old photograph of your father in his Czarist uniform. I have asked my sister Helen to look for it.* Asher had served in the Red Army and was wounded. He was now an electro-welder, a moody-looking man with strong teeth. He went with Moses to visit the Dead Sea. It was sultry. They sat down in the mouth of a salt mine to cool off. Asher said, "Don't you have a picture of my father?"

Dear Mr. President, I listened to your recent optimistic message on the radio and thought that in respect to taxes there was little to justify your optimism. The new legislation is highly discriminatory and many believe it will only aggravate unemployment problems by accelerating automation. This means that more adolescent gangs will dominate the underpoliced streets of big cities. Stresses of overpopulation, the race question. . .

Dear Doktor Professor Heidegger, I should like to know what you mean by the expression "the fall into the quotidian." When did this fall occur? Where were we standing when it happened?

Mr. Emmett Strawforth, U.S. Public Health Service, he wrote. *Dear Emmett, I saw you on television making a damn fool of yourself. Since we were undergraduates together (M. E. Herzog '38) I feel free to tell you what I think of your philosophy.*

Herzog crossed this out and readdressed his letter to the *New York Times. Again a government scientist, Dr. Emmett Strawforth, has come forward with the Philosophy of Risk in the controversy over fallout, to which has now been added the problem of chemical pesticides, contamination of ground water, etc. I am as deeply concerned with the social and ethical reasoning of scientists as I am with those other forms of poisoning. Dr. Strawforth on Rachel Carson, Dr. Teller on the genetic effects of radioactivity. Recently Dr. Teller argued that the new fashion of tight pants, by raising body temperatures, could affect the gonads more than fallout. People greatly respected in their generation often turn out to be dangerous lunatics. Take Field Marshal Haig. He drowned hundreds*

49

of thousands of men in the mudholes of Flanders. Lloyd George was obliged to sanction this because Haig was such an important and respected leader. Such people simply have to be allowed to do their stuff. How paradoxical it is that a man who uses heroin may get a 20-year sentence for what he does to himself. . . . They'll see what I mean.

Dr. Strawforth says we must adopt his Philosophy of Risk with regard to radioactivity. Since Hiroshima (and Mr. Truman calls people Bleeding Hearts when they question his Hiroshima decision) life in civilized countries (because they survive through a balance of terror) stands upon a foundation of risk. So argues Dr. Strawforth. But then he compares human life to Risk Capital in business. What an idea! Big business takes no chances, as the recent stockpiling investigation showed. I should like to call your attention to one of de Tocqueville's prophecies. He believed modern democracies would produce less crime, more private vice. Perhaps he should have said less private crime, more collective crime. Much of this collective or organizational crime has the object precisely of reducing risk. Now I know it's no cinch to manage the affairs of this planet with its population exceeding 2 billion. The number itself is something of a miracle and throws our practical ideas into obsolescence. Few intellectuals have grasped the social principles behind this quantitative transformation.

Ours is a bourgeois civilization. I am not using this term in its Marxian sense. Chicken! *In the vocabularies of modern art and religion it is bourgeois to consider that the universe was made for our safe use and to give us comfort, ease, and support. Light travels at a quarter of a million miles per second so that we can see to comb our hair or to read in the paper that ham hocks are cheaper than yesterday. De Tocqueville considered the impulse toward well-being as one of the strongest impulses of a democratic society. He can't be blamed for underestimating the destructive powers generated by this same impulse.* You must be out of your mind to write to the *Times* like this! There are millions of bitter Voltairean types whose souls are filled with angry satire and who keep looking for the keenest, most poisonous word. You could send in a poem instead, you nitwit. Why should you be more right out of sheer distraction than they are out of organization? You ride in their trains, don't you? Distraction didn't build the railroad. Go on, write a poem, and kill 'em with bitterness. They print little poems as fillers on the editorial page. But he continued his letter, nevertheless. *Nietzsche, Whitehead, and John Dewey wrote on the question of Risk. . . . Dewey tells us that mankind distrusts its own nature and tries to find stability beyond or above, in religion or philosophy. To him the past often means the erroneous.* But Moses checked himself. Come to the point. But what was the point? The point was that there were people who could destroy mankind and that they were foolish and arrogant, crazy, and must be begged not to do it. Let the enemies of life step down. Let each man now examine his heart. Without a great change of heart, I would not trust myself in a position of authority. Do I love mankind? Enough to spare it, if I should be in a position to blow it to hell? Now let us all dress in our shrouds and walk on Washington and Moscow. Let us lie down, men, women, and children, and cry, "Let life continue—we may not deserve it, but let it continue."

In every community there is a class of people profoundly dangerous to the rest. I don't mean the criminals. For them we have punitive sanctions. I mean the leaders. Invariably the most dangerous people seek the power. While in the parlors of indignation the right-thinking citizen brings his heart to a boil.

Mr. Editor, we are bound to be the slaves of those who have power to destroy us. I am not speaking of Strawforth any more. I knew him at school. We played ping-pong at the Reynolds Club. He had a white buttocky face with a few moles, and fat curling thumbs that put a cheating spin on the ball. Clickety-clack over the green table. I don't believe his I.Q. was so terribly high, though maybe it was, but he worked hard at his math and chemistry. While I was fiddling in the fields. Like the grasshoppers in Junie's favorite song.

> Grasshoppers three a-fiddling went.
> Hey-ho, never be still.
> They paid no money towards their rent
> But all day long with elbows bent
> They fiddled a song called Rillabyrillaby
> They fiddled a song called Rillabyrill.

Delighted, Moses began to grin. His face wrinkled tenderly at the thought of his children. How well kids understand what love is! Marco was entering an age of silence and restraint with his father, but Junie was exactly as Marco had been. She stood on her father's lap to comb his hair. His thighs were trodden by her feet. He embraced her small bones with fatherly hunger while her breath on his face stirred his deepest feelings.

He had been wheeling the child's stroller on the Midway, saluting students and faculty with a touch to the brim of his green velours hat, a mossier green than the slopes and hollow lawns. Under the tucks of her velvet bonnet, the little girl had very much her Papa's looks, so he thought. He smiled at her with large creases, dark eyes, while reciting nursery rhymes:

> "There was an old woman
> Who flew in a basket
> Seventeen times as high as the moon."

"More," the child said.

> "And where she was going
> Nobody could tell you
> For under her arm she carried a broom."

"More, more."

The warm lake wind drove Moses westward, past the gray gothic buildings. He had had the child at least, while mother and lover were undressing in a bedroom somewhere. And if, even in that embrace of lust and treason, they had life and nature on their side, he would quietly step aside. Yes, he would bow out.

The conductor (one of an ancient vanishing breed, this gray-faced conductor) took the ticket from Herzog's hatband. As he punched it, he seemed about to say something. Perhaps the straw hat carried him back to old times. But Herzog was finishing his letter. *Even if Strawforth were a philosopher-king, should we give him the power to tamper with the genetic foundations of life, pollute the atmosphere and the waters of the earth? I know it is cranky to be indignant. But . . .*

The conductor left a punched cardboard slip under the metal of the seat number and went away, leaving Moses still writing on his valise. He might have gone to the club car, of course, where there were tables, but there he'd have to buy drinks, talk to people. Besides, he had one of his most essential letters to write, to Dr. Edvig, the psychiatrist in Chicago.

So, Edvig, Herzog wrote, *you turn out to be a crook too! How pathetic!* But this was no way to begin. He started over. *My dear Edvig, I have news for you.* Ah, yes, much better this way. A provoking thing about Edvig was that he behaved as if he were the one with all the news—this calm Protestant Nordic Anglo-Celtic Edvig with his grizzled little beard, clever, waving, mounting hair, and glasses, round, clean, and glittering. *Admittedly, I came to you in a bad way. Madeleine made psychiatric treatment a condition of our staying together. If you remember, she said I was in a dangerous mental state. I was allowed to choose my own psychiatrist. Naturally I picked one who had written on Barth, Tillich, Brunner, etc. Especially since Madeleine, though Jewish, had had a Christian phase as a Catholic convert and I hoped you might help me to understand her. Instead, you went for her yourself. You did, it's undeniable, the more you learned from me that she was beautiful, had a brilliant mind, by no means sane, and was religious, to boot.* And she and Gersbach managed and planned every step I took. They figured a headshrinker could help to ease me out—a sick man, exceptionally neurotic, perhaps even hopeless. Anyway the cure would keep me busy, absorbed in my own case. Four afternoons a week they knew where I was, on the couch, and so were safe in bed. *I was near the point of breakdown, the day I came to see you—wet weather, trickling snow, the overheated bus.* The snow certainly made my heart no cooler. The street plastered with yellow leaves. That elderly person in her green plush hat, unturbulent green, and like a deadly bag in soft folds on her head. But it was not such a bad day at that. Edvig said I was not off my rocker. Simply a reactive-depressive.

"But Madeleine says I'm insane. That I . . ." Eager and trembling, his sore spirit distorted his face, swelled his throat, painfully. But he was encouraged by the kindness of Edvig's bearded smile. He then did his best to draw Edvig out, but all he would tell him that day was that depressives tended to form frantic dependencies and to become hysterical when cut off, when threatened with loss. "And of course," he added, "from what you tell me, you haven't been guiltless. And she sounds like an angry person to begin with. When did she lapse from the Church?"

53

"I'm not sure. I thought she was through long ago. But last Ash Wednesday she had the soot on her forehead. I said 'Madeleine, I thought you stopped being a Catholic. But what do I see between your eyes, ashes?' But she said, 'I don't know what you're talking about.' She tried to pass it off as one of my delusions, or something. But it was no delusion. It was a spot. I swear it was at least half a spot. But her attitude seems to be, a Jew like me, what would I know about this stuff."

Herzog could see that Edvig was fascinated by every word about Madeleine. Nodding, he raised his head, his chin rose at every sentence, he touched his neat beard, his lenses glittered, he smiled. "You feel she's a Christian?"

"She feels I'm a Pharisee. She says so."

"Ah?" Edvig sharply commented.

"Ah, what?" Moses said. "You agree with her?"

"How can I? I scarcely know you. But what do you think of the question?"

"Do you think that any Christian in the twentieth century has the right to speak of Jewish Pharisees? From a Jewish standpoint, you know, this hasn't been one of your best periods."

"But do you think your wife has a Christian outlook?"

"I think she has some home-brewed otherworldly point of view." Herzog sat straighter in his chair, and pronounced his words with slight portentousness, perhaps. "I don't agree with Nietzsche that Jesus made the whole world sick, infected it with his slave morality. But Nietzsche himself had a Christian view of history, seeing the present moment always as some crisis, some fall from classical greatness, some corruption or evil to be saved from. I call that Christian. And Madeleine has it, all right. To some extent many of us do. Think we have to recover from some poison, need saving, ransoming. Madeleine wants a savior, and for her I'm no savior."

This was the kind of thing Edvig apparently expected from Moses. Shrugging and smiling, he took it all as analytic material and seemed very pleased. He was a fair, mild man; his shoulders had a certain slender squareness. Old-fashioned, with pink nearly colorless frames, his glasses made him drably, humbly, thoughtful and medical.

By degrees, and I don't quite know how it happened, Madeleine became the principal figure in the analysis, and dominated it as she dominated me. And came to dominate you. I began to notice how impatient you were to meet her. Because of the unusual facts of the case you said you had to interview her. By and by you were deep in discussions of religion with her. And finally, you were treating her, too. You said you could see why she had fascinated me. And I said, "I told you she was extraordinary. She's brilliant, the bitch, a terror!" So you knew, at least, if I was stoned out of my skull (as they say), it was by no ordinary woman. As for Mady, she enriched her record by conning you. It all added to her depth. And because she was getting her Ph.D. in Russian religious history (I guess), your sessions with her, at twenty-five bucks a throw, were for several months a course of lectures on Eastern Christianity. After this, she began to develop strange symptoms.

First, she accused Moses of hiring a private detective to spy on her. She began this accusation with the slightly British diction he had learned to recognize as a sure sign of trouble. "I should have thought," she said, "you'd have been far too clever to engage such an obvious type."

"Engage," said Herzog. "Whom have I engaged?"

"I mean that horrible man—that stinking, fat man in the sports coat." Madeleine, absolutely sure of herself, flashed him one of her terrible looks. "I defy you to deny this. And it's simply beneath contempt."

Seeing how pale she had become, he cautioned himself to be careful and above all not to mention the British manner. "But, Mady, this is simply a mistake."

"It is no mistake. I never dreamed you might be capable of this."

"But I don't know what you're talking about."

Her voice began to rise and tremble. She said fiercely, "You son-ofabitch! Don't give me this soft treatment. I know all your fucking tricks." Then she shrieked, "This must stop! I will not have a dick tailing me!" Staring, those marvelous eyes grew red.

"But why would I have you followed, Mady? I don't understand. What could I find out?"

"Now that man dogged my steps around F-Field's, all afternoon." She often stammered when she was enraged. "I waited in the l-l-ladies' room half an hour, and when I came out he was still there. Then in the I.C. tunnel . . . when I was buying f-f-flowers."

"Maybe it was only some fellow trying to pick you up. It's got nothing to do with me."

"That was a dick!" She clenched her fists. Her lips were frighteningly thin, and her whole body trembled. "He was sitting on the screen porch next door this afternoon when I got home."

Moses, pale, said, "You point him out, Mady. I'll go right up to him. . . . Just show the man to me."

Edvig termed this a paranoid episode, and Herzog said, "Really?" He took this in for a moment and then exclaimed, with a burst of feeling, looking at the doctor with large eyes, "Do you really think this was a delusion? Do you mean to tell me she's disturbed? Insane?"

Edvig said, conservatively, measuring his words, "One incident like this doesn't indicate insanity. I meant precisely what I said, a paranoid episode."

"But it's she who's sick, sicker than I am."

Ah, poor girl! It was a clinical matter. She was really unwell. Toward the sick, Moses was always especially compassionate. He assured Edvig, "If she really is as you say, I'll have to watch my step. I must try to take care of her."

Charity, as if it didn't have enough trouble in this day and age, will always be suspected of morbidity—sado-masochism, perversity of some sort. All higher or moral tendencies lie under suspicion of being rackets. Things we simply honor with old words, but betray or deny in our very nerves. At any rate, Edvig did not congratulate Moses on his pledge to look after Madeleine.

"What I must do," said Edvig, "is inform her of this tendency."

But it did not seem to disturb Madeleine to be warned professionally against paranoid delusions. She said it wasn't exactly news to her that she was abnormal. In fact, she took the whole thing calmly. "Anyway, it'll never be boring," was what she said to Herzog.

The trouble was not over yet. For a week or two, Field's delivery truck was bringing jewelry, cigarette boxes, coats and dresses, lamps, carpets, almost daily. Madeleine could not recall making these purchases. In ten days she ran up a twelve-hundred-dollar bill. All these articles were choice, very beautiful—there was some satisfaction in that. She did things in style, even when unbalanced. As he sent them back, Moses felt very tender toward her. Edvig predicted that she would never lapse into a true psychosis, but would have such spells for the rest of her life. It was melancholy for Moses, but perhaps his sighs expressed some satisfaction too. It was possible.

The deliveries presently stopped. Madeleine turned back to her graduate studies. But one night, in the disorderly bedroom, when they were both naked, and Herzog, lifting the sheet, made a sharp remark about the old books underneath (big, dusty volumes of an ancient Russian encyclopedia), it was too much for her. She began to scream at him, and threw herself on the bed, tearing off blankets and sheets, slamming books on the floor, then attacking the pillows with her nails, giving a wild, choked scream. There was a plastic cover on the mattress, and this she clutched and twisted, still cursing him shrilly, inarticulate, an odd white grime in the corners of her mouth.

Herzog picked up the overturned lamp. "Madeleine—don't you think you ought to take something . . . for this?" Stupidly, he reached out a hand to soothe her, and at once she straightened and hit him in the face, too clumsily to hurt him. She jumped at him with her fists, not pummeling womanlike, but swinging like a street fighter with her knuckles. Herzog turned and took these blows on his back. It was necessary. She was sick.

Maybe it's just as well that I didn't hit her. I might have won back her love. But I can tell you that my meekness during these crises infuriated her, as if I was trying to beat her at the religious game. I know you discussed agapé with her, and similar high ideas, but the least sign of the same in me put her in a frenzy. She thought I was a faker. For in her paranoid mind I was disintegrated into my primitive elements. This is why I suggest her attitude might have changed if I had belted her. Paranoia is perhaps the normal state of mind in savages. And if my soul, out of season, out of place, experienced these higher emotions, I could get no credit for them anyway. Not from you, with your attitudes toward good intentions. I've read your stuff about the psychological real-

ism of Calvin. I hope you don't mind my saying that it reveals a lousy, cringing, grudging conception of human nature. This is how I see your Protestant Freudianism.

Edvig sat calmly through Herzog's description of the assault in the bedroom, smiling a bit. Then he said, "Why do you suppose it happened?"

"Something about the books, maybe. Interference with her studies. If I say the house is dirty, it stinks, she thinks I'm criticizing her mind and forcing her back into housework. Disrespectful of her rights as a person . . ."

Edvig's emotional responses were unsatisfactory. When he needed a feeling reaction, Herzog had to get it from Valentine Gersbach. Accordingly, he took his troubles to him. But first, ringing Gersbach's doorbell, he had to face the coldness (he couldn't understand it) of Phoebe Gersbach, who answered. She was looking very gaunt, dry, pale, strained. Of course—the Connecticut landscape raced, rose, contracted, opened its depths, and the Atlantic water shone—of course, Phoebe knew her husband was sleeping with Madeleine. And Phoebe had only one business in life, one aim, to keep her husband and protect her child. Answering the bell, she opened the door on foolish, feeling, suffering Herzog. He had come to see his friend.

Phoebe was not strong; her energy was limited; she must have been past the point of irony. And as for pity, what would she have pitied him for? Not adultery—that was too common to be taken seriously by either of them. Anyway, to her, having Madeleine's body could never seem a big deal. She might have pitied Herzog's stupid eggheadedness, his clumsy way of putting his troubles into high-minded categories; or simply his suffering. But she probably had only enough feeling for the conduct of her own life, and no more. Moses was sure that she blamed him for aggravating Valentine's ambitions—Gersbach the public figure, Gersbach the poet, the television-intellectual, lecturing at the Hadassah on Martin Buber. Herzog himself had introduced him to cultural Chicago.

"Val's in his room," she said. "Excuse me, I've got to get the kid ready for Temple."

Gersbach was putting up bookshelves. Deliberate, heavy, slow-moving, he measured the wood, the wall, and jotted figures on the plaster. He handled the level masterfully, looked over the toggle bolts. With his thick, ruddy-dark, judicious face and his broad chest and his artificial leg which made him stand tilted, he concentrated on the choice of a bit for the electric drill as he listened to Herzog's account of Madeleine's strange assault.

"We were getting into bed."

"Well?" He made an effort to be patient.

"Both naked."

"Did you try anything?" said Gersbach. A severe note entered his voice.

"Me? No. She's built a wall of Russian books around herself. Vladimir of Kiev, Tikhon Zadonsky. In my bed! It's not enough they persecuted my ancestors! She ransacks the library. Stuff from the bottom of the stacks nobody has taken out in fifty years. The sheets are full of crumbs of yellow paper."

"Have you been complaining again?"

"Maybe I have, a little. Eggshells, chop bones, tin cans under the table, under the sofa. . . . It's bad for June."

"There's your mistake! Right there—she can't bear that nagging, put-upon tone. If you expect me to help straighten this out, I've got to tell you. You and she—it's no secret from anybody—are the two people I love most. So I must warn you, *chaver,* get off the lousy details. Just knock off all chicken shit, and be absolutely level and serious."

"I know," said Herzog, "she's going through a long crisis—finding herself. And I know I have a bad tone, sometimes. I've gone over this ground with Edvig. But Sunday night . . ."

"Are you sure you didn't make a pass?"

"No. It so happens we had intercourse the night before."

Gersbach seemed extremely angry. He gazed at Moses with burning ruddy-dark eyes and said, "I didn't ask you that. My question was only about Sunday night. You've got to learn what the score is, God damn it! If you don't level with me, I can't do a frigging thing for you."

"Why shouldn't I level with you?" Moses was astonished by this vehemence, by Gersbach's fierce, glowing look.

"You don't. You're damn evasive."

Moses considered the charge under Gersbach's intense red-brown gaze. He had the eyes of a prophet, a *Shofat,* yes, a judge in Israel, a king. A mysterious person, Valentine Gersbach. "We had intercourse the night before. But as soon as it was done she turned on the light, picked up one of those dusty Russian folios, put it on her chest, and started to read away. As I was leaving her body, she was reaching for the book. Not a kiss. Not a last touch. Only her nose, twitching."

Valentine gave a faint smile. "Maybe you should sleep separately."

"I could move into the kid's room, I suppose. But June is restless as it is. She wanders around at night in her Denton sleepers. I wake up and find her by my bed. Often wet. She's feeling the strain."

"Now knock it off, about the kid. Don't use her in this."

Herzog bowed his head. He felt threatened by tears. Gersbach sighed and walked along his wall slowly, bending and straightening like a gondolier. "I explained to you last week . . ." he said.

"You'd better tell me once more. I'm in a state," said Herzog.

"Now you listen to me. We'll go over the ground again."

Grief greatly damaged—it positively wounded—Herzog's handsome face. Anyone he had ever injured by his conceit might now feel revenged to see how ravaged he looked. The change was almost ludicrous. And the lectures Gersbach read him—those were so spirited, so vehement, gross, they were ludicrous, too, a parody of the intellectual's desire for higher meaning, depth, quality. Moses sat by the window in raw sunlight, listening. The drapery with gilt-grooved rods lay on the table with planks and books. "One thing you can be sure, *bruder*," said Valentine. "I have no ax to grind. In this thing, I just have no prejudice." Valentine loved to use Yiddish expressions, to misuse them, rather. Herzog's Yiddish background was genteel. He heard with instinctive snobbery Valentine's butcher's, teamster's, commoner's accent, and he put himself down for it—My God! those ancient family prejudices, absurdities from a lost world. "Let's cut out all the *shtick*," said Gersbach. "Let's say you're a crumb. Let's say even you're a criminal. There's nothing—nothing!—you could do to shake my friendship. That's no shit, and you know it! I can take what you've done to me."

Moses, astonished again, said, "What have I done to you?"

"Hell with that. *Hob es in drerd*. I know Mady is a bitch. And maybe you think I never wanted to kick Phoebe in the ass. That *klippa*! But that's the female nature." He shook his abundant hair into place. It had fiery-dark depths. At the back it was brutally barbered. "You've taken care of her for some time, okay, I know. But if she's got a disgusting father and a *kvetsch* of a mother, what else should a man do? And expect nothing in return."

"Well, of course. But I spent twenty grand in about a year. Everything I inherited. Now we've got this rotten hole on Lake Park with the I.C. trains passing all night. The pipes stink. The house is all trash and garbage and Russian books and the kid's unwashed clothes. And there I am, returning Coke bottles and vacuuming, burning paper and picking up veal bones."

"The bitch is testing you. You're an important professor, invited to conferences, with an international correspondence. She wants you to admit her importance. You're a *ferimmter mensch.*"

Moses, to save his soul, could not let this pass. He said quietly, "*Berimmter.*"

"*Fe—be,* who cares. Maybe it's not so much your reputation as your egotism. You could be a real *mensch.* You've got it in you. But you're effing it up with all this egotistical shit. It's a big deal— such a valuable person dying for love. Grief. It's a lot of bull!"

Dealing with Valentine was like dealing with a king. He had a thick grip. He might have held a scepter. He *was* a king, an emotional king, and the depth of his heart was his kingdom. He appropriated all the emotions about him, as if by divine or spiritual right. He could do more with them, and therefore he simply took them over. He was a big man, too big for anything but the truth. (Again, the truth!) Herzog had a weakness for grandeur, and even bogus grandeur (was it ever entirely bogus?).

They went out to clear their heads in the fresh winter air. Gersbach in his great storm coat, belted, bareheaded, exhaling vapor, kicking through the snow with the all-battering leg. Moses held down the brim of his dead-green velours hat. His eyes couldn't bear the glitter.

Valentine spoke as a man who had risen from terrible defeat, the survivor of sufferings few could comprehend. His father had died of sclerosis. He'd get it, too, and expected to die of it. He spoke of death majestically—there was no other word for it—his eyes amazingly spirited, large, rich, keen, or, thought Herzog, like the broth of his soul, hot and shining.

"Why when I lost my leg," said Gersbach. "Seven years old, in Saratoga Springs, running after the balloon man; he blew his little *fifel*. When I took that short cut through the freight yards, crawling under cars. Lucky the brakeman found me as soon as the wheel took off my leg. Wrapped me in his coat and rushed me to the hospital. When I came to, my nose was bleeding. Alone in the room." Moses listened, white, the frost did not change his color. "I leaned over," Gersbach went on, as if relating a miracle. "A drop of blood fell on the floor, and as it splashed I saw a little mouse under the bed who seemed to be staring at the splash. It backed away, it moved its tail and whiskers. And the room was just full of bright sunlight. . . ." (There are storms on the sun itself, but here all is peaceful and temperate, thought Moses.) "It was a little world, underneath the bed. Then I realized that my leg was gone."

Valentine would have denied that the tears in his eyes were for himself. No: curse *that,* he'd have said. Not for him. They were for that little kid. There were stories about himself, too, that Moses had told a hundred times, so he couldn't complain of Gersbach's repetitiveness. Each man has his own batch of poems. But Gersbach almost always cried, and it was strange, because his long curling coppery lashes stuck together; he was tender but he looked rough, his face broad and rugged, heavy-bristled, and his chin positively brutal. And Moses recognized that under his own rules the man who had suffered more was more special, and he conceded willingly that Gersbach had suffered harder, that his agony under the wheels of the boxcar must have been far deeper than anything Moses had ever suffered. Gersbach's tormented face was stony white, pierced by the radiant bristles of his red beard. His lower lip had almost disappeared beneath the upper. His great, his hot sorrow! Molten sorrow!

Dr. Edvig, Herzog wrote, *Your opinion, repeated many times, is that Madeleine has a deeply religious nature. At the time of her conversion, before we were married, I went to church with her more than once. I clearly remember . . . In New York . . .*

At her insistence. One morning when Herzog brought her to the church door in a cab she said he had to come in. He must. She said no relationship between them was possible if he didn't respect her faith. "But I don't know anything about churches," said Moses.

She got out of the cab and went up the stairs quickly, expecting that he would follow. He paid the driver and caught up with her.

62

She pushed the swinging door open with her shoulder. She put her hand in the font and crossed herself, as if she'd been doing it all her life. She'd learned that in the movies, probably. But the look of terrible eagerness and twisted perplexity and appeal on her face—where did that come from? Madeleine in her gray suit with the squirrel collar, her large hat, hurried forward on high heels. He followed slowly, holding his salt-and-pepper topcoat at the neck as he took off his hat. Madeleine's body seemed gathered upward in the breast and shoulders, and her face was red with excitement. Her hair was pulled back severely under the hat but escaped in wisps to form sidelocks. The church was a new building—small, cold, dark, the varnish shining hard on the oak pews, and blots of flame standing motionless near the altar. Madeleine genuflected in the aisle. Only it was more than genuflection. She sank, she cast herself down, she wanted to spread herself on the floor and press her heart to the boards—he recognized that. Shading his face on both sides, like a horse in blinders, he sat in the pew. What was he doing here? He was a husband, a father. He was married, he was a Jew. Why was he in church?

The bells tinged. The priest, quick and arid, rattled off the Latin. In the responses, Madeleine's high clear voice led the rest. She crossed herself. She genuflected in the aisle. And then they were in the street again and her face had recovered its normal color. She smiled and said, "Let's go to a nice place for breakfast."

Moses told the cabbie to go to the Plaza.

"But I'm not dressed for it," she said.

"In that case I'll take you to Steinberg's Dairy, which I prefer anyway."

But Madeleine was putting on lipstick, and fluffing out her blouse, and checking her hat. How lovely she could be! Her face was gay and round, pink, the blue of her eyes was clear. Very different from the terrifying menstrual ice of her rages, the look of the murderess. The doorman ran down from his rococo shelter in front of the Plaza. The wind was blowing hard. She swept into the lobby. Palms and pink-toned carpets, gilding, footmen . . .

I don't quite understand what you mean by "religious." A religious woman may find she doesn't love her lover or her husband. But what if she should hate him? What if she should wish continually for his death? What if she should wish it most fervently when

63

they were making love? What if in the act of love he should see that wish shining in her blue eyes like a maiden's prayer? Now, I am not simple-minded, Dr. Edvig. I often wish I were. It hardly does much good to have a complex mind without actually being a philosopher. I don't expect a religious woman to be lovable, a saintly pussycat. But I would like to know how you decided that she is deeply religious.

Somehow I got into a religious competition. You and Madeleine and Valentine Gersbach all talking religion to me—so I tried it out. To see how it would feel to act with humility. As though such idiotic passivity or masochistic crawling or cowardice were humility, or obedience, not terrible decadence. Loathsome! O, patient Griselda Herzog! I put up the storm windows as an act of love, and left my child well provided, paying the rent and the fuel and the phone and insurance, and packing my valise. As soon as I was gone, Madeleine, your saint, sent my picture to the cops. If I ever set foot on the porch again to see my daughter, she was going to call the squad car. She had a warrant ready. The kid was brought to me, and taken home, by Valentine Gersbach, who also gave me advice and consolation, religion. He brought me books (by Martin Buber). He commanded me to study them. I sat reading I and Thou, Between God and Man, The Prophetic Faith *in a nervous fever. Then we discussed them.*

I'm sure you know the views of Buber. It is wrong to turn a man (a subject) into a thing (an object). By means of spiritual dialogue, the I-It relationship becomes an I-Thou relationship. God comes and goes in man's soul. And men come and go in each other's souls. Sometimes they come and go in each other's beds, too. You have dialogue with a man. You have intercourse with his wife. You hold the poor fellow's hand. You look into his eyes. You give him consolation. All the while, you rearrange his life. You even make out his budget for years to come. You deprive him of his daughter. And somehow it is all mysteriously translated into religious depth. And finally your suffering is greater than his, too, because you are the greater sinner. And so you've got him, coming and going. You told me my hostile suspicions of Gersbach were unfounded, even, you hinted, paranoid. Did you know he was Madeleine's lover? Did she tell you? No, or you wouldn't have said that. She had good reason to fear being followed by a private in-

vestigator. There was nothing at all neurotic about it. Madeleine, your patient, told you what she liked. You knew nothing. You know nothing. She snowed you completely. And you fell in love with her yourself, didn't you? Just as she planned. She wanted you to help her dump me. She would have done it in any case. She found you, however, a useful instrument. As for me, I was your patient. . . .

DEAR *Governor Stevenson,*
Herzog wrote, gripping his seat in the hurtling train, *Just a word with you, friend. I supported you in 1952. Like many others I thought this country might be ready for its great age in the world and intelligence at last assert itself in public affairs—a little more of Emerson's* American Scholar, *the intellectuals coming into their own. But the instinct of the people was to reject mentality and its images, ideas, perhaps mistrusting them as foreign. It preferred to put its trust in visible goods. So things go on as before with those who think a great deal and effect nothing, and those who think nothing evidently doing it all. You might as well be working for them, I suppose. I am sure the Coriolanus bit was painful, kissing the asses of the voters, especially in cold states like New Hampshire. Perhaps you did contribute something useful in the last decade, showing up the old-fashioned self-intensity of the "humanist," the look of the "intelligent man" grieving at the loss of his private life, sacrificed to public service. Bah! The general won because he expressed low-grade universal potato love.*

Well, Herzog, what do you want? An angel from the skies? This train would run him over.

Dear Ramona, you mustn't think because I've taken a powder, briefly, that I don't care for you. I do! I feel you close about me, much of the time. And last week, at that party, when I saw you across the room in your hat with flowers, your hair crowded down close to your bright cheeks, I had a glimpse of what it might be like to love you.

He exclaimed mentally, Marry me! Be my wife! End my troubles! —and was staggered by his rashness, his weakness, and by the characteristic nature of such an outburst, for he saw how very neurotic and typical it was. We must be what we are. That is necessity. And what are we? Well, here he was trying to hold on to Ramona as he ran from her. And thinking that he was binding her, he bound himself, and the culmination of this clever goofiness might be to entrap himself. Self-development, self-realization, happiness —these were the titles under which these lunacies occurred. Ah, poor fellow!—and Herzog momentarily joined the objective world in looking down on himself. He too could smile at Herzog and despise him. But there still remained the fact. *I* am Herzog. I have to *be* that man. There is no one else to do it. After smiling, he must return to his own Self and see the thing through. But there was a brainstorm for you—the third Mrs. Herzog! This was what infantile fixations did to you, early traumata, which a man could not molt and leave empty on the bushes like a cicada. No true individual has existed yet, able to live, able to die. Only diseased, tragic, or dismal and ludicrous fools who sometimes hoped to achieve some ideal by fiat, by their great desire for it. But usually by bullying all mankind into believing them.

From many points of view, Ramona truly was a desirable wife. She was understanding. Educated. Well situated in New York. Money. And sexually, a natural masterpiece. What breasts! Lovely ample shoulders. The belly deep. Legs brief and a little bowed but for that very reason especially attractive. It was all there. Only he was not through with love and hate elsewhere. Herzog had unfinished business.

Dear Zinka, I dreamed about you last week. In my dream we were taking a walk in Ljubljana, and I had to get my ticket for Trieste. I was sorry to leave. But it was better for you that I should. It was snowing. Actually, it did snow, not only in the dream. Even when I got to Venice. This year I covered half the world, and saw people in such numbers—it seems to me I saw everybody but the dead. Whom perhaps I was looking for. *Dear Mr. Nehru, I think I have a most important thing to tell you. Dear Mr. King, The Negroes of Alabama filled me with admiration. White America is in danger of being depoliticalized. Let us hope this example by Negroes will penetrate the hypnotic trance of the majority. The political question in modern democracies is one of the reality of public questions. Should all of these become matters of fantasy the old political order is ended. I for one wish to go on record recognizing the moral dignity of your group. Not the Powells, who want to be as corrupt as white demagogues, nor the Muslims building on hate.*

Dear Commissioner Wilson—I sat next to you at the Narcotics Conference last year—Herzog, a stocky fellow, dark eyes, scar on his neck, grizzled, in an Ivy League suit (selected by his wife), a bad cut (far too youthful for my figure). *I wonder if you will allow me to make a few observations on your police force? It's not the fault of any single person that civil order can't be maintained in a community. But I am concerned. I have a small daughter who lives near Jackson Park, and you know as well as I do the parks are not properly policed. Gangs of hoodlums make it worth your life to go in. Dear Mr. Alderman, Must the Army have its Nike missile site on the Point? Perfectly futile, I believe, obsolete, and taking up space. Plenty of other sites in the city. Why not move this useless junk to some blighted area?*

Quickly, quickly, more! The train rushed over the landscape. It swooped past New Haven. It ran with all its might toward Rhode Island. Herzog, now barely looking through the tinted, immovable, sealed window felt his eager, flying spirit streaming out, speaking, piercing, making clear judgments, uttering final explanations, necessary words only. He was in a whirling ecstasy. He felt at the same time that his judgments exposed the boundless, baseless bossiness and willfulness, the nagging embedded in his mental constitution.

Dear Moses E. Herzog, Since when have you taken such an interest in social questions, in the external world? Until lately, you led a life of innocent sloth. But suddenly a Faustian spirit of discontent and universal reform descends on you. Scolding. Invective.

Dear Sirs, The Information Service was kind enough to send a package from Belgrade containing articles of winter wear. I did not want to take my long-johns to Italy, the paradise of exiles, *and regretted it. It was snowing when I got to Venice. I couldn't get into the vaporetto with my valise.*

Dear Mr. Udall, A petroleum engineer I met recently in a Northwest jet told me our domestic oil reserves were almost used up and that plans had been completed for blasting the polar caps with hydrogen bombs to get at the oil beneath. What about that?

Shapiro!

Herzog had a lot to explain to Shapiro, and he was certainly waiting for his explanations. Shapiro was not good-humored although his face wore a good-humored look. His nose was sharp and angry and his lips appeared to be smiling away their anger. His cheeks were white and plump, and his thin hair was combed straight back, glistening in the Rudolph Valentino or Ricardo

68

Cortez style of the twenties. He had a dumpy figure, but wore natty clothes.

Still, Shapiro was in the right this time. *Shapiro, I should have written sooner to tell you . . . to apologize . . . to make amends. . . .* But I have a splendid excuse—trouble, sickness, disorder, afflictions. *You've written a fine monograph. I hope I made that clear in my review. My memory abandoned me complete in one place, and I was all wrong about Joachim da Floris.* You and Joachim must both forgive me. I was in a terrible state. Having agreed to review Shapiro's study before the trouble broke, Herzog couldn't get out of it. He dragged the heavy volume with him all over Europe in his valise. It caused much pain in his side; he feared a hernia from it, and also ran up considerable overweight charges. Herzog kept reading away at it for the sake of the discipline, and under a growing burden of guilt. Abed in Belgrade, at the Metropol, with bottles of cherry juice, the trolley cars whizzing past in the frozen night. *Finally, in Venice, I sat down and wrote my review.*

My excuse for the botch I made now follows:

I assume, since he's at Madison, Wisconsin, *you've heard that I blew up in Chicago last October. We left the house in Ludeyville some time ago. Madeleine wanted to finish her degree in Slavonic languages. She had about ten courses in linguistics to take, and she got interested also in Sanskrit. Perhaps you can guess how she would work at things—her interests, passions. Do you remember that when you came to see us in the country two years ago, we discussed Chicago?* Whether it would be safe to live in that slum.

Shapiro in his stylish pin-striped suit, pointed shoes, as if dressed for dinner, sat on Herzog's lawn. He has the profile of a thin man. His nose is sharp but his throat sags and his cheeks hang a little toward the lips. Shapiro is very courtly. And he was impressed with Madeleine. He thought her so beautiful, so intelligent. Well, she is. The conversation was spirited. Shapiro had come to see Moses ostensibly to get "advice"—actually to ask a favor—but he was enjoying Madeleine's company. She excited him and he was laughing as he drank his quinine water. The day was hot but he didn't loosen his conservative necktie. His sharp black shoes glistened; and he has fat feet, with bulging insteps. On the grass, mowed by himself, Moses sat in torn wash pants. Stirred by

Madeleine, Shapiro was particularly lively, almost shrieking when he laughed, and his laughter becoming more frequent, wilder, uncaused. His manner at the same time grew more formal, measured, judicious. He spoke in long sentences, Proustian he may have thought—actually Germanic, and filled with incredible bombast. "On balance, I should not venture to assay the merit of the tendency without more mature consideration," he was saying. Poor Shapiro! What a brute he was! That snarling, wild laugh of his, and the white froth forming on his lips as he attacked everyone. Madeleine was greatly stirred by him too, and on her high manners. They found each other exceedingly stimulating.

She came from the house with the bottles and glasses on the tray—cheese, liver paste, crackers, ice, herring. She had on blue trousers and a yellow Chinese blouse, the coolie hat I bought her on Fifth Avenue. She said she was subject to sunstroke. Stepping quickly, she advanced from the shadow of the house into the sparkling grass, the cat leaping from her path, the bottles and glasses clinking. She hastened because she didn't want to miss any of the conversation. As she bent to set things out on the lawn table, Shapiro couldn't keep his eyes from the shape of her behind in the tight cotton-knit fabric.

Madeleine, "stuck away in the woods," was avid for scholarly conversation. Shapiro knew the literature of every field—he read *all* the publications; he had accounts with book dealers all over the world. When he found that Madeleine was not only a beauty but was preparing for her doctoral examination in Slavonic languages, he said, "How delightful!" And it was he himself who knew, betraying the knowledge by affectation, that for a Russian Jew from Chicago's West Side that "How delightful!" was inappropriate. A German Jew from Kenwood might have gotten away with it—old money, in the dry-goods business since 1880. But Shapiro's father had had no money, and peddled rotten apples from South Water Street in a wagon. There was more of the truth of life in those spotted, spoiled apples, and in old Shapiro, who smelled of the horse and of produce, than in all of these learned references.

Madeleine and the dignified visitor were talking about the Russian Church, Tikhon Zadonsky, Dostoevski, and Herzen. Shapiro made a great production of learned references, correctly pronouncing all foreign words whether in French, German, Serbian,

Italian, Hungarian, Turkish, or Danish, snapping them out and laughing—that hearty, sucking, snarling, undirected laugh, teeth moist, head worked back onto his shoulders. Ha! The thorns crackled. ("Like the crackling of thorns under a pot is the laughter of fools.") The cicadas in great numbers were singing. That year, they came out of the ground.

Under such stimulation, Mady's face did strange things. The tip of her nose moved, and her brows, which needed no help from cosmetics, rose with nervous eagerness, repeatedly, as if she were trying to clear her eyesight. Dr. Edvig said this was a diagnostic trait of paranoia. Beneath the huge trees, surrounded by the Berkshire slopes, with not another house in sight to spoil the view, the grass was fresh and dense, the slender, fine grass of June. The red-eyed cicadas, squat forms vividly colored, were wet after molting, sopping, immobile; but drying, they crept, hopped, tumbled, flew, and in the high trees kept up a continuous chain of song, shrilling.

Culture—ideas—had taken the place of the Church in Mady's heart (a strange organ that must be!). Herzog sat thinking his own thoughts on the grass in Ludeyville, his wash pants torn, feet bare, but his face that of an educated Jewish gentleman with fine lips, dark eyes. He watched his wife, on whom he doted (with a troubled, angry heart, another oddity among hearts) as she revealed the wealth of her mind to Shapiro.

"My Russian is not what it could be," said Shapiro.

"But how much you know about my subject," Madeleine said. She was very happy. The blood glowed in her face, and her blue eyes were warm and brilliant.

They opened a new subject—the Revolution of 1848. Shapiro had sweated through his starched collar. Only a dollar-crazed Croatian steelworker would have bought such a striped shirt. And what were his views of Bakunin, Kropotkin? Did he know Comfort's work? He did. Did he know Poggioli? Yes. He didn't feel that Poggioli had done full justice to certain important figures—Rozanov, for instance. Though Rozanov was cracked on certain questions, like the Jewish ritual bath, still he was a great figure, and his erotic mysticism was highly original—highly. Leave it to those Russians. What hadn't they done for Western Civilization, all the while repudiating the West and ridiculing it! Madeleine, Herzog thought, became almost dangerously excited. He could tell, when her voice grew reedy, when her throat sounded positively like a clarinet, that she was bursting with ideas and feelings. And if Moses did not join in, if he sat there, in her own words, like a clunk, bored, resentful, he proved he didn't respect her intelligence. Now Gersbach always boomed along in conversation. He was so emphatic in style, so impressive in his glances, looked so clever that you forgot to inquire whether he was making sense.

The lawn was on an elevation with a view of fields and woods. Formed like a large teardrop of green, it had a gray elm at its small point, and the bark of the huge tree, dying of dutch blight, was purplish gray. Scant leaves for such a vast growth. An oriole's nest, in the shape of a gray heart, hung from twigs. God's veil over things makes them all riddles. If they were not all so particular, detailed, and very rich I might have more rest from them. But I am a prisoner of perception, a compulsory witness. They are too exciting. Meantime I dwell in yon house of dull boards. Herzog was worried about that elm. Must he cut it down? He hated to do it. Meanwhile the cicadas all vibrated a coil in their bellies, a horny posterior band in a special chamber. Those billions of red eyes from the enclosing woods looked out, stared down, and the steep waves of sound drowned the summer afternoon. Herzog had seldom heard anything so beautiful as this massed continual harshness.

Shapiro mentioned Soloviëv—the younger one. Did he really have a vision, in the British Museum, of all places? It so happened that Madeleine had made a study of the younger Soloviëv, and this was her opportunity. She had enough confidence now in Shapiro to speak freely—it would be appreciated, genuinely. She gave a brief lecture on the career and thought of this dead Russian. Her offended look passed over Moses. She complained that he never really listened to her. *He* wanted to shine all the time. But that wasn't it. He had heard her lecture on this subject many times, and far into the night. He didn't dare say he was sleepy. Anyway, it had to be *quid pro quo,* given these conditions—buried in the remote Berkshires—for he had to discuss knotty points of Rousseau and Hegel with her. He relied completely on her intellectual judgments. Before Soloviëv, she had talked of no one but Joseph de Maistre. And before de Maistre—Herzog made up the list—the French Revolution, Eleanor of Aquitaine, Schliemann's excavations at Troy, extrasensory perception, then tarot cards, then Christian Science, before that, Mirabeau; or was it mystery novels (Josephine Tey), or science fiction (Isaac Asimov)? The intensity was always high. If she had one constant interest it was murder mysteries. Three or four a day, she'd read.

Black and hot under the green, the soil gave off its dampness. Herzog felt it in his bare feet.

From Soloviëv, Mady naturally turned to Berdyaev, and while speaking of *Slavery and Freedom*—the concept of *Sobornost*—she opened the jar of pickled herring. Saliva spurted to Shapiro's lips. Quickly, he pressed his folded handkerchief to the corners of his mouth. Herzog remembered him as a greedy eater. In the cubicle they had shared at school, he used to chew his pumpernickel-and-onion sandwiches with an open mouth. Now at the smell of spice and vinegar Shapiro's eyes flooded, though he managed to keep his portly, good-humored, sharp-nosed, refined look as he pressed the handkerchief to his shaven jowls. His plump hairless hand—his quivering fingers. "No, no," he said, "thank you very much, Mrs. Herzog. Delightful! But I have a stomach condition." Condition! He had ulcers. Vanity kept him from saying it; the psychosomatic implications were unflattering. Later that afternoon, he vomited in the wash basin. He must have eaten squid, thought Herzog, who had to do the cleaning up. Why didn't he use the toilet bowl—too stout to bend?

But that was in the aftermath of his visit. Before that, Moses recalled, there was a visit from the Gersbachs, Valentine and Phoebe. They stopped their little car under the catalpa tree—then in flower, though last year's pods still hung from the twigs. Out came Valentine, in his swaying stride, and Phoebe, pale at every season of the year, calling after him in her complaining voice, "Val —Va-al." She was returning a casserole she had borrowed, one of Madeleine's great iron pots, red as lobster shell—Descoware, made in Belgium. These visits often gave Herzog a depressed feeling he couldn't account for. Madeleine sent him for more folding chairs. Perhaps it was the rotted honey fragrance of the white catalpa bells that got him. Faintly lined with pink within, heavy with pollen dust, they dropped on the gravel. Too beautiful! Little Ephraim

Gersbach was making a pile of bells. Moses was glad to go for the chairs, into the musty disorder of the house, down to the stony deaf security of the cellar. He took his time about the chairs.

When he returned, they were speaking of Chicago. Gersbach, standing with his hands in his hip pockets, his face just shaved and his plumelike hair revealing heavy copper depths, was saying that his advice was to get the hell out of this backwater. Nothing interesting had happened here since the Battle of Saratoga, over the hills, for Christ's sake. Phoebe, looking tired and pale, smoked her cigarette, faintly smiling, and hoping, probably, to be let alone. Among assertive, learned, or eloquent people, she seemed to feel her dowdiness and insufficiency. Actually she was far from stupid. She had fine eyes, a bosom, good legs. If only she didn't make herself look like the head nurse, letting her dimples lengthen into disciplinary creases.

"Chicago, by all means!" said Shapiro. "That's the school for graduate studies. A little woman like Mrs. Herzog is just what the old place needs, too."

Fill your big mouth with herring, Shapiro! Herzog thought, and mind your own fucking business. Madeleine gave her husband a rapid sidelong look. She was flattered, happy. She wanted him to be reminded, if he had forgotten, how high a value other people set upon her.

Anyway, Shapiro, I was in no mood for Joachim da Floris and the hidden destiny of Man. Nothing seemed especially hidden—it was all painfully clear. Listen, you said long ago, already pompous as a young student, that someday we would "join issue," meaning there were important differences between us even then. I think it must have started in that seminar on Proudhon and the long arguments we had, back and forth with old Larson, about the decay of the religious foundations of civilization. Are all the traditions used up, the beliefs done for, the consciousness of the masses not yet ready for the next development? Is this the full crisis of dissolution? Has the filthy moment come when moral feeling dies, conscience disintegrates, and respect for liberty, law, public decency, all the rest, collapses in cowardice, decadence, blood? Old Proudhon's visions of darkness and evil can't be passed over. But we mustn't forget how quickly the visions of genius become the canned goods of the intellectuals. The canned sauerkraut of Spengler's

"Prussian Socialism," the commonplaces of the Wasteland outlook, the cheap mental stimulants of Alienation, the cant and rant of pipsqueaks about Inauthenticity and Forlornness. I can't accept this foolish dreariness. We are talking about the whole life of mankind. The subject is too great, too deep for such weakness, cowardice—too deep, too great, Shapiro. It torments me to insanity that you should be so misled. A merely aesthetic critique of modern history! After the wars and mass killings! You are too intelligent for this. You inherited rich blood. Your father peddled apples.

I don't pretend that my position, on the other hand, is easy. We are survivors, in this age, so theories of progress ill become us, because we are intimately acquainted with the costs. To realize that you are a survivor is a shock. At the realization of such election, you feel like bursting into tears. As the dead go their way, you want to call to them, but they depart in a black cloud of faces, souls. They flow out in smoke from the extermination chimneys, and leave you in the clear light of historical success—the technical success of the West. Then you know with a crash of the blood that mankind is making it—making it in glory though deafened by the explosions of blood. Unified by the horrible wars, instructed in our brutal stupidity by revolutions, by engineered famines directed by "ideologists" (heirs of Marx and Hegel and trained in the cunning of reason), perhaps we, modern humankind (can it be!), have done the nearly impossible, namely, learned something. You know that the decline and doom of civilization refuses to follow the model of antiquity. The old empires are shattered but those same one-time powers are richer than ever. I don't say that the prosperity of Germany is altogether agreeable to contemplate. But there it is, less than twenty years after the demonic nihilism of Hitler destroyed it. And France? England? No, the analogy of the decline and fall of the classical world will not hold for us. Something else is happening, and that something lies closer to the vision of Comte—the results of rationally organized labor—than to that of Spengler. Of all the evils of standardization in the old bourgeois Europe of Spengler, perhaps the worst was the standardized pedantry of the Spenglers themselves—this coarse truculence born in the Gymnasium, in cultural drill administered by an old-fashioned bureaucracy.

I intended in the country to write another chapter in the history

*of Romanticism as the form taken by plebeian envy and ambition
in modern Europe. Emergent plebeian classes fought for food,
power, sexual privileges, of course. But they fought also to inherit
the aristocratic dignity of the old regimes, which in the modern
age might have claimed the right to speak of decline. In the sphere
of culture the newly risen educated classes caused confusion between aesthetic and moral judgments. They began with anger over
the industrial defilement of landscapes (Ruskin's British "Vales
of Tempe") and ended by losing sight of the old-fashioned moral
characteristics of the Ruskins. Reaching at last the point of denying
the humanity of the industrialized, "banalized" masses. It was easy
for the Wastelanders to be assimilated to totalitarianism. Here the
responsibility of artists remains to be assessed. To have assumed,
for instance, that the deterioration of language and its debasement
was tantamount to dehumanization led straight to cultural fascism.*

*I planned also to consider the whole question of models, of
imitatio, in the history of civilization. After long study of the ancien
régime I was ready to risk a theory concerning the effects of the
high traditions of the court, the politics, the theater of Louis XIV
on French (and therefore European) personality. Circumstances
of bourgeois privacy in the modern age deprived individuals of
scope for Grand Passions, and it is here that one of the most fascinating but least amiable tendencies of the Romantics develops.
(One of the results of this sort of personal drama is that, to the
colonial world, Western Civilization dramatized itself as Aristocratic.) I had a chapter in progress, when you visited, called "The
American Gentleman," a short history of social climbing. And there
was I, myself, in Ludeyville, as Squire Herzog. The Graf Pototsky of the Berkshires. It was quite a funny twist of events, Shapiro.
While you and Madeleine were tossing your heads, coquetting,
bragging, showing off your clean sharp teeth—the learned badinage
—I was trying to take stock of my position. I understood that
Madeleine's ambition was to take my place in the learned world. To
overcome me. She was reaching her final elevation, as queen of the
intellectuals, the castiron bluestocking. And your friend Herzog
writhing under this sharp elegant heel.*

*Ah, Shapiro, the victor of Waterloo drew apart to shed bitter
tears for the dead (slain under his orders). Not so my ex-Missis.*

She does not live between two contradictory Testaments. She is stronger than Wellington. She wants to live in the delirious professions, as Valéry calls them—trades in which the main instrument is your opinion of yourself and the raw material is your reputation or standing.

As for your book, there is too much imaginary history in it. Much of it is simply utopian fiction. I will never change my mind about that. Nevertheless, I thought your idea about milleniarianism and paranoia very good. Madeleine, by the way, lured me out of the learned world, got in herself, slammed the door, and is still in there, gossiping about me.

It was not terribly original, this idea of Shapiro's, but he did a good clear job. *In my review I tried to suggest that clinical psychologists might write fascinating histories. Put professionals out of business. Megalomania for the Pharaohs and Caesars. Melancholia in the Middle Ages. Schizophrenia in the eighteenth century. And then this Bulgarian, Banowitch, seeing all power struggles in terms of paranoid mentality*—a curious, creepy mind, that one, convinced that madness always rules the world. The Dictator must have living crowds and also a crowd of corpses. The vision of mankind as a lot of cannibals, running in packs, gibbering, bewailing its own murders, pressing out the living world as dead excrement. Do not deceive yourself, dear Moses Elkanah, with childish jingles and Mother Goose. Hearts quaking with cheap and feeble charity or oozing potato love have not written history. Shapiro's snarling teeth, his salivating greed, the dagger of an ulcer in his belly give him true insights, too. Fountains of human blood that squirted from fresh graves! Limitless massacre! I never understood it!

I took a list of the traits of paranoia from a psychiatrist recently—I asked him to jot them down for me. It might aid my understanding, I thought. He did this willingly. I put the scribbled paper in my wallet and studied it like the plagues of Egypt. Just like "DOM, SFARDEYA, KINNIM" in the Haggadah. It read "Pride, Anger, Excessive 'Rationality,' Homosexual Inclinations, Competitiveness, Mistrust of Emotion, Inability to Bear Criticism, Hostile Projections, Delusions." It's all ·there—all! I've thought about Mady in every category, and though the portrait isn't yet complete

77

I know I can't abandon a tiny child to her. Mady is no Daisy. Daisy is a strict, moody woman, but dependable. Marco has come through all right.

Abandoning the letter to Shapiro—it raised too many painful thoughts, and this was precisely the sort of thing he must avoid if he was not to lose the benefit of a holiday—he turned to his brother Alexander. *Dear Shura,* he wrote, *I think I owe you 1500 bucks. How about making it a round 2000. I need it. In the process of pulling myself together.* Shura was a generous brother. The Herzogs had their characteristic family problems, but stinginess was not one of their traits. Moses knew that the rich man would push a button and say to his secretary, "Send a check to screwloose Moses Herzog." His handsome stout white-haired brother in his priceless suit, vicuña coat, Italian hat, his million-dollar shave and rosy manicured fingers with big rings, looking out of his limousine with princely hauteur. Shura knew everyone, paid off everyone, and despised everyone. Toward Moses his contempt was softened by family feeling. Shura was your true disciple of Thomas Hobbes. Universal concerns were idiocy. Ask nothing better than to prosper in the belly of Leviathan and set a hedonistic example to the community. It amused Shura that his brother Moses should be so fond of him. Moses loved his relatives quite openly and even helplessly. His brother Willie, his sister Helen, even the cousins. It was childish of him; he knew that. He could only sigh at himself, that he should be so undeveloped on that significant side of his nature. He sometimes tried to think, in his own vocabulary, whether this might be his archaic aspect, prehistoric. Tribal, you know. Associated with ancestor worship and totemism.

Also, as I have been having legal troubles, I wonder whether you could recommend a lawyer. Perhaps one of Shura's own legal staff who would not charge Moses for his services.

He now composed a letter in his head to Sandor Himmelstein, the Chicago lawyer who had looked after him last autumn, after Madeleine put him out of the house. *Sandor! Last time we were in touch, I wrote from Turkey. Of all places!* And yet that suited Sandor, in a way; it was Arabian Nights country and Sandor himself might have come out of a bazaar, for all that he had his office on the fourteenth floor of the Burnham Building, up the street

78

from City Hall. Herzog had met him in the steam bath at Postl's Health Club, at Randolph and Wells. He was a short man, misshapen from the loss of part of his chest. In Normandy, he always said. He had probably been a sort of large dwarf when he enlisted. It must have been possible to get a commission in the Judge Advocate's branch though a dwarf. It made Herzog uneasy, perhaps, that he had been discharged from the Navy owing to his asthma and never saw action. Whereas this dwarf and hunchback was disabled by a mine near the beachhead. The wound had made a hunchback of him. Anyway, that was Sandor, with a proud, sharp, handsome face, pale mouth and sallow skin, grand nose, thin gray hair. *In Turkey I was in sad condition.* Partly, again, the weather. Spring was struggling to come in, but the winds changed. The sky closed over the white mosques. It snowed. The trousered, mannish Turkish women veiled their stern faces. I never expected to see them striding so powerfully. Coal had been dumped in the street, but the laborers had not appeared to shovel it, so the furnace was out. Herzog drank plum brandy and tea in the café, and chafed his hands and worked his toes inside his shoes to keep the blood going. He was worried about his circulation at that time. To see the early flowers covered by snow increased his gloom.

I sent you this belated bread-and-butter note, to thank you and Bea for taking me under your roof. Acquaintances, not old friends. I'm sure I was a terrible house guest. Sick and angry—broken by this lousy grief. Taking pills for my insomnia but still unable to sleep, going about drugged, and the whisky gave me tachycardia. I should have been in a padded cell. *Gratitude! I was deeply grateful.* But the politic gratitude of weakness, of the sufferer, furious underneath. Sandor took me over. I was inept. He moved me into his house, far south, ten blocks from the Illinois Central. Mady had kept the car, claiming she needed it for Junie, to take her to the zoo and the like.

Sandor said, "You won't mind sleeping next to the booze, I guess," for the cot was unfolded beside the bar. The room was full of Carmel Himmelstein's high-school crowd. "Get out!" Sandor cried shrilly at the adolescents. "Can't see through the goddamn cigarette smoke! Look at these Coke bottles filled with butts." He turned on the air-conditioner, and Moses, still red with the cold of the day, but with white circles under his eyes, held his valise, the same valise that now lay in his lap. Sandor cleared the glasses from several shelves. "Unpack, kid," he said. "Put your stuff here. We eat in twenty minutes. Good chow. Sauerbraten. Bea's specialty."

Obedient, Moses set out his things—toothbrush, razor, Desenex powder, sleeping pills, his socks, Shapiro's monograph, and an old pocket edition of Blake's poems. The slip of paper on which Dr. Edvig had listed the traits of paranoia was his bookmark.

After dinner, that first night in the Himmelsteins' living room, Herzog began reluctantly to understand that in accepting Sandor's hospitality he had made still another characteristic mistake.

"You'll get over this. That's all right. You'll make it," said Sandor. "I'll put my dough on you. You're my boy."

And Beatrice, with her black hair and her pretty pink mouth which needed no rouge, said, "Moses, we know how you must feel."

"The bitches come and the bitches go," said Sandor. "My whole practice, almost, is these bitches. You should know what they carry on, and what happens in this city of Chicago." He shook his heavy head and his lips came together with the pressure of disgust. "If she wants to go, fuck her! Let her go! You'll be okay. So you were a sucker! Big deal! Every man is a sucker for some type of broad. I always got clobbered by the blue-eyed kind, myself. But I had the sense to fall in love with this beautiful pair of brown eyes. Isn't she great?"

"She certainly is." It had to be said. And it was actually not too difficult. Moses had not lived forty-odd years without learning to get through these moments. Among narrow puritans, this is lying; but with civilized people only civility.

"I'll never know what she saw in a wreck like me. Anyway, Moses, you just stay with us for a while. At a time like this, you shouldn't be without friends. Sure, I know you have family of your own in this town. I see your brothers at Fritzl's. I talked to your middle brother just the other day."

"Willie."

"He's a fine fellow—very active in Jewish life, too," said Sandor. "Not like that *macher,* Alexander. Always some scandal about him. Now he's connected with the Juice racket, and next with Jimmy Hoffa, and then he's in with the Dirksen bunch. Well, okay, your brothers are big shots. But they'd make you eat your heart out. Here nobody'll ask any questions."

"With us you can just let yourself go," said Beatrice.

"Well, I don't understand this thing at all," said Moses. "Mady and I had our ups and downs from the start. But things were improving. Last spring we discussed the marriage and whether we were getting along well enough to continue—a practical question came up: whether I should tie myself up with a lease. She said that as soon as she finished her thesis we'd have a second child. . . ."

"I'll tell you," said Sandor. "It's your own frigging fault, too, if you want my opinion."

"Mine? What do you mean?"

"Because you're a highbrow and married a highbrow broad. Somewhere in every intellectual is a dumb prick. You guys can't answer your own questions—still, I see hope for you, Mose."

"What hope?"

"You're not like those other university phonies. You're a *mensch*. What good are those effing eggheads! It takes an ignorant bastard like me to fight liberal causes. Those silk-stocking Yale squares may have a picture of Learned Hand in the office, but when it comes to getting mixed up in Trumbull Park, or fighting those yellowbellies in Deerfield or standing up for a man like Tompkins—" Sandor was proud of his record in the case of Tompkins, a Negro in the postal service whom he had defended.

"Well, I suppose they were out to get Tompkins because he was a Negro," said Herzog. "But unfortunately, he was a drunk. You told me that yourself. And there was a question as to his competence."

"Don't go around repeating that," said Sandor. "It'll be used the wrong way. You going to blab what I told you confidentially? It was a question of justice. Aren't there any white drunks on civil service? Not much!"

"Sandor—Beatrice. I feel terrible. Another divorce—out again, at my time of life. I can't take it. I don't know . . . it feels like death."

"Shush, what are you talking!" said Sandor. "It's pitiful because of the kid, but you'll get over it."

At that time, when you thought, and I agreed, that I shouldn't be alone, perhaps I really should have been alone, Herzog wrote.

"Look, I'll handle the whole thing for you," Sandor assured him. "You'll come out of all this dreck smelling like a roast. Leave it to me, will you? Don't you trust me? You think I'm not leveling with you?"

I ought to have taken a room at the Quadrangle Club.

"You can't be left to yourself," said Sandor. "You're not the type. A human being! A *mensch!* Your heart has been shat on. And you have about as much practical sense as my ten-year-old, Sheldon, you poor bastard."

"I'm going to shake this off. I'm not going to be a victim. I hate the victim bit," said Moses.

Himmelstein sat in his wing chair, his feet tucked under his short belly. His eyes were moist, the color of freshly sliced cucumber, with fine lashes. He chewed a cigar. His ugly nails were polished. He had his manicure at the Palmer House. "A strong-minded bitch," he said. "Terrifically attractive. Loves to make up her mind. Once decided, decided forever. What a will power. It's a type."

"Still, she must have loved you once, Moses," said Bea. She spoke very, very slowly—that was her manner. Her dark brown eyes were set within strong orbital bones. Her lips were pink and vivid. Moses did not want to meet her gaze; he would have to hold it long and earnestly and nothing would come of it. He knew he had her sympathy but that she could never approve of him.

"I don't think she loved me," said Moses.

"I'm sure she did."

It was the middle-class female solidarity, defending a nice girl from charges of calculation and viciousness. Nice girls marry for love. But should they fall out of love, they must be free to love another. No decent husband will oppose the heart. This is orthodox. Not utterly bad. But a new orthodoxy. Anyway, thought Moses, he was in no position to quarrel with Beatrice. He was in her house, taking comfort from her.

"You don't know Madeleine," he said. "When I met her, she needed a lot of help. The sort only a husband can provide . . ."

I know how long—endless—people's stories are when they have grievances. And how tedious for everyone.

"I happen to think she's a nice person," said Bea. "At first she looked stuck-up and acted suspicious, but when I got to know her she turned out to be friendly and very nice. Basically, she must be a good person."

"Shit! People are nice, most of them. You've got to give 'em a chance," said Sandor, sallow and handsome.

"Mady planned it all out," said Herzog. "Why couldn't she break off before I signed the lease?"

"Because she has to keep a roof over the kid's head," said Sandor. "What do you expect?"

"What I *expect?*" Herzog stood up, struggling for words. His face was white, his eyes dilated, fixed. He stared at Sandor, who was seated like a sultan, the small heels gathered under his bulging belly. Then he became aware that Beatrice with her pretty, lusterless look was warning him not to anger Sandor. His blood pressure was liable to shoot up dangerously when he was crossed.

Herzog wrote, *I was thankful for your friendship. I was in a state, though. One of those states in which one makes great, impossible demands. In anger people become dictatorial. Hard to take.* I was trapped there. Sleeping next to the bar. My heart went out to poor Tompkins. No wonder he hit the bottle when Sandor took him over.

"You're not going to fight for the kid's custody, are you?" Sandor said to Herzog.

"Suppose I do?"

"Well," said Sandor, "speaking as a lawyer, I can see you with a jury. They'll look at Madeleine, blooming and lovely, then you, haggard and gray-haired, and bam! there goes your custody suit. That's the jury system. Dumber than cave men, those bastards—I know this isn't easy for you to hear, but I better say it. Guys at our time of life must face facts."

"Facts!" said Herzog, faint, groping, outraged.

"I know," said Sandor. "I'm ten years older. But after forty it's all the same. If you can get it up once a week, you should be grateful."

Beatrice tried to restrain Sandor, but he said, "Shut up." He then turned to Moses again, shaking his head so that it gradually sank toward his disfigured breast, and his shoulder blades jutted behind, coracoid through the white-on-white shirt. "What the fuck does *he* know what it is to face facts. All he wants is everybody should love him. If not, he's going to scream and holler. All

83

right! After D-Day, I lay smashed up in that effing limey hospital—a cripple. Why, Christ! I had to walk out under my own power. And what about his pal Valentine Gersbach? *There's* a man for you! That gimpy redhead knows what real suffering is. But he lives it up—three men with six legs couldn't get around like that effing peg-leg. It's okay, Bea—Moses can take it. Otherwise, he'd be just another Professor Jerk. I wouldn't even bother with the sonofabitch."

Herzog was incoherent with anger. "What do you mean? Should I die because of my hair? What *about* the child?"

"Now, don't stand there rubbing your hands like a goddamn fool—Christ, I hate a fool," Sandor shouted. His green eyes were violently clear, his lips were continually tensing. He must have been convinced that he was cutting the dead weight of deception from Herzog's soul, and his long white fingers, thumbs and forefingers worked nervously.

"What! Die? Hair? What the hell are you babbling! I only said they'd give the kid to a young mother."

"Madeleine put you up to that. She planted this, too. To keep me from suing."

"She *nothing!* I'm trying to tell you for your own good. This time, she calls the shots. She wins, and you lose. Maybe she wants somebody else."

"Does she? Did she tell you that?"

"She told me nothing. I said *maybe*. Now calm down. Pour him a drink, Bea. Out of his own bottle. He doesn't like Scotch."

Beatrice went to fetch Herzog's own bottle of Guckenheimer's 86 proof.

"Now," said Sandor, "stop this baloney. Don't be a clown, man." His look changed, and he let some kindness flow toward Herzog. "Well, when you suffer, you really suffer. You're a real, genuine old Jewish type that digs the emotions. I'll give you that. I understand it. I grew up on Sangamon Street, remember, when a Jew was still a Jew. I know about suffering—we're on the same identical network."

Herzog the passenger noted, *For the life of me, I couldn't understand. I often thought I was going to have apoplexy, to burst. The more comfort you gave me, the closer I came to death's door. But what was I doing? Why was I in your house?*

It must have been funny how I grieved. Looking from my room at the leafless weeds in back. Brown, delicate frames of ragweed. Milkweed with the discharged pods gaping. Or else gazing at the dark gray face of the television.

On Sunday morning, early, Sandor called Herzog into the living room. "Man," he said, "I found one hell of an insurance policy for you."

Moses, tying his robe about him as he came from his bed by the bar, didn't understand.

"What?"

"We can get you a terrific policy to cover the kid."

"What's this about?"

"I told you last week but you must've been thinking of other things. If you get sick, have an accident, lose an eye, even if you go nuts, Junie will be protected."

"But I'm going to Europe, and I have travel insurance."

"That's if you die. But here, even if you have a mental break-down and have to go to an institution the kid still gets her monthly support."

"Who says I'm breaking down?"

"Listen, you think I'm doing this for myself? I'm in the middle here," said Sandor, stamping a bare foot on the thick pile of the carpet.

Sunday, with gray fog from the lake and the ore boats lowing like waterborne cattle. You could hear the emptiness of the hulls. Herzog would have given anything to be a deckhand bound for Duluth.

"Either you want my legal advice or you don't," said Sandor. "I want to do the best for all of you. True?"

"Well, here I am to prove it. You've taken me into your house."

"Okay, so let's talk sense. With Madeleine you're not going to have trouble. She gets no alimony. She'll be married soon. I took her to lunch at Fritzel's, and guys who haven't given Sandor H. the time of day for years came running with a hard-on, tripping over themselves. That includes the rabbi of my temple. She's some dish."

"You're a lunatic. And I know what she is."

"What do you mean—she's less of a whore than most. We're all whores in this world, and don't you forget it. I know damn well *I'm* a whore. And you're an outstanding shnook, I realize. At least the eggheads tell me so. But I bet you a suit of clothes you're a whore, too."

"Do you know what a mass man is, Himmelstein?"

Sandor scowled. "How's that?"

"A mass man. A man of the crowd. The soul of the mob. Cutting everybody down to size."

"What soul of the mob! Don't get highfalutin. I'm talking facts, not shit."

"And you think a fact is what's nasty."

"Facts *are* nasty."

"You think they're true because they're nasty."

"And you—it's all too much for you. Who told you you were such a prince? Your mother did her own wash; you took boarders; your old man was a two-bit moonshiner. I know you Herzogs and your *Yiches*. Don't give me that hoity-toity. I'm a Kike myself and got my diploma in a stinking night school. Okay? Now let's both knock off this crap, dreamy boy."

Herzog, subdued, much shaken, had no answer. What had he come here for? Help? A forum for his anger? Indignation for his injustices? But it was Sandor's forum, not his. This fierce dwarf with protruding teeth and deep lines in his face. His lopsided breast protruded from his green pajama top. But this was Sandor's bad, angry state, thought Herzog. He could be attractive, too, generous, convivial, even witty. The lava of that heart may have pushed those ribs out of shape, and the force of that hellish tongue made his teeth protrude. Very well, Moshe Herzog—if you must be pitiable, sue for aid and succor, you will put yourself always, inevitably, in the hands of these angry spirits. Blasting you with their "truth." This is what your masochism means, *mein zisse n'shamele*. The good are attracted by men's perceptions and think not for themselves. You must cleanse the gates of vision by self-knowledge, by experience. Besides which, opposition is true friendship. So they tell me.

"You want to take care of your own kid, don't you?" said Sandor.

"Sure I do. But you told me the other day that I might as well forget about her, that she'd grow up a stranger to me."

"That's right. She won't even know you next time you see her."

Sandor was thinking of his own kids, those hamsters; not my daughter, made of finer clay. *She* won't forget me. "I don't believe it," said Herzog.

"As the lawyer, I have a social obligation to the child. I've got to protect her."

"*You?* I'm her father."

"You may crack up. Or else die."

"Mady is just as liable to die. Why don't we write the insurance on her?"

"She'd never let you. That's not part of the woman's deal. It's the man's deal."

"Not this man's. Madeleine swings her weight like a male. She made all these decisions to take the kid and throw me in the street. She thinks she can be both mother and father. I'll pay the premiums on *her* life."

Sandor suddenly began to yell. "I don't give a shit about her. I don't give a shit about you. I'm looking after that child."

"What makes you so sure I'll die first?"

"And is this the woman you love?" Sandor said in a lower tone. Apparently, he had remembered his dangerously high blood pressure. An elaborate effort occurred which involved his pale eyes, and his lips, and which pitted his chin. He said more evenly, "I'd take that policy myself if I could pass the physical. It would give me pleasure to croak and leave my Bea a rich widow. I'd like that."

"Then she could go to Miami, and dye her hair."

"That's right. While I turn green like an old penny, in my box, and she screws around. I don't grudge her."

"All right, Sandor—" said Herzog. He wanted to end this talk. "Just now I don't feel like making arrangements for my death."

"What's so great about your effing death?" Sandor cried. His figure straightened. He stood very close to Herzog, who was somewhat frightened by his shrillness and stared down, wide-eyed, at the face of his host. It was strong-cut and coarsely handsome. The small mustache bristled, a fierce green, milky poison rose to his eyes; his mouth twisted. "I'm getting out of this case!" Himmelstein began to scream.

"What's the matter with you!" Herzog said. "Where's Beatrice! Beatrice!"

But Mrs. Himmelstein only shut her bedroom door.

"She'll go to a shyster firm!"

"For God's sake, stop screaming."

"They'll kill you."

"Sandor, quit this."

"Put you over a barrel. Tear your hide off."

Herzog held his ears. "I can't stand it."

"Tie your guts in knots. Sonofabitch. They'll put a meter on your nose, and charge you for breathing. You'll be locked up back and front. Then you'll think about death. You'll pray for it. A coffin will look better to you than a sports car."

"But I didn't leave Madeleine."

"I've done this to guys myself."

"What harm did I do her."

"The court doesn't care. You signed papers—did you read them?"

"No, I took your word."

"They'll throw the book at you in court. She's the mother—the female. She's got the tits. They'll crush you."

"But I'm not guilty of anything."

"She hates you."

Sandor no longer screamed. He had resumed his normal loudness. "Jesus! You don't know anything," he said. "You an educated man? Thank God my old pa didn't have the dough to send me to the U. of C. I worked in the Davis Store and went to John Marshall. Education? It's a laugh! You don't know what goes on."

Moses was shaken. He began to reconsider. "All right—" he said.

"What's all right?"

"I'll take a policy on my life."

"Not as a favor to me!"

"Not as a favor . . ."

"It's a big bite—four hundred and eighteen bucks."

"I'll find the money."

Sandor said, "All right, my boy. Finally you make some sense. Now what about some breakfast—I'll cook porridge." In his green paisley pajamas he set off for the kitchen on his long, slipperless feet. Following in the corridor, Herzog heard a cry from Sandor at the kitchen sink. "Look at this crap! Not a pot—not a dish—there isn't a spoon that's clean. It stinks of garbage. It's just a sewer here!" The old dog, obese and bald, escaped in fear, claws rapping on the tiles—clickclick, clickclick. "Spendthrift bitches!" he shouted at the women of his house. "Frigging lice! All they're good for is to wag their asses at the dress shops and play gidgy in the bushes. Then they come home, and gorge cake and leave plates smeared with chocolate in the sink. That's what gives them the pimples."

"Easy, Sandor."

"Do I ask for much? The old veteran cripple runs up and down City Hall, from courtroom to courtroom—out to Twenty-sixth and California. For them! Do they care if I have to suck up to all kinds of pricks to get a little business?" Sandor began to rake out the sink. He threw eggshells and orange rinds into the corner beside the garbage pail—coffee grounds. He worked himself into a rage and began to smash dishes and glassware. His long fingers, like those of a hunchback, gripped the plates soiled with icing. Without losing beauty of gesture—amazing!—he shattered them on the wall. He knocked over the dish drainer and the soap powder, and then he wept with anger. And also at himself, that he should have such emotions. His open mouth and jutting teeth! The long hairs streamed from his disfigured breast.

"Moses—they're killing me! Killing their father!"

The daughters lay listening in their rooms. Young Sheldon was in Jackson Park with his scout troup. Beatrice did not appear.

"We don't have to have porridge," said Herzog.

"No, I'll wash a pot." He was still shedding tears. Under the torrential tap his manicured fingers scrubbed the aluminum with steel wool.

When he grew calmer, he said, "You know, Moses, I've been to a psychiatrist about these effing dishes. They cost me twenty bucks an hour. Moses, what am I going to do with my kids. Sheldon's going to be all right. Tessie's maybe not so bad. But Carmel! I don't know how to handle her. I'm afraid the boys are getting into her pants already. Prof, while you're here, I don't ask anything from you" (in return for bed and board, he meant) "but I'd appreciate it if you'd take an interest in her mental development. This is her chance to know an intellectual—a famous person—an authority. Will you talk to her?"

"About what?"

"Books—ideas. Take her for a walk. Discuss with her. Please, Moses, I'm begging you!"

"Well, of course I'll talk to her."

"I asked the rabbi—but what good are these reform rabbis? I know I'm a vulgar bastard, The Terrible-Tempered Mr. Bang. I work for these kids. . . ."

He squeezes the poor. Buys credit paper from merchants who sell fancy goods on installments to prostitutes on the South Side. And it's all very well for me to surrender my daughter, but his little hamsters have to have elevating discourses.

"If Carmel was a little older, I'd say, marry her."

Moses, pale and startled, said, "She's a very attractive girl. Far too young, of course."

Sandor put his long arm about Herzog's waist and drew him close. "Don't be such a rolling stone, Prof. Start leading a normal life. Where the hell haven't you been—Canada, Chicago, Paris, New York, Massachusetts. Your brothers have done okay right here, in this town. Of course, what's good enough for Alexander and Willie isn't good enough for a *macher* like you. Moses E. Herzog—he has no money in the bank, but you can look up his name in the library."

"I hoped that Madeleine and I would settle down."

"Out in the sticks? Don't be nuts. With that chick? Are you kidding? Come back to the home town. You're a West Side Jew. I used to see you as a kid in the Jewish People's Institute. Slow down. Stop knocking yourself out. I love you better than my own effing family. You never pulled that phony Harvard stuff on me. Stick with the folks—with good hearts. With love. Jesus! What d'ye say?" He drew away his big handsome sallow head a little distance, to look into Herzog's eyes, and Herzog felt the circuit of affection enclosing them again. Himmelstein's face with its long yellow grooves was joyful. "Can you sell that dump in the Berkshires?"

"I might."

"Hell, it's settled then. Take a loss if you have to. They've ruined Hyde Park, but you don't want to live with those longhair shmoes anyhow. Rent in my neighborhood."

Though he was tired out, and suffering at heart like a fool, Herzog listened like a child to a tale.

"Get yourself a housekeeper closer to your own age. And a good lay, too. What's wrong with that? Or we'll find you a gorgeous brownskin housekeeper. No more Japs for you."

"What do you mean?"

"You know what I mean. Or maybe what you need is a girl who survived the concentration camps, and would be grateful for a good home. And you and I will lead the life. We'll go to the Russian bath on North Avenue. They hit me at Omaha Beach, but screw 'em all, I'm still going. We'll live it up. We'll find an orthodox shul —enough of this Temple junk. You and me—we'll track down a good *chazan*. . . ." Forming his lips so that the almost invisible mustache thinly appeared, Sandor began to sing, *"Mi pnei chatoenu golino m'artzenu."* And for our sins we were exiled from our land. "You and me, a pair of old-time Jews." He held Moses with his dew-green eyes. "You're my boy. My innocent kind-hearted boy."

He gave Moses a kiss. Moses felt the potato love. Amorphous, swelling, hungry, indiscriminate, cowardly potato love.

"Oh, you sucker," Moses cried to himself in the train. "Sucker!"

I left you money for an emergency. You turned it all over to Madeleine to buy clothes. Were you her lawyer, or mine?

I might have understood, from the way he spoke of his female clients and assaulted all the men. But my God! how did I get into all of that? Why did I become involved with him at all? I must have wanted such absurd things to happen to me. I was so far gone in foolishness that even they, those Himmelsteins, knew more than I. And showed me the facts of life, and taught me the truth.

Revenged with hate on my own proud inanities.

In the mild end of the afternoon, later, at the waterside in Woods Hole, waiting for the ferry, he looked through the green darkness at the net of bright reflections on the bottom. He loved to think about the power of the sun, about light, about the ocean. The purity of the air moved him. There was no stain in the water, where schools of minnows swam. Herzog sighed and said to himself, "Praise God—praise God." His breathing had become freer. His heart was greatly stirred by the open horizon; the deep colors; the faint iodine pungency of the Atlantic rising from weeds and mollusks; the white, fine, heavy sand; but principally by the green transparency as he looked down to the stony bottom webbed with golden lines. Never still. If his soul could cast a reflection so brilliant, and so intensely sweet, he might beg God to make such use of him. But that would be too simple. But that would be too childish. The actual sphere is not clear like this, but turbulent, angry. A vast human action is going on. Death watches. So if you have some happiness, conceal it. And when your heart is full, keep your mouth shut also.

He had moments of sanity, but he couldn't maintain the balance for very long. The ferry came, he boarded it, pulling his hat tight in the sea wind, slightly shamefaced because he enjoyed this typical moment of a holiday. The cars were loaded in a cloud of blowing sand and marl while Herzog looked down from the upper deck. During the crossing he rested his feet on his up-ended valise, taking the sun, watching the boats through half-lidded eyes.

In Vineyard Haven he caught a cab at the dock. It turned right on the main street parallel to the harbor, lined with big trees—water, sails on the right, and the road passing under leaves filled with sun. Big gilt letters shone on red store fronts. The shopping center was as bright as a stage set. The taxi went slowly, as if the old engine had a heart condition. It passed the public library, and pillared driveways, great lyre-shaped elm trees and sycamores with patches of white bark—he noted the sycamores. These trees held an important place in his life. The green of evening was settling in, and the blue of the water, when your eyes turned from the shadows of the grass, seemed paler and paler. The cab turned right again, toward the shore, and Herzog got out, missing half of the driver's directions as he paid. "Down the stairs—up again. I get it. Okay." He saw Libbie waiting on the porch in a bright dress, and waved to her. She blew him a kiss.

At once he knew that he had made a mistake. Vineyard Haven was not the place for him. It was lovely, and Libbie was charming, one of the most charming women in the world. But I should never have come. It just isn't right, he thought. He appeared to be looking for the wooden treads on the slope, hesitating, a strong-looking man, holding his valise in a double grip like a player about to throw a forward pass. His hands were broad, heavily veined; not the hands of a man whose occupation was mental, but of a born bricklayer or housepainter. The breeze swelled out his light clothes and then fitted them tightly to his body. And what a look he had—such a face! Just then his state of being was so curious that he was compelled, himself, to see it—eager, grieving, fantastic, dangerous, crazed and, to the point of death, "comical." It was enough to make a man pray to God to remove this great, bone-breaking burden of selfhood and self-development, give himself, a failure, back to the species for a primitive cure. But this was becoming the up-to-date and almost conventional way of looking at any single life. In this view the body itself, with its two arms and vertical length, was compared to the Cross, on which you knew the agony of consciousness and separate being. For that matter, he had been taking this primitive cure, administered by Madeleine, Sandor, et cetera; so that his recent misfortunes might be seen as a collective project, himself participating, to destroy his vanity and his pretensions to a personal life so that he might disintegrate and suffer and hate, like so many others, not on anything so distinguished as a cross, but down in the mire of post-Renaissance, post-humanistic, post-Cartesian dissolution, next door to the Void. Everybody was in the act. "History" gave everyone a free ride. The very Himmelsteins, who had never even read a book of metaphysics, were touting the Void as if it were so much salable real estate. This little demon was impregnated with modern ideas, and one in particular excited his terrible little heart: you must sacrifice your poor, squawking, niggardly individuality—which may be nothing anyway (from an analytic viewpoint) but a persistent infantile megalomania, or (from a Marxian point of view) a stinking little bourgeois property—to historical necessity. And to truth. And truth is true only as it brings down more disgrace and dreariness upon human beings, so that if it shows anything except evil it is illusion, and not truth. But of course he, Herzog, predictably bucking such trends, had characteristically, obstinately, defiantly, blindly but without sufficient courage or intelligence tried to be a *marvelous* Herzog, a Herzog who, perhaps clumsily, tried to live out marvelous qualities vaguely comprehended. Granted he had gone too far, beyond his talents and his powers, but this was the cruel difficulty of a man who had strong impulses, even faith, but lacked clear ideas. What if he failed? Did that really mean that there was no faithfulness, no generosity, no sacred quality? Should he have been a plain, unambitious Herzog? No. And Madeleine would never have married such a type. What she had been looking for, high and low, was precisely an ambitious Herzog. In order to trip him, bring him low, knock him sprawling and kick out his brains with a murderous bitch foot. Oh, what a confusion he had made—what a waste of intelligence and feeling! When he thought of the endless anxious tedium of courtship and marriage with all that he had invested in arrangements—merely in practical measures, in trains and planes and hotels and department stores, and banks where he had banked, in hospitals, in doctors and drugs, in debts; and, for himself, the nights of rigid insomnia, the yellow boring afternoons, the trials by sexual combat, and all the horrible egomania of it, he wondered that he had survived at all. He wondered, even, why he should have wanted to survive. Others in his generation wore themselves out, died of strokes, of cancer, willed their own deaths, conceivably. But he, despite all blunders, fucky-knuckles that he was, he must be cunning, tough. He survived. And for what? What was he hanging around for? To follow this career of *personal relationships* until his strength at last gave out? Only to be a smashing success in the private realm, a king of hearts? Amorous Herzog, seeking love, and embracing his Wandas, Zinkas, and Ramonas, one after another? But this is a female pursuit. This hugging and heartbreak is for women. The occupation of a man is in duty, in use, in civility, in politics in the Aristotelian sense. Now then, why am I arriving here, in Vineyard Haven, on a *holiday* no less! Heartbroken, and gussied up, with my Italian pants and my fountain pens, and my grief—to bother and pester poor Libbie, and exploit her affections, forcing her to pay off because I was so kind and decent when *her* last husband, Erikson, went off his rocker and tried to stab her and take the gas himself? At which time, yes, I was very helpful. But if she hadn't been so very beautiful, sexual, and obviously attracted to me, would I have been such a willing friend and helper? And it's not much to be pleased with that I bother her now, a bride of a few months, with my troubles. Have I come to collect the quid pro quo? Turn around, Moshe-Hanan, and catch the next ferry back. All you needed was a train ride. It has turned the trick.

Libbie came down the path to greet him, and gave him a kiss. She was dressed for the evening in an orange or poppy-colored cocktail dress. It took Moses an extra moment to determine whether the fragrance he smelled came from the nearby bed of peonies or from her neck and shoulders. She was unaffectedly happy to see him. By fair means or not, he had made a friend of her.

"How are you!"

"I'm not going to stay," said Herzog. "It's not right."

"What are you talking about? You've been traveling for hours. Come inside and meet Arnold. Sit down and have a drink. You *are* funny."

She laughed at him, and he was obliged to laugh with her. Sissler came out on the porch, a man in his fifties, untidy and sleepy but cheerful, and began to make welcoming sounds in his deep voice. He had on a pair of large pink slacks with a rubberized waistband.

"He says he's already on his way back, Arnold. I told you he was funny."

"You traveled all this way to tell us? Come in—come in. I was going to light a fire. It gets colder in an hour and people are coming to dinner. What about a drink? Scotch or bourbon? Maybe you'd like a swim instead?" Sissler gave him a broad, amiable, wrinkled, black-eyed smile. These eyes were small and there were spaces between his teeth; he was bald, his back hair was thick and projected like one of those large tree mushrooms that grow on the mossy side of a trunk. Libbie had married a comfortable, wise old dog, the kind who always turned out to have large reserves of understanding and humanity. In the brighter light of the seaward side of the house she looked extremely well, happy, her face tanned and smooth. On her mouth she wore poppy-colored lipstick, and gold-mesh jewelry on her arm, a heavy gold chain on her neck. She had aged a little—she must be thirty-eight or thirtynine, was his guess, but her dark, close-set eyes, which gave her a fluid and merged gaze (she had a delicate, lovely nose), were clearer than he had ever seen them. She was in the time of life when the later action of heredity begins, the blemishes of ancestors appear—a spot, or the deepening of wrinkles, at first increasing a woman's beauty. Death, the artist, very slow, putting in his first touches. Now to Sissler it couldn't matter less. He had already accepted this, would rumble on in his Russian accent, and be the same forthright businessman to the day of his death. When that moment came, because of his bunchy back hair, he would have to die lying on his side.

Ideas that depopulate the world.

But as Herzog accepted a drink, and heard himself in a clear voice saying thanks, and saw how he sat down in a chintz-covered chair, his psychological reading suggested that it might not be Sissler whose deathbed he saw in this vision, but some other person who had a wife. Maybe it was even himself who was dying in fantasy. He had had a wife—two wives—and been the object of such death-flavored fantasies himself. Now: the first requirement of stability in a human being was that the said human being should really desire to exist. This is what Spinoza says. It is necessary for happiness (*felicitas*). He can't behave well (*bene agere*), or live well (*bene vivere*), if he himself doesn't want to live. But if it's also natural, as psychology says, to kill mentally (one thought-murder a day keeps the psychiatrist away), then the desire to exist is not steady enough to support a good life. Do I want to exist, or want to die? But at this social moment he couldn't expect to answer such questions, and he swallowed freezing bourbon from the clinking glass instead. The whisky went down, burning pleasurably in his chest like a tangled string of fire. Below he saw the pock-marked beach, and flaming sunset on the water. The ferry was returning. As the sun went down, its wide hull suddenly filled with electric lights. In the calm sky a helicopter steered toward Hyannis Port, where the Kennedys lived. Big doings there, once. The power of nations. What do we know about it? Moses felt a sharp pang at the thought of the late President. (I wonder what I would say to a President in actual conversation.) He smiled a little as he remembered his mother boasting to Aunt Zipporah about him. "What a little tongue it has. Moshele could talk to the President." But at that time the President was Harding. Or was it Coolidge? Meantime the conversation was going on. Sissler was trying to make Moses feel at home—I must seem obviously shook up—and Libbie looked concerned.

"Ah, don't worry about me," said Moses. "I'm just a little excited by things." He laughed. Libbie and Sissler exchanged a look, but grew easier. "This is a fine house you have. Is it rented?"

"I own it," said Sissler.

"Is that so. Wonderful place. Summer only, isn't it? You could winterize it easily."

"It would cost fifteen grand, or more," said Sissler.

"That much? I suppose labor and materials are higher on this island."

"I could do the work myself, sure," said Sissler. "But we come here to rest. I understand you're a property owner, too."

"Ludeyville, Mass," said Herzog.

"Where is that?"

"Berkshires. Near the Connecticut corner of the state."

"Must be a beautiful spot of country."

"Oh, it's beautiful all right. Too remote, though. Far from everything."

"What about another drink?"

Perhaps Sissler thought the liquor would calm him.

"Moses probably wants to clean up after his trip," said Libbie.

"I'll show him his room."

Sissler carried Herzog's valise up.

"This is a fine old staircase," said Moses. "Couldn't duplicate it today for thousands. They put a lot of work into it, for a summer house."

"Sixty years ago they still had craftsmen," said Sissler. "Take a look at the doors—bird's-eye maple. Here's where you are. I think you got everything here—towels, soap. Some neighbors are coming this evening. One single lady. A singer. Miss Elisa Thurnwald. Divorced."

The room was wide and comfortable, and had a view of the bay. The bluish beacons of the two points, East and West Chop, were lighted.

"This is a fine spot," said Herzog.

"Unpack. Make yourself at home. Don't be in any hurry to go. I know you were a good friend to Libbie when she was up against it. She told me how you protected her from that blowtop, Erikson. He even tried to stab the poor kid. She didn't have anybody but you to turn to."

"As a matter of fact, Erikson had nobody else to turn to, either."

"What's the diff?" Sissler said, with his rugged face a little averted but only so that his small shrewd eyes might see Herzog from the angle required for the fullest consideration. "You stood up for her. To me that's everything. Not just because I love the kid, either, but because there's so many creeps in circulation. You got trouble, I can see that. Jumping out of your skin. You got a soul—

97

haven't you, Moses." He shook his head, smoking his cigarette with two stained fingers pressed to his mouth, his voice rumbling. "Can't dump the sonofabitch, can we? Terrible handicap, a soul."

Moses answered in a low voice. "I'm not even sure I've got the thing still."

"I would say yes. Well . . ." He turned his wrist to catch the last of the light on his gold watch. "You got time to rest up a little."

He left, and Moses lay on the bed a while—a good mattress, a clean comforter. He lay for a quarter of an hour without thinking, lips parted, legs and arms extended, breathing quietly as he gazed at the figures of the wallpaper until they were hidden in darkness. When he stood up it was not to wash and dress but to write a farewell note on the maple desk. There was stationery in the drawer.

Have to go back. Not able to stand kindness at this time. Feelings, heart, everything in strange condition. Unfinished business. Bless you both. And much happiness. Toward end of summer, perhaps, if you will give me a rain check. Gratefully, Moses.

He stole from the house. The Sisslers were in the kitchen. Sissler was making a clatter with the ice trays. Moses rapidly descended and was out of the screen door with frantic swiftness, softly. He passed through the bushes into the neighboring lot. Up the path, and back to the ferry slip. He took a cab to the airport. All he could get at this hour was a Boston flight. He took it and caught a plane for Idlewild at Boston airport. At eleven P.M. he was lying in his own bed, drinking warm milk and eating a peanut-butter sandwich. It had cost him a pretty penny, all of this travel.

He kept Geraldine Portnoy's letter always on his bed table, and he picked it up now and reread it before he fell asleep. He tried to remember how he had felt when he had first read it, in Chicago, after some delay.

Dear Mr. Herzog, I am Geraldine Portnoy, Lucas Asphalter's friend. You may remember. . . . May remember? Moses had read faster (the script was feminine—progressive-school printing turned cursive and the i's dotted with curious little open circles), trying to swallow the whole letter at once, turning the pages to see whether the gist of the thing was underscored anywhere. *Actually I took your course in Romantics as Social Philosophers. We differed about*

Rousseau and Karl Marx. I have come around to your view, that Marx expressed metaphysical hopes for the future of mankind. I took what he said about materialism far too literally. My view! It's common, and why does she want to make me dangle like this—why doesn't she get on with it? He had tried again to find the point, but all those circular open dots fell on his vision like snow and masked the message. *You probably never noticed me, but I liked you, and as a friend of Lucas Asphalter—he just adores you, he says you are just a feast of the most human qualities—I have of course heard a lot about you, growing up in Lucas' old neighborhood, and how you played basketball in the Boys' Brotherhood of the Republic, in the good old Chicago days on Division Street. An uncle of mine by marriage was one of the coaches—Jules Hankin.* I think I do recall Hankin. He wore a blue cardigan, and parted his hair in the middle. *I don't want you to get me wrong. I don't want to meddle in your affairs. And I am not an enemy of Madeleine's. I sympathize with her, too. She is so vivacious, intelligent, and such a charmer, and has been so warm and frank with me. For quite a while, I admired her and as a younger woman was very pleased by her confidences.* Herzog flushed. Her confidences would include his sexual disgrace. *And as a former student, I was of course intrigued to hear of your private life, but was also surprised by her freedom and willingness to talk, and soon saw she wanted to win me over, for some reason. Lucas warned me to look out for something dikey, but then any intense feeling between members of the same sex is often, and unjustly, under suspicion. My scientific background has taught me to make more cautious generalizations, and resist this creeping psychoanalysis of ordinary conduct. But she did want to win me to her side, although far too subtle to pour it on, as they say. She told me that you had very fine human and intellectual qualities, though neurotic and with an intolerable temper which often frightened her. However, she added, you could be great, and after two bad, loveless marriages perhaps you would devote yourself to the work you were meant to do. Emotional relationships you were not really good at. It was soon obvious that she would never have given herself to a man who lacked distinction of intelligence or feeling. Madeleine said that for the first time in her life she knew clearly what she was doing. Until now it was all*

99

confusion and there were even gaps of time she couldn't account for. In marrying you, she was in this mixup and might have remained so but for a certain break. It is extremely exciting to talk with her, she gives a sense of a significant encounter—with life—a beautiful, brilliant person with a fate of her own. Her experiences are rich, or pregnant. . . . What is this? Herzog had thought. Is she going to tell me that Madeleine is going to have a child? Gersbach's child! No! How wonderful—what luck for me. If she has a kid out of wedlock, I can petition for Junie's custody. Eagerly, he had devoured the rest of the page, turned over. No, Madeleine was not pregnant. She'd be far too clever to let that happen. She owed her survival to intelligence. It was part of her sickness to be shrewd. She was not pregnant, then. *I was not merely a graduate student who helped with the child, but a confidante. Your little girl is greatly attached to me, and I find her a most extraordinary child. Exceptional, really. I love Junie with more than the usual affection, oh far more, than one has for the children one meets in this way. I understand the Italians are supposed to be the most child-oriented culture in the West (judge by the figure of the Christ child in Italian painting), but obviously Americans have their own craze about child psychology. Everything is done for children, ostensibly. To be fair, I think Madeleine is not bad with little June, basically. She tends to be authoritarian. Mr. Gersbach, who has an ambiguous position in this household, is very amusing to the child, on the whole. She calls him Uncle Val, and I often see him giving her a piggyback, or tossing her in the air.* Here Herzog had set his teeth, angry, scenting danger. *But I have to report one disagreeable thing, and I talked this over with Lucas. This is that, coming to Harper Avenue the other night, I heard the child crying. She was inside Gersbach's car, and couldn't get out, and the poor little thing was shaking and weeping. I thought she had shut herself in while playing, but it was after dark, and I didn't understand why she would be outside, alone, at bedtime.* Herzog's heart had pounded with dangerous thick beats at these words. *I had to calm her, and then I found out that her Mama and Uncle Val were having a quarrel inside, and Uncle Val had taken her by the hand and led her out to the car, and told her to play a while. He shut her up and went back in the house. I can see him* mount the stairs while Junie screams in fright. I'll kill him for that —so help me, if I don't! He reread the concluding lines. *Luke says you have a right to know such things. He was going to phone but I felt it would be upsetting and harmful to hear this over the phone. A letter gives one a chance to consider—think matters over, and reach a more balanced view. I don't think Madeleine is a bad mother, actually.*

HE was at his letter-writing again in the morning. The little desk at the window was black, rivaling the blackness of his fire escape, those rails dipped in asphalt, a heavy cosmetic coat of black, rails equidistant but appearing according to the rules of perspective. He had letters to write. He was busy, busy, in pursuit of objects he was only now, and dimly, beginning to understand. His first message today, begun half-consciously as he was waking up, was to Monsignor Hilton, the priest who had brought Madeleine into the Church. Sipping his black coffee, Herzog in his cotton paisley robe narrowed his eyes and cleared his throat, already aware of the anger, the pervasive indignation he felt. The Monsignor should know what effect he had on the people he tampered with. *I am the husband, or ex-husband, of a young woman whom you converted, Madeleine Pontritter, the daughter of the well-known impresario. Perhaps you remember, she took instruction from you some years ago and was baptized by you. A recent Radcliffe graduate, and very beautiful. . . .* Was Madeleine really such a great beauty, or did the loss of her make him exaggerate—did it make his suffering more notable? Did it console him that a beautiful woman had dumped him? But she had done it for that loud, flamboyant, ass-clutching brute Gersbach. Nothing can be done about the sexual preferences of women. That's ancient wisdom. Nor of men. Quite objectively, however, she was a beauty. So was Daisy, in her time. I myself was once handsome, but spoiled my looks with conceit . . . *Her complexion healthy and pink, fine dark hair gathered in a bun behind and a fringe on her forehead, a slender neck, heavy blue eyes and a Byzantine nose which came straight down from the brow. The bangs concealed a forehead of considerable intellectual power, the will of a demon,* or else outright mental disorder. *She had a great sense of style. As soon as she began to take instruction she bought crosses and medals and rosaries, and suitable clothes. But then, she was just a girl, really, just out of college. Still, I believe she understood many things better than I. And I want you to know, Monsignor, that I am not writing with the purpose of exposing Madeleine, or attacking you. I simply believe you may be interested to find out what may happen, or actually does happen, when people want to save themselves from . . . I suppose the word is nihilism.*

Now then, what does happen? What actually did happen? Herzog tried to understand, staring at the brick walls to which he had fled again from the Vineyard. I had that room in Philadelphia—that one-year job—and I was commuting to New York three or four times a week on the Pennsylvania train, to visit Marco. Daisy swore there would be no divorce. And, for a time, I was shacked up with Sono Oguki, but she didn't answer my purpose. Not *serious* enough. I wasn't getting much work done. Routine classes in Philadelphia. They were bored with me, and I with them. Papa got wind of my dissolute life, and was angry. Daisy wrote him all about it, but it was none of Papa's business. What actually happened? I gave up the shelter of an orderly, purposeful, lawful existence because it bored me, and I felt it was simply a slacker's life. Sono wanted me to move in with her. But I thought that would make me a squaw man. So I took my papers and books, and my Remington office machine with the black hood, and my records and oboe and music down to Philadelphia.

Dragging back and forth on the train, wearing himself out—the best sacrifice he could offer. He went to visit his little boy, and faced the anger of his ex-wife. Daisy would try to be stolid. It did great harm to her looks. She met Moses at the top of the stairs, her arms crossed, turning herself into a square figure with green eyes and chopped hair, waiting to say he must bring Marco home within two hours. He had a horror of these meetings. Of course she always knew exactly what he was doing, whom he was seeing, and now and then would say, "How's Japan?" or "How's the Pope?" It was not funny. She had good qualities, but a sense of humor was not among them.

Moses prepared for his outings with Marco. The time passed heavily otherwise. On the train he memorized facts about the Civil War—dates, names, battles—so that while Marco was eating his hamburger at the Zoo Cafeteria, where they always went, they could talk. "Now it's time to tell you about Beauregard," he said. "This part is very exciting." But Herzog could only try to fix his mind on General Beauregard or on Island Number 10 or Andersonville. He was thinking how to deal with Sono Oguki, whom he was deserting for Madeleine—it felt like a desertion. The woman was waiting for him to call; he knew that. And he was often tempted, when Madeleine was too busy with the Church and refused to see him, to drop in and have a talk, nothing more, with Sono. This confusion was ugly, and he despised himself for creating it. Was this all the work a man could find to do?

Losing self-respect! Lacking clear ideas!

He could see that Marco sympathized with his confused father. He played the game with Moses, asking more questions about the Civil War simply because it was all that he had to offer. The child would not reject his well-meant gift. There was love in that, thought Herzog, wrapped in his paisley cotton, his coffee turning cold. These children and I love one another. But what can I give them? Marco would look at him with clear eyes, his pale child's face, the Herzog face, freckled, his hair crew-cut, by his own choice, and somewhat alien. He had his Grandmother Herzog's mouth. "Well, okay, kid, I've got to go back to Philadelphia now," said Herzog. He felt, on the contrary, nothing necessary about this return to Philadelphia. Philadelphia was entirely a mistake. What need *was* there to ride that train? Was it necessary, for instance, to see Elizabeth and Trenton? Were they waiting for him to look at them? Was his single cot in Philadelphia expecting him? "It's just about train time, Marco." He pulled out his pocket watch, a gift twenty years ago from his father. "Take care on the subway. And around the neighborhood, too. Don't go down into Morningside Park. There are gangs down there."

He repressed the impulse to dial Sono Oguki's number from a sidewalk booth and got on the subway instead, which carried him to Penn Station. In his long brown coat, tight in the shoulders and misshapen by the books stuffed into the pockets, he walked the underground tunnel of shops—flowers, cutlery, whisky, doughnuts and grilled sausages, the waxy chill of the orangeade. Laboriously he climbed into the light-filled vault of the station, the great windows dustily dividing the autumn sun—the stoop-shouldered sun of the garment district. The mirror of the gum machine revealed to Herzog how pale he was, unhealthy—wisps from his coat and wool scarf, his hat and brows, twisting and flaming outward in the overfull light and exposing the sphere of his face, the face of a man who was keeping up a front. Herzog smiled at this earlier avatar of his life, at Herzog the victim, Herzog the would-be lover, Herzog the man on whom the world depended for certain intellectual work, to change history, to influence the development of civilization. Several boxes of stale paper under his bed in Philadelphia were going to produce this very significant result.

So, by the expanding iron gate with its crimson plaque, lettered in gold, Herzog holding his unpunched ticket marched down to the train. His shoelaces were dragging. Ghosts of an old physical pride were still about him. On the lower level the cars, smoky red, were waiting. Was he coming or going? At times he didn't know.

The books in his pockets were Pratt's short history of the Civil War and several volumes of Kierkegaard. Although he had given up tobacco, Herzog was still drawn to the smoker. He liked the fumes. Sitting in a dirty plush seat he took out a book and read *For dying means that it is all over, but dying the death means to experience death,* trying to think what this might signify. If . . . Yes . . . No . . . on the other hand, if existence is nausea then faith is an uncertain relief. Or else—be demolished by suffering and you will feel the power of God as he restores you. Fine reading for a depressive! Herzog, at his desk, smiled. He let his head fall into his hands, almost silently laughing. But on the train he was laboriously studying, totally serious. All who live are in despair.(?) And that is the sickness *unto* death.(?) It is that a man refuses to be what he is.(?)

He closed the book as the train reached the junk heaps of New Jersey. His head was hot. He found coolness by pressing the large Stevenson button on his lapel to his cheek. The smoke in the car was sweet, rotten, rich. He sucked it deep into his lungs—a stirring foulness; he raptly breathed in the swampiness of old pipes. The wheels were speeding with a sharp racket, biting the rails. The cold fall sun flamed over the New Jersey mills. Volcanic shapes of slag, rushes, dumps, refineries, ghostly torches, and presently the fields and woods. The short oaks bristled like metal. The fields turned blue. Each radio spire was like a needle's eye with a drop of blood in it. The dull bricks of Elizabeth fell behind. At dusk Trenton approached like the heart of a coal fire. Herzog read the municipal sign—TRENTON MAKES, THE WORLD TAKES!

At nightfall, in a cold electric glitter, came Philadelphia.

Poor fellow, his health was not good.

Herzog was grinning as he thought of the pills he had taken, and the milk he had drunk in the night. By his bed in Philadelphia there often stood a dozen bottles. He sipped milk to calm his stomach.

Living amid great ideas and concepts, insufficiently relevant to the present, day-by-day, American conditions. You see, Monsignor, if you stand on television in the ancient albs and surplices of the Roman church there are at least enough Irishmen, Poles, Croatians watching in saloons to understand you, lifting elegant arms to heaven and glancing your eyes like a silent movie star— Richard Barthelmess or Conway Tearle; the R.C. working class takes great pride in him. *But I, a learned specialist in intellectual history, handicapped by emotional confusion . . . Resisting the argument that scientific thought has put into disorder all considerations based on value . . . Convinced that the extent of universal space does not destroy human value, that the realm of facts and that of values are not eternally separated. And the peculiar idea entered my (Jewish) mind that we'd see about this! My life would prove a different point altogether. Very tired of the modern form of historicism which sees in this civilization the defeat of the best hopes of Western religion and thought, what Heidegger calls the second Fall of Man into the quotidian or ordinary. No philosopher knows what the ordinary is, has not fallen into it deeply enough. The question of ordinary human experience is the principal question of these modern centuries, as Montaigne and Pascal, otherwise in disagreement, both clearly saw.—The strength of a man's virtue or spiritual capacity measured by his ordinary life.*

One way or another the no doubt mad idea entered my mind that my own actions had historic importance, and this (fantasy?) made it appear that people who harmed me were interfering with an important experiment.

Herzog tragically sipping milk in Philadelphia, a frail hopeful lunatic, tipping the carton to quiet his stomach and drown his unquiet mind, courting sleep. He was thinking of Marco, Daisy, Sono Oguki, Madeleine, the Pontritters, and now and then of the difference between ancient and modern tragedy according to Hegel, the inner experience of the heart and the deepening of individual character in the modern age. His own individual character cut off at times both from facts and from values. But modern character is inconstant, divided, vacillating, lacking the stonelike certitude of archaic man, also deprived of the firm ideas of the seventeenth century, clear, hard theorems.

Moses wanted to do what he could to improve the human condition, at last taking a sleeping pill, to preserve himself. In the best interests of everyone. But when he met his Philadelphia class in the morning, he could hardly see his lecture notes. His eyes were swollen and his head asleep, but his anxious heart beat faster than ever.

Madeleine's father, a powerful personality, first-rate intelligence, many of the peculiar and grotesque vanities of theatrical New York in him, however, told me I might do her a great deal of good. He said, "Well, it's about time she quit hanging around with queers. She's like a lot of bluestocking college girls—all her friends are homosexuals. She's got more faggots at her feet than Joan of Arc. It's a good sign that she's interested in you." But the old man also thought him a poor fish. That psychological fact was not concealed. He had come to see Pontritter in his studio—Madeleine had said, "My father insists on having a talk with you. I wish you'd stop in." He found Pontritter dancing the samba or the cha-cha (Herzog didn't know one from the other) with his own instructress, a middle-aged Filipino woman who had once belonged to a well-known tango team (Ramon and Adelina). Adelina had put on weight in the middle, but her long legs were thin. Her makeup didn't much lighten her dark face. Pontritter, this immense figure of a man with single white fibers growing from his tanned scalp (he used a sun lamp all winter) was making tiny steps in his canvas, rope-soled slippers. His seat-fallen trousers moved from side to side as he swayed his wide hips. His blue eyes were severe. The music played, sucking and knocking, tiny, rapping, scraping steel-band rhythms. When it stopped, Pontritter said with somewhat distant interest, "You Moses Herzog?"

"That's right."

"In love with my daughter?"

"Yes."

"It isn't doing much for your health, I see."

"I haven't been too well, Mr. Pontritter."

"Everyone calls me Fitz. This is Adelina. Adelina—Moses. He's laying my daughter. I thought I'd never live to see the day. Well, congratulations . . . Hope Sleeping Beauty will wake up."

"'Allo, guapo," said Adelina. There was nothing personal in this greeting. Adelina's eyes were concentrated on the lighting of her cigarette. She took a match from Pontritter's hand. Herzog remembered thinking how purely external that match game was, under the studio skylight. Artificial heat or none at all.

Later in the day, he had a talk with Tennie Pontritter, too. As Tennie spoke of her daughter, tears quickly came to her eyes. She had a smooth, long-suffering countenance, slightly tearful even when she smiled, and most mournful when you met her by chance, as Moses did on Broadway, and saw her face—she was above the average height—coming toward him, large, smooth, kindly, with permanent creases of suffering beside her mouth. She invited him to sit with her in Verdi Square, the tattered grass plot railed in and always surrounded by a seated throng of dying old men and women, and by begging cripples, lesbians swaggering like truck drivers and fragile Negro homosexuals with dyed hair and earrings.

"I don't have much influence with my daughter," said Tennie. "I love her dearly, of course. It hasn't been easy. I had to stand by Fitz. He was blacklisted for years. I couldn't be disloyal. After all, he is a great artist. . . ."

"I believe it. . . ." Herzog muttered. She had waited for him to accept this.

"He's a giant," said Tennie. She had learned to say such things with utter conviction. Only a Jewish woman of a good, culture-respecting background—her father had been a tailor and a member of the Arbeiter-Ring, a Yiddishist—could sacrifice her life to a great artist as she had done. "In a mass society!" she said. She looked at him still with the same sisterly gentleness and appeal. "A money society!" He wondered at this. Madeleine had told him, very bitter toward her parents, that the old man needed fifty thousand a year, and that he got it, too, the old Svengali, out of women and stage-struck suckers. "So Mady thinks I let her down. She doesn't understand—hates her father. I can tell you this, Moses, I think people must trust you instinctively. I see that Mady does, and she's *not* a trusting girl. So I think she must be in love with you."

"*I* am, with her," said Moses, emotionally.

"You must love her—I think you do. . . . Things are so complicated."

"That I'm older—married? Is that what you mean?"

"You won't hurt her, will you? No matter what she thinks, I am her mother. I have a mother's heart, whatever she says." She began crying, softly. "Oh, Mr. Herzog . . . I'm always between the two of them. I know we haven't been conventional parents. She feels I just turned her out into the world. And there's nothing *I* can do. It's up to you. You'll have to give the child the only thing that can help her." Tennie took off her elaborate glasses, now making no effort to disguise her weeping. Her face, her nose reddened, and her eyes, shaped to make what seemed to Moses a crooked appeal, darkened blindly with tears. There was a measure of hypocrisy and calculation in Tennie's method, but behind this, again, was real feeling for her daughter and her husband; and behind this real feeling there was something still more meaningful and somber. Herzog was all too well aware of the layers upon layers of reality—loathsomeness, arrogance, deceit, and then—God help us all!—truth, as well. He understood he was being manipulated by Madeleine's worried mother. Thirty years the bohemian wife, the platitudes of that ideology threadbare, cynically exploited by old Pontritter, Tennie remained faithful, chained in the dull silver "abstract" jewelry that she wore.

But it would never happen to her daughter, if she could help it. And Madeleine was just as determined that it should not. And this was where Moses came in, on the bench in Verdi Square. His face was shaven, his shirt was clean, his nails clean, his legs, somewhat heavy in the thighs, were crossed, and he listened to Tennie very thoughtfully—for a man whose mind had stopped working. It was too full of his grand projects to think anything clearly. Of course he understood that Tennie was setting him up, and that he was a sucker for just the sort of appeal she made. He had a weakness for good deeds, and she flattered this weakness, asking him to save this headstrong deluded child of hers. Patience, loving-kindness, and virility would accomplish this. But Tennie flattered him even more subtly. She was telling Moses that he could bring stability into the life of this neurotic girl and cure her by his steadiness. Among this crowd of the aged, dying, and crippled, Tennie making her appeal to Moses for his help, stirred his impure sympathies intensely. Repulsively. His heart felt sick. "I adore Madeleine, Tennie," he said. "You don't have to worry. I'll do everything possible."

An eager, hasty, self-intense, and comical person.

Madeleine had an apartment in an old building, and Herzog stayed with her when he was in town. They slept together on the studio sofa with the morocco cover. Moses pressed her body all night with fervor, exaltation. She was not so fervent, but then she was a recent convert. Besides, one lover is always more moved than the other. Sometimes she had tears of anger and misery in her eyes and complained of her sinfulness. Still, she wanted it, too.

At seven in the morning, seeming to anticipate the alarm clock by a split second, she stiffened, and when it rang she was already exclaiming with suffocated anger, "Damn!" and striding to the bathroom.

The fixtures were old-fashioned in this place. These had been luxury apartments in the 1890s. The broad-mouthed faucets ran a shattering stream of cold water. She dropped her pajama top so that she was bare to the waist, and washed herself with a cloth, purifying herself with angry vigor, her blue-eyed face growing red, her breasts pink. Silent, barefooted, wearing his trench coat as a robe, Herzog came in and sat on the edge of the tub, watching.

The tiles were a faded cherry color, and the toothbrush rack, the fixtures, were ornate, old nickel. The water stormed from the faucet, and Herzog watched as Madeleine transformed herself into an older woman. She had a job at Fordham, and the first requirement, to her mind, was to look sober and mature, long in the Church. His open curiosity, the fact that he familiarly shared the bathroom with her, his nakedness under the trench coat, his pallid morning face in this setting of disgraced Victorian luxury—it all vexed her. She did not look at him while making her preparations. Over her brassière and slip she put a high-necked sweater, and to protect the shoulders of the sweater she wore a plastic cape. It kept the makeup from crumbling on the wool. Now she began to apply her cosmetics—the bottles and powders filled the shelves above the toilet. Whatever she did, it was with unhesitating speed and efficiency, headlong, but with the confidence of an expert. Engravers, pastry cooks, acrobats on the trapeze worked in this manner. He thought she was too reckless at it—going too fast, about to have a spill, but that never happened. First she spread a layer of cream on her cheeks, rubbing it into her straight nose, her childish chin and soft throat. It was gray, pearly bluish stuff. That was the base. She fanned it with a towel. Over this she laid the makeup. She worked with cotton swabs, under the hairline, about the eyes, up the cheeks and on the throat. Despite the soft rings of feminine flesh, there was already something discernibly dictatorial about that extended throat. She would not let Herzog caress her face downward—it was bad for the muscles. Seated, watching, on the edge of the luxurious tub, he put on his pants, tucked in his shirt. She took no notice of him; she was trying in some way to be rid of him as her daytime life began.

She put on a pale powder with her puff, still at the same tilting speed, as if desperate. Then she turned swiftly to examine the work—right profile, left profile—bracing at the mirror, holding her hands as if to support her bust but not actually touching it. She was satisfied with the powder. She put touches of Vaseline on her lids. She dyed the lashes with a tiny coil. Moses participated in all this, intensely, silently. Still without pauses or hesitations, she put a touch of black in the outer corner of each eye, and redrew the line of her brows to make it level and earnest. Then she picked up a pair of large tailor's shears and put them to her bangs. She seemed to have no need to measure; her image was fixed in her will. She cut as if discharging a gun, and Herzog felt an impulse of alarm, short-circuited. Her decisiveness fascinated him, and in such fascination he discovered his own childishness. He, an able-bodied person seated on the edge of the pompous old tub, the enamel wreathed with hairlike twistings like cooked rhubarb, absorbed in this transformation of Madeleine's face. She primed her lips with waxy stuff, then painted them a drab red, adding more years to her age. This waxen mouth just about did it. She moistened a finger on her tongue, and brushed a few last touches on. That was it. She looked with level-browed gravity in the mirror and seemed satisfied. Yes, this was just right. She put on a long heavy tweed skirt, which hid her legs. High heels tilted her ankles slightly. And now the hat. It was gray, with a low crown, wide-brimmed.

When she drew it over her sleek head she became a woman of forty—some white, hysterical, genuflecting hypochondriac of the church aisles. The wide brim over her anxious forehead, her childish intensity, her fear, her religious will—the pity of the whole thing! While he, the worn, unshaven, sinful Jew, endangering her redemption—his heart ached. But she barely gave him a glance. She had put on the jacket with the squirrel collar and was reaching under to adjust the shoulder pads. That hat! It was made like coil basketry of one long gray tape, about half an inch wide, like the hat worn by the Christian lady who had read the Bible with him in the hospital ward in Montreal. "The wind bloweth where it listeth, and thou hearest the sound thereof. . . ." There was even a hatpin. The job was finished. Her face was smooth and middle-aged. Only the eyeballs hadn't been touched, and the tears seemed about to spring from them. She looked angry—furious. She wanted him there at night. She would even, half with rancor, take his hand and put it on her breast as they were falling asleep. But in the morning she would have liked him to disappear. And he was not used to this; he was used to being a favorite. But he was dealing with a new female generation, that was what he told himself. To her he was a fatherly, graying, patient seducer (he could not believe it!). But the parts had been distributed. She had her white convert's face and Herzog couldn't refuse to play opposite.

"You should have some breakfast," he said.

"No. It'll make me late."

The pastes had dried on her skin. She put on a big pectoral cross. She had been a Catholic for only three months, and already because of Herzog she couldn't be confessed, not by Monsignor, anyway.

Conversion was a theatrical event for Madeleine. Theater—the art of upstarts, opportunists, would-be aristocrats. Monsignor himself was an actor. One role, but a fat one. *Obviously she had religious feeling, but the glamour and the social climbing were more important. You are famous for converting celebrities, and she went to you.* Nothing but the best for our Mady. *The Jewish interpretation of the high-minded Christian lady or gentleman is a curious chapter in the history of social theater.* The Dignities continually replenished from below. Where would any distinguished person come from, if not the masses? With the devotion and fire of transcendent resentment. *I don't deny that it did much for me as well. It reflected very favorably on me to be involved in such an issue.*

"You'll get sick going to work on an empty stomach. Have breakfast with me and I'll pay your cab fare out to Fordham."

Decisively, but awkwardly, she left the bathroom, her stride hampered by the long ugly skirt. She wanted to fly, but with the cartwheel hat, the tweeds, the religious medals, the large pectoral cross, her heavy heart, getting off the ground was not easy.

He trailed her through the mirror-paneled room, past framed prints of Flemish altarpieces, gilt, green, and red. The doorknobs and locks were immobilized by many coats of paint. Madeleine tugged, impatiently. Herzog coming up behind her jerked open the white front door. They went down a corridor where bags of garbage were put out on the once luxurious carpet, and down in the decayed elevator, out of the trapped air of the black shaft into the porphyry façade of the moldy lobby, into the crowded street.

"Aren't you coming? What are you doing?" said Madeleine.

Perhaps he was not yet fully awake. Herzog was loitering for a moment near the fish store, arrested by the odor. A thin muscular Negro was pitching buckets of ground ice into the deep window. The fish were packed together, backs arched as if they were swimming in the crushed, smoking ice, bloody bronze, slimy black-green, gray-gold—the lobsters were crowded to the glass, feelers bent. The morning was warm, gray, damp, fresh, smelling of the river. Pausing on the metal doors of the sidewalk elevator, Moses received the raised pattern of the steel through his thin shoe soles; like Braille. But he did not interpret a message. The fish were arrested, lifelike, in the white, frothing, ground ice. The street was overcast, warm and gray, intimate, unclean, flavored by the polluted river, the sexually stirring brackish tidal odor.

"I can't wait for you, Moses," said Madeleine, peremptory, over her shoulder.

They went into the restaurant and sat at the yellow formica table.

"What were you dawdling for?"

"Well, my mother came from the Baltic provinces. She loved fish."

But Madeleine was not to be interested in Mother Herzog,

twenty years dead, however mother-bound this nostalgic gentle-man's soul might be. Moses, thinking, ruled against himself. He was a fatherly person to Madeleine—he couldn't expect her to consider *his* mother. She was one of the *dead* dead, without effect on the new generation.

On the yellow-plated table was a red flower. The sharp dots of the blossom in a metal holder, or choker, sunk to the neck. Curious to know whether it was plastic too, Herzog touched it. Finding it real, he quickly drew back his fingers. Madeleine was watching.

"You *know* I'm in a hurry," she said.

She was fond of English muffins. He ordered them. She called after the waitress, "Tear mine. Please don't slice them." She tilted her chin to Moses, then, and said, "Moses, is my makeup on all right—on my neck?"

"With your complexion, you don't need any of this."

"But is it ragged?"

"No. Am I going to see you later?"

"I'm not sure. I've been invited for cocktails out at Fordham—for one of the missionaries."

"But afterwards—I can catch a late train to Philly."

"I promised Mother. . . . She's having trouble again with the old man."

"I thought it was all settled—divorce."

"She's such a slave!" said Madeleine. "She can't let go, and neither will he. It's to his advantage. She still goes to that rotten acting school after hours and keeps his books. He's the great thing in her life—another Stanislavsky. She sacrificed herself and if he's not a great genius what was it all for! Therefore he *is* a great genius. . . ."

"I've heard people say what a brilliant director he was."

"He has *something*," said Madeleine. "Almost a female kind of insight. And he drugs people—it's evil the way he does it. Tennie says he spends about fifty thousand a year just on himself alone. He uses all his genius to burn that money."

"It sounds to me as though she's keeping his books for your sake—trying to save what she can for you."

"He'll leave nothing but lawsuits and debts. . . ." She set her teeth in the toasted muffin—they were girlish, short. But then, she

114

did not eat. She put the muffin down, and her eyes filled in their strange manner.

"What's wrong? Eat."

She pushed away the plate, however. "I've asked you not to phone me, up at Fordham. It upsets me. I have to keep the two things separate."

"I'm sorry. I won't."

"I've been beside myself. I'm ashamed to go to Monsignor for confession."

"Won't another priest do?"

She put down her cup with a sharp crack of clumsy restaurant china. A pale lipstick mark was on the rim. "The last priest bawled hell out of me about you. He asked how long *had* I been in the Church? Why *was* I baptized if I was going to act like this within a few months!" The great eyes of the middle-aged woman she had made herself up to be accused him. Across her white face were the straight brows she had given herself. He thought he could see the true outline beneath.

"God! I'm sorry," said Moses. He looked contrite. "I don't want to make trouble." This was certainly untrue. On the contrary, he was bent on making trouble. He thought difficulty was the whole object. She wanted Moses and the Monsignor to struggle over her. It heightened the sexual excitement. He fought her apostasy in the sack. And certainly the Monsignor made female converts with his burning eyes.

"I feel miserable—miserable," she said. "It'll be Ash Wednesday soon, and I can't take Communion till I confess."

"That's awkward. . . ." Moses really did sympathize with her, but he wouldn't offer to bow out.

"And what about marriage? How can we marry?"

"Things can be worked out—the Church is a wise old institution."

"At the office they talk about Joe DiMaggio, when he wanted to marry Marilyn Monroe. And the Tyrone Power case—one of his last marriages was performed by a prince of the Church. The other day there was another thing in Leonard Lyons about Catholic divorces." Madeleine read all the gossip columnists. Her bookmarks in St. Augustine and in her missal were clippings from the *Post* and *Mirror*.

"Favorable?" asked Moses, doubling his muffin over and pressing it—it was buttered too thickly.

Madeleine's large, violet eyes seemed swollen. Her thoughts were strained with these difficulties, many times analyzed. "I have an appointment with an Italian priest in the Society for the Propagation of the Faith. He's a canon-law expert. I phoned him yesterday."

In the Church twelve weeks, she already knew everything.

"It would be easier if Daisy would divorce me," said Herzog.

"She's *got* to give you a divorce." Madeleine's voice rose sharply. Herzog found himself looking at the face which had been prepared for the Jesuits, uptown. But something had happened—some string had tightened and twisted in her breast, and her figure grew rigid. Her fingertips whitened as she pressed the edge of the table and glared at him, her lips thinning and the color darkening under the tubercular pallor of her makeup. "What makes you think I intend to have a lifelong affair with you? I want some action."

"But Mady—you know how I feel. . . ."

"Feel? Don't give me that line of platitudes about feelings. I don't believe in it. I believe in God—sin—death—so don't pull any sentimental crap on me."

"No—now listen." He put on his fedora, as if he hoped to derive some authority from it.

"I want to be married," she said. "This other stuff is just balls! My mother had to live a bohemian life. She worked, while Pontritter carried on. He bribed me with nickels when I saw him with one of his broads. You know how I learned my ABC's? From Lenin's *State and Revolution*. Those people are insane!"

Probably so, Herzog mentally agreed. But now Madeleine wants white Christmases and Easter bunnies and to live perhaps in one of those streets of brick, semi-detached parochial houses in the dull wilderness of Queens borough, fussing over Communion dresses, with a steady Irish husband who sweeps up the crumbs at the biscuit factory.

"Maybe I have become a fanatic about conventional things," said Madeleine. "But I won't have it any other way. You and I have got to marry in the Church, otherwise I quit. Our children will be baptized and brought up in the Church." Moses gave a dumb half-nod. Compared with her he felt static, without temperament. The powdered fragrance of her face stirred him (my gratitude for art, was his present reflection, any sort of art).

"My childhood was a grotesque nightmare," she went on. "I was bullied, assaulted, ab-ab-ab . . ." she stammered.

"Abused?"

She nodded. She had told him this before. He could not bring this sexual secret of hers to light.

"It was a grown man," she said. "He paid me to keep it quiet."

"Who was he?"

Her eyes were sullenly full and her pretty mouth desperately vengeful but silent.

"It happens to many, many people," he said. "Can't base a whole life on that. It doesn't mean that much."

"What—a whole year of amnesia not mean much? My fourteenth year is blacked out."

She couldn't accept this broad-minded consolation from Herzog. Perhaps it seemed to her a kind of indifference. "My parents damn near destroyed me. All right—it doesn't matter now," she said. "I believe in my Savior, Jesus Christ. I'm not afraid of d-death now, Moses. Pon said we all died and rotted in the grave. Saying that to a girl of six or seven. He ought to be punished for it. But now I'm willing to go on living, and to bring children into the world, provided that I have something to tell them when they ask me about death and the grave. But don't expect me to go along in the ordinary loose way—without rules. No! It'll be these rules or nothing."

Moses watched her as though he were submerged, through the vitreous distortion of deep water.

"Do you hear me?"

"Oh, yes," he said. "Yes. I do."

"I've got to go now. Father Francis is never a minute late." She picked up her handbag and hurried away, her cheeks shaken by the abruptness of her steps. She wore very high heels.

Rushing into the subway on one of those mornings, she caught a heel in the hem of her skirt and fell, injuring her back. She limped up to the street and took a taxi to the office but Father Francis sent her to the doctor, who taped her heavily and told her to go home. There she found Moses, still half dressed, having a thoughtful cup of coffee (he was thinking continually, but nothing clear resulted).

"Help me!" Madeleine said.

"What happened?"

"I fell in the subway. I'm hurt." Her voice was piercing.

"You'd better lie down," he said. He unpinned her hat, and carefully unbuttoned her jacket and sweater, took off her skirt and slip. The clear, pink color of her body was disclosed below the makeup line at the base of her neck. He took off the pectoral cross.

"Get me pajamas." She was shivering. The broad tapes had a strongly medicated smell. He led her to the bed and lay down with her to warm and comfort her, just as she wanted him to. There was a March snow, that grimy day. He did not go back to Philadelphia.

"I punished myself for my sins," Madeleine repeated.

I thought it might interest you to learn the true history of one of your converts, Monsignor. Ecclesiastical dolls—gold-threaded petticoats, whining organ pipes. The actual world, to say nothing of the infinite universe, demanded a sterner, a real masculine character.

Like whose? thought Herzog. Mine, for instance? And, instead of concluding this letter to Monsignor, he wrote out, for his own use, one of June's favorite nursery rhymes.

> *I love little pussy, her coat is so warm*
> *And if I don't hurt her, she'll do me no harm.*
> *I'll sit by the fire and give her some food,*
> *And pussy will love me because I am good.*

That's more like it, he thought. Yes. You must aim the imagination also at yourself, point-blank.

But when all was said and done, Madeleine didn't marry in the Church, nor did she baptize her daughter. Catholicism went the way of zithers and tarot cards, bread-baking and Russian civilization. And life in the country.

———

With Madeleine, Herzog had made his second attempt to live in the country. For a big-city Jew he was peculiarly devoted to country life. He had forced Daisy to endure a freezing winter in eastern Connecticut while he was writing *Romanticism and Christianity,* in a cottage where the pipes had to be thawed with candles and freezing blasts penetrated the clapboard walls while Herzog brooded over his Rousseau or practiced on the oboe. The instrument had been left to him at the death of Aleck Hirshbein, his roommate at Chicago, and Herzog with his odd sense of piety (much heavy love in Herzog; grief did not pass quickly, with him) taught himself to play the instrument and, come to think of it, the sad music must have oppressed Daisy even more than the months of cold fog. Perhaps Marco's character had been affected by the experience, too; at times he showed a streak of melancholy.

But with Madeleine it was going to be altogether different. She dropped from the Church and after a struggle with Daisy and her lawyers and his own, and under pressure from Tennie and Madeleine, Moses was divorced and remarried. The wedding supper was cooked by Phoebe Gersbach. Herzog, at his desk, gazing at great scrolls of cloud (the sky unusually clear for New York), remembered the Yorkshire pudding and the home-made cake. Phoebe baked incomparable banana cakes, light, moist, white icing. A doll bride and groom. And Gersbach, boisterous, yucking it up, poured whisky, wine, pounded the table, danced, stumping, with the bride. He wore one of his favorite loose sports shirts, which opened on his big chest and slipped away from his shoulders softly. Male decolleté. There were no other guests.

The house in Ludeyville was bought when Madeleine became pregnant. It seemed the ideal place to work out the problems Herzog had become involved with in *The Phenomenology of Mind* —the importance of the "law of the heart" in Western traditions, the origins of moral sentimentalism and related matters, on which he had distinctly different ideas. He was going—he smiled secretly now, admitting it—to wrap the subject up, to pull the carpet from under all other scholars, show them what was what, stun them, expose their triviality once and for all. It was not simple vanity, but a sense of responsibility that was the underlying motive. That he would say for himself. He was a *bien pensant* type. He took seriously Heinrich Heine's belief that the words of Rousseau had turned into the bloody machine of Robespierre, that Kant and Fichte were deadlier than armies. He had a small foundation grant, and his twenty-thousand-dollar legacy from Father Herzog went into the country place.

He turned into its caretaker. Twenty thousand and more would have gone down the drain if he hadn't thrown himself into the work—Papa's savings, representing forty years of misery in America. I don't understand how it was possible, thought Herzog. I was in a fever when I wrote the check. I didn't even look.

But after the papers were signed he inspected the house as if for the first time. It was unpainted, gloomy, with rotting Victorian ornaments. Nothing on the ground floor but a huge hole like a shell crater. The plaster was coming down—moldy, thready, sickening stuff hung from the laths. The old fashioned knob-and-tube wiring was dangerous. Bricks were dropping from the foundations. The windows leaked.

Herzog learned masonry, glazing, plumbing. He sat up nights studying the *Do-It-Yourself Encyclopedia,* and with hysterical passion he painted, patched, tarred gutters, plastered holes. Two coats of paint counted for nothing on old, open-grained wood. In the bathroom the nails hadn't been set and their heads worked through the vinyl tiles, which came loose like playing cards. The gas radiator was suffocating. The electric heater blew fuses. The tub was a relic; it rested on four metal talons, toylike. You had to crouch in it and sponge yourself. Still, Madeleine had come back from Sloane's Bath Shop with luxurious fixtures, scallop-shell silver soap dishes and bars of Ecusson soap, thick Turkish towels. Herzog worked in the rusty slime of the toilet tank, trying to get the cock and ball to work. At night he heard the trickle that was exhausting the well.

A year of work saved the house from collapse.

In the cellar was another lavatory with thick walls like a bunker. In summer the crickets liked it best, and so did Herzog. Here he loitered over a ten-cent bargain Dryden and Pope. Through a chink he saw the fiery morning of high summer, the wicked spiny green of vines, and the tight, shapely heads of wild roses, the huge elm in front, dying on him, the oriole's nest, gray and heart-shaped. He read, "I am His Highness' dog at Kew." But Herzog had a touch of arthritis in the neck. The stony cell became too damp. He removed the top of the tank with a grating noise and pulled the rubber fitting to release the water. The parts were rusty, stiff.

> . . . His Highness' dog at Kew,
> Pray tell me, Sir, whose dog are you?

Mornings he tried to reserve for brainwork. He corresponded with the Widener Library to try to get the *Abhandlungen der Königlich Sächsischen Gesellschaft der Wissenschaft*. His desk was covered with unpaid bills, unanswered letters. To raise money, he took on hackwork. University presses sent manuscripts for his professional judgment. They lay in bundles, unopened. The sun grew hot, the soil was damp and black, and Herzog looked with despair on the thriving luxuriant life of the plants. He had all this paper to get through, and no help. The house was waiting—huge, hollow, urgent. QUOS VULT PERDERE DEMENTAT, he lettered in dust. The gods were working on him, but they hadn't demented him enough yet.

In commenting on monographs, Moses' very hand rebelled. Five minutes at a letter and he got writer's cramp. His look turned wooden. He was running out of excuses. *I regret the delay. A bad case of poison ivy has kept me from my desk.* Elbows on his papers, Moses stared at half-painted walls, discolored ceilings, filthy windows. Something had come over him. He used to be able to keep going, but now he worked at about two per cent of efficiency, handled every piece of paper five or ten times and misplaced everything. It was too much! He was going under.

He picked up the oboe. In his dark study, vines clutching the bulging screen, Herzog played Handel and Purcell—jigs, bourrées, contredanses, his face puffed out, fingers fleet on the keys, the music hopping and tumbling, absent-minded and sad. Below, the washing machine ran, two steps clockwise, one step counter. The kitchen was foul enough to breed rats. Egg yolks dried on the plates, coffee turned green in the cups—toast, cereal, maggots breeding in marrow bones, fruit flies, house flies, dollar bills, postage stamps and trading stamps soaking on the formica counter.

Madeleine, to get away from his music, slammed the screen door, slammed the car door. The motor roared. The Studebaker had a split in the muffler. She started down the slope. Unless you remembered to bear right the tailpipe would scrape on the rocks. Herzog played softer as he waited for the sound. That muffler would come off one of these days, but he had stopped mentioning it to her. He had too many subjects of this sort. They made her angry. Through a cover of honeysuckle that bent the screen inward he watched for her to reappear on the second curve of the slope. Pregnancy had thickened her features but she was still beautiful. Such beauty makes men breeders, studs and servants. As she drove, her nose worked involuntarily under the sight-obscuring fringe of her hair (all part of the process of steering). Her fingers, some elegant, some nail-bitten, gripped the agate steering wheel. He declared it was unsafe for a pregnant woman to drive. He thought she must at least get a driver's license. She said if a state trooper stopped her, she could sweet-talk him.

When she was gone, he dried the oboe, looked over the reeds, shut the frowzy plush case. He wore fieldglasses about his neck. Once in a while he tried to examine a bird. Usually it was gone before he could get it in focus. Abandoned, he sat at his desk, a flush door on wrought-iron legs. Philodendrons grew from the base of his lamp, twining about the iron. With a rubber band he shot wads of paper at the horseflies on the paint-streaked windows. He was not a skillful painter. He tried a spray gun at first, attaching it to the rear of the vacuum cleaner, a very efficient blower. Muffled in rags to protect the lungs, Moses sprayed ceilings, but the gun speckled the windows and banisters and he went back to the brush. Dragging the ladder and buckets and rags and thinners, scraping with his putty knife, he patched and painted, reaching left, right, above, this stretch, beyond, way out, to the corner, to the molding, his taut hand trying to achieve a straight line, laying paint on in big strokes or in an agony of finesse. Spattered and streaming sweat when the frenzy wore off, he went into the garden. Stripped naked, he fell in the hammock.

Meanwhile, Madeleine toured the antique shops with Phoebe Gersbach, or brought home loads of groceries from the Pittsfield supermarkets. Moses was continually after her about money. Beginning his reproaches, he tried to keep his voice low. It was always something trivial that set him off—a bounced check, a chicken that had rotted in the icebox, a new shirt torn up for rags. Gradually his feelings became very fierce.

"When are you going to stop bringing home this junk, Madeleine —these busted commodes, these spinning wheels."

"We have to furnish the place. I can't stand these empty rooms."

"Where's all the dough going? I'm working myself sick." He felt black with rage inside.

"I pay the bills—what do you think I do with it?"

"You said you had to learn to handle money. No one ever trusted you. Well, you're being trusted now and the checks are bouncing. The dress shop just phoned—Milly Crozier. Five hundred bucks on a maternity outfit. Who's going to be born—Louis Quatorze?"

"Yes, I know, your darling mother wore flour sacks."

"You don't need a Park Avenue obstetrician. Phoebe Gersbach used the Pittsfield hospital. How can I get you to New York from here? It's three and a half hours."

"We'll go ten days before."

"What about all this work?"

"You can carry your Hegel to the city. You haven't cracked a book in months anyway. The whole thing is a neurotic mess. These bushels of notes. It's grotesque how disorganized you are. You're no better than any other kind of addict—sick with abstractions. Curse Hegel, anyway, and this crappy old house. It needs four servants, and you want me to do all the work."

Herzog made himself dull by repeating what was right. He was maddening, too. He realized it. He appeared to know how everything ought to go, down to the smallest detail (under the category of "Free Concrete Mind," misapprehension of a universal by the developing consciousness—reality opposing the "law of the heart," alien necessity gruesomely crushing individuality, *und-soweiter*). Oh, Herzog granted that he was in the wrong. But all he asked, it seemed to him, was a bit of cooperation in his effort, benefiting everyone, to work toward a meaningful life. Hegel was curiously significant but also utterly cockeyed. Of course. That was the whole point. Simpler and without such elaborate metaphysical rigmarole was Spinoza's Prop. XXXVII; man's desire to have others rejoice in the good in which he rejoices, not to make others live according to his way of thinking—*ex ipsius ingenio*.

Herzog, mulling over these ideas as he all alone painted his walls in Ludeyville, building Versailles as well as Jerusalem in the green hot Berkshire summers. Time and again he was brought down from the ladder to the telephone. Madeleine's checks were bouncing.

"Jesus Christ!" he cried out. "Not again, Mady!"

She was ready for him in a bottle-green maternity blouse and knee-length stockings. She was becoming very stout. The doctor had warned her not to eat candy. On the sly, she greedily devoured enormous Hershey bars, the thirty-cent size.

"Can't you add! There's not a damn reason in the world for these checks to come back." Moses glared at her.

"Oh—here we go with this same petty stuff."

"It's not petty. It's damn serious. . . ."

"I suppose you'll start on my upbringing now—my lousy, free-loading bohemian family, all chiselers. And you gave me your good name. I know this routine backwards."

"Do I repeat myself? Well, so do you, Madeleine, with these checks."

"Spending your dead father's money. Dear Daddy! That's what you choke on. Well, he was *your* father. I don't ask you to share *my* horrible father. So don't try to force your old man down my throat."

"We've got to have a little order in these surroundings."

Madeleine said quickly, firmly, and accurately, "You'll never get the surroundings *you* want. Those are in the twelfth century somewhere. Always crying for the old home and the kitchen table with the oilcloth on it and your Latin book. Okay—let's hear your sad old story. Tell me about your poor mother. And your father. And your boarder, the drunkard. And the old synagogue, and the bootlegging, and your Aunt Zipporah . . . Oh, what balls!"

"As if you didn't have a past of your own."

"Oh, balls! So now we're going to hear how you SAVED me. Let's hear it again. What a frightened puppy I was. How I wasn't strong enough to face life. But you gave me LOVE, from your big heart, and rescued me from the priests. Yes, cured me of menstrual cramps by servicing me so good. You SAVED me. You SACRIFICED your freedom. I took you away from Daisy and your son, and your Japanese screw. Your important time and money and attention." Her wild blue glare was so intense that her eyes seemed twisted.

"Madeleine!"

"Oh—shit!"

"Just think a minute."

"Think? What do you know about thinking?"

"Maybe I married you to improve my mind!" said Herzog. "I'm learning."

"Well, I'll teach you, don't worry!" said the beautiful, pregnant Madeleine between her teeth.

Herzog noted, from a favorite source—*Opposition is true friendship. His house, his child, yea, all that a man hath will he give for wisdom.*

The husband—a beautiful soul—the exceptional wife, the angelic child and the perfect friends all dwelt in the Berkshires together. The learned professor sat at his studies. . . . Oh, he had really been asking for it. Because he insisted on being the ingénu whose earnestness made his own heart flutter—*zisse n'shamele,* a sweet little soul, Tennie had called Moses. At forty; to earn such a banal reputation! His forehead grew wet. Such stupidity deserved harsher punishment—a sickness, a jail sentence. Again, he was only being "lucky" (Ramona, food and wine, invitations to the seashore). Still, extreme self-abuse was not really interesting to him, either. It was not the most relevant thing. *Not* to be a fool might not be worth the difficult alternatives. Anyway, who was that non-fool? Was it the power-lover, who bent the public to his will—the scientific intellectual who administered a budget of billions? Clear eyes, a hard head, a penetrating political intelligence —the organizational realist? Now wouldn't it be nice to be one? But Herzog worked under different orders—doing, he trusted, the work of the future. The revolutions of the twentieth century, the liberation of the masses by production, created private life but gave nothing to fill it with. This was where such as he came in. The progress of civilization—indeed, the survival of civilization—depended on the successes of Moses E. Herzog. And in treating him as she did, Madeleine injured a great project. This was, in the eyes of Moses E. Herzog, what was so grotesque and deplorable about the experience of Moses E. Herzog.

A very special sort of lunatic expects to inculcate his principles. Sandor Himmelstein, Valentine Gersbach, Madeleine P. Herzog, Moses himself. *Reality instructors. They want to teach you—to punish you with—the lessons of the Real.*

Moses, a collector of pictures, had kept a photograph of Madeleine, aged twelve, in riding habit. She was posed with the horse, about to mount, a stocky long-haired girl with fat wrists and desperate dark shadows under her eyes, premature signs of suffering and of a craving for revenge. In jodhpurs, boots, and bowler she had the hauteur of the female child who knows it won't be long before she is nubile and has the power to hurt. This is mental politics. The strength to do evil is sovereignty. She knew more at twelve than I did at forty.

Now Daisy had been a very different sort of person —cooler, more regular, a conventional Jewish woman. Herzog had photographs of her, too, in his foot locker under the bed, but there was no need to examine pictures, he could evoke her face at will—slant green eyes, large ones, kinky, golden but lusterless hair, a clear skin. Her manner was shy but also rather stubborn. Without difficulty, Herzog saw her as she had appeared on a summer morning beneath the El on 51st Street, Chicago, a college student with grimy texts—Park and Burgess, Ogburn and Nimkoff. Her dress was simple, thin-striped green-and-white seersucker, square at the neck. Beneath its laundered purity, she had small white shoes, bare legs, and her hair was held at the top by a barrette. The red streetcar came from the slums to the west. It clanged, swayed, wallowed, its trolley shedding thick green sparks, tatters of paper flying in its wake. Moses had stood behind her on the carbolic-reeking platform when she gave her transfer slip to the conductor. From her bare neck and shoulders he inhaled the fragrance of summer apples. Daisy was a country girl, a Buckeye who grew up near Zanesville. She was childishly systematic about things. It sometimes amused Moses to recall that she had a file card, clumsily printed out, to cover every situation. Her awkward form of organization had had a certain charm. When they were married she put his pocket money in an envelope, in a green metal file bought for budgeting. Daily reminders, bills, concert tickets were pinned by thumbtacks to the bulletin board. Calendars were marked well in advance. Stability, symmetry, order, containment were Daisy's strength.

Dear Daisy, I have a few things to say to you. By my irregularity and turbulence of spirit I brought out the very worst in Daisy. *I* caused the seams of her stockings to be so straight, and the buttons to be buttoned symmetrically. *I* was behind those rigid curtains and underneath the square carpets. Roast breast of veal every Sunday with bread stuffing like clay was due to *my* disorders, my huge involvement—huge but evidently formless—in the history of thought. She took Moses' word for it that he was seriously occupied. Of course a wife's duty was to stand by this puzzling and often disagreeable Herzog. She did so with heavy neutrality, recording her objections each time—once but not more. The rest was silence—such heavy silence as he felt in Connecticut when he was finishing *Romanticism and Christianity.*

The chapter on "Romantics and Enthusiasts" nearly did him in—it almost ended them both. (The Enthusiastic reaction against the scientific mode of suspending belief, intolerable to the expressive needs of certain temperaments.) Here Daisy picked up and left him alone in Connecticut. She had to go back to Ohio. Her father was dying. Moses read the literature of Enthusiasm in his cottage, by the small nickel-trimmed kitchen stove. Wrapped in a blanket like an Indian, he listened to the radio—debated the pros and cons of Enthusiasm with himself.

It was a winter of rocklike ice. The pond like a slab of halite—green, white, resonant ice, bitterly ringing underfoot. The trickling mill dam froze in twisting pillars. The elms, giant harp shapes, made cracking noises. Herzog, responsible to civilization in his icy outpost, lying in bed in an aviator's helmet when the stoves were out, fitted together Bacon and Locke from one side and Methodism and William Blake from the other. His nearest neighbor was a clergyman, Mr. Idwal. Idwal's automobile, a Model A Ford, was running when Herzog's Whippet had frozen solid. They drove to the market together. Mrs. Idwal made graham-cracker pies filled with chocolate gelatin, and left them, neighborly, on Moses' table. He returned from his solitary walks on the pond, in the woods, and found pies in big Pyrex plates on which he warmed his numb cheeks and fingertips. In the morning, eating gelatin pie for breakfast, he saw Idwal, ruddy and small, with steel spectacles, in his bedroom swinging Indian clubs, doing knee-bends in his long underwear. His wife sat in her parlor, hands folded, the spidery design of lace curtains thrown on her face by sunlight. Moses was invited to play his oboe, accompanying Mrs. Idwal, who played a melodeon, on Sunday evenings while the farm families sang hymns. And were they farmers? No, they were the country poor—odd-job people. The little parlor was hot, the air bad, the hymns pierced with Jewish melancholy by Moses and his reeds.

His relations with the Reverend and Mrs. Idwal were excellent until the minister started to give him testimonials by orthodox rabbis who had embraced the Christian faith. The photos of these rabbis in fur hats, bearded, were put down with the pies. The large eyes of those men and especially their lips thrust out from foaming beards began to seem crazy to Moses, and he thought it time to get away from the snowbound cottage. He was afraid for his own sanity, living like this, especially after the death of Daisy's father. Moses thought he saw him, met him in the woods, and when he opened doors he encountered his father-in-law, vivid and characteristic, waiting by a table or sitting in the bathroom.

Herzog made a mistake in rejecting Idwal's rabbis. The clergyman was keener than ever to convert him and dropped in every afternoon for theological discussions until Daisy returned. Sad, clear-eyed, mostly mute, resistant. But a wife. And the child! The thaws began—ideal for making snowmen. Moses and Marco lined the drive with them. Little anthracite eyes glittered even by starlight. In spring the blackness of night was filled with shrilling cheepers. Herzog's heart began to warm toward the country. The blood-colored sunsets of winter and solitude were behind him. They didn't seem so bad now that he had survived them.

Survival! he noted. *Till we figure out what's what. Till the chance comes to exert a positive influence.* (Personal responsibility for history, a trait of Western culture, rooted in the Testaments, Old and New, the idea of the continual improvement of human life on this earth. What else explained Herzog's ridiculous intensity?) *Lord, I ran to fight in Thy holy cause, but kept tripping, never reached the scene of the struggle.*

He saw through this as well. If nothing else, he was too rich in diseases to be satisfied with such a description. From the middle height of New York, looking down, seeing lunchtime crowds like ants upon smoked glass, Herzog, wrapped in his wrinkled robe and sipping cold coffee, set apart from daily labor for greater achievements, but at present without confidence in his calling, tried now and again to get back to work. *Dear Dr. Mossbach, I*

*am sorry you are not satisfied with my treatment of T. E. Hulme
and his definition of Romanticism as "split religion." There is
something to be said for his view. He wanted things to be clear,
dry, spare, pure, cool, and hard. With this I think we can all
sympathize. I too am repelled by the "dampness," as he called it,
and the swarming of Romantic feelings. I see what a villain Rousseau was, and how degenerate (I do not complain that he was un-
gentlemanly; it ill becomes me). But I do not see what we can
answer when he says "Je sens mon cœur et je connais les hommes."
Bottled religion, on conservative principles—does that intend to
deprive the heart of such powers—do you think? Hulme's followers
made sterility their truth, confessing their impotence. This was
their passion.*

Still fighting it out, Herzog was fairly deadly in polemics. His
polite formulas often carried much spleen. His docile ways, his
modest conduct—he didn't deceive himself. The certainty of being
right, a flow of power, rose in his bowels and burned in his legs.
Queer, the luxurious victories of anger! There was passionate satire
in Herzog. Still he knew that the demolition of error was not *it*. He
began to have a new horror of winning, of the victories of untram-
meled autonomy. *Man has a nature, but what is it? Those who have
confidently described it, Hobbes, Freud, et cetera, by telling us what
we are "intrinsically," are not our greatest benefactors. This is
true also for Rousseau. I sympathize with Hulme's attack on the
introduction by the Romantics of Perfection into human things,
but do not like his narrow repressiveness, either. Modern science,
least bothered with the definition of human nature, knowing only
the activity of investigation, achieves its profoundest results
through anonymity, recognizing only the brilliant functioning of intellect. Such truth as it finds may be nothing to live by, but perhaps
a moratorium on definitions of human nature is now best.*

Herzog abandoned this theme with characteristic abruptness.

Dear Nachman, he wrote. *I know it was you I saw on 8th St.
last Monday. Running away from me.* Herzog's face darkened. *It
was you. My friend nearly forty years ago—playmates on Napoleon Street. The Montreal slums.* In a beatnik cap, on the razzle-
dazzle street of lion-bearded homosexuals wearing green eye
paint, there, suddenly, was Herzog's childhood playmate. A heavy
nose, hair white, thick unclean glasses. The stooped poet took one

look at Moses and ran away. On gaunt legs, under urgent pressure, he fled to the other side of the street. He turned up his collar and stared into the window of the cheese shop. *Nachman! Did you think I'd ask for the money you owe me? I wrote that off, long ago. It meant very little to me, in Paris after the War. I had it then.*

Nachman had come to Europe to write poetry. He was living in the Arab slum on Rue St. Jacques. Herzog was installed in comfort on the Rue Marbeuf. Wrinkled and dirty, Nachman, his nose red from weeping, his creased face the face of a dying man, appeared at Herzog's door one morning.

"What's happened!"

"Moses, they've taken my wife away—my little Laura."

"Wait a minute—what's up?" Herzog was perhaps a little cold, then, repelled by such excesses.

"Her father. The old man from the floor-covering business. Spirited her away. The old Sorcerer. She'll die without me. The child can't bear life without me. And I can't live without her. I've got to get back to New York."

"Come in. Come in. We can't talk in this lousy hallway."

Nachman entered the little drawing room. It was a furnished apartment in the style of the twenties—spitefully correct. Nachman seemed hesitant to sit down, in his gutter-stained pants. "I've been to all the lines already. There's space on the *Hollandia* tomorrow. Lend me dough or I'm ruined. You're my only friend in Paris."

Honestly, I thought you'd be better off in America.

Nachman and Laura had been wandering up and down Europe, sleeping in ditches in the Rimbaud country, reading Van Gogh's letters aloud to each other—Rilke's poems. Laura was not too strong in the head, either. She was thin, soft-faced, the corners of her pale mouth turned down. She caught the flu in Belgium.

"I'll pay you every penny." Nachman wrung his hands. His fingers had grown knobby—rheumatic. His face was coarse—slack from illness, suffering, and absurdity.

I felt it would be cheaper in the long run to send you back to New York. In Paris I was stuck with you. You see, I don't pretend that I was altruistic. Perhaps, thought Herzog, the sight of *me* frightened *him*. Have I changed even more than he has? Was Nachman horrified to see Moses? *But we did play in the street together. I learned the* aleph-beth *from your father, Reb Shika.*

Nachman's family lived in the yellow tenement just opposite. Five years old, Moses crossed Napoleon Street. Up the wooden staircase with slanted, warped treads. Cats shrank into corners or bolted softly upstairs. Their dry turds crumbled in the darkness with a spicy odor. Reb Shika had a yellow color, Mongolian, a tiny handsome man. He wore a black satin skullcap, a mustache like Lenin's. His narrow chest was clad in a winter undershirt— Penman's woollens. The Bible lay open on the coarse table cover. Moses clearly saw the Hebrew characters—DMAI OCHICHO—the blood of thy brother. Yes, that was it. God speaking to Cain. Thy brother's blood cries out to me from the earth.

At eight, Moses and Nachman shared a bench in the cellar of the synagogue. The pages of the Pentateuch smelled of mildew, the boys' sweaters were damp. The rabbi, short-bearded, his soft big nose violently pitted with black, scolding them. "You, Rozavitch, you slacker. What does it say here about Potiphar's wife, *V'tispesayu b'vigdi . . .*"

"And she took hold of . . ."

"Of what? *Beged.*"

"*Beged.* A coat."

"A garment, you little thief. *Mamzer!* I'm sorry for your father. Some heir he's got! Some *Kaddish!* Ham and pork you'll be eating, before his body is in the grave. And you, Herzog, with those behemoth eyes—*V'yaizov bigdo b'yodo.*"

"And he left it in her hands."

"Left what?"

"*Bigdo,* the garment."

"You watch your step, Herzog, Moses. Your mother thinks you'll be a great *lamden*—a rabbi. But I know you, how lazy you are. Mothers' hearts are broken by *mamzeirim* like you! Eh! Do I know you, Herzog? Through and through."

The only refuge was the W.C., where the disinfectant camphor balls dwindled in the green trough of the urinal, and old men came down from the shul with webby eyes nearly blind, sighing, grumbling snatches of liturgy as they waited for the water to come.

Urine-rusted brass, scaly green. In an open stall, pants dropped to his feet, sat Nachman playing the harmonica. "It's a Long, Long Way to Tipperary." "Love Sends a Little Gift of Roses." The peak of his cap was warped. You heard the saliva in the cells of the tin instrument as he sucked and blew. The bowler-hatted elders washed their hands, gave their beards a finger-combing. Moses observed them.

Almost certainly, Nachman ran away from the power of his old friend's memory. Herzog persecuted everyone with it. It was like a terrible engine.

Last time we met—how many years ago was that?—I went with you to visit Laura. Laura was then in an insane asylum. Herzog and Nachman had transferred at six or seven corners. It was a thousand bus stops out on Long Island. In the hospital the women in green cotton dresses wandered in the corridors on soft shoes, murmuring. Laura had bandaged wrists. It was her third suicide attempt that Moses knew of. She sat in a corner, holding her breasts in her arms, wanting to talk of French literature only. Her face was moony, lips however moving quickly. Moses had to agree with what he understood nothing of—the shape of Valéry's images.

Then he and Nachman left, toward sunset. They crossed the cement yard after an autumn rainfall. From the building, a crowd of ghosts in green uniforms watched the visitors depart. Laura, at the grill, raised her taped wrist, a wan hand. Good-by. Her long thin mouth silently said, Good-by, good-by. The straight hair fell beside her cheeks—a stiff childish figure with female swellings. Nachman was hoarsely saying, "My innocent darling. My bride. They've put her away, the grim ones, the *machers*—our masters. Imprisoned her. As if to love me proved she was mad. But I shall be strong enough to protect our love," said gaunt, furrowed Nachman. His cheeks were sunken. Under the eyes his skin was yellow.

"Why does she keep trying to kill herself?" said Moses.

"The persecution of her family. What do you think? The bourgeois world of Westchester! Wedding announcements, linens, charge accounts, that was what her mother and father expected of her. But this is a pure soul that understands only pure things. She is a stranger here. The family only wants to part us. In New York we were wanderers too. When I came back—thanks to you, and I'll repay you, I'll work!—we didn't have money to rent a room. How could I take a job? Who would look after her? So friends gave us shelter. Food. A cot to lie down. To make love."

Herzog was very curious, but he merely said, "Oh?"

"I wouldn't tell anyone but you, old friend. We had to take care. In our ecstasies we had to warn each other to be more moderate. It was like a holy act—we mustn't make the gods jealous. . . ." Nachman spoke in a throbbing, droning voice. "Good-by, my blessed spirit—my dear one. Good-by." He blew kisses at the window with painful sweetness.

On the way to the bus, he went on lecturing in his unreal way, fervent and dull. "So back of it all is bourgeois America. This is a crude world of finery and excrement. A proud, lazy civilization that worships its own boorishness. You and I were brought up in the old poverty. I don't know how American you've become since the old days in Canada—you've lived here a long time. But I will never worship the fat gods. Not I. I'm no Marxist, you know. I keep my heart with William Blake and Rilke. But a man like Laura's father! You understand! Las Vegas, Miami Beach. They wanted Laura to catch a husband at the Fountainblue, a husband with money. At the edge of doom, beside the last grave of mankind, they will still be counting their paper. Praying over their balance sheets. . . ." Nachman went on with boring persistent power. He had lost teeth, and his jaw was smaller, his gray cheeks were bristly. Herzog could still see him as he had been at six. In fact he could not dismiss his vision of the two Nachmans, side by side. And it was the child with his fresh face, the smiling gap in his front teeth, the buttoned blouse and the short pants that was real, not this gaunt apparition of crazy lecturing Nachman. "Perhaps," he was saying, "people wish life to end. They have polluted it. Courage, honor, frankness, friendship, duty, all made filthy. Sullied. So that we loathe the daily bread that prolongs useless existence. There was a time when men were born, lived, and died. But do you call these men? We are only creatures. Death himself must be tired of us. I can see Death coming before God to say 'What shall I do? There is no more grandeur in being Death. Release me, God, from this meanness.' "

"It isn't as bad as you make out, Nachman," Moses remembered answering. "Most people are unpoetical, and you consider this a betrayal."

"Well, childhood friend, you have learned to accept a mixed condition of life. But I have had visions of judgment. I see mainly the obstinacy of cripples. We do not love ourselves, but persist in stubbornness. Each man is stubbornly, stubbornly himself. Above all himself, to the end of time. Each of these creatures has some secret quality, and for this quality he is prepared to do anything. He will turn the universe upside down, but he will not deliver his quality to anyone else. Sooner let the world turn to drifting powder. This is what my poems are about. You don't think highly of my New Psalms. You're blind, old friend."

"Maybe."

"But a good man, Moses. Rooted in yourself. But a good heart. Like your mother. A gentle spirit. You got it from her. I was hungry and she fed me. She washed my hands and sat me at the table. That I remember. She was the only one who was kind to my Uncle Ravitch, the drunkard. I sometimes say a prayer for her."

Yiskor elohim es nishmas Imi . . . the soul of my mother.

"She's been dead a long time."

"And I pray for you, Moses."

The bus on giant tires advanced through sunset-colored puddles over leaves, ailanthus twigs. Its route was interminable, through the low, brick, suburban, populous vastness.

But fifteen years later, on 8th Street, Nachman ran away. He looked old, derelict, stooped, crooked as he sprinted to the cheese shop. Where is his wife? He must have beat it to avoid explanations. His mad sense of decency told him to shun such an encounter. Or has he forgotten everything? Or would he be glad to forget it? But I, with *my* memory—all the dead and the mad are in my custody, and I am the nemesis of the would-be forgotten. I bind others to my feelings, and oppress them.

Was Ravitch actually your uncle, or only a landtsman? I was never certain.

Ravitch boarded with the Herzogs on Napoleon Street. Like a tragic actor of the Yiddish stage, with a straight drunken nose and a bowler pressing on the veins of his forehead, Ravitch, in an apron, worked at the fruit store near Rachel Street in 1922.

There at the market in zero weather he was sweeping a mixed powder of sawdust and snow. The window was covered with large ferns of frost, and against it pressed the piled blood-oranges and russet apples. And that was melancholy Ravitch, red with drink and cold. The project of his life was to send for his family, a wife and two children who were still in Russia. He'd have to find them first, for they were lost during the Revolution. Now and then he soberly cleaned himself up and went to the Hebrew Immigrants' Aid Society to make an inquiry. But nothing ever happened. He drank his pay—a *shicker*. No one judged himself more harshly. When he came out of the saloon he stood wavering in the street, directing traffic, falling among horses and trucks in the slush. The police were tired of throwing him in the drunk tank. They brought him home, to Herzog's hallway, and pushed him in. Ravitch, late at night, sang on the freezing stairs in a sobbing voice.

> *"Alein, alein, alein, alein*
> *Elend vie a shtein*
> *Mit die tzen finger—alein"*

Jonah Herzog got out of bed and turned on the light in the kitchen, listening. He wore a Russian sleeping suit of linen with a pleated front, the last of his gentleman's wardrobe from Petersburg. The stove was out, and Moses, in the same bed with Willie and Shura, sat up, the three of them, under the lumpy wads of the quilt, looking at their father. He stood under the bulb, which had a spike at the end like a German helmet. The large loose twist of tungsten filament blazed. Annoyed and pitying, Father Herzog, with his round head and brown mustache, looked upward. The straight groove between his eyes came and went. He nodded and mused.

> "Alone, alone, alone, alone
> Solitary as a stone
> With my ten fingers—alone"

Mother Herzog spoke from her room, "Yonah—help him in."
"All right," said Father Herzog, but he waited.
"Yonah . . . It's a pity."
"Pity on us, too," said Father Herzog. "Damn it. You sleep,

you're free from misery awhile, and he wakes you up. A Jewish drunkard! He can't even do *that* right. Why can't he be *freilich* and cheerful when he drinks, eh? No, he has to cry and tear your heartstrings. Well, curse him." Half laughing, Father Herzog cursed the heartstrings, too. "It's enough that I have to rent a room to a miserable *shicker*."

> *"Al tastir ponecho mimeni*
> I'm broke without a penny.
> Do not hide Thy countenance from us
> Vich nobody can deny."

Ravitch, tuneless and persistent, cried in the black, frozen staircase.

> "O'Brien
> *Lo mir trinken a glesele vi-ine*
> *Al tastir ponecho mimeni*
> I'm broke without a penny
> Vich nobody can deny."

Father Herzog, silent and wry, laughed under his breath.
"Yonah—I beg you. *Genug schon*."
"Oh, give him time. Why should I *schlepp* out my guts."
"He'll wake the whole street."
"He'll be covered with vomit, his pants filled."
But he went. He pitied Ravitch, too, though Ravitch was one of the symbols of his changed condition. In Petersburg there were servants. In Russia, Father Herzog had been a gentleman. With forged papers of the First Guild. But many gentlemen lived on forged papers.

The children still gazed into the empty kitchen. The black cookstove against the wall, extinct; the double gas ring connected by rubber pipe to the meter. A Japanese reed mat protected the wall from cooking stains.

It amused the boys to hear how their father coaxed drunken Ravitch to get on his feet. It was family theater. *"Nu, landtsman?* Can you walk? It's freezing. Now, get your crooked feet on the step—*schneller, schneller*." He laughed with his bare breath. "Well, I think we'll leave your *dreckische* pants out here. Phew!" The boys pressed together in the cold, smiling.

Papa supported him through the kitchen—Ravitch in his filthy drawers, the red face, dropped hands, the bowler, the drunken grief of his closed eyes.

As for my late unlucky father, J. Herzog, he was not a big man, one of the small-boned Herzogs, finely made, round-headed, keen, nervous, handsome. In his frequent bursts of temper he slapped his sons swiftly with both hands. He did everything quickly, neatly, with skillful Eastern European flourishes: combing his hair, buttoning his shirt, stropping his bone-handled razors, sharpening pencils on the ball of his thumb, holding a loaf of bread to his breast and slicing toward himself, tying parcels with tight little knots, jotting like an artist in his account book. There each canceled page was covered with a carefully drawn X. The 1s and 7s carried bars and streamers. They were like pennants in the wind of failure. First Father Herzog failed in Petersburg, where he went through two dowries in one year. He had been importing onions from Egypt. Under Pobedonostsev the police caught up with him for illegal residence. He was convicted and sentenced. The account of the trial was published in a Russian journal printed on thick green paper. Father Herzog sometimes unfolded it and read aloud to the entire family, translating the proceedings against Ilyona Isakovitch Gerzog. He never served his sentence. He got away. Because he was nervy, hasty, obstinate, rebellious. He came to Canada, where his sister Zipporah Yaffe was living.

In 1913 he bought a piece of land near Valleyfield, Quebec, and failed as a farmer. Then he came into town and failed as a baker; failed in the dry-goods business; failed as a jobber; failed as a sack manufacturer in the War, when no one else failed. He failed as a junk dealer. Then he became a marriage broker and failed— too short-tempered and blunt. And now he was failing as a bootlegger, on the run from the provincial Liquor Commission. Making a bit of a living.

In haste and defiantly, with a clear tense face, walking with mingled desperation and high style, a little awkwardly dropping his weight on one heel as he went, his coat, once lined with fox, turned dry and bald, the red hide cracking. This coat sweeping open as he walked, or marched his one-man Jewish march, he was saturated with the odor of the Caporals he smoked as he covered Montreal in his swing—Papineau, Mile-End, Verdun, Lachine, Point St. Charles. He looked for business opportunities—bankruptcies, job lots, mergers, fire sales, produce—to rescue him from illegality. He could calculate percentages mentally at high speed, but he lacked the cheating imagination of a successful businessman. And so he kept a little still in Mile-End, where goats fed in the empty lots. He traveled on the tramcar. He sold a bottle here and there and waited for his main chance. American rum-runners would buy the stuff from you at the border, any amount, spot cash, if you could get it there. Meanwhile he smoked cigarettes on the cold platforms of streetcars. The Revenue was trying to catch him. Spotters were after him. On the roads to the border were hijackers. On Napoleon Street he had five mouths to feed. Willie and Moses were sickly. Helen studied the piano. Shura was fat, greedy, disobedient, a plotting boy. The rent, back rent, notes due, doctors' bills to pay, and he had no English, no friends, no influence, no trade, no assets but his still—no help in all the world. His sister Zipporah in St. Anne was rich, very rich, which only made matters worse.

Grandfather Herzog was still alive, then. With the instinct of a Herzog for the grand thing, he took refuge in the Winter Palace in 1918 (the Bolsheviks allowed it for a while). The old man wrote long letters in Hebrew. He had lost his precious books in the upheaval. Study was impossible now. In the Winter Palace you had to walk up and down all day to find a *minyan*. Of course there was hunger, too. Later, he predicted that the Revolution would fail and tried to acquire Czarist currency, to become a millionaire under the restored Romanoffs. The Herzogs received packets of worthless rubles, and Willie and Moses played with great sums. You held the glorious bills to the light and you saw Peter the Great and Catherine in the watermarked rainbow paper. Grandfather Herzog was in his eighties but still strong. His mind was powerful and his Hebrew calligraphy elegant. The letters were read aloud in Montreal by Father Herzog—accounts of cold, lice, famine, epidemics, the dead. The old man wrote, "Shall I ever see the faces of my children? And who will bury me?" Father Herzog approached the next phrase two or three times, but could not find his full voice. Only a whisper came out. The tears were in his eyes and he suddenly put his hand over his mustached mouth and hurried from the room. Mother Herzog, large-eyed, sat with the children in the primitive kitchen which the sun never entered. It was like a cave with the ancient black stove, the iron sink, the green cupboards, the gas ring.

Mother Herzog had a way of meeting the present with a partly averted face. She encountered it on the left but sometimes seemed to avoid it on the right. On this withdrawn side she often had a dreaming look, melancholy, and seemed to be seeing the Old World—her father the famous *misnagid,* her tragic mother, her brothers living and dead, her sister, and her linens and servants in Petersburg, the dacha in Finland (all founded on Egyptian onions). Now she was cook, washerwoman, seamstress on Napoleon Street in the slum. Her hair turned gray, and she lost her teeth, her very fingernails wrinkled. Her hands smelled of the sink.

Herzog was thinking, however, how she found the strength to spoil her children. She certainly spoiled me. Once, at nightfall, she was pulling me on the sled, over crusty ice, the tiny glitter of snow, perhaps four o'clock of a short day in January. Near the grocery we met an old baba in a shawl who said, "Why are you pulling him, daughter!" Mama, dark under the eyes. Her slender cold face. She was breathing hard. She wore the torn seal coat and a red pointed wool cap and thin button boots. Clusters of dry fish hung in the shop, a rancid sugar smell, cheese, soap—a terrible dust of nutrition came from the open door. The bell on a coil of wire was bobbing, ringing. "Daughter, don't sacrifice your strength to children," said the shawled crone in the freezing dusk of the street. I wouldn't get off the sled. I pretended not to understand. One of life's hardest jobs, to make a quick understanding slow. I think I succeeded, thought Herzog.

Mama's brother Mikhail died of typhus in Moscow. I took the letter from the postman and brought it upstairs—the long latchstring ran through loops under the banister. It was washday. The copper boiler steamed the window. She was rinsing and wringing in a tub. When she read the news she gave a cry and fainted. Her lips turned white. Her arm lay in the water, sleeve and all. We two were alone in the house. I was terrified when she lay like that, legs spread, her long hair undone, lids brown, mouth bloodless, deathlike. But then she got up and went to lie down. She wept all day. But in the morning she cooked the oatmeal nevertheless. We were up early.

My ancient times. Remoter than Egypt. No dawn, the foggy winters. In darkness, the bulb was lit. The stove was cold. Papa shook the grates, and raised an ashen dust. The grates grumbled and squealed. The puny shovel clinked underneath. The Caporals gave Papa a bad cough. The chimneys in their helmets sucked in the wind. Then the milkman came in his sleigh. The snow was spoiled and rotten with manure and litter, dead rats, dogs. The milkman in his sheepskin gave the bell a twist. It was brass, like the winding-key of a clock. Helen pulled the latch and went down with a pitcher for the milk. And then Ravitch, hung-over, came from his room, in his heavy sweater, suspenders over the wool to keep it tighter to the body, the bowler on his head, red in the face, his look guilty. He waited to be asked to sit.

The morning light could not free itself from gloom and frost. Up and down the street, the brick-recessed windows were dark, filled with darkness, and schoolgirls by twos in their black skirts marched toward the convent. And wagons, sledges, drays, the horses shuddering, the air drowned in leaden green, the dung-stained ice, trails of ashes. Moses and his brothers put on their caps and prayed together,

"*Ma tovu ohaleha Yaakov. . . .*"
"How goodly are thy tents, O Israel."

Napoleon Street, rotten, toylike, crazy and filthy, riddled, flogged with harsh weather—the bootlegger's boys reciting ancient prayers. To this Moses' heart was attached with great power. Here was a wider range of human feelings than he had ever again been able to find. The children of the race, by a never-failing miracle, opened their eyes on one strange world after another, age after age, and uttered the same prayer in each, eagerly loving what they found. What was wrong with Napoleon Street? thought Herzog. All he ever wanted was there. His mother did the wash, and mourned. His father was desperate and frightened, but obstinately fighting. His brother Shura with staring disingenuous eyes was plotting to master the world, to become a millionaire. His brother Willie struggled with asthmatic fits. Trying to breathe he gripped the table and rose on his toes like a cock about to crow. His sister Helen had long white gloves which she washed in thick suds. She wore them to her lessons at the conservatory, carrying a leather music roll. Her diploma hung in a frame. *Mlle. Hélène Herzog . . . avec distinction.* His soft prim sister who played the piano.

On a summer night she sat playing and the clear notes went through the window into the street. The square-shouldered piano had a velveteen runner, mossy green as though the lid of the piano were a slab of stone. From the runner hung a ball fringe, like hickory nuts. Moses stood behind Helen, staring at the swirling pages of Haydn and Mozart, wanting to whine like a dog. Oh, the music! thought Herzog. He fought the insidious blight of nostalgia in New York—softening, heart-rotting emotions, black spots, sweet for one moment but leaving a dangerous acid residue. Helen played. She wore a middy and a pleated skirt, and her pointed shoes cramped down on the pedals, a proper, vain girl. She frowned while she played—her father's crease appeared between her eyes. Frowning as though she performed a dangerous action. The music rang into the street.

Aunt Zipporah was critical of this music business. Helen was not a genuine musician. She played to move the family. Perhaps to attract a husband. What Aunt Zipporah opposed was Mama's ambition for her children, because she wanted them to be lawyers, gentlemen, rabbis, or performers. All branches of the family had the caste madness of *yichus*. No life so barren and subordinate that it didn't have imaginary dignities, honors to come, freedom to advance.

Zipporah wanted to hold Mama back, Moses concluded, and she blamed Papa's failure in America on these white gloves and piano lessons. Zipporah had a strong character. She was witty, grudging, at war with everyone. Her face was flushed and thin, her nose shapely but narrow and grim. She had a critical, damaging, nasal voice. Her hips were large and she walked with wide heavy steps. A braid of thick glossy hair hung down her back.

Now Uncle Yaffe, Zipporah's husband, was quiet-spoken, humorously reserved. He was a small man but strong. His shoulders were wide, and he wore a black beard like King George V. It grew tight and curly on his brown face. The bridge of his nose was dented. His teeth were broad, and one was capped with gold. Moses had smelled the tart flavor of his uncle's breath as they played checkers. Over the board, Uncle Yaffe's broad head with short black twisted hair, a bit bald, was slightly unsteady. He had a mild nervous tremor. Uncle Yaffe, from the past, seemed to find out his nephew at this very instant of time and to look at him with the brown eyes of an intelligent, feeling, satirical animal. His glance glittered shrewdly, and he smiled with twisted satisfaction at the errors of young Moses. Affectionately giving me the business.

In Yaffe's junkyard in St. Anne the ragged cliffs of scrap metal bled rust into the puddles. There was sometimes a line of scavengers at the gate. Kids, greenhorns, old Irishwomen, or Ukrainians and redmen from the Caughnawaga reservation, came with pushcarts and little wagons, bringing bottles, rags, old plumbing or electrical fixtures, hardware, paper, tires, bones to sell. The old man, in his brown cardigan, stooped, and his strong trembling hands sorted out what he had bought. Without straightening his back he could pitch pieces of scrap where they belonged—iron here, zinc there, copper left, lead right, and Babbitt metal by the shed. He and his sons made money during the War. Aunt Zipporah bought real estate. She collected rents. Moses knew that she carried a bankroll in her bosom. He had seen it.

"Well, *you* lost nothing by coming to America," Papa said to her.

Her first reply was to stare sharply and warningly at him. Then she said, "It's no secret how **we** started out. By labor. Yaffe took a pick and shovel on the CPR until we saved up a little capital. But you! No, you were born in a silk shirt." With a glance at Mama, she went on, "You got used to putting on style, in Petersburg, with servants and coachmen. I can still see you getting off the train from Halifax, all dressed up among the greeners. *Gott meiner!* Ostrich feathers, taffeta skirts! *Greenhorns mit strauss federn!* Now forget the feathers, the gloves. Now—"

"That seems like a thousand years ago," said Mama. "I have forgotten all about servants. I am the servant. *Die dienst bin ich.*"

"Everyone must work. Not suffer your whole life long from a fall. Why must your children go to the conservatory, the Baron de Hirsch school, and all those special frills? Let them go to work, like mine."

"She doesn't want the children to be common," said Papa.

"My sons are not common. They know a page of *Gemara,*

142

too. And don't forget we come from the greatest Hasidic rabbis. Reb Zusya! Herschele Dubrovner! Just remember."

"No one is saying . . ." said Mama.

To haunt the past like this—to love the dead! Moses warned himself not to yield so greatly to this temptation, this peculiar weakness of his character. He was a depressive. Depressives cannot surrender childhood—not even the pains of childhood. He understood the hygiene of the matter. But somehow his heart had come open at this chapter of his life and he didn't have the strength to shut it. So it was again a winter day in St. Anne, in 1923—Aunt Zipporah's kitchen. Zipporah wore a crimson crepe de Chine wrapper. Discernible underneath were voluminous yellow bloomers and a man's undershirt. She sat beside the kitchen oven, her face flushing. Her nasal voice often rose to a barbed little cry of irony, of false dismay, of terrible humor.

Then she remembered that Mama's brother Mikhail was dead, and she said, "Well—about your brother—what was the matter?"

"We don't know," said Papa. "Who can imagine what a black year they're making back home." (It was always *in der heim,* Herzog reminded himself.) "A mob broke into his house. Cut open everything, looking for *valuta.* Afterwards, he caught typhus, or God knows what."

Mama's hand was over her eyes, as though she were shading them. She said nothing.

"I remember what a fine man he was," said Uncle Yaffe. "May he have a *lichtigen Gan-Eden.*"

Aunt Zipporah, who believed in the power of curses, said, "Curse those Bolsheviks. They want to make the world *horav.* May their hands and feet wither. But where are Mikhail's wife and children?"

"No one knows. The letter came from a cousin—Shperling, who saw Mikhail in the hospital. He barely recognized him."

Zipporah said a few more pious things, and then in a more normal manner she added, "Well, he was an active fellow. Had plenty of money, in his time. Who knows what a fortune he brought back from South Africa."

"He shared with us," said Mama. "My brother had an open hand."

"It came easily," said Zipporah. "It's not as if he had to work hard for it."

"How do you know?" said Father Herzog. "Don't let your tongue run away with you, my sister."

But Zipporah couldn't be restrained now. "He made money out of those miserable black Kaffirs! Who knows how! So you had a dacha in Shevalovo. Yaffe was away in the service, in the Kavkaz. I had a sick child to nurse. And you, Yonah, were running around Petersburg spending two dowries. Yes! You lost the first ten thousand rubles in a month. He gave you another ten. I can't say what else he was doing, with Tartars, gypsies, whores, eating horsemeat, and God only knows what abominations went on."

"What kind of malice is in you?" said Father Herzog, angry.

"I have nothing against Mikhail. He never harmed me," Zipporah said. "But he was a brother who gave, so I am a sister who doesn't give."

"No one said it," Father Herzog said. "But if the shoe fits, you can wear it."

Engrossed, unmoving in his chair, Herzog listened to the dead at their dead quarrels.

"What do you expect?" said Zipporah. "With four children, if I started to give, and indulged your bad habits, it would be endless. It's not my fault you're a pauper here."

"I am a pauper in America, that's true. Look at me. I haven't got a copper to bless my naked skin. I couldn't pay for my own shroud."

"Blame your own weak nature," said Zipporah. *"Az du host a schwachen natur, wer is dir schuldig?* You can't stand alone. You leaned on Sarah's brother, and now you want to lean on me. Yaffe served in the Kavkaz. *A finsternish!* It was too cold for dogs to howl. Alone, he came to America and sent for me. But you—you want *alle sieben glicken*. You travel in style, with ostrich feathers. You're an *edel-mensch*. Get your hands dirty? Not you."

"It's true. I didn't shovel manure *in der heim*. That happened in the land of Columbus. But I did it. I learned to harness a horse. At three o'clock in the morning, twenty below in the stable."

Zipporah waved this aside. "And now, with your still? You had to escape from the Czar's police. And now the Revenue? And you have to have a partner, a *goniff*."

"Voplonsky is an honest man."

"Who—that *German?*" Voplonsky was a Polish blacksmith. She called him a German because of his pointed military mustaches and the German cut of his overcoat. It hung to the ground. "What have you in common with a blacksmith? You, a descendant of Herschel Dubrovner! And he, a Polisher *schmid* with red whiskers! A rat! A rat with pointed red whiskers and long crooked teeth and reeking of scorched hoof! Bah! Your partner. Wait and see what he does to you."

"I'm not so easy to take in."

"No? Didn't Lazansky swindle you? He gave it to you in the real Turkish style. And didn't he beat your bones also?"

That was Lazansky, in the bakery, a giant teamster from the Ukraine. A huge ignorant man, an *amhoretz* who didn't know enough Hebrew to bless his bread, he sat on his narrow green delivery wagon, ponderous, growling "Garrap" to his little nag and flicking with the whip. His gross voice rolled like a bowling ball. The horse trotted along the bank of the Lachine Canal. The wagon was lettered

LAZANSKY—PATISSERIES DE CHOIX

Father Herzog said, "Yes, it's true he beat me."

He had come to borrow money from Zipporah and Yaffe. He did not want to be drawn into a quarrel. She had certainly guessed the purpose of this visit and was trying to make him angry so that she might refuse him more easily.

"Ai!" said Zipporah. A brilliantly shrewd woman, her many gifts were cramped in this little Canadian village. "You think you can make a fortune out of swindlers, thieves, and gangsters. You? You're a gentle creature. I don't know why you didn't stay in the Yeshivah. You wanted to be a gilded little gentleman. I know these hooligans and *razboiniks*. They don't have skins, teeth, fingers like you but hides, fangs, claws. You can never keep up with these teamsters and butchers. Can you shoot a man?"

Father Herzog was silent.

"If, God forbid, you had to shoot . . ." cried Zipporah. "Could you even hit someone on the head? Come! Think it over. Answer me, *gazlan*. Could you give a blow on the head?"

Here Mother Herzog seemed to agree.

"I'm no weakling," said Father Herzog, with his energetic face and brown mustache. But of course, thought Herzog, all of Papa's violence went into the drama of his life, into family strife, and sentiment.

"They'll take what they like from you, those *leite*," said Zipporah. "Now, isn't it time you used your head? You do have one—*klug bist du*. Make a legitimate living. Let your Helen and your Shura go to work. Sell the piano. Cut expenses."

"Why shouldn't the children study if they have intelligence, talent," said Mother Herzog.

"If they're smart, all the better for my brother," said Zipporah. "It's too hard for him—wearing himself out for spoiled princes and princesses."

She had Papa on her side, then. His craving for help was deep, bottomless.

"Not that I don't love the children," said Zipporah. "Come here, little Moses, and sit on your old *tante*'s knee. What a dear little *yingele*." Moses on the bloomers of his aunt's lap—her red hands held him at the belly. She smiled with harsh affection and kissed his neck. "Born in my arms, this child." Then she looked at brother Shura, who stood beside his mother. He had thick, blocky legs and his face was freckled. "And you?" said Zipporah to him.

"What's wrong?" said Shura, frightened and offended.

"Not too young to bring in a dollar."

Papa glared at Shura.

"Don't I help?" said Shura. "Deliver bottles? Paste labels?"

Papa had forged labels. He would say cheerfully, "Well, children, what shall it be—White Horse? Johnnie Walker?" Then we'd all call out our favorites. The paste pot was on the table.

In secret, Mother Herzog touched Shura's hand when Zipporah turned her eyes on him. Moses saw. Breathless Willie was scampering outside with his cousins, building a snow fort, squeaking and throwing snowballs. The sun came lower and lower. Ribbons of red from the horizon wound over the ridges of glazed snow. In the blue shadow of the fence, the goats were feeding. They belonged to the seltzer man next door. Zipporah's chickens were about to roost. Visiting us in Montreal, she sometimes brought a fresh egg. One egg. One of the children might be sick. A fresh egg had a world of power. Nervous and critical, with awkward feet and heavy hips, she mounted the stairs on Napoleon Street, a stormy woman, a daughter of Fate. Quickly and nervously she kissed her fingertips and touched the mezuzah. Entering, she inspected Mama's housekeeping. "Is everybody well?" she said. "I brought the children an egg." She opened her big bag and took out the present, wrapped in a piece of Yiddish newspaper (*Der Kanader Adler*).

A visit from Tante Zipporah was like a military inspection. Afterwards, Mama laughed and often ended by crying, "Why is she my enemy! What does she want? I have no strength to fight her." The antagonism, as Mama felt it, was mystical—a matter of souls. Mama's mind was archaic, filled with old legends, with angels and demons.

Of course Zipporah, that realist, was right to refuse Father Herzog. He wanted to run bootleg whisky to the border, and get into the big time. He and Voplonsky borrowed from moneylenders, and loaded a truck with cases. But they never reached Rouses Point. They were hijacked, beaten up, and left in a ditch. Father Herzog took the worse beating because he resisted. The hijackers tore his clothes, knocked out one of his teeth, and trampled him.

He and Voplonsky the blacksmith returned to Montreal on foot. He stopped at Voplonsky's shop to clean up, but there was not much he could do about his swollen bloody eye. He had a gap in his teeth. His coat was torn and his shirt and undergarment were bloodstained.

That was how he entered the dark kitchen on Napoleon Street. We were all there. It was gloomy March, and anyway the light seldom reached that room. It was like a cavern. We were like cave dwellers. "Sarah!" he said. "Children!" He showed his cut face. He spread his arms so we could see his tatters, and the white of his body under them. Then he turned his pockets inside out—empty. As he did this, he began to cry, and the children standing about him all cried. It was more than I could bear that anyone should lay violent hands on him—a father, a sacred being, a king. Yes, he was a king to us. My heart was suffocated by this horror. I thought I would die of it. Whom did I ever love as I loved them?

Then Father Herzog told his story.

"They were waiting for us. The road was blocked. They dragged us from the truck. They took everything."

"Why did you fight?" said Mother Herzog.

"Everything we had . . . all I borrowed!"

"They might have killed you."

"They had handkerchiefs over their faces. I thought I recognized . . ."

Mama was incredulous. *"Landtsleit?* Impossible. No Jews could do this to a Jew."

"No?" cried Papa. "Why not! Who says not! Why shouldn't they!"

"Not Jews! Never!" Mama said. "Never. Never! They couldn't have the heart. Never!"

"Children—don't cry. And poor Voplonsky—he could barely creep into bed."

"Yonah," said Mama, "you must give up this whole thing."

"How will we live? We have to live."

He began to tell the story of his life, from childhood to this day. He wept as he told it. Put out at four years old to study, away from home. Eaten by lice. Half starved in the Yeshivah as a boy. He shaved, became a modern European. He worked in Kremenchug for his aunt as a young man. He had a fool's paradise in Petersburg for ten years, on forged papers. Then he sat in prison with common criminals. Escaped to America. Starved. Cleaned stables. Begged. Lived in fear. A *baal-chov*—always a debtor. Shadowed by the police. Taking in drunken boarders. His wife a servant. And this was what he brought home to his children. This was what he could show them—his rags, his bruises.

Herzog, wrapped in his cheap paisley robe, brooded with clouded eyes. Under his bare feet was a small strip of carpet. His elbows rested on the fragile desk and his head hung down. He had written only a few lines to Nachman.

I suppose, he was thinking, that we heard this tale of the Herzogs ten times a year. Sometimes Mama told it, sometimes he. So we had a great schooling in grief. I still know these cries of the soul. They lie in the breast, and in the throat. The mouth wants to open wide and let them out. But all these are antiquities—yes, Jewish antiquities originating in the Bible, in a Biblical sense of personal experience and destiny. What happened during the War abolished Father Herzog's claim to exceptional suffering. We are on a more brutal standard now, a new terminal standard, indifferent to persons. Part of the program of destruction into which the human spirit has poured itself with energy, even with joy. These personal histories, old tales from old times that may not be worth remembering. I remember. I must. But who else—to whom can this matter? So many millions—multitudes—go down in terrible pain. And, at that, moral suffering is denied, these days. Personalities are good only for comic relief. But I am still a slave to Papa's pain. The way Father Herzog spoke of himself! That could make one laugh. His *I* had such dignity.

"You must give it up," Mama cried. "You must!"

"What should I do, then! Work for the burial society? Like a man of seventy? Only fit to sit at deathbeds? *I?* Wash corpses? *I?* Or should I go to the cemetery and wheedle mourners for a nickel? To say *El malai rachamim. I?* Let the earth open and swallow me up!"

"Come, Yonah," said Mama in her earnest persuasive way. "I'll put a compress on your eye. Come, lie down."

"How can I?"

"No, you must."

"How will the children eat?"

"Come—you must lie down awhile. Take off that shirt."

She sat by the bed, silent. He lay in the gray room, on the iron bedstead, covered with the worn red Russian blanket—his handsome forehead, his level nose, the brown mustache. As he had from that dark corridor, Moses now contemplated those two figures.

Nachman, he began again to write, but stopped. How was he to reach Nachman with a letter? He would do better to advertise in the *Village Voice.* But, then, to whom would he send the other letters he was drafting?

He concluded that Nachman's wife was dead. Yes, that must be it. That slender, thin-legged girl with the dark brows that rose high and recurved again beside her eyes, and the wide mouth which curved down at the corners—she had committed suicide, and Nachman ran away because (who could blame him) he would have had to tell Moses all about it. Poor thing, poor thing—she too must be in the cemetery.

THE telephone rang—five, eight, ten peals. Herzog looked at his watch. The time astonished him—nearly six o'clock. Where had the day gone? The phone went on ringing, drilling away at him. He didn't want to pick it up. But there were two children, after all—he *was* a father, and he must answer. He reached for the instrument, therefore, and heard Ramona—the cheerful voice of Ramona calling him to a life of pleasure on the thrilling wires of New York. And not simple pleasure but metaphysical, transcendent pleasure—pleasure which answered the riddle of human existence. That was Ramona—no mere sensualist, but a theoretician, almost a priestess, in her Spanish costumes adapted to American needs, and her flowers, her really beautiful teeth, her red cheeks, and her thick, kinky, exciting black hair.

"Hello—Moses? What number is this?"

"This is the Armenian Relief."

"Oh, Moses! It's you!"

"I'm the only man you know old enough to remember the Armenian Relief."

"Last time you said it was the City Morgue. You must be feeling more cheerful. This is Ramona. . . ."

"Of course." Who else has the voice that lifts so light from height to height with foreign charm. "The Spanish lady."

"La navaja en la liga."

"Why, Ramona, I never felt less threatened by knives."

"You sound positively high."

"I haven't spoken to a soul all day."

"I meant to call you, but the shop was very busy. Where were you yesterday?"

"Yesterday? Where *was* I—let me see. . . ."

"I thought you took a powder."

"Me? How could that be?"

"You mean, you wouldn't run out on me?"

Run out on fragrant, sexual, high-minded Ramona? Never in a million years. Ramona had passed through the hell of profligacy and attained the seriousness of pleasure. For when will we civilized beings become really serious? said Kierkegaard. Only when we have known hell through and through. Without this, hedonism and frivolity will diffuse hell through all our days. Ramona, however, does not believe in any sin but the sin against the body, for her the true and only temple of the spirit.

"But you did leave town yesterday," said Ramona.

"How do you know—are you having me tailed by a private eye?"

"Miss Schwartz saw you in Grand Central with a valise in your hand."

"Who? That little Miss Schwartz, in your shop?"

"That's right."

"Well, what do you know . . ." Herzog would not discuss it further.

Ramona said, "Perhaps some lovely woman scared you on the train, and you turned back to your Ramona."

"Oh . . ." said Herzog.

Her theme was her power to make him happy. Thinking of Ramona with her intoxicating eyes and robust breasts, her short but gentle legs, her Carmen airs, thievishly seductive, her skill in the sack (defeating invisible rivals), he felt she did not exaggerate. The facts supported her claim.

"Well, were you running away?" she said.

"Why should I? You're a marvelous woman, Ramona."

"In that case you're being very odd, Moses."

"Well, I suppose I am one of the odder beasts."

"But I know better than to be proud and demanding. Life has taught me to be humble."

Moses shut his eyes and raised his brows. Here we go.

"Perhaps you feel a natural superiority because of your education."

"Education! But I don't know anything. . . ."

"Your accomplishments. You're in *Who's Who*. I'm only a merchant—a petit-bourgeois type."

"You don't really believe this, Ramona."

"Then why do you keep aloof, and make me chase you? I realize you want to play the field. After great disappointments, I've done it myself, for ego-reinforcement."

"A high-minded intellectual ninny, square . . ."

"Who?"

"Myself, I mean."

She went on. "But as one recovers self-confidence, one learns the simple strength of simple desires."

Please, Ramona, Moses wanted to say—you're lovely, fragrant, sexual, good to touch—everything. But these lectures! For the love of God, Ramona, shut it up. But she went on. Herzog looked up at the ceiling. The spiders had the moldings under intensive cultivation, like the banks of the Rhine. Instead of grapes, encapsulated bugs hung in clusters.

I brought all this on myself by telling Ramona the story of my life—how I rose from humble origins to complete disaster. But a man who has made so many mistakes can't afford to ignore the corrections of his friends. Friends like Sandor, that humped rat. Or like Valentine, the moral megalomaniac and prophet in Israel. To all such, one is well advised to listen. Scolding is better than nothing. At least it's company.

Ramona paused, and Herzog said, "It's true—I have a lot to learn."

But I am diligent. I work at it and show steady improvement. I expect to be in great shape on my deathbed. The good die young, but I have been spared to build myself up so that I may end my life as good as gold. The senior dead will be proud of me. . . . I will join the Y.M.C.A. of the immortals. Only, in this very hour, I may be missing eternity.

"Are you listening?" said Ramona.

"Of course."

"What did I just say."

"That I have to trust my instincts more."

"I said I wanted you to come to dinner."

"Oh."

"If only I were a bitch! Then you'd hang on every word."

"But I was going to ask you . . . to come to an Italian restaurant." He was clumsily inventing. At times he was cruelly absentminded.

"I've shopped already," said Ramona.

"But how, if that snooping Miss Schwartz with the blue spectacles saw me running away in Grand Central . . . ?"

152

"Did I expect you? I figured you had to go to New Haven for the day—to the Yale library, or some such place. . . . Please come. Join me for dinner. I'll have to eat alone if you don't."

"Why, where's your aunt?"

Ramona had her father's elderly sister living with her.

"She's gone to visit the cousins in Hartford."

"Ah—I see." He thought that old Aunt Tamara must be well used to taking these trips on short notice.

"My aunt understands such things," said Ramona. "Besides, she likes you so much."

And she thinks I'm a fine new prospect. Besides, one must make sacrifices for a husbandless niece who has a troubled love life. Just before meeting Herzog, Ramona had broken off with an assistant television producer named George Hoberly who was hard hit, in a pitiable state—close to hysteria. As Ramona explained it, old Aunt Tamara was Hoberly's great sympathizer—advised him, consoled him as well as an old woman could. At the same time, she was almost as excited about Herzog as Ramona herself. Meditating on Aunt Tamara, Moses thought he now could better understand Aunt Zelda. The female passion for secrecy and double games. For we must eat our fruit from the wily serpent's jaws.

Still, Herzog observed that Ramona had genuine family feeling, and of this he approved. She seemed really fond of her aunt. Tamara was the daughter of a Polish Czarist official something-or-other (what harm could there be in making him a general?). Ramona said about her, "She is very *jeune fille Russe*"—an excellent description. Aunt Tamara was docile, girlish, sensitive, impulsive. Whenever she spoke of Papá and Mamá and her teachers and the Conservatoire her dry breast filled, and the collarbones stood out tightly. She seemed still to be trying to decide whether to have a concert career against her Papá's wishes. Herzog, listening with serious looks, could not establish whether she had given a recital at the Salle Gaveau or wanted to give a recital. Old women from Eastern Europe with dyed hair and senseless cameo brooches had easy access to his affections.

"Well, then, are you coming or not?" said Ramona. "Why are you so hard to pin down?"

"I shouldn't go out—I have a lot to do—letters to write."

"What letters! You're such a mystery man. What are these important letters? Business? Perhaps you should discuss it with me, if it is business. Or a lawyer, if you don't trust me. But you have to eat, anyway. Or perhaps you don't eat when you're alone."

"Of course I do."

"Well, then?"

"Okay," said Herzog. "Expect me soon. I'll bring a bottle of wine."

"No, no! Don't do that. I've got some on ice."

He put down the phone. She was emphatic about the wine. Perhaps he had given the impression that he was a little stingy. Or else he had awakened a feeling of protectiveness in her, an effect he often produced. He wondered at times whether he didn't belong to a class of people secretly convinced they had an arrangement with fate; in return for docility or ingenuous good will they were to be shielded from the worst brutalities of life. Herzog's mouth formed a soft but twisted smile as he considered whether he really had inwardly decided years ago to set up a deal—a psychic offer—meekness in exchange for preferential treatment. Such a bargain was feminine, or, extended to trees, animals, childlike. None of these self-judgments had any terror for him; no percentage now in quarreling with what one was. There was the thing—the composite, the mystical achievement of natural forces and his own spirit. He opened the paisley Hong Kong robe and looked at his naked body. He was no child. And the house in Ludeyville, a disaster in every other way, had kept him fit. Wrestling with that old ruin in an effort to recover his legacy made his arms muscular. Extended the lease of narcissism a little while. Gave him strength to carry a heavy-buttocked woman to the bed. Oh, yes—still in fleeting moments the young and glossy stud—such as he really had never been. There were more faithful worshipers of Eros than Moses Elkanah Herzog.

But why was Ramona so firm about wine? Maybe she was afraid he'd turn up with California sauterne. Or, no, she believed in the aphrodisiac power of her own brand. That might be it. Or else he harped more on the subject of money than he knew. A last possibility was that she wanted to surround him with luxuries.

Glancing at his watch, Herzog, with an appearance of efficiency or purpose, failed, anyway, to fix the time in his mind. What he did observe, stooping to the window to get an angle over roofs and walls, was that the sky was reddening. He was astonished that a whole day had been spent scrawling a few letters. And what ridiculous, angry letters! The spite and frenzy in them! Zelda! Sandor! Why write to them at all? And the Monsignor! Between the lines of Herzog's letter the Monsignor would only see a mad, reasoning face, just as Moses saw the brick of those walls between these rods caked in asphalt black. Endless repetition threatens sanity.

Suppose that I am absolutely right and the Monsignor, for instance, absolutely wrong. If I am right, the problem of the world's coherence, and all responsibility for it, becomes mine. How will it make out when Moses E. Herzog has his way? No, why should I take that on myself? The Church has universal understanding. This I consider a harmful, Prussian delusion. Readiness to answer all questions is the infallible sign of stupidity. Did Valentine Gersbach ever admit ignorance of any matter? He was a regular Goethe. He finished all your sentences, rephrased all your thoughts, explained everything.

. . . *I want you to know, Monsignor, that I am not writing with the purpose of exposing Madeleine, or to attack you.* Herzog tore up the letter. Untrue! He despised the Monsignor, wanted to murder Madeleine. Yes, he was capable of killing her. And yet, while filled with horrible rage, he was able also to shave and dress, to be the citizen on the town for an evening of pleasure, groomed, scented, and his face sweetened for kisses. He did not flinch from these criminal fantasies. It's the certainty of punishment that stops me, Herzog thought.

Time to clean up. He turned from the desk and the deepening light of the afternoon and dropping the robe entered the bathroom and turned on the water in the basin. He drank, in the obscurity of the cool tiled room. New York has the sweetest water in the world, for a metropolis. Then he began to soap his face. He could look forward to a good dinner. Ramona knew how to cook, and how to set a table. There would be candles, linen napkins, flowers. Perhaps the flowers were being rushed from the shop now, in evening traffic. On the windowsill of Ramona's dining room pigeons roosted. You heard wings flapping in the airshaft. As for the menu, on a summer evening like this she'd probably prepare vichyssoise, then shrimp Arnaud—New Orleans style. White asparagus. A cool dessert. Rum-flavored ice cream with raisins? Brie and cold-water biscuits? He was judging by previous dinners. Coffee. Brandy. And, all the time, Egyptian music on the phonograph in the adjoining room—Mohammad al Bakkar playing "Port Said" with zithers, drums, and tambourines. In that room was a Chinese rug, the light of the green lamp deep and quiet. Here also she had fresh flowers. If I had to work all day in a flower shop, I wouldn't want to be pursued by the smell of flowers at night. On the coffee table she had art books and international magazines. Paris, Rio, Rome, all were represented. Invariably, also, the latest presents from Ramona's admirers were displayed. Herzog always read the little cards. For what other reason did she leave them? George Hoberly for whom she was cooking shrimp Arnaud last spring still sent her gloves, books, theater tickets, opera glasses. You could trace his love-crazed wanderings up and down New York by the labels. Ramona said he didn't know what he was doing. Herzog was sorry for him.

The bluish-green carpet, the Moorish knickknacks and arabesques, the wide comfortable sofa-bed, the Tiffany lamp with glass like plumage, the deep armchairs by the windows, the downtown view of Broadway and Columbus Circle. And after dinner, when they were settling down here with coffee and brandy, Ramona would ask whether he wouldn't like to take off his shoes. Why not? A free foot on a summer night eases the heart. And by and by, going by precedents, she'd ask why he was so abstracted—was he thinking of his children? Then he'd say . . . he was shaving now, scarcely glancing in the mirror, finding the stubble with his fingertips . . . he'd say that he was no longer so worried about Marco. The boy had a firm character. He was one of the more stable breed of Herzogs. Ramona then would give him level-headed advice about his little daughter. Moses would say how could he abandon her to those psychopaths? Could she doubt that they were psychopaths? Did she want to look again at the letter from Geraldine—the frightful letter that told what they were doing? And there would follow another discussion of Madeleine, Zelda, Valentine Gersbach, Sandor Himmelstein, the Monsignor, Dr. Edvig, Phoebe Gersbach. Against his will, like an addict struggling to kick the habit, he would tell again how he was swindled, conned, manipulated, his savings taken, driven into debt, his trust betrayed by wife, friend, physician. If ever Herzog knew the loathsomeness of a *particular* existence, knew that the *whole* was required to redeem every separate spirit, it was then, in his terrible passion, which he tried, impossibly, to share, telling his story. Then, in the midst of it, the realization would come over him that he had no right to tell, to inflict it, that his craving for confirmation, for help, for justification, was useless. Worse, it was unclean. (For some reason the French word suited him better, and he said *"Immonde!"* and again, more loudly, *"C'est immonde!"*) However, Ramona would tenderly sympathize with him. No doubt she genuinely pitied him, though the injured are, for primitive reasons, unattractive and even ludicrous. In a spiritually confused age, however, a man who could feel as he did might claim a certain distinction. He was beginning to see that his particular brand of short-sightedness, lack of realism, and apparent ingenuousness conferred a high status on him. For Ramona it evidently surrounded him with glamour. And provided that he remain *macho* she would listen with glistening eyes, with more sympathy, and more, and more. She transformed his miseries into sexual excitements and, to give credit where it was due, turned his grief in a useful direction. Cannot agree with Hobbes that where there is no overawing power men have no pleasure (*voluptas*) in keeping company but instead (*molestia*) a great deal of grief. There is always an overawing power, namely, one's terror. To set aside these theoretical considerations, however, when he was done, having drunk four or five glasses of Armagnac from the Venetian decanter, far above the Puerto Rican disorders of the street, it would be Ramona's turn. You treat me right, I treat you right.

He continued shaving, like a blind man, by touch and by sound, the sound of bristle and blade.

Ramona was highly experienced at entertaining gentlemen. The shrimp, wine, flowers, lights, perfumes, the rituals of undressing, the Egyptian music whining and clanging, bespoke practice, and he regretted that she'd had to live this way, but it flattered him, also. Ramona was astonished that any woman should find fault with Moses. He told her that he was often a flat failure with Madeleine. It might be the release of his angry feeling against Mady that improved his performance. At this Ramona looked severe.

"I don't know—it might be *me*—have you considered that?" she said. "Poor Moses—unless you're having a bad time with a woman you can't believe you're being serious."

Moses rinsed his face with pleasant witch hazel, a brimming

handful, and blew upon his cheeks from the corners of his mouth. He tuned in Polish dance music on the small transistor radio on the glass shelf over the sink, and powdered his feet. Then he gave in for a while to the impulse to dance and leap on the soiled tiles, some of which came free from the grout and had to be kicked under the tub. It was one of his oddities in solitude to break out in song and dance, to do queer things out of keeping with his customary earnestness. He danced out the number until the Polish commercial—"Ochyne-pynch-ochyne, Pynch Avenue, Flushing." He mimicked the announcer in the ivory yellow gloom of the tile bathroom—the water closet, as he anachronistically called it. He was ready to go for another polka when he discovered, breathing hard, that the sweat was rolling down his sides, and that another dance would make a shower necessary. He didn't have the time or patience for that. He couldn't bear the thought of drying himself—one of those killing chores he had always hated.

He put on clean drawers, socks. In stocking feet he trod the toes of his shoes to bring out a dull shine. Ramona did not like his taste in shoes. Before the window of the Bally shop on Madison Avenue she pointed at a pair of ankle-high Spanish boots and said, "That's what you need—those vicious-looking black things." Smiling, she looked upward so that he was confronted by the brightness of her eyes. She had marvelous, slightly curved white teeth. Her lips would part and close over these significant teeth, and she had a short, curved, French nose, small and fine; hazel eyes; thick vivid black hair. The weight of her face was mainly in the lower part. A slight defect, in Herzog's view. Nothing serious.

"You want me to dress up like a flamenco dancer?" said Herzog.

"You ought to use a little imagination about clothes—encourage certain aspects of your character."

You would think—Herzog smiled broadly—he was a piece of human capital badly invested. To her surprise, perhaps, he agreed with her. Almost cheerfully, he agreed. Strength, intelligence, feeling, opportunity had been wasted on him. What he could not see, however, was that such Spanish shoes—which, by the way, greatly appealed to his childish taste—would improve his character. And we must improve. Must!

He put on trousers. Not the Italian pants: they'd be uncomfortable after dinner. One of the new poplin shirts was next. He removed all the pins. Then he put on the madras jacket. He bent down to see what he could see of the harbor through the small opening of the bathroom window. Nothing in particular. Only a sense of water bounding the overbuilt island. It was a movement of orientation that he was making, like the glance at his watch which did not tell him the time. And next came his specific self, an apparition in the square mirror. How did he look? Oh, terrific—you look exquisite, Moses! Smashing! The primitive self-attachment of the human creature, that sweet instinct for the self, so deep, so old it may have a cellular origin. As he breathed, he was aware of it, quiet but far-reaching, all through his system, a pleasing hunger in his remotest nerves. *Dear Professor Haldane* . . . No, that was not Herzog's man at this moment. *Dear Father Teilhard de Chardin, I have tried to understand your notion of the inward aspect of the elements. That sense organs, even rudimentary sense organs, could not evolve from molecules described by mechanists as inert. Thus matter itself should perhaps be studied as evolving consciousness . . . is the carbon molecule lined with thought?*

His shaven face, muttering in the mirror—great shadows under the eyes. That's okay, he thought; if the light's not too bright, you're still a grand-looking man. For a while yet, you can get women. All but that bitch, Madeleine, whose face looks either beautiful or haggy. Go, then—Ramona will feed you, give you wine, remove your shoes, flatter you, smooth down your hackles, kiss you, pinch your lip with her teeth. Then uncover the bed, turn down the lights, and go into the essentials. . . .

He was half elegant, half slovenly. That had always been his style. If he knotted his tie with care, his shoelaces dragged. His brother Shura, immaculate in his tailored clothes, manicured and barbered at the Palmer House, said this was done on purpose. Once it had perhaps been his boyish defiance, but by now it was an established part of the daily comedy of Moses E. Herzog. Ramona often said, "You're not a true, puritanical American. You have a talent for sensuality. Your mouth gives you away." Herzog could not help putting his fingers to his lip when it was mentioned. But then he laughed the whole thing off. What remained to bother him was that she did not recognize him as an American. That hurt! What else was he? In the Service his mates had also considered him a foreigner. The Chicagoans questioned him suspiciously. "What's on State and

Lake? How far west is Austin Avenue?" Most of them seemed to come from the suburbs. Moses knew the city much better than they, but even this was turned against him. "Ah, you just memorized everything. You're a spy. That proves. One of them smart Jews. Come clean, Mose—they're gonna drop you by parachute—right?" No, he became a communications officer, discharged for asthma. Choked by fog, in the Gulf of Mexico, on maneuvers, losing contact owing to his hoarseness. Except that the whole fleet heard him groan, "We're lost! Fucked!"

But in Chicago, in 1934, he was class orator at the McKinley High School, his text taken from Emerson. He didn't lose his voice then, telling the Italian mechanics, Bohemian barrel makers, Jewish tailors *The main enterprise of the world, for splendor . . . is the upbuilding of a man. The private life of one man shall be a more illustrious monarchy . . . than any kingdom in history. Let it be granted that our life, as we lead it, is common and mean. . . . Beautiful and perfect men we are not now. . . . The community in which we live will hardly bear to be told that every man should be open to ecstasy or a divine illumination.* If he had lost craft and crew somewhere near Biloxi, that didn't mean he wasn't in earnest about beauty and perfection. He believed his American credentials were in good order. Laughing, but pained, too, he remembered that a Chief Petty Officer from Alabama had asked him, "Wheah did you loin to speak English—at the Boilitz Scho-ool?"

No, what Ramona meant, as a compliment, was that he had not lived the life of an ordinary American. No, his peculiarities had governed him from the start. Did he see any great value or social distinction in this? Well, he had to endure these peculiarities, so there was no reason why he shouldn't make use of them, a little.

But, speaking of ordinary Americans, what sort of mother would Ramona make? Would she be able to take a little girl to Macy's parade? Moses tried to imagine Ramona, a priestess of Isis, in a tweed suit, watching the procession of floats.

Dear McSiggins. I read your monograph, "The Ethical Ideas of the American Business Community." A field day for McSiggins. *Interesting. Would have appreciated closer investigation of hypocrisy, public and private, in the American accounting system. Nothing to prevent the individual American from claiming as much merit as he likes. By degrees, in Populistic philosophy, goodness has become a free commodity like air, or nearly free, like a subway ride. Best of everything for everybody—help yourself. No one much cares. The honest look, recommended by Ben Franklin as a business asset, has a predestinarian, Calvinistic background. You don't cast doubts on another man's election. You may damage his credit rating. As belief in damnation vanishes, it leaves behind solid formations of Reliable Appearances.*

Dear General Eisenhower. In private life perhaps you have the leisure and inclination to reflect on matters for which, as Chief Executive, you obviously had no time. The pressure of the Cold War . . . which now so many people agree was a phase of political hysteria, and the journeys and speeches of Mr. Dulles rapidly changing in this age of shifting perspectives from their earlier appearance of statesmanship to one of American wastefulness. I happened to be in the press gallery at the UN the day you spoke of the risk of error in precipitating nuclear war. That day I put down a deposit on a chandelier, an old gas fixture, really, on Second Avenue. Another ten bucks squandered on Ludeyville. *I was present also when Premier Khrushchev pounded the desk with his shoe. Amid such crises, in such an atmosphere, there was obviously no time for the more general questions of the sort I have been concerned with.* Indeed, put my life into. But what do you want him to do about that? *I gather from the book by Mr. Hughes, however, and from your letter to him expressing concern about "spiritual values" that I may not be wasting your time in calling your attention to the report of your own Committee on National Aims, published at the end of your administration. I wonder whether the people you appointed to it were the best for the job—corporation lawyers, big executives, the group now called the Industrial Statesmen. Mr. Hughes has noted how you were shielded from distressing opinions, insulated, as it were. Perhaps you will be asking yourself who your present correspondent is, whether a liberal, an egghead, a bleeding heart, or a nut of some kind. So let us say he is a thoughtful person who believes in civil usefulness. Intelligent people without influence feel a certain self-contempt, reflecting the contempt of those who hold real political or social power, or think they do.* Can you make it all clear, in few words? It's well known he hates long, complicated documents. *A collection of loyal, helpful statements to inspire us in the struggle against the Communist enemy is not what we needed. The old proposition of Pascal (1623-1662) that man is a reed, but a thinking reed, might be taken with a different emphasis by the modern citizen of a democracy. He thinks, but he feels like a reed bending before centrally generated winds.* Ike would certainly pay no attention to this. Herzog tried another approach. *Tolstoi (1828-1910) said, "Kings are history's slaves." The higher one stands in the scale of power, the more his actions are determined. To Tolstoi, freedom is entirely personal. That man is free whose condition is simple, truthful—real. To be free is to be released from historical limitation. On the other hand, GWF Hegel (1770-1831) understood the essence of human life to be derived from history. History, memory—that is what makes us human, that, and our knowledge of death: "by man came death." For knowledge of death makes us wish to extend our lives at the expense of others. And this is the root of the struggle for power.* But that's all wrong! thought Herzog, not without humor in his despair. I'm bugging all these people—Nehru, Churchill, and now Ike, whom I apparently want to give a Great Books course. Nevertheless, there was much earnest feeling in this, too. *No civil order, no higher development of mankind. The goal, however, is freedom. And what does a man owe to the State? It was with such considerations, reading your Committee's report on National Aims,* that I seem to have been stirred fiercely by a desire to communicate, or by the curious project of attempted communication. Or bent by a disguised passion, offering these ideas about Death and History to the commander of SHAEF, like mocking flowers grown in the soil of fever and unacted violence. Suppose, after all, we are simply a kind of beast, peculiar to this mineral lump that runs around in orbit to the sun, then why such loftiness, such great standards? *that I thought of the variation on Gresham's famous Law: Public life drives out private life. The more political our society becomes (in the broadest sense of "political"—the obsessions, the compulsions of collectivity) the more individuality seems lost. Seems, I say, because it has millions of secret resources. More plainly, national purpose is now involved with the manufacture of commodities in no way essential to human life, but vital to the political survival of the country. Because we are now all sucked into these phenomena of Gross National Product, we are forced to accept the sacred character of certain absurdities or falsehoods whose high priests not so long ago were mere pitchmen, and figures of derision—sellers of snake-oil. On the other hand there is more "private life" than a century ago, when the working day lasted fourteen hours. The whole matter is of the highest importance since it has to do with invasion of the private sphere (including the sexual) by techniques of exploitation and domination.*

His tragic successor would have been interested, but not Ike. Nor Lyndon. Their governments could not function without intellectuals—physicists, statisticians—but these are whirling lost in the arms of industrial chiefs and billionaire brass. Kennedy was not about to change this situation, either. Only he seemed to have acknowledged, privately, that it existed.

A new idea possessed Moses. He would offer an outline to Pulver, Harris Pulver, who had been his tutor in 1939 and was now the editor of *Atlantic Civilization*. Yes, tiny, nervous Pulver with his timid, whole-souled blue eyes, his crumbled teeth, the profile of Gizeh's mummy as pictured in Robinson's *Ancient History,* the taut skin hectically spotted with high color. Herzog loved this man in his own immoderate, heart-flooded way. *Listen, Pulver,* he wrote, *a marvelous idea for a much-needed essay on the "inspired condition"! Do you believe in transcendence downward as well as upward? (The terms originate with Jean Wahl.) Shall we concede the impossibility of transcendence? It all involves historical analysis. I would argue that we have fashioned a new utopian history, an idyll, comparing the present to an imaginary past, because we hate the world as it is. This hatred of the present has not been well understood. Perhaps the first demand of emerging consciousness in this mass civilization is expressive. The spirit, released from servile dumbness, spits dung and howls with anguish stored during long ages. Perhaps the fish, the newt, the horrid scampering ancestral mammal find their voice and add their long experience to this cry. Taking up the suggestion, Pulver, that evolution is nature becoming self-aware—in man, self-awareness has been accompanied at this stage with a sense of the loss of more general natural powers, of a price paid by instinct, by sacrifices of freedom, impulse (alienating labor, et cetera). The drama of this stage of human development seems to be the drama of disease, of self-revenge. An age of special comedy. What we see is not simply the leveling de Tocqueville predicted, but the plebeian stage of evolutionary self-*

awareness. Perhaps the revenge taken by numbers, by the species, on our impulses of narcissism (but also on the demand for freedom) is inevitable. In this new reign of multitudes, self-awareness tends to reveal us to ourselves as monsters. This is undoubtedly a political phenomenon, an action taken against personal impulse or against the personal demand for adequate space and scope. The individual is obliged, or put under pressure, to define "power" as it is defined in politics, and to work out the personal consequences of this for himself. Thus he is provoked to take revenge upon himself, a revenge of derision, contempt, denial of transcendence. This last, his denial, is based upon former conceptions of human life or on images of man at present impossible to maintain. But the problem as I see it is not one of definition but of the total reconsideration of human qualities. Or perhaps even the discovery of qualities. I am certain that there are human qualities still to be discovered. Such discovery or recovery is only hampered by definitions which hold mankind down at the level of pride (or masochism), asserting too much and then suffering from self-hatred as a consequence.

But you will be wondering what happened to "the inspired condition." This is thought to be attainable only in the negative and is so pursued in philosophy and literature as well as in sexual experience, or with the aid of narcotics, or in "philosophical," "gratuitous" crime and similar paths of horror. (It never seems to occur to such "criminals" that to behave with decency to another human being might also be "gratuitous.") Intelligent observers have pointed out that "spiritual" honor or respect formerly reserved for justice, courage, temperance, mercy, may now be earned in the negative by the grotesque. I often think that this development is possibly related to the fact that so much of "value" has been absorbed by technology itself. It is "good" to electrify a primitive area. Civilization and even morality are implicit in technological transformation. Isn't it good to give bread to the hungry, to clothe the naked? Don't we obey Jesus in shipping machinery to Peru or Sumatra? Good is easily done by machines of production and transportation. Can virtue compete? New techniques are in themselves bien pensant *and represent not only rationality but benevolence. Thus a crowd, a herd of* bien pensants *has been driven into nihilism, which, as is now well known, has Christian and moral roots and for its wildest frenzies offers a "constructive" rationale. (See Polyani, Herzog, et al.)*

Romantic individuals (a mass of them by now) accuse this mass civilization of obstructing their attainment of beauty, nobility, integrity, intensity. I do not want to sneer at the term Romantic. Romanticism guarded the "inspired condition," preserved the poetic, philosophical, and religious teachings, the teachings and records of transcendence and the most generous ideas of mankind, during the greatest and most rapid of transformations, the most accelerated phase of the modern scientific and technical transformation.

Finally, Pulver, to live in an inspired condition, to know truth, to be free, to love another, to consummate existence, to abide with death in clarity of consciousness—without which, racing and conniving to evade death, the spirit holds its breath and hopes to be immortal because it does not live—is no longer a rarefied project. Just as machinery has embodied ideas of good, so the technology of destruction has also acquired a metaphysical character. The practical questions have thus become the ultimate questions as well. Annihilation is no longer a metaphor. Good and Evil are real. The inspired condition is therefore no visionary matter. It is not reserved for gods, kings, poets, priests, shrines, but belongs to mankind and to all of existence. And therefore—

Therefore, Herzog's thoughts, like those machines in the lofts he had heard yesterday in the taxi, stopped by traffic in the garment district, plunged and thundered with endless—infinite!—hungry, electrical power, stitching fabric with inexhaustible energy. Having seated himself again in his striped jacket he was gripping the legs of his desk between his knees, his teeth set, the straw hat cutting his forehead. He wrote, *Reason exists! Reason . . .* he then heard the soft dense rumbling of falling masonry, the splintering of wood and glass. *And belief based on reason. Without which the disorder of the world will never be controlled by mere organization. Eisenhower's report on National Aims, if I had had anything to do with it, would have pondered the private and inward existence of Americans first of all. . . . Have I explained that my article would be a review of this report?* He thought intensely, deeply, and wrote, *Each to change his life. To change!*

Thus I want you to see how I, Moses E. Herzog, am changing.

I ask you to witness the miracle of his altered heart—how, hearing the sounds of slum clearance in the next block and watching the white dust of plaster in the serene air of metamorphic New York, he communicates with the mighty of this world, or speaks words of understanding and prophecy, having arranged at the same time a comfortable and entertaining evening—food, music, wine, conversation, and sexual intercourse. Transcendence or no transcendence. All work and no games is bad medicine. Ike went trout fishing and played golf; my needs are different. (More in Herzog's vein of wide-eyed malice.) The erotic must be admitted to its rightful place, at last, in an emancipated society which understands the relation of sexual repression to sickness, war, property, money, totalitarianism. Why, to get laid is actually socially constructive and useful, an act of citizenship. So here I am in the gathering dusk, the striped jacket on my back, sweating again after my wash, shaved, powdered, taking my underlip in my teeth nervously, as if anticipating what Ramona will do to it. Powerless to reject the hedonistic joke of a mammoth industrial civilization on the spiritual desires, the high cravings of a Herzog, on his moral suffering, his longing for the good, the true. All the while his heart is *contemptibly* aching. He would like to give this heart a shaking, or put it out of his breast. Evict it. Moses hated the humiliating comedy of heartache. But can thought wake you from the dream of existence? Not if it becomes a second realm of confusion, another more complicated dream, the dream of intellect, the delusion of total *explanations*.

He had gotten a significant warning once from Daisy's mother, Polina, when he had fallen in love for a while with his Japanese friend Sono, and Polina, the old Russian Jewish suffragette—fifty years a modern woman in Zanesville, Ohio (from 1905 to 1935 Daisy's father drove a soda-pop-and-seltzer truck there)—descended on him. Neither Polina nor Daisy actually knew anything about Sono Oguki then. (What a lot of romances! thought Herzog. One after another. Were those my real career?) But . . . Polina flew in, gray-haired and wide-hipped, with her bag of knitting, an elegant, determined person. She arrived with a Quaker Oats box filled with apple strudel for Herzog—he still felt a pang at the loss of her strudel; it was truly great. But he was aware that his greed for it was childlike, and that there were adult questions to be decided.

Polina had the peculiar stiffness and severity of the emancipated woman of her generation. Once a beauty, she was now very dry in appearance, with gold octagonal glasses and the sparse white hairs of an old woman at the corners of her mouth.

They spoke in Yiddish. "What are you going to become?" said Polina, *"ein ausvurf—ausgelassen?"* Outcast—dissolute? The old lady was Tolstoian, puritanical. She did eat meat, however, and she was a tyrant. She was frugal, arid, clean, respectable and domineering. But there was nothing so tart, sweet, soft, and fragrant as her strudel made with brown sugar and green apples. It was extraordinary how much sensuality went into her baking. And she never gave Daisy the recipe. "Well, what about it?" said Polina. "First one woman and then another, then another. Where will it end? You can't abandon a wife, a son for these women—whores."

I should never have had these "explanations" with her, thought Moses. Was it a point of honor to explain myself to everyone? But how could I explain? I myself didn't understand, didn't have a clue.

He stirred. He'd better be on his way. It was growing late. He was expected uptown. But he was not yet ready to leave. He took a new sheet of paper and wrote *Dear Sono.*

She had gone back to Japan long ago. When was it? He turned his eyes upward as he tried to calculate the length of time, and he saw the white clouds rolling above Wall Street and the harbor. *I don't blame you for going home.* She was a person of means. She owned a house in the country, too. Herzog had seen the colored photographs—an Oriental countryside with rabbits, hens, piglets, her own hot spring in which she bathed. She had a picture of the village blind man who came to massage her. She loved massages, believed in them. She had often massaged Moses, and he had massaged her.

You were right about Madeleine, Sono. I shouldn't have married her. I should have married you.

But Sono had never really learned to speak English. For two years, she and Moses had conversed in French—*petit nègre.* He wrote, *Ma chère, Ma vie est devenue un cauchemar affreux. Si tu savais!* At McKinley High School, from a forbidding spinster, Miss Miloradovitch, he had learned his French. The most useful course I took.

Sono had seen Madeleine only once, but once was enough. She warned me as I sat in her broken Morris chair. "Moso, méfie toi. Prend garde, Moso."

She had a tender heart, and Herzog knew that if he wrote her of the sadness of his life, she would certainly cry. Instantaneous tears. They had a way of appearing without the usual Western preliminaries. Her black eyes rose from the surface of her cheeks in the same way that her breasts rose from the surface of her body. No, he would not write her sad news of any sort, he decided. Instead, he allowed himself to picture her as she might be now (it was morning in Japan), bathing in her steaming spring, her small mouth open, singing. She bathed often, and sang as she washed, her eyes upcast and her lips dainty and tremulous. The songs were sweet and odd, narrow, steep, at times with catlike sounds.

During the troubled time when he was being divorced from Daisy and he came to visit Sono in her West Side apartment, she would immediately run the little tub and fill it with Macy's bath salts. She unbuttoned Moses' shirt, took off his clothes, and when she had him settled ("Easy now, it's hot") in the swirling, foaming, perfumed water she let drop her petticoat and got in behind him, singing that vertical music of hers.

> "Chin-chin
> Je te lave le dos
> Mon Mo-so."

As a young girl she had gone to live in Paris, and she was caught there by the War. She was down with pneumonia when the American troops entered and was still sick when she was repatriated via the Trans-Siberian Railroad. She no longer cared for Japan, she said; the West had spoiled her for life in Tokyo, and her rich father allowed her to study design in New York.

She told Herzog that she was not sure she believed in God, but that if he did she would also try to have faith. If on the other hand he was a Communist she was prepared to become one, too. Because "Les Japonaises sont très fidèles. Elles ne sont pas comme les Américaines. Bah!" Still, American women also amused her. She often entertained the Baptist ladies who were her sponsors with the Immigration Department. She prepared shrimp or raw fish for them or treated them to the tea ceremony. Moses sometimes sat waiting on the stoop of the brownstone opposite when the ladies were slow to leave. Sono with great enjoyment—she was greedy for intrigue (the abysses of female secrecy!)—would come to the window and give him the high sign, pretending to water her plants. She grew little ginkgo trees and cactuses in yoghurt containers.

On the West Side, she occupied three rooms with high ceilings; at the back there grew an ailanthus tree, and one of the front windows contained a giant air-conditioner; it must have weighed a ton. Fourteenth Street bargains filled the apartment—an overstuffed chesterfield, bronze screens, lamps, nylon drapes, masses of wax flowers, articles of wrought iron and twisted wire and glass. Here Sono went back and forth busily on bare feet, coming down on her heels sturdily. Her lovely body was covered unbecomingly in knee-length bargain negligees bought on the stands near Seventh Avenue. Every purchase involved her in a battle with the other bargain hunters. Excitedly holding her soft throat she would tell Herzog with sharp cries what had happened. "Chéri! J'avais déjà choisi mon tablier. Cette femme s'est foncée sur moi. Woo! Elle était noire! Moooan dieu! Et grande! Derrière immense. Immense poitrine. Et sans soutien-gorge. Tout à fait comme Niagara Fall. En chair noire." Sono puffed out her cheeks and crooked her arms as though suffocating with fat, thrusting out her belly, then displaying her rump. "Je disais, 'No, no, leddy. I here first.' Elle avait les bras comme ça—enflés. Et quelle gorge! Il y avait du monde au balcon. 'No!' je disais. 'No, no, leddy.'" Proudly Sono showed her nostrils, made her eyes heavy and dangerous. She set a hand on her hip. Herzog in the broken Morris chair from the Catholic Salvage said, "That's the stuff, Sono. They can't push the Samurai around on Fourteenth Street."

Abed, he had touched Sono's eyelids experimentally, as she lay smiling. Those strange, complex, soft, pale lids would keep the imprint of a touch for quite a while. *To tell the truth, I never had it so good,* he wrote. *But I lacked the strength of character to bear such joy.* That was hardly a joke. When a man's breast feels like a cage from which all the dark birds have flown—he is free, he is light. And he longs to have his vultures back again. He wants his customary struggles, his nameless, empty works, his anger, his afflictions and his sins. In this parlor of Oriental luxury, making a principled quest—*principled,* mind you—for life-giving pleasure, solving for Moses E. Herzog the puzzle of the body (curing himself of the fatal disorder of worldliness which rejects worldly happiness, this Western plague, this mental leprosy), he seemed to have found his object. But often he sat morose, depressed, in the Morris chair. Well, curse such sadness! But she liked even that. She saw me with the eyes of love, and she said, "Ah! T'es mélancolique—c'est très beau!" It may be that guilt and sadness made me look Oriental. A morose, angry eye, a long upper lip—what people used to call the Chinese Gleep. It was *beau* to her. And no wonder she thought I might be a Communist. The world should love lovers; but not theoreticians. Never theoreticians! Show them the door. Ladies, throw out these gloomy bastards! Hence, loathéd melancholy! In dark Cimmerian desart ever dwell.

Sono's three tall rooms in the brownstone apartment were hung with transparent bargain curtains, like the Far East in the movies. There were many interiors. The inmost was the bed, with sheets of spearmint green, or washed-out chlorophyll, unmade, everything in disorder. After the bath, Herzog's body was red. When she had dried and powdered him, she dressed him in a kimono, her pleased but still slightly unwilling Caucasian doll. The stiff cloth cramped him under the arms as he sat on the pillows. She brought him tea in her best cups. He listened to her talk. She would tell him the latest scandals of the Tokyo press. A woman had mutilated her unfaithful lover and was found with the missing parts in her obi. A locomotive engineer slept through a signal and killed a hundred and fifty-four people. Her father's concubine was now driving a Volkswagen. She parked at the gate of the house, for she was not allowed into the yard. And Herzog thought . . . is this really possible? Have all the traditions, passions, renunciations, virtues, gems, and masterpieces of Hebrew discipline and all the rest of it—rhetoric, a lot of it, but containing true facts—brought me to these untidy green sheets, and this rippled mattress? As if anyone cared what he was doing here. As if it affected the fate of the world in any way. It was his own business. "I got a right," Herzog whispered, though his face neither changed nor moved. Very good. The Jews were strange to the world for a great length of time, and now the world is being strange to them in return. Sono brought out a bottle and spiked his tea with cognac or Chivas Regal. When she had taken a few nips herself she gave a playful growl. Herzog could not help laughing. Sono then brought out her scrolls. Fat merchants made love to slender girls who looked away comically as they submitted. Moses and Sono sat cross-legged on the bed. She pointed to things, winking and exclaiming and pressing her round face to his.

Something was always frying or brewing in her kitchen, a dark closet rank with fish and soy sauce, seaweed vermicelli, old tea leaves. The plumbing was often out of order. She wanted Herzog to have a talk with the Negro janitor, who would only laugh at her when she demanded service. Sono kept two cats; their pan was never clean. When Herzog was in the subway, coming to see her, he already began to smell those odors of her apartment. Their darkness passed through his heart. He violently desired Sono, and just as violently did not want to go. Even now he felt the fever, remembered the smells, experienced the difficulty. He shivered when he rang her bell. The chain rattled, she pulled open the large door and threw her arms about his neck. Her face was elaborately made up, and she smelled of musk. The cats tried to make an escape. She captured them, and then she cried out—always the same cry—

"Moso! Je viens de rentrer!"

She was breathless. She had run to meet him and beat him home by seconds. Why? Why did she always have to be just under the wire? Perhaps to show that she had an independent and active life; she did not sit waiting. The tall door with the curved top admitted him. Sono secured it again with bolt and chain (precautions of a woman living alone; but she said the super tried to let himself in without knocking). Herzog with a beating heart but composed face entered, looked around with pale-faced dignity at the hangings (sienna, crimson, green) and the fireplace stuffed with the wrappings of her latest purchases, the draftsman's table where she did her homework and where the cats perched. He smiled at eager Sono, and sat down in the Morris chair. "Mauvais temps, eh chéri?" she said, and she began at once to cheer him. She took off his miserable shoes, telling him where she had been. Some lovely Christian Science ladies had invited her to a concert at the Cloisters. She had seen a double feature at the Thalia—Danielle Darrieux, Simone Signoret, Jean Gabin, et Harry Bow-wow. The Nippon-America Society invited her to the United Nations building, where she presented flowers to the Nizam of Hyderabad. Through a Japanese trade mission she also met Mr. Nasser and Mr. Sukarno and the Secretary of State and the President. Tonight she had to go to a night club with the foreign minister of Venezuela. Moses had learned not to doubt her. She always produced a night-club photograph in which she sat beautiful and laughing in a low-cut gown. She had Mendès-France's autograph on a menu. She would never ask Herzog to take her to the Copacabana. This was a mark of her respect for his deep gravity. "T'es philosophe. O mon philosophe, mon professeur d'amour. T'es très important. Je le sais." She rated him higher than kings and presidents.

As she put the kettle on for Herzog's tea, she never failed to describe the events of her day from the kitchen at the top of her voice. She saw a three-legged dog which made a truck swerve into a pushcart. A cabdriver wanted to give her his parrot, but the cats would kill it. She could not accept such a responsibility. A panhandling old woman—vieille mendiante—got her to buy a copy of the *Times* for her. That was all the old creature wanted, this morning's *Times*. A policeman said he would give Sono a ticket for jaywalking. A man had exposed himself behind a subway pillar. "Ooooh, c'était honteux—quelle chose!" She measured with her hands from her own body. "One foots, Moso. Très laide."

"Ça t'a plu," Moses said smiling.

"Oh no! Moso, no! Elle était vilain." She was, however, delightfully excited. Moses looked at her gently, suspiciously as well, perhaps, lying back elegantly in the broken reclining chair. The fever he had felt as he was coming had now begun to subside. Even the smells were never quite so bad as he had anticipated. The cats were less jealous of him. They came to be petted. He grew used to their Siamese mewing, more passionate and hungry than that of American cats.

Then she said, "Et cette blouse—combien j'ai payé? Dis-moi."

"You paid—let me see—you paid three bucks for it."

"No, no," she cried, "sixty sen'. Solde!"

"Impossible. Why, that thing is worth five bucks. You must be the greatest shopper in New York."

Gratified, she gave him a brilliant wink and took off his socks, chafing his feet. She brought him tea and poured a double shot of Chivas Regal into it. For him she kept the best of everything.

"Veux-tu scrombled eggs, chéri-koko. As-tu faim?" A cold rain was killing desolate New York with its green icy spikes. *When I pass Northwest Orient Airlines, I always mean to price a ticket to Tokyo.* She put soy sauce on the eggs. Herzog ate and drank. All the food was salty. He swallowed a great deal of tea. "We take bath," said Sono, and began to unbutton his shirt. "Tu veux?"

Teas and baths—the steam of boiling water loosened the wallpaper from the green plaster behind. The great console radio through a cloth-of-gold speaker played the music of Brahms. The cats were cuffing shrimp shells under the chairs.

"Oui—je veux bien," he said.

She went to run the water. He heard her singing as she sprinkled the lilac salts and bubble-bath powder.

I wonder who's scrubbing her now.

Sono asked for no great sacrifices. She did not want me to work for her, to furnish her house, support her children, to be regular at meals or to open charge accounts in luxury shops; she asked only that I should be with her from time to time. But some people are at war with the best things of life and pervert them into fantasies and dreams. The Yiddish French we spoke was funny but innocent. She told me no such broken truths and dirty lies as I heard in my own language, and my simple declarative sentences couldn't do her much harm. Other men have forsaken the West, looking for just this. It was delivered to me in New York City.

The bath was not without its occasional trials. At times, Sono examined Herzog's body for signs that he was unfaithful. Lovemaking, she was strongly convinced, turned men lean. "Ah!" she would say. "Tu as maigri. Tu fais amour?" He denied it but she shook her head, continuing to smile, though her face became puffy and bitter. She refused to believe him. But she would forgive him, at last. Her good humor returning, she put him in the tub, climbing in behind him. Singing, or growling mock orders at him in military Japanese. But peace had come. They bathed. She put her feet forward for him to soap. She dipped water in a plastic dish and poured it over his head. Draining the tub at last, she turned on the shower to rinse away the suds, and they stood together smiling under the spray. "Tu seras bien propre, chéri-koko."

Yes, she kept me very clean. With amusement and with sorrow, Herzog recalled it all.

They dried themselves with Turkish towels from 14th Street. She dressed him in the kimono, kissing his chest. He kissed the palms of her hands. Her eyes were tender, shrewd, they showed a thrifty light at times; she knew where to invest her sensuality and how to increase it. She sat him on the bed, and there she served him tea. Her concubine. They sat cross-legged, sipping from the small cups, looking at the scrolls. The door was bolted, the telephone off the hook. Tremulous, Sono's face came near, and she touched his cheek with her chub lips. They helped each other out of the Oriental garments. "Doucement, chéri. Oh, lentement. Oh!" Turning up her eyes so that he saw only the whites.

She tried to explain to me once that earth and the planets were sucked from the sun by a passing star. As if a dog should trot by a bush and set free worlds. And in those worlds life appeared, and within that life such as we—souls. And even stranger creatures than we, she said. I liked to hear this, but I didn't understand her well. I know I kept her from returning to Japan. For my sake, she disobeyed her father. Her mother died, and Sono did not mention it for weeks. And once she said, "Je ne crains pas la mort. Mais tu me fais souffrir, Moso." I hadn't called her in a month. She had had pneumonia again. No one had come to see her. She was weak and pale, and she cried and said, "Je souffre trop." But she did not let him comfort her; she had heard that he was seeing Madeleine Pontritter.

She did, however, say, "Elle est méchante, Moso. Je suis pas jalouse. Je ferai amour avec un autre. Tu m'as laissée. Mais elle a les yeux très, très froids."

He wrote, *Sono, you were right. I thought you might like to know. Her eyes are very cold.* Still, they are her eyes, and what is she to do about them? It would not be practical for her to hate herself. Luckily, God sends a substitute, a husband.

———

Ah, in the midst of such realizations, a man needs some comfort. Herzog once more set off on his visit to Ramona. As he stood at the door with the long metal shank of the police lock in his hand, his memory sought a certain song title. Was it "Just One More Kiss"? Not that. Nor "The Curse of an Aching Heart." "Kiss Me Again." That was it. It struck him very funny, and laughter made him clumsy as he set up the complicated lock to protect his worldly goods. Three thousand million human beings exist, each with *some* possessions, each a microcosmos, each infinitely precious, each with a peculiar treasure. There is a distant garden where curious objects grow, and there, in a lovely dusk of green, the heart of Moses E. Herzog hangs like a peach.

I need this outing like a hole in the head, he thought as he turned the key. Still, he was going, wasn't he. He was pocketing the key. And now ringing for the elevator. He listened to the sound of the power, the cables threshing. He went down alone, humming "Kiss Me," and trying to capture, as if it were an elusive fragile thread, the reason why these old songs were running through his head. Not the obvious reason. (He had an aching heart, was going forth to be kissed.) The recondite reason (if that was worth finding). He was glad to reach the open air, to breathe. He dried the sweatband of the straw hat with his handkerchief—it was hot in the shaft. And who wore such a hat, such a blazer? Why, Lou Holtz, of course, the old vaudeville comic. He sang, "I picked a lemon in the garden of love, where they say only *peaches* grow." Herzog's face again quickened with a smile. The old Oriental Theatre in Chicago. Three hours of entertainment for two bits.

At the corner he paused to watch the work of the wrecking crew. The great metal ball swung at the walls, passed easily through brick, and entered the rooms, the lazy weight browsing on kitchens and parlors. Everything it touched wavered and burst, spilled down. There rose a white tranquil cloud of plaster dust. The afternoon was ending, and in the widening area of demolition was a fire, fed by the wreckage. Moses heard the air, softly pulled toward the flames, felt the heat. The workmen, heaping the bonfire with wood, threw strips of molding like javelins. Paint and varnish smoked like incense. The old flooring burned gratefully—the funeral of exhausted objects. Scaffolds walled with pink, white, green doors quivered as the six-wheeled trucks carried off fallen brick. The sun, now leaving for New Jersey and the west, was surrounded by a dazzling broth of atmospheric gases. Herzog observed that people were spattered with red stains, and that he himself was flecked on the arms and chest. He crossed Seventh Avenue and entered the subway.

Out of the burning, the dust, down the stairs he hurried underground, listening for a train, fingers examining the coins in his pocket, seeking a subway token. He inhaled the odors of stone, of urine, bitterly tonic, the smells of rust and of lubricants, felt the presence of a current of urgency, speed, of infinite desire, possibly related to the drive within himself, his own streaming nervous vitality. (Passion? Perhaps hysteria? Ramona might relieve him by sexual means.) He took a long breath, inhaling the musty damp air endlessly, on and on, stabbed in both shoulders as his chest expanded, but continuing. Then he let the air out slowly, very slowly, down, down, into his belly. He did it again, again, and felt better for it. He dropped his fare in the slot where he saw a whole series of tokens lighted from within and magnified by the glass. Innumerable millions of passengers had polished the wood of the turnstile with their hips. From this arose a feeling of communion—brotherhood in one of its cheapest forms. This was serious, thought Herzog as he passed through. The more individuals are destroyed (by processes such as I know) the worse their yearning for collectivity. Worse, because they return to the mass agitated, made fervent by their failure. Not as brethren, but as degenerates. Experiencing a raging consumption of potato love. Thus occurs a second distortion of the divine image, already so blurred, wavering, struggling. The real question! He stood looking down at the tracks. The most real question!

Rush hour was just ended. Almost empty local cars were scenes of rest and peace, conductors reading the papers. Waiting for his uptown express, Herzog made a tour of the platform, looking at the mutilated posters—blacked-out teeth and scribbled whiskers, comical genitals like rockets, ridiculous copulations, slogans and exhortations. *Moslems, the enemy is White. Hell with Goldwater, Jews! Spicks eat* SHIT. *Phone, I will go down on you if I like the sound of your voice.* And by a clever cynic, *If they smite you, turn the other face.* Filth, quarrelsome madness, the prayers and wit of the crowd. Minor works of Death. Trans-descendence—that was the new fashionable term for it. Herzog carefully examined all such writings, taking his own public-opinion poll. He assumed the unknown artists were adolescents. Taunting authority. Immaturity, a new political category. Problems connected with the increasing mental emancipation of untrained unemployables. Better the Beatles. Further occupying the idle moment, Herzog looked at the penny scale The mirror was wired—could not be smashed except by an ingenious maniac. The benches were bolted down, the candy-vending machines padlocked.

A note to Willie the Actor, the famous bank robber now serving a life sentence. *Dear Mr. Sutton, The study of locks.* Mechanical devices and Yankee genius . . . He began again, *Second only to Houdini,* Willie never carried a gun. In Queens, once, he used a toy pistol. Disguised as a Western Union messenger, he entered the bank and took it over with his cap gun. The challenge was irresistible. Not the money, really, but the problem of getting in, and the companion problem of escape. Narrow-shouldered, with sunk cheeks and the mothy, dapper mustache, blue baggy eyes above, Willie lay thinking of banks. On his inadoor bed in Brooklyn, sucking a cigarette, wearing his hat and a pair of pointed shoes, he had visions of roofs leading to roofs, of power lines, sewer connections, vaults. All locks opened at his touch. Genius cannot let the world be. He had buried his loot in Flushing Meadows, in tin cans. He might have retired. But he took a walk, he saw a bank, a creative opportunity. This time he was caught and went to prison. But he planned a great getaway, made an elaborate mental survey and drew a master plan, crawled through pipes, dug under walls. He almost had it made. The stars were in view. But the screws were waiting when he broke through the earth. They carried him back —this insignificant person, the escape artist; one of the greatest, *and not very far behind Houdini, either. Motive: The power and completeness of all human systems must be continually tested, outwitted, at the risk of freedom, of life.* Now he is a lifer. They say he owns a set of the Great Books, corresponds with Bishop Sheen. . . .

Dear Dr. Schrodinger, In What Is Life? *you say that in all of nature only man hesitates to cause pain. As destruction is the master-method by which evolution produces new types, the reluctance to cause pain may express a human will to obstruct natural law. Christianity and its parent religion, a few short millennia, with frightful reverses . . .* The train had stopped, the door was already shutting when Herzog roused himself and squeezed through. He caught a strap. The express flew uptown. It emptied and refilled at Times Square, but he did not sit down. It was too hard to fight your way out again from a seat. Now, where were we? *In your remarks on entropy . . . How the organism*

maintains itself against death—in your words, against thermo-
dynamic equilibrium . . . Being an unstable organization of mat-
ter, the body threatens to rush away from us. It leaves. It is real.
It! Not we! Not I! This organism, while it has the power to hold
its own form and suck what it needs from its environment, attract-
ing a negative stream of entropy, the being of other things which
it uses, returning the residue to the world in simpler form. Dung.
Nitrogenous wastes. Ammonia. But reluctance to cause pain cou-
pled with the necessity to devour . . . a peculiar human trick
is the result, which consists in admitting and denying evils at the
same time. To have a human life, and also an inhuman life. In
fact, to have everything, to combine all elements with immense
ingenuity and greed. To bite, to swallow. At the same time to pity
your food. To have sentiment. At the same time to behave brutally.
It has been suggested (and why not!) that reluctance to cause pain
is actually an extreme form, a delicious form of sensuality, and
that we increase the luxuries of pain by the injection of a moral
pathos. Thus working both sides of the street. Nevertheless, there
are moral realities, Herzog assured the entire world as he held
his strap in the speeding car, *as surely as there are molecular*
and atomic ones. However, it is necessary today to entertain the
very worst possibilities openly. In fact we have no choice as to
that. . . .

This was his station, and he ran up the stairs. The revolving
gates rattled their multiple bars and ratchets behind him. He hastened by the change booth where a man sat in a light the color of
strong tea, and up the two flights of stairs. In the mouth of the
exit he stopped to catch his breath. Above him the flowering glass,
wired and gray, and Broadway heavy and blue in the dusk, almost
tropical; at the foot of the downhill Eighties lay the Hudson, as
dense as mercury. On the points of radio towers in New Jersey
red lights like small hearts beat or tingled. In midstreet, on the
benches, old people: on faces, on heads, the strong marks of decay: the big legs of women and blotted eyes of men, sunken mouths
and inky nostrils. It was the normal hour for bats swooping raggedly (Ludeyville), or pieces of paper (New York) to remind
Herzog of bats. An escaped balloon was fleeing like a sperm,
black and quick into the orange dust of the west. He crossed the
street, making a detour to avoid a fog of grilled chicken and sau-

sage. The crowd was traipsing over the broad sidewalk. Moses took a keen interest in the uptown public, its theatrical spirit, its performers—the transvestite homosexuals painted with great originality, the wigged women, the lesbians looking so male you had to wait for them to pass and see them from behind to determine their true sex, hair dyes of every shade. Signs in almost every passing face of a deeper comment or interpretation of destiny—eyes that held metaphysical statements. And even pious old women who trod the path of ancient duty, still, buying kosher meat.

Herzog had several times seen George Hoberly, Ramona's friend before him, following him with his eyes from one or another of these doorways. He was thin, tall, younger than Herzog, correctly dressed in Ivy League Madison Avenue clothes, dark glasses on his lean, sad face. Ramona, with the accent on "nothing," said she felt nothing but pity for him. His two attempted suicides probably made her realize how indifferent she was to him. Moses had learned from Madeleine that when a woman was done with a man she was done with him utterly. But tonight it occurred to him that, since Ramona was keen on men's styles and often tried to guide his choices, Hoberly might be wearing the clothes she had picked for him. He is vainly appealing, in the trappings of his former happiness and love, like the trained mouse in the frustration experiment. Even being phoned by the police and running to Bellevue in the middle of the night to be by his side now bores Ramona. The whole feeling-and-sensation market has shot up—shock, scandal priced out of range for the average man. You have to do more than take a little gas, or slash the wrists. Pot? Zero! Daisy chains? Nothing! Debauchery? A museum word from prelibidinous times! The day is fast approaching—Herzog in his editorial state—when only proof that you are despairing will entitle you to the vote, instead of the means test, the poll tax, the literacy exam. You must be forlorn. Former vices now health measures. Everything changing. Public confession of each deep wound which at one time was borne as if nothing were amiss. A good subject: the history of composure in Calvinistic societies. When each man, feeling fearful damnation, had to behave as one of the elect. All such historic terrors—every agony of spirit—must at last be released. Herzog began to be almost eager to see Hoberly, to have another look at that face wasted by suffering, insomnia, nights of pills and drink, of prayer—his dark glasses, his almost brimless fedora. Unrequited love. Nowadays called hysterical dependency. There were times when Ramona spoke of Hoberly with great sympathy. She said she had been crying over one of his letters or gifts. He kept sending her purses and perfumes, and long extracts from his journal. He had even sent her a large sum in cash. This she turned over to Aunt Tamara. The old lady opened a savings account for him. Let the money gather a little interest, at least. Hoberly was attached to the old woman. Moses, too, was fond of her.

He rang Ramona's bell and the buzzer opened the lobby door at once. She was considerate that way. One more delicate attention. The arrival of her lover was never routine. The elevator let people out—a fellow with a heavy front, one eye shut, smoking a strong cigar; a woman with two chihuahuas, red nail polish matching the harness of the dogs. And perhaps in the whirling fumes of the street, through two glass doors, his rival watched him. Moses rode up. On the fifteenth floor Ramona had the door ajar, on the chain. She didn't want to be surprised by the wrong man. When she saw Moses, she unbolted and took his hand, drawing him to her side. She offered her face to him. Herzog found it full, and very hot. Her perfume sprang out at him. She wore a white satin blouse, cut to suggest the wrapping of a shawl and showing her bust. Her face was flushed; she did not need the added color of rouge. "I'm glad to see you, Ramona. I'm very glad," he said. He hugged her, discovering in himself a sudden eagerness, a hunger for contact. He kissed her.

"So—you're glad to see me?"

"I am! I am!"

She smiled and shut the door, bolting it again. She led Herzog by the hand along the uncarpeted hall where her heels made a military clatter. It excited him. "Now," she said, "let's have a look at Moses in his finery." They stopped before the gilt, ornate mirror. "You have a great straw hat. And what a coat—Joseph's coat of stripes."

"You approve?"

"I certainly do. It's a beautiful jacket. You look Indian in it, with your dark coloring."

"I may join the Bhave group."

"Which is that?"

"Sharing large estates among the poor. I'll give away Ludeyville."

"You'd better consult me before you start another give-away program. Shall we have a drink? Perhaps you'd like to wash up while I get the drinks."

"I shaved before leaving the house."

"You look hot, as if you've been running, and you've got soot on your face."

He must have leaned against a subway pillar. Or perhaps it was a smudge from the wreckage bonfire. "Yes, I see."

"I'll get you a towel, dear," said Ramona.

In the bathroom, Herzog turned his tie to the back of his neck to keep it from drooping into the basin. This was a luxurious little room, with indirect lighting (kindness to haggard faces). The long tap glittered, the water rushed forth. He sniffed the soap. *Muguet.* The water felt very cold on his nails. He recalled the old Jewish ritual of nail water, and the word in the Haggadah, *Rachatz!* "Thou shalt wash." It was obligatory also to wash when you returned from the cemetery (*Beth Olam*—the Dwelling of the Multitude). But why think of cemeteries, of funerals, now? Unless . . . the old joke about the Shakespearean actor in the brothel. When he took off his pants, the whore in bed gave a whistle. He said, "Madam, we come to bury Caesar, not to praise him." How schoolboy jokes clung to you!

He opened his mouth under the tap and let the current run also into his shut eyes, gasping with satisfaction. Broad disks of iridescent brightness swam under his lids. He wrote to Spinoza, *Thoughts not causally connected were said by you to cause pain. I find that is indeed the case. Random association, when the intellect is passive, is a form of bondage. Or rather, every form of bondage is possible then. It may interest you to know that in the twentieth century random association is believed to yield up the deepest secrets of the psyche.* He realized he was writing to the dead. To bring the shades of great philosophers up to date. But then why shouldn't he write to the dead? He lived with them as much as with the living—perhaps more; and besides, his letters to the living were increasingly mental, and anyway, to the Unconscious, what was death? Dreams did not recognize it. *Believing that reason can make steady progress from disorder to harmony and that the con-*

quest of chaos need not be begun anew every day. How I wish it! How I wish it were so! How Moses prayed for this!

As for his relation to the dead, it was very bad indeed. He really believed in letting the dead bury their own dead. And that life was life only when it was understood clearly as dying. He opened the large medicine chest. They used to build on the grand scale, in old New York. Fascinated, he studied Ramona's bottles—skin freshener, estrogenic deep-tissue lotion, Bonnie Belle antiperspirant. Then this crimson prescription—twice daily for upset stomach. He smelled it and thought it must contain belladonna—calming for the stomach, mydriatic in the eyes. Made of deadly night-shade. There were also pills for menstrual cramp. Somehow, he didn't think Ramona was the type. Madeleine used to scream. He had to take her in a taxi to St. Vincent's where she cried for a Demerol injection. These forceps-looking things he thought must be for curling the eyelashes. They looked like the snail tongs in a French restaurant. He sniffed the scouring mitten. Especially for the elbows and heels, he thought, to rub away the bumps. He pressed the toilet lever with his foot; it flushed with silent power; the toilets of the poor always made noise. He applied a little brilliantine to the dry ends of his hair. His shirt was damp, of course, but she was wearing perfume enough for them both. And how was he otherwise? All things considered, not too bad. Ruin comes to beauty, inevitably. The space-time continuum reclaims its elements, taking you away bit by bit, and then again comes the void. But better the void than the torment and boredom of an incorrigible character, doing always the same stunts, repeating the same disgraces. But these instants of disgrace and pain could seem eternal, so that if a man could capture the eternity of these painful moments and give them a different content, he would achieve a revolution. How about that!

Wrapping the palm of his hand tightly in the towel, like a barber, Herzog wiped the drops of moisture at his hairline. Next he thought he would weigh himself. He used the toilet first, to make himself a little lighter, and stripped off his shoes without bending, climbing on the scale with an elderly sigh. Between his toes, the pointer swept past the 170 mark. He was regaining the weight he had lost in Europe. He forced his feet into the shoes again, treading down the backs, and returned to Ramona's sitting room—her sitting and sleeping room. She was waiting with two glasses of Campari. Its taste was bittersweet and its odor a little gassy—from the gas main. But all the world was drinking it, and Herzog drank it too. Ramona had chilled the glasses in the freezer.

"*Salud.*"

"*Sdrutch!*" he said.

"Your necktie is hanging down your back."

"Is it?" He pulled it to the front again. "Forgetful. I once tucked my jacket into the back of my trousers, coming from the gentlemen's room, and walked in to teach a class."

Ramona seemed astonished that he would tell such a story on himself. "Wasn't that dreadful?"

"Not too good. But it should have been very liberating for the students. Teacher is mortal. Besides, the humiliation didn't destroy him. This should have been more valuable than the course itself. In fact, one of the young ladies told me later I was very human —such a relief to us all. . . ."

"What is funny is how completely you answer any question. You are a funny man." Engagingly affectionate; her fine large teeth, tender dark eyes, enriched by black lines, smiled upon him. "It's the way you try to sound rough or reckless, though—like a guy from Chicago—that's even more amusing."

"Why amusing?"

"It's an act. Swagger. It's not really you." She refilled his glass and stood up to go to the kitchen. "I've got to look after the rice. I'll put on some Egyptian music to keep you cheerful." A wide patent-leather belt set off her waist. She bent over the phonograph.

"The food smells delicious."

Mohammad al Bakkar and his band began with drums and tambourines, and then a clatter of wires and braying wind instruments. A guttural pimping voice began to sing, "Mi Port Said . . ." Herzog, alone, looked at the books and theater programs, magazines and pictures. A photograph of Ramona as a little girl stood in a Tiffany frame—seven years old, a wise child leaning on a bank of plush, her finger pressing on her temple. He remembered the pose. A generation ago it used to get them. Little Einsteins. Prodigious wisdom in children. Pierced ears, a locket, a kiss-me curl, and the kind of early sensuality in tiny girls which he recalled very well.

Aunt Tamara's clock began to chime. He went into her parlor to look at its old-fashioned porcelain face with long gilt lines, like cat whiskers, and listened to the bright quick notes. Beneath it was the key. To own a clock like this you had to have regular habits—a permanent residence. Raising the window shade of this little European parlor with its framed scenes of Venice and friendly Dutch porcelain inanities, you saw the Empire State Building, the Hudson, the green, silver evening, half of New York lighting up. Thoughtful, he pulled the shade down again. This—this asylum was his for the asking, he believed. Then why didn't he ask? Because today's asylum might be the dungeon of tomorrow. To listen to Ramona, it was all very simple. She said she understood his needs better than he, and she might well be right. Ramona never hesitated to express herself fully, and there was something unreserved, positively operatic about some of her speeches. Opera. Heraldry. She said her feelings for him had depth and maturity and that she had an enormous desire to help him. She told Herzog that he was a better man than he knew—a deep man, beautiful (he could not help wincing when she said this), but sad, unable to take what his heart really desired, a man tempted by God, longing for grace, but escaping headlong from his salvation, often close at hand. This Herzog, this man of many blessings, for some reason had endured a frigid, middlebrow, castrating female in his bed, given her his name and made her the instrument of creation, and Madeleine had treated him with contempt and cruelty as if to punish him for lowering and cheapening himself, for lying himself into love with her and betraying the promise of his soul. What he really must do, she went on, in this same operatic style—unashamed to be so fluent; he marveled at this—was to pay his debt for the great gifts he had received, his intelligence, his charm, his education, and free himself to pursue the meaning of life, not by disintegration, where he would never find it, but humbly and yet proudly continuing his learned studies. She, Ramona, wanted to add riches to his life and give him what he pursued in the wrong places. This she could do by the art of love, she said—the art of love which was one of the sublime achievements of the spirit. It was love she meant by riches. What he had to learn from her—while there was time; while he was still virile, his powers substantially intact—was how to renew the spirit through the flesh (a precious vessel in which the spirit rested). Ramona—bless her!—was as florid in these sermons as in her looks. Oh, what a sweet orator she was! But where were we? Ah, yes, he was to continue his studies, aiming at the meaning of life. He, Herzog, overtake life's meaning! He laughed into his hands, covering his face.

But (sobering) he knew that he elicited these speeches by his airs. Why did little Sono cry, "O mon philosophe—mon professeur d'amour!"? Because Herzog behaved like a philosophe who cared only about the very highest things—creative reason, how to render good for evil, and all the wisdom of old books. Because he thought and cared about belief. (Without which, human life is simply the raw material of technological transformation, of fashion, salesmanship, industry, politics, finance, experiment, automatism, et cetera, et cetera. The whole inventory of disgraces which one is glad to terminate in death.) Yes, he looked like, behaved like, Sono's philosophe.

And after all, why was he here? He was here because Ramona also took him seriously. She thought she could restore order and sanity to his life, and if she did that it would be logical to marry her. Or, in her style, he would desire to be united with her. And it would be a union that really unified. Tables, beds, parlors, money, laundry and automobile, culture and sex knit into one web. Everything would at last make sense, was what she meant. Happiness was an absurd and even harmful idea, unless it was really comprehensive; but in this exceptional and lucky case where each had experienced the worst sorts of morbidity and come through by a miracle, by an instinct for survival and delight which was positively religious—there was simply no other way to talk about her life, said Ramona, except in terms of Magdalene Christianity—comprehensive happiness was possible. In that case, it was a duty; to refuse to answer the accusations against happiness (that it was a monstrous and selfish delusion, an absurdity) was cowardly, a surrender to malignancy, capitulating to the death instinct. Here was a man, Herzog, who knew what it was to rise from the dead. And she, Ramona, she knew the bitterness of death and nullity, too. Yes, she too! But with him she experienced a real Easter. She knew what Resurrection was. He might look down his conscious nose at sensual delight, but with her, when their clothes were off, he knew what it was. No amount of sublimation could replace that erotic happiness, that knowledge.

Not even tempted to smile, Moses listened earnestly, bowing his head. Some of it was current university or paperback chatter and some was propaganda for marriage, but, after such debits were entered against her, she was genuine. He sympathized with her, respected her. It was all real enough. She had something genuine at heart.

When he jeered in private at the Dionysiac revival it was himself he made fun of. Herzog! A prince of the erotic Renaissance, in his *macho* garments! And what about the kids? How would they like a new stepmother? And Ramona, would she take Junie to see Santa Claus?

"Ah, this is where you are," said Ramona. "Aunt Tamara would be flattered if she knew you were interested in her Czarist museum."

"These old-time interiors," said Herzog.

"Isn't it touching?"

"They drugged you with schmaltz."

"The old woman is so fond of you."

"I like her, too."

"She says you brighten up the house."

"That *I* . . ." He smiled.

"Why not? You have a tender trusting face. You can't bear to hear that, can you. Why not?"

"I put the old woman out when I come," he said.

"You're wrong. She loves these trips. She puts on a hat, and gets dressed up. It's such a thing for her to go to the railroad station. Anyway . . ." Ramona's tone changed. "She needs to get away from George Hoberly. He's become her problem now." For a brief instant she was downcast.

". . . Sorry," said Herzog. "Has it been bad lately?"

"Poor man . . . I feel so sorry for him. But come, Moses, dinner is all ready and I want you to open the wine." In the dining room she handed him the bottle—Pouilly Fuissé, well chilled—and the French corkscrew. With competent hands and strong purpose, his neck reddening as he exerted himself, he pulled the cork. Ramona had lighted the candles. The table was decorated with spiky red gladiolas in a long dish. On the windowsill the pigeons stirred and grumbled; they fluttered and went to sleep again. "Let me help you to this rice," said Ramona. She took the plate, good bone china with a cobalt rim (the steady spread of luxury into all ranks of society since the fifteenth century, noted by the famous Sombart, inter alia). But Herzog was hungry, and the dinner was delicious. (He would become austere hereafter.) Tears of curious, mixed origin came into his eyes as he tasted the shrimp remoulade. "Awfully good—my God, how good!" he said.

"Haven't you eaten all day?" said Ramona.

"I haven't seen food like this for some time. Prosciutto and Persian melon. What's this? Watercress salad. Good Christ!"

She was pleased. "Well, eat," she said.

After the shrimp Arnaud and salad, she offered cheese and cold-water biscuits, rum-flavored ice cream, plums from Georgia, and early green grapes. Then brandy and coffee. In the next room, Mohammad al Bakkar kept singing his winding, nasal, insinuating songs to the sounds of wire coathangers moved back and forth, and drums, tambourines and mandolins and bagpipes.

"What have you been doing?" said Ramona.

"Me? Oh, all kinds of things. . . ."

"Where did you go on the train? Were you running away from me?"

"Not from you. But I suppose I was running."

"You're still a little afraid of me, aren't you."

"I wouldn't say that. . . . Confused. Trying to be careful."

"You're used to difficult women. To struggle. Perhaps you like it when they give you a bad time."

"Every treasure is guarded by dragons. That's how you can tell it's valuable. . . . Do you mind if I unbutton my collar? It seems to be pressing on an artery."

"But you came right back. Perhaps that was because of me."

Moses was strongly tempted to lie to her, to say, "Yes, Ramona, it was you." Strict and literal truthfulness was a trivial game and might even be a disagreeable neurotic affliction. Ramona had Moses' complete sympathy—a woman in her thirties, successful in business, independent, but still giving such suppers to gentlemen friends. But in times like these, how should a woman steer her heart to fulfillment? In emancipated New York, man and woman, gaudily disguised, like two savages belonging to hostile tribes, confront each other. The man wants to deceive, and then to disengage himself; the woman's strategy is to disarm and detain him. And this is Ramona, a woman who knows how to look after herself. Think how it is with some young thing, raising mascara-ringed eyes to heaven, praying, "Oh, Lord, let no bad man come unto my chubbiness."

Besides which, Herzog realized that to eat Ramona's shrimp and drink her wine, and then sit in her parlor listening to the straggling lustfulness of Mohammad al Bakkar and his Port Said specialists, thinking such thoughts, was not exactly commendable. *And Monsignor Hilton, what is priestly celibacy? A more terrible discipline is to go about and visit women, to see what the modern world has made of carnality. How little relevance certain ancient ideas have. . . .*

But at least one thing became clear. To look for fulfillment in another, in interpersonal relationships, was a feminine game. And the man who shops from woman to woman, though his heart aches with idealism, with the desire for pure love, has entered the female realm. After Napoleon fell, the ambitious young man carried his power drive into the boudoir. And there the women took command. As Madeleine had done, as Wanda might as easily have done. And what about Ramona? And Herzog, formerly a silly young thing, now becoming a silly old thing, by accepting the design of a *private life* (approved by those in authority) turned himself into something resembling a concubine. Sono made this entirely clear, with her Oriental ways. He had even joked about it with her, trying to explain how unprofitable his visits to her appeared to him at last. *"Je bêche, je sème, mais je ne récolte point."* He joked—but no, he was no concubine, not at all. He was a difficult, aggressive man. As for Sono, she was trying to instruct him, to show how a man should treat a woman. The pride of the peacock, the lust of the goat, and the wrath of the lion are the glory and wisdom of God.

"Wherever you were going, with your valise, your fundamentally healthy instincts brought you back. They're wiser than you," said Ramona.

"Maybe . . ." said Herzog. "I am going through a change of outlook."

"Thank goodness you haven't destroyed your birthright yet."

"I haven't been really independent. I find I've been working for others, for a number of ladies."

"If you can conquer your Hebrew puritanism . . ."

"Developing the psychology of a runaway slave."

"It's your own fault. You look for domineering women. I'm trying to tell you that you've met a different type in me."

"I know I have," he said. "And I think the world of you."

"I wonder. I don't think you understand." Here she showed some resentment. "About a month ago you told me I ran a sexual circus. As if I were an acrobat of some kind."

"Why, Ramona, that meant nothing."

"It implied that I had known too many men."

"Too many? No, Ramona. I don't look at it that way. If anything, it does a lot for my self-esteem to be able to keep up."

"Why, the very idea of keeping up betrays you. It makes me angry to hear you say that."

"I know. You want to put me on a higher level and bring out the Orphic element in me. But I've tried to be a pretty mediocre person, if the truth be told. I've done my job, kept up my end, performed my duty, and waited for the old quid pro quo. What I had coming, naturally, was a sock on the head. I thought I had entered into a secret understanding with life to spare me the worst. A perfectly bourgeois idea. On the side, I was just flirting a little with the transcendent."

"There's nothing so ordinary about marrying a woman like Madeleine or having a friend like Valentine Gersbach."

His indignation rose, and he tried to check it. Ramona was being considerate, giving him a chance to sound off to release spleen. This was not what he had come for. And anyway he was growing tired of his obsession. Besides, she had troubles of her own. And the poet said that indignation was a kind of joy, but was he right? There is a time to speak and a time to shut up. The only truly interesting side of the matter was the intimate design of the injury, the fact that it was so penetrating, custom-made exactly to your measure. It's fascinating that hatred should be so personal as to be almost loving. The knife and the wound aching for each other. Much of course depends upon the vulnerability of the intended. Some cry out, and some swallow the thrust in silence. About the latter you could write the inner history of mankind. How did Papa feel when he found that Voplonsky was in cahoots with the hijackers? He never said.

Herzog wondered whether he would succeed in holding all this in, tonight. He hoped he would. But Ramona often encouraged him to give in to it. She not only spread a supper but invited him to sing.

"I don't think of them as exactly a mediocre pair," she said.

"I sometimes see all three of us as a comedy team," said Herzog, "with me playing straight man. People say that Gersbach imitates me—my walk, my expressions. He's a second Herzog."

"Anyway, he convinced Madeleine that he was superior to the original," said Ramona. She lowered her eyes. They moved and then came to rest beneath the lids. By candlelight, he observed this momentary disquiet of her face. Perhaps she thought she had spoken tactlessly.

"Madeleine's greatest ambition, I think, is to fall in love. This is the deepest part of the joke about her. Then there's her grand style. Her tics. To give the bitch her due, she is beautiful. She adores being the center of attention. In one of those fur-trimmed suits she struts in, with her deep color and blue eyes. And when she has an audience and begins spellbinding, there's a kind of flat pass she makes with the palm of her hand, and her nose twitches like a little rudder, and by and by one brow joins in and begins to rise, rise."

"You make her sound adorable," said Ramona.

"We lived together on a high level, all of us. Except Phoebe. She merely went along."

"What is she like?"

"She has attractive features but she looks severe. She comes on like the head nurse."

"She didn't care for you?"

". . . Her husband was a cripple. He knows how to make the most of it, emotionally, with his lurid sob stuff. She had bought him cheap because he was factory damaged. New and perfect, she could never have afforded such a luxury. He knew and she knew and we knew. Because this is an age of insight. The laws of psychology are known to all educated people. Anyway, he was only a one-legged radio announcer but she had him to herself. Then

Madeleine and I arrived, and a glamorous life began in Ludeyville."

"It must have upset her when he began to imitate you."

"Yes. But if I was going to be swindled the best way was to do
the job in my own style. Poetic justice. Philosophical piety describes the style."

"When did you first notice?"

"When Mady began to stay away from Ludeyville. A few times
she holed up in Boston. She said she simply had to be alone and
think things over. So she took the kid—just an infant. And I asked
Valentine to go and reason with her."

"And this was when he began to give you those lectures?"

Herzog tried to smile away the quick-welling rancor whose
source had been touched. He might not be able to control it. "They
all lectured. Everyone lectured. People legislate continually by
means of talk. I have Madeleine's letters from Boston. I have letters
from Gersbach, too. All kinds of documents. I even have a bundle
of letters written by Madeleine to her mother. They came in the
mail."

"But what did Madeleine say?"

"She's quite a writer. She writes like Lady Hester Stanhope. First
of all, she said I resembled her father in too many ways. That when
we were in a room together *I* seemed to swallow and gulp up all
the air and left nothing for her to breathe. I was overbearing, infantile, demanding, sardonic, and a psychosomatic bully."

"Psychosomatic?"

"I had pains in my belly in order to dominate her, and got my
way by being sick. They all said that, all three of them. Madeleine
had another lecture about the only basis for a marriage. A marriage was a tender relationship resulting from the overflow of feeling, and all the rest of that. She even had a lecture about the right
way to perform the conjugal act."

"Incredible."

"She must have been describing what she had learned from
Gersbach."

"You don't need to go into it," said Ramona. "I'm sure she
made it as painful as possible."

"In the meantime, I was supposed to wind up this study of mine,
and become the Lovejoy of my generation—that's the silly talk of

scholarly people, Ramona, I didn't think of it that way. The more Madeleine and Gersbach lectured me, the more I thought that my only purpose was to lead a quiet, regular life. She said this quietness was more of my scheming. She accused me of being on 'a meek kick,' and said that I was now trying to keep her in line by a new tactic."

"How curious! What were you supposed to be doing?"

"She thought I had married her in order to be 'saved,' and now I wanted to kill her because she wasn't doing the job. She said she loved me, but couldn't do what I demanded, because this was so fantastic, and so she was going to Boston one more time to think it all through and find a way to save this marriage."

"I see."

"About a week later, Gersbach came to the house to pick up some of her things. She had phoned him from Boston. She needed her clothes. And money. He and I took a long walk in the woods. It was early autumn—sunny, dusty, marvelous . . . melancholy. I helped him over the rough ground. He poles his way along, with that leg. . . ."

"As you told me. Like a gondolier. And what did he say?"

"He said he didn't know how the fuck he would survive this terrible trouble between the two people he loved most in the world. He repeated that—the two people who meant more to him than wife and child. It was tearing him to pieces. His faith in things was going to be smashed."

Ramona laughed, and Herzog joined her.

"And then?"

"Then?" said Herzog. He remembered the tremor in Gersbach's dark-red powerful face which seemed at first brutal, the face of a butcher, until you came to understand the depth and subtlety of his feelings. "Then we went back to the house and Gersbach packed her things. And what he had mainly come for—her diaphragm."

"You don't mean it!"

"Of course I mean it."

"But you seem to accept it. . . ."

"What I accept is that my idiocy inspired them, and sent them to greater heights of perversity."

"Didn't you ask her what this meant?"

"I did. She said I had lost my right to an answer. It was more of the same from me—pettiness. Then I asked her whether Valentine had become her lover."

"And what kind of answer did you get?" Ramona's curiosity was greatly excited.

"That I didn't understand what Gersbach had given me— the kind of love, the kind of feeling. I said, 'But he took the thing from the medicine chest.' And she said, 'Yes, and he stays overnight with June and me when he comes to Boston, but he's the brother I never had, and that's all.' I hesitated to accept this, so she added, 'Now don't be a fool, Moses. You know how coarse he is. He's not my type at all. Our intimacy is a different kind altogether. Why, when he uses the toilet in our little Boston apartment it fills up with his stink. I know the smell of his shit. Do you think I could give myself to a man whose shit smells like that!' That was her answer."

"How frightful, Moses! Is that what she said? What a strange woman. She's a strange, strange creature."

"Well, it shows how much we know about one another, Ramona. Madeleine wasn't just a wife, but an education. A good, steady, hopeful, rational, diligent, dignified, childish person like Herzog who thinks human life is a subject, like any other subject, has to be taught a lesson. And certainly anyone who takes dignity seriously, old-fashioned individual dignity, is bound to get the business. Maybe dignity was imported from France. Louis Quatorze. Theater. Command. Authority. Anger. Forgiveness. *Majesté*. The plebeian, bourgeois ambition was to inherit this. It all belongs in the museum now."

"But I thought Madeleine herself was always so dignified."

"Not always. She could turn against her own pretensions. And don't forget, Valentine is a great personality, too. Modern consciousness has this great need to explode its own postures. It teaches the truth of the creature. It throws shit on all pretensions and fictions. A man like Gersbach can be gay. Innocent. Sadistic. Dancing around. Instinctive. Heartless. Hugging his friends. Feeble-minded. Laughing at jokes. Deep, too. Exclaiming 'I *love* you!' or 'This I *believe*.' And while moved by these 'beliefs' he steals you blind. He makes realities nobody can understand. A radio-astronomer will sooner understand what's happening in space ten billion light years away than what Gersbach is fabricating in his brain."

"You're far too excited about it," said Ramona. "My advice is to forget them both. How long did this stupidity go on?"

"Years. Several years, anyway. Madeleine and I got together again, a while after this. And then she and Valentine ran my life for me. I didn't know a thing about it. All the decisions were made by them—where I lived, where I worked, how much rent I paid. Even my mental problems were set by them. They gave me my homework. And when they decided that I had to go, they worked out all the details—property settlement, alimony, child support. I'm sure Valentine thought he acted in my best interests. He must have held Madeleine back. He knows he's a good man. He understands, and when you understand you suffer more. You have higher responsibilities, responsibilities that come with suffering. I couldn't take care of my wife, poor fish. He took care of her. I wasn't fit to bring up my own daughter. He has to do it for me, out of friendship, out of pity and sheer greatness of soul. He even agrees that Madeleine is a psychopath."

"No, you can't mean it!"

"I do. 'The poor crazy bitch,' he'd say. 'My heart goes out to that cracked broad!' "

"So he's mysterious, too. What a strange pair!" she said.

"Of course he is," said Herzog.

"Moses," said Ramona. "Let's stop talking about this, please. I feel there's something wrong in it. . . . Wrong for us. Now come . . ."

"You haven't heard it all. There's Geraldine's letter, telling how they mistreat the kid."

"I know. I've read it. Moses, no more."

"But . . . Yes, you're right," said Herzog. "Okay, I'll stop it right now. I'll help you clear the table."

"There's no need to."

"I'll wash the dishes."

"No, you certainly will not wash dishes. You're a guest here. I intend to put them all in the sink, for tomorrow."

He thought, I prefer to accept as a motive not the thing I fully understand but the thing I partly understand. Utter clarity of explanation to me is false. However, I must take care of June.

"No, no, Ramona, there's something about washing dishes that calms me. Now and then, anyway." He fixed the drain, put in soap powder, ran the water, hung his coat on the knob of a cupboard, tucked up his sleeves. He refused the apron Ramona offered. "I'm an old hand. I won't splash."

As even Ramona's fingers were sexual, Herzog wanted to see how she would do ordinary tasks. But the kitchen towel in her hands as she dried the glasses and silver looked natural. So she was not simply pretending to be a homebody. Herzog had at times wondered whether it wasn't Aunt Tamara who prepared the shrimp remoulade before she slipped out. The answer was no. Ramona did her own cooking.

"You should be thinking about your future," said Ramona. "What are you planning to do next year?"

"I can pick up a job of some sort."

"Where?"

"I can't decide whether to be near my son Marco, in the east, or go back to Chicago to keep an eye on June."

"Listen, Moses, it's no disgrace to be practical. Is it a point of honor or something, not to think clearly? You want to win by sacrificing yourself? It doesn't work, as you ought to know by now. Chicago would be a mistake. You'd only suffer."

"Perhaps, and suffering is another bad habit."

"Are you joking?"

"Not at all," he said.

"It's hard to imagine a more masochistic situation. Everybody in Chicago knows your story by now. You'd be in the middle of it. Fighting, arguing, getting hurt. That's too humiliating for a man like you. You don't respect yourself enough. Do you want to be torn to pieces? Is that what you're offering to do for little June?"

"No, no. What good is that? But can I turn the child over to those two? You read what Geraldine said." He knew that letter by heart, and was prepared to recite it.

"Still, you can't take the child from her mother."

"She's my kind. She has my genes. She's a Herzog. They're mentally alien types."

He grew tense again. Ramona tried to draw him away from this subject.

"Didn't you tell me that your friend Gersbach has become a kind of figure in Chicago?"

"Yes, yes. He started out in educational radio, and now he's all over the place. On committees, in the papers. He gives lectures to the Hadassah . . . readings of his poems. In the Temples. He's joining the Standard Club. He's on television! Fantastic! He was such a provincial character, he thought there was only one railroad station in Chicago. And now he's turned out to be a terrific operator —covers the city in his Lincoln Continental, wearing a tweed coat of a sort of salmon-puke color."

"You're getting into a state just thinking about it," said Ramona. "Your eyes get feverish."

"Gersbach hired a hall, did I tell you?"

"No."

"He sold tickets to a reading of his poems. My friend Asphalter told me about it. Five dollars for the front seats, three bucks at the back of the hall. Reading a poem about his grandfather who was a street sweeper, he broke down and cried. Nobody could get out. The hall was locked."

Ramona could not help laughing.

"Ha-ha!" Herzog let out the water, wringing the rag, sprinkling scouring powder. He scrubbed and rinsed the sink. Ramona brought him a slice of lemon for the fishy smell. He squeezed it over his hands. "Gersbach!"

"Still," said Ramona earnestly. "You ought to get back to your scholarly work."

"I don't know. I feel I'm stuck with it. But what else is there for me to do?"

"You only say that because you're agitated. You'll think differently when you're calm."

"Maybe."

She led the way to her room. "Shall I play more of that Egyptian music? It has a good effect." She went to the machine. "And why don't you take your shoes off, Moses. I know you like to remove them in this weather."

"It does relieve my feet. I think I will. They're already unlaced."

The moon was high over the Hudson. Distorted by window glass, distorted by summer air, appearing bent by its own white power, it floated also in the currents of the river. The narrow rooftops below were pale, long figures of constriction beneath the moon. Ramona turned the record over, and now a woman was singing to the music of al Bakkar's band *"Viens, viens dans mes bras—je te donne du chocolat."*

Sitting on the hassock beside him, Ramona took his hand. "But what they tried to make you believe," she said. "It just isn't true."

This was what he was aching to hear from her. "What do you mean?"

"I know something about men. As soon as I saw you I realized how much of you was unused. Erotically. Untouched, even."

"I've been a terrible flop at times. A total flop."

"There are some men who should be protected . . . by law, if necessary."

"Like fish and game?"

"I am not really joking," she said. He saw plainly, clearly, how kind she was. She felt for him. She knew he was in pain, and what the pain was, and she offered the consolation he had evidently come for. "They tried to make you feel that you were old and finished. But let me explain one fact. An old man smells old. Any woman can tell you. When an old man takes a woman in his arms she can smell a stale, dusty kind of thing, like old clothes that need an airing. If the woman has let things go as far as that, and doesn't want to humiliate him when she finds that he really is quite old (people do disguise themselves and it's hard to guess), she will probably go on with it. And that is so awful! But Moses, you are chemically youthful." She put her bare arms about his neck. "Your skin has a delicious odor. . . . What does Madeleine know. She's nothing but a packaged beauty."

He thought what a fine achievement he had made of his life that—aging, vain, terribly narcissistic, suffering without proper dignity—he was taking comfort from someone who really didn't have too much of it to spare him. He had seen her when she was tired, upset and weak, when the shadows came over her eyes, when the fit of her skirt was wrong and she had cold hands, cold lips parted on her teeth, when she was lying on her sofa, a woman of short frame, very full, but after all, a tired, short woman whose breath had the ashen flavor of fatigue. The story then told itself—struggles and disappointments; an elaborate system of theory and eloquence at the bottom of which lay the simple facts of need, a woman's need. She senses that I am for the family. For I am a family type, and she wants me for her family. Her idea of family behavior appeals to me. She was brushing his lips back and forth with hers. She was leading him (somewhat aggressively) away from hatred and fanatical infighting. Her head thrown back, she breathed quickly with excitement, skill, purpose. She began to bite his lip and he drew back, but only from surprise. She held fast to his lip, taking in more of it, and the result was a leap of sexual excitement in Herzog. She was unbuttoning his shirt. Her hand was on his skin. She also reached behind, turning on the hassock, to undo the back of her blouse with the other hand. They held each other. He began to stroke her hair. The scent of lipstick and the odor of flesh came from her mouth. But suddenly they interrupted their kissing. The phone was ringing.

"Oh, lord!" said Ramona. "Lord, lord!"

"Are you going to answer?"

"No, it's George Hoberly. He must have seen you arrive, and he wants to spoil things for us. We mustn't allow him to. . . ."

"I'm not in favor of it," said Herzog.

She turned over the phone and silenced it with the switch at the base. "He had me in tears again, yesterday."

"He wanted to give you a sports car, last I heard."

"Now he's urging me to take him to Europe. I mean, he wants me to show him Europe."

"I didn't know he had that sort of money."

"He doesn't. He'd have to borrow. It would cost ten thousand dollars, staying at the Grand Hotels."

"I wonder what he's trying to get across?"

"What do you mean?" Ramona found something suspect in Herzog's tone.

"Nothing . . . nothing. Only that he thinks you have the sort of money a tour like that would take."

"Money has nothing to do with it. There's simply nothing more in the relationship."

"What was there to begin with?"

"I thought there was something. . . ." Her hazel eyes gave him an odd look; they reproved him; or, more in sadness, asked him why he wanted to say such queer things. "Do you want to make an issue of this?"

"What's he doing in the street?"

198

"It's not my fault."

"He made his great pitch for you, and failed, so now he thinks he's under a curse and wants to kill himself. He'd be better off at home, on his sofa, drinking a can of beer, watching Perry Mason."

"You're too severe," said Ramona. "Maybe you think I'm giving him up for you and it makes you uneasy. You feel you're pushing him out and will have to be his replacement."

Herzog paused, reflecting, and leaned back in his chair. "Perhaps," he said. "But I think it's that while in New York I am the man inside, in Chicago the man in the street is me."

"But you're not in the least like George Hoberly," said Ramona with that musical lift he very much liked to hear. Her voice, when it was drawn up from her breast, and changed its tone in her throat—that gave Moses great pleasure. Another man might not react to its intended sensuality, but he did. "I took pity on George. For that reason it could never be anything but a temporary relationship. But you—you aren't the kind of man a woman feels sorry for. You aren't weak, whatever else. You have strength. . . ."

Herzog nodded. Once more he was being lectured. And he didn't really mind it. That he needed straightening out was only too obvious. And who had more right than a woman who gave him asylum, shrimp, wine, music, flowers, sympathy, gave him room, so to speak, in her soul, and finally the embrace of her body? We must help one another. In this irrational world, where mercy, compassion, heart (even if a *little* fringed with self-interest), all rare things—hard-won in many human battles fought by rare minorities, victories whose results should never be taken for granted, for they were seldom reliable in anyone—rare things, were often debunked, renounced, repudiated by every generation of skeptics. Reason itself, logic, urged you to kneel and give thanks for every small sign of true kindness. The music played. Surrounded by summer flowers and articles of beauty, even luxury, under the soft green lamp, Ramona spoke to him earnestly—he looked affectionately at her warm face, its ripe color. Beyond, hot New York; an illuminated night which did not need the power of the moon. The Oriental rug and its flowing designs held out the hope that great perplexities might be resolved. He held Ramona's soft cool arm in his fingers. His shirt was open on his chest. He was smiling, nodding a little as he listened to her. Much of what she said was perfectly right. She was a clever woman and, even better, a dear woman. She had a good heart. And she had on black lace underpants. He knew she did.

"You have great capacity for life," she was saying. "And you're a very loving man. But you must try to break away from grudges. They'll eat you up."

"I think that's true."

"I know you think I theorize too much. But I've taken more than one beating myself—a terrible marriage, and a whole series of bad relationships. Look—you have the strength to recover, and it's sinful not to use it. Use it now."

"I see what you mean."

"Maybe it's biology," said Ramona. "You have a powerful system. You know what? The woman in the bakery told me yesterday I was looking so changed—my complexion, my eyes, she said. 'Miss Donsell, you must be in love.' And I realized it was because of you."

"You do look changed," said Moses.

"Prettier?"

"Lovely," he said.

Her color deepened still more. She took his hand and placed it inside her blouse, looking steadily at him, eyes growing fluid. Bless the girl! What pleasure she gave him. All her ways satisfied him— her French-Russian-Argentine-Jewish ways. "Let's take off your shoes, too," he said.

Ramona turned out all the lights except the green lamp by the bed. She whispered, "I'll be right back."

"Would you switch off that whining Egyptian, please? He needs his tongue wiped with a dishrag."

She stopped the phonograph with a touch, and said, "Just a few minutes," softly closing the door.

"A few minutes" was a figure of speech. She was long at her preparations. He had gotten used to waiting, saw the point of it, and was no longer impatient. Her reappearance was always dramatic and worth waiting for. In substance, however, he understood that she was trying to teach him something and he was trying (the habit of obedience to teaching being so strong in him) to learn from her. But how was he to describe this lesson? The description might begin with his wild internal disorder, or even with the fact that he was quivering. And why? Because he let the entire world press upon him. For instance? Well, for instance, what it means to be a man. In a city. In a century. In transition. In a mass. Transformed by science. Under organized power. Subject to tremendous controls. In a condition caused by mechanization. After the late failure of radical hopes. In a society that was no community and devalued the person. Owing to the multiplied power of numbers which made the self negligible. Which spent military billions against foreign enemies but would not pay for order at home. Which permitted savagery and barbarism in its own great cities. At the same time, the pressure of human millions who have discovered what concerted efforts and thoughts can do. As megatons of water shape organisms on the ocean floor. As tides polish stones. As winds hollow cliffs. The beautiful supermachinery opening a new life for innumerable mankind. Would you deny them the right to exist? Would you ask them to labor and go hungry while you enjoyed delicious old-fashioned Values? You—you yourself are a child of this mass and a brother to all the rest. Or else an ingrate, dilettante, idiot. There, Herzog, thought Herzog, since you ask for the instance, is the way it runs. On top of that, an injured heart, and raw gasoline poured on the nerves. And to this, what does Ramona answer? She says, get your health back. *Mens sana in corpore sano.* Constitutional tension of whatever origin needed sexual relief. Whatever the man's age, history, condition, knowledge, culture, development, he had an erection. Good currency anywhere. Recognized by the Bank of England. Why should his memories injure him now? Strong natures, said F. Nietzsche, could forget what they could not master. Of course he also said that the semen reabsorbed was the great fuel of creativity. Be thankful when syphilitics preach chastity.

Oh, for a change of heart, a change of heart—a true change of heart!

Into that there was no way to con yourself. Ramona wanted him to go the whole hog (*pecca fortiter!*) Why was he such a Quaker in love-making? He said that after his disappointments of recent date he was glad enough to perform at all, simple missionary style. She said that made him a rarity in New York. A woman had her problems here. Men who seemed decent often had very special tastes. She wanted to give him his pleasure in any way he might choose. He said she would never turn an old herring into a dolphin. It was odd that Ramona should sometimes carry on like one of those broads in a girlie magazine. For which she advanced the most high-minded reasons. An educated woman, she quoted him Catullus and the great love poets of all times. And the classics of psychology. And finally the Mystical Body. And so she was in the next room, joyously preparing, stripping, perfuming. She wanted to please. He had only to be pleased and to let her know it, and then she would grow simpler. How glad she would be to change! How it would relieve her if he said, "Ramona, what's all this for?" But then, would I have to marry her?

The idea of marriage made him nervous, but he thought it through. Her instincts were good, she was practical, capable, and wouldn't injure him. A woman who squandered her husband's money, all psychiatric opinion agreed, was determined to castrate him. On the practical side—and he found it very exciting to have practical thoughts—he couldn't stand the disorder and loneliness of bachelorhood. He liked clean shirts, ironed handkerchiefs, heels on his shoes, all the things Madeleine despised. Aunt Tamara wanted Ramona to have a husband. There must be a few Yiddish words left in the old girl's memory—*shiddach, tachliss*. He could be a patriarch, as every Herzog was meant to be. The family man, father, transmitter of life, intermediary between past and future, instrument of mysterious creation, was out of fashion. Fathers obsolete? Only to masculine women—wretched, pitiful bluestockings. (How bracing it was to think shrewdly!) He knew that Ramona was keen about scholarship, his books and encyclopedia articles, Ph.D., University of Chicago, and would want to be Frau Professor Herzog. Amused, he saw how they would arrive at white-tie parties at the Hotel Pierre, Ramona in long gloves and introducing Moses with her charming, lifted voice: "This is my husband, Professor Herzog." And he himself, Moses, a different man, radiating well-being, swimming in dignity, affable to one and all. Giving his back hair a touch. What a precious pair they'd make, she with her tics and he with his! What a vaudeville show! Ramona would get revenge on people who had once given her a hard time. And he? He too would get back at his enemies. *Yemach sh'mo!* Let their names be blotted out! They prepared a net for my steps. They digged a pit before me. Break their teeth, O God, in their mouth!

His face, his eyes especially, dark, intent, he took off his pants, further loosened his shirt. He wondered what Ramona would say if he offered to go into the flower business. Why not? More contact with life, meeting customers. The privations of scholarly isolation had been too much for a man of his temperament. He had read lately that lonely people in New York, shut up in their rooms, had taken to calling the police for relief. "Send a squad car, for the love of God! Send someone! Put me in the lockup with somebody! Save me. Touch me. Come. Someone—please come!"

Herzog couldn't say definitely that he would not finish his study. The chapter on "Romantic Moralism" had gone pretty well, but the one called "Rousseau, Kant, and Hegel" had him stopped cold. What if he should actually become a florist? It was an outrageously over-priced business, but that didn't need to be his problem. He saw himself in striped trousers, suede shoes. He'd have to get used to odors of soil and flowers. Thirty-some years ago, when he was dying of pneumonia and peritonitis, his breath was poisoned by the sweetness of red roses. They were sent, probably stolen, by his brother Shura who worked, then, for the florist on Peel Street. Herzog thought he might be able to stand the roses now. That pernicious thing, fragrant beauty, shapely red. You had to have strength to endure such things or by intensity they might pierce you inside and you might bleed to death.

At this moment Ramona appeared. She thrust the door open and stood, letting him see her in the lighted frame of bathroom tile. She was perfumed and, to the hips, she was naked. On her hips she wore the black lace underthing, that single garment low on her belly. She stood on spike-heeled shoes, three inches high. Only those, and the perfume and lipstick. Her black hair.

"Do I please you, Moses?"

"Oh, Ramona! Of course! How can you ask! I'm delighted!"

Looking downward, she laughed in a low voice. "Oh, yes. I see I please you." She held back the hair from her forehead as she bent a little to examine the effect of her nudity on him—how he reacted to the sight of her breasts and female hips. Open wide, her eyes were intensely black. She held him by the wrist, where his veins were large, and drew him toward the bed. He began to kiss her. He thought, It never makes sense. It is a mystery.

"Why don't you take off your shirt. You won't really need it, Moses."

They both laughed, she at his shirt, he at her costume. It was a stunner! No wonder clothes were so important to Ramona, they were the setting of that luxurious jewel, her nakedness. His laughter as it became silent, internal, was all the deeper. Her black lace pants might be utter foolishness, but they had the desired result. Her methods might be crude, but her calculations were correct. He was laughing, but it got him. His wit was tickled but his body burned.

"Touch me, Moses. Should I touch, too?"

"Oh, please, yes."

"Aren't you glad you didn't run away from me?"

"Yes, yes."

"How does this feel."

"Sweet. Very, very sweet."

"If only you would learn to trust your instincts . . . The lamp, too? Would you rather in the dark?"

"No, never mind the lamp now, Ramona."

"Moses, dear Moses. Tell me you belong to me. Tell me!"

"I belong to you, Ramona!"

"To me only."

"Only!"

"Thank God a person like you exists. Kiss my breasts. Darling Moses. Oh! Thank God."

———————

Both slept deeply, Ramona without stirring. Herzog was awakened once, by a jet plane—something screaming with great power at a terrible height. Not fully roused, he got out of bed and sat heavily in the striped chair, prepared at once to write another message—perhaps to George Hoberly. But when the noise of the plane passed the thought went, too. His eyes were filled by the still, hot, flutterless night—the city, its lights.

Ramona's face, relaxed by love-making and sleep, had a rich color. In one hand she held the frilled binding of the summer blanket, and her head was raised on the pillows in a thinking posture—it reminded him of that photograph of the pensive child in the next room. One leg was free from the covers—the inside of the thigh with its wealth of soft skin and faint ripples—sexually fragrant. Her instep had a lovely fleshy curve. Her nose was curved too. And then there were her plump, pressed toes, in descending size. Herzog, smiling at the sight of her, went back to bed with sleepy clumsiness. He stroked her thick hair and fell asleep.

HE took Ramona to her shop after breakfast. She was wearing a tight red dress, and they were hugging and kissing in the taxi. Moses was stirred and laughed a great deal, saying to himself more than once, "How lovely she is! And I'm making it." On Lexington Avenue he got out with her and they embraced on the sidewalk (since when did middle-aged men behave so passionately in public places?). Ramona's rouge was superfluous, her face was glowing, even burning, and she pressed him with her breasts as she kissed him; the waiting cabbie and Miss Schwartz, Ramona's assistant, both were watching.

Was this perhaps the way to live? he wondered. Had he had trouble enough, and paid his debt to suffering and earned the right to ignore what anyone might think? He clasped Ramona closer, felt that she was swelling, bursting, heart in the body, body in the tight-fitting red dress. She gave him still another perfumed kiss. On the sidewalk before the window of her shop were daisies, lilacs, small roses, flats with tomato and pepper seedlings for transplanting, all freshly watered. There stood the green pot with its perforated brass spout. Drops of water assumed blurred shapes on the cement. In spite of the buses which glazed the air with stinking gases, he could smell the fresh odor of soil, and he heard the women passing by, the rapid knocking of their heels on the crusty pavement. So between the amusement of the cabbie and the barely controlled censure of Miss Schwartz's eyes behind the leaves, he went on kissing Ramona's painted, fragrant face. Within the great open trench of Lexington Avenue, the buses pouring poison but the flowers surviving, garnet roses, pale lilacs, the cleanliness of the white, the luxury of the red, and everything covered by the gold overcast of New York. Here, on the street, as far as character and disposition permitted, he had a taste of the life he might have led if he had been simply a loving creature.

But as soon as he was alone in the rattling cab, he was again the inescapable Moses Elkanah Herzog. Oh, what a thing I am—what a *thing!* His driver raced the lights on Park Avenue, and Herzog considered what matters were like: I fall upon the thorns of life, I bleed. And then? I fall upon the thorns of life, I bleed. And what next? I get laid, I take a short holiday, but very soon after I fall upon those same thorns with gratification in pain, or suffering in joy—who knows what the mixture is! What good, what lasting good is there in me? Is there nothing else between birth and death but what I can get out of this perversity—only a favorable balance of disorderly emotions? No freedom? Only impulses? And what about all the good I have in my heart—doesn't it mean anything? Is it simply a joke? A false hope that makes a man feel the illusion of worth? And so he goes on with his struggles. But this good is no phony. I know it isn't. I swear it.

Again, he was greatly excited. His hands shook as he opened the door of his apartment. He felt he must do something, something practical and useful, and must do it at once. His night with Ramona had given him new strength, and this strength itself revived his fears, and, with the rest, the fear that he might break down, that these strong feelings might disorganize him utterly.

He took off his shoes, his jacket, loosened his collar, opened his front-room windows. Warm currents of air with the slightly contaminated odor of the harbor lifted his shabby curtains and the window shade. This flow of air calmed him slightly. No, the good in his heart evidently didn't count for much, for here, at the age of forty-seven, he was coming home after a night out with a lip made sore by biting and kissing, his problems as unsolved as ever, and what else did he have to show for himself at the bar of judgment? He had had two wives; there were two children; he had once been a scholar, and in the closet his old valise was swelled like a scaly crocodile with his uncompleted manuscript. While he delayed, others came up with the same ideas. Two years ago a Berkeley professor named Mermelstein had scooped him, confounding, overwhelming, stunning everyone in the field, as Herzog had meant to do. Mermelstein was a clever man, and an excellent scholar. At least he must be free from personal drama and able to give the world an example of order, thus deserving a place in the human community. But he, Herzog, had committed a sin of some kind against his own heart, while in pursuit of a grand synthesis.

What this country needs is a good five-cent synthesis.

What a catalogue of errors! Take his sexual struggles, for instance. Completely wrong. Herzog, going to brew himself some coffee, blushed as he measured the water in the graduated cup. It's the hysterical individual who allows his life to be polarized by simple extreme antitheses like strength–weakness, potency–impotence, health–sickness. He feels challenged but unable to struggle with social injustice, too weak, so he struggles with women, with children, with his "unhappiness." Take a case like that of poor George Hoberly—Hoberly, that sobbing prick! Herzog washed off the ring inside his coffee cup. Why did Hoberly rush in a fever to the luxury shops of New York for intimate gifts, for tributes to Ramona? Because he was crushed by failure. See how a man will submit his whole life to some extreme endeavor, often crippling, even killing himself in his chosen sphere. Now that it can't be political, it's sexual. Maybe Hoberly felt he had not satisfied her in bed. But that didn't seem likely, either. Trouble with the member, even a case of ejaculatio praecox, would not throw a woman like Ramona. If anything, such humiliations would challenge or intrigue her, bring out her generosity. No, Ramona was humane. She simply didn't want this desperate character to cast *all* his burdens on her. It's possible that a man like Hoberly by falling apart intends to bear witness to the failure of individual existence. He proves it *can't work*. He pushes love to the point of absurdity to discredit it forever. And in that way prepares to serve the Leviathan of organization even more devotedly. But another possibility was that a man bursting with unrecognized needs, imperatives, desires for activity, for brotherhood, desperate with longing for reality, for God, could not wait but threw himself wildly upon anything resembling a hope. And Ramona did look like a hope; she *chose* to. Herzog knew how that was, since he himself had sometimes given people hope. Emitting a secret message: *"Rely on me."* This was probably a matter simply of instinct, of health or vitality. It was his vitality that led a man from lie to lie, or induced him to hold out hopes to others. (Destructiveness created lies of its own, but that was another matter.) What I seem to do, thought Herzog, is to inflame myself with my drama, with ridicule, failure, denunciation, distortion, to inflame myself voluptuously, esthetically, until I reach a sexual climax. And that climax looks like a resolution and an answer to many "higher" problems. In so far as I can trust Ramona in the role of prophetess, it is that. She has read Marcuse, N. O. Brown, all those neo-Freudians. She wants me to believe the body is a spiritual fact, the sinstrument of the soul. Ramona is a dear woman, and very touching, but this theorizing is a dangerous temptation. It can only lead to more high-minded mistakes.

He watched the coffee beating in the cracked dome of the percolator (comparable to the thoughts in his skull). When the brew looked dark enough, he filled his cup and breathed in the fumes. He decided to write Daisy saying that he would visit Marco on Parents' Day, not plead weakness. Enough malingering! He decided also that he must have a talk with lawyer Simkin. Immediately.

He ought to have phoned Simkin earlier, knowing his habits. The ruddy, stout Machiavellian old bachelor lived with his mother and a widowed sister and several nephews and nieces on Central Park West. The apartment itself was luxurious, but he slept on an army cot in the smallest of the rooms. His night table was a pile of legal volumes and here he worked and read, far into the night. The walls were covered from top to bottom by abstract-expressionist paintings, unframed. At six Simkin rose from his cot and drove his Thunderbird to a small East Side restaurant—he found out the most authentic places, Chinese, Greek, Burmese, the darkest cellars in New York; Herzog had often eaten with him. After a breakfast of onion rolls and Nova Scotia, Simkin liked to lie down on the black Naugahyde sofa in his office, cover himself with an afghan knitted by his mother, listening to Palestrina, Monteverdi, as he elaborated his legal and business strategies. At eight or so he shaved his large cheeks with Norelco, and by nine, having left instructions for his staff, he was out, visiting galleries, attending auctions.

Herzog dialed, and found Simkin in. At once—it was a ritual—Simkin began complaining. It was June, the month for weddings, two junior members of the firm were absent—honeymooning. What idiots! "Well, Professor," he said, "I haven't seen you in a while. What's on your mind?"

"First, Harvey, I ought to ask whether you can advise me. You are a friend of Madeleine's family, after all."

"Let's say, instead, that I have a relationship with them. For you I have sympathy. No Pontritter needs my sympathy, least of all Madeleine, that bitch."

"Recommend another lawyer if you want to keep out of it."

"Lawyers can be expensive. You aren't rolling in money, I take it."

Of course, Herzog reflected, Harvey is curious. He'd like to know as much as possible about my situation. Am I being sensible? Ramona wants me to consult her lawyer. But that might commit me to something else again. Besides, her lawyer would want to protect Ramona from me. "When are you free, Harvey?" said Herzog.

"Listen—I picked up two paintings by a Yugoslavian primitive —Pachich. He's just in from Brazil."

"Can we meet for lunch?"

"Not today. Lately the Angel of Death has taken charge. . . ." Herzog recognized the peculiar notes of Jewish comedy that Simkin loved, his elaborate shows of dread, his cosmic mock dismay. "Getting and spending I lay waste my powers. . . ." Simkin went on.

"Half an hour."

"Let's have dinner at Macario's. I'll bet you never even heard of it. . . . I thought not. You *are* a hick." He shouted harshly to his secretary, "Bring me that column Earl Wilson wrote about Macario. You hear me, Tilly?"

"Are you busy all day long?"

"I have to go to court. Those schmucks are in Bermuda with their brides while I fight the *Moloch-ha-movos* alone. Do you know what you pay for one serving of spaghetti al burro at Macario's? Guess."

I must go along, Herzog reflected. He rubbed his brows with thumb and forefinger. "Three-fifty?"

"Is that your idea of expensive? Five dollars and fifty cents!"

"My God, what do they put in it?"

"Sprinkled with gold dust, not cheese. No, seriously, I have to try a case today. I—myself. And I loathe courtrooms."

"Let me pick you up in a cab and drive you downtown. I'll be right over."

"But I'm waiting for the client here. I'll tell you what, if I have a few minutes to spare later . . . You sound very nervous. My cousin Wachsel is in the District Attorney's office. I'll leave word with him. . . . Well, as long as my guy isn't here yet, why don't you tell me what it's all about."

"It's about my daughter."

"You want to sue for custody?"

"Not necessarily. I'm concerned about her. I don't know how the child is."

"Besides which, you'd like to get revenge, I imagine."

"I send the support money regularly and always ask after June, but never a word in reply. Himmelstein, the lawyer in Chicago, said I wouldn't stand a chance in a custody suit. But I don't know how the girl is being brought up. I do know they shut her up in the car when she bothers them. How far do they go?"

"Do you think Madeleine is an unfit mother?"

"Of course I think so, but I hesitate to rush between the kid and her mother."

"Is she living with this guy, your buddy? Remember when you were running away to Poland last year and made your will? You named him executor and guardian."

"I did? Yes . . . I remember now. I guess I did."

He could hear the lawyer coughing, and knew it was a feigned cough; Simkin was laughing. You could hardly blame him. Herzog himself was somewhat amused by his sentimental faith in "best friends," and could not help thinking how much he must have added to Gersbach's pleasure by his gullibility. Obviously, thought Moses, I wasn't fit to look after my own interests, and proved my incompetence every day. A stupid prick!

"I was kind of surprised when you named him," said Simkin.

"Why, did you know anything?"

"No, but there was something about his looks, his clothes, his loud voice, and his phony Yiddish. And such an exhibitionist! I didn't like the way he hugged you. Even kissed you, if I recall. . . ."

"That's his exuberant Russian personality."

"Oh, I'm not saying he's queer, exactly," Simkin said. "Well, is Madeleine shacked up with this gorgeous guardian? You could at least investigate. Why don't you hire a private investigator?"

"A detective! Of course!"

"The idea grabs you?"

"It certainly does! Why didn't I think of it myself?"

"Do you have the kind of money that takes? Now that's *real* money!"

"I go back to work in a few months."

"Even so, what can you earn?" Simkin always spoke of Moses' earnings with a ring of sadness. Poor intellectuals, so badly treated. He seemed to wonder why Herzog did not resent this. But Herzog still accepted Depression standards.

"I can borrow."

"Private investigation costs a tremendous amount. I'll explain it to you." He paused. "The big corporations have created a new aristocracy under the present tax structure. Cars, planes, hotel suits—fringe benefits. Also restaurants, theaters, et cetera, good private schools have been priced out of range for the low-salaried man. Even the cost of prostitution. The deductible medical expense has enriched psychiatrists, so even suffering costs more now. As for the various dodges in insurance, real estate, et cetera, I could tell you about them, too. Everything is subtler. Large organizations have their own C.I.A. Scientific spies who steal secrets from other corporations. Anyhow, detectives get big fees from the carriage trade, so that when you low-income fellows come along you have to deal with the worst element in this racket. Many a plain blackmailer calls himself a private investigator. Now I could give you a piece of useful advice. Do you want it?"

"Yes—yes, I do. But . . ." Herzog hesitated.

"But what's my angle?" Simkin, as Herzog had intended, put the question for him. "I suppose you're the only person in New York who doesn't know how Madeleine turned on me—such slanders! And I was like an uncle to her. Living in lofts, among those theater types, the child was like a frightened puppy. I took pity on Mady. I gave her dolls, I took her to the circus. When she was old enough to enter Radcliffe, I paid for her wardrobe. But then when she was converted by that dude monsignor I tried to talk to her; and she called me a hypocrite and crook. She said I was a social climber, using her father's connections, and nothing but an ignorant Jew. Ignorant! I took the Latin medal at Boys' High in 1917. All right. But then she injured a little cousin of mine, an epileptic girl, a sickly, immature, innocent frail mouse of a woman who couldn't take care of herself—never mind the awful details."

"What did she do?"

"That's another long story."

"So you're not protecting Madeleine any more. I didn't hear what she said against you."

"Maybe you don't remember it. She gave me some pretty sharp wounds, believe me. Never mind that. I'm a greedy old money-grubber—I don't claim I'm a candidate for sainthood, but . . . Well, that's just the frenzy of the world. Maybe you don't always take cognizance, Professor, being absorbed in the true the good and the beautiful like Herr Goethe."

"Okay, Harvey. I know I'm not a realist. I haven't got the strength to make all the judgments a man must make to be realistic. What advice were you going to give me?"

"Here's something to think about, as long as my stinking client hasn't arrived. If you really want to bring suit . . ."

"Himmelstein said a jury would take one look at my gray hairs and give a verdict against me. Perhaps I could dye my hair."

"Get a clean-cut gentile lawyer from one of the big firms. Don't have a lot of Jews yelling in the court. Give your case dignity. Then you subpoena all the principals, Madeleine, Gersbach, Mrs. Gersbach, and put them on the stand under oath. Warn them of perjury. If the questions are asked in the right way, and I'm willing to coach your clean-cut lawyer, and mastermind the whole trial, you'll never have to touch a hair of your head."

With his sleeve, Herzog wiped the sweat that broke out on his forehead. He was suddenly very hot. The heat, which pricked his skin, also released the scent of Ramona's body which he had absorbed. It was mixed with his own odors.

"Are you with me?"

"I'm listening, go on," said Herzog.

"They'll have to come clean, and they themselves will make your whole case for you. We can ask Gersbach when this affair with Madeleine started, how he got you to bring him to the Midwest—you did, didn't you?"

"I got him the job. I rented the house for them. I arranged to have the garbage-disposal unit installed in the sink. I measured the windows so that Phoebe could decide whether to bring her drapes from Massachusetts."

Simkin made one of his token exclamations of astonishment. "Well, which woman is he living with?"

"That I don't really know. I'd like to confront him myself—could I conduct the examination in court?"

"That's not feasible. But the lawyer can ask your questions for you. You could crucify that cripple. And Madeleine—she's had it all her own way so far. It never enters her mind that you have any rights. Wouldn't she come down to earth with a bang!"

"I often think, if she died I'd get my daughter back. There are times when I know I could look at Madeleine's corpse without pity."

"They tried to murder *you*," Simkin said. "In a manner of speaking, they meant to." Herzog sensed that his words about Madeleine's death had excited Simkin and made him eager to hear more. He wants me to say that I actually feel capable of murdering them both. Well, it's true. I've tested it in my mind with a gun, a knife, and felt no horror, no guilt. None. And I could never imagine such a crime before. So perhaps I might kill them. But I'll say no such thing to Harvey.

Simkin went on: "In court, you must prove they have an adulterous relationship to which the child is exposed. In itself, sexual intimacy doesn't count. An Illinois court gave custody to a call girl, the mother, because whatever tricks she performed, she saved them for hotel rooms. The courts don't expect to stop the whole sexual revolution of our time. But if the fucking is at home and the child exposed to it, the judicial attitude is different. Damage to the little psyche."

Herzog listened, looking through the window with a hard gaze, and tried to master the spasms of his stomach and the twisted, knotted sensations of his heart. The telephone seemed to pick up the sound of his blood, rhythmic, thin, and quick, washing within his skull. Perhaps it was only a nervous reflex of his eardrums. The membranes appeared to shiver.

"Understand," said Simkin, "it would hit all the Chicago papers."

"I've got nothing to lose, I'm practically forgotten in Chicago. The scandal would hit Gersbach, not me," said Herzog.

"How do you figure?"

"He's on the make everywhere and cultivates all the Chicago hotshots—clergymen, newspapermen, professors, television guys, federal judges, Hadassah ladies. Jesus Christ, he never lets up. He organizes new combinations on television. Like Paul Tillich and Malcolm X and Hedda Hopper on one program."

"I thought the fellow was a poet and a radio announcer. Now he sounds like a TV impresario."

"He's a poet in mass communications."

"He really has got you, hasn't he. By golly, if this isn't something in your bloodstream."

"Well, how would you like it if you woke up to see that all your best tries were nothing but sleepwalking?"

"But I don't understand this Gersbach's game."

"I'll tell you. He's a ringmaster, popularizer, liaison for the elites. He grabs up celebrities and brings them before the public. And he makes all sorts of people feel that he has exactly what they've been looking for. Subtlety for the subtle. Warmth for the warm. For the crude, crudity. For the crooks, hypocrisy. Atrocity for the atrocious. Whatever your heart desires. Emotional plasma which can circulate in any system."

Simkin was perfectly delighted with such an outburst, Herzog knew. He even understood that the lawyer was winding him up, putting him on. But that did not stop him. "I've tried to see him as a type. Is he an Ivan the Terrible? Is he a would-be Rasputin? Or the poor man's Cagliostro? Or a politician, orator, demagogue, rhapsode? Or some kind of Siberian shaman? Those are often transvestites or androgynes. . . ."

"Do you mean to say that those philosophers you've studied for so many years are all frustrated by one Valentine Gersbach?" said Simkin. "All those years of Spinoza—Hegel?"

"You're ribbing me, Simkin."

"Sorry. That wasn't a good joke."

"I don't mind. It seems true. Like taking swimming lessons on the kitchen table. Well, I can't answer for the philosophers. Maybe power philosophy, Thomas Hobbes, could analyze him. But when I think of Valentine I don't think of philosophy, I think of the books I devoured as a boy, on the French and Russian revolutions. And silent movies, like *Mme. Sans Gêne*—Gloria Swanson. Or Emil Jannings as a Czarist general. Anyway, I see the mobs breaking into the palaces and churches and sacking Versailles, wallowing in cream desserts or pouring wine over their dicks and dressing in purple velvet, snatching crowns and miters and crosses. . . ."

Herzog knew very well when he talked like this that he was again in the grip of that eccentric, dangerous force that had been capturing him. It was at work now, and he felt himself bending. At any moment he might hear a crack. He must stop this. He heard Simkin laughing softly and steadily to himself with, probably, one small hand placed in restraint on his fat chest, and wrinkles of cheerful satire in play about his bushy eyes and hairy ears. "Emancipation resulting in madness. Unlimited freedom to choose and play a tremendous variety of roles with a lot of coarse energy."

"I never saw a man pour wine over his dick in any movie— when did you ever see that?" said Simkin. "At the Museum of Modern Art? Besides, in your mind, you don't identify yourself with Versailles or the Kremlin or the old regime, or anything like that, do you?"

"No, no, of course not. It's nothing but a metaphor, and probably not a good one. I only meant to say that Gersbach won't let anything go, he tries everything on. For instance, if he took away my wife, did he have to suffer my agony for me, too? Because he could do even that better? And if he's such a tragic-love figure, practically a demigod in his own eyes, does he have to be also the greatest of fathers and family men? His wife says he's an ideal husband. Her only complaint was that he was so horny. She said he was on top of her every night. She couldn't keep up the pace."

"Who did she complain to?"

"Why, to her best friend, Madeleine, of course. Who else? And the truth is that Valentine is a family man, along with everything else. He alone knew how I felt about my kid and wrote me weekly reports about her, faithfully, with real kindliness. Until I found out he gave me the grief he was consoling me for."

"What did you do then?"

"I looked all over Chicago for him. Finally, I sent him a telegram from the airport as I was leaving. I wanted to say that I'd kill him on sight. But Western Union doesn't accept such messages. So I wired five words—Dirt Enters At The Heart. The first letters spell death."

"I'm sure he was bowled over by the threat."

Herzog did not smile. "I don't know. He is superstitious. But as I said, he is a family man. He fixes the appliances at home. When the kid needs a snowsuit he shops for it. He goes to Hillman's basement and brings back rolls and pickled herring in his shopping bag. In addition, he's a sportsman—college boxing champ at Oneonta, despite his wooden leg, he says. With pinochle players he plays pinochle, with rabbis it's Martin Buber, with the Hyde Park Madrigal Society he sings madrigals."

"Well," said Simkin, "he's nothing but a psychopath on the make, boastful and exhibitionistic. A bit clinical, maybe, except that he's a recognizable Jewish type. One of those noisy crooks with a booming voice. What kind of car does this promoter poet drive?"

"A Lincoln Continental."

"Heh, heh."

"But as soon as he slams the door of his Continental he begins to talk like Karl Marx. I heard him at the Auditorium with an audience of two thousand people. It was a symposium on desegregation, and he let loose a blast against the affluent society. That's how it is. If you've got a good job, about fifteen grand a year, and health insurance, and a retirement fund, and maybe some stock as well, why shouldn't you be a radical too? Literate people appropriate all the best things they can find in books, and dress themselves in them just as certain crabs are supposed to beautify themselves with seaweed. And then there was the audience, a comfortable audience of conventional business people and professionals who look after their businesses and specialties well enough, but seem confused about everything else and come to hear a speaker express himself confidently, with emphasis and fire, direction and force. With a head like a flaming furnace, a voice like a bowling alley, and the wooden leg drumming the stage. To me he's a curiosity, like a Mongolian idiot singing *Aïda*. But to *them* . . ."

"By golly, you are worked up," said Simkin. "Why are you suddenly talking about the opera? As you describe him, it's perfectly plain to me the fellow is an actor, and I know damn well Madeleine is an actress. That I've always realized. But take it easy. This exaggeration is bad for you. You eat yourself alive."

Moses was silent, shutting his eyes for a moment. Then he said, "Well, maybe so . . ."

"Wait up, Moses, I think my client is here."

"Oh, all right, I won't keep you. Let's have your cousin's number and I'll meet you downtown later."

"This can't wait."

"No, I have to reach a decision today."

"Well, I'll try to find a little time. Now taper off."

"I need fifteen minutes," said Herzog. "I'll prepare all my questions."

Moses as he took Wachsel's number was thinking that perhaps the best thing he could do was to stop asking people for advice and help. That in itself might change the entire picture. He printed Wachsel's number more legibly on the pad. In the background he heard Simkin shouting rudely at his client. Something about an ant-eater . . . ?

He unbuttoned his shirt and let it fall behind him to the bathroom floor. Then he ran the water in the sink. The crude oval of the basin was smooth and beautiful in the gray light. He touched the almost homogeneous whiteness with his fingertips and breathed in the water odors and the subtle stink rising from the throat of the waste pipe. Unexpected intrusions of beauty. This is what life is. He bent his head under the flowing tap and sighed with shock and then with pleasure. *Dear M. de Jouvenel, If the aims of political philosophy be as you say to civilize power, to impress the brute, to improve his manners and harness his energy to constructive tasks, I would like to say,* he was no longer addressing de Jouvenel, *that the sight of James Hoffa on your television show the other night made me realize how terrible a force angry single-mindedness can be. I was sorry for the poor professors on your panel whom he was chewing up. I'll tell you what I would have said to Hoffa. "What makes you think realism must be brutal?"* Herzog's hands were on the taps; the left now shut off the warm water, the right increased the pressure of the cold. It poured over his scalp and his neck. He was shivering with the extreme violence of thought and feeling.

At last he straightened his dripping head and wrapped it in the towel, rubbing and shaking his head in an effort to recover some degree of calm. As he was doing this, it occurred to him that this going into the bathroom to pull himself together was one of his habits. He seemed to feel that here he was more effective, more master of himself. In fact, he remembered, for a few weeks in Ludeyville he required Madeleine to make love on the bathroom floor. She complied, but he could see when she lay down on the old tiles that she was in a rage. Much good could come of that. This is how the all-powerful human intellect employs itself when it has no real occupation. And now he pictured the November rain dropping from the sky on his half-painted house in Ludeyville. The sumacs spilled the red Chinese paper of their leaves, and in the shivering woods the hunters were banging away at the deer—bang, bang, bang—driving home with dead animals. The gun-smoke was slow to rise from the woods' edge. Moses knew that in her heart his recumbent wife was cursing him. He tried to make his lust comical, to show how absurd it all was, easily the most wretched form of human struggle, the very essence of slavery.

Then suddenly Moses recalled something quite different that had happened at Gersbach's house just outside Barrington about a month later. Gersbach was lighting the Chanukah candles for his little son, Ephraim, garbling the Hebrew blessing, then dancing with the boy. Ephraim was buttoned into his clumsy sleepers, and Valentine, powerful and gimpy, undaunted by mutilation—that was his great charm; sulk because he was a cripple? Screw that! He was dancing, pounding, clapping his hands, his flamboyant hair, always brutally barbered at the neck, moving up and down, and he looked at the boy with fanatical tenderness, eyes dark and hot. Whenever that look came over him the ruddy color of his face seemed to be drawn entirely into his brown eyes and it made his cheeks seem almost porous. I might have guessed already, from Mady's look, that spurt of breath that came from her when she laughed spontaneously. That look was deep. Strange. A look like a steel binder bent open. She loves that actor.

Oneself is simply grotesque! Herzog stated it impulsively, though with pain, and his mind immediately looking for formal stability, catching (as he was lathering, clipping the blade into his injector razor) at ideas, of Professor Hocking's latest book *whether justice on this earth can or cannot be general, social, but must originate within each heart. Subjective monstrosity must be overcome, must be corrected by community, by useful duty. And, as you indicate, private suffering transformed from masochism. But we know this. We know, we know, know it! Creative suffering, as you think . . . at the core of Christian belief.* Now what is it? Herzog urged himself to be clearer. What really is on my mind? Probably this: shall I put those two on the stand under oath, torture them, hold a blowtorch to their feet? Why? They have a right to each other; they seem even to belong together. Why, let them alone. But what about justice?—Justice! Look who wants justice! Most of mankind has lived and died without—totally without it. People by the billions and for ages sweated, gypped, enslaved, suffocated, bled to death, buried with no more justice than cattle. But Moses E. Herzog, at the top of his lungs, bellowing with pain and anger, has to have justice. It's his *quid pro quo,* in return for all he has suppressed, his right as an Innocent Party. *I love little pussy her coat is so warm, and I'll sit by the fire and give her some food, and pussy will love me because I am good.* So now his rage is so great and deep, so murderous, bloody, positively rapturous, that his arms and fingers ache to strangle them. So much for his boyish purity of heart. Social organization, for all its clumsiness and evil, has accomplished far more and embodies more good than I do, for at least it sometimes gives justice. I am a mess, and talk about justice. I owe the powers that created me a human life. And where is it! Where is that human life which is my only excuse for surviving! What have I to show for myself? Only this! His face was before him in the blotchy mirror. It was bearded with lather. He saw his perplexed, furious eyes and he gave an audible cry. *My God! Who is this creature? It considers itself human. But what is it? Not human of itself. But has the longing to be human. And like a troubling dream, a persistent vapor. A desire. Where does it all come from? And what is it? And what can it be! Not immortal longing. No, entirely mortal, but human.*

As he was putting on his shirt he made plans to visit his son on Parents' Day. The Trailways Bus for Catskill left the West Side Terminal at seven A.M. and made the trip on the Thruway in less than three hours. He remembered two years ago milling on the dusty playing field with kids and parents, the coarse boards of the barracks, the tired goats and hamsters, leafless bushes, and the spaghetti served on paper plates. By one o'clock he would be utterly beat, and the hours before bus time would be difficult and sad, but he must do everything possible for Marco. As for Daisy, it would spare her a trip. She had been having troubles of her own, her old mother having grown senile. Herzog knew of this from many sources, and it affected him strangely to hear that his former mother-in-law, handsome, autocratic, every inch the suffragist and "modern woman" with her pince-nez and abundant gray hair, had lost her self-control. She had got it into her head that Moses had divorced Daisy because she was a streetwalker, carried the yellow ticket—Polina in her delusions became a Russian again. Fifty years in Zanesville, Ohio, melted away when she pleaded with Daisy to stop "going with men." Poor Daisy had to listen to this every morning after she had sent the boy off to school and was herself leaving for work. An utterly steady, reliable woman, responsible to the point of grimness. Daisy was a statistician for the Gallup Poll. For Marco's sake she tried to make the house cheerful, but she had no talent for this, and the parakeets and the plants and goldfish and gay reproductions of Braque and Klee from the Museum of Modern Art seemed to increase its sadness. Similarly, in her neatness, the straight seams of her stockings, her face with its powder and the brows realigned with pencil to give a more spirited expression, Daisy never overcame her heavy-heartedness. After cleaning the bird cage and feeding all her little creatures and watering the plants, she still had to face her senile mother in the entryway. And Polina commanded her to give up this life of shame. Then she began, "Daisy, I beg you." And at last she pleaded on her knees, getting down with difficulty, a broad-hipped old woman, the white braids hanging, her gray head long and slender—much feminine delicacy still in the shape of that head—and the pince-nez swinging on the silk cord. "You can't go on like this, my child."

Daisy tried to raise her from the ground. "All right, Mama. I'll change. I promise."

"Men are waiting for you, in the street."

"No, no, Mama."

"Yes, men. This is a social evil. You'll catch a disease. You'll die a terrible death. You must stop. Moses will come back if you do."

"All right. Please stand up, Mama. I'll stop."

"There are other ways to make a living. Please, Daisy, I beg you."

"No more, Mama. Come, sit down."

Shaky and clumsy, with awkward haunches and feeble knees, old Polina rose from the floor and Daisy guided her to her chair. "I'll send them all away. Come, Mama. I'll turn on the television. You want to watch the cooking school? Dione Lucas, or the Breakfast Club?" The sun came through the venetian blinds. The sputtering, flickering images on the screen looked yellow. And gray, genteel Polina, this high-principled old woman, iron at the core, knitted all day before the TV. The neighbors looked in on her. Cousin Asya came from the Bronx now and then. On Thursdays the cleaning woman was there. But Polina, now in her eighties, at last had to be placed in a home for the aged somewhere on Long Island. So this is how the strongest characters end!

Oh, Daisy, I am very sorry about this. I pity . . .

One sad thing after another, Herzog thought. His shaved cheeks stinging, he rubbed them with witch hazel, drying his fingers on his shirttails. He took up hat, coat, and necktie and hurried down the gloomy stairway to the street—the elevator was far too slow. At the hack stand he found a Puerto Rican driver who was touching up his sleek black hair with a pocket comb.

Moses knotted his tie in the back seat. The cabbie turned around to look. He studied him.

"Where to, Sport?"

"Downtown."

"You know, I think I got a coincident to tell you." They ran eastward toward Broadway. The driver was observing him in the mirror as he drove. Herzog also bent forward and deciphered the name beside the meter: Teodoro Valdepenas. "Early in the morning," said Valdepenas, "I seen a guy on Lexington Avenue dressed like you, with the exact same model coat. The hat."

"Did you see his face?"

"No . . . the face I didn't see." The taxi rattled into Broadway, and sped toward Wall Street.

"Where, on Lexington?"

"Like the sixties."

"What was the fellow doing?"

"Kissing a broad in a red dress. That's why I didn't see the face. And what I mean *kissing!* Was it you?"

"It must have been me."

"How do you like that!" Valdepenas slapped the wheel. "Boy! Out of millions. I took a guy from La Guardia, over the Triboro and the East River Drive and left him off at Seventy-second and Lexington. I seen you kissing a broad and then I get you two hours afterwards."

"Like catching the fish that swallowed the queen's ring," said Herzog.

Valdepenas turned slightly to look at Herzog over his shoulder. "That was a real nice-looking broad. Stacked! Terrific! Your wife?"

"No. I'm not married. She's not married."

"Well, boy, you're all right. When I get old I'm going to be doing just like you. Why stop! And believe you me, I stay away from young chicks already. You waste your time with a broad under twenty-five. I quit on that type. A woman over thirty-five is just beginning to be serious. That's the kind that puts down the best stuff. . . . Where are you going?"

"The City Courthouse."

"You a lawyer? A cop?"

"How could I be a detective in this coat?"

"Hombre, detectives even go in drag now. What do I care! Listen to me. I got real burned up at a young chick last mont'. She just lies on the bed chewing gum and reading a magazine. Like she's saying 'Do me something!' I said, 'Listen, Teddy's here. What's this gum? Magazines?' She said, 'All right, let's get it over.' How's that for an attitude! I said, 'In my hack, that's where I hurry. You ought to get a punch in the teeth for talkin' like that.' And I'll tell you something. She was a no-good lay. A broad eighteen don't know even how to shit!"

Herzog laughed, largely from astonishment.

"That's right, ain't it?" said Valdepenas. "You ain't no kid."

"No, I'm not."

"A woman over forty really appreciates . . ." They were at Broadway and Houston. A boozer, stubble-faced, jaws strong and arrogant, waited with a filthy rag to wipe the windshields of passing cars, holding out his hand for tips. "Look how that bum operates here," said Valdepenas. "He smears the glass. The fat guys pay out. They shiver in their pupick. They're scared not to. I seen these Bowery slobs spit on cars. They better not lay a hand on my hack. I keep a tire tool right here, boy. I'd bust the sonofabitch on the head!"

On slanting Broadway lay the heavy shadow of summer. Second-hand desks and swivel chairs, old green filing cases were exposed on the sidewalk—aquarium green, dill-pickle green. And now financial New York closed in, ponderous and sunless. Just below was Trinity Church. Herzog remembered that he had promised to show Marco the grave of Alexander Hamilton. He had described to him the duel with Burr, the bloody body of Hamilton brought back on a summer morning in the bottom of a boat. Marco listened, pale and steady, his freckled Herzog face revealing little. Marco never seemed to wonder at the immense (the appalling!) collection of facts in his father's head. At the aquarium Herzog supplied the classification of fish scales—"the cotenoid, the placoid . . ." He knew where the coelacanth had been caught, the anatomy of a lobster's stomach. He offered all this to his son—we must stop this, Herzog decided—guilty conduct, an overemotional father, a bad example. I try too hard with him.

Valdepenas was still talking when Moses paid him. He answered cheerfully, but by rote. He had stopped listening. Oratorical lechery, momentarily amusing. "Keep sockin' away, Doc."

"See you again, Valdepenas."

He turned to face the vast gray court building. Dust swirled on the broad stairway, the stone was worn. Going up, Herzog found a bouquet of violets, dropped from the hand of a woman. Perhaps a bride. Little perfume remained in them, but they made him remember Massachusetts—Ludeyville. By now the peonies were wide open, the mock-orange bushes fragrant. Madeleine sprayed the lavatory with syringa deodorant. These violets smelled to him like female tears. He gave them burial in a trashcan, hoping they had not dropped from a disappointed hand. He went through the four-bladed revolving door into the lobby, fishing in his shirt pocket for the folded slip of paper with Wachsel's phone number. It was still too early to call. Simkin and his client hadn't had time enough to get downtown.

With time on his hands Herzog wandered in the huge dark corridors upstairs where swinging padded doors with small oval windows led into courtrooms. He peered into one of these; the broad mahogany seats looked restful. He entered, respectfully removing his hat and nodding at the magistrate, who took no notice of him. Broad and bald, all face, deep voiced, resting his fist on documents—Mr. Judge. The chamber, with ornate ceiling, was immense, the walls buff but somber. When one of the police attendants opened the door behind the bench you saw the bars of the detention cells. Herzog crossed his legs (with a certain style: his elegance never deserted him even when he scratched himself), and, dark-eyed, attentive, averted his face slightly as he prepared to listen, a tendency inherited from his mother.

Very little seemed at first to be happening. A small group of lawyers and clients almost casually talked things over, arranged details. Raising his voice, the magistrate interrupted.

"But just a minute, here. Do you say . . . ?"

"He says . . ."

"Let me hear the man himself. Do you say . . . ?"

"No, sir, I don't."

The magistrate demanded, "Well what do you mean, then? Counsel, what is this supposed to mean?"

"My client's plea is still the same—not guilty."

"I did not . . ."

"Mistuh judge, he did," a Negro voice said, without insistence.

". . . Dragged this man, drunk, off St. Nicholas Avenue, into the cellar of premises at—what is the exact address? With intention to rob." This was the magistrate's overriding basso; he had a broad New York accent.

From behind, Herzog was now able to make out the defendant in this case. He was the Negro in filthy brown pants. His legs appeared to be trembling with nervous strength. He might have been about to run a race; he even crouched slightly, in the big cocoa-brown pants, as if at the starting line. But about ten feet before him were the shining prison bars. The plaintiff wore a bandage on his head.

"How much money did you have in your pocket?"

"Sixty-eight cents, your honor," the bandaged man said.

"And did he force you to enter the basement?"

The defendant said, "No, suh."

"I didn't ask you. Now keep your mouth shut." The magistrate was vexed.

The injured man now turned his bandaged head. Herzog saw a

black, dry, elderly face, eyes red-rimmed. "No suh. He said he given me a drink."

"Did you know him?"

"No, suh, but he was given me a drink."

"And you went with this stranger to the cellar at—address? Bailiff, where are those papers?" Moses now became aware how the magistrate diverted himself and the courtroom loafers with a show of temperament. These were dull routines otherwise. "What happened down in the cellar?" He studied the forms the bailiff had passed him.

"He hit me."

"Without warning? Where was he standing, behind you?"

"I couldn't see. The blood started to comin' down. In my eyes. I couldn't see."

Those tense legs desired their freedom. They were ready for flight.

"And he took the sixty-eight cents?"

"I grabbed him and started in to holler. Then he give me another lick."

"What did you hit this man with?"

"Your honor, my client denies that he struck him," the lawyer said. "They are acquaintances. They were out drinking together."

The black face, framed in bandages, heavy-lipped, dry, eyes red, stared at the lawyer. "I don't know him."

"Any of those blows might have killed this fellow."

"Assault with intent to rob," Herzog heard. The magistrate added, "I assume plaintiff was drunk to begin with."

That is—his blood was well thinned with whisky as it dropped into the coal dust. Whisky-blood was bound to be shed in some such way. The criminal began to go, the same wolfish tension within his voluminous, ridiculous pants. The cop, with pads of police fat on his cheeks, looked almost kindly as he led him to the cells. Lard-faced, he held the door open and sent him on his way with a pat on the shoulder.

A new group stood before the magistrate, a plainclothesman testifying. "At seven-thirty-eight P.M. at a urinal in the lower level men's lavatory, Grand Central Station . . . this man (name given) standing in the adjacent space reached over and placed his hand upon my organ of sex at the same time saying . . ." The detective, a specialist in men's toilets, Herzog thought, loitering there, a bait. By the speed and expertness of the testimony you knew it was routine. "I therefore arrested him for violations. . . ." Before the plainclothesman had finished listing the ordinances by number, the magistrate was saying, "Guilty—not guilty?"

The offender was a tall young foreigner; a German. His passport was shown. He wore a long brown leather coat tightly belted, and his small head was covered with curls; his brow was red. He turned out to be an intern in a Brooklyn hospital. Here the magistrate surprised Herzog, who had taken him for the ordinary gross, grunting, ignorant political magistrate, putting on an act for the idlers on the benches (including Herzog). But, both hands tugging at the neck of his black robe, demonstrating by this gesture, thought Herzog, that he wanted the accused man's lawyer to stop, he said, "Better advise your client if he pleads guilty he'll never practice medicine in the U.S.A."

That mass of flesh rising from the opening of the magistrate's black cloth, nearly eyeless, or whale-eyed, was, after all, a human head. The hollow, ignorant voice, a human voice. You don't destroy a man's career because he yielded to an impulse in that ponderous stinking cavern below Grand Central, in the cloaca of the city, where no mind can be sure of stability, where policemen (perhaps themselves that way given) tempt and trap poor souls. Valdepenas had reminded him that cops now went in drag to lure muggers, or mashers, and if they could become transvestites in the name of the law, what else would they think of! The deeper creativity of police imagination . . . He opposed this perverse development in law enforcement. Sexual practices of any sort, provided they didn't disturb the peace, provided they didn't injure minor children, were a private matter. Except for the children. Never children. There one must be strict.

Meanwhile he watched keenly. The case of the intern was continued, and the principals in an attempted robbery appeared at the bar. The prisoner was a boy; though his face was curiously lined, some of its grooves feminine, others masculine enough. He wore a soiled green shirt. His dyed hair was long, stiff, dirty. He had pale round eyes and he smiled with empty—no, worse than empty—cheerfulness. His voice, when he answered questions, was high-pitched, ice-cold, thoroughly drilled in its affectations.

"Name?"

"Which name, your honor?"

"Your own name."

"My boy's-name or my girl's-name?"

"Oh, I see. . . ." The magistrate, alerted by this, swept the courtroom, rounding up his audience with his glance. *Now hear this.* Moses leaned forward. "Well, which are you, a boy or a girl?"

The cold voice said, "It depends what people want me for. Some want a boy, and others a girl."

"Want what?"

"Want sex, your honor."

"Well, what's your boy's-name?"

"Aleck, your honor. Otherwise I'm Alice."

"Where do you work?"

"Along Third Avenue, in the bars. I just sit there."

"Is that how you make your living?"

"Your honor, I'm a prostitute."

Idlers, lawyers, policemen grinning, and the magistrate himself relishing the scene deeply—only one stout woman standing by with bare, heavy arms did not participate in this. "Wouldn't it be better for your business if you washed?" the magistrate said. Oh, these actors! thought Moses. Actors all!

"Filth makes it better, judge." The icy soprano voice was unexpectedly sharp and prompt. The magistrate showed intense satisfaction. He brought his large hands together, asking, "Well, what's the charge?"

"Attempted holdup with toy pistol Fourteenth Street Notions and Drygoods. He told the cashier to hand over the money and she struck him and disarmed him."

"A toy! Where's the cashier?"

She was the stout woman with the thick arms. Her head was dense with graying quills. Her shoulders were thick. Earnestness seemed to madden her pug-nosed face.

"That's me, your honor. Marie Poont."

"Marie? You're a brave woman, Marie, and a quick thinker. Tell us how it happened."

"He only made in his pocket like a gun, and gave me a bag to fill with money." A heavy and simple spirit, Herzog saw; a mesomorph, in the catchword; the immortal soul encased in this somatic vault. "I knew it was a trick."

"What did you do?"

"I have a baseball bat, your honor. The store sells them. I gave a slam on the arm."

"Good for you! Is this what happened, Aleck?"

"Yes sir," he answered in his clear, chill voice. Herzog tried to guess the secret of this alert cheerfulness. What view of things was this Aleck advancing? He seemed to be giving the world comedy for comedy, joke for joke. With his dyed hair, like the winter-beaten wool of a sheep, and his round eyes, traces of mascara still on them, the tight provocative pants, and something sheeplike, too, even about his vengeful merriment, he was a dream actor. With his bad fantasy he defied a bad reality, subliminally asserting to the magistrate, "Your authority and my degeneracy are one and the same." Yes, it must be something like that, Herzog decided. Sandor Himmelstein declared with rage that every living soul was a whore. Of course the magistrate had not spread his legs literally; but he must have done all that was necessary within the power structure to get appointed. Still, nothing about him denied such charges, either. His face was illusionless, without need of hypocrisy. Aleck was the one who claimed glamour, even a certain amount of "spiritual" credit. Someone must have told him that fellatio was the path to truth and honor. So this bruised, dyed Aleck *also* had an idea. He was purer, loftier than any square, did not lie. It wasn't only Sandor who had such ideas—strange, minimal ideas of truth, honor. Realism. Nastiness in the transcendent position.

There was a narcotics record. That was to be expected. He need the money for the dope, was that it?

"That was it, your honor," said Aleck. "I almost didn't try because this lady looked so butch. I knew she might be tough. But I took a chance anyway."

Unless spoken to, Marie Poont said nothing. Her head hung forward.

The magistrate said, "Aleck, if you keep this up you'll be in Potter's Field. . . . I give you four-five years."

In the grave! Eyes really empty, and this strained sweetness rotted from the lips. Well, Aleck, how about that? Will you think—be serious? But where would it get Aleck to be serious? What could he hope from it? Now he was going back to the cell, and he called out, "G'by all. Good-by." Sugary and lingering. "By-ee." An icy voice. They pushed him out.

The magistrate shook his head. These fairies, what a bunch! He fetched up a handkerchief from the black gown and wiped his neck, raising his chin and catching the gold of many lights on his face. He was smiling. Marie Poont still waited, and he said, "Thank you, Miss. And you may go now."

Herzog discovered that he had been sitting, legs elegantly crossed, the jagged oval rim of his hat pressed on his thigh, his striped jacket still buttoned and strained by his eager posture, that he had been watching all that happened with his look of intelligent composure, of charm and sympathy—like the old song, he thought, the one that goes, "There's flies on me, there's flies on you, but there ain't no flies on Jesus." A man who looked so fine and humane would be outside police jurisdiction, immune to lower forms of suffering and punishment. Herzog shifted his weight on the bench, forcing his hand into his pocket. Did he have a dime for the phone? He must call Wachsel. But he couldn't reach his coins (was he getting fat?) and he stood up. As soon as he was on his feet, he realized that there was something the matter with him. He felt as though something terrible, inflammatory, bitter, had been grated into his bloodstream and stung and burned his veins, his face, his heart. He knew he was turning white, although the pulses beat violently in his head. He saw that the magistrate was staring at him, as though Herzog owed him the courtesy of a nod in leaving his courtroom. . . . But he turned his back, and hurried into the corridor, thrusting aside the swinging doors. He opened his collar, struggling with the stiff buttonhole of the new shirt. The sweat broke out on his face. He began to breathe more normally as he stood beside the broad high window. It had a metal grille at its base. Through this a draft of cooler air passed, and the dust silently circulated under the folds of the green-black window blind. Some of Herzog's dearest friends, not to mention his Uncle Arye—his own father, come to think of it—had died of heart failure, and there were times when Herzog thought he might be having an attack too. But no, he was really very strong and healthy, and no . . . What was he saying? He finished his sentence, however: no such luck. He must live. Complete his assignment, whatever that was.

The burning within his chest subsided. It had felt like swallowing a mouthful of poison. But he now grasped the floating suspicion that this poison rose from within. He knew in fact that it did. What produced it? Must he suppose that something once good in him had spoiled, gone bad? Or was it originally bad? His own evil? To see people in the hands of the law agitated him. The red forehead of the medical student, the trembling legs of the Negro he found horrible. But he was suspicious of his own reaction, too. There were people, Simkin, for instance, or Himmelstein, or Dr. Edvig, who believed that in a way Herzog was rather simple, that his humane feelings were childish. That he had been spared the destruction of certain sentiments as the pet goose is spared the ax. Yes, a pet goose! Simkin seemed to see him as he saw that sickly innocent girl, the epileptic cousin whom Madeleine supposedly injured. Young Jews, brought up on moral principles as Victorian ladies were on pianoforte and needlepoint, thought Herzog. And I have come here today for a look at something different. That evidently is my purpose.

I willfully misread my contract. I never was the principal, but only on loan to myself. Evidently I continue to believe in God. Though never admitting it. But what else explains my conduct and my life? So I may as well acknowledge how things are, if only because otherwise I can't even be described. My behavior implies that there is a barrier against which I have been pressing from the first, pressing all my life, with the conviction that it is necessary to press, and that something must come of it. Perhaps that I can eventually pass through. I must always have had such an idea. Is it faith? Or is it simply childishness, expecting to be loved for doing your bidden task? It is, if you're looking for the psychological explanation, childish and classically depressive. But Herzog didn't believe that the harshest or most niggardly explanation, following the law of parsimony, was necessarily the truest. Eager impulses, love, intensity, passionate dizziness that make a man sick. How long can I stand such inner beating? The front wall of this body will go down. My whole life beating against its boundaries, and the force of balked longings coming back as stinging poison. Evil, evil, evil . . . ! Excited, characteristic, ecstatic love turning to evil.

————

He was in pain. He should be. Quite right. If only because he had required so many people to lie to him, many, many, beginning, naturally, with his mother. Mothers lie to their children from demand. But perhaps his mother had been struck, too, by the amount of melancholy, her own melancholy, she saw in Moses. The family look, the eyes, those eye-lights. And though he recalled his mother's sad face with love, he couldn't say, in his soul, that he wanted to see such sadness perpetuated. Yes, it reflected the deep experience of a race, its attitude toward happiness and toward mortality. This somber human case, this dark husk, these indurated lines of submission to the fate of being human, this splendid face showed the responses of his mother's finest nerves to the greatness of life, rich in sorrow, in death. All right, she was beautiful. But he hoped that things would change. When we have come to better terms with death, we'll wear a different expression, we human beings. Our looks will change. *When* we come to terms!

Nor had she always lied to spare his feelings. He remembered that late one afternoon she led him to the front-room window because he asked a question about the Bible: how Adam was created from the dust of the ground. I was six or seven. And she was about to give me the proof. Her dress was brown and gray—thrush-colored. Her hair was thick and black, the gray already streaming through it. She had something to show me at the window. The light came up from the snow in the street, otherwise the day was dark. Each of the windows had colored borders—yellow, amber, red—and flaws and whorls in the cold panes. At the curbs were the thick brown poles of that time, many-barred at the top, with green glass insulators, and brown sparrows clustered on the crossbars that held up the iced, bowed wires. Sarah Herzog opened her hand and said, "Look carefully, now, and you'll see what Adam was made of." She rubbed the palm of her hand with a finger, rubbed until something dark appeared on the deep-lined skin, a particle of what certainly looked to him like earth. "You see? It's true." A grown man, in the present, beside the big color-less window, like a static sail outside Magistrate's Court, Herzog did as she had done. He rubbed, smiling; and it worked; a bit of the same darkness began to form in his palm. Now he stood staring into the black openwork of the brass grille. Maybe she offered me this proof partly in a spirit of comedy. The wit you can have only when you consider death very plainly, when you consider what a human being really is.

The week of her death, also in winter. This happened in Chicago, and Herzog was sixteen years old, nearly a young man. It occurred on the West Side. She was dying. Evidently Moses wanted no part of that. He was already a free-thinker. Darwin and Haeckel and Spencer were old stuff to him. He and Zelig Koninski (what had happened to that gilded youth?) disdained the branch library. They bought thick books of all sorts out of the thirty-nine-cent barrel at Walgreen's—*The World as Will and Idea* and *The Decline of the West*. And what was going on! Herzog knitted his brows to force his memory to work. Papa had the night job, and slept days. You had to tiptoe through the house. If you woke him he was furious. His overalls, reeking of linseed oil, were hung behind the bathroom door. At three in the afternoon, half dressed, he came out for his tea, silent, his face filled with stern anger. But by and by he became an entrepreneur again, doing business out of his hat on Cherry Street, opposite the Negro whorehouse, among the freight trains. He had a roll-top desk. He shaved his mustache. And then Mama started to die. And I was in the kitchen winter nights, studying *The Decline of the West*. The round table was covered with an oilcloth.

That was a frightful January, streets coated with steely ice. The moon lay on the glazed snow of the back yards where clumsy lumber porches threw their shadows. Under the kitchen was the furnace room. The janitor stoked the fire, his apron a burlap sack, his Negro beard gritty with the soft coal. The shovel scraped on the cement, and then clanged in the mouth of the furnace. He would slam the metal door shut with his shovel. And then he carried ashes out in bushels—old peach baskets. As often as I could, I hugged the laundry girls, down in the tub room. But I was poring over Spengler now, struggling and drowning in the oceanic visions of that sinister kraut. First there was antiquity, for which all men

233

sigh—beautiful Greece! Then the Magian era, and the Faustian. I learned that I, a Jew, was a born Magian and that we Magians had already had our great age, forever past. No matter how hard I tried, I would never grasp the Christian and Faustian world idea, forever alien to me. Disraeli *thought* he could understand and lead the British, but he was totally mistaken. I had better resign myself to Destiny. A Jew, a relic as lizards are relics of the great age of reptiles, I might prosper in a false way by swindling the *goy*, the laboring cattle of a civilization dwindled and done for. Anyway, it was an age of spiritual exhaustion—all the old dreams were dreamed out. I was angry; I burned like that furnace; reading more, sick with rage.

When I looked away from the dense print and its insidious pedantry, my heart infected with ambition, and the bacteria of vengeance, Mama was entering the kitchen. Seeing light under the door, she came the whole length of the house, from the sickroom. Her hair had to be cut during her illness, and this made those eyes hard to recognize. Or no, the shortness of her hair merely made their message simpler: *My son, this is death.*

I chose not to read this text.

"I saw the light," she said. "What are you doing up so late?" But the dying, for themselves, have given up hours. She only pitied me, her orphan, understood I was a gesture-maker, ambitious, a fool; thought I would need my eyesight and my strength on a certain day of reckoning.

A few days afterward, when she had lost the power to speak, she was still trying to comfort Moses. Just as when he knew she was breathless from trudging with his sled in Montreal but would not get up. He came into her room when she was dying, holding his school books, and began to say something to her. But she lifted up her hands and showed him her fingernails. They were blue. As he stared, she slowly began to nod her head up and down as if to say, "That's right, Moses, I am dying now." He sat by the bed. Presently she began to stroke his hand. She did this as well as she could; her fingers had lost their flexibility. Under the nails they seemed to him to be turning already into the blue loam of graves. She had begun to change into earth! He did not dare to look but listened to the runners of children's sleds in the street, and the grating of peddlers' wheels on the knotted ice, the hoarse call of the apple peddler and the rattle of his steel scale. The steam whispered in the vent. The curtain was drawn.

In the corridor outside Magistrate's Court, he thrust both hands into his trousers pockets and drew up his shoulders. His teeth were on edge. A bookish, callow boy. And then, he thought, there was the funeral. How Willie cried in the chapel! It was his brother Willie, after all, who had the tender heart. But . . . Moses shook his head to be rid of such thoughts. The more he thought, the worse his vision of the past.

He waited his turn at the phone booth. The instrument, when he got it, was humid from the many mouths and ears that used it. Herzog rang the number Simkin had given him. Wachsel said no, he had no messages from Simkin, but Mr. Herzog was welcome to come up and wait. "No, thanks, I'll phone again," Herzog said. He had absolutely no ability to wait in offices. He never had been able to wait for anything. "You don't happen to know—is he in the building somewhere?"

"I know he's here, all right," said Wachsel. "I have an idea it's a criminal case. And that would be . . ." He rattled off a list of room numbers.

Herzog fixed on a few of these. He said, "I'll go and have a look around and call you again in half an hour, if you don't mind."

"No, I don't mind. We're open for business all day! Whyn't you try the eighth floor. Little Napoleon—with that voice you should be able to hear him through the walls."

In the first courtroom Herzog entered after getting this suggestion there was a jury trial. He was one of a small number of people in the polished wooden rows. Within a few minutes he had forgotten Simkin entirely.

A young couple, a woman and the man she had been living with in a slum hotel, uptown, were being tried for the murder of her son, a child of three. She had had the boy by another man who deserted her, said the lawyer in his presentation. Herzog observed how gray and elderly all these lawyers were, people of another generation and a different circle of life—tolerant, comfortable people. The defendants could be identified by their looks and clothing. The man wore a stained and frayed zipper jacket and she, a redheaded woman, with a wide ruddy face, had on a brown print house dress. Both sat stolid, to all appearances unmoved by the testimony, he with his low sideburns and blond mustache, she with blunt freckled cheekbones and long, hidden eyes.

She came from Trenton, born lame. Her father was a garage mechanic. She had a fourth-grade education, I.Q. 94. An older brother was the favorite; she was neglected. Unattractive, sullen, clumsy, wearing an orthopedic boot, she became delinquent at an early age. Her record was before the court, the lawyer went on, even, mild and pleasant. An angry uncontrollable girl, from first grade. There were affidavits from teachers. There were also medical and psychiatric records, and a neurological report to which the lawyer particularly wished to call the court's attention. This showed his client had been diagnosed by encephalogram as having a brain lesion capable of altering her behavior radically. She was known to have violent epileptoid fits of rage; her tolerance for emotions controlled from the affected lobe was known to be very low. Because she was a poor crippled creature, she had often been molested, later sexually abused by adolescent boys. Indeed, her file in children's court was very thick. Her mother loathed her, had refused to attend the trial, was quoted as saying, "This is no kid of mine. We wash our hands of her." The defendant was made pregnant at nineteen by a married man who lived with her several months, then went back to his wife and family. She refused to give the child for adoption, lived for a while in Trenton with it, and then moved to Flushing, where she cooked and cleaned for a family. On one of her weekends she met the other defendant, at the time employed as porter in a lunchroom on Columbus Avenue, and decided to live with him at the Montcalme Hotel on 103rd Street—Herzog had often passed the place. You could smell the misery of it from the street; its black stink flowed out through open windows—bedding, garbage, disinfectant, roach killer. His mouth was dry and he sat forward, straining to hear.

The medical examiner was on the stand. Had he seen the dead child? Yes. Did he have a report to make? He did. He gave the date and circumstances of the examination. A hefty, bald, solemn man with fleshy and deliberate lips, he held his notes in both hands like a singer—the experienced, professional witness. The child, he said, was normally formed but seemed to have suffered from malnutrition. There were signs of incipient rickets, the teeth were already quite carious, but this was sometimes a symptom that the mother had had toxemia in pregnancy. Were any unusual marks visible on the child's body? Yes, the little boy had apparently been beaten. Once, or repeatedly? In his opinion, often beaten. The scalp was torn. There were unusually heavy bruises on the back and legs. The shins were discolored. Where were the bruises heaviest? On the belly, and especially in the region of the genitals, where the boy seemed to have been beaten with something capable of breaking the skin, perhaps a metal buckle or the heel of a woman's shoe. "And what internal findings did you make?" the prosecutor went on. There were two broken ribs, one an older break. The more recent one had done some damage to the lung. The boy's liver had been ruptured. The hemorrhage caused by this may have been the immediate cause of death. There was also a brain injury. "In your opinion, then, the child died violently?" "That is my opinion. The liver injury would have been enough."

All this seemed to Herzog exceptionally low-pitched. All—the lawyers, the jury, the mother, her tough friend, the judge—behaved with much restraint, extremely well controlled and quiet-spoken. Such calm—inversely proportionate to the murder? he was thinking. Judge, jury, lawyers and the accused, all looked utterly unemotional. And he himself? He sat in his new madras coat and held his hard straw hat. He gripped his hat strongly and felt sick at heart. The ragged edge of the straw made marks on his fingers.

A witness was sworn, a solid-looking man of thirty-five or so, in a stylish oxford gray summer suit, of Madison Avenue cut. His face was round, full, jowly, but his head had little height above the ears and was further flattened by his butch haircut. He made very good gestures, pulling up his trouser legs as he sat, freeing his shirt cuffs and leaning forward to answer questions with measured, earnest, masculine politeness. His eyes were dark. You could see his scalp furrow as he frowned, weighing his answers. He identified himself as a salesman in the storm-window business, screens and storm windows. Herzog knew what he meant—aluminum sashes with triple tracks: he had read the ads. The witness lived in Flushing. Did he know the accused woman? She was asked to stand, and she did, a short hobbling figure, dark-red hair frizzy, the long eyes recessed, skin freckled, lips thick and dun-colored. Yes, he knew her, she had lived in his house eight months ago, not exactly employed by him, no, she was a distant cousin of his wife, who felt sorry for her and gave her a room—he had built a small apartment in the attic; separate bathroom, air-conditioner. She was asked to help with housework, naturally, but she also took off and left the boy for days at a time. Did he ever know her to mistreat the child? The kid was never clean. You never wanted to hold him on your lap. He had a cold sore, and his wife at last put salve on it, as the mother would not. The child was quiet, undemanding, clung to its mother, a frightened little boy, and he had a bad smell. Could the witness further describe the mother's attitude? Well, on the road, they were driving to visit the grandmother and stopped at Howard Johnson's. Everyone ordered. She had a barbecued beef sandwich and when it came began to eat and fed the child nothing. Then he himself (indignant) gave the boy some of his meat and gravy.

I fail to understand! thought Herzog, as this good man, jowls silently moving, got off the stand. I fail to . . . but this is the difficulty with people who spend their lives in humane studies and therefore imagine once cruelty has been described in books it is ended. Of course he really knew better—understood that human beings *would* not live so as to be understood by the Herzogs. Why should they?

But he had no time to think of this. The next witness was already sworn, the clerk at the Montcalme; a bachelor in his fifties; slack lips, large creases, damaged cheeks, hair that looked touched up, voice deep and melancholy, with a sinking rhythm to every sentence. The sentences sank down, down, until the last words were lost in rumbling syllables. An alcoholic once, judged Herzog from the look of his skin, and there was a certain faggotty prissi-ness in his speech, too. He said he had kept an eye on this "un-fortunate pair." They rented a housekeeping room. The woman drew Relief money. The man had no occupation. The police came a few times to ask about him. And the boy, could he tell the court anything about him? Mostly that the child cried a lot. Tenants complained, and when he investigated he found the kid was kept shut in a closet. For discipline, was what the defendant told him. But toward the end the boy cried less. On the day of his death, however, there was a lot of noise. He heard something falling, and shrieks from the third floor. Both the mother and the boy were screaming. Someone was fooling with the elevator, so he ran upstairs. Knocked at the door, but she was screaming too loud to hear. So he opened and stepped in. Would he tell the court what he saw? He saw the woman with the boy in her arms. He thought she was hugging him, but to his astonishment she threw him from her with both arms. He was hurled against the wall. This made the noise he had been hearing below. Was anyone else present? Yes, the other defendant was lying on the bed, smoking. And was the child now screaming? No, at this time he was lying silent on the floor. Did the clerk then speak? He said he was frightened by the look of the woman, her swollen face. She turned red, crimson, and screamed with all her might, and she stamped her foot, the one with the built-up heel, he noticed, and he was afraid she would go for his eyes with her nails. He then went to call the police. Soon the man came downstairs. He explained that her boy was a problem child. She could not toilet-train him. He drove her wild sometimes the way he dirtied himself. And the crying all night! So they were talking when the squad car came. And found the child dead? Yes, he was dead when they arrived.

"Cross-examination?" said the bench. The defense lawyer waived examination with a movement of long white fingers, and the judge said, "You may step down. That will be all."

When the witness stood, Herzog stood up, too. He had to move, had to go. Again he wondered whether he was going to come down with sickness. Or was it the terror of the child that had gotten into him? Anyway, he felt stifled, as if the valves of his heart were not closing and the blood were going back into his lungs. He walked heavily and quickly. Turning once in the aisle, he saw only the lean gray head of the judge, whose lips silently moved as he read one of his documents.

Reaching the corridor, he said to himself, "Oh my God!" and in trying to speak discovered an acrid fluid in his mouth that had to be swallowed. Then stepping away from the door he stumbled into a woman with a cane. Black-browed, her hair very black though she was middle-aged, she pointed downward with the cane, instead of speaking. He saw that she wore a cast with metal clogs on the foot and that her toenails were painted. Then getting down the loathesome taste, he said, "I'm sorry." He had a sick repulsive headache, piercing and ugly. He felt as if he had gotten too close to a fire and scalded his lungs. She did not speak at all but was not ready to let him off. Her eyes, prominent, severe, still kept him standing, identifying him thoroughly, fully, deeply, as a fool. Again—silently—*Thou fool!* In the red-striped jacket, the hat tucked under his arm, hair uncombed, eyes swollen, he waited for her to go. When she left at last, going, cane, cast, clogs, down the speckled corridor, he concentrated. With all his might—mind and heart—he tried to obtain something for the murdered child. But what? How? He pressed himself with intensity, but "all his might" could get nothing for the buried boy. Herzog experienced nothing but his own *human feelings,* in which he found nothing of use. What if he felt moved to cry? Or pray? He pressed hand to hand. And what did he feel? Why he felt himself—his own trembling hands, and eyes that stung. And what was there in modern, post . . . post-Christian America to pray for? Justice—justice and mercy? And pray away the monstrousness of life, the wicked dream it was? He opened his mouth to relieve the pressure he felt. He was wrung, and wrung again, and wrung again, again.

The child screamed, clung, but with both arms the girl hurled it against the wall. On her legs was ruddy hair. And her lover, too, with long jaws and zooty sideburns, watching on the bed. Lying down to copulate, and standing up to kill. Some kill, then cry. Others, not even that.

NEW YORK could not hold him now. He had to go to Chicago to see his daughter, confront Madeleine and Gersbach. The decision was not reached; it simply arrived. He went home and changed from the new clothes in which he had been diverting himself, into an old seersucker suit. Luckily, he had not unpacked when he came back from the Vineyard. He checked the valise quickly and left the apartment. Characteristically, he was determined to act without clearly knowing what to do, and even recognizing that he had no power over his impulses. He hoped that on the plane, in the clearer atmosphere, he would understand why he was flying.

The superjet carried him to Chicago in ninety minutes, due west, flying against the rotation of the planet and giving him an extension of afternoon and sunlight. Beneath, the white clouds were foaming. And the sun, like the spot that inoculated us against the whole of disintegrating space. He looked into the blue vacancy and at the sharp glitter of wingborne engines. When the plane bucked, he held his lip with his teeth. Not that he feared flying, but it occurred to him that if the ship were to crash, or simply explode (as had happened over Maryland recently, when human figures were seen to spill and fall like shelled peas), Gersbach would become June's guardian. Unless Simkin tore up the will. *Dear Simkin, shrewd Simkin, tear up that will!* There would also be two insurance policies, one bought by Father Herzog for his son Moshe. Only see how this child, young Herzog, had turned out—wrinkled, perplexed, pain at heart. I'm telling myself the truth. As heaven is my witness. The stewardess offered him a drink, which he refused with a shake of the head. He felt incapable of looking into the girl's pretty, healthful face.

As the jet landed, Herzog turned back his watch. He hurried from gate 38 and down the long corridor to the auto rental office. To identify himself, he had an American Express card, his Massachusetts driver's license, his university credentials. He himself would have been suspicious of such diverse addresses, to say nothing of the soiled, wrinkled seersucker suit worn by this applicant,

Moses Elkanah Herzog; but the official who took his application, a sweet-mannered, bosomy, curly, fat-nosed little woman (even in his present state Herzog felt moved to smile faintly) only asked whether he wanted a convertible or a hard-top. He chose the hard-top, teal blue, and drove off, trying to find his way under the greenish glare of the lamps and dusty sunlight amid unfamiliar signs. He followed the winding cloverleaf into the Expressway and then joined the speeding traffic—in this zone, 60 m.p.h. He did not know these new sections of Chicago. Clumsy, stinking, tender Chicago, dumped on its ancient lake bottom; and this murky orange west, and the hoarseness of factories and trains, spilling gases and soot on the newborn summer. Traffic was heavy coming from the city, not on Herzog's side of the road, and he held the right lane looking for familiar street names. After Harlem Avenue he was in the city proper and knew his way. Leaving the Expressway at Montrose, he turned east and drove to his late father's house, a small two-story brick building, one of a row built from a single blueprint—the pitched roof, the cement staircase inset on the right side, the window boxes the length of the front-room windows, the lawn a fat mound of grass between the sidewalk and the foundation; along the curb, elms and those shabby cottonwoods with blackened, dusty, wrinkled bark, and leaves that turned very tough by midsummer. There were also certain flowers, peculiar to Chicago, crude, waxy things like red and purple crayon bits, in a special class of false-looking natural objects. These foolish plants touched Herzog because they were so graceless, so corny. He was reminded of his father's devotion to his garden, when old Herzog became a property owner toward the end of his life—how he squirted his flowers at evening with the hose and how rapt he looked, his lips quietly pleased and his straight nose relishing the odor of the soil. To right and left, as Herzog emerged from the rented hard-top, the sprinklers turned and danced, scattering bright drops, fizzing out iridescent veils. And this was the house in which Father Herzog had died a few years ago, on a summer night, sitting up in bed suddenly, saying, *"Ich shtarb!"* And then he died, and that vivid blood of his turned to soil, in all the shrunken passages of his body. And then the body, too—ah, God!—wastes away; and leaves its bones, and even the bones at last wear away and crumble to dust in that shallow place of deposit. And thus humanized, this planet in its galaxy of stars and worlds goes from void to void, infinitesimal, aching with its unrelated significance. *Unrelated?* Herzog, with one of his Jewish shrugs, whispered, *"Nu, maile. . . ."* Be that as it may.

In any case, here was his late father's house in which the widow lived, Moses' very ancient stepmother, quite alone in this small museum of the Herzogs. The bungalow belonged to the family. No one wanted it now. Shura was a multimillionaire, he made that obvious enough. Willie had gone far in his father's construction-materials business—owned a fleet of those trucks with tremendous cylinder bodies that mixed cement en route to the job where it was funneled, pumped (Moses was vague about it) into the rising skyscrapers. Helen, if her husband was not in Willie's class, was at least well off. She rarely spoke of money any more. And he himself? He had about six hundred dollars in the bank. Still, for his purposes, he had what he needed. Poverty was not his portion; unemployment, slums, the perverts, thieves, victims in court, the horror of the Montcalme Hotel and its housekeeping rooms, smelling of decay and deadly bug juice—these were not for him. He could still take the superjet to Chicago when he had the impulse, could rent a teal-blue Falcon, drive to the old house. Thus he realized with peculiar clarity his position in the scale of prerogatives—of affluence, of insolence, of untruth, if you like. And not only his position, but when lovers quarreled they had a Lincoln Continental to shut a weeping child up in.

Face white, mouth grim, he mounted the stairs in the shadow of approaching sunset, and pressed the button. It had a crescent moon in the middle which lighted up at night.

The chimes rang inside, those chromium tubes above the door, xylophone metal, that played "Merrily We Roll Along," all but the last two notes. He had long to wait. The old woman, Taube, always had been slow, even in her fifties, thorough, deliberate, totally unlike the dexterous Herzogs—they had all inherited their father's preposterous quickness and elegance, something of the assertiveness of that one-man march with which old Herzog had defiantly paraded through the world. Moses was rather fond of Taube, he told himself; perhaps to feel differently toward her would have been too troubling. The unsteady gaze of her round prominent eyes was possibly caused by a radical resolve to be slow, a life-long program of delay and stasis. Creepingly, she accomplished every last goal she set herself. She ate, or sipped, slowly. She did not bring the cup to her mouth but moved her lips out toward it. And she spoke very slowly, to give her shrewdness scope. She cooked with fingers that did not grip firmly but was an excellent cook. She won at cards, poking along, but won. All questions she asked two or three times, and repeated the answers half to herself. With the same slowness she braided her hair, she brushed her exposed teeth, or chopped figs, dates, and senna leaves for her digestion. Her lip grew pendulous as she aged and her neck gradually thickened at the shoulders so that she had to hold her head forward somewhat. Oh, she was very old now, in her eighties and far from well. She was arthritic; one eye had a cataract. But unlike Polina she had a clear mind. No doubt her troubles with Father Herzog, stormier and more hot-headed and fractious as he aged, had strengthened her brain.

The house was dark, and anyone but Moses would have gone away, assuming there was no one at home. He, however, waited, knowing she would presently open. In his youth he had watched her take five minutes to open a bottle of soda—an hour to spread the dough over the table when she baked. Her strudel was like jeweler's work, and filled with red and green gems of preserves. At last he heard her at the door. Links of brass chain rose in the narrow opening. He saw old Taube's dark eyes, more somber now, and more extruded. The glass winter door still separated her from Moses. He knew it would also be locked. The old people had been guarded and suspicious in their own house. Moreover, Moses knew the light was behind him; he might not be recognized. And he was not the same Moses, anyway. But, although she studied him like a stranger, she had already identified him. Her intellect was not slow, whatever else.

"Who is it?"

"It's Moses. . . ."

"I don't know you. I'm alone. Moses?"

"Tante Taube—Moses Herzog. Moshe."

"Ah—Moshe."

Slow lame fingers released the catch. The door was shut to free the links from strain, and then opened, and—merciful God!— what a face he saw, how grooved with woe and age, lined downward at the mouth! As he came in she raised feeble hands to embrace him. "Moshe . . . Come in I'll make a light. Shut the door, Moshe."

He found the switch and turned on the very dim bulb of the entry hall. It shed a pinkish color; the old-fashioned glass of the fixture reminded him of the *ner tamid,* the vigil light in the synagogue. He shut the door on the watered fragrance of lawns as he entered. The house was close and faintly sour with furniture polish. The remembered luster was there in the faint twilit parlor —cabinets and tables, with inlaid tops, the brocaded sofa in its gleaming protective plastic, the Oriental rug, the drapes perfect and rigid on the windows with laterally rigid venetian blinds. A lamp went on behind him. He discovered on the console phonograph a smiling picture of Marco as a little boy, bare-kneed, on a bench, a fresh face, and charming, dark hair combed forward. And next to it was he himself in a photo taken when he got his M.A., handsome but somewhat jowly. His younger face expressed the demands of ingenuous conceit. A man in years he then was, but in years only, and in his father's eyes stubbornly un-European, that is, innocent by deliberate choice. Moses refused to know evil. But he could not refuse to experience it. And therefore others were appointed to do it to him, and then to be accused (by him) of wickedness. Among the rest was a picture of Father Herzog in his last incarnation—an American citizen—handsome, smooth-shaven, with none of his troubled masculine defiance, his one-time impetuousness or passionate protest. Still, to see Father Herzog's face in his own house melted Moses. Tante Taube was coming up with slow steps. She kept no photograph of herself here. Moses knew that she had been a stunning girl, despite her Habsburg lip; and even in her fifties when he first knew her as the Widow Kaplitzky she had had thick handsome strong brows and a heavy braid of animal brown; a soft if somewhat slack figure held rigid by her "gorselette." She didn't want to be reminded of her beauty or her former vigor.

"Let me look at you," she said, coming before him. Her eyes were puffy, but steady enough. He stared at her, and tried to prevent the horror from coming into his face. He guessed that it was putting in her plates that had delayed her. She had new ones, poorly made—no arch but a straight line of teeth. Like a woodchuck, he thought. Her fingers were disfigured, with loose skin that had worked forward over the nails. But those fingertips were painted. And what changes did she see in him? "Ach, Moshe, you changed."

He limited his answer to a nod. "And how are you?"

"You see. The living dead."

"You live alone?"

"I had a woman—Bella Ockinoff from the fish store. You knowed her. But she was not clean."

"Come, Tante, sit down."

"Oh, Moshe," she said, "I can't sit, I can't stand, can't lay. Better, already, next to Pa. Pa is better off than me."

"Is it so bad?" Herzog must have betrayed more emotion than he knew, for he now found her eyes examining him rather sharply, as if she did not believe that his feeling was for her and tried to find the real source of it. Or was it the cataract that gave her that expression? He guided her to a chair, holding her arm, and sat on the plastic-covered sofa. Under the tapestry. Pierrot. Clair de Lune. Venetian moonlight. All that phooey banality that oppressed him in his student days. It had no special power over him now. He was another man and had different purposes. The old woman, he saw, was trying to find what he had come for. She sensed that he was strongly agitated, missed his habitual vagueness, the proud air of abstraction in which M. E. Herzog, Ph.D., had once been clothed. *Them days is gone forever.*

"You working hard, Moshe?"

"Yes."

"Making a living?"

"Oh, yes."

The old woman bowed her head a moment. He saw the scalp, her thin gray hair. Exiguous. The organism had done all it could.

He clearly understood that she was communicating her right to live in this Herzog property, even though by staying alive she was depriving him of this remaining part of the estate.

"It's okay, I don't grudge you, Tante Taube," he said.

"What?"

"Just go on living, and don't worry about the property."

"You're not dressed well, Moshe. What's the matter, is it a hard time?"

"No. I wore an old suit for the plane."

"You got business in Chicago?"

"Yes, Tante."

"The children all right? Marco?"

"He's at camp."

"Daisy didn't married yet?"

"No."

"You have to pay her alimony?"

"Not very much."

"I was not a bad stepmother? Tell the truth."

"You were a good stepmother. You were very good."

"I did mine best," she said, and in this meekness he glimpsed her old disguises—the elaborate and powerful role she had played with Father Herzog as the patient Widow Kaplitzky, once wife of Kaplitzky the prominent wholesaler, childless, his only darling, wearing a locket set with little rubies and traveling in Pullman drawing rooms—the Portland Rose, the 20th Century—or on the *Berengaria*, first class. As the second Mrs. Herzog she did not have an easy life. She had good reason to mourn Kaplitzky. *"Gottseliger* Kaplitzky," she always called him. And she once had told Moses, *"Gottseliger* Kaplitzky didn't want I should have children. The doctor thought it would be bad for mine heart. And every time . . . Kaplitzky-*alehoshalom* took care on everything. I didn't even looked."

Recalling this, Herzog very briefly laughed. Ramona would like "I didn't even looked." She always looked, bent close, held back a falling lock of hair, cheeks flushing, greatly amused by his shyness. As last night, lying down, opening her arms to him . . . He must wire her. She would not understand his disappearance. And then the blood began to beat in his head. He remembered why he was here.

He sat near the very spot where Father Herzog, the year before his death, had threatened to shoot him. The cause of his rage was money. Herzog was broke, and asked his father to underwrite a loan. The old man questioned him narrowly, about his job, his expenses, his child. He had no patience with Moses. At that time I was living in Philadelphia, alone, making my choice (it was no choice!) between Sono and Madeleine. Perhaps he had even heard I was about to be converted to Catholicism. Someone started such a rumor; it may have been Daisy. I was in Chicago then because Papa had sent for me. He wanted to tell me about the changes in his will. Day and night, he thought how he would divide his estate, and thought accordingly of each of us, what we deserved, how we would use it. At odd times, he'd telephone and tell me I had to come right away. I'd sit up all night on the train. And he'd take me into a corner and say, "I want you to hear, once and for all. Your brother Willie is an honest man. When I die, he'll do as we agreed." "I believe it, Papa."

But he lost his temper every time, and when he wanted to shoot me it was because he could no longer bear the sight of me, that look of mine, the look of conceit or proud trouble. The elite look. I don't blame him, thought Moses as Taube slowly and lengthily described her ailments. Papa couldn't bear such an expression on the face of his youngest son. I aged. I wasted myself in stupid schemes, *liberating* my spirit. His heart ached angrily because of me. And Papa was not like some old men who become blunted toward their own death. No, his despair was keen and continual. And Herzog again was pierced with pain for his father.

He listened awhile to Taube's account of her cortisone treatments. Her large, luminous, tame eyes, the eyes that had domesticated Father Herzog, were not watching Moses now. They gazed at a point beyond him and left him free to recall those last days of Father Herzog. We walked to Montrose together to buy cigarettes. It was June, warm like this, the weather bright. Papa wasn't exactly making sense. He said he should have divorced the Widow Kaplitzky ten years ago, that he had hoped to enjoy the last years of his life—his Yiddish became more crabbed and quaint in these conversations—but he had brought his iron to a cold forge. *A kalte kuzhnya, Moshe. Kein fire.* Divorce was impossible because he owed her too much money. "But you have money now, don't you?" said Herzog, blunt with him. His father stopped, staring into his face. Herzog was stunned to see in full summer light how much disintegration had already taken place. But the remaining elements, incredibly vivid, had all their old power over Moses—the straight nose, the furrow between the eyes, the brown and green colors in those eyes. "I need my money. Who'll provide for me—you? I may bribe the Angel of Death a long time yet." Then he bent his knees a little—Moses read that old signal; he had a lifetime of skill in interpreting his father's gestures: those bent knees meant that something of great subtlety was about to be revealed. "I don't know when I'll be delivered," Father Herzog whispered. He used the old Yiddish term for a woman's confinement—*kimpet*. Moses did not know what to say, and his answering voice was not much above a whisper. "Don't torment yourself, Papa." The horror of this second birth, into the hands of death, made his eyes shine, and his lips silently pressed together. Then Father Herzog said, "I have to sit down, Moshe. The sun is too hot for me." He did, suddenly, appear very flushed, and Moses supported him, eased him down on the cement embankment of a lawn. The old man's look was now one of injured male pride. "Even I feel the heat today," said Moses. He placed himself between his father and the sun.

"I may go next month to St. Joe for the baths," Taube was saying. "To the Whitcomb. It's a nice place."

"Not alone?"

"Ethel and Mordecai want to go."

"Oh . . . ?" He nodded, to keep her going. "How is Mordecai?"

"How can he be in his age?" Moses was attentive until she was well started and then he returned to his father. They had had lunch on the back porch that day, and that was where the quarrel began. It had seemed to Moses, perhaps, that he was here as a prodigal son, admitting the worst and asking the old man's mercy, and so Father Herzog saw nothing except a stupid appeal in his son's face—incomprehensible. "Idiot!" was what the old man had shouted. "Calf!" Then he saw the angry demand underlying Moses' look of patience. "Get out! I leave you nothing! Everything to Willie and Helen! You . . . ? Croak in a flophouse." Moses rising, Father Herzog shouted, "Go. And don't come to my funeral."

"All right, maybe I won't."

Too late, Tante Taube had warned him to keep silent, raising her brows—she had still had brows then. Father Herzog rose stumbling from the table, his face distorted, and ran to get his pistol.

"Go, go! Come back later. I'll call you," Taube had whispered to Moses, and he, confused, reluctant, burning, stung because his misery was not recognized in his father's house (his monstrous egotism making its peculiar demands)—he reluctantly got up from the table. "Quick, quick!" Taube tried to get him to the front door, but old Herzog overtook them with the pistol.

He cried out, "I'll kill you!" And Herzog was startled not so much by this threat, which he did not believe, as by the return of his father's strength. In his rage he recovered it briefly, though it might cost him his life. The strained neck, the grinding of his teeth, his frightening color, even the military Russian strut with which he lifted the gun—these were better, thought Herzog, than his sinking down during a walk to the store. Father Herzog was not made to be pitiful.

"Go, go," said Tante Taube. Moses was weeping then.

"Maybe you'll die first," Father Herzog shouted.

"Papa!"

Half hearing Tante Taube's slow description of Cousin Mordecai's approaching retirement, Herzog grimly recovered the note of that cry. *Papa—Papa.* You lout! The old man in his near-demented way was trying to act out the manhood you should have had. Coming to his house with that Christianized smirk of the long-suffering son. Might as well have been an outright convert, like Mady. He should have pulled the trigger. Those looks were agony to him. He deserved to be spared, in his old age.

And then there was Moses with puffy weeping eyes, in the street, waiting for his cab, while Father Herzog hastily walked up and back before these windows, staring at him in agony of spirit—yes, you got that out of him. Walking quickly there, back and forth in his hasty style, dropping his weight on the one heel. The pistol thrown down. Who knows whether Moses shortened his life by the grief he gave him. Perhaps the stimulus of anger lengthened it. He could not die and leave this half-made Moses yet.

They were reconciled the following year. And then more of the same. And then . . . death.

"Should I make a cup of tea?" said Tante Taube.

"Yes, please, I'd like that if you feel up to it. And I also want to look in Papa's desk."

"Pa's desk? It's locked. You want to look in the desk? Everything belongs to you children. You could take the desk when I die."

"No, no!" he said, "I don't need the desk itself, but I was passing from the airport and thought I'd see how you were. And now that I'm here, I'd like to have a look in the desk. I know you don't mind."

"You want something, Moshe? You took your Mama's silver coin case the last time."

He had given it to Madeleine.

"Is Papa's watch chain still in there?"

"I think Willie took it."

He frowned with concentration. "Then what about the rubles?" he asked. "I'd like them for Marco."

"Rubles?"

"My grandfather Isaac bought Czarist rubles during the Revolution, and they've always been in the desk."

"In the desk? I surely never seen them."

"I'd like to look, while you make a cup of tea, Tante Taube. Give me the key."

"The key . . . ?" Questioning him before, she had spoken more quickly, but now she receded again into slowness, raising a mountain of dilatory will in his way.

"Where do you keep it?"

"Where? Where did I put it? Is it in Pa's dresser? Or somewheres else? Let me remember. That's how I am now, it's hard to remember. . . ."

"I know where it is," he said, suddenly rising.

"You know where it is? So where is it?"

"In the music box, where you always used to keep it."

"In the music . . . ? Pa took it from there. He locked up my social-security checks when they came. He said all the money *he* should have. . . ."

Moses knew he had guessed right. "Don't bother, I'll get it," he said. "If you'll put the kettle on. I'm very thirsty. It's been a hot, long day."

He helped her to rise, holding her flaccid arm. He was having his way—a poor sort of victory and filled with dangerous consequences. Going forward without her, he entered the bedroom. His father's bed had been removed. Hers stood alone with its ugly bedspread—some material that reminded him of a coated tongue. He breathed the old spice, the dark, heavy air, and lifted the lid of the music box. In this house he had only to consult his memory to find what he wanted. The mechanism released its little notes as the cylinder turned within, the small spines picking out the notes from *Figaro*. Moses was able to supply the words:

> *Nel momento*
> *Della mia cerimonia*
> *Io rideva di me*
> *Senza saperlo.*

His fingers recognized the key.

Old Taube in the dark outside the bedroom said, "Did you found it?"

He answered, "It's here," and spoke in a low, mild voice, not to make matters worse. The house was hers, after all. It was rude to invade it. He was not ashamed of this, he only recognized with full objectivity that it was not right. But it had to be done.

"Do you want me to put the kettle on?"

"No, a cup of tea I can still make."

He heard her slow steps in the passage. She was going to the kitchen. Herzog quickly made for the small sitting room. The drapes were drawn. He turned on the lamp beside the desk. In seeking the switch he tore the ancient silk of the shade, releasing a fine dust. The name of this color was old rose—he felt certain of it. He opened the cherry-wood secretary, braced the wide leaf on its runners, drawing them out from either side. Then he went back and shut the door, first making sure Taube had reached the kitchen. In the drawers he recognized each article—leather, paper, gold. Swift and tense, veins standing out on his head, and tendons on the hands, he groped, and found what he was looking for— Father Herzog's pistol. An old pistol, the barrel nickel-plated. Papa had bought it to keep on Cherry Street, in the railroad yards. Moses flipped the gun open. There were two bullets. This was it, then. He rapidly clicked it shut and put it in his pocket. There it made too large a bulge. He took out his wallet and replaced it with the gun. The wallet he buttoned in his hip pocket.

Now he began to search for those rubles. Those he found in a small compartment with old passports, ribbons sealed in wax, like gobs of dried blood. *La bourgeoise Sarah Herzog avec ses enfants, Alexandre huit ans, Hélène neuf ans et Guillaume trois ans*, signed by Count Adlerberg *Gouverneur de St. Petersbourg*. The rubles were in a large billfold—his playthings of forty years ago. Peter the Great in a rich coat of armor, and a splendid imperial Catherine. Lamplight revealed the watermarks. Recalling how he and Willie used to play casino for these stakes, Herzog uttered one of his short laughs, then made a nest of these large bills in his pocket for the pistol. He thought it must be less conspicuous now.

"You got what you want?" Taube asked him in the kitchen.

"Yes." He put the key on the enameled metal table.

He knew it was not proper that he should think her expression sheeplike. This figurative habit of his mind crippled his judgment, and was likely to ruin him some day. Perhaps the day was near; perhaps this night his soul would be required of him. The gun weighed on his chest. But the protuberant lips, great eyes, and pleated mouth *were* sheeplike, and they warned him he was taking too many chances with destruction. Taube, a veteran survivor, to be heeded, had fought the grave to a standstill, balking death itself by her slowness. All had decayed but her shrewdness and her incredible patience; and in Moses she saw Father Herzog again, nervy and hasty, impulsive, suffering. His eye twitched as he bent toward her in the kitchen. She muttered, "You got a lot of trouble? Don't make it worser, Moshe."

"There's no trouble, Tante. I have business to take care of. . . . I don't think I can wait for tea, after all."

"I put out Pa's cup for you."

Moses drank tap water from his father's teacup.

"Good-by, Tante Taube, keep well." He kissed her forehead.

"Remember I helped you?" she said. "You shouldn't forget. Take care, Moshe."

He left by the back door; it made departure simpler. Honeysuckle grew along the rainspout, as in his father's time, and fragrant in the evening—almost too rich. Could any heart become quite petrified?

———

He gunned his motor at the stoplight, trying to decide which was the faster route to Harper Avenue. The new Ryan Expressway was very quick but it would land him in the thick of the Negro traffic on West 51st Street, where people promenaded, or cruised in their cars. There was Garfield Boulevard, much better; however, he was not sure he could find his way through Washington

Park after dark. He decided to follow Eden's to Congress Street and Congress to the Outer Drive. Yes, that would be fastest. What he would do when he got to Harper Avenue he hadn't yet decided. Madeleine had threatened him with arrest if he so much as showed his face near the house. The police had his picture, but that was sheer bunk, bunk and paranoia, the imperiousness of imaginary powers that had once impressed him. But there was now a real matter between him and Madeleine, a child, a reality—June. Out of cowardice, sickness, fraud, by a bungling father out of a plotting bitch, something genuine! This little daughter of his! He cried out to himself as he raced up the ramp of the Expressway that nobody would harm *her*. He accelerated, moving in his lane with the rest of the traffic. The thread of life was stretched tight in him. It quivered crazily. He did not fear its breaking so much as his failing to do what he should. The little Falcon was storming. He thought his speed was terrible until a huge trailer truck passed him on the right, when he realized that this was not the time to risk a traffic ticket—not with a pistol in his pocket—and lifted his foot from the pedal. Peering left and right, he recognized that the new Expressway had been cut through old streets, streets he knew. He saw the vast gas tanks, crowned with lights, from a new perspective, and the rear of a Polish church with a Christ in brocades exhibited in a lighted window, like a showcase. The long curve eastbound passed over the freight yards, burning with sunset dust, rails streaking westward; next, the tunnel under the mammoth post office; next, the State Street honky-tonks. From the last slope of Congress Street the distortions of dusk raised up the lake like a mild wall crossed by bands, amethyst, murky blue, irregular silver, and a slate color at the horizon, boats hanging rocking inside the breakwater, and helicopters and small aircraft whose lights teetered overhead. The familiar odor of the fresh water, bland but also raw, reached him as he sped south. It did not seem illogical that he should claim the privilege of insanity, violence, having been made to carry the rest of it—name-calling and gossip, railroading, pain, even exile in Ludeyville. That property was to have been his madhouse. Finally, his mausoleum. But they had done something else to Herzog—unpredictable. It's not everyone who gets the opportunity to kill with a clear conscience. They had opened the way to justifiable murder. They deserved to die. He had a right to kill them.

They would even know why they were dying; no explanation necessary. When he stood before them they would have to submit. Gersbach would only hang his head, with tears for himself. Like Nero—*Qualis artifex pereo*. Madeleine would shriek and curse. Out of hatred, the most powerful element in her life, stronger by far than any other power or motive. In spirit she was his murderess, and therefore he was turned loose, could shoot or choke without remorse. He felt in his arms and in his fingers, and to the core of his heart, the sweet exertion of strangling—horrible and sweet, an orgastic rapture of inflicting death. He was sweating violently, his shirt wet and cold under his arms. Into his mouth came a taste of copper, a metabolic poison, a flat but deadly flavor.

When he reached Harper Avenue he parked around the corner, and entered the alley that passed behind the house. Grit spilled on the concrete; broken glass and gravelly ashes made his steps loud. He went carefully. The back fences were old here. Garden soil spilled under the slats, and shrubs and vines came over their tops. Once more he saw open honeysuckle. Even rambler roses, dark red in the dusk. He had to cover his face when he passed the garage because of the loops of briar that swung over the path from the sloping roof. When he stole into the yard he stood still until he could see his way. He must not stumble over a toy, or a tool. A fluid had come into his eyes—very clear, only somewhat distorting. He wiped it away with fingertips, and blotted, too, with the lapel of his coat. Stars had come out, violet points framed in roof shapes, leaves, strut wires. The yard was visible to him now. He saw the clothesline—Madeleine's underpants and his daughter's little shirts and dresses, tiny stockings. By the light of the kitchen window he made out a sandbox in the grass, a new red sandbox with broad ledges to sit on. Stepping nearer, he looked into the kitchen. Madeleine was there! He stopped breathing as he watched her. She was wearing slacks and a blouse fastened with a broad red leather and brass belt he had given her. Her smooth hair hung loose as she moved between the table and the sink, cleaning up after dinner, scraping dishes in her own style of abrupt efficiency. He studied her straight profile as she stood at the sink, the flesh under her chin as she concentrated on the foam in the sink, tempering the water. He could see the color in her cheeks, and almost the blue of her eyes. Watching, he fed his rage, to keep it steady, up to full strength.

She was not likely to hear him in the yard because the storm windows had not been taken down—not, at least, those he had put up last fall at the back of the house.

He moved into the passageway. Luckily the neighbors were not at home, and he did not have to worry about their lights. He had had his look at Madeleine. It was his daughter he wanted to see now. The dining room was unoccupied—after-dinner emptiness, Coke bottles, paper napkins. Next was the bathroom window, set higher than the rest. He remembered, however, that he had used a cement block to stand on, trying to take out the bathroom screen until he had discovered there was no storm window to replace it. The screen was still in, therefore. And the block? It was exactly where he had left it, among the lilies of the valley on the left side of the path. He moved it into place, the scraping covered by the sound of water in the tub, and stood on it, his side pressed to the building. He tried to muffle the sound of his breathing, opening his mouth. In the rushing water with floating toys his daughter's little body shone. His child! Madeleine had let her black hair grow longer, and now it was tied up for the bath with a rubber band. He melted with tenderness for her, putting his hand over his mouth to cover any sound emotion might cause him to make. She raised her face to speak to someone he could not see. Above the flow of water he heard her say something but could not understand the words. Her face was the Herzog face, the large dark eyes *his* eyes, the nose his father's, Tante Zipporah's, his brother Willie's nose, and the mouth his own. Even the bit of melancholy in her beauty—that was his mother. It was Sarah Herzog, pensive, slightly averting her face as she considered the life about her. Moved, he watched her, breathing with open mouth, his face half covered by his hand. Flying beetles passed him. Their heavy bodies struck the screen but did not attract her notice.

Then a hand reached forward and shut off the water—a man's hand. It was Gersbach. He was going to bathe Herzog's daughter! Gersbach! His waist was now in sight. He came into view stalking beside the old-fashioned round tub, bowing, straightening, bowing—his Venetian hobble, and then, with great trouble, he began to kneel, and Herzog saw his chest, his head, as he arranged himself. Flattened to the wall, his chin on his shoulder, Herzog saw Gersbach roll up the sleeves of his paisley sports shirt, put back his thick glowing hair, take the soap, heard him say, not unkindly, "Okay, cut out the monkeyshines," for Junie was giggling, twisting, splashing, dimpling, showing her tiny white teeth, wrinkling her nose, teasing. "Now hold still," said Gersbach. He got into her ears with the washrag as she screamed, cleaned off her face, the nostrils, wiped her mouth. He spoke with authority, but affectionately and with grumbling smiles and occasionally with laughter he bathed her—soaped, rinsed, dipping water in her toy boats to rinse her back as she squealed and twisted. The man washed her tenderly. His look, perhaps, was false. But he had no *true* expressions, Herzog thought. His face was all heaviness, sexual meat. Looking down his open shirt front, Herzog saw the hair-covered heavy soft flesh of Gersbach's breast. His chin was thick, and like a stone ax, a brutal weapon. And then there were his sentimental eyes, the thick crest of hair, and that hearty voice with its peculiar fraudulence and grossness. The hated traits were all there. But see how he was with June, scooping the water on her playfully, kindly. He let her wear her mother's flowered shower cap, the rubber petals spreading on the child's head. Then Gersbach ordered her to stand, and she stooped slightly to allow him to wash her little cleft. Her father stared at this. A pang went through him, but it was quickly done. She sat again. Gersbach ran fresh water on her, cumbersomely rose and opened the bath towel. Steady and thorough, he dried her, and then with a large puff he powdered her. The child jumped up and down with delight. "Enough of this wild stuff," said Gersbach. "Put on those p-j's now."

She ran out. Herzog still saw faint wisps of powder, that floated over Gersbach's stooping head. His red hair worked up and down. He was scouring the tub. Moses might have killed him now. His left hand touched the gun, enclosed in the roll of rubles. He might have shot Gersbach as he methodically salted the yellow sponge rectangle with cleansing powder. There were two bullets in the chamber. . . . But they would stay there. Herzog clearly recognized that. Very softly he stepped down from his perch, and passed without sound through the yard again. He saw his child in the kitchen, looking up at Mady, asking for something, and he edged through the gate into the alley. Firing this pistol was nothing but a thought.

The human soul is an amphibian, and I have touched its

sides. Amphibian! It lives in more elements than I will ever know; and I assume that in those remote stars matter is in the making which will create stranger beings yet. I seem to think because June looks like a Herzog, she is nearer to me than to them. But how is she near to me if I have no share in her life? Those two grotesque love-actors have it all. And I apparently believe that if the child does not have a life resembling mine, educated according to the Herzog standards of "heart," and all the rest of it, she will fail to become a human being. This is sheer irrationality, and yet some part of my mind takes it as self-evident. But what in fact can she learn from them? From Gersbach, when he looks so sugary, repulsive, poisonous, not an individual but a fragment, a piece broken off from the mob. To shoot him!—an absurd thought. As soon as Herzog saw the actual person giving an actual bath, the reality of it, the tenderness of such a buffoon to a little child, his intended violence turned into *theater,* into something ludicrous. He was not ready to make such a complete fool of himself. Only self-hatred could lead him to ruin himself because his heart was "broken." How could it be broken by such a pair? Lingering in the alley awhile, he congratulated himself on his luck. His breath came back to him; and how good it felt to breathe! It was worth the trip.

Think! he noted to himself in the Falcon, on a pad under the map light. *Demographers estimate that at least half of all the human beings ever born are alive now, in this century. What a moment for the human soul! Characteristics drawn from the genetic pool have, in statistical probability, reconstituted all the best and all the worst of human life. It's all around us. Buddha and Lao-tse must be walking the earth somewhere. And Tiberius and Nero. Everything horrible, everything sublime, and things not imagined yet. And you, part-time visionary, cheerful, tragical mammal. You and your children and children's children . . . In ancient days, the genius of man went largely into metaphors. But now into facts . . . Francis Bacon. Instruments.* Then with inexpressible relish he added, *Tante Zipporah told Papa he could never use a gun on anyone, never keep up with teamsters, butchers, sluggers, hooligans, razboiniks. "A gilded little gentleman." Could he hit anyone on the head? Could he shoot?*

Moses could confidently swear that Father Herzog had never—

not once in his life—pulled the trigger of this gun. Only threatened. As he threatened me with it. Taube defended me then. She "saved" me. Dear Aunt Taube! A cold forge! Poor Father Herzog!

But he was not yet willing to call it a day. He had to have a talk with Phoebe Gersbach. It was essential. And he decided not to phone her and give her an opportunity to prepare herself, or even refuse to see him. He drove directly to Woodlawn Avenue—a dreary part of Hyde Park, but characteristic, *his* Chicago: massive, clumsy, amorphous, smelling of mud and decay, dog turds; sooty façades, slabs of structural *nothing,* senselessly ornamented triple porches with huge cement urns for flowers that contained only rotting cigarette butts and other stained filth; sun parlors under tiled gables, rank areaways, gray backstairs, seamed and ruptured concrete from which sprang grass; ponderous four-by-four fences that sheltered growing weeds. And among these spacious, comfortable, dowdy apartments where liberal, benevolent people lived (this was the university neighborhood) Herzog did in fact feel at home. He was perhaps as midwestern and unfocused as these same streets. (Not so much determinism, he thought, as a lack of determining elements—the absence of a formative power.) But it was all typical, and nothing was lacking, not even the sound of roller skates awkwardly gritting on the pavement beneath new summer leaves. Two poky little girls under the green transparency of street lamps, skating in short skirts, and with ribbons in their hair.

A nervous qualm went through him now that he was at Gersbach's gate, but he mastered it and went up the walk, rang the bell. Phoebe approached quickly. She called, "Who is it?" and seeing Herzog through the glass was silent. Was she scared?

"It's an old friend," said Herzog. A moment passed, Phoebe, despite the firmness of her mouth, hesitating, eyes large-lidded beneath her bangs. "Won't you let me in?" Moses asked. His tone made refusal unthinkable. "I won't take much of your time," he said as he was entering. "We do have a few matters to discuss, though."

"Come in the kitchen, will you."

"Sure . . ." She didn't want to be surprised talking to him in the front room or overheard by little Ephraim, who was in his bedroom. In the kitchen she shut the door and asked Herzog to sit. The chair her eyes were looking at was beside the refrigerator. There he would not be seen from the kitchen window. With a faint smile he sat down. From the extreme composure of her slender face he knew how her heart must be pounding, working perhaps even more violently than his. An orderly person, self-controlled in high degree, clean—the head nurse—she tried to maintain a businesslike look. She was wearing the amber beads he had brought her from Poland. Herzog buttoned up his jacket to make sure the butt of his gun did not show. The sight of a weapon would certainly frighten her to death.

"Well, how are you, Phoebe?"

"We're all right."

"Comfortably settled? Liking Chicago? Little Ephraim still in the Lab School?"

"Yes."

"And the Temple? I see that Val taped a program with Rabbi Itzkowitz—what did he call it? 'Hasidic Judaism, Martin Buber, *I and Thou*.' Still the Buber kick! He's very thick with these rabbis. Maybe he wants to swap wives with a rabbi. He'll work his way round from 'I and Thou' to 'Me and You'—'You and Me, Kid!' But I suppose you'd draw the line there. You wouldn't go along with everything."

Phoebe made no answer and remained standing.

"Maybe you think I'll leave sooner if you don't sit. Come, Phoebe, sit down. I promise you I haven't come to make scenes. I have only one purpose here, in addition to wanting to see an old friend. . . ."

"We're not really old friends."

"Not by calendar years. But we were so close out in Ludeyville. That is true. You have to think of duration—Bergsonian duration. We have known each other in duration. Some people are *sentenced* to certain relationships. Maybe every relationship is either a joy or a sentence."

"You earned your own sentence, if that's how you want to think about it. We had a quiet life till you and Madeleine descended on Ludeyville and forced yourself on me." Phoebe, her face thin but hot, eyelids unmoving, sat down on the edge of the chair Herzog had drawn forward for her.

"Good. Say what you think, Phoebe. That's what I want. Sit back. Don't be afraid. I'm not looking for trouble. We've got a problem in common."

Phoebe denied this. She shook her head, with a stubborn look, all too vigorously. "I'm a plain woman. Valentine is from upstate New York."

"Just a rube. Yes. Knows nothing about fancy vices from the big city. Didn't even know how to dial a number. Had to be led step by step into degeneracy by me—Moses E. Herzog."

Stiff and hesitant, she turned her body aside in her abrupt way. Then she came to a decision and turned to him again with the same abruptness. She was a pretty woman, but stiff, very stiff, bony, without self-confidence. "You never understood a thing about him. He fell for you. Adored you. Tried to become an intellectual because he wanted to help you—saw what a terrible thing you had done in giving up your respectable university position and how reckless you were, rushing out to the country with Madeleine. He thought she was ruining you and tried to set you on the right track again. He read all those books so you'd have somebody to talk to, out in the sticks, Moses. Because you needed help, praise, flattery, support, affection. It never was enough. You wore him out. It nearly killed him trying to back you up."

"Yes . . . ? What else? Go on," said Herzog.

"It's still not enough. What do you want from him now? What are you here for? More excitement? Are you still greedy for excitement?"

Herzog no longer smiled. "Some of what you say is right enough, Phoebe. I was certainly floundering in Ludeyville. But you take the wind out of me when you say you were leading a perfectly ordinary life up there in Barrington. Until Mady and I came along with the books and the theatrical glamour, high-level mental life, scattering big-shot ideas and blowing whole ages of history. You were scared by us because we—Mady especially—gave him confidence. As long as he was only a small-time gimpy radio announcer, he might bluff at being a big shot, but you had him where you wanted him. Because he is a bluffer and a screwball, a kind of freak, but *yours*. Then he got bolder. He gave his exhibitionism scope. Quite right, I'm an idiot. You were even right to dislike me, if only because I wouldn't see what was happening and in that way put another burden on you. But why didn't you say something? You watched the whole thing going on. It went on for years, and you said nothing. I wouldn't have been so indifferent if I saw the same thing happening to *you*."

Phoebe hesitated to speak of this and turned even paler. She said, at last, "It's not my fault that you refuse to understand the system other people live by. Your ideas get in the way. Maybe a weak person like me has no choice. I couldn't do anything for you. Especially last year. I was seeing a psychiatrist, and he advised me to keep away. To keep away from you, most of all from you and all your trouble. He said I wasn't strong enough, and you know it's true—I'm not strong enough."

Herzog considered this—Phoebe was weak, that was certainly the truth. He decided to get to the point. "Why don't you divorce Valentine?" he said.

"I see no reason why I should." Her voice immediately recovered strength.

"He's deserted you, hasn't he?"

"Val? I don't know why you say that! I'm not deserted."

"Where is he now—this evening? This minute?"

"Downtown. On business."

"Oh, come on, don't pull that stuff on me, Phoebe. He's living with Madeleine. Do you deny it?"

"I most certainly do. I can't imagine how you ever got such a fantastic idea."

Moses leaned with one arm against the refrigerator as he shifted in his chair and took out a handkerchief—the scrap of kitchen towel from his New York apartment. He wiped his face.

"If you would sue for divorce," he explained, "as you have every right to do, you could name Madeleine for adultery. I'd help raise the money. I'd underwrite the whole cost. I want Junie. Don't you see? Together we could nail them. You've let Madeleine drive you here and there. As if you were a nanny goat."

"That's the old devil in you talking again, Moses."

Nanny goat was a mistake; he was making her more obstinate. But, anyway, she was going to follow her own line. She'd never share any plan of his.

"Don't you want me to have custody of June?"

"I'm indifferent to that."

"You have your own war with Madeleine, I suppose," he said. "Fighting over the man. A cat fight—a female sex fight. But she'll beat you. Because she's a psychopath. I know you've got reserve strength. But she's a nut, and nuts win. Besides, Valentine doesn't want you to get him."

"I really don't understand what you're saying."

"He'll lose his value to Madeleine as soon as you withdraw. After the victory, she'll have to throw him out."

"Valentine comes home every night. He's never out late. He should be here soon. . . . When I'm even a little delayed somewhere, why, he gets frantic with worry. He phones all over the city."

"Perhaps that's just hope," said Moses. "Hope disguised as concern. Don't you know how that is? If you get killed in an accident, he cries and packs up and moves in with Madeleine for good."

"That's your devil speaking again. My child is going to keep *his* father. You still want Madeleine, don't you!"

"Me? Never! All that hysterical stuff is finished. No, I'm glad to be rid of her. I don't even loathe her much any more. And she's welcome to all she chiseled from me. She must have been banking my money all along. Okay! Let her keep it with my blessing. Bless the bitch! Good luck and good-by. I bless her. I wish her a busy, useful, pleasant, dramatic life. Including *love*. The best people fall in love, and she's one of the best, therefore she loves this fellow. They both *love*. She's not good enough to bring up the kid, though. . . ."

If he were a wild pig, and those bangs of hers a protective hedge —Phoebe's brown eyes were as vigilant as that. And yet Moses was sorry for her. They bullied her—Gersbach; Madeleine through Gersbach. But Phoebe herself meant to win this contest. It must be inconceivable to her that one should set such modest, such minimal goals—table, market, laundry, child—and still lose the struggle. Life couldn't be as indecent as that. Could it? Another hypothesis: sexlessness was her strength; she wielded the authority of the superego. Still another: she acknowledged the creative depth of modern degeneracy, all the luxuriant vices of emancipated swingers, and thus accepted her situation as a poor, neurotic, dry unfortunate, mud-stuck, middle-class woman. To her, Gersbach was no ordinary man, and because of his richness of character, his spiritual-erotic drive, or God knows what foot-smelling meta-physics, he required two wives or more. Maybe these two women lent this piece of orange-tufted flesh to each other for widely different needs. For three-legged copulation. For domestic peace.

"Phoebe," he said. "Admitting you're weak—but how weak are you? Excuse me. . . . I find this pretty funny. You have to deny *everything,* and keep up a perfect appearance. Can't you admit even a tiny bit?"

"What good would that do you?" she asked sharply. "And also, what are you prepared to do for me?"

"I? I'd help . . ." he began. But he checked himself. It was true, he couldn't offer much. He really was useless to her. With Gersbach she could still be a wife. He came home. She cooked, ironed, shopped, signed checks. Without him, she could not exist, cook, make beds. The trance would break. Then what?

"Why do you come to me, if you want custody of your daughter? Either do something by yourself or forget it. Let me alone, now, Moses."

This, too, was perfectly just. Silent, he stared hard at her. The early and native tendency of his mind, lately acting without inhibitions, found significance in small bloodless marks on her face. As if death had tried her with his teeth and found her still unripe.

"Well, thank you for this talk, Phoebe. I'm going." He stood up. There was a softer kindliness in Herzog's expression, not often seen. Rather awkwardly he took Phoebe's hand, and she could not move fast enough to avoid his lips. He drew her closer and kissed her on the head. "You're right. This was an unnecessary visit." She freed her fingers.

"Good-by, Moses." She spoke without looking at him. He would not get more from her than she was able to spare. ". . . You've been treated like dirt. That's true. But it's all over. You should get away. Just get away from this now."

The door was shut.

Crumbs of decency—all that we paupers can spare one another. No wonder "personal" life is a humiliation, and to be an individual contemptible. The historical process, putting clothes on our backs, shoes on the feet, meat in the mouth, does infinitely more for us by the indifferent method than anyone does by intention, Herzog wrote in the rented Falcon. *And since these good commodities are the gifts of anonymous planning and labor, what intentional goodness can achieve (when the good are amateurs) becomes the question. Especially if, in the interests of health, our benevolence and love demand exercise, the creature being emotional, passionate, expressive, a relating animal. A creature of deep peculiarities, a web of feeling intricacies and ideas now approaching a level of organization and automatism where he can hope to be free from human dependency. People are practicing their future condition already. My emotional type is archaic. Belongs to the agricultural or pastoral stages . . .*

Herzog could not say what the significance of such generalities might be. He was only vastly excited—in a streaming state—and intended mostly to restore order by turning to his habit of thoughtfulness. Blood had burst into his psyche, and for the time being he was either free or crazy. But then he realized that he did not need to perform elaborate abstract intellectual work—work he had always thrown himself into as if it were the struggle for survival. But not thinking is not necessarily fatal. Did I really believe that I would die when thinking stopped? Now to fear such a thing—that's really crazy.

He went to spend the night with Lucas Asphalter, telephoning from a sidewalk booth to invite himself over. "I won't be in the way, will I? Have you got anybody there with you? No? I want you to do me a special favor. I can't phone Madeleine to ask to see the child. She hangs up on me as soon as she recognizes my voice Will you call and arrange for me to pick up June tomorrow?"

"Why, of course," said Asphalter. "I'll do it now and have the answer for you when you get here. Did you just blow in, on impulse? Unplanned?"

"Thank you, Luke. Please do it now."

He left the booth reflecting that he really must rest tonight, try to get some sleep. At the same time, he hesitated somewhat to lie down and shut his eyes; tomorrow he might not be able to recover his state of simple, free, intense realization. He therefore drove slowly, stopping at Walgreen's, where he bought a bottle of Cutty Sark for Luke and playthings for June—a toy periscope through which she could look over the sofa, around corners, a beach ball you inflated with your breath. He even found time to send a wire to Ramona from the yellow Western Union office at Blackstone and 53rd. *Chicago business two days* was his message. *Much love.* Trust her, she'd find comfort while he was away, not be despondent in "desertion" as he would have been—his childish disorder, that infantile terror of death that had bent and buckled his life into these curious shapes. Having discovered that everyone must be indulgent with bungling child-men, pure hearts in the burlap of innocence, and willingly accepting the necessary quota of consequent lies, he had set himself up with his emotional goodies— truth, friendship, devotion to children (the regular American worship of kids), and potato love. So much we know now. But this— even this—is not the whole story, either. It only begins to approach the start of true consciousness. The necessary premise is that a man is somehow more than his "characteristics," all the emotions, strivings, tastes, and constructions which it pleases him to call "My Life." We have ground to hope that a Life is something more than such a cloud of particles, mere facticity. Go through what is comprehensible and you conclude that only the incomprehensible gives any light. This was by no means a "general idea" with him now. It was far more substantial than anything he saw in this intensely lighted telegraph office. It all seemed to him exceptionally clear. What made it clear? Something at the very end of the line. Was that thing Death? But death was not the incomprehensible accepted by his heart. No, far from it.

He stopped to gaze at the fine hand beating its way over the face of the clock, the yellow furniture of another era—no wonder large corporations raked in such profits; high charges, old equipment, no competitors, now that Postal Telegraph was knocked out. They certainly got more mileage out of these yellow desks than Father Herzog did out of the same kind of furniture on Cherry Street. That was across from the cat-house. When the madame didn't pay them off the cops threw the whores' beds out of the second-story windows. The women shrieked Negro curses as they were pushed into the wagon. Father Herzog, the businessman, musing at these aliens of vice and brutality, police and barbarous obese women, stood among such tables—standard second-hand equipment acquired in warehouse sales. Here my ancestral fortune was founded.

In front of Asphalter's house he locked the Falcon for the night, leaving Junie's gifts in the trunk. He felt certain she would love the periscope. There was much to be seen in that house on Harper Avenue. Let the child find life. The plainer the better, perhaps.

He was met on the staircase by Asphalter.

"I've been waiting for you."

"Is something wrong?" said Herzog.

"No, no, don't worry. I'm picking June up at noon tomorrow. She goes to a play school, half-days."

"Wonderful," Herzog said. "No trouble?"

"With Madeleine? None at all. She doesn't want to see you. Otherwise, you can visit with your little girl to your heart's content."

"She doesn't want me to come with a court order. Legally, she's in a dubious position, with that crook in the house. Well, let's have a look at you." They entered the apartment where the light was better. "You've grown a bit of a beard, Luke."

Nervously and shyly Asphalter touched his chin, looking away. He said, "I'm brazening it out."

"Compensation for the sudden unfortunate baldness?" said Herzog.

"Fighting a depression," said Asphalter. "Thought a change of image might be good . . . Excuse my pad."

Asphalter had always lived in such graduate-student filth. Herzog looked about. "If I ever have another windfall I'll buy you some bookshelves, Luke. About time you got rid of these old crates. This scientific literature is heavy stuff. But look, you've got clean sheets on the studio couch for me. This is very kind of you, Luke."

"You're an old friend."

"Thanks," said Herzog. To his surprise he found difficulty in speaking. A swift rush of feeling, out of nowhere, caught his throat. His eyes filled up. The potato love, he announced to himself. It's here. To advert to his temperament, call things by the correct name, restored his control. Self-correction refreshed him. "Luke, did you get my letter."

"Letter? Did you send me one? I sent you a letter."

"Never saw it. What was it about?"

"About a job. Remember Elias Tuberman?"

"The sociologist who married that gym teacher?"

"Don't joke. He's general editor of Stone's Encyclopedia, and has a million to spend on revision. I'm in charge of the biology. He's looking for you to take over in history."

"Me?"

"He said he read your book on Romanticism and Christianity over again. Didn't think too highly of it in the fifties when it came out, but must have been blind. It's a monument, he says."

Herzog looked grave. He began to make up several answers but abandoned them all. "I don't know whether I'm still a scholar. When I left Daisy, apparently I quit that, too."

"And Madeleine snatched it right up."

"Yes. They divvied me up. Valentine took my elegant ways and Mady's going to be the professor. Isn't she coming up for her orals?"

"Right away."

Remembering now the death of Asphalter's monkey, Herzog said, "What got into you, Luke? You didn't catch T.B. from your pet, did you?"

"No, no. I've taken the tuberculin test regularly. No."

"You must have been out of your mind, giving Rocco mouth-to-mouth respiration. That's letting eccentricity go too far."

"Did they report that too?"

"Of course. How else would I know? How did it get into the papers?"

"One of the little bastards in Physiology picks up a few bucks by spying for the *American*."

"Didn't you know the monkey was tubercular?"

"I knew he was ailing, but had no idea. And I certainly wasn't expecting to be so hard hit by his death." Herzog was not prepared for the solemnity of Asphalter's look. His new beard was vari-colored but his eyes were even blacker than the hair he had lost. "It really threw me into a spin. I thought that palling around with Rocco was a gag. I didn't realize how much he meant to me. But the truth is, I realized that no other death in the world could have affected me so much. I had to ask myself whether the death of my brother would have shook me up half as much. I think not. We're all some kind of nut or other, I realize. But . . ."

"You don't mind if I smile," Herzog apologized. "I can't help it."

"What else can you do?"

"A man could do worse than to love his monkey," said Herzog. *"Le cœur a ses raisons.* You've seen Gersbach. He was a dear friend of mine. And Madeleine *loves* him. What have you got to be ashamed of? It's one of those painful emotional comedies. Did you ever read Collier's story about the man who married a chimpanzee? *His Monkey Wife.* An excellent story."

"I've been horribly depressed," said Asphalter. "It's better now; but for about two months I did no work, and I was glad I had no wife or kids to hide these crying jags from."

"All because of that monkey?"

"I stopped going to the lab. I doctored myself with tranquilizers, but that couldn't continue. I had to face the music, finally."

"And you went to Doctor Edvig?" Herzog was laughing.

"Edvig? No, no. Another headshrinker. He calmed me down. But that was only two hours a week. The rest of the time, I was shaking. So I got some books out of the library. . . . Have you read the book by that Hungarian woman Tina Zokóly about what to do in these crises?"

"No. What does she say?"

"She prescribes certain exercises."

Moses was interested. "What are they?"

"The main one is facing your own death."

"How do you do that?"

Asphalter tried to maintain an ordinary, conversational, descriptive tone. Obviously it was a very difficult thing for him to talk about. Irresistible, though.

"You pretend you have already died," Asphalter began.

"The worst has happened. . . . Yes?" Herzog turned his head as if to hear better, listen more intently. His hands were folded in his lap, his shoulders had dropped with fatigue, his feet were turned inward. The musty bookish room with a clamp-light affixed to one of the crates and the stirring of leaves in the summer street brought Herzog some peace. *True things in grotesque form,* he was thinking. He knew how that was. He felt for Asphalter.

"The blow has fallen. The agony is over," said Asphalter. "You're dead, and you have to lie as if dead. What's it like in the casket? Padded silk."

"Ah? So you construct it all. Must be pretty hard. I see. . . ." Moses sighed.

"It takes practice. You have to feel and not feel, be and not be. You're present and absent both. And one by one the people in your life come and look. Father. Mother. Whoever you loved, or hated."

"And what then." Herzog, wholly absorbed, looked at him more obliquely than ever.

"And then you ask yourself, 'What have you got to say to them now? What do you feel for them?' Now there's nothing to say but what you really thought. And you don't say it to them because you're dead, but only to yourself. Reality, not illusions. Truth, not lies. It's over."

"Face death. That's Heidegger. What comes out of this?"

"As I gaze up from my coffin, at first I can keep my attention on my death, and on my relations with the living, and then other things come in—every time."

"You begin to get tired?"

"No, no. Time after time, I see the same things." Lucas laughed nervously, painfully. "Did we know each other when my father owned the flophouse on West Madison Street?"

"Yes, I used to see you at school."

"When the Depression hit, we had to move into the old hotel ourselves. My father made an apartment on the top story. The Haymarket Theatre was a few doors away, do you remember?"

"The burlesque house? Oh yes, Luke. I used to cut school to watch the bumps and grinds."

"Well, first of all, what I begin to see is the fire that broke out in that building. We were trapped in the loft. My brother and I wrapped up the younger kids in blankets and stood by the windows. Then the hook-and-ladder company came and rescued us. I had my little sister. The firemen took us down, one by one. Last of all was my Aunt Rae. She weighed nearly two hundred pounds. Her dress flew up as the fireman carried her. He was very red in the face from the weight and strain. A great Irish face. And I was standing below and watched her buttocks coming slowly nearer—that tremendous rear part, and the huge cheeks, so pale and helpless."

"And is this what you see when you play dead? A fat-assed old auntie saved from death."

"Don't laugh," said Asphalter, himself grimly laughing. "That's one of the things I see. Another is the burlesque broads from next door. Between turns, they didn't have anything to do. The picture was running—Tom Mix. They got bored in their dressing rooms. So they'd come out in the street and play baseball. They loved it. They were all big hearty cornfed girls, they needed exercise. I'd sit on the curb and watch them play."

"They were in their burlesque costumes?"

"All powdered and rouged. Their hair done up. And their tits heaving as they pitched and batted and ran the bases. They played piggy-move-up—softball. Moses, I swear to you . . ." Asphalter pressed his hands to his bearded cheeks, and his voice shook. His fluid black eyes were bewildered, painfully smiling. Then he drew his chair back, out of the light. Perhaps he was about to cry. I hope he won't, thought Herzog. His heart went out to him.

"Don't feel so bad, Luke. Now listen to me. Maybe I can tell you something about this. At least I can tell you how I see it. A man may say, 'From now on I'm going to speak the truth.' But the truth hears him and runs away and hides before he's even done speaking. There is something funny about the human condition, and civilized intelligence makes fun of its own ideas. This Tina Zokóly has got to be kidding, too."

"I don't think so."

"Then it's the old *memento mori,* the monk's skull on the table, brought up to date. And what good is that? It all goes back to those German existentialists who tell you how good dread is for you, how it saves you from distraction and gives you your freedom and makes you authentic. God is no more. But Death is. That's their story. And we live in a hedonistic world in which happiness is set up on a mechanical model. All you have to do is open your fly and grasp happiness. And so these other theorists introduce the tension of guilt and dread as a corrective. But human life is far subtler than any of its models, even these ingenious German models. Do we need to study *theories* of fear and anguish? This Tina Zokóly is a nonsensical woman. She tells you to practice overkill on yourself, and your intelligence answers her with wit. But you're pushing matters. This is self-ridicule to the degree of anguish. Bitterer and bitterer. Monkeys and buttocks and chorus girls playing piggy-move-up."

"I was hoping we could have a talk about this," said Asphalter.

"Don't abuse yourself too much, Luke, and cook up these fantastic plots against your feelings. I know you're a good soul, with real heartaches. And you believe the world. And the world tells you to look for truth in grotesque combinations. It warns you also to stay away from consolation if you value your intellectual honor. On this theory truth is punishment, and you must take it like a man. It says truth will harrow your soul because your inclination as a poor human thing is to lie and to live by lies. So if you have anything else waiting in your soul to be revealed you'll never learn about it from these people. Do you have to think yourself into a coffin and perform these exercises with death? As soon as thought begins to deepen it reaches death, first thing. Modern philosophers would like to recover the old-fashioned dread of death. The new attitude which makes life a trifle not worth anyone's anguish threatens the heart of civilization. But it isn't a question of dread, or any such words at all. . . . Still, what can thoughtful people and humanists do but struggle toward suitable words? Take me, for instance. I've been writing letters helter-skelter in all directions. More words. I go after reality with language. Perhaps I'd like to change it all into language, to force Madeleine and Gersbach to have a *Conscience*. There's a word for you. I must be trying to keep tight the tensions without which human beings can no longer be called human. If they don't suffer, they've gotten away from me. And I've filled the world with letters to prevent their escape. I want them in human form, and so I conjure up a whole environment and catch them in the middle. I put my whole heart into these constructions. But they are constructions."

"Yes, but you deal with human beings. What have I got to show? Rocco?"

"But let's stick to what matters. I really believe that brotherhood is what makes a man human. If I owe God a human life, this is where I fall down. 'Man liveth not by Self alone but in his brother's face. . . . Each shall behold the Eternal Father and love and joy abound.' When the preachers of dread tell you that others only distract you from metaphysical freedom then you must turn away from them. The real and essential question is one of our employment by other human beings and their employment by us. Without this true employment you never dread death, you cultivate it. And consciousness when it doesn't clearly understand what to live for, what to die for, can only abuse and ridicule itself. As you do with the help of Rocco and Tina Zokóly, as I do by writing impertinent letters. . . . I feel dizzy. Where's that bottle of Cutty Sark? I need a shot."

"You need to go to sleep. You look ready to cave in."

"I don't feel bad at all," said Herzog.

"I've got some things to do, anyway. Go to sleep. I haven't finished grading all my exams."

"I guess I am folding," Moses said. "The bed looks good."

"I'll let you sleep late. Plenty of time," said Asphalter. "Good night, Moses." They shook hands.

AT last he embraced his daughter, and she pressed his cheeks with her small hands and kissed him. Hungry to feel her, to breathe in her childish fragrance, to look in her face, her black eyes, touch her hair, the skin under her dress, he pressed her little bones, stammering, "Junie, sweetie. I've missed you." His happiness was painful. And she with all her innocence and childishness and with the pure, or amorous, instinct of tiny girls, kissed him on the lips, her careworn, busted, germ-carrying father.

Asphalter stood by, smiling but feeling somewhat awkward, his bald scalp perspiring, his new parti-colored beard looking hot. They were on the long gray staircase of the Museum of Science in Jackson Park. Busloads of children were entering, black and white flocks, herded by teachers and parents. The bronze-trimmed glass doors flashed in and out, and all these little bodies, redolent of milk and pee, blessed heads of all hues, shapes, the promise of the world to come, in the eyes of benevolent Herzog, its future good and evil, hurried in and out.

"My sweet June. Papa missed you."

"Poppy!"

"You know, Luke," Herzog spoke out with a burst, his face both happy and twisted. "Sandor Himmelstein told me this kid would forget me. He was thinking of his own Himmelstein breed—guinea pigs, hamsters."

"Herzogs are made of finer clay?" Asphalter put it in the interrogative form. But it was courteous, he meant it kindly. ". . . I can meet you right at this spot at four p.m.," he said.

"Only three and a half hours? Where does she get off! Well, all right, I won't quarrel. I don't want any conflict. There's another day tomorrow."

Once of his units of mental extension swelling and passing, a lengthy aside (Much heartbreak to relinquish this daughter. To become another lustful she-ass? Or a melancholy beauty like Sarah Herzog, destined to bear children ignorant of her soul and her soul's God? Or would humankind find a new path, making his type—he would be glad of that!—obsolete? In New York, after giving a lecture, he had been told by a young executive who came up rapidly, "Professor, Art is for Jews!" Seeing this slender, blond, and violent figure before him, Herzog had only nodded and said, "It used to be usury"), departed with another of those twinges. That's the new realism, he thought. "Luke? Thank you. I'll be here at four. Now don't you spend the day brooding."

Moses carried his daughter into the museum to see the chickens hatching. "Did Marco send you a postcard, baby?"

"Yes. From the camp."

"You know who Marco is?"

"My big brother."

So Madeleine was not trying to estrange her from the Herzogs, whatever course of madness she was running.

"Have you gone down in the coal mine, here in the museum?"

"It scared me."

"Do you want to see the chickies?"

"I seen them."

"Don't you want to see them more?"

"Oh, yes. I like them. Uncle Val took me last week."

"Do I know Uncle Val?"

"Oh, Papa! You fooler." She hugged his neck, snickering.

"Who is he?"

"He's my stepfather, Papa. You *know* it."

"Is that what Mama tells you?"

"He's my stepfather."

"Was he the one who locked you up in the car?"

"Yes."

"And what did you do?"

"I was crying. But not long."

"And do you like Uncle Val?"

"Oh, yes, he's fun. He makes faces. Can you make good faces?"

"Some," he said. "I have too much dignity to make good faces."

"You tell better stories."

"I expect I do, sweetheart."

"About the boy with the stars."

So she remembered his best inventions. Herzog nodded his head, wondering at her, proud of her, thankful. "The boy with all the freckles?"

"They were like the sky."

"Each freckle was just like a star, and he had them all. The Big Dipper, Little Dipper, Orion, the Bear, the Twins, Betelgeuse, the Milky Way. His face had each and every star on it, in the right position."

"Only one star nobody knew."

"They took him to all the astronomers."

"I saw astronomers on television."

"And the astronomers said, 'Pooh, pooh, an interesting coincidence. A little freak.' "

"More. More."

"At last he went to see Hiram Shpitalnik, who was an old old old man, very tiny, with a long beard down to his feet. He lived in a hatbox. And he said, 'You must be examined by *my* grandfather.' "

"He lived in a walnut shell."

"Exactly. And all his friends were bees. The busy bee has no time for sorrow. Great-grandfather Shpitalnik came out of the shell with a telescope, and looked at Rupert's face."

"The boy's name was Rupert."

"Old Shpitalnik had the bees lift him into position, and he looked and said it *was* a real star, a new discovery. He had been watching for that star. . . . Now, here are the chicks." He held the child on the railing, to his left, so that she would not press against the pistol, wrapped in her great-grandfather's rubles. These were in his right breast pocket still.

"They're yellow," she said.

"They keep it hot and bright in there. See that egg wobble? The chick is trying to get out. Soon his bill will go through the shell. Watch."

"Papa, you don't shave at our house any more, why not?"

He must stiffen his resistance to heartache now. A kind of necessary hardness was demanded. Otherwise it was as the savage described the piano, "You fight 'im 'e cry." And this Jewish art of tears must be suppressed. In measured words he answered, "I have my razor in another place. What does Madeleine say?"

"She says you didn't want to live with us any more."

He kept his anger from the child. "Did she? Well, I always want to be with you. I just can't."

"Why?"

"Because I'm a man, and men have to work, and be in the world."

"Uncle Val works. He writes poems and reads them to Mama."

Herzog's sober face brightened. "Splendid." She had to listen to his trash. Bad art and vice hand in hand. "I'm glad to hear it."

"He looks ooky when he says them."

"And does he cry?"

"Oh, yes."

Sentiment and brutality—never one without the other, like fossils and oil. This news is priceless. It's sheer happiness to hear it.

June had bent her head, and held her wrists to her eyes.

"What's the matter darling?"

"Mama said I shouldn't talk about Uncle Val."

"Why?"

"She said you'd be very very angry."

"But I'm not. I'm laughing my head off. All right. We won't talk about him. I promise. Not one word."

An experienced father, he prudently waited until they reached the Falcon before he said, "I have presents for you in the trunk!"

"Oh, Papa—what did you bring!"

Against the clumsy, gray, gaping Museum of Science she looked so fresh, so new (her milk teeth and sparse freckles and big expectant eyes, her fragile neck). And he thought how she would inherit this world of great instruments, principles of physics and applied science. She had the brains for it. He was already intoxicated with pride, seeing another Madame Curie in her. She loved the periscope. They spied on each other from the sides of the car, hiding behind tree trunks and in the arches of the comfort station. Crossing the bridge on the Outer Drive they walked by the lake. He let her take off her shoes and wade, drying her feet afterward in his shirttail, carefully brushing out the sand between her toes. He bought her a box of Cracker Jack which she nibbled on the grass. The dandelions had blown their fuses and were all loose silk; the turf was springy, neither damp as in May nor dry and hard as in August, when the sun would scorch it. The mechanical mower was riding in circles, barbering the slopes, raising a spray of clippings. Lighted from the south the water was a marvelous, fresh heavy daylight blue; the sky rested on the mild burning horizon, clear except toward Gary, where the dark thin pillars of the steel hearths puffed out russet and sulphur streams of smoke. By now the lawns at Ludeyville, uncut for two years, must be simply hay-fields, and local hunters and lovers were breaking in again, most likely, shattering windows, lighting fires.

"I want to go to the aquarium, Papa," said June. "Mama said you should take me."

"Oh, did she? Well, come on then."

The Falcon had grown hot in the sun. He opened the windows to cool it. He had an extraordinary number of keys, by now, and must organize them better in his pockets. There were his New York house keys, the key Ramona had given him, the Faculty Men's Lounge key from the university, and the key to Asphalter's apart-ment, as well as several Ludeyville keys. "You must sit in the back seat, honey. Creep in, now, and pull down your dress because the plastic is very hot." The air from the west was drier than the east air. Herzog's sharp senses detected the difference. In these days of near-delirium and wide-ranging disordered thought, deeper cur-rents of feeling had heightened his perceptions, or made him instill something of his own into his surroundings. As though he painted them with moisture and color taken from his own mouth, his blood, liver, bowels, genitals. In this mingled way, therefore, he was aware of Chicago, familiar ground to him for more than thirty years. And out of its elements, by this peculiar art of his own organs, he created his version of it. Where the thick walls and buckled slabs of pave-ment in the Negro slums exhaled their bad smells. Farther West, the industries; the sluggish South Branch dense with sewage and glittering with a crust of golden slime; the Stockyards, deserted; the tall red slaughterhouses in lonely decay; and then a faintly buzzing dullness of bungalows and scrawny parks; and vast shopping cen-ters; and the cemeteries after these—Waldheim, with its graves for Herzogs past and present; the Forest Preserves for riding parties, Croatian picnics, lovers' lanes, horrible murders; airports; quarries; and, last of all, cornfields. And with this, infinite forms of activity—Reality. Moses had to see reality. Perhaps he was somewhat spared from it so that he might see it better, not fall asleep in its thick em-brace. Awareness was his work; extended consciousness was his line, his business. Vigilance. If he borrowed time to take his tiny daughter to see the fishes he would find a way to make it up to the vigilance-fund. This day was just like—he braced himself and faced it—like the day of Father Herzog's funeral. Then, too, it was flowering weather—roses, magnolias. Moses, the night before, had cried, slept, the air was wickedly perfumed; he had had luxuriant dreams, painful, evil, and rich, interrupted by the rare ecstasy of nocturnal emission—how death dangles freedom before the enslaved instincts: the pitiful sons of Adam whose minds and bodies must answer strange signals. Much of my life has been spent in the effort to live by more coherent ideas. I even know which ones.

"Papa, you must turn here. This is where Uncle Val always turns."

"Okay." He observed in the mirror that the slip had distressed her. She had mentioned Gersbach again. "Hey, Pussycat," he said. "If you say anything about Uncle Val to me, I'll never tell. I'll never ask you any questions about him. Now don't you ever worry about it. It's all silliness."

He had been no older than June when Mother Herzog instructed him to say nothing about that still in Verdun. He remembered the contraption well. Those pipes were beautiful. And the reeking mash. If he was not mistaken, Father Herzog emptied sacks of stale rye bread into the vat. In any case, secrets were not too bad.

"There's nothing wrong with a few secrets," he said.

"I know lots of them." She stood directly behind him in the back seat and stroked his head. "Uncle Val is very nice."

"Why of course he is."

"But I don't like him. He doesn't smell good."

"Ha, ha! Well, we'll get him a bottle of perfume and make him smell terrific."

He held her hand as they mounted the aquarium staircase, feeling himself to be the father whose strength and calm judgment she could trust. The center court of the building, whitened by the skylight, was very warm. The splashing pool and luxuriant plants and soft tropical fishy air forced Moses to take a grip on himself, to keep up his energy.

"What do you want to see first?"

"The big turtles."

They went up and down the obscure gold and green alleys.

"This fast little fish is called the humuhumuu-elee-elee, from Hawaii. This slithering beast is the sting ray and has teeth and venom in its tail. And these are lampreys, related to hagfish, they fasten their sucker mouths on other fish and drink until they kill them. Over there you see the rainbow fish. No turtles in this aisle, but look at those great things at the end. Sharks?"

"I saw the dolphins at Brookfield," said June. "They wear sailor hats, ring a bell. They can dance on their tails and play basketball."

Herzog picked her up and carried her. These children's outings, perhaps because they were pervaded with so much emotion, were always exhausting. Often, after a day with Marco, Moses had to put a cold compress on his eyes and lie down. It seemed his fate to be the visiting father, an apparition who faded in and out of the children's lives. But this peculiar sensitivity about meeting and parting had to be tamed. Such trembling sorrow—he tried to think what term Freud had for it: partial return of repressed traumatic material, ultimately traceable to the death instinct?—should not be imparted to children, not that tremulous lifelong swoon of death. This same emotion, as Herzog the student was aware, was held to be the womb of cities, heavenly as well as earthly, mankind being unable to part with its beloved or its dead in this world or the next. But to Moses E. Herzog as he held his daughter in his arms, looking through aqueous green at the hagfish and smooth sharks with their fanged bellies, this emotion was nothing but tyranny. For the first time he took a different view of the way in which Alexander V. Herzog had run Father Herzog's funeral. No solemnity in the chapel. Shura's portly, golf-tanned friends, bankers and corporation presidents, forming an imposing wall of meat as heavy in the shoulders, hands, and cheeks as they were thin in the hair. Then there was the cortege. City Hall had sent a motorcycle escort in recognition of Shura Herzog's civic importance. The cops ran ahead with screaming sirens, booting cars and trucks aside so that the hearse could speed through lights. No one ever got to Waldheim so fast. Moses said to Shura, "While he lived, Papa had the cops at his back. Now . . ." Helen, Willie, all four children in the limousine, laughed softly at this remark. Then as the coffin was lowered and Moses and the others wept, Shura said to him, "Don't carry on like a goddamn immigrant." I embarrassed him with his golfing friends, the corporation presidents. Maybe I was not entirely in the right. Here he was the good American. I still carry European pollution, am infected by the Old World with feelings like Love—Filial Emotion. Old stuporous dreams.

"There is the turtle!" June shouted. The thing rose from the depths of the tank in its horny breastplate, the beaked head lazy, the eyes with aeons of indifference, the flippers slowly striving, pushing at the glass, the great scales pinkish yellow or, on the back, bearing beautiful lines, black curved plates mimicking the surface tension of water. It trailed a fuzz of parasitic green.

For comparison they went back to the Mississippi River turtles in the pool at the center; their sides were red-straked; they dozed on their logs and paddled in company with catfish over a bottom shaded by ferns, strewn with pennies.

The child had now had enough, and so had her father. "I think we'll go and get you a sandwich. It's lunchtime," he said.

They left the parking lot carefully enough, Herzog later thought. He was a circumspect driver. But getting his Falcon into the main stream of traffic he should perhaps have reckoned with the long curve from the north on which the cars picked up speed. A little Volkswagen truck was on his tail. He touched the brakes, meaning to slow up and let the other driver pass. But the brakes were all too new and responsive. The Falcon stopped short and the small truck struck it from behind and rammed it into a utility pole. June screamed and clutched at his shoulders as he was thrown forward, against the steering wheel. The kid! he thought; but it was not the kid he had to worry about. He knew from her scream that she was not hurt, only frightened. He lay over the wheel, feeling weak, radically weak; his eyes grew dark; he felt that he was losing ground to nausea and numbness. He listened to June's screams but could not turn to her. He notified himself that he was passing out, and he fainted away.

They spread him out on the grass. He heard a locomotive very close—the Illinois Central. And then it seemed somewhat farther off, blundering in the weeds across the Drive. His vision at first was bothered by large blots, but these dwindled presently to iridescent specks. His pants had worked themselves up. He felt a chill in his legs.

"Where's June? Where's my daughter?" He raised himself and saw her between two Negro policemen, looking at him. They had his wallet, the Czarist rubles, and the pistol, of course. There it was. He closed his eyes again. He felt the nausea return as he considered what he had gotten himself into. "Is she all right?"

"She's okay."

"Come here, Junie." He leaned forward and she walked into his arms. As he felt her, kissed her scared face, he had a sharp pain in his ribs. "Papa lay down for a minute. It's nothing." But she had seen him lying on this grass. Just past the new building beyond the Museum. Stretched limp, looking dead, probably, while the cops went through his pockets. His face felt bloodless, hollow, stiff, its sensations intensely reduced, and this frightened him. From the pricking of his hair at the roots he thought it must be turning white all at once. The police were giving him a few minutes to come to himself. The blue light of the squad car flashed, revolving. The driver of the small truck was staring at him, angry. A little beyond, the grackles were walking, feeding, the usual circle of lights working flexibly back and forth about their black necks. Over his shoulder Herzog was aware of the Field Museum. If only I were a mummy in that cellar! he thought.

The cops had him. Their silent looks gave him this information. Because he was holding Junie they waited; they might not be too rough with him just yet. Already stalling for time, he acted more dazed than he really felt. The cops could be very bad, he had seen them at work. But that was in the old days. Perhaps times had changed. There was a new Commissioner. He had sat close to Orlando Wilson at a Narcotics Conference last year. They had shaken hands. Of course it wasn't worth mentioning; anyway, nothing would antagonize these two big Negro cops more than hints of influence. For them, he was part of today's haul, and with his rubles, the gun, he couldn't hope that they would simply let him go. And there was the teal-blue Falcon crumpled against the utilities pole. The traffic rushing by, the road with its blazing cars.

"You Moses?" the older of the two Negroes asked. There it was —that note of deadly familiarity that you heard only when immunity was lost.

"Yes, I'm Moses."

"This your chile?"

"Yes—my little girl."

"You better put your handkercher to your head. You got a little cut, Moses."

"Is that so?" This explained the pricking under his hair. Unable to locate his handkerchief—the scrap of towel—he unknotted his silk tie and folded it, pressed the broad end to his scalp. "Nothing to it," he said. The child had hidden her head in his shoulder. "Sit down by Papa, sweetheart. Sit on the grass right next to me. Papa's head hurts a little." She obeyed. Her docility, her feeling for him, what seemed to him the wise, tender sense of the child, her sympathy, moved him, pressed his guts. He put a protective, wide, eager hand on her back. Sitting forward, he held the tie to his scalp.

"You got the permit for this gun, Moses?" The cop pursed his large lips as he waited for the answer, brushing the small bristles of his mustache upward with his fingernail. The other policeman spoke with the driver of the Volkswagen truck, who was wildly angry. Sharp-faced, his nose sharp and red, he was glaring at Moses, saying, "You're going to take that guy's license away, aren't you?" Moses thought, I'm in bad because of the pistol, and this fellow wants to pour it on. Warned by this indignation, Herzog held his own feelings in.

"I asked you once, I ask you again, Moses, you got a permit?"

"No sir, I haven't."

"Two bullets in here. Loaded weapon, Moses."

"Officer, it was my father's gun. He died, and I was taking it back to Massachusetts." His answers were as brief and patient as he could make them. He knew he would have to repeat his story, over and over.

"What's this money here?"

"Worthless, officer. Like Russian Confederate money. Stage money. Another souvenir."

Not devoid of sympathy, the policeman's face also expressed a fatigued skepticism. He was heavy-lidded, and on his silent, thick mouth there was a sort of smile. Sono's lips had looked a little like this when she questioned him about the other women in his life. Well—the variety of oddities, alibis, inventions, fantasies the police ran into every day . . . Herzog, making his reckonings as intelligently as he could, though he had a heavy weight of responsibility and dread inside him, believed it might not be so easy for this cop to type him. There were labels to fit him, naturally, but a harness cop like this would not be familiar with them. Even now there was possibly some tinge of pride in this reflection, so tenacious was human foolishness. "Lord, let the angels praise thy name. Man is a foolish thing, a foolish thing. Folly and sin play all his game. . . ." Herzog's head ached and he could remember no more verses. He lifted the tie from his scalp. No sense in letting it stick; it would pull away the clot. June had put her head in his lap. He covered her eyes from the sun.

"We have to diagram this accident." The copper in his shiny pants squatted beside Herzog. From his fat, bulging hips his own gun hung low. Its brown butt of cross-hatched metal and the cartridge belt looked very different from Father Herzog's big, clumsy Cherry Street revolver. "I don't see the title of this Falcon, here."

The small car was staved in at both ends, the hood gaping like a mussel shell. The engine itself could not be damaged much; no fluids had trickled out. "It's rented. I picked it up at O'Hare. The papers are in the glove compartment," said Herzog.

"We got to get these facts, here." The policeman opened a folder and began to mark the thick paper of a printed form with his yellow pencil. "You come out of this parking lot—what speed?"

"I was creeping. Five, eight miles an hour—I just nosed out."

"You didn't see this fellow coming?"

"No. The curve was hiding him, I suppose. I don't know. But he was right on my bumper when I got into the lane." He bent forward, trying to change his position and ease the pain in his side. He had already arranged with his mind to disregard it. He stroked June's cheek. "At least she wasn't hurt," he said.

"I just lifted her out the back window. The door got jammed. I looked her over. She's okay." The mustached Negro frowned, as if to make plain that he did not owe Herzog—a man with a loaded gun—any explanations whatever. For it was the possession of this clumsy horse pistol with two cartridges, not the accident, that would be the main charge against him.

"I'd have blown my brains out if anything happened to her."

The squatting cop, to judge by his silence, had no concern with what Moses might have done. To speak of any use of the revolver, even against himself, was not very smart. But he was still somewhat stunned and dizzy, brought down, as he pictured it, from his strange, spiraling flight of the last few days; and the shock, not to say desperation, of this sudden drop. His head still swam. He decided that this foolishness must stop, or things would go even worse. Running to Chicago to protect his daughter, he almost killed her. Coming to offset the influence of Gersbach, and to give her the benefit of his own self—man and father, et cetera—what did he do but bang into a pole. And then the child saw him dragged out fainting, cut on the head, the revolver and the rubles sliding from his pocket. No, weakness, or sickness, with which he had copped a plea all his life (alternating with arrogance), his method of preserving equilibrium—the Herzog gyroscope—had no further utility. He seemed to have come to the end of *that*.

The driver of the Volkswagen utilities truck, in a green jumper, was giving his account of the accident. Moses tried to make out the letters stitched in yellow thread over his pocket. Was he from the gas company? No telling. He was laying the whole guilt on him, of course. It was very inventive—creative. The story deepened every moment. Oh, the grandeur of self-justification, thought Herzog. What genius it brought out in these mortals, even the most red-nosed. The ripples in this fellow's scalp followed a different pattern from the furrows in his forehead. You could make out his former hairline by this means. A certain number of skimpy hairs remained.

"He just cut out in front of me. No signal, nothing. Whyn't you give him the drunk test? That's drunken driving."

"Well, now, Harold," the older Negro said. "What was your speed?"

"Why, Jesus! I was way below the limit."

"A lot of these company drivers like to give private cars the business," said Herzog.

"First he cut in front, then he slammed his brake."

"You mashed him pretty hard. That means you were crowdin' him."

"That's right. Looks like to me . . ." The senior policeman pointed two, three, five times with the rubber tip of his pencil before he spoke another word; he made you consider the road (there Herzog seemed to see the rushing of the Gadarene swine, multicolored and glittering, not yet come to their cliff). "Looks to me, you were pushin' him, Harold. He couldn't get in the next lane so he thought he'd slow and give you a chance to pass. Hit the brake too hard, and you clobbered him. I see from the staple marks on your license you already got two moving violations."

"That's right, and that's why I've been extra careful."

God keep this anger from burning up your scalp, Harold. A very unbecoming red color, and all ridges, like a dog's palate.

"Looks like to me, if you hadn't been on top of him, you wouldn't have hit him so flush. You'd 'a tried to turn, and got him on the right. Got to write you a ticket, Harold."

Then, to Moses, he said, "I got to take you in. You gonna be booked for misdemeanor."

"This old gun?"

"Loaded . . ."

"Why, it's nothing. I have no record—never been booked."

They waited for him to get to his feet. Sharp-nosed, the Volkswagen-truck driver knitted his ginger brows at him and, under his red, angry stare, Herzog stood and then picked up his daughter. She lost her barrette as he lifted her. Her hair came free beside her cheeks, quite long. He could not bend again to hunt for the tortoise-shell clip. The door of the squad car, parked on a slope, opened wide for him. He could now feel for himself what it was like to be in custody. No one was robbed, no one had died. Still he felt the heavy, deadly shadow lying on him. "And this is just like you, Herzog," he said to himself. He could not escape self-accusation. For this big, nickel-plated pistol, whatever he had vaguely intended yesterday to do with it, he should have left today in the flight bag under Asphalter's sofa. When he had put on his jacket in the morning and felt the awkward weight on his chest, then and there he might have stopped being quixotic. For he was not a quixote, was he? A quixote imitated great models. What models did he imitate? A quixote was a Christian, and Moses E. Herzog was no Christian. This was the post-quixotic, post-Copernican U.S.A., where a mind freely poised in space might discover relationships utterly unsuspected by a seventeenth-century man sealed in his smaller universe. There lay his twentieth-century advantage. Only—they walked over the grass toward the wheeling blue light—in nine-tenths of his existence he was exactly what others were before him. He took the revolver (his purpose as intense as it was diffuse) because he was his father's son. He was almost certain Jonah Herzog, afraid of the police, of revenue inspectors, or of hoodlums, could not stay away from these enemies. He pursued his terrors and challenged them to blast him (Fear: could he take it? Shock: would he survive?). Ancient Herzogs with their psalms and their shawls and beards would never have touched a revolver. Violence was for the goy. But they were gone, vanished, archaic men. Jonah, for a buck, had bought a gun, and Moses, this morning, had thought, "Oh, hell—why not," and, buttoning the jacket, went down to his car.

"What are we going to do about this Falcon?" he asked the police. He stopped. But they pushed him on, saying, "Don't you worry about that. We'll take care of it."

He saw the tow truck coming up with its crane and hook. It too had the blue light spinning above its cab.

"Listen," he said, "I have to get this kid home."

"She'll get home. She ain't in no danger."

"But I'm supposed to turn her over at four."

"You got almost two hours."

"But isn't this going to take longer than an hour? I'd certainly appreciate it if you'd let me look after her first."

"Get goin', Moses. . . ." Grimly kind, the senior patrolman moved him along.

"She hasn't eaten lunch."

"You in worse shape than she is."

"Come on, now."

He shrugged and crumpled the stained necktie, letting it drop at the roadside. The cut was not serious; it had stopped bleeding. He handed June in, and when he was seated in the fiery heat of the blue plastic rear, he took her on his lap. Is this, by chance, the reality you have been looking for, Herzog, in your earnest Herzog way? Down in the ranks with other people—ordinary life? By yourself you can't determine which reality is real? Any philosopher can tell you it's based, like all rational judgment, on common proof. Only this particular way of doing it was perverse. But it was only human. You burn the house to roast the pig. It was the way humankind always roasted pigs.

He explained to June, "We're going for a ride, darling." She nodded and was silent. Her face was tearless, clouded, and this was far worse. It hurt him. It tore his heart. As if Madeleine and

Gersbach weren't enough, *he* had to come running with his eager love and excitement, hugging, kissing, periscopes, anxious emotions. She had to see him bleeding from the head. His eyes smarted, and he shut them with thumb and forefinger. The doors slammed. The motor gave a raw snort and raced smoothly, and the dry rich summer air began to flow in, flavored with exhaust gas. It aggravated his nausea like a forced draft. When the car left the lake front he opened his eyes on the yellow ugliness of 22nd Street. He recognized the familiar look of summer damnation. Chicago! He smelled the hot reek of chemicals and inks coming from the Donnelly plant.

She had watched the cops going through his pockets. At her age he had seen everything vividly. And everything was beautiful or frightful. He was spattered forever with things that bled or stank. He wondered if she must remember just as keenly. As he remembered chicken slaughtering, as he remembered those fiery squawks when the hens were dragged from the lath coops, the shit and sawdust and heat and fowl-musk, and the birds tossed when their throats were cut to bleed to death head down in tin racks, their claws going, going, working, working on the metal shield. Yes, that was on Roy Street next to the Chinese laundry where the vermilion tickets fluttered, lettered with black symbols. And this was near the lane—Herzog's heart began to pound; he felt feverish—where he was overtaken by a man one dirty summer evening. The man clapped his hand over his mouth from the back. He hissed something to him as he drew down his pants. His teeth were rotten and his face stubbled. And between the boy's thighs this red skinless horrible thing passed back and forth, back and forth, until it burst out foaming. The dogs in the back yards jumped against the fences, they barked and snarled, choking on their saliva—the shrieking dogs, while Moses was held at the throat by the crook of the man's arm. He knew he might be killed. The man might strangle him. How did he know! He guessed. So he simply stood there. Then the man buttoned his army coat and said, "I'm going to give you a nickel. But I have to change this dollar." He showed him the bill and told him to wait where he was. Moses watched him recede in the mud of the lane, stooping and gaunt in the long coat, walking swiftly, with bad feet; bad feet, evil feet, Moses remembered; almost running. The dogs stopped barking, and he waited, afraid to stir. At last he fetched up his wet pants and went home.

He sat on the stoop awhile and then turned up at supper as if nothing had happened. Nothing! He washed his hands at the sink with Willie and came to the table. He ate his soup.

And later when he was in the hospital and the good Christian lady came, the one with the button shoes and the hatpin like a trolley-rod, the soft voice and grim looks, she asked him to read for her from the New Testament, and he opened and read, "Suffer the little children to come unto me." Then she turned to another place, and it said, "Give and it shall be given unto you. Good measure . . . shall men give into your bosom."

Well, there is a piece of famous advice, grand advice even if it is German, to forget what you can't bear. The strong can forget, can shut out history. Very good! Even if it is self-flattery to speak of strength—these aesthetic philosophers, they take a posture, but power sweeps postures away. Still, it's true you can't go on transposing one nightmare into another, Nietzsche was certainly right about that. The tender-minded must harden themselves. Is this world nothing but a barren lump of coke? No, no, but what sometimes seems a system of prevention, a denial of what every human being knows. I love my children, but I am the world to them, and bring them nightmares. I had this child by my enemy. And I love her. The sight of her, the odor of her hair, this minute, makes me tremble with love. Isn't it mysterious how I love the child of my enemy? But a man doesn't need happiness for *himself*. No, he can put up with any amount of torment—with recollections, with his own familiar evils, despair. And this is the unwritten history of man, his unseen, negative accomplishment, his power to do without gratification for himself provided there is something great, something into which his being, and all beings, can go. He does not need meaning as long as such intensity has scope. Because then it is self-evident; it *is* meaning.

But all this has got to stop. By *this* he meant such things as this ride in the squad car. His filial idea (practically Chinese) of carrying an ugly, useless revolver. To hate, to be in a position to do something about it. Hatred is self-respect. If you want to hold your head up among people . . .

Here was South State Street; here movie distributors used to hang their garish posters: Tom Mix plunging over a cliff; now it's only a smooth empty street where they sell glassware to bars. But what is the philosophy of this generation? Not God is dead, that point was passed long ago. Perhaps it should be stated Death is God. This generation thinks—and this is its thought of thoughts—that nothing faithful, vulnerable, fragile can be durable or have any true power. Death waits for these things as a cement floor waits for a dropping light bulb. The brittle shell of glass loses its tiny vacuum with a burst, and that is that. And this is how we teach metaphysics on each other. "You think history is the history of loving hearts? You fool! Look at these millions of dead. Can you pity them, feel for them? You can nothing! There were too many. We burned them to ashes, we buried them with bulldozers. History is the history of cruelty, not love, as soft men think. We have experimented with every human capacity to see which is strong and admirable and have shown that none is. There is only practicality. If the old God exists he must be a murderer. But the one true god is Death. This is how it is—without cowardly illusions." Herzog heard this as if it were being spoken slowly inside his head. His hand was wet and he released June's arm. Perhaps what had made him faint was not the accident but the premonition of such thoughts. The nausea was only apprehension, excitement, the unbearable intensity of these ideas.

The car stopped. As if he had come to police headquarters in a rocking boat, over the water, he wavered when he got out on the sidewalk. Proudhon says, "God is *the* evil." But after we search in the entrails of world revolution for *la foi nouvelle,* what happens? The victory of death, not of rationality, not of rational faith. Our own murdering imagination turns out to be the great power, our human imagination which starts by accusing God of murder. At the bottom of the whole disaster lies the human being's sense of a grievance, and with this I want nothing more to do. It's easier not to exist altogether than accuse God. Far more simple. Cleaner. But no more of that!

They handed his daughter out to him and escorted them to the elevator, which seemed roomy enough for a squadron. Two men who had been pinched—two other men in custody—went up with him. This was 11th and State. He remembered it. Dreadful here. Armed men came in, got out. As he was ordered, he followed the stout Negro policeman with the huge hands and wide hips down the corridor. Others walked behind him. He would need a lawyer and he thought, naturally, of Sandor Himmelstein. He laughed to think what Sandor would say. Sandor himself used police methods, clever psychology, the same as in the Lubianka, the same the world over. First he emphasized the brutal, then when he got the desired results he relaxed, could afford to be nicer. His words were memorable. He had screamed that he would drop from the case and let the shysters take Moses over, lock him up back and front, close his mouth, shut his bowels, put a meter on his nose and charge him by the breath. Yes, yes, those were unforgettable words, the words of the teacher of Reality. They were indeed. "You'll be glad to think of your death, then. You'll step into your coffin as if it were a new sports car." And then, "I'll leave my wife a rich widow, not too old to screw around, either." This he often repeated. It amused Herzog, now. Flushed, grimy, his shirt blood-spotted, he thought of it, grinning. I shouldn't look down on old Sandor for being so tough. This is his personal, brutal version of the popular outlook, the American way of life. And what has my way been? I love little pussy, her coat is so warm, and if I don't hurt her she'll do me no harm, which represents the childish side of the same creed, from which men are wickedly awakened, and then become snarling realists. Get smart, sucker! Or Tante Taube's version of innocent realism: "*Gottseliger* Kaplitzky took care on everything. I never even looked." But Tante Taube was canny as well as sweet. Between oblivion and oblivion, the things we do and the things we say . . . But now he and June had been brought into a big but close room, and he was being booked by another Negro policeman, a sergeant. He was well along in years, smoothly wrinkled. His creases were extruded, not internal. His color was dark yellow, Negro gold. He conferred with the arresting policeman and then looked at the gun, took out the two bullets, whispered more questions to the cop in shiny pants who bent down to whisper secretly.

"Okay, you," he then said to Moses. He put on his Ben Franklin spectacles, two colonial tablets in thin gold frames. He took up his pen.

"Name?"

"Herzog—Moses."

"Middle initial?"

"E. Elkanah."

"Address?"

"Not living in Chicago."

The sergeant, fairly patient, said again, "Address?"

"Ludeyville, Mass., and New York City. Well, all right, Ludeyville, Massachusetts. No street number."

"This your child?"

"Yes, sir. My little daughter June."

"Where does she live?"

"Here in the city, with her mother, on Harper Avenue."

"You divorced?"

"Yes, sir. I came to see the child."

"I see. You want to put her down?"

"No, officer—sergeant," he corrected himself, smiling agreeably.

"You're bein' booked, Moses. You weren't drunk were you? Did you have a drink today?"

"I had one last night, before I went to sleep. Nothing today. Do you want me to take an alcohol test?"

"It won't be necessary. There's no traffic charge against you. We're booking you on account of this gun."

Herzog pulled down his daughter's dress.

"It's just a souvenir. Like the money."

"What kind of dough is this?"

"It's Russian, from World War I."

"Just empty your pockets, Moses. Put your stuff down so's I can check it over."

Without protest, he laid down his money, his notebooks, pens, the scrap of handkerchief, his pocket comb, and his keys.

"Seems to me you've got a mess of keys, Moses."

"Yes, sir, but I can identify them all."

"That's okay. There's no law against keys, exceptin' if you're a burglar."

"The only Chicago key is this one with the red mark on it. It's the key to my friend Asphalter's apartment. He's supposed to meet me at four o'clock, by the Rosenwald Museum. I've got to get her to him."

"Well, it ain't four, and you ain't goin' anywhere yet."

"I'd like to phone and head him off. Otherwise, he'll stand waiting."

"Well, now, Moses, why ain't you bringin' the kid straight back to her mother?"

"You see . . . we're not on speaking terms. We've had too many scraps."

"Appears to me you might be scared of her."

Herzog was briefly resentful. The remark was calculated to provoke him. But he couldn't afford to be angry now. "No, sir, not exactly."

"Then maybe she's scared of you."

"This is how we arranged it, with a friend to go between. I haven't seen the woman since last autumn."

"Okay, we'll call your buddy and the kid's mama, too."

Herzog exclaimed, "Oh, don't call her!"

"No?" The sergeant gave him an odd smile, and rested for a moment in his chair as if he had gotten from him what he wanted. "Sure, we'll bring her down here and see what she's got to say. If she's got a complaint in against you, why, it's worse than just illegal possession of firearms. We'll have you on a bad charge, then."

"There isn't any complaint, sergeant. You can check that in the files without making her come all this way. I'm the support of this child, and never miss a check. That's all Mrs. Herzog can tell you."

"Who'd you buy this revolver from?"

There it was again, the natural insolence of the cops. He was being goaded. But he kept himself steady.

"I didn't buy it. It belonged to my father. That and the Russian rubles."

"You're just sentimental?"

"That's right. I'm a sentimental s.o.b. Call it that."

"You sentimental about these here, too?" He tapped each of the bullets, one, two. "All right, we'll make those phone calls. Here, Jim, write the names and numbers."

He spoke to the copper who had brought Herzog in. He had been standing by, fat-cheeked, teasing the bristles of his mustache with his nail, pursing his lips.

"You may as well take my address book, the red one there. Bring it back, please. My friend's name is Asphalter."

"And the other name's Herzog," said the sergeant. "On Harper Avenue, ain't it?"

Moses nodded. He watched the heavy fingers turning the pages of his Parisian leather address book with its scribbles and blots. "It'll put me in bad if you notify the child's mother," he said, making a last attempt to persuade the sergeant. "Why wouldn't it be the same to you if my friend Asphalter came here?"

"Go on, Jim."

The Negro marked the places with red pencil, and went. Moses made a special effort to keep a neutral look—no defiance, no special pleading, nothing of the slightest personal color. He remembered that he once believed in the appeal of a direct glance, driving aside differences of position, accident, one human being silently opening his heart to another. The recognition of essence by essence. He smiled inwardly at this. Sweet dreams, those! If he tried looking into his eyes, the sergeant would throw the book at him. So Madeleine was coming. Well, let her come. Perhaps that was what he wanted after all, a chance to confront her. Straight-nosed and pale, he looked intently at the floor. June changed her position in his arms, stirring the pain in his ribs. "Papa's sorry, sweetheart," he said. "Next time we'll go see the dolphins. Maybe the sharks were bad luck."

"You can sit down if you want," said the sergeant. "You look a little weak in the legs, Moses."

"I'd like to phone my brother to send his lawyer. Unless I don't need a lawyer. If I have to post a bond . . ."

"You'll have to post one, but I can't say how big, yet. Plenty of bondsmen settin' here." He motioned with the back of the hand, or with a wag of his wrist, and Moses turned and saw all sorts of people ranged behind him, along the walls. In fact, there were two men, he now noticed, loitering near, bondsmen by their natty appearance. He neutrally recognized that they were sizing him up as a risk. They had already seen his plane ticket, his keys, pens, rubles, and his wallet. His own car, wrecked on the Drive, would have secured a small bond. But a rented car? A man from out of state, in a dirty seersucker, no necktie? He didn't look good for a few hundred bucks. If it's no more than that, he reflected, I can probably swing it without bothering Will, or Shura. Some fellows always make a nice impression. I never had that ability. Due to my feelings. A passionate heart, a bad credit risk. Asked to make this practical judgment on myself, I wouldn't make it any differently.

It came back to him how he used to be banished to left field when sides were chosen in the sand lot, and when the ball came and he missed it because he was musing about something everyone would cry out, *"Hey! Ikey-Moe. Butterfingers! Fucky-knuckles! You lookin' at the butterflies? Ikey-Fishbones. Fishbones!"* Although silent, he participated in the derision.

His hands were clasped about his daughter's heart, which was beating quickly and lightly.

"Now, Moses, why you been carryin' a loaded gun. To shoot somebody?"

"Of course not. And, please, sergeant, I don't like the kid to hear such things."

"You the one that brought it along, not me. Maybe you just wanted to scare somebody. You sore at somebody?"

"No, sergeant, I was only going to make a paperweight of it. I forgot to take out the bullets, but that's because I don't know much about guns so it didn't occur to me. Will you let me make a phone call?"

"By and by. I ain't ready to. Sit down while I take care of other business. You sit and wait for the kid's mama to come."

"Could I get a container of milk for her?"

"Give Jim, here, two bits. He'll fetch it."

"With a straw, eh, June? You'd like to drink it with a straw." She nodded and Herzog said, "Please, a straw with it, if you don't mind."

"Papa?"

"Yes, June."

"You didn't tell me about the most-most."

For an instant he did not remember. "Ah," he said, "you mean that club in New York where people are the most of everything."

"That's the story."

She sat between his knees on the chair. He tried to make more room for her. "There's this association that people belong to. They're the most of every type. There's the hairiest bald man, and the baldest hairy man."

"The fattest thin lady."

"And the thinnest fat woman. The tallest dwarf and the smallest giant. They're all in it. The weakest strong man, and the strongest weak man. The stupidest wise man and the smartest blockhead. Then they have things like crippled acrobats, and ugly beauties."

"And what do they do, Papa?"

"On Saturday night they have a dinner-dance. They have a contest."

"To tell each other apart."

"Yes, sweetheart. And if you can tell the hairiest bald man from the baldest hairy man, you get a prize."

Bless her, she enjoyed her father's nonsense, and he must amuse her. She leaned her head on his shoulder and smiled, drowsy, with small teeth.

The room was hot and close. Herzog, sitting off to one side, took in the case of the two men who had come up in the elevator with him. A pair of plainclothesmen giving testimony—the Vice Squad, he soon realized. They had brought a woman too. He hadn't noticed her before. A prostitute? Yes, obviously, for all her respectable middle-class airs. In spite of his own troubles, Herzog looked on and found himself listening keenly. The plainclothesman was saying, "They were having a hassle in this woman's room."

"Sip your milk, June dear," said Herzog. "Is it cold? Drink it nice and easy, darling."

"You heard them from the corridor?" said the sergeant. "What's it about?"

"This fellow was yelling about a pair of earrings."

"What about earrings? The ones she's wearing? Where'd you get them?"

"I bought them. From him. It was just business."

"On payments, which you didn't make."

"You were gettin' paid."

"He was takin' it out in trade. I see," the sergeant said.

"The way it figures," said the plainclothesman, explaining with a heavy, dull face, "he brought this other fellow along and after she did the trick he tried to get the ten bucks for himself because she owed him on the earrings. She wouldn't give up the money."

"Sergeant!" the second man pleaded. "What do I know! I'm from out of town."

From the town of Nineveh, with those twisting swarthy brows. Moses watched with interest, whispering occasionally to the child to divert her attention. The woman looked oddly familiar, despite her smeary makeup, emerald eye shadow, dyed hair, the thickening pride of her nose. He wanted very much to ask her a question. Had she attended McKinley High School? Did she sing in the Glee Club? Me too! Don't you remember? Herzog? Herzog who gave the class oration—who spoke on Emerson?

"Papa, the milk won't come."

"Because you've chewed the straw. Let's get the kinks out of it."

"We got to get out of here, sergeant," said the jewel salesman. "We got people waiting for us."

The wives! thought Herzog. The wives were waiting!

"You two fellows related?"

The jewel salesman said, "He's my brother-in-law, just visiting from Louisville."

The wives, one of them a sister, were waiting. And he, too, Herzog, was waiting, light-headed with anticipation. Could this really be Carlotta from the Glee Club who sang the contralto solo in "Once More with Joy" (from Wagner)? It was not impossible. Look at her now. Why would anyone want to give a broad like this a bang? Why! He knew well enough why. Look at the heavy veins in her legs, and look at those breasts, huddled together. They looked as if they had been washed but not ironed. And that slightly herring-eyed look, and her fat mouth. But he knew why. Because she had dirty ways, that was why. Lewd knowledge.

At this moment Madeleine arrived. She came in, saying, "Where is my child . . . !" Then she saw June on Herzog's lap and crossed the room quickly. "Come here to me, baby!" She lifted the milk container and put it aside, and took up the girl in her arms. Herzog felt the blood beating in his eardrums, and a great pressure at the back of the head. It was necessary that Madeleine should see him, but her look was devoid of intimate recognition. Coldly she turned from him, her brow twitching. "Is the child all right?" she said.

The sergeant motioned to the Vice Squad to make way. "She's fine. If she had even a scratch on her we'd have taken her to

Michael Reese." Madeleine examined June's arms, her legs, felt her with nervous hands. The sergeant beckoned to Moses. He came forward, and he and Mady faced each other across the desk.

She wore a light blue linen suit and her hair fell loose behind her. The word to describe her conduct was *masterful*. Her heels had made a commanding noise clearly audible in this buzzing room. Herzog took a long look at her blue-eyed, straight, Byzantine profile, the small lips, the chin that pressed on the flesh beneath. Her color was deep, a sign with her that consciousness was running high. He thought he could make out a certain thickening in her face—incipient coarseness. He hoped so. It was only right that some of Gersbach's grossness should rub off on her. Why shouldn't it? He observed that she was definitely broader behind. He imagined what clutching and rubbing was the cause of that. Uxorious business—but that was not the right word. . . . Amorous.

"Is this the girl's daddy, lady?"

Madeleine still refused to grant him a look of recognition. "Yes," she said, "I divorced him. Not long ago."

"Does he live in Massachussetts?"

"I don't know where he lives. It's none of my business."

Herzog marveled at her. He could not help admiring the perfection of her self-control. She never hesitated. When she took the milk from Junie she knew precisely where to drop the container, though she had been only an instant in the room. By now she had certainly made an inventory of all the objects on the desk, including the rubles, and the gun, of course. She had never seen it, but she could identify the Ludeyville keys by the round magnetic clasp of the ring, and she would realize the pistol belonged to him. He knew her ways so well, all her airs, the patrician style, the tic of her nose, the crazy clear hauteur of the eyes. As the sergeant questioned her, Moses, in his slightly dazed but intense way, unable to restrain associations, wondered whether she still gave off those odors of feminine secretions—the dirty way she had with her. That personal sweet and sour fragrance of hers, and her fire-blue eyes, her spiky glances and her small mouth ready with any wickedness would never again have the same power over him. Still, it gave him a headache merely to look at her. The pulses in his skull were quick and regular, like the tappets of an engine beating in their film of dark oil. He saw her with great vividness—the smoothness of her breast, bared by the square-cut dress, the smoothness of her legs, Indian brown. Her face, especially the forehead, was altogether too smooth, too glabrous for his taste. The whole burden of her severity was carried there. She had what the French called *le front bombé;* in other terms, a pedomorphic forehead. Ultimately unknowable, the processes behind it. See, Moses? We don't know one another. Even that Gersbach, call him any name you like, charlatan, psychopath, with his hot phony eyes and his clumsy cheeks, with the folds. He was unknowable. And I myself, the same. But hard ruthless action taken against a man is the assertion by evildoers that he is fully knowable. They put me down, ergo they claimed final knowledge of Herzog. They *knew* me! And I hold with Spinoza (I hope he won't mind) that to demand what is impossible for any human being, to exercise power where it can't be exercised, is tyranny. Excuse me, therefore, sir and madam, but I reject your definitions of me. Ah, this Madeleine is a strange person, to be so proud but not well wiped—so beautiful but distorted by rage—such a mixed mind of pure diamond and Woolworth glass. And Gersbach who sucked up to me. For the symbiosis of it. Symbiosis and trash. And she, as sweet as cheap candy, and just as reminiscent of poison as chemical sweet acids. But I make no last judgment. That's for them, not me. I came to do harm, I admit. But the first bloodshed was mine, and so I'm out of this now. Count me out. Except in what concerns June. But for the rest, I withdraw from the whole scene as soon as I can. Good-by to all.

"Well, he give you a hard time?" Herzog who had been listening subliminally heard the sergeant put this question.

He said tersely to Madeleine, "Watch it, if you please. Let's not have unnecessary trouble."

She ignored this. "He bothered me, yes."

"He make any threats?"

Herzog waited, tense, for her reply. She would consider the support money—the rent. She was canny, a superbly cunning, very canny woman. But there was also the violence of her hatred, and that hatred had a fringe of insanity.

"No, not directly to me. I haven't seen him since last October."

"To who, then?" The sergeant pressed her.

Madeleine evidently would do what she could to weaken his

position. She was aware that her relations with Gersbach offered grounds for a custody suit and she would therefore make the most of his present weakness—his idiocy. "His psychiatrist," she said, "saw fit to warn me."

"Saw fit! Of what!" said Herzog.

Still she spoke only to the sergeant. "He said he was concerned. Doctor Edvig is his name if you want to talk to him. He felt it necessary to advise me . . ."

"Edvig is a sucker—he's a fool," said Herzog.

Madeleine's color was very high, her throat flushed, like pink—like rose quartz, and the curious tinge had come into her eyes. He knew what this moment was to her—happiness! Ah, yes, he said to himself, Ikey-Fishbones has dropped another pop fly in left field. The other team is scoring—clearing all bases. She was making brilliant use of error.

"Do you recognize this gun?" The sergeant held it in his yellow palm, turning it over with delicate fingers like a fish—a perch.

The radiance of her look as it rested on the gun was deeper than any sexual expression he had ever seen on her face. "It's his, isn't it?" she said. "The bullets, too?" He recognized the hard clear look of joy in her eyes. Her lips were pressed shut.

"He had it on him. Do you know it?"

"No, but I'm not surprised."

Moses was watching June now. Her face was clouded again; she seemed to frown.

"Did you ever file a complaint against Moses, here?"

"No," said Mady. "I didn't actually do that." She took a sharp breath. She was about to plunge into something.

"Sergeant," said Herzog. "I told you there was no complaint. Ask her if I've ever missed a single support check."

Madeleine said, "I did give his photograph to the Hyde Park police."

He warned her that she was going too far. "Madeleine!" he said.

"Shut it up, Moses," said the sergeant. "What was that for, lady?"

"In case he prowled around the house. To alert them."

Herzog shook his head, partly at himself. He had made the kind of mistake today that belonged to an earlier period. As of today it was no longer characteristic. But he had to pay an earlier reckoning. When will you catch up with yourself! he asked himself. When will that day come!

"Did he ever prowl?"

"He was never seen, but I know damn well he did. He's jealous and a troublemaker. He has a terrible temper."

"You never signed a complaint, though?"

"No. But I expect to be protected from any sort of violence."

Her voice went up sharply, and as she spoke, Herzog saw the sergeant take a new look at her, as if he were beginning to make out her haughty peculiarities at last. He picked up the Ben Franklin glasses with the tablet-shaped lenses. "There ain't going to be any violence, lady."

Yes, Moses thought, he's beginning to see how it is. "I never intended to use that gun except to hold papers down," he said.

Madeleine now spoke to Herzog for the first time, pointing with a rigid finger to the two bullets and looking him in the eyes. "One of those was for me, wasn't it!"

"You think so? I wonder where you get such ideas? And who was the other one for?" He was quite cool as he said this, his tone was level. He was doing all he could to bring out the hidden Madeleine, the Madeleine he knew. As she stared at him her color receded and her nose began to move very slightly. She seemed to realize that she must control her tic and the violence of her stare. But by noticeable degrees her face became very white, her eyes smaller, stony. He believed he could interpret them. They expressed a total will that he should die. This was infinitely more than ordinary hatred. It was a vote for his nonexistence, he thought. He wondered whether the sergeant was able to see this. "Well, who do you think that second imaginary shot was for?"

She said no more to him, only continued to stare in the same way.

"That'll be all now, lady. You can take your child and go."

"Good-by, June," said Moses. "You go home now. Papa'll see you soon. Give us a kiss, now, on the cheek." He felt the child's lips. Over her mother's shoulder, June reached out and touched him. "God bless you." He added, as Madeleine strode away, "I'll be back."

"I'll finish bookin' you now, Moses."

"I've got to post bond? How much?"

"Three hundred. American, not this stuff."

"I wish you'd let me make a call."

As the sergeant silently directed him to take one of his own dimes, Moses still had the time to note what a powerful police-face he had. He must have Indian blood—Cherokee, perhaps, or Osage; an Irish ancestor or two. His sallow gold skin with heavy seams descending, the austere nose and prominent lips for impassivity, and the many separate, infinitesimal gray curls on his scalp for dignity. His rugged fingers pointed to the phone booth.

Herzog was tired, dragged out, as he dialed his brother, but far from downcast. For some reason he believed he had done well. He was running true to form, yes; more mischief; and Will would have to bail him out. Still, he was not at all heavy-hearted but, on the contrary, felt rather free. Perhaps he was too tired to be glum. That may have been it, after all—the metabolic wastes of fatigue (he was fond of these physiological explanations; this one came from Freud's essay on Mourning and Melancholia) made him temporarily light-hearted, even gay.

"Yes."

"Will Herzog in?"

Each recognized the other's voice.

"Mose!" said Will.

Herzog could do nothing about the feelings stirred by hearing Will. They came to life suddenly at hearing the old tone, the old name. He loved Will, Helen, even Shura, though his millions had made him remote. In the confinement of the metal booth the sweat burst out instantly on his neck.

"Where've you been, Mose? The old woman called last night. I couldn't sleep afterwards. Where are you?"

"Elya," said Herzog, using his brother's family name, "don't worry. I haven't done anything serious, but I'm down at Eleventh and State."

"At Police Headquarters?"

"Just a minor traffic accident. No one hurt. But they're holding me for three hundred bucks bond, and I haven't got the money on me."

"For heaven's sake, Mose. Nobody's seen you since last summer. We've been worried sick. I'll be right down."

He waited in the cell with two other men. One was drunk and

sleeping in his soiled skivvies. The other was a Negro boy, not old enough to shave. He wore a fawn-colored expensive suit and brown alligator shoes. Herzog said hello, but the boy chose not to answer. He stuck to his own misery, and looked away. Moses was sorry for him. He leaned against the bars, waiting. The wrong side of the bars—he felt it with his cheek. And here were the toilet bowl, the bare metal bunk, and the flies on the ceiling. This, Herzog realized, was not the sphere of *his* sins. He was merely passing through. Out in the streets, in American society, that was where he did his time. He sat down calmly on the bunk. Of course, he thought, he'd leave Chicago immediately, and he'd come back only when he was ready to do June good, genuine good. No more of this hectic, heart-rent, theatrical window-peering; no more collision, fainting, you-fight-'im-'e-cry encounters, confrontations. The drone of trouble coming from the cells and corridors, the bad smell of headquarters, the wretchedness of faces, the hand that turned the key of no better hope than the hand of this stuporous sleeper in his urine-stained underpants—the man who has eyes, nostrils, ears, let him hear, smell, see. The man who has intellect, heart, let him consider.

Sitting as comfortably as the pain in his ribs would permit, Herzog even jotted a few memoranda to himself. They were not very coherent or even logical, but they came quite naturally to him. This was how Moses E. Herzog worked, and he wrote on his knee with cheerful eagerness, *Clumsy, inexact machinery of civil peace. Paleotechnic, as the man would say. If a common primal crime is the origin of social order, as Freud, Róheim et cetera believe, the band of brothers attacking and murdering the primal father, eating his body, gaining their freedom by a murder and united by a blood wrong, then there is some reason why jail should have these dark, archaic tones. Ah, yes, the wild energy of the band of brothers, soldiers, rapists, etc. But all that is nothing but metaphor. I can't truly feel I can attribute my blundering to this thick unconscious cloud. This primitive blood-daze.*

The dream of man's heart, however much we may distrust and resent it, is that life may complete itself in significant pattern. Some incomprehensible way. Before death. Not irrationally but incomprehensibly fulfilled. Spared by these clumsy police guardians, you get one last chance to know justice. Truth.

Dear Edvig, he noted quickly. *You gave me good value for my money when you explained that neuroses might be graded by the inability to tolerate ambiguous situations. I have just read a certain verdict in Madeleine's eyes, "For cowards, Not-being!" Her disorder is super-clarity. Allow me modestly to claim that I am much better now at ambiguities. I think I can say, however, that I have been spared the chief ambiguity that afflicts intellectuals, and this is that civilized individuals hate and resent the civilization that makes their lives possible. What they love is an imaginary human situation invented by their own genius and which they believe is the only true and the only human reality. How odd! But the best-treated, most favored and intelligent part of any society is often the most ungrateful. Ingratitude, however, is its social function. Now there's an ambiguity for you! . . . Dear Ramona, I owe you a lot. I am fully aware of it. Though I may not be coming back to New York right away, I intend to keep in touch. Dear God! Mercy! My God!* Rachaim olenu . . . melekh maimis. . . . *Thou King of Death and Life . . . !*

His brother observed, as they were leaving police headquarters, "You don't seem too upset."

"No, Will."

Above the sidewalk and the warm evening gloom the sky carried the long gilt trails of jets, and the jumbled lights of honky-tonks, just north of 12th Street, were already heaving up and down, a pale mass in which the street seemed to end.

"How do you feel?"

"I feel fine," said Herzog. "How do I look?"

His brother said discreetly, "You could do with a little rest. Why don't we stop and have you looked at by my doctor."

"I don't think that's necessary. This small cut on my head stopped bleeding almost immediately."

"But you've been holding your side. Don't be a fool, Mose."

Will was an undemonstrative man, substantial, shrewd, quiet, shorter than his brother but with thicker, darker hair. In a family of passionately expressive people like Father Herzog and Aunt Zipporah Will had developed a quieter, observant, reticent style.

"How's the family, Will—the kids?"

"Fine . . . What have you been doing, Moses?"

"Don't go by appearances. There's less to worry about than meets the eye. I'm really in very good shape. Do you remember when we got lost at Lake Wandawega? Floundering in the slime, cutting our feet on those reeds? That was really dangerous. But this is nothing."

"What were you doing with that gun?"

"You know I'm no more capable of firing it at someone than Papa was. You took his watch chain, didn't you? I remembered those old rubles in his drawer and then I took the revolver too. I shouldn't have. At least I ought to have emptied it. It was just one of those dumb impulses. Let's forget it."

"All right," said Will. "I don't mean to embarrass you. That's not the point."

"I know what it is," Herzog said. "You're worried." He had to lower his voice to control it. "I love you too, Will."

"Yes, I know that."

"But I haven't behaved very sensibly. From your standpoint . . . Well, from any reasonable standpoint. I brought Madeleine to your office so you could see her before I married her. I could tell you didn't approve. I didn't approve of her myself. And she didn't approve of me."

"Why did you marry her?"

"God ties all kinds of loose ends together. Who knows why! He couldn't care less about my welfare, or my ego, that thing of value. All you can say is, 'There's a red thread spliced with a green, or blue, and I wonder why.' And then I put all that money into the house in Ludeyville. That was simply crazy."

"Perhaps not," said Will. "It is real estate, after all. Have you tried to sell it?" Will had great faith in real estate.

"To whom? How?"

"List it with an agent. Maybe I'll come and look it over."

"I'd be grateful," said Herzog. "I don't think any buyer in his right mind would touch it."

"But let me call Doctor Ramsberg, Mose, and have him examine you. Then come home and have some dinner with us. It would be a treat for the family."

"When could you come to Ludeyville?"

"I've got to go to Boston next week. Then Muriel and I were going out to the Cape."

"Come by way of Ludeyville. It's close to the Turnpike. I'd consider it a tremendous favor. I have to sell that house."

"Have dinner with us, and we can talk about it."

"Will—no. I'm not up to it. Just look at me. I'm stinking dirty, and I'd upset everyone. Like a lousy lost sheep." He laughed. "No, some other time when I'm feeling a little more normal. I look as if I'd just arrived in this country. A D.P. Just as we arrived from Canada at the old Baltimore and Ohio Station. On the Michigan Central. God, we were filthy with the soot."

William did not share his brother's passion for reminiscence. He was an engineer and technologist, a contractor and builder; a balanced, reasonable person, he was pained to see Moses in such a state. His lined face was hot, uneasy; he took a handkerchief from the inner pocket of his well-tailored suit and pressed it to his forehead, his cheeks, under the large Herzog eyes.

"I'm sorry, Elya," said Moses, more quietly.

"Well—"

"Let me straighten myself up a bit. I know you're concerned about me. But that's just it. I'm sorry to worry you. I really am all right."

"Are you?" Will sadly looked at him.

"Yes, I'm at an awful disadvantage here—dirty, foolish, just bailed out. It's just ridiculous. Everything will look a lot different in the East, next week. I'll meet you in Boston, if you like. When I've got myself in better order. There's nothing you can do now but treat me like a jerk—a child. And that's not right."

"I'm not making any judgments on you. You don't have to come home with me, if that embarrasses you. Although we're your own family . . . But there's my car, across the street." He gestured toward his dark-blue Cadillac. "Just come along to the doctor so I can be sure you weren't hurt in the accident. Then you can do what you think best."

"All right. Fair enough. There's nothing wrong. I'm sure of it."

He was not entirely surprised, however, to learn that he had a broken rib. "No lung puncture," the doctor said. "Six weeks or so in tape. And you'll need two or three stitches in your head. That's the whole story. No heavy lifting, straining, chopping, or other violent exercise. Will tells me you're a country gentleman. You've got a farm in the Berkshires? An estate?"

The doctor with grizzled backswept hair and small keen eyes looked at him with thin-lipped amusement.

"It's in bad repair. Miles from a synagogue," said Herzog.

"Ha, your brother likes to kid," Dr. Ramsberg said. Will faintly smiled. Standing with folded arms he favored one heel, somewhat like Father Herzog, and had a bit of the old man's elegance but not his eccentricities. He had no time for such stuff, thought Herzog, running a big business. No great interest in it. Other things absorb. He's a good man, a very good man. But there's a strange division of functions that I sense, in which I am the specialist in . . . in spiritual self-awareness; or emotionalism; or ideas; or nonsense. Perhaps of no real use or relevance except to keep alive primordial feelings of a certain sort. He mixes grout to pump into these new high-risers all over town. He has to be political, and deal, and wangle and pay off and figure tax angles. All that Papa was inept in but dreamed he was born to do. Will is a quiet man of duty and routine, has his money, position, influence, and is just as glad to be rid of his private or "personal" side. Sees me spluttering fire in the wilderness of this world, and pities me no doubt for my temperament. Under the old dispensation, as the stumbling, ingenuous, burlap Moses, a heart without guile, in need of protection, a morbid phenomenon, a modern remnant of other-worldliness—under that former dispensation I would need protection. And it would be gladly offered by him—by the person who "knows-the-world-for-what-it-is." Whereas a man like me has shown the arbitrary withdrawal of proud subjectivity from the collective and historical progress of mankind. And that is true of lower-class emotional boys and girls who adopt the aesthetic mode, the mode of rich sensibility. Seeking to sustain their own version of existence under the crushing weight of *mass*. What Marx described as that "material weight." Turning this thing, "my personal life," into a circus, into gladiatorial combat. Or tamer forms of entertainment. To make a joke of your "shame," your ephemeral dimness, and show why you deserve your pain. The white modern lights of the small room were going round, wheeling. Herzog himself felt that he was rotating with them as the doctor wound the medicinal-smelling tapes tightly about his chest. Now, to get rid of all such falsehoods . . .

"I have an idea my brother could do with some rest," said Will. "What's your opinion, doctor?"

"He looks as if he's been going pretty hard, that's true."

"I'm going to spend a week at Ludeyville," Moses said.

"What I mean is complete rest—bed rest."

"Yes, I know I seem to be in a state. But it's not a bad state."

"Still," said Herzog's brother, "you worry me."

A loving brute—a subtle, spoiled, loving man. Who can make use of him? He craves use. Where is he needed? Show him the way to make his sacrifice to truth, to order, peace. Oh, that mysterious creature, that Herzog! awkwardly taped, helped into his wrinkled shirt by brother Will.

HE reached his country place the following afternoon, after taking a plane to Albany, from there the bus to Pittsfield, and then a cab to Ludeyville. Asphalter had given him some Tuinal the night before. He slept deeply and was feeling perfectly fine, despite his taped sides.

The house was two miles beyond the village, in the hills. Beautiful, sparkling summer weather in the Berkshires, the air light, the streams quick, the woods dense, the green new. As for birds, Herzog's acres seemed to have become a sanctuary. Wrens nested under the ornamental scrolls of the porch. The giant elm was not quite dead, and the orioles lived in it still. Herzog had the driver stop in the mossy roadway, boulder-lined. He couldn't be sure the house was approachable. But no fallen trees blocked the path, and although much of the gravel had washed down in thaws and storms the cab might easily have gotten through. Moses, however, didn't mind the short climb. His chest was securely armored in tape and his legs were light. He had bought some groceries in Ludeyville. If hunters and prowlers had not eaten it, there was a supply of canned goods in the cellar. Two years ago he had put up tomatoes and beans and raspberry preserves, and before leaving for Chicago he had hidden his wine and whisky. The electricity of course was turned off but perhaps the old hand pump could be made to work. There was always cistern water to fall back on. He could cook in the fireplace; there were old hooks and trivets—and here (his heart trembled) the house rose out of weeds, vines, trees, and blossoms. Herzog's folly! Monument to his sincere and loving idiocy, to the unrecognized evils of his character, symbol of his Jewish struggle for a solid footing in White Anglo-Saxon Protestant America ("The land was ours before we were the land's," as that sententious old man declared at the Inauguration). I too have done my share of social climbing, he thought, with hauteur to spare, defying the Wasps, who, because the government gave much of this continent away to the railroads, stopped boiling their own soap circa 1880, took European tours, and began to complain of the Micks and the Spicks and the Sheenies. What a struggle I waged!—left-handed but fierce. But enough of that—here I am. *Hineni!* How marvelously beautiful it is today. He stopped in the overgrown yard, shut his eyes in the sun, against flashes of crimson, and drew in the odors of catalpa-bells, soil, honeysuckle, wild onions, and herbs. Either deer or lovers had lain in this grass near the elm, for it was flattened. He circled the house to see whether it was much damaged. There were no broken windows. All the shutters, hooked from within, were undisturbed. Only a few of the posters he had put up warning that this property was under police protection had been torn down. The garden was a thick mass of thorny canes, roses and berries twisted together. It looked too hopeless—past regretting. He would never have the strength to throw himself into such tasks again, to hammer, paint, patch, splice, prune, spray. He was here only to look things over.

The house was as musty as he had expected. He opened a few windows and shutters in the kitchen. The debris of leaves and pine needles, webs, cocoons, and insect corpses he brushed away. What was needed, immediately, was a fire. He had brought matches. One of the benefits of a riper age was that you became clever about such things—foresightful. Of course he had a bicycle—he could ride to the village to buy what he had forgotten. He had even been smart enough to set the bike on its saddle, to spare the tires. There was not much air in them, but they'd get him down to the Esso station. He carried in a few pine logs, kindling, and started a small blaze first, to make sure of the draft. Birds or squirrels might have nested in the flues. But then he remembered that he had climbed out on the roof to fasten wire mesh over the chimneys— part of his frenzy of efficient toil. He laid on more wood. The old bark dropped away and disclosed the work of insects underneath— grubs, ants, long-legged spiders ran away. He gave them every opportunity to escape. The black, dry branches began to burn with yellow flames. He heaped on more logs, secured them with the andirons, and continued his examination of the house.

The canned food had not been touched. There was fancy-goods bought by Madeleine (always the best of everything), S. S. Pierce terrapin soup, Indian pudding, truffles, olives, and then grimmer-looking victuals bought by Moses himself at Army surplus sales— beans, canned bread, and the like. He made his inventory with a sort of dreamy curiosity about his onetime plan for solitary self-sufficiency—the washer, dryer, the hot-water unit, pure white and gleaming forms into which he had put his dead father's dollars, ugly green, laboriously made, tediously counted, divided in agony among the heirs. Well, well, thought Herzog, he shouldn't have sent me to school to learn about dead emperors. "My name is Ozymandias, king of kings:/Look on my works, ye Mighty, and despair!" But self-sufficiency and solitude, gentleness, it all was so tempting, and had sounded so innocent, it became smiling Herzog so well in the description. It's only later you discover how much viciousness is in these hidden heavens. *Unemployed consciousness,* he wrote in the pantry. *I grew up in a time of widespread unemployment, and never believed there might be work for me. Finally, jobs appeared, but somehow my consciousness remained unemployed. And after all,* he continued beside the fire, *the human intellect is one of the great forces of the universe. It can't safely remain unused. You might almost conclude that the boredom of so many human arrangements (middle-class family life, for instance) has the historical aim of freeing the intellect of newer generations, sending them into science. But a terrible loneliness throughout life is simply the plankton on which Leviathan feeds. . . . Must reconsider. The soul requires intensity. At the same time virtue bores mankind. Read Confucius again. With vast populations, the world must prepare to turn Chinese.*

Herzog's present loneliness did not seem to count because it was so consciously cheerful. He peered through the chink in the lavatory where he used to hide away with his ten-cent volume of Dryden and Pope, reading "I am His Highness' dog at Kew" or "Great wits to madness sure are near allied." There, in the same position as in former years, was the rose that used to give him comfort—as shapely, as red (as nearly "genital" to his imagination) as ever. Some good things do recur. He was a long time peering at it through the meeting of masonry and lumber. The same damp-loving grasshoppers (giant orthoptera) still lived in this closet of masonry and plywood. A struck match revealed them. Among the pipes.

It was odd, the tour he made through his property. In his own room he found the ruins of his scholarly enterprise strewn over the desk and the shelves. The windows were so discolored as to seem stained with iodine, and the honeysuckles outside had almost pulled the screens down. On the sofa he found proof that the place was indeed visited by lovers. Too blind with passion to hunt in darkness for the bedrooms. But they'll get curvature of the spine using Madeleine's horsehair antiques. For some reason it particularly pleased Herzog that his room should be the one chosen by the youth of the village—here among bales of learned notes. He found girls' hairs on the curving armrests, and tried to imagine bodies, faces, odors. Thanks to Ramona he had no need to be greatly envious, but a little envy of the young was quite natural too. On the floor was one of his large cards with a note in which he had written *To do justice to Condorcet* . . . He hadn't the heart to read further and turned it face down on the table. For the present, anyway, Condorcet would have to find another defender. In the dining room were the precious dishes that Tennie wanted, crimson-rimmed bone china, very handsome. He wouldn't need that. The books, muslin-covered, were undisturbed. He lifted the cloth and glanced at them with no special interest. Visiting the little bathroom, he was entertained to see the lavish fittings Madeleine had bought at Sloane's, scalloped silver soap dishes and flashing towel racks too heavy for the plaster, even after they were fastened with toggle bolts. They were drooping now. The shower stall, for Gersbach's convenience—the Gersbachs had had no shower in Barrington—was thoughtfully equipped with a handrail. "If we're going to put it in, let's make it so Valentine can use it," Mady had said. Ah, well—Moses shrugged. A strange odor in the toilet bowl attracted his notice next, and raising the wooden lid he found the small beaked skulls and other remains of birds who had nested there after the water was drained, and then had been entombed by the falling lid. He looked grimly in, his heart aching somewhat at this accident. There must be a broken window in the attic, he inferred from this, and other birds nesting in the house. Indeed, he found owls in his bedroom, perched on the red valances, which they had streaked with droppings. He gave them every opportunity to escape, and, when they were gone, looked for a nest. He found the young owls in the large light fixture over the bed where he and Madeleine had known so much misery and hatred. (Some delight as well.) On the mattress much nest litter had fallen—straws, wool threads, down, bits of flesh (mouse ends) and streaks of excrement. Unwilling to disturb these flat-faced little creatures, Herzog pulled the mattress of his marriage bed into June's room. He opened more windows, and the sun and country air at once entered. He was surprised to feel such contentment . . . contentment? Whom was he kidding, this was joy! For perhaps the first time he felt what it was to be free from Madeleine. Joy! His servitude was ended, and his heart released from its grisly heaviness and encrustation. Her absence, no more than her absence itself, was simply sweetness and lightness of spirit. To her, at 11th and State, it had been happiness to see him in trouble, and to him in Ludeyville it was a delicious joy to have her removed from his flesh, like something that had stabbed his shoulders, his groin, made his arms and his neck lame and cumbersome. *My dear sage and imbecilic Edvig. It may be that the remission of pain is no small part of human happiness. In its primordial and stupider levels, where now and then a closed valve opens again. . . .* Those strange lights, Herzog's brown eyes, so often overlaid with the film or protective chitin of melancholy, the by-product of his laboring brain, shone again.

It cost him some effort to turn over the mattress on the floor of June's old room. He had to move aside some of her cast-off toys and kiddie furniture, a great stuffed blue-eyed tiger, the potty chair, a red snowsuit, perfectly good. He recognized also the grandmother's bikini, shorts, and halters, and, among other oddities, a washrag which Phoebe had stitched with his initials, a birthday present, a possible hint that his ears were not clean. Beaming, he pushed it aside with his foot. A beetle escaped from beneath. Herzog, lying under the open window with the sun in his face, rested on the mattress. Over him the great trees, the spruces in the front yard, showed their beautiful jaggedness and sent down the odor of heated needles and gum.

It was here, until the sun passed from the room, that he began in earnest, from tranquil fullness of heart, to consider another series of letters.

Dear Ramona. Only "Dear"? Come, Moses, open up a little. *Darling Ramona. What an excellent woman you are.* Here he paused to consider whether he should say he was in Ludeyville. In her Mercedes she could drive from New York in three hours, and it was probable that she would. God's blessing on her short but perfect legs, her solid, well-tinted breasts, and her dashing curved teeth and gypsy brows and curls. *La devoradora de hombres.*

He decided, however, to date his letter Chicago and ask Lucas to remail it. What he wanted now was peace—peace and clarity. *I hope I didn't upset you by copping out. But I know you're not one of those conventional women it takes a month to appease because of a broken date. I had to see my daughter, and my son. He's at Camp Ayumah, near Catskill. It's turning into a busy summer. Several interesting developments. I hesitate to make too many assertions yet, but at least I can admit what I never stopped asserting anyway, or feeling. The light of truth is never far away, and no human being is too negligible or corrupt to come into it.* I don't see why I shouldn't say that. *But to accept ineffectuality, banishment to personal life, confusion . . . Why don't you try this out, Herzog, on the owls next door, those naked owlets pimpled with blue. Since the last question, also the first one, the question of death, offers us the interesting alternatives of disintegrating ourselves by our own wills in proof of our "freedom," or the acknowledging that we owe a human life to this waking spell of existence, regardless of the void. (After all, we have no positive knowledge of that void.)*

Should I say all this to Ramona? Some women think that earnestness is wooing. She'll want a child. She'll want to breed with a man who talks to her like this. *Work. Work. Real, relevant work.* . . . He paused. But Ramona was a willing worker. According to her lights. And she loved her work. He smiled affectionately on his sunlit mattress.

Dear Marco. I've come up to the old homestead to look things over and relax a bit. The place is in pretty good shape, considering. Perhaps you'd like to spend some time here with me, only the two of us—roughing it—after camp. We'll talk about it Parents' Day. I'm looking forward to that, eagerly. Your little sister whom I saw in Chicago yesterday is very lively and as pretty as ever. She received your postcard.

Do you remember the talks we had about Scott's Antarctic Expedition, and how poor Scott was beaten to the Pole by Amundsen? You seemed interested. This is a thing that always gets me. There was a man in Scott's party who went out and lost himself to give the others a chance to survive. He was ailing, footsore, couldn't keep up any longer. And do you remember how by chance they found a mound of frozen blood, the blood of one of their

314

slaughtered ponies, and how thankful they were to thaw and drink it? The success of Amundsen was due to his use of dogs instead of ponies. The weaker were butchered and fed to the stronger. Otherwise the expedition would have failed. I have often wondered at one thing. Hungry as they were, the dogs would sniff at the flesh of their own and back away. The skin had to be removed before they would eat it.

Maybe you and I could take a trip at Xmas to Canada just to get the feel of genuine cold. I am a Canadian, too, you know. We could visit Ste. Agathe, in the Laurentians. Expect me on the 16th, bright and early.

Dear Luke—Be so kind as to post these enclosures. I hope to hear your depression is over. I think your visions of the aunt being rescued by the fireman and of the broads playing piggy-move-up are signs of psychological resiliency. I predict your recovery. As for me. . . . As for you, thought Herzog, you will not tell him how you feel now, all this overflow! It wouldn't make him happier. Keep it to yourself if you feel exalted. Anyway, he may think you've simply gone off your nut.

But if I am out of my mind, it's all right with me.

My dear Professor Mermelstein. I want to congratulate you on a splendid book. In some matters you scooped me, you know, and I felt like hell about it—hated you one whole day for making a good deal of my work superfluous (Wallace and Darwin?). However, I well know what labor and patience went into such a work—so much digging, learning, synthesizing, and I'm all admiration. When you are ready to print a revised edition—or perhaps another book —it would be a great pleasure to talk over some of these questions. There are parts of my projected book I'll never return to. You may do what you like with those materials. In my earlier book (to which you were kind enough to refer) I devoted one section to Heaven and Hell in apocalyptic Romanticism. I may not have done it to your taste, but you ought not to have overlooked it completely. You ought to have a look at the monograph by that fat natty brute Egbert Shapiro, "From Luther to Lenin, A History of Revolutionary Psychology." His fat cheeks give him a great resemblance to Gibbon. It is a valuable piece of work. I was greatly impressed by the section called Millenarianism and Paranoia. It should not be ignored that modern power-systems do offer a re-

semblance to this psychosis. A gruesome and crazy book on this has been written by a man named Banowitch. Fairly inhuman, and filled with vile paranoid hypotheses such as that crowds are fundamentally cannibalistic, that people standing secretly terrify the sitting, that smiling teeth are the weapons of hunger, that the tyrant is mad for the sight of (possibly edible?) corpses about him. It seems quite true that the making of corpses has been the most dramatic achievement of modern dictators and their followers (Hitler, Stalin, etc.). Just to see—Herzog tried this on, experimenting—whether Mermelstein didn't have a vestige of old Stalinism about him. But this fellow Shapiro is something of an eccentric, and I mention him as an extreme case. How we all love extreme cases and apocalypses, fires, drownings, stranglings, and the rest of it. The bigger our mild, basically ethical, safe middle classes grow the more radical excitement is in demand. Mild or moderate truthfulness or accuracy seems to have no pull at all. Just what we need now! ("When a dog is drowning, you offer him a cup of water," Papa used to say, bitterly.) In any case, if you had read that chapter of mine on apocalypse and Romanticism you might have looked a little straighter at that Russian you admire so much—Isvolsky? The man who sees the souls of monads as the legions of the damned, simply atomized and pulverized, a dust storm in Hell; and warns that Lucifer must take charge of collectivized mankind, devoid of spiritual character and true personality. I don't deny this makes some sense, here and there, though I do worry that such ideas, because of the bit of suggestive truth in them, may land us in the same old suffocating churches and synagogues. I was somewhat bothered by borrowings and references which I considered "hit and run," or the use of other writers' serious beliefs as mere metaphors. For instance, I liked the section called "Interpretations of Suffering" and also the one called "Toward a Theory of Boredom." This was an excellent piece of research. But then I thought the treatment you gave Kierkegaard was fairly frivolous. I venture to say Kierkegaard meant that truth has lost its force with us and horrible pain and evil must teach it to us again, the eternal punishments of Hell will have to regain their reality before mankind turns serious once more. I do not see this. Let us set aside the fact that such convictions in the mouths of safe, comfortable people playing at crisis, alienation, apocalypse and desperation, make me sick. We must get it out of our heads that this is a doomed time, that we are waiting for the end, and the rest of it, mere junk from fashionable magazines. Things are grim enough without these shivery games. People frightening one another—a poor sort of moral exercise. But, to get to the main point, the advocacy and praise of suffering take us in the wrong direction and those of us who remain loyal to civilization must not go for it. You have to have the power to employ pain, to repent, to be illuminated, you must have the opportunity and even the time. With the religious, the love of suffering is a form of gratitude to experience or an opportunity to experience evil and change it into good. They believe the spiritual cycle can and will be completed in a man's existence and he will somehow make use of his suffering, if only in the last moments of his life, when the mercy of God will reward him with a vision of the truth, and he will die transfigured. But this is a special exercise. More commonly suffering breaks people, crushes them, and is simply unilluminating. You see how gruesomely human beings are destroyed by pain, when they have the added torment of losing their humanity first, so that their death is a total defeat, and then you write about "modern forms of Orphism" and about "people who are not afraid of suffering" and throw in other such cocktail-party expressions. Why not say rather that people of powerful imagination, given to dreaming deeply and to raising up marvelous and self-sufficient fictions, turn to suffering sometimes to cut into their bliss, as people pinch themselves to feel awake. I know that my suffering, if I may speak of it, has often been like that, a more extended form of life, a striving for true wakefulness and an antidote to illusion, and therefore I can take no moral credit for it. I am willing without further exercise in pain to open my heart. And this needs no doctrine or theology of suffering. We love apocalypses too much, and crisis ethics and florid extremism with its thrilling language. Excuse me, no. I've had all the monstrosity I want. We've reached an age in the history of mankind when we can ask about certain persons, "What is this Thing?" No more of that for me—no, no! I am simply a human being, more or less. I am even willing to leave the more or less in your hands. You may decide about me. You have a taste for metaphors. Your otherwise admirable work is marred by them. I'm sure you can come up with a grand metaphor for me. But don't forget to say that I will never expound suffering for anyone or call for Hell to make us seri-

ous and truthful. I even think man's perception of pain may have grown too refined. But that is another subject for lengthy treatment.

Very good, Mermelstein. Go, and sin no more. And Herzog, perhaps somewhat sheepish over this strange diatribe, rose from the mattress (the sun was moving away) and went downstairs again. He ate several slices of bread, and baked beans—a cold bean sandwich, and afterward carried outside his hammock and two lawn chairs.

Thus began his final week of letters. He wandered over his twenty acres of hillside and woodlot, composing his messages, none of which he mailed. He was not ready to pedal to the post office and answer questions in the village about Mrs. Herzog and little June. As he knew well, the grotesque facts of the entire Herzog scandal had been overheard on the party line and become the meat and drink of Ludeyville's fantasy life. He had never restrained himself on the telephone; he was too agitated. And Madeleine was far too patrician to care what the hicks were overhearing. Anyway, she had been throwing him out. It reflected no discredit on her.

Dear Madeleine—You are a terrific one, you are! Bless you! What a creature! To put on lipstick, after dinner in a restaurant, she would look at her reflection in a knife blade. He recalled this with delight. *And you, Gersbach, you're welcome to Madeleine. Enjoy her—rejoice in her. You will not reach me through her, however. I know you sought me in her flesh. But I am no longer there.*

Dear Sirs, The size and number of the rats in Panama City, when I passed through, truly astonished me. I saw one of them sunning himself beside a swimming pool. And another was looking at me from the wainscoting of a restaurant as I was eating fruit salad. Also, on an electric wire which slanted upward into a banana tree, I saw a whole rat-troupe go back and forth, harvesting. They ran the wire twenty times or more without a single collision. My suggestion is that you put birth-control chemicals in the baits. Poisons will never work (for Malthusian reasons; reduce the population somewhat and it only increases more vigorously). But several years of contraception may eliminate your rat problem.

Dear Herr Nietzsche—My dear sir, May I ask a question from the floor? You speak of the power of the Dionysian spirit to endure the sight of the Terrible, the Questionable, to allow itself the luxury of Destruction, to witness Decomposition, Hideousness, Evil. All this the Dionysian spirit can do because it has the same power of recovery as Nature itself. Some of these expressions, I must tell you, have a very Germanic ring. A phrase like the "luxury of Destruction" is positively Wagnerian, and I know how you came to despise all that sickly Wagnerian idiocy and bombast. Now we've seen enough destruction to test the power of the Dionysian spirit amply, and where are the heroes who have recovered from it? Nature (itself) and I are alone together, in the Berkshires, and this is my chance to understand. I am lying in a hammock, chin on breast, hands clasped, mind jammed with thoughts, agitated, yes, but also cheerful, and I know you value cheerfulness—true cheerfulness, not the seeming sanguinity of Epicureans, nor the strategic buoyancy of the heartbroken. I also know you think that deep pain is ennobling, pain which burns slow, like green wood, and there you have me with you, somewhat. But for this higher education survival is necessary. You must outlive the pain. Herzog! you must stop this quarrelsomeness and baiting of great men. No, really, Herr Nietzsche, I have great admiration for you. Sympathy. You want to make us able to live with the void. Not lie ourselves into good-naturedness, trust, ordinary middling human considerations, but to question as has never been questioned before, relentlessly, with iron determination, into evil, through evil, past evil, accepting no abject comfort. The most absolute, the most piercing questions. Rejecting mankind as it is, that ordinary, practical, thieving, stinking, unilluminated, sodden rabble, not only the laboring rabble, but even worse the "educated" rabble with its books and concerts and lectures, its liberalism and its romantic theatrical "loves" and "passions"—it all deserves to die, it will die. Okay. Still, your extremists must survive. No survival, no Amor Fati. Your immoralists also eat meat. They ride the bus. They are only the most bus-sick travelers. Humankind lives mainly upon perverted ideas. Perverted, your ideas are no better than those of the Christianity you condemn. Any philosopher who wants to keep his contact with mankind should pervert his own system in advance to see how it will really look a few decades after adoption. I send you greetings from this mere border of grassy temporal light, and wish you happiness, wherever you are. Yours, under the veil of Maya, M.E.H.

Dear Dr. Morgenfruh. Dead for some time now. *This is Herzog, Moses E.* Discover yourself. *We played billiards in Madison, Wisconsin.* Tell him more. *Until Willie Hoppe arrived to demonstrate, and put us to shame.* The great billiard artist got absolute obedience from those three balls; as if he whispered to them, stroked them a little with his cue, and they would part and kiss again. And old Morgenfruh with his bald head and fine, humorous, curved nose and foreign charm, applauding, getting up all his breath to exclaim "Bravo." Morgenfruh played the piano and made himself weep. Helen played Schumann better but she had less at stake. She frowned at the music as if to show that it was dangerous, but that she could tame it. Morgenfruh, however, groaned, sitting at the keys in his fur coat. Next he sang along, and lastly he cried— it overcame him. He was a splendid old man, only partly fraudulent, and what more can you ask of anyone? *Dear Dr. Morgenfruh, Latest intelligence from the Olduvai Gorge in East Africa gives grounds to suppose that man did not descend from a peaceful arboreal ape, but from a carnivorous, terrestrial type, a beast that hunted in packs and crushed the skulls of prey with a club or femoral bone. It sounds bad, Morgenfruh, for the optimists, for the lenient hopeful view of human nature. The work of Sir Solly Zuckerman on the apes in the London Zoo, of which you spoke so often, has been superseded. Apes in their own habitat are less sexually driven than those in captivity. It must be that captivity, boredom, breeds lustfulness. And it may also be that the territorial instinct is stronger than the sexual. Abide in light, Morgenfruh. I will keep you posted from time to time.*

Despite the hours he spent in the open he believed he still looked pale. Perhaps this was because the mirror of the bathroom door into which he stared in the morning reflected the massed green of the trees. No, he did not look well. His excitement must be a great drain on his strength, he thought. And then there was the persistently medicinal smell of the tapes on his chest to remind him that he was not quite well. After the second or third day he stopped sleeping on the second floor. He didn't want to drive the owls out of the house and leave a brood to die in the old fixture with the triple brass chain. It was bad enough to have those tiny skeletons in the toilet bowl. He moved downstairs, taking with him a few useful articles, an old trench coat and rain hat, his boots ordered from Gokey's in St. Paul—marvelous, flexible, handsome snakeproof boots; he had forgotten that he had them. In the storeroom he made other interesting discoveries, photographs of the "happy days," boxes of clothing, Madeleine's letters, bundles of canceled checks, elaborately engraved wedding announcements, and a recipe book belonging to Phoebe Gersbach. The photographs were all of him. Madeleine had left those behind, taking the others. Interesting—her attitude. Among the abandoned dresses were her expensive maternity outfits. The checks were for large sums, and many of these were paid to Cash. Had she secretly been saving? He wouldn't put it past her. The announcements made him laugh; Mr and Mrs Pontritter were giving their daughter in marriage to Mr Moses E Herzog Ph D.

In one of the closets he found a dozen or so Russian books under a stiff painter's drop cloth. Shestov, Rozanov—he rather liked Rozanov, who was, luckily, in English. He read a few pages of *Solitaria*. Then he looked over the paint situation—old brushes, thinners, evaporated, crusted buckets. There were several cans of enamel, and Herzog thought, What if I should paint up the little piano? I could send it out to Chicago, to Junie. The kid is really highly musical. As for Madeleine, she'll have to take it in, the bitch, when it's delivered, paid for. She can't send it back. The green enamel seemed to him exactly right, and he wasted no time but found the most usable brushes and set himself to work, full of eagerness, in the parlor. *Dear Rozanov.* He painted the lid of the piano with absorption; the green was light, beautiful, like summer apples. *A stupendous truth you say, heard from none of the prophets, is that private life is above everything. More universal than religion. Truth is higher than the sun. The soul is passion. "I am the fire that consumeth." It is joy to be choked with thought. A good man can bear to listen to another talk about himself. You can't trust the people who are bored by such talk. God has gilded me all over. I like that, God has gilded me all over.* Very touching, this man, though extremely coarse at times, and stuffed with violent prejudices. The enamel covered well but it would probably need a second coat, and he might not have enough paint for that.

Putting down the brush he gave the piano lid time to dry, considering how to get the instrument out of here. He couldn't expect one of the giant interstate vans to climb this hill. He would have to hire Tuttle from the village to come in his pick-up truck. The cost would amount to something like a hundred dollars, but he must do everything possible for the child, and he had no serious problems about money. Will had offered him as much as he needed to get through the summer. *A curious result of the increase of historical consciousness is that people think explanation is a necessity of survival. They have to explain their condition. And if the unexplained life is not worth living, the explained life is unbearable, too. "Synthesize or perish!" Is that the new law? But when you see what strange notions, hallucinations, projections, issue from the human mind you begin to believe in Providence again. To survive these idiocies . . . Anyway the intellectual has been a Separatist. And what kind of synthesis is a Separatist likely to come up with?* Luckily for me, I didn't have the means to get too far away from our common life. I am glad of that. I mean to share with other human beings as far as possible and not destroy my remaining years in the same way. Herzog felt a deep, dizzy eagerness to *begin*.

He had to get water from the cistern; the pump was too rusty; he had primed it and worked the handle but only tired himself. The cistern was full. He raised the iron lid with a pry bar and put down a bucket. It made a good sound, dropping, and you couldn't get softer water anywhere, but it had to be boiled. There was always a chipmunk or two, a rat, dead at the bottom though it looked pure enough when you drew it up, pure, green water.

He went to sit under the trees. *His* trees. He was amused, resting here on his American estate, twenty thousand dollars' worth of country solitude and privacy. He did not feel an owner. As for the twenty grand, the place was certainly not worth more than three or four. Nobody wanted these old-fashioned houses on the fringes of the Berkshires, not the fashionable section where there were music festivals and modern dancing, riding to hounds or other kinds of snobbery. You couldn't even ski on these slopes. No one came here. He had only gentle, dotty old neighbors, Jukes and Kallikaks, rocking themselves to death on their porches, watching television, the nineteenth century quietly dying in this remote green hole. Well, this was his own, his hearth; these were *his* birches, catalpas, horse chestnuts. His rotten dreams of peace. The patrimony of his children—a sunken corner of Massachusetts for Marco, the little piano for June painted a loving green by her solicitous father. That, too, like most other things he would probably botch. But at least he would not die here, as he had once feared. In former summers, when cutting the grass, he would sometimes lean on the mower, overheated, and think, What if I were to die suddenly, of a heart attack? Where will they put me? Maybe I should pick my own spot. Under the spruce? That's too close to the house. Now he reflected that Madeleine would have had him cremated. *And these explanations are unbearable, but they have to be made. In the seventeenth century the passionate search for absolute truth stopped so that mankind might transform the world. Something practical was done with thought. The mental became also the real. Relief from the pursuit of absolutes made life pleasant. Only a small class of fanatical intellectuals, professionals, still chased after these absolutes. But our revolutions, including nuclear terror, return the metaphysical dimension to us. All practical activity has reached this culmination: everything may go now, civilization, history, meaning, nature. Everything! Now to recall Mr. Kierkegaard's question . . .*

To Dr. Waldemar Zozo: You, Sir, were the Navy psychiatrist who examined me in Norfolk, Va., about 1942, and told me I was unusually immature. I knew that, but professional confirmation caused me deep anguish. In anguish I was not immature. I could call upon ages of experience. I took it all very seriously then. Anyway, I was subsequently discharged for asthma, not childishness. I fell in love with the Atlantic. O the great reticulated, mountain-bottomed sea! *But the sea fog paralyzed my voice, and for a communications officer it was the end. However, in your cubicle, as I sat naked, pale, listened to the sailors at drill in the dust, heard what you told me about my character, felt the Southern heat, it was unsuitable that I should wring my hands. I kept them lying on my thighs.*

From hatred at first, but later because I became objectively interested, I followed your career in the journals. Your article "Existential Unrest in the Unconscious" recently beguiled me. It was really quite a classy piece of work. You don't mind if I speak to you in this way, I hope. I am really in an unusually free condition of mind. "*In paths untrodden,*" as Walt Whitman marvelously put it. "*Escaped from the life that exhibits itself . . .*" Oh, that's a plague, the life that exhibits itself, a real plague! There comes a time when every ridiculous son of Adam wishes to arise before the rest, with all his quirks and twitches and tics, all the glory of his self-adored ugliness, his grinning teeth, his sharp nose, his madly twisted reason, saying to the rest—in an overflow of narcissism which he interprets as benevolence—"I am here to witness. I am come to be your exemplar." Poor dizzy spook! . . . Escaped, anyway, as Whitman says, from the life that exhibits itself and "talked to by tongues aromatic." . . . But here is a further interesting fact. I recognized you last spring in the Primitive Art Museum on 54th Street. How my feet ached! I had to ask Ramona to sit down. I said to the lady I had come with, "Isn't that Dr. Waldemar Zozo?" She happened also to know you, and brought me up to date: You were quite rich, a collector of African antiquities, your daughter a folk singer, and much else. I realized sharply how I still loathed you. I thought I had forgiven you, too. Isn't that interesting? Seeing you, your white turtle-necked shirt and dinner jacket, your Edwardian mustache, your damp lips, the back hair trained over your bald spot, your barren paunch, apish buttocks (chemically old!) I recognized with joy how I abhorred you. It sprang fresh from my heart after 22 years!

His mind took one of its odd jumps. He opened a clean page in his grimy notebook, and in the twig-divided shade of a wild cherry, infested with tent caterpillars, he began to make notes for a poem. He was going to try an Insect Iliad for Junie. She couldn't read, but maybe Madeleine would allow Luke Asphalter to take the child to Jackson Park and read the installments to her as he received them. Luke knew a lot of natural history. It would do him good, too. Moses, pale with this heartfelt nonsense, stared at the ground with brown eyes, standing round-shouldered, the notebook held behind him as he thought it over. He could make the Trojans ants. The Argives might be water-skaters. Luke might find them for her along the edge of the lagoon, where those stupid caryatides were posted. The water-skaters, therefore, with long velvet hairs beaded with glittering oxygen. Helen, a beautiful wasp. Old Priam a cicada, sucking sap from the roots and with his trowel-shaped belly plastering the tunnels. And Achilles a stag-beetle with sharp spikes and terrible strength, but doomed to a brief life though half a god. At the edge of the water he cried out to his mother

> *Thus spoke Achilles*
> *And Thetis heard him in the ooze,*
> *Sitting beside her ancient father*
> *In glorious debris, enough for all.*

But this project was quickly abandoned. It wasn't a good idea, really not. For one thing, he wasn't stable enough, he could never keep his mind at it. His state was too strange, this mixture of clairvoyance and spleen, *esprit de l'escalier,* noble inspirations, poetry and nonsense, ideas, hyperesthesia—wandering about like this, hearing forceful but indefinite music within, seeing things, violet fringes about the clearest objects. His mind was like that cistern, soft pure water sealed under the iron lid but not entirely safe to drink. No, he was better occupied painting the piano for the child. Go! let the fiery claw of imagination take up the green brush. Go! But the first coat was not dry yet, and he wandered out to the woods, eating a piece of bread from the package he carried in his trench-coat pocket. He was aware that his brother might now show up at any time. Will had been disturbed by his appearance. It was unmistakable. And I had better look out, thought Herzog, people do get put away, and seem even to intend it. I have wanted to be cared for. I devoutly hoped Emmerich would find me sick. But I have no intention of doing that—I am responsible, responsible to reason. This is simply temporary excitement. Responsible to the children. He walked quietly into the woods, the many leaves, living and fallen, green and tan, going between rotted stumps, moss, fungus disks; he found a hunters' path, also a deer trail. He felt quite well here, and calmer. The silence sustained him, and the brilliant weather, the feeling that he was easily contained by everything about him *Within the hollowness of God,* as he noted, *and deaf to the final multiplicity of facts,* as well as, *blind to ultimate distances. Two billion light-years out. Supernovae.*

> *Daily radiance, trodden here*
> *Within the hollowness of God*

To God he jotted several lines.
How my mind has struggled to make coherent sense. I have not

been too good at it. But have desired to do your unknowable will, taking it, and you, without symbols. Everything of intensest significance. Especially if divested of me.

Returning once more to practical considerations, he must be very careful with Will and talk to him only in the most concrete terms about concrete matters, like this property, and look as ordinary as possible. If you wear a wise look, he warned himself, you'll be in trouble, and fast. No one can bear such looks any longer, not even your brother. Therefore, watch your face! Certain expressions burn people up, and especially the expression of wisdom, which can lead you straight to the loony bin. You will have earned it!

He lay down near the locust trees. They bloomed with a light, tiny but delicious flower—he was sorry to have missed that. He recognized that with his arms behind him and his legs extended any way, he was lying as he had lain less than a week ago on his dirty little sofa in New York. But was it only a week—five days? Unbelievable! How different he felt! Confident, even happy in his excitement, stable. The bitter cup would come round again, by and by. This rest and well-being were only a momentary difference in the strange lining or variable silk between life and void. *The life you gave me has been curious,* he wanted to say to his mother, *and perhaps the death I must inherit will turn out to be even more profoundly curious. I have sometimes wished it would hurry up, longed for it to come soon. But I am still on the same side of eternity as ever. It's just as well, for I have certain things still to do. And without noise, I hope. Some of my oldest aims seem to have slid away.* But I have others. *Life on this earth can't be simply a picture.* And terrible forces in me, including the force of admiration or praise, powers, including loving powers, very damaging, making me almost an idiot because I lacked the capacity to manage them. *I may turn out to be not such a terrible hopeless fool as everyone, as you, as I myself suspected.* Meantime, to lay off certain persistent torments. To surrender the hyperactivity of this hyperactive face. But just to put it out instead to the radiance of the sun. *I want to send you, and others, the most loving wish I have in my heart. This is the only way I have to reach out—out where it is incomprehensible. I can only pray toward it. So . . . Peace!*

For the next two days—or were there three?—Herzog did nothing but send such messages, and write down songs, psalms, and utterances, putting into words what he had often thought but, for the sake of form, or something of the sort, had always suppressed. Once in a while he found himself painting the little piano again, or eating bread and beans in the kitchen, or sleeping in the hammock, and he was always slightly surprised to discover how he had been occupied. He looked at the calendar one morning, and tried to guess the date, counting in silence, or rather groping over nights and days. His beard informed him better than his brain. His bristles felt like four days' growth, and he thought it best to be clean-shaven when Will arrived.

He built a fire and heated a pan of water, lathered his cheeks with brown laundry soap. Clean-shaven, he was extremely pale. His face had become much thinner, too. He had just put down his razor when he heard the smooth noise of an engine at the foot of the drive. He ran into the garden to meet his brother.

Will was alone in his Cadillac. The great car got up the hill slowly, scraping its underbelly on rocks and bending the tall growth of weeds and canes. Will was a masterful driver. He might be short but there was nothing timid about him, and as for the beautiful Italian Plum finish of the Cadillac he was not the sort of man to fret about a few scratches. On level ground, under the elm, the car stood idling. Two Chinese fangs of vapor came from the rear, and William got out, his face lined in the sun. He took in the house, Moses approaching eagerly. What must Will feel? Moses wondered. He must be appalled. What else could he be?

"Will! How are you?" He embraced his brother.

"How are you, Moses. Are you feeling all right?" Will might act as conservative as he pleased. He could never conceal his real emotions from his brother.

"I just shaved. I always look white after shaving, but I feel well. Honest, I do."

"You've lost weight. Maybe ten pounds, since you left Chicago. It's too much," said Will. "How's your rib?"

"Doesn't bother me a bit."

"And the head?"

"Fine. I've been resting. Where's Muriel? I thought she was coming, too."

"She took the plane. I'm going to meet her in Boston."

Will had learned to conduct himself with restraint. A Herzog, he had a good deal to hold down. Moses could remember a time when Willie, too, had been demonstrative, passionate, explosive, given to bursts of rage, flinging objects on the ground. Just a moment —what was it, now, that he had thrown down? A brush! That was it! The broad old Russian shoe brush. Will slammed it to the floor so hard the veneer backing fell off, and beneath were the stitches, ancient waxed thread, maybe even sinew. But that was long ago. Thirty-five years ago, easily. And where had it gone, the wrath of Willie Herzog? my dear brother? Into a certain poise and quiet humor, part decorousness, part (possibly) slavery. The explosions had become implosions, and where light once was darkness came, bit by bit. It didn't matter. The sight of Will stirred Moses' love for him. Will looked tired and wrinkled; he had been on the road a long time, he needed something to eat, and a rest. He had taken this long trip because he was concerned about him, Moses. And how considerate of him not to bring Muriel.

"How was the drive, Will? Are you hungry? Shall I open a can of tuna?"

"You're the one that doesn't seem to have eaten. I had something on the road."

"Well, come, sit down a while." He led him toward the lawn chairs. "It was lovely here when I took care of the grounds."

"So this is the house? No, I don't want to sit, thanks. I'd rather move around. Let's see it."

"Yes, this is the famous house, the house of happiness," said Moses, but he added, "As a matter of fact, I *have* been happy here. None of this ingratitude."

"It seems well built."

"From a builder's viewpoint it's terrific. Imagine what it would cost today. The foundations would hold the Empire State Building. And I'll show you the hand-hewn chestnut beams. Old mortice and tenon. No metal at all."

"It must be hard to heat."

"Not so hard. Electric baseboards."

"I wish I were selling you the current. Make a fortune . . . But it is a beautiful spot, I'll give you that. These trees are fine. How many acres have you got?"

"Forty. But surrounded by abandoned farms. Not a neighbor in two miles."

"Oh . . . Is that good?"

"Very private, I mean."

"What are your taxes?"

"One-eighty-six or so. Never over one-ninety."

"And the mortgage?"

"There's only a small principal. Payments and interest are two hundred and fifty a year."

"Very good," said Will approvingly. "But now tell me, how much money have you put into this place, Mose?"

"I've never totaled it up. Twenty grand, I guess. More than half of it in improvements."

Will nodded. His arms crossed, he gazed upward at the structure with his partly averted face—he too had this hereditary peculiarity. Only his eyes were quietly and firmly shrewd, not dreaming. Moses, however, saw without the slightest difficulty what Will was thinking.

He expressed it to himself in Yiddish. *In drerd aufn deck. The edge of nowhere. Out on the lid of Hell.*

"In itself, it's a fine-looking piece of property. It may turn out to be a pretty reasonable investment at that. Of course, the location *is* a bit peculiar. Ludeyville isn't on the map."

"No, not on the Esso map," Moses conceded. "The state of Massachusetts knows where it is, naturally."

Both brothers smiled slightly, without looking at each other.

"Let's look over the interior," said Will.

Moses gave him a tour of the house, beginning in the kitchen. "It needs an airing."

"It is a bit musty. But handsome. The plaster is in excellent condition."

"You need a cat to police the fieldmice. They winter in here. I'm fond of them but they chew everything. Even book bindings. They seem to love glue. And wax. Paraffin. Candles. Anything like that."

Will showed him great politeness. He did not confront him harshly with fundamentals, as Shura would have done. There was a certain sweet decency in Will. Helen had it, too. Shura would have said, "What a jerk you were to sink so much dough into this old barn." Well, that was simply Shura's way. Moses loved them all, notwithstanding.

"And the water supply?" said Will.

"Gravity-fed, from the spring. We have two old wells, too. One of them was ruined by kerosene. Someone let a whole tankful of kerosene leak out and soak down. But it doesn't matter. The water supply is excellent. The cesspool is well built. Could accommodate twenty people. You wouldn't need orange trees."

"Meaning what?"

"It means that at Versailles Louis Quatorze planted oranges because the excrement of the court made the air foul."

"How nice to have an education," said Will.

"To be pedantic, you mean," said Herzog. He spoke with a great deal of caution, taking special pains to give an impression of completest normalcy. That Will was studying him—Will who had become the most discreet and observant of the Herzogs—was transparently plain. Moses thought he could bear his scrutiny fairly well. His haggard, just-shaven cheeks were against him; as was the whole house (the skeletons in the toilet bowl, the owls in the fixtures, the half-painted piano, the remains of meals, the wife-deserted atmosphere); his "inspired" visit to Chicago was bad, too. Very bad. It must be noticeable, also, that he was in an extraordinary state, eyes dilated with excitement, the very speed of his pulses possibly visible in his large irises. *Why must I be such a throb-hearted character . . . But I am. I am, and you can't teach old dogs. Myself is thus and so, and will continue thus and so. And why fight it? My balance comes from instability. Not organization, or courage, as with other people. It's tough, but that's how it is. On these terms I, too—even I!—apprehend certain things. Perhaps the only way I'm able to do it. Must play the instrument I've got.*

"You've been painting this piano, I see."

"For June," said Herzog. "A present. A surprise."

"What?" Will laughed. "Are you planning to send it from here? Why it'll cost two hundred bucks in freight. And it would have to be fixed up, tuned. Is it such a great piano?"

"Madeleine bought it at auction for twenty-five bucks."

"Take my word for it, Moses, you can buy a nice old piano right in Chicago, at a warehouse sale. Lots of old instruments like this, kicking around."

"Yes . . . ? Only I like this color." This apple, parrot green, the special Ludeyville color. Moses' eyes were fixed upon his work with a certain inspired persistency. He was near a point of open impulsiveness, and some peculiarity might now dart forth. He couldn't allow that to happen. Under no circumstances must he utter a single word that might be interpreted as irrational. Things already looked bad enough. He glanced away from the piano into the clear shade of the garden, and tried to become as clear as *that*. He deferred to his brother's opinion. "Okay. Next trip, I'll get her a piano."

"What you've got here is an excellent summer house," said Will. "A little lonely, but nice. If you can clean it up."

"It can be lovely here. But you know, we might make it a Herzog summer resort. For the family. Everyone put in a little money. Cut the brush. Build a swimming pool."

"Oh, sure. Helen hates travel, you know that. And Shura is just the man to come up here where there are no race horses, or card games, or other tycoons, or broads."

"There are trotter races at the Barrington Fair. . . . No, I guess that's not such a good idea, either. Well, perhaps we could make it into a nursing home. Or move it to another location."

"Not worth it. I've seen mansions wrecked for slum clearance or for new superhighways. This isn't worth dismantling. Can't you rent it out?"

Herzog silently grinned, staring with piercing humor at Will.

"All right, Mose, the only other suggestion is that you put it up for sale. You won't get your money out of it."

"I could go to work and become rich. Make a ton of money, just to keep this house."

"Yes," said Will. "You might." He spoke gently to his brother.

"Odd situation I've gotten into, Will—isn't it?" said Moses. "For me. For us—the Herzogs, I mean. It seems a strange point to arrive at after all the other points. In this lovely green hole . . . You're worried about me, I see."

Will, troubled but controlled, one of the most deeply familiar and longest-loved of human faces, looked at him in a way that could not be mistaken. "Of course I'm worried. Helen too."

"Well, you mustn't be distressed about me. I'm in a peculiar state, but not in a bad one. I'd open my heart to you, Will, if I could

331

find the knob. There's no reason to be upset about me. By God, Will, I'm about to cry! How did that happen? I won't do it. It's only love. Or something that bears down like love. It probably is love. I'm in no shape to buck it. I don't want you to think anything wrong."

"Mose—why should I?" Will spoke in a low voice. "I have something deep-in for you, too. I feel about the way you do. Just because I'm a contractor doesn't mean I can't understand what you mean. I didn't come to do you harm, you know. That's right, Mose, take a chair. You look out on your feet."

Moses sat on the old sofa, which gave off dust as soon as you touched it.

"I'd like to see you less agitated. You must get some food and sleep. Probably a little medical care. A few days in the hospital, taking it easy."

"Will, I'm excited, not sick. I don't want to be treated as though I were sick in the head. I'm grateful that you came." Silently and stubbornly he sat, persisting, putting down his violent, choking craving for tears. His voice was dim.

"Take your time," said Will.

"I . . ." Herzog found his voice again and said distinctly, "I want to be straight about one thing. I'm not turning myself over to you out of weakness, or because I can't make my own way. I don't mind taking it easy in some hospital for a few days. If you and Helen decided that that was what I should do, I see no objection. Clean sheets and a bath and some hot food. Sleep. That's all pleasant. But only a few days. I have to visit Marco at camp on the sixteenth. That's Parents' Day and he's expecting me."

"Fair enough," said Will. "That's no more than right."

"Only a while back, in New York, I had fantasies about being put in the hospital."

"You were only being sensible," said his brother. "What you need is supervised rest. I've thought about it, too, for myself. Once in a while, we all get that way. Now"—he looked at his watch—"I asked my physician to phone a local hospital. In Pittsfield."

As soon as Will had spoken, Moses sat forward on the sofa. He could not find words. He only made a negative sign with his head. At this, Will's face changed, too. He seemed to think he had pronounced the word hospital too abruptly, that he ought to have been more gradual, circumspect.

"No," said Moses, still shaking his head. "No. Definitely."

Now Will was silent, still with the pained air of a man who had made a tactical error. Moses could easily imagine what Will had said to Helen, after he had bailed him out, and what a worried consultation they had had about him. ("What shall we do? Poor Mose—maybe it's all driven him mad. Let's at least get a professional opinion about him.") Helen was great on professional opinions. The veneration with which she said "professional opinion" had always amused Moses. And so they had approached Will's internist to ask if he would, discreetly, arrange something in the Berkshire area. "But I thought we already agreed," said Will.

"No, Will. No hospitals. I know you and Helen are doing what brother and sister should. And I'm tempted to go along. To a man like me, it's a seductive idea. 'Supervised rest.' "

"And why not? If I'd found some improvement in you I might not have brought it up," said Will. "But look at you."

"I know," said Moses. "But just as I begin to be a little rational you want to hand me over to a psychiatrist. It *was* a psychiatrist you and Helen had in mind, wasn't it?"

Will was silent, taking counsel with himself. Then he sighed and said, "What harm could there be in it?"

"Was it any more fantastic for me to have these wives, children, to move to a place like this than for Papa to have been a bootlegger? We never thought he was mad." Moses began to smile. ". . . Do you remember, Will—he had those phony labels printed up: White Horse, Johnnie Walker, Haig and Haig, and we'd sit at the table with the paste-pot, and he'd flash those labels and say, 'Well, children, what should we make today?', and we'd start to cry out and squeak 'White Horse,' 'Teacher's.' And the coal stove was hot. It dropped embers like red teeth in the ash. He had those dark green lovely bottles. They don't make glass like that, in those shapes, any more. My favorite was White Horse."

Will laughed softly.

"Going to the hospital would be fine," said Herzog. "But it would be just the wrong thing to do. It's about time I stopped laboring with this curse—I think, I figure things out. I see exactly what I should avoid. Then, all of a sudden, I'm in bed with that very thing, and making love to it. As with Madeleine. She seems to have filled a special need."

"How do you figure that, Moses?" Will joined him on the sofa, and sat beside him.

"A very special need. I don't know what. She brought ideology into my life. Something to do with catastrophe. After all, it's an ideological age. Maybe she wouldn't make a father of anyone she liked."

Will smiled at Moses' way of putting it. "But what do you intend to do here now?"

"I may as well stay on. I'm not far from Marco's camp. Yes, that's it. If Daisy'll let me, I'll bring him here next month. What I'll do is this, if you'll drive me and my bike into Ludeyville, I'll have the lights and the phone turned on. Tuttle'll come up and mow the place. Maybe Mrs. Tuttle will clean up for me. That's what I'll do." He stood up. "I'll get the water running again, and buy some solid food. Come, Will, give me a lift down to Tuttle's."

"Who is this Tuttle?"

"He runs everything. He's the master spirit of Ludeyville. A tall fellow. He's shy, to look at, but that's only more of his shrewdness. He's the demon of these woods. He can have the lights burning here within an hour. He knows all. He overcharges, but very, very shyly."

Tuttle was standing beside his high, lean, antiquated gas pumps when Will drove up. Thin, wrinkled, the hairs on his corded forearms bleached meal-white, he wore a cotton paint cap and between his false teeth (to help him kick the smoking habit, as he had once explained to Herzog) he kept a plastic toothpick. "I knew you was up in the place, Mr. Herzog," he said. "Welcome back."

"How did you know?"

"I saw the smoke onto your chimney, that's the first of all."

"Yes? And what's the second?"

"Why, a lady's been tryin' to get you on the telephone."

"Who?" said Will.

"A party in Barrington. She left the number."

"Only her number?" said Herzog. "No name?"

"Miss Harmona, or Armona."

"Ramona," said Herzog. "Is she in Barrington?"

"Were you expecting someone?" Will turned to him in the seat.

"No one but you."

Will insisted on knowing more. "Who is she?"

Somewhat unwillingly, and with an evasive look, Moses answered, "A lady—a woman." Then, putting off his reticence—why, after all, should he be nervous about it?—he added, "A woman, a florist, a friend from New York."

"Are you going to return her call?"

"Yes, of course." He observed the white listening face of Mrs. Tuttle in the dark store. "I wonder," he said to Tuttle. ". . . I want to open the house. I have to get the current on. Maybe Mrs. Tuttle will help me clean the place a bit."

"Oh, I think she might."

Mrs. Tuttle wore tennis shoes and, under her dress, the edge of her nightgown showed. Her polished fingernails were tobacco-stained. She had gained much weight in Herzog's absence, and he noted the distortion of her pretty face, the heaviness of her neglected dark hair and the odd distant look in her gray eyes, as if the fat of her body had an opiate effect on her. He knew that she had monitored his conversations with Madeleine on the party line. Probably she had heard all the shameful, terrible things that had been said, listened to the rant and the sobbing. Now he was about to invite her to come to work, to sweep the floors, make his bed. She reached for a filter cigarette, lit it like a man, stared through smoke with tranced gray eyes and said, "Why, I think so, yes. It's my day off from the mortel. I been working as a chambermaid over in the new mortel on the highway."

"Moses!" said Ramona, on the telephone. "You got my message. How lovely you're in your place. Everybody in Barrington says if you want things done in Ludeyville, call Tuttle."

"Hello, Ramona. Didn't my wire from Chicago reach you?"

"Yes, Moses. It was very considerate. But I didn't think you'd stay away long, and I had a feeling about your house in the country. Anyway, I had to visit old friends in Barrington, so I drove up."

"Really?" said Herzog. "What day of the week is this?"

Ramona laughed. "How typical. No wonder women lose their heads over you. It's Saturday. I'm staying with Myra and Eduardo Misseli."

"Oh, the fiddler. I only know him to nod to at the super-market."

"He's a charming man. Do you know he's studying the art of violin-making? I've been in his shop all morning. And I thought I must have a look at the Herzog estate."

"My brother is with me—Will."

"Oh, splendid," said Ramona, in her lifted voice. "Is he staying with you?"

"No, he's passing through."

"I'd love to meet him. The Misselis are giving a little party for me. After dinner."

Will stood beside the booth, listening. Earnest, worried, his dark eyes discreetly appealed to Moses to make no more mistakes. I can't promise that, thought Moses. I can only tell him that I don't contemplate putting myself in the hands of Ramona or any woman, at this time. Will's gaze held a family look, a brown light as clear as any word.

"No, thank you," said Herzog. "No parties. I'm not up to them. But look, Ramona . . ."

"Should I run up?" said Ramona. "It's silly, being on the phone like this. You're only eight minutes away."

"Well, perhaps," said Herzog. "It occurs to me I have to come down to Barrington anyway, to shop, and to have my phone recon-nected."

"Oh, you're planning to stay awhile in Ludeyville?"

"Yes. Marco'll be joining me. Just a moment, Ramona." Her-zog put a hand over the instrument and said to Will, "Can you take me into Barrington?" Will of course said yes.

Ramona was waiting, smiling, a few minutes later. She stood beside her black Mercedes in shorts and sandals. She wore a Mexi-can blouse with coin buttons. Her hair glittered, and she looked flushed. The anxiety of the moment threatened her self-control. "Ramona," said Moses, "this is Will."

"Oh, Mr. Herzog, what a pleasure to meet Moses' brother."

Will, though wary of her, was courteous nevertheless. He had a quiet, tidy social manner. Herzog was grateful to him for the charm-ing reserve of his courtesy to Ramona. Will's glance was sym-pathetic. He smiled, but not too much. Obviously he found Ramona impressively attractive. "He must have been expecting a dog," thought Herzog.

"Why, Moses," said Ramona, "you've cut yourself shaving. And badly. Your whole jaw is scraped."

"Ah?" He touched himself with vague concern.

"You look so much like your brother, Mr. Herzog. The same fine head, and those soft hazel eyes. You're not staying?"

"I'm on my way to Boston."

"And I simply had to get out of New York. Aren't the Berkshires marvelous? Such green!"

Love-bandit, the tabloids used to print over such dark heads. In the twenties. Indeed, Ramona did look like those figures of sex and swagger. But there was something intensely touching about her, too. She struggled, she fought. She needed extraordinary courage to hold this poise. In this world, to be a woman who took matters into her own hands! And this courage of hers was unsteady. At times it trembled. She pretended to look for something in her purse because her cheek quivered. The perfume of her shoulders reached his nostrils. And, as almost always, he heard the deep, the cosmic, the idiotic masculine response—*quack*. The progenitive, the lustful quacking in the depths. *Quack. Quack.*

"You won't come to the party then?" said Ramona. "And when am I going to see your house?"

"Why, I'm having it cleaned up a little," said Herzog.

"Then can't we . . . Why don't we have dinner together?" she said. "You, too, Mr. Herzog. Moses can tell you that my shrimp remoulade is rather good."

"It's better than that. I never ate better. But Will has to go on, and you're on a holiday, Ramona, we can't have you cooking for three. Why don't you come out and have dinner with me?"

"Oh," said Ramona with a new rise of gaiety. "You want to entertain me?"

"Well, why not? I'll get a couple of swordfish steaks."

Will looked at him with his uncertain smile.

"Wonderful. I'll bring a bottle of wine," said Ramona.

"You'll do nothing of the sort. Come up at six. We'll eat at seven and you can still get back to your party in plenty of time."

Musically (was it a deliberate effect? Moses could not decide),

Ramona said to Will, "Then good-by, Mr. Herzog. I hope we shall meet again." Turning to get into her Mercedes, she put her hand momentarily on Moses' shoulder. "I expect a good dinner. . . ."

She wanted Will to be aware of their intimacy, and Moses saw no reason to deny her this. He pressed his face to hers.

"Shall we say good-by here, too?" said Moses as she drove off. "I can take a cab back. I don't want to make you late."

"No, no, I'll run you up to Ludeyville."

"I'll go in here and get my swordfish. Some lemon, too. Butter. Coffee."

They were on the last slope before Ludeyville when Will said, "Am I leaving you in good hands, Mose?"

"Is it safe to go, you mean? I think you can, with confidence. Ramona's not so bad."

"Bad? What do you mean? She's stunning. But so was Madeleine."

"I'm not being left in anyone's hands."

With a mild, soft look of irony, sad and affectionate, Will said, "Amen. But what about this ideology. Doesn't she have some?"

"This will do, here, in front of Tuttle's. They'll take me in the pickup, bike and all. Yes, I think she has some. About sex. She's pretty fanatical about it. But I don't mind that."

"I'll get out and make certain of the directions," said Will.

Tuttle, as they walked slowly past him, told Moses, "I think we'll have that current onto your house in a few minutes."

"Thanks . . . Here, Will, take a little of this arborvitae to chew. It's a very pleasant taste."

"Don't decide anything now. You can't afford any more mistakes."

"I've asked her to dinner. Only that. She goes back to the party at Misseli's—I'm not going with her. Tomorrow is Sunday. She's got a business in New York, and she can't stay. I won't elope with her. Or she with me, as you see it."

"You have a strange influence on people," said Will. "Well, good-by, Mose. Maybe Muriel and I will stop by on our way west."

"You'll find me unmarried."

"If you didn't give a goddamn, it wouldn't matter. You could marry five more wives. But with your intense way of doing everything . . . and your talent for making a fatal choice."

338

"Will, you can go with an easy mind. I tell you . . . I promise. Nothing like that will happen. Not a chance. Good-by, and thanks. And as for the house . . ."

"I'll be thinking about that. Do you need money?"

"No."

"You're sure? You're telling the truth? Remember, you're talking to your brother."

"I know whom I'm talking to." He took Will by the shoulders and kissed him on the cheek. "Good-by, Will. Take the first right as you leave town. You'll see the turnpike sign."

When Will had gone, Moses waited for Mrs. Tuttle in the seat by the arborvitae, having his first leisurely look at the village. *Everywhere on earth, the model of natural creation seems to be the ocean. The mountains certainly look that way, glossy, plunging, and that haughty blue color. And even these scrappy lawns. What keeps these red brick houses from collapse on these billows is their inner staleness. I smell it yawning through the screens. The odor of souls is a brace to the walls. Otherwise the wrinkling of the hills would make them crumble.*

"You got a gorgeous old place here, Mr. Herzog," said Mrs. Tuttle as they drove in her old car up the hill. "It must've cost you a penny to improve it. It's a shame you don't use it more."

"We've got to get the kitchen cleaned up so I can cook a meal. I'll find you the brooms and pails and such."

He was groping in the dark pantry when the lights went on. *Tuttle is a miracle man,* he thought. *I asked him at about two. It must be four-thirty, five.*

Mrs. Tuttle, a cigarette in her mouth, tied her head up in a bandanna. Beneath the hem of her dress the peach nylon of her nightgown nearly touched the floor. In the stone cellar Herzog found the pump switch. At once he heard the water rising, washing into the empty pressure tank. He connected the range. He turned on the refrigerator; it would take a while to get cold. Then it occurred to him to chill the wine in the spring. After that, he took up the scythe to clear the yard, so that Ramona would have a better view of the house. But after he had cut a few swathes his ribs began to ache. He didn't feel well enough for this sort of work. He lay stretched in the lawn chair, facing south. As soon as the sun lost its main strength the hermit thrushes began, and while they sang their sweet fierce music threatening trespassers, the blackbirds would begin to gather in flocks for the night, and just toward sunset they would break from these trees in waves, wave after wave, three or four miles in one flight to their waterside nests.

To have Ramona coming troubled him slightly, it was true. But they would eat. She would help him with the dishes, and then he'd see her to her car.

I will do no more to enact the peculiarities of life. This is done well enough without my special assistance.

Now on one side the hills lost the sun and began to put on a more intense blue color; on the other they were still white and green. The birds were very loud.

Anyway, can I pretend I have much choice? I look at myself and see chest, thighs, feet—a head. This strange organization, I know it will die. And inside—something, something, happiness . . . "Thou movest me." That leaves no choice. Something produces intensity, a holy feeling, as oranges produce orange, as grass green, as birds heat. Some hearts put out more love and some less of it, presumably. Does it signify anything? There are those who say this product of hearts is knowledge. "Je sens mon cœur et je connais les hommes." But his mind now detached itself also from its French. I couldn't say that, for sure. My face too blind, my mind too limited, my instincts too narrow. But this intensity, doesn't it mean anything? Is it an idiot joy that makes this animal, the most peculiar animal of all, exclaim something? And he thinks this reaction a sign, a proof, of eternity? And he has it in his breast? But I have no arguments to make about it. "Thou movest me." "But what do you want, Herzog?" "But that's just it—not a solitary thing. I am pretty well satisfied to be, to be just as it is willed, and for as long as I may remain in occupancy."

Then he thought he'd light candles at dinner, because Ramona was fond of them. There might be a candle or two in the fuse box. But now it was time to get those bottles from the spring. The labels had washed off, but the glass was well chilled. He took pleasure in the vivid cold of the water.

Coming back from the woods, he picked some flowers for the table. He wondered whether there was a corkscrew in the drawer. Had Madeleine taken it to Chicago? Well, maybe Ramona had a corkscrew in her Mercedes. An unreasonable thought. A nail could be used, if it came to that. Or you could break the neck of the bottle as they did in old movies. Meanwhile, he filled his hat from the rambler vine, the one that clutched the rainpipe. The spines were still too green to hurt much. By the cistern there were yellow day lilies. He took some of these, too, but they wilted instantly. And, back in the darker garden, he looked for peonies; perhaps some had survived. But then it struck him that he might be making a mistake, and he stopped, listening to Mrs. Tuttle's sweeping, the rhythm of bristles. Picking flowers? He was being thoughtful, being lovable. How would it be interpreted? (He smiled slightly.) Still, he need only know his own mind, and the flowers couldn't be used; no, they couldn't be turned against him. So he did not throw them away. He turned his dark face toward the house again. He went around and entered from the front, wondering what further evidence of his sanity, besides refusing to go to the hospital, he could show. Perhaps he'd stop writing letters. Yes, that was what was coming, in fact. The knowledge that he was done with these letters. Whatever had come over him during these last months, the spell, really seemed to be passing, really going. He set down his hat, with the roses and day lilies, on the half-painted piano, and went into his study, carrying the wine bottles in one hand like a pair of Indian clubs. Walking over notes and papers, he lay down on his Recamier couch. As he stretched out, he took a long breath, and then he lay, looking at the mesh of the screen, pulled loose by vines, and listening to the steady scratching of Mrs. Tuttle's broom. He wanted to tell her to sprinkle the floor. She was raising too much dust. In a few minutes he would call down to her, "Damp it down, Mrs. Tuttle. There's water in the sink." But not just yet. At this time he had no messages for anyone. Nothing. Not a single word.

II

THE AUTHOR SPEAKS

SAUL BELLOW: AN INTERVIEW
BY GORDON LLOYD HARPER

The interview "took place" over a period of several weeks. Beginning with some exploratory discussions during May of 1965, it was shelved during the summer, and actually accomplished during September and October. Two recording sessions were held, totaling about an hour and a half, but this was only a small part of the effort Mr. Bellow gave to this interview. A series of meetings, for over five weeks, was devoted to the most careful revision of the original material. Recognizing at the outset the effort he would make for such an interview, he had real reluctance about beginning it at all. Once his decision had been reached, however, he gave a remarkable amount of his time freely to the task—up to two hours a day, at least twice and often three times a week throughout the entire five-week period. It had become an opportunity, as he put it, to say some things which were important but which weren't being said.

Certain types of questions were ruled out in early discussions. Mr. Bellow was not interested in responding to criticisms of his work which he found trivial or stupid. He quoted the Jewish proverb that a fool can throw a stone into the water which ten wise men cannot recover. Nor did he wish to discuss what he considered his personal writing habits, whether he used a pen or typewriter, how hard he pressed on the page. For the artist to give such loving attention to his own shoelaces was dangerous, even immoral. Finally, there were certain questions that led into too "wide

From *Writers at Work: Third Series* (New York: The Viking Press, 1967).
First published in *The Paris Review*, No. 36 (Winter 1966).

spaces" for this interview, subjects for fuller treatment on other occasions.

The two tapes were made in Bellow's University of Chicago office on the fifth floor of the Social Sciences Building. The office, though large, is fairly typical of those on the main quadrangles: much of it rather dark with one brightly lighted area, occupied by his desk, immediately before a set of three dormer windows; dark-green metal bookcases line the walls, casually used as storage for a miscellany of books, magazines, and correspondence. A set of *The Complete Works of Rudyard Kipling* ("It was given to me") shares space with examination copies of new novels and with a few of Bellow's own books, including recent French and Italian translations of *Herzog*. A table, a couple of typing stands, and various decrepit and mismatched chairs are scattered in apparently haphazard fashion throughout the room. A wall rack just inside the door holds his jaunty black felt hat and his walking cane. There is a general sense of disarray, with stacks of papers, books, and letters lying everywhere. When one comes to the door, Bellow is frequently at his typing stand, rapidly pounding out on a portable machine responses to some of the many letters he gets daily. Occasionally a secretary enters and proceeds to type away on some project at the far end of the room.

During the two sessions with the tape recorder, Bellow sat at his desk, between the eaves with project prominently into the room, backlighted by the dormer windows which let in the bright afternoon sun from the south. Four stories below lie Fifty-ninth Street and Chicago's Midway, their automobile and human noises continually penetrating the office. As the questions were asked, Bellow listened carefully and often developed an answer slowly, pausing frequently to think out the exact phrasing he sought. His answers were serious, but full of his special quality of humor. He took obvious pleasure in the amusing turns of thought with which he often concluded an answer. Throughout, he was at great pains to make his ideas transparent to the interviewer, asking repeatedly if this was clear or if he should say more on the subject. His concentration during these sessions was intense enough to be tiring, and both tapes were brought to a close with his confessing to some exhaustion.

Following each taping session, a typescript of his remarks was prepared. Bellow worked over these typed sheets extensively with pen and ink, taking as many as three separate meetings to do a complete revision. Then another typescript was made, and the process started over. This work was done when the interviewer could be present, and again the changes were frequently tested on him. Generally these sessions occurred at Bellow's office or at his apartment, overlooking the Outer Drive and Lake Michigan. Once, however, revisions were made while he and the interviewer sat on a Jackson Park bench on a fine October afternoon, and one typescript was worked on along with beer and hamburgers at a local bar.

Revisions were of various sorts. Frequently there were slight changes in meaning: "That's what I really meant to say." Other alterations tightened up his language or were in the nature of stylistic improvements. Any sections which he judged to be excursions from the main topic were deleted. Most regretted by the interviewer were prunings that eliminated certain samples of the characteristic Bellow wit: In a few places he came to feel he was simply "exhibiting" himself, and these were scratched out. On the other hand, whenever he could substitute for conventional literary diction an unexpected colloquial turn of phrase—which often proved humorous in context—he did so.

INTERVIEWER: Some critics have felt that your work falls within the tradition of American naturalism, possibly because of some things you've said about Dreiser. I was wondering if you saw yourself in a particular literary tradition.

BELLOW: Well, I think that the development of realism in the nineteenth century is still the major event of modern literature. Dreiser, a realist of course, had elements of genius. He was clumsy, cumbersome, and in some respects a poor thinker. But he was rich in a kind of feeling which has been ruled off the grounds by many contemporary writers—the kind of feeling that every human being intuitively recognizes as primary. Dreiser has more open access to primary feelings than any American writer of the twentieth century. It makes a good many people uncomfortable that his emotion has not found a more developed literary form. It's true his art may be too "natural." He sometimes conveys his understanding by masses of words, verbal approximations. He blunders, but generally in the direction of truth. The result is that we are moved in an unmediated way by his characters, as by life, and then we say that his novels are simply torn from the side of life, and therefore not novels. But we can't escape reading them. He somehow conveys, without much refinement, depths of feeling that we usually associate with Balzac or Shakespeare.

INTERVIEWER: This realism, then, is a particular kind of sensibility, rather than a technique?

BELLOW: Realism specializes in *apparently* unmediated experiences. What stirred Dreiser was simply the idea that you could bring unmediated feeling to the novel. He took it up naïvely without going to the trouble of mastering an art. We don't see this because he makes so many familiar "art" gestures, borrowed from the art fashions of his day, and even from the slick magazines, but he is really a natural, a primitive. I have great respect for his simplicities and I think they are worth more than much that has been praised as high art in the American novel.

INTERVIEWER: Could you give me an example of what you mean?

BELLOW: In a book like *Jennie Gerhardt* the delicacy with which Jennie allows Lester Kane to pursue his conventional life while she herself lives unrecognized with her illegitimate daughter, the depth of her understanding, and the depth of her sympathy and of her truthfulness impress me. She is not a sentimental figure. She has a natural sort of honor.

INTERVIEWER: Has recent American fiction pretty much followed this direction?

BELLOW: Well, among his heirs there are those who believe that clumsiness and truthfulness go together. But cumbersomeness does not necessarily imply a sincere heart. Most of the "Dreiserians" lack talent. On the other hand, people who put Dreiser down, adhering to a "high art" standard for the novel, miss the point.

INTERVIEWER: Aside from Dreiser, what other American writers do you find particularly of interest?

BELLOW: I like Hemingway, Faulkner, and Fitzgerald. I think of Hemingway as a man who developed a significant manner as an artist, a life-style which is important. For his generation, his language created a life-style, one which pathetic old gentlemen are still found clinging to. I don't think of Hemingway as a great novelist. I like Fitzgerald's novels better, but I often feel about Fitzgerald that he couldn't distinguish between innocence and social climbing. I am thinking of *The Great Gatsby*.

INTERVIEWER: If we go outside American literature, you've mentioned that you read the nineteenth-century Russian writers with a good deal of interest. Is there anything particular about them that attracts you?

BELLOW: Well, the Russians have an immediate charismatic appeal—excuse the Max Weberism. Their conventions allow them to express freely their feelings about nature and human beings. We have inherited a more restricted and imprisoning attitude toward the emotions. We have to work around puritanical and stoical restraints. We lack the Russian openness. Our path is narrower.

INTERVIEWER: In what other writers do you take special interest?

BELLOW: I have a special interest in Joyce; I have a special interest in Lawrence. I read certain poets over and over again. I can't say where they belong in my theoretical scheme; I only know that I have an attachment to them. Yeats is one such poet. Hart Crane is another. Hardy and Walter de la Mare. I don't know what these have in common—probably nothing. I know that I am drawn repeatedly to these men.

INTERVIEWER: It's been said that one can't like *both* Lawrence and Joyce, that one has to choose between them. You don't feel this way?

BELLOW: No. Because I really don't take Lawrence's sexual theories very seriously. I take his art seriously, not his doctrine. But he himself warned us repeatedly not to trust the artist. He said trust the work itself. So I have little use for the Lawrence who wrote *The Plumed Serpent* and great admiration for the Lawrence who wrote *The Lost Girl*.

INTERVIEWER: Does Lawrence at all share the special feeling you find attractive in Dreiser?

BELLOW: A certain openness to experience, yes. And a willingness to trust one's instinct, to follow it freely—that Lawrence has.

INTERVIEWER: You mentioned before the interview that you would prefer not to talk about your early novels, that you feel you are a different person now from what you were then. I wonder if this is all you want to say, or if you can say something about how you have changed.

BELLOW: I think that when I wrote those early books I was timid. I still felt the incredible effrontery of announcing myself to the world (in part I mean the WASP world) as a writer and an artist. I had to touch a great many bases, demonstrate my abilities, pay my respects to formal requirements. In short, I was afraid to let myself go.

INTERVIEWER: When do you find a significant change occurring?

BELLOW: When I began to write *Augie March*. I took off many of these restraints. I think I took off too many, and went too far, but I was feeling the excitement of discovery. I had just increased my freedom, and like any emancipated plebeian I abused it at once.

INTERVIEWER: What were these restraints that you took off in *Augie March*?

BELLOW: My first two books are well made. I wrote the first quickly but took great pains with it. I labored with the second and tried to make it letter-perfect. In writing *The Victim* I accepted a Flaubertian standard. Not a bad standard, to be sure, but one which, in the end, I found repressive—repressive because of the circumstances of my life and because of my upbringing in Chicago as the son of immigrants. I could not, with such an instrument as I developed in the first two books, express a variety of things I knew intimately. Those books, though useful, did not give me a form in which I felt comfortable. A writer should be able to express himself easily, naturally, copiously in a form which frees his mind, his energies. Why should he hobble himself with formalities? With a borrowed sensibility? With the desire to be "correct"? Why should I force myself to write like an Englishman or a contributor to *The New Yorker*? I soon saw that it was simply not in me to be a mandarin. I should add that for a young man in my position there were social inhibitions, too. I had good reason to fear that I would be put down as a foreigner, an interloper. It was made clear to me when I studied literature in the university that as a Jew and the son of Russian Jews I would probably never have the right *feeling* for Anglo-Saxon traditions, for English words. I realized even in college that the people who told me this were not necessarily disinterested friends. But they had an effect on me, nevertheless. This was something from which I had to free myself. I fought free because I had to.

INTERVIEWER: Are these social inhibitors as powerful today as they were when you wrote *Dangling Man*?

BELLOW: I think I was lucky to have grown up in the Middle West, where such influences are less strong. If I'd grown up in the East and attended an Ivy League university, I might have been damaged more badly. Puritan and Protestant America carries less weight in Illinois than in Massachusetts. But I don't bother much with such things now.

INTERVIEWER: Did another change in your writing occur between *Augie March* and *Herzog*? You've mentioned writing *Augie March* with a great sense of freedom, but I take it that *Herzog* was a very difficult book to write.

BELLOW: It was. I had to tame and restrain the style I developed in *Augie March* in order to write *Henderson* and *Herzog*. I think both those books reflect that change in style. I wouldn't really know how to describe it. I don't care to trouble my mind to find an exact description for it, but it has something to do with a kind of readiness to record impressions arising from a source of which we know little. I suppose that all of us have a primitive prompter or commentator within, who from earliest years has been advising us, telling us what the real world is. There is such a commentator in me. I have to prepare the ground for him. From this source come words, phrases, syllables; sometimes only sounds, which I try to interpret, sometimes whole paragraphs, fully punctuated. When E. M. Forster said, "How do I know what I think until I see what I say?" he was perhaps referring to his own prompter. There is that observing instrument in us—in childhood at any rate. At the sight of a man's face, his shoes, the color of light, a woman's mouth or perhaps her ear, one receives a word, a phrase, at times nothing but a nonsense syllable from the primitive commentator.

INTERVIEWER: So this change in your writing—

BELLOW:—was an attempt to get nearer to that primitive commentator.

INTERVIEWER: How do you go about getting nearer to him, preparing the way for him?

BELLOW: When I say the commentator is primitive, I don't mean that he's crude; God knows he's often fastidious. But he won't talk until the situation's right. And if you prepare the ground for him with too many difficulties underfoot, he won't say anything. I must be terribly given to fraud and deceit because I sometimes have great difficulty preparing a suitable ground. This is why I've had so much trouble with my last two novels. I appealed directly to my prompter. The prompter, however, has to find the occasion perfect—that is to say, truthful, and necessary. If there is any superfluity or inner falsehood in the preparations, he is aware of it. I have to stop. Often I have to begin again, with the first word. I can't remember how many times I wrote *Herzog*. But at last I did find the acceptable ground for it.

INTERVIEWER: Do these preparations include your coming to some general conception of the work?

BELLOW: Well, I don't know exactly how it's done. I let it alone a good deal. I try to avoid common forms of strain and distortion. For a long time, perhaps from the middle of the nineteenth century, writers have not been satisfied to regard themselves simply as writers. They have required also a theoretical framework. Most often they have been their own theoreticians, have created their own ground as artists, and have provided an exegesis for their own works. They have found it necessary to take a position, not merely to write novels. In bed last night I was reading a collection of articles by Stendhal. One of them amused me very much, touched me. Stendhal was saying how lucky writers were in the age of Louis XIV not to have anyone take them very seriously. Their obscurity was very valuable. Corneille had been dead for several days before anyone at court considered the fact important enough to mention. In the nineteenth century, says Stendhal, there would have been several public orations, Corneille's funeral covered by all the papers. There are great advantages in not being taken *too* seriously. Some writers are excessively serious about themselves. They accept the ideas of the "cultivated public." There is such a thing as overcapitalizing the A in artist. Certain writers and musicians understand this. Stravinsky says the composer should practice his trade exactly as a shoemaker does. Mozart and Haydn accepted commissions—wrote to order. In the nineteenth century, the artist loftily waited for Inspiration. Once you elevate yourself to the rank of a cultural institution, you're in for a lot of trouble.

Then there is a minor modern disorder—the disease of people who live by an image of themselves created by papers, television, Broadway, Sardi's, gossip, or the public need for celebrities. Even buffoons, prize fighters, and movie stars have caught the bug. I avoid these "images." I have a longing, not for downright obscurity—I'm too egotistical for that—but for peace, and freedom from meddling.

INTERVIEWER: In line with this, the enthusiastic response to *Herzog* must have affected your life considerably. Do you have any thoughts as to why this book became and remained the best seller it did?

BELLOW: I don't like to agree with the going view that if you write a best seller it's because you betrayed an important principle or sold your soul. I know that sophisticated opinion believes this. And although I don't take much stock in sophisticated opinion, I have examined my conscience. I've tried to find out whether I had unwittingly done wrong. But I haven't yet discovered the sin. I do think that a book like *Herzog*, which ought to have been an obscure book with a total sale of eight thousand, has such a reception because it appeals to the unconscious sympathies of many people. I know from the mail I've received that the book described a common predicament. *Herzog* appealed to Jewish readers, to those who had been divorced, to those who talk to themselves, to college graduates, readers of paperbacks, autodidacts, to those who yet hope to live awhile, etc.

INTERVIEWER: Do you feel there were deliberate attempts at lionizing by the literary tastemakers? I was thinking that the recent deaths of Faulkner and Hemingway have been seen as creating a vacuum in American letters, which we all know is abhorrent.

BELLOW: Well, I don't know whether I would say a vacuum. Perhaps a pigeonhole. I agree that there is a need to keep the pigeonholes filled and that people are uneasy when there are vacancies. Also the mass media demand material—grist—and literary journalists have to create a major-league atmosphere in literature. The writers don't offer to fill the pigeonholes. It's the critics who want figures in the pantheon. But there are many people who assume that every writer must be bucking for the niche. Why should writers wish to be rated—seeded—like tennis players? Handicapped like racehorses? What an epitaph for a novelist: "He won all the polls"!

INTERVIEWER: How much are you conscious of the reader when you write? Is there an ideal audience that you write for?

BELLOW: I have in mind another human being who will understand me. I count on this. Not on perfect understanding, which is Cartesian, but on approximate understanding, which is Jewish. And on a meeting of sympathies, which is human. But I have no ideal reader in my head, no. Let me just say this, too. I seem to have the blind self-acceptance of the eccentric who can't conceive that his eccentricities are not clearly understood.

INTERVIEWER: So there isn't a great deal of calculation about rhetoric?

BELLOW: These are things that can't really be contrived. People who talk about contrivance must think that a novelist is a man capable of building a skyscraper to conceal a dead mouse. Skyscrapers are not raised simply to conceal mice.

INTERVIEWER: It's been said that contemporary fiction sees man as a victim. You gave this title to one of your early novels, yet there seems to be very strong opposition in your fiction to seeing man as simply determined or futile. Do you see any truth to this claim about contemporary fiction?

BELLOW: Oh, I think that realistic literature from the first has been a victim literature. Pit any ordinary individual—and realistic literature concerns itself with ordinary individuals—against the external world, and the external world will conquer him, of course. Everything that people believed in the nineteenth century about determinism, about man's place in nature, about the power of productive forces in society, made it inevitable that the hero of the realistic novel should not be a hero but a sufferer who is eventually overcome. So I was doing nothing very original by writing another realistic novel about a common man and calling it *The Victim*. I suppose I was discovering independently the essence of much of modern realism. In my innocence, I put my finger on it. Serious realism also contrasts the common man with aristocratic greatness. He is overborne by fate, just as the great are in Shakespeare or Sophocles. But this contrast, inherent in literary tradition, always damages him. In the end the force of tradition carries realism into parody, satire, mock-epic—Leopold Bloom.

INTERVIEWER: Haven't you yourself moved away from the suggestion of plebeian tragedy toward a treatment of the sufferer that has greater comic elements? Although the concerns and difficulties are still fundamentally serious, the comic elements in *Henderson*, in *Herzog*, even in *Seize the Day* seem much more prominent than in *Dangling Man* or *The Victim*.

BELLOW: Yes, because I got very tired of the solemnity of complaint, altogether impatient with complaint. Obliged to choose between complaint and comedy, I choose comedy, as more energetic, wiser, and manlier. This is really one reason why I dislike my own early novels. I find them plaintive, sometimes querulous. *Herzog* makes comic use of complaint.

INTERVIEWER: When you say that you are obliged to choose

between complaint and comedy, does it mean this is the only choice—that you are limited to choosing between just these two alternatives?

BELLOW: I'm not inclined to predict what will happen. I may feel drawn to comedy again, I may not. But modern literature was dominated by a tone of elegy from the twenties to the fifties, the atmosphere of Eliot in "The Waste Land" and that of Joyce in *A Portrait of the Artist as a Young Man*. Sensibility absorbed this sadness, this view of the artist as the only contemporary link with an age of gold, forced to watch the sewage flowing in the Thames, every aspect of modern civilization doing violence to his (artist-patrician) feelings. This went much farther than it should have been allowed to go. It descended to absurdities, of which I think we have had enough.

INTERVIEWER: I wonder if you could say something about how important the environments are in your works. I take it that for the realist tradition the context in which the action occurs is of vital importance. You set your novels in Chicago, New York, as far away as Africa. How important are these settings for the fiction?

BELLOW: Well, you present me with a problem to which I think no one has the answer. People write realistically but at the same time they want to create environments which are somehow desirable, which are surrounded by atmospheres in which behavior becomes significant, which display the charm of life. What is literature without these things? Dickens's London is gloomy, but also cozy. And yet realism has always offered to annihilate precisely such qualities. That is to say, if you want to be ultimately realistic you bring artistic space itself in danger. In Dickens, there is no void beyond the fog. The environment is human, at all times. Do you follow me?

INTERVIEWER: I'm not sure I do.

BELLOW: The realistic tendency is to challenge the human significance of things. The more realistic you are the more you threaten the grounds of your own art. Realism has always both accepted and rejected the circumstances of ordinary life. It accepted the task of writing about ordinary life and tried to meet it in

356

some extraordinary fashion. As Flaubert did. The subject might be common, low, degrading; all this was to be redeemed by art. I really do see those Chicago environments as I represent them. They suggest their own style of presentation. I elaborate it.

INTERVIEWER: Then you aren't especially disturbed by readers of *Henderson*, for example, who say that Africa really isn't like that? One sort of realist would require a writer to spend several years on location before daring to place his characters there. You're not troubled by him, I take it?

BELLOW: Perhaps you should say "factualist" rather than "realist." Years ago, I studied African ethnography with the late Professor Herskovits. Later he scolded me for writing a book like *Henderson*. He said the subject was much too serious for such fooling. I felt that my fooling was fairly serious. Literalism, factualism, will smother the imagination altogether.

INTERVIEWER: You have on occasion divided recent American fiction into what you call the "cleans" and the "dirties." The former, I gather, tend to be conservative and easily optimistic, the latter the eternal nay-sayers, rebels, iconoclasts. Do you feel this is still pretty much the picture of American fiction today?

BELLOW: I feel that both choices are rudimentary and pitiful, and though I know the uselessness of advocating any given path to other novelists, I am still inclined to say, Leave both these extremes. They are useless, childish. No wonder the really powerful men in our society, whether politicians or scientists, hold writers and poets in contempt. They do it because they get no evidence from modern literature that anybody is thinking about any significant question. What does the radicalism of radical writers nowadays amount to? Most of it is hand-me-down bohemianism, sentimental populism, D. H. Lawrence-and-water, or imitation Sartre. For American writers radicalism is a question of honor. They must be radicals for the sake of their dignity. They see it as their function, and a noble function, to say Nay, and to bite not only the hand that feeds them (and feeds them with comic abundance, I might add) but almost any other hand held out to them. Their radicalism, however, is contentless. A genuine radicalism, which

357

truly challenges authority, we need desperately. But a radicalism of posture is easy and banal. Radical criticism requires knowledge, not posture, not slogans, not rant. People who maintain their dignity as artists, in a small way, by being mischievous on television, simply delight the networks and the public. True radicalism requires homework—thought. Of the cleans, on the other hand, there isn't much to say. They seem faded.

INTERVIEWER: Your context is essentially that of the modern city, isn't it? Is there a reason for this beyond the fact that you come out of an urban experience?

BELLOW: Well, I don't know how I could possibly separate my knowledge of life, such as it is, from the city. I could no more tell you how deeply it's gotten into my bones than the lady who paints radium dials in the clock factory can tell you.

INTERVIEWER: You've mentioned the distractive character of modern life. Would this be most intense in the city?

BELLOW: The volume of judgments one is called upon to make depends upon the receptivity of the observer, and if one is very receptive, one has a terrifying number of opinions to render— "What do you think about this, about that, about Viet Nam, about city planning, about expressways, or garbage disposal, or democracy, or Plato, or pop art, or welfare states, or literacy in a 'mass society'?" I wonder whether there will ever be enough tranquillity under modern circumstances to allow our contemporary Wordsworth to recollect anything. I feel that art has something to do with the achievement of stillness in the midst of chaos. A stillness which characterizes prayer, too, and the eye of the storm. I think that art has something to do with an arrest of attention in the midst of distraction.

INTERVIEWER: I believe you once said that it is the novel which must deal particularly with this kind of chaos, and that as a consequence certain forms appropriate to poetry or to music are not available to the novelist.

BELLOW: I'm no longer so sure of that. I think the novelist can avail himself of similar privileges. It's just that he can't act with the same purity or economy of means as the poet. He has to traverse a very muddy and noisy territory before he can arrive at a pure conclusion. He's more exposed to the details of life.

INTERVIEWER: Is there anything peculiar about the *kind* of distractions you see the novelist having to confront today? Is it just that there are more details, or is there quality different today from what it used to be?

BELLOW: The modern masterpiece of confusion is Joyce's *Ulysses*. There the mind is unable to resist experience. Experience in all its diversity, its pleasure and horror, passes through Bloom's head like an ocean through a sponge. The sponge can't resist; it has to accept whatever the waters bring. It also notes every microorganism that passes through it. This is what I mean. How much of this must the spirit suffer, in what detail is it obliged to receive this ocean with its human plankton? Sometimes it looks as if the power of the mind has been nullified by the volume of experiences. But of course this is assuming the degree of passivity that Joyce assumes in *Ulysses*. Stronger, more purposeful minds can demand order, impose order, select, disregard, but there is still the threat of disintegration under the particulars. A Faustian artist is unwilling to surrender to the mass of particulars.

INTERVIEWER: Some people have felt your protagonists are seeking the answer to a question that might be phrased, How is it possible today for a good man to live? I wonder if you feel there is any single recurring question like this in the novels?

BELLOW: I don't think that I've represented any really good men; no one is thoroughly admirable in any of my novels. Realism has restrained me too much for that. I should *like* to represent good men. I long to know who and what they are and what their condition might be. I often represent men who desire such qualities but seem unable to achieve them on any significant scale. I criticize this in myself. I find it a limitation.

INTERVIEWER: I'm sorry; what exactly is this limitation?

BELLOW: The fact that I have not discerned those qualities or that I have not shown them in action. Herzog wants very much to have effective virtues. But that's a source of comedy in the book. I think I am far more concerned with another matter, and I don't approach this as a problem with a ready answer. I see it rather as a piece of research, having to do with human characteristics or qualities which have no need of justification. It's an odd thing to do, it shouldn't be necessary to "justify" certain things. But there are many skeptical, rebellious, or simply nervous writers all around us, who, having existed a full twenty or thirty years in this universe, denounce or reject life because it fails to meet their standards as philosophical intellectuals. It seems to me that they can't know enough about it for confident denial. The mystery is too great. So when they knock at the door of mystery with the knuckles of cognition it is quite right that the door should open and some mysterious power should squirt them in the eye. I think a good deal of *Herzog* can be explained simply by the implicit assumption that existence, quite apart from any of our judgments, has value, that existence is worth-ful. Here it is possible, however, that the desire to go on with his creaturely career vulgarly betrays Herzog. He wants to live? What of it! The clay that frames him contains this common want. Simple *aviditas vitae*. Does a man deserve any credit for this?

INTERVIEWER: Would this help to explain, then, why many of the difficulties which Herzog's mind throws up for him throughout the novel don't ever seem to be *intellectually* resolved?

BELLOW: The book is not anti-intellectual, as some have said. It simply points to the comic impossibility of arriving at a synthesis that can satisfy modern demands. That is to say, full awareness of all major problems, together with the necessary knowledge of history, of science and philosophy. That's why Herzog paraphrases Thomas Marshall, Woodrow Wilson's vice-president, who said what this country needs is a good five-cent cigar. (I think it was Bugs Baer who said it first.) Herzog's version: What this country needs is a good five-cent synthesis.

INTERVIEWER: Do you find many contemporary writers attempting to develop such syntheses or insisting that significant fiction provide them?

BELLOW: Well, I don't know that too many American novelists, young or old, are tormenting their minds with these problems.

Europeans do. I don't know that they can ever reach satisfactory results on the grounds they have chosen. At any rate, they write few good novels. But that leads us into some very wide spaces.

INTERVIEWER: Do the ideas in *Herzog* have any other major roles to play? The "anti-intellectual" charge seems to come from people who don't feel the ideas are essential either in motivating the action, the decisions Herzog makes, or in helping him to come through at the end.

BELLOW: To begin with, I suppose I should say something about the difference in the role ideas play in American literature. European literature—I speak now of the Continent—is intellectual in a different sense from ours. The intellectual hero of a French or a German novel is likely to be a philosophical intellectual, an ideological intellectual. We here, intellectuals—or the educated public—know that in our liberal democracy ideas become effective within an entirely different tradition. The lines are less clearly drawn. We do not expect though to have results, say, in the moral sphere, or in the political, in quite the way a Frenchman would. To be an intellectual in the United States sometimes means to be immured in a private life in which one thinks, but thinks with some humiliating sense of how little thought can accomplish. To call therefore for a dramatic resolution in terms of ideas in an American novel is to demand something for which there is scarcely any precedent. My novel deals with the humiliating sense that results from the American mixture of private concerns and intellectual interests. This is something which most readers of the book seem utterly to have missed. Some, fortunately, have caught it. But in part *Herzog* is intended to bring to an end, under blinding light, a certain course of development. Many people feel a "private life" to be an affliction. In some sense it is a genuine affliction; it cuts one off from a common life. To me, a significant theme of *Herzog* is the imprisonment of the individual in a shameful and impotent privacy. He feels humiliated by it; he struggles comically with it; and he comes to realize at last that what he considered his intellectual "privilege" has proved to be another form of bondage. Anyone who misses this misses the point of the book. So that to say that Herzog is not motivated in his acts by ideas is entirely false. Any *Bildungsroman*—and *Herzog* is, to use that heavy German term, a *Bildungsroman*—concludes with the first step. The first *real* step. Any man who has rid himself of superfluous ideas in order to take that first step has done something significant. When people complain of a lack of ideas in novels, they may mean that they do not find familiar ideas, fashionable ideas. Ideas outside the "canon" they don't recognize. So, if what they mean is ideas à la Sartre or ideas à la Camus, they are quite right: There are few such in *Herzog*. Perhaps they mean that the thoughts of a man fighting for sanity and life are not suitable for framing.

INTERVIEWER: Herzog rejects certain of these fashionable ideas, doesn't he—the ideas à la Sartre or à la Camus?

BELLOW: I think he tests them first upon his own sense of life and against his own desperate need for clarity. With him these thoughts are not a game. Though he may laugh as he thinks them, his survival depends upon them. I didn't have him engage in full combat with figures like Sartre. If he had chosen to debate with Sartre in typical Herzogian fashion he would perhaps have begun with Sartre's proposition that Jews exist only because of anti-Semitism, that the Jew has to choose between authentic and in-authentic existence, that authentic existence can never be detached from this anti-Semitism which determines it. Herzog might have remembered that for Sartre, the Jew exists because he is hated, not because he has a history, not because he has origins of his own—but simply because he is designated, created, in his Jewishness by an outrageous evil. Sartre offers a remedy for those Jews who are prepared to make the authentic choice: He extends to them the invitation to become Frenchmen. If this great prince of contemporary European philosophy offers Herzog ideas such as this to embrace (or dispute), who can blame him for his skepticism toward what is called, so respectfully, Thought, toward contemporary intellectual fare? Often Herzog deals with ideas in negative fashion. He needs to dismiss a great mass of irrelevancy and nonsense in order to survive. Perhaps this was what I meant earlier when I said that we were called upon to make innumerable judgments. We can be consumed simply by the necessity to discriminate between multitudes of propositions. We have to dismiss a great number of thoughts if we are to have any creaturely or human life at all. It seems at times that we are on trial seven days a week answering the questions, giving a clear account of ourselves. But when does one live? How does one live if it is necessary to render ceaseless judgments?

INTERVIEWER: Herzog's rejection of certain ideas has been widely recognized, but—

BELLOW:—why he rejects them is not at all clear. Herzog's skepticism toward ideas is very deep. Though Jews are often accused of being "rootless" rationalists, a man like Herzog knows very well that habit, custom, tendency, temperament, inheritance, and the power to recognize real and human facts have equal weight with ideas.

INTERVIEWER: You've spoken also of the disabling effects of basing a novel on ideas. Does this mean structuring a novel according to a philosophical conception?

BELLOW: No, I have no objection to that, nor do I have any objection to basing novels on philosophical conceptions or anything else that works. But let us look at one of the dominant ideas of the century, accepted by many modern artists—the idea that humankind has reached a terminal point. We find this terminal assumption in writers like Joyce, Céline, Thomas Mann. In *Doktor Faustus* politics and art are joined in the destruction of civilization. Now here is an idea found in some of the greatest novelists of the twentieth century. How good is this idea? Frightful things have happened, but is the apocalyptic interpretation true? The terminations did not fully terminate. Civilization is still here. The prophecies have not been borne out. Novelists are wrong to put an interpretation of history at the base of artistic creation—to speak "the last word." It is better that the novelist should trust his own sense of life. Less ambitious. More likely to tell the truth.

INTERVIEWER: Frequently in your fiction the hero strives to avoid being swallowed up by other people's ideas or versions of reality. On occasion you seem to present him with something like

363

the whole range of contemporary alternatives—say, in *Augie March* or *Herzog*. Was this one of your intentions?

BELLOW: All these matters are really so complicated. Of course these books are somewhat concerned with free choice. I don't think that they pose the question successfully—the terms are not broad enough. I think I have let myself off easily. I seem to have asked in my books, How can one resist the controls of this vast society *without* turning into a nihilist, avoiding the absurdity of empty rebellion? I have asked, Are there other, more good-natured forms of resistance and free choice? And I suppose that, like most Americans, I have involuntarily favored the more comforting or melioristic side of the question. I don't mean that I ought to have been more "pessimistic," because I have found "pessimism" to be in most of its forms nearly as empty as "optimism." But I am obliged to admit that I have not followed these questions to the necessary depth. I can't blame myself for not having been a stern moralist; I can always use the excuse that I'm after all nothing but a writer of fiction. But I don't feel satisfied with what I have done to date, except in the comic form. There is, however, this to be added—that our French friends invariably see the answers to such questions, and all questions of truth, to be overwhelmingly formidable, uncongenial, hostile to us. It may be, however, that truth is not always so punitive. I've tried to suggest this in my books. There may be truths on the side of life. I am quite prepared to admit that being habitual liars and self-deluders, we have good cause to fear the truth, but I'm not at all ready to stop hoping. There may be some truths which are, after all, our friends in the universe.

DEEP READERS OF THE WORLD, BEWARE

Interviewed as he was getting on the train for Boston, E. M. Forster was asked how he felt on the eve of his first visit to Harvard. He replied that he had heard that there were some particularly deep readers of his books to be found in Cambridge. He expected to be questioned closely by them, and this worried him. The reason is perfectly understandable.

In this age of ours serious people are more serious than they ever were, and lightness of heart like Mr. Forster's is hard to find. To the serious a novel is a work of art; art has a role to play in the drama of civilized life; civilized life is set upon a grim and dangerous course—and so we may assume if we are truly serious that no good novelist is going to invite us to a picnic merely to eat egg salad and chase butterflies over the English meadows or through the Tuscan woods. Butterflies are gay, all right, but in them lies the secret of metamorphosis. As for eggs, life's mystery hides in the egg. We all know that. So much for butterflies and egg salad.

It would be unjust to say that the responsibility for this sort of thing belongs entirely to the reader. Often the writer himself is at fault. He doesn't mind if he *is* a little deeper than average. Why not?

Nevertheless deep reading has gone very far. It has become dangerous to literature.

"Why, sir," the student asks, "does Achilles drag the body of Hector around the walls of Troy?" "That sounds like a stimulating question. Most interesting. I'll bite," says the professor. "Well, you see, sir, the *Aeneid* is full of circles—shields, chariot wheels, and other round figures. And you know what Plato said about circles. The Greeks were all mad for geometry." "Bless you," says the professor, "for such a beautiful thought. You have exquisite sensibility. Your approach is both deep and serious. Still I always believed that Achilles did it because he was so angry."

It would take an unusual professor to realize that Achilles *was* angry. To many teachers he would represent much, but he would not *be* anything in particular. To be is too obvious. Our professor however is a square, and the bright student is annoyed with him. Anger! What good is anger? Great literature is subtle, dignified, profound. Homer is as good as Plato any time; and if Plato thought, Homer must surely have done so too, and thought just as beautifully, circle for circle.

Things are not what they seem. And anyway, unless they represent something large and worthy, writers will not bother with them. Any deep reader can tell you that picking up a bus transfer is the *Reisemotiv* when it happens in a novel. A travel folder signifies Death. Coal holes represent the Underworld. Soda crackers are the Host. Three bottles of beer are—it's obvious. The busy mind can hardly miss at this game, and every player is a winner.

Are you a Marxist? Then Herman Melville's *Pequod* in *Moby Dick* can be a factory, Ahab the manager, the crew the working class. Is your point of view religious? The *Pequod* sailed on Christmas morning, a floating cathedral headed south. Do you follow Freud or Jung? Then your interpretations may be rich and multitudinous. I recently had a new explanation of *Moby Dick* from the young man in charge of an electronic brain. "Once and for all," he said, "that whale is everybody's mother wallowing in her watery bed. Ahab has the Oedipus complex and wants to slay the hell out of her."

This is deep reading. But it is only fair to remember that the best novelists and poets of the century have done much to promote it. When Mairy (in James Joyce's *Ulysses*) loses the pin for her drawers, she doesn't know what to do to keep them up; the mind of Bloom goes from grammar to painting, from painting to religion. It is all accomplished in a few words. Joyce's genius holds all the elements in balance.

The deep reader, however, is apt to lose his head. He falls wildly on any particle of philosophy or religion and blows it up bigger than the *Graf Zeppelin*. Does Bloom dust Stephen's clothes and brush off the wood shavings? They are no ordinary shavings but the shavings from the true Cross.

What else? All the little monkish peculiarities at which Robert Browning poked fun in "Soliloquy in a Spanish Cloister," crossing knife and fork on the platter at the end of a meal and the rest of it, have become the pillars of the new system.

Are we to attach meaning to whatever is grazed by the writer? Is modern literature Scripture? Is criticism Talmud, theology? Deep readers of the world, beware! You had better be sure that your seriousness is indeed high seriousness and not, God forbid, low seriousness.

A true symbol is substantial, not accidental. You cannot avoid it, you cannot remove it. You can't take the handkerchief from *Othello*, or the sea from *The Nigger of the Narcissus*, or the disfigured feet from *Oedipus Rex*. You can, however, read *Ulysses* without suspecting that wood shavings have to do with the Crucifixion or that the name Simon refers to the sin of simony or that the hunger of the Dubliners at noon parallels that of the Lestrigonians. These are purely peripheral matters; fringe benefits, if you like. The beauty of the book cannot escape you if you are any sort of reader, and it is better to approach it from the side of naïveté than from that of culture-idolatry, sophistication, and snobbery. Of course it's hard in our time to be as naïve as one would like. Information does filter through. It *leaks*, as we have taken to saying. Still, the knowledge of even the sophisticated is rather thin, and even the most wised-up readers, stuffed to the ears with arcana, sometimes prove to be fairly simple people.

Perhaps the deepest readers are those who are least sure of themselves. An even more disturbing suspicion is that they prefer meaning to feeling. What, *again* about the feelings? Yes, it's too bad. I'm sorry to have to ring in this tiresome subject, but there's no help for it. The reason why the schoolboy takes refuge in circles is that the wrath of Achilles and the death of Hector are too much for him. He is doing no more than most civilized people do when confronted with passion and death. They contrive somehow to avoid them.

The practice of avoidance is so widespread that it is probably not fair to single out any group for blame. But if nothing is to be said or done, we might as well make ready to abandon literature altogether. Novels are being published today which consist entirely of abstractions, meanings, and while our need for meaning is certainly great our need for concreteness, for particulars, is even greater. We need to see how human beings act after they have appropriated or assimilated the meanings. Meanings themselves are a dime a dozen. In literature humankind becomes abstract when we begin to dislike it. And . . .

Interruption by a deep reader: Yes, yes, we know all that. But just look at the novels of the concrete and the particular, people opening doors and lighting cigarettes. Aren't they boring? Besides, do you want us to adopt a program to curtail the fear of feeling and to pretend to *like* the creature of flesh and bone?

Certainly not. No programs.

A pretty pass we have come to!

We must leave it to imagination and to inspiration to redeem the concrete and the particular and to recover the value of flesh and bone. Meanwhile, let Plato have his circles and let the soda crackers be soda crackers and the wood shavings be wood shavings. They are mysterious enough as it is.

DISTRACTIONS OF A FICTION WRITER

On the one hand literature, tragic as well as comic, belongs in the realm of happiness; on the other hand writers are often unhappy and distracted. They have never been examined so earnestly before. The writer hasn't often in the past been called upon to give an account of himself. When the poet tries to come between Brutus and Cassius during their quarrel they throw him out. They don't ask him to give historical reasons for being a poet. He is too unimportant for that. And I believe his unimportance in that day to have been one of his advantages. Now there are people who devote themselves to the study of poets and who badger and investigate them. Poets and other writers are asked—they ask themselves—many serious and weighty questions. Which means either that society has a larger stake in literature than it used to have, or that it can't resist meddling with anything related to happiness with a view to doing it some damage.

What are some of these questions—or charges or indictments?

Let us say that the writer (in this case a novelist) is in the customary solitude of his room, and that he is under a strain and that his writing is not at its best. Today it is hard for him to declare with Joseph Conrad that the world is a temple. He would have to assert, "It *is* a temple." And that would already be a mistake. The feeling of sacredness is beyond price, but the assertion has very little value. Therefore the novelist will make no assertion for the sake of strengthening himself. He will rather ask, "Why didn't you choose a different sort of work, something you could do wholeheartedly every day? Why do you write fiction? You can't build a business on inspirations. Besides, what makes you think it's wanted? Maybe it's an unhistorical and superfluous occupation you've chosen. The whole world is in motion, blazing. And what are you doing? You're doing nothing commensurate. Only sitting here alone, oddly faithful to things you learned as a boy. They taught you the Palmer method in school, so here you are still covering pages with words. You go on about men and women, families and marriages, divorces, crime and flight, murders, weddings, wars, rises and declines, simplicities and complexities, blessedness and agony, and it's all largely imaginary. Who asks you to write such things? What the devil are you doing here? What's all this about dead and nonexistent people—Priams and Hecubas? Who is this Hecuba anyway and what are you to her? You're a foolish busybody," says the writer to himself. "Adding book to book. What for? Aren't there enough books? Even King Solomon was already complaining that there was a 'sufficiency' of them. You are practicing a peculiar and, some say, an obsolete art. You may have an inherited Jewish taste for such things."

Such are the questions or doubts or charges. I believe they can be answered. And though it is sad and possibly harmful that they must be heard, it is not necessarily fatal. Eros manages somehow to survive analysis; and somehow imagination survives criticism. In either case the rising of an imperious need abolishes all the questions. "Do you feel it necessary to do this? Then, for the love of God, do it," says the need. If it argues at all.

As a young man Rilke made a pilgrimage to Russia to see Tolstoy. As I have heard the story, he followed the impatient old man around filling his ears with his problems about writing. Tolstoy couldn't bear it. He had exchanged art for religion, and all this seemed very trifling to him. *"Vous voulez écrire?"* he said. *"Eh bien, écrivez donc! Écrivez!"* What else is there to say? Do it if you must, and don't fuss so about it.

Nevertheless, there are certain distractions.

The novelist is distracted; he writes for someone and that someone is sure to be distracted. The Wedding Guest is distracted when the Ancient Mariner stops him. The Mariner lets his two companions go and holds the Guest with his glittering eye. Amid the distractions of merrymaking the Bride is led to the altar, ready to forswear all others. The Guest can only tear his hair as he hears the loud bassoon. He is cut off from his beloved distractions by the power of art and he cannot choose but hear. This is the position we are all in; we resist the spell but we also desire it.

"Why should I end my distractions for you?" That is the question asked of the writer. For there are more things that solicit the attention of the mind than there ever were before. The libraries and museums are full, great storehouses with their thousands of masterpieces in every style. Their vast wealth excites our ambition. It can make a Dr. Faustus out of many an educated man. It menaces him with death by distraction. But everyone on every level is exposed to this danger. The giant producers of goods need our defenseless attention. They catch us on the run and through the eyes and ears fill us with the brand names of cars and cigarettes and soaps. And then news and information distract us. Bad art distracts us. Genuine culture is also, as I've already noted, distracting. Lastly, there are the inner demands of memory, desire, fantasy, anxiety, and the rest. These are perhaps the most tyrannical. The great outer chaos drives us inward, and in our own small kingdoms we indulge our favorite distractions.

The following quotation shows the elementary forms of common distraction. It is taken from a popular booklet, *The Handbook of Beauty*, by Constance Hart. The chapter title is "Double-Duty Beauty Tricks":

While doing housework: You can keep your face creamed, your hair in pin curls; you can practice good standing and walking posture; when you're sitting at the kitchen counter peeling potatoes you can do your ankle exercises and foot strengtheners, and also practice good sitting posture. . . . *While telephoning* (at home, of course): You can do neck exercises; brush your hair; do ankle exercises, eye exercises, foot strengtheners, and chin-and-neck exercises; practice good standing or sitting posture; even massage your gums (while listening to the other person). . . . *While reading or watching TV:* You can brush your hair; massage your gums; do your ankle and hand exercises and foot strengtheners; do some bust and back exercises; massage your scalp; use the abrasive treatment for removing superfluous hair.

Here we see basic distraction. Here even personal beauty is put on the Taylor system of industrial efficiency. All this simultaneous writhing and plucking suggests both Willow Run and the torments of Hell. Such grim energy can only be drawn from the feeling that life's shortness requires us to combine our activities, combine and combine and multiply the levels of consciousness and those of muscular coordination layer upon layer, on a sandwich principle. We are not perfect. We must perfect ourselves, we must exhaust ourselves. Maybe, too, there is a perverse desire for freedom in this. Dominated by no single activity, we are free; free but not tranquil; at leisure, but not idle, since all the while we strive for perfection. No, the face, the neck, the bust, the skin, the mind are not good as they are and we must tirelessly improve them. By so doing we deny the power of death over us because as long as we're getting better there's no reason why we should die. But I think the ruling principle behind all of this can be stated as follows: Don't give yourself wholly to any single thing. Divide and multiply.

What a fate to marry a woman who follows such instructions! But what shall we say about the fate of the author whose novel she holds in her hand—if she has a hand to spare. How is he to get her attention? Can he hold her with his glittering eye? Why, he himself suffers from such diseases. He, like everyone else, is subject to vanity, not willingly. He also is deafened by the noise of life, by cries and claims and counter-claims and fantasy and desire and ambition for perfection, by false hope and error and fear of death.

But distraction is not necessarily inimical to the imagination. Novels are floated upon distraction. They begin in the midst of it. On the first page of *Anna Karenina* we are told "All was confusion in the house of the Oblonskys." Distraction is one of the subjects of Tolstoy's masterpiece. Society is in Tolstoy's view a system of distractions. Anna and Vronsky are drawn apart by its disapproval of their union. Vronsky grows bored; he has no proper work or a center of attention, for love, or the purest sort of attention to another, can't be sustained day by day. Love is not an occupation. Therefore Vronsky falls away. Anna's brother Oblonsky makes a last attempt to obtain his brother-in-law Karenin's consent to a divorce. Anna's life depends on this.

"After an excellent dinner with unlimited cognac ... Oblonsky arrived at the Countess Lydia Ivanovna's," says Tolstoy. In the course of the evening Oblonsky falls asleep and when he awakes he steals out of the house, forgetting the appeal he was to have made to Karenin. Next morning he receives Karenin's final refusal.

I don't see how we can avoid blaming Oblonsky for his sister's suicide. A normally decent man, no worse than most, hearty, a good liver, he loves his sister, yes, but he is unable to keep his attention fixed upon her need. He is not a monster of selfishness, he is distracted. The attention is supplied by Tolstoy in the writing of the novel. His method is one of deliberate slowness and simplification, a contemplative slowness which brings order and unity out of confusion. We never go from distraction to attention (of a certain sort) without experiencing a triumphant emotion. Distractions give force to a work of art by their resolution, and the novelist works more deeply with distractions than any other kind of artist. Many events fall upon us, assail us with claims on our time and our judgment; waves of disintegrative details wash over us and threaten to wear away all sense of order and proportion. The novelist begins at a great depth of distraction and difficulty. Sometimes, as in James Joyce's *Ulysses*, he risks total immersion in distraction. I don't say that the novelist knows what order is; but he relies upon his imagination to lead him toward it. In a work of art the imagination is the sole source of order. There are critics who assume that you must begin with order if you are to end with it. Not so. A novelist begins with disorder and disharmony, and he goes toward order by an unknown process of the imagination. And anyway, the order he achieves is not the order that ideas have. Critics need to be reminded of this, I think. Art is the speech of artists. The rules are not the same as those in science or philosophy. No one knows what the power of the imagination comes from or how much distraction it can cope with. We are now told that it has reached its limit. The distraction is supposed to be too broad for love and too deep for beauty and too agonizing for any order. And so we are told by critics that the novel is dead. These people can't know what the imagination is or what its powers are. I wish I could believe in their good-natured objectivity. But I can't. I should like to disregard them, but that is a little difficult because they have a great deal of power. Not real power, perhaps, but power of a sort. And they can be very distracting.

But the deadly earnestness with which they lower the boom! On what, after all? On flowers. On mere flowers.

It occurs to a man that he is a writer. He doesn't obtain a certificate, like a doctor, or take the bar examination, like a lawyer; nor does he apprentice himself like a tool-and-die maker or get into a union like a bricklayer. A novel is written by a man who thinks of himself as a novelist. Unless he makes such an assumption about himself he simply can't do it. The thing is impossible. He has to encounter the world in a particular way. He goes within a sort of tissue which floats about the mind when he is well or collapses upon it when he isn't. It's hard to say exactly where this tissue comes from or what it is, but it is a sign of his autonomy. He has called himself out and anointed himself. No prophet picked him. And so he has neither supernatural nor social assistance. Now aren't we Americans fond of self-made men? Of some of them, yes. And to this peculiar self-election of the man who goes about calling himself a novelist there is no visible barrier, at least. Well, then, let's say that the anointee is carried away by the force of his imagination; he gives utterance to the images it brings him, and with a certain arrogance he assumes that what he writes needs to be read and will be read. The origin of this arrogance, if arrogance is what it is, is rather mysterious too. In fact, from any sensible, rational point of view the whole thing is bewildering. Still, as it begins privately and harms no one, there are no objections. None will be heard as long as the interests of power are not touched.

Society doesn't do much to encourage this self-elected man; on the contrary it subjects him to many negative pressures. Is it angry with the imagination? Does it perhaps hate it? That may well be. At any rate it holds the imagination under suspicion. For there are always leading activities which society needs and sponsors. Sometimes it is the lawgiver who is in the highest place, and sometimes the priest, and sometimes the general. With us it is the businessman, the administrator, the political leader, the military man. These have the power; they are the representative men; in them manhood is mirrored. They honor themselves and are universally honored and imitated as the possessors of power and virtue. They rule armies and industries and publishing empires and build atomic reactors and legislate for us all. A modern writer, when he comes to speak of their powers, is forced to speak vaguely because he doesn't really know what they're doing. Any connection between art and authority has for some time been broken. Who now is Cromwell's secretary? Was it Mr. Stephen Early? Is it Mr. Haggerty? Well then, if it is true that the writer has no actual connection with power, and that he is separated from the main current of things not only by the lack of certain dignities but also because he is compelled by his self-authorization to live in a manner different from most other men, why doesn't he by the daring of his imagination alone make a leap into the councils of state or into the Pentagon or a cabinet meeting? Oddly enough he doesn't even expect it of himself. He accepts timidly all the restrictions of the rule of experience. The demons of first-hand knowledge, documentation, and naturalistic accuracy have seized him. *The Red Badge of Courage* was probably the last American novel to be taken wholly from the imagination, and there are indignant letters in the old *Dial* by Civil War veterans denouncing Crane for the technical errors which, not then experienced in war, he had made. We are a nation devoted to facts, and we don't like to waste time with books that give the wrong dope about shipwrecks on the coast of Bohemia. We like to get things straight. Otherwise we feel that we are wasting valuable time. And if a man writes a book we think we are justified in asking him, as though we were about to hire him, about his qualifications and his experience. For we really feel that experience is intrinsically valuable and we have the same acquisitive attitude towards it as towards other things of value. Experience can never be bad, we seem to believe; the more one has had the better. While this attitude may be justified in some respects, I think it ought to be pointed out that the disorder of experience is distraction. Imagination may do with experience or with nonexperience precisely what it likes. By refusing to write anything with which he is not thoroughly familiar the American writer confesses the powerlessness of the imagination and accepts its relegation to an inferior place.

"All the qualities of a man acquire dignity when he knows that the service of the collectivity that owns him needs them," wrote William James in his essay, "The Moral Equivalent of War." Well, the writer certainly must think that if the collectivity knew what its best interests were it would see that it needed him as much as it does—let's not go so far as to say the secretaries of State or Defense—but as much as it needs psychiatrists, who deal also with the confusions of experience, or television directors. But since the writer of novels has found the oil and anointed himself he need not deceive himself about the "collectivity." He can't feel that it needs him. Not unless he creates a sensation or makes a great fortune. For of course money will turn the trick. "If," continues William James, "if proud of the collectivity, his own pride rises in proportion." There doesn't seem to be much of this pride around. In modern times the feelings and thoughts of writers have gone counter to the general direction. If they have gone with the collectivity—the mass—it has been on the terms of the mass and not their own.

American writers have often described themselves as loafers, vagabonds, beggars, and bums. Thoreau sits apart from the economy in idleness beside Walden Pond. Walt Whitman describes himself as one of the "roughs." Vachel Lindsay wrote *A Handy Guide for Beggars* out of his experiences as a preacher of his Gospel of Beauty. Writers have stood aside from the ordinary duties of their fellow citizens. I don't perhaps so much mean duties as I mean the routines of the mill towns, the mining towns, and the great cities. Others get up in the morning and ride in crowds to their work. Not the self-anointed writer. He sits up in his room, writing, a freer man. Or is he freer? Is he free? Perhaps he feels a weak and treasonable fear in his soul at doing something so hard to explain to the others, the early morning passengers on the Milwaukee Avenue streetcar.

"I loaf and invite my soul," says Walt Whitman.

Well, perhaps his counterpart today does, too. Perhaps. I hope so, because his imagination requires the tranquil attitude. But chances are that he is working, bitterly working, in an effort to meet his brothers of the office and factory sympathetically. The odds are good that he is literally a brother and comes out of the same mass. And now for some strange reason he is trying to throw a bridge from this same place, from a room in Chicago to, let us say, Ahab, to Cervantes, to Shakespeare, to the Kings of the old Chronicles, to Genesis. For he says, "Aren't we still part of the same humanity, children of Adam?" So he invites his soul away from distractions.

But sometimes he can feel in the very streets that the energies of the population have been withdrawn to mass activity, industry, and money. At midday in an American city you are aware of a certain emptiness about the houses. You hear the organ groaning in dissolution as the scenes of the soap opera change in the kitchen below, beneath the table where you sit writing. And sometimes the suspicion arises that maybe the Studebaker, maybe the Bendix have absorbed man's highest powers. Can the intellectual, esthetic, moral genius of the human race have come to a stop? That's impossible. Aeronautical engineers have just shown that the globe can be circumnavigated in a forty-five-hour nonstop flight. That is genius—to lift man and metal from the ground and send them around the face of the earth. Before such an achievement nobody ought to be bored and no one ought to feel isolated. The shuddering of the organ, the vacant dullness of a world that is (temporarily) not a temple have no great importance. The smell of beer on the dark stairs is nothing. The absence of a human contact is merely temporary. The page in the typewriter describing a certain conversation that never actually took place is an offering placed on the alter of certain gods who—who aren't around just now. But they'll be back, for in time everyone will miss them. Remember Thoreau sitting beside his pond. The industry of his neighbors failed to separate his connection with nature. "You are," the writer may tell himself, "joined to your fellows in a better way. For in actual fact how well are they joined to one another? They form a very loose, friable mass. The comradeship of the assembly line isn't very thick; nor that of the bowling alley, community club, tavern, package store. Camps and barracks were different. But there you drew sneers and hatred if you read books or spoke in your own style. Remember your loyalty to the human spirit, and don't drag after the mob protesting that you're not a writer at all but a fisherman or farmer. It would be fear only that made you say such things; the shame of being divorced by difference from other men, and also the fear of the savage strength of the many."

Thus the fiction writer may talk to himself—when he's distracted. For when he is actually at work the excitement of the imagination carries him and he needs no justification as a vagabond or dedicated idler who by his example will recall his money-chasing brethren to sit down with him and feel their hearts and tell sad tales, and be tranquil before the beauty of the external world, and all the rest of it. No, then he is too busy.

But once in a while, he is visited by the thought that he is sitting still in the midst of the most widespread destruction. Man's hatred of himself has led in this century to the wildest of wars and demolition of the human image in camps and jails built for that purpose. Bodies stacked like firewood we have seen; and the bodies of the massacred exhumed for the gold in their teeth, we have seen too. And even the so-called years of peace have been years of war. The buying and consumption of goods that keep the economy going the writer sitting in his room may envision as acts of duty, of service, of war. By our luxury we fight, too, eating and drinking and squandering to save our form of government which survives because it produces and sells vast quantities of things. This sort of duty or service, he thinks, may well destroy our souls. They are taken from us and put to strange uses. Under it all perhaps, he reflects, is a hatred of individual being. "Let it be obliterated," is the secret message that we hear. And many in their hearts answer, "Yea, so be it." It may be that this is the hidden purpose of the frantic distraction to which we are exposed. If that is the case, the writer, like the minister of a religion, feels that perhaps he is anachronistic.

"The priest departs, the divine literatus comes," said Walt Whitman. He felt that the office of the poet absorbed the sacerdotal one. In *Democratic Vistas* he gave the poet the responsibility of creating a type of man, an archetype he called it, and he offered himself as a model or representative. We have to begin somewhere. Touch me, he said, and you touch a man. I am not different from others; they are not different from me. What I assume you shall assume. This is not always understood for the act of love that it was. Between the radically unlike there is no love. So the creation of an archetype was to belong to the poet—and the humanist, the scholar. Well, now, where are these people? You can see them around the country in various places, most commonly in colleges and universities. They are different, though many of them try not to be. They are powerless. The universities are the warehouses of culture. Let us imagine a man who lives in Akron, Ohio, and teaches the history of the Italian Renaissance. It is dreadful to think what he has to reconcile. Or he teaches ethics, and takes part in departmental politics. He behaves shabbily and his own heart cannot bear the contrast. What I am trying to say is that certain ideas can't be held idly. Attempted containment of them is ruin. Lying in his bed in his impoverished attic, Raskolnikov is ashamed of the thoughts of mastery that come into his head; this shame, like a radioactive material, eats through the wall of moral restraint, and issues destructively. He commits a double murder. But it is not only ideas of evil that become destructive. Ideas of good, held in earnest, may be equally damaging to the passive thinker. His passivity puts him in self-contempt. This same contempt may estrange him from the ideas of good. He lives below them and feels dwarfed. On certain occasions a hero in thought, he has become abject in fact and he cannot be blamed for feeling that he is not doing a man's work. He reads about man's work in the paper. Men are planning new bond issues, molding public opinion, solving the crisis of the Suez Canal. Men are active. Ideas are passive. Ideas are held in contempt. Literature in these circumstances is contemptible. Of course it is pleasant to have some poets around. All great empires have had them. We are a great empire and need some too. And so Herod sits in his vast palace of advertising and publicity, and once in a while he hears the voice of John from the dungeon. He doesn't even bother to cut off his head.

The writer has no connection with power, and yet he keeps thinking about it. I offer a few eighteenth- and nineteenth-century declarations in evidence. "Poets are the unacknowledged legislators of the world." "Give me the making of the songs of a nation and I care not who makes its laws." "Above all previous lands a great original literature is surely to become the justification and reliance (in some respects the sole reliance) of American democracy."

But I should like to point out that impotence has received more attention from modern writers than any other subject. I use the word impotence rather loosely to include the loss or defect of the sympathetic power, the failure of feeling (what Elizabeth Bowen has called "the death of the heart") as well as literal incapacity. Here is a brief list:

Oblomov: he spends his life in bed.

Moreau in Flaubert's *The Sentimental Education*: a life spent on trifles, utterly spoiled.

Captain Ahab: "I have lost the low enjoying power." He means that he is distracted. Natural beauty is recognized by his mind but it doesn't move him.

Clym Yeobright in *The Return of the Native*: empty of the feeling which Eustacia desires.

The hero of Henry James's "The Beast in the Jungle": empty of feeling.

Dostoevsky's hero or anti-hero in *Notes from the Underground*:

his spite, his coldness, his venom, combined with the largeness of his mind, give him an exceptional stature.

Leopold Bloom: the distracted and impotent man.

I could add hundreds more to this list, from Lawrence or Proust or Hemingway and their innumerable imitators. They all tell the same story. The dread is great, the soul is small, man might be godlike but he is wretched; the heart should be open but it is sealed by fear. If man, wretched by nature, is represented, what we have here is only accurate reporting. But if it is man in the image of God, man a little lower than the angels, who is impotent, the case is not the same. And it is the second assumption, the sub-angelic one, that writers generally make. For they are prone, as Nietzsche said in *Human, All Too Human*, to exaggerate the value of human personality. I don't know whether exaggeration is quite the word, but what it suggests we can certainly agree with. Why should wretched man need power or wish to inflate himself with imaginary glory? If this is what power signifies it can only be vanity to suffer from impotence. On the nobler assumption he should have at least sufficient power to overcome ignominy and to complete his own life. His suffering, feebleness, servitude then have a meaning. This is what writers have taken to be the justification of power. It should reveal the greatness of man. And if no other power will do this, the power of the imagination will take the task upon itself.

"That undisturbed, innocent, somnambulatory production by which alone anything great can thrive, is no longer possible. Our talents at present lie before the public. The daily criticisms which appear in fifty different places, and the gossip that is caused by them amongst the public, prevent the appearance of any sound production. . . . he who does not keep aloof from all this, and isolate himself by main force, is lost" (Goethe: *Conversations with Eckermann*).

So, if the writer is wise, he will avoid certain books and papers and magazines and social circles. But perhaps wisdom won't help. Everybody talks. The cat is already out of the bag. You go to a party and a psychiatrist tells you that *his* analyst believes literature is dying. This is an act of aggression. But how can a novelist be expected to stay away from parties? He must go, and he must inevitably hear the worst, exposing his somnambulatory innocence to grave dangers. Once more the boom is lowered on the flowers. But they will grow again. There is man's own greatness, and then there is the greatness of his imbecility—both are eternal.

It's only natural that writers should have their enemies. It's the rule of life, among writers as among snakes, mice, and lice. The subtler creatures have subtler enemies. The subtlest of enemies are those who get you over to their own side. You read the authoritative words of an eminent critic; they sound reasonable; you half agree, and then are distracted and stiflingly depressed.

Finished! We have heard this from Valéry and from T. S. Eliot, from Ortega and from Oswald Spengler, and most recently from the summit of Morningside Heights. We are supposed to be done for. The great dinosaurs are gone; only vestigial Gila monsters remain. Oh, to have once more the unimportance of that poor poet whom Brutus and Cassius threw out! For every poet now there are a hundred custodians and doctors of literature and dozens of undertakers measuring away at coffins. If only, says D. H. Lawrence in a poem, man were as much man as the lizard is lizard! If only the novelist, though merely a degenerate Gila monster, were at least a true Gila monster! He would sit in the sun undistracted and catch flies.

The novelist has been trained to take words seriously, and he thinks he is hearing words of high seriousness. He believes it is the voice of high seriousness saying, "Obsolete. Finished." But what if it were to prove to be the voice of low seriousness instead?

Scholars and critics are often curiously like property owners. They have their lots surveyed. Here the property begins and there it ends. A conservative instinct in them, which every lover of order will recognize and respect, resists extension, calls for limits. And why not? Besides, it's awfully fine to be an epigone. It tickles one so in the self-esteem. But how odd it is that these words "obsolete" and "finished" should never be spoken with regret or pain. The accent is rather one of satisfaction. And this is all the more strange because if the critics are wrong their opinions will do harm. They are certain to be destructive.

The students of literature line up with the epigones. "Thank God!" they say. "It's over. We have a field. We can study." Well, it does seem logical that the thing should have an end. The libraries and the second-hand stores are very full, as I've already observed. Isn't it enough that the physical universe overwhelms us with its immensities; must the works of man flood us as well? But I wonder whether novels can be studied with much profit or even read if we don't continue to write them. Not professional study but imagination keeps imagination alive. Samuel Butler offers a theory to which I subscribe. ". . . all things which come to much," he says, "whether they be books, buildings, pictures or living beings are suggested by others of their kind." I wonder what historical reasons there are for this process of suggestion to stop. And what will happen to *Anna Karenina* or to the *Iliad* if they are never read by those to whom they may suggest others of their kind? Literature, all of it, will then be extinct.

"The novel has died a victim to the loss of an agreed picture of the Universe, which has faded with the stifling of Christianity by non-dogmatic idealism and crude materialism." Thus writes Mr. J. M. Cohen in his recent *History of Western European Literature*. His is the bluntest, flattest, most Spartan statement of the position, and I like it because there is something wonderfully bureaucratic about it. The "agreed picture of the Universe" appeals especially to me. I like the stoutness of it. It reminds me of the textbooks I studied in college. "The Crusades were begun because . . ." "The following developments made possible the beginning of the Renaissance in Italy . . ." It is always like that, blunt, plain, and positive. Textbooks told us what the prerequisites were for a flourishing literature. The end of feudalism, the rise of the burghers, the Reformation, the Age of Reason, the growth of science (et cetera) made possible the great century of the novel. The method has worked so well (obviously) in explaining the past that now scholars have decided to project it into the future. This is a new branch of the historians' art—*made* history.

Ever since M. Jourdain, the bourgeois gentleman, discovered that his everyday speech was Prose, writers have written Literature, painters have painted Art, musicians have composed Music, and now culture-historians create Culture epoch by epoch, past, present, and future.

An agreed picture of the Universe? What is that? And when we have come to know what it means (if we can) must we believe that novels have become poor because they lack it? It has recently been well argued by J. Bronowski in *The Nation* that the imagination of the scientist is not vastly different from that of the artist. Does the scientific imagination also have need of an agreed picture of the Universe? Science quickly changes the agreed pictures. And why does it survive so well the stifling of Christianity?

"Probably all of us, to some extent, share in the misconception of modern literature that dominates illiterate minds," wrote my late friend Isaac Rosenfeld, "that it is divisive and fragmented, reflecting the breakdown of the social order, the decay of capitalism and bourgeois civilization . . . such minds, not necessarily of low intelligence, and often brilliant on ground far removed from the arts, betray a fear of modernity; they recoil from experience before it has deeply touched them and never receive more than the disintegrative impression. . . . Yet our age is perhaps the most highly systematizing one in history . . . The mind that flees disorder is frightened by a multiplicity of choice even more than by chaos; in fact this is its basic image of chaos . . . it forces a reductive and equalizing system on experience."

The argument that the novel is dying or dead is made by men who shut the door on multiplicity and distraction. They suppose the distraction to be too great for the imagination to overcome. When they speak of an agreed picture what they mean is that we are a mass civilization, doomed to be shallow and centerless. Question: "And what if the soul doesn't accept?" Answer: "It had better. Its acceptance is historically determined." But this smells of bars and prisons. And we started out to talk of literature and happiness! How busy the grimmer impulses are!

Why were we born? What are we doing here? Where are we

going? In its eternal naïveté the imagination keeps coming back to these things. It does this when we have an agreed picture and when we haven't. For it isn't an agreed picture that makes man interesting to himself. It isn't history and it isn't culture; the interest is intrinsic. And it's not unfair to ask those literary people who argue that the novel is dead whether their own feelings are fresh or tired. Life quickly wears us out; there is good reason to be tired. But this is not a matter for the tired to settle.

But we are living in what they call an eschatological age. Whole worlds have become as light as Ping-Pong balls. At lunch we talk about good and evil, death and immortality, and over cocktails metaphysical questions are raised as if the world, like the bottles, might be empty by dinner time. Then why should so minor a thing as The Novel escape its moment of question?

A lot of things have been called obsolete. I brooded over Spengler in college. As a Jew I was, in his vocabulary, a Magian and therefore obsolete. Toynbee, unless I am mistaken, has a similar view of Jews, that they are a sort of fossil. Marx and Engels, too, were prophets of obsolescence. For Stalin the kulaks were obsolete; for Hitler, all the inferior breeds of men. In the dustbins of various reform movements are found numerous orthodoxies called obsolete. And we all know—what else does Mr. Cohen mean when he speaks of the stifling of Christianity?—that God has been called obsolete. I don't mean to say that there is no such thing as obsolescence. I merely wish to show that the term *obsolete*, derived from evolutionary thought, has a place of some importance in the history of modern persecution. Far, far down in the scale of power, far from Rome and Berlin and Leningrad, in certain academic and critical circles we hear it said that a particular kind of imagination is now obsolete. The objective conditions necessary for its existence are supposedly gone. I've never heard it stated in these circles that money is obsolete or that social advancement and distinction are obsolete. Apparently these things are hardier and don't require the same agreement as to the nature of the Universe.

Well, such an issue can never be settled in debate. Neither the denials of academic people nor the affirmations of writers can make much difference. "To believe in the existence of human beings as such is love," says Simone Weil. This is what makes the difference. It is possible—all too possible—to say when we have read one more modern novel, "So what? What do I care? You yourself, the writer, didn't really care." It is, all too often, like that. But this caring or believing or love alone matters. All the rest, obsolescence, historical views, manners, agreed views of the Universe, is simply nonsense and trash. If we don't care, don't immediately care, then perish books both old and new, and novelists, and governments, too. If we do care, if we believe in the existence of others, then what we write is necessary.

The writer asks himself, "Why shall I write this next thing?" It is still possible, despite all theories to the contrary, to answer, "Because it *is* necessary." A book, any book, may easily be superfluous. But to manifest love—can this be superfluous? Is there so much of it about us? Not so much. It is still rare, still wonderful. It is still effective against distraction.

A COMMENT ON "FORM AND DESPAIR"

Harold Rosenberg is entirely right when he describes the inherited apparatus of modern fiction. And when he says, "The groove worn by the reiterated sentiment of the doom of the West works automatically to make the expression of any other kind of outlook extraordinarily difficult," he earns the gratitude of every writer of independent imagination. The "doom of the West" is the Established Church in modern literature.

In what I am about to say I shall take no data to be well-known. Can anyone today easily adopt an optimistic view of modern history? The question answers itself. It is, however, the negative view that has become the "easy" one. To demonstrate this, anyone can

First appeared in *Location*, Summer 1964. Copyright © 1964 by Saul Bellow.

run up for himself, at short notice, a list of terms taken seriously by the whole intellectual community: bureaucracy, alienation, mass media, anomie, privation of instinctual needs, etc. Lists of optimistic terms do not come quite so spontaneously. I have no wish to be frivolous about this. I want to suggest simply that the facility with which lists like the first can be whipped up does not inspire the imagination with confidence.

In two words, this is simpleminded historicism. On the one side the doom-of-the-West shows us—or instructs us to make out— solid ages of authority or faith. On the other side, it depicts us as estranged, debased, negligible, speaking demotic dialects, and blowing cigar smoke over the fabrics of enchantment. It alleges that we have been torn from meaningful communities regulated by custom and hierarchy, stabilized by estates, and are born instead into howling urban wastes. This is by now a familiar story. It is usual for modern writers to describe the technical and political transformation of Western society by telling it once more. Eliot, Joyce, Pound, Wyndham Lewis, Thomas Mann, Céline (the list would be endless) have differed in details but agreed in substance that such indeed was the modern story. Rosenberg believes that this hollow-man version of things was in its days vanguardist. I do not quite agree, but since some of these were men of genius I shall not grudge them a nice rubric. In any case we have their legacy, and few modern novelists of serious pretensions approach contemporary experience without making a filial bow to their sainted ancestors. They take no independent view of contemporary facts.

Now the modern novel is predominantly realistic, and realism is based upon our common life. It is a literature of ordinary human beings in ordinary circumstances, against a contemporary background. Everything in a modern novel stems from the novelist's judgment of the "ordinary." Common labor and humble life had their brief decades of glorification at the beginning of the modern era. But after the Cotter and the Leech Gatherer came the Man in the Crowd. In its Western form, realism made the ordinary man extraordinarily limited—weak, sick, paltry, subject to devouring illusion. (Here I need only cite the name of Flaubert.) Tolstoy, it is

387

true, tells us that the life of Ivan Ilyich was "most ordinary and therefore most terrible," but by "ordinary" he appears to mean "conventional," for Ivan Ilyich's powers of analysis and synthesis are anything but ordinary.

In the West, a dislike of modern civilization, partly of romantic origin, has been built into realism, so that to name certain ordinary objects is already to derogate them. Common commodities, chain stores, cheap hotels, empty city lots, subway cars, graveyards for automobiles, Main Street, Coney Island, these are recognized as soon as they are mentioned because realism has given them a color which is not easily changed. The "objectivity" of realism is therefore simply a convention; from the beginning, it has judged its facts. These judgments were founded on a given view of modern civilization, and the successors of Flaubert have never seriously considered any other view. Their attitude toward the facts is fixed by their tradition, and this tradition expresses an esthetic horror of the conditions of modern life. It is not I alone who invoke the classics. They are negatively invoked by the rejection of modern civilization, and this rejection is based upon all that we have *not*, on a Nietzschean, a Burckhardtian antiquity or on the family life of the Russian gentry of the nineteenth century.

Modern literature is engaged in a debate about the capacities of the sort of human being Western civilization has produced. But no—I retract the word *debate*. Since Flaubert, "the myth of the diminished man" has not often been challenged. A view of ordinary human nature has been synthesized by the Joyces, Hemingways, Gides, Moravias, Camus', etc. The collective effort of the intellectual classes of all civilized countries has from decade to decade in this century created limits for the ordinary man, or conventions for his representation in literature and history.

III

OPINIONS OF CRITICS

IRVING HOWE

Irving Howe, editor of this volume, is Distinguished Professor of English at Hunter College of the City University of New York. He is the author of numerous books of literary and social criticism, among them *Politics and the Novel*, *Decline of the New*, *Steady Work*, and *The Critical Point*. His most recent work is a social history of immigrant Jews, *World of Our Fathers*.

DOWN AND OUT IN NEW YORK AND CHICAGO
Saul Bellow, Professor Herzog and Mr. Sammler

Where shall a contemporary novel begin? Perhaps unavoidably: with the busted hero reeling from a messy divorce and moaning in a malodorous furnished room; picking at his psyche's wounds like a boy at knee scabs; rehearsing the mightly shambles of ambition ("how I rose from humble origins to complete disaster"); cursing the heart-and-ball breakers, both wives and volunteers, who have, he claims, laid him low; snarling contempt at his own self-pity with a Johnsonian epigram, "Grief, Sir, is a species of idleness"; and yet, amidst all this woe, bubbling with intellectual hope, as also with intellectual gas, and consoling himself with the truth that indeed "there were worse cripples around."

This is Moses Herzog, Saul Bellow's hero-patsy. Herzog is a representative man of the sixties, eaten away by those "personal relations" which form the glory and the foolishness of a post-political intelligentsia. He is a good scholar, but cannot complete his books. He rips off imaginary letters to great men, finessing their wisdom and patronizing their mistakes. He is a lady-killer, "aging" at forty-seven and worried about his potency. He is a loving father twice-divorced, who each time has left behind him a child as a token of good will. He is a true-blue Jewish groaner, but perversely groans against fashionable despair. Inside or outside our skins, we all know Herzog: *Hypocrite lecteur—mon semblable—mein schlemiel*. Hungering for a life of large significance, eager for "a politics in the Aristotelian sense," he nevertheless keeps melting into the mercies of women, each of whom, in sequence, really understands him.

All of Bellow's books—whether melancholy realism, moral fable, or picaresque fantasia—represent for him a new departure, a chosen risk in form and perception. Bellow has the most powerful mind among contemporary American novelists, or at least he is the American novelist who best assimilates his intelligence to creative purpose. This might have been foreseen at the beginning of his career, for he has always been able to turn out a first-rate piece of discursive prose; what could not have been foreseen was that he would also become a virtuoso of fictional technique and language.

Behind Bellow's writing there is always a serious intention, but as he grows older he becomes increasingly devoted to the idea of the novel as sheer spectacle. His last few books constitute a hectic and at times ghastly bazaar of contemporary experience; they ring with the noise of struggle; characters dash in and out, glistening with bravura; adventures pile up merrily, as if the decline of the West had not been definitely proclaimed; the male characters plunge and rise, mad for transcendence; the women (a little tiresomely) are all very beautiful and mostly very damaging. And the language spins.

Before and, I hope, after everything else has been said, *Herzog* should be praised as a marvelously animated performance. The minor figures are drawn as sharp caricature, without the distraction of psychological probe or nuance, and sometimes, when Bellow's zest becomes compulsive, a little overfocused. There are foul-mouth lawyers, boiling with drug-store wisdom and "potato love";

a sadly ineffectual father fumbling at bootleggery; a professor who loves, solely but purely, his monkey. There are Herzog's ladies of the season: Sono, a Japanese doll who soothes the spirit and, Oriental-style, washes the back of Master Moses in an Upper West Side bathtub, while cooing at him in baby French, "mon professeur d'amour," and Ramona, bravely marching into middle age with an overload of "understanding" and graduate credentials in sex, who "entered a room provocatively . . . one hand touching her thigh, as though she carried a knife in her garter belt."

And then the demons, the evil spirits: Madeleine, the wife who betrays; Valentine Gersbach, the best friend with whom she does it.

A talentless buffoon-double of the talented hero, Valentine Gersbach (what a name!) booms out the latest highbrow cant in his great bearish voice and ends by lecturing to Hadassah clubs on Martin Buber. Toward Valentine Bellow is merciless, yet one is seldom troubled by this open display of aggression; for there is no pretense in this novel that we are being shown a world which exists, self-sufficient, apart from the neurotic inflammations of the central figure. Gersbach is a clown, a windbag, a traitor, the kind of man who makes intellectuals wish they were dead when they hear him parroting their words; yet he is utterly alive, one waits for him to reappear on the page, and finally even he wins a moment of humane redemption: Secretly, angrily, Herzog watches Gersbach bathing his (Herzog's) little girl and must admit to himself that the act, though done by a betrayer, is yet done with tenderness.

Madeleine is drawn with pure venom, a sentiment capable of generating in writers, as in other men, great quantities of energy. She is, naturally, a beauty; she piddles in Russian intellectual history and Catholic conversion; she outmaneuvers the slumping Herzog not merely at sexual games (where she has, after all, the advantage of youth) but also in intellectual competition. When Herzog complains about her extravagance, her arrogance, her paranoia, she replies with the great modern rationale: "Anyway, it'll never be boring." A moony schoolgirl meets Madeleine, and describes her in a phrase embodying the great modern cant: "She gives a sense of significant encounter." With her postures of depth, screeches of enthusiasm, learned references, and distinguished airs, Madeleine is the female pseudointellectual done, and done in, once and for all. The portrait is unjust, an utter libel, but a classic of male retaliation.

Herzog himself is not, in the traditional sense, a novelistic character at all. He is observed neither from a cool distance nor through intimate psychological penetration. We experience him intensely, entering his very bones; yet, trapped as we are in his inner turmoil, we cannot be certain that finally we know him. For Bellow has not provided a critical check: There is no way of learning what any of the other characters, by way of Jamesian correction, might think or feel about Herzog. Bellow offers not a full-scale characterization but a full-length exposure of a state of being. We do not see Herzog acting in the world, we are made captive in the world of Herzog. The final picture is that of Herzog in cross-section, bleeding from the cut.

In one sense, then, there is a complete identification between Bellow and Herzog: The consciousness of the character forms the enclosing medium of the novel. But in a more important respect Bellow manages skillfully to avoid the kind of identification which might lead one to conclude that he "favors" his central character or fails to see through his weaknesses and falsities—a fault that could radically distort the line of vision by which everything is to be considered. That Herzog cannot accurately perceive the other figures in the novel and that we are closely confined to his sense of them is true and, in ways I shall later suggest, a limitation. But not a crippling limitation. For it soon becomes clear that, while totally committed to Herzog's experience, Bellow is not nearly so committed to his estimate of that experience.

Things, to be sure, do not always work out neatly. There are sections in which the malice toward Madeleine gets out of hand, so much so that one suspects Bellow of settling private scores. And while the device of having Herzog compose imaginary letters is often amusing—

Dear Doktor Professor Heidegger, I should like to know what you mean by the expression "the fall into the quotidian." When did this fall occur? Where were we standing when it happened?

—one becomes somewhat irked at being unable, at times, to grasp which of the letters are serious, that is, Bellow's opinions, and which are not, that is, Herzog's conniptions. Ambiguity? No doubt. We all know about this prime blessing of modern literature; but there are occasions when the uses of ambiguity can themselves be anbiguous, shading off into confusion or evasiveness.

For the most part, however, *Herzog* marks a notable advance in technique over Bellow's previous books. He has become a master of something that is rarely discussed in criticism because it is hard to do more than point toward it: the art of timing, which concerns the massing, centering, and disposition of the characters and creates a sense of delight in the sheer motion of the narrative.

Bellow has also found a good solution to a technical problem which keeps arising in the contemporary novel. Most readers, I imagine, groan a little when they see a novelist wheeling into position one of those lengthy and leaden flashbacks in which, we know in advance, the trauma will be unveiled that is to explain the troubles of time-present. These flashbacks, by now one of the dreariest conventions of the novel, result in a lumpiness of narrative surface and blockage of narrative flow. But Bellow has managed to work out a form in which the illusion of simultaneity of time—a blend of past with the present-moving-into-future—is nicely maintained. Instead of the full-scale flashback, which often rests on the mistaken premise that a novelist needs to provide a psychiatric or sociological casebook on his characters, Bellow allows the consciousness of his narrator to flit about in time, restlessly, nervously, thereby capturing essential fragments of the past as they break into the awareness of the present. Through these interlockings of time—brief, dramatic, and made to appear simultaneous—he creates the impression of a sustained rush of experience.

395

Bellow began his career as a novelist of somber intellectuality: His impressive early book *The Victim* asks almost to be read as a fable concerning the difficulties of attempting a secure moral judgment in our day. With *Augie March* he made a sharp turn, casting aside the urban contemplativeness and melancholy of his previous work, and deciding to regard American life as wonderfully "open," a great big shapeless orange bursting with the juices of vitality. Though in some ways his most virtuoso performance, *Augie March* suffers from a programmatic exuberance: It is fun to watch the turns and tricks the suddenly acrobatic Bellow can execute, yet hard to suppress a touch of anxiety concerning his heartbeat.

With *Augie March* Bellow also began to work out a new fictional style, for which there may be some predecessors—possibly Daniel Fuchs and Nathanael West—but which in the main is an original achievement. By now it has come to be imitated by many American Jewish novelists as well as by a few Gentiles trying wistfully to pass, but none of these manages it nearly so well as Bellow himself.

What Bellow did was to leave behind him the bleak neutrality of naturalistic prose and the quavering sensibility of the Jamesian novel: The first, he seemed to feel, was too lifeless and the second insufficiently masculine. Beginning with *Augie March*—but none of this applies to his masterful novella *Seize the Day*—Bellow's prose becomes strongly antiliterary, a roughing up of diction and breaking down of syntax in order to avoid familiar patterns and expectations. The prose now consists of a rich, thick impasto of verbal color in which a splatter of sidewalk eloquence is mixed with erudite by-play. Together with this planned coarsening of texture, there is a great emphasis on speed, a violent wrenching and even forcing of images, all the consequence of his wish to break away from the stateliness of the literary sentence. Analytic refinement is sacrificed to sensuous vigor, careful psychological notation to the brawling of energy, syntactical qualification to kinesthetic thrust. (One is reminded a bit of action painting.) Psychology is out, absolutely out: For to psychologize means to reflect, to hesitate, to qualify, to modulate, to analyze. By contrast, the aim of Bellow's neobaroque style is to communicate sensations of immediacy and intensity, even when dealing with abstract intellectual topics—to communicate, above all, the sense that men are still alive. Toward this end he is prepared to yield niceties of phrasing, surface finish, sometimes even coherence of structure.

It is a style admirably suited to the flaming set piece, the rapid vignette, the picaresque excursion. But it is not so well suited to a sustained and complex action, or a lengthy flow of experience, or a tragic plot, or what George Moore, in discussing the nature of fiction, called the "rhythmic sequence of events." In *Augie March* there is a run of action but hardly a plot; in *Herzog*, a superbly realized situation but hardly a developing action; and in both of these novels, as well as in *Henderson*, not much of a "rhythmic sequence of events." That is why, I think, none of them has a fully satisfying denouement, an organic fulfillment of the action. In principle these books could continue forever, and that is one reason Bellow finds it hard to end them. He simply stops, much against one's will.

Finally, Bellow's style draws heavily from the Yiddish, not so much in borrowed diction as in underlying intonation and rhythm. Bellow's relation to Yiddish is much more easy and authoritative than that of most other American Jewish writers. The jabbing interplay of ironies, the intimate vulgarities, the strange blend of sentimental and sardonic which characterizes Yiddish speech are lassoed into Bellow's English so that what we get is not a sick exploitation of folk memory but a vibrant linguistic and cultural transmutation. (Precisely at the moment when Yiddish is dying off as an independent language, it has experienced an astonishing, and not always happy, migration into American culture. In two or three decades students of American literature may have to study Yiddish for reasons no worse than those for which students of English literature study Anglo-Saxon.)

One of the most pleasing aspects of *Herzog* is that Bellow has brought together his two earlier manners: the melancholy and the bouncy, the "Russian" and the "American," *Seize the Day* and *Augie March*. *Herzog* is almost free of the gratuitous verbalism which marred *Augie March*, yet retains its vividness and richness of texture.

There is a similar marshaling of Bellow's earlier themes. For some years now he has been obsessed with that fatigue of spirit which hangs so dismally over contemporary life. *Seize the Day* shows a man utterly exhausted, unable so much as to feel his despair until the wrenching final page. *Augie March* shows a man composing a self out of a belief in life's possibilities. Of the two books *Seize the Day* seems to me the more convincing and authentic, perhaps because despair is easier to portray than joy, perhaps because the experience of our time, as well as its literature, predisposes us to associate truth with gloom. In any case, what seems notable about *Herzog* is that nothing is here blinked or evaded, rhetoric does not black out reality (Herzog declares himself "aging, vain, terribly narcissistic, suffering without proper dignity"); yet the will to struggle, the insistence upon human possibility, is maintained, and not as a mere flourish but as the award of agony. Herzog learns that

> . . . to look for fullfillment in another . . . was a feminine game. And the man who shops from woman to woman, though his heart aches with idealism, with the desire for pure love, has entered the female realm.

Not, perhaps, a very remarkable lesson, but worth learning when the cost comes high. More importantly, Herzog says about himself, wryly but truthfully, that he is a man who "thought and cared about belief." That is the first step toward salvation.

For all its vividness as performance, *Herzog* is a novel driven by an idea. It is a serious idea, though in my judgment neither worked out with sufficient care nor worked into the grain of the book with sufficient depth. Herzog, he tells us, means to write something that will deal "with a new angle on the modern condition, showing how life could be lived by renewing universal connections, overturning the last of the Romantic errors about the uniqueness of the Self, revising the old Western, Faustian ideology. . . ." This time clearly speaking for Bellow, Herzog declares himself opposed to

> The canned sauerkraut of Spengler's "Prussian Socialism," the commonplaces of the Wasteland outlook, the cheap mental stimulants of Alienation, the cant and rant of pipsqueaks about Inauthenticity and Forlornness. I can't accept this foolish dreariness. We are talking about the whole life of mankind. The subject is too great, too deep for such weakness, cowardice. . . .

And in the magazine *Location* Bellow has written a sharp attack on "the 'doom of the West' [which] is the Established Church in modern literature." It is a Church, he says, which asserts the individual to be helpless among the impersonal mechanisms and sterilities of modern life; it cultivates self-pity and surrender; and it is wrong.

Bellow has touched on something real. Talk about "the decline of the West" can be elitist rubbish. The posture of alienation, like any other, can collapse into social accommodation. Cries of despair can become mere notes of fashion. Where the motif of alienation in the literature of modernism during the late nineteenth and early twentieth centuries signified an act of truth, courage, and sometimes rebellion too, now it can easily become the occasion for a mixture of private snobbism and public passivity. Yet may not all ideas suffer this sort of outcome in a culture which seems endlessly capable of assimilating and devitalizing everything? Suppose Bellow's assault upon alienation becomes fashionable: Will it not then suffer a public fate similar to that of the ideas he attacks?

Bellow is being just a little too cavalier in so readily disposing of a central theme of modernist literature. Surely, as it was manifested in the work of writers like Joyce, Flaubert, Eliot, and Baudelaire, the sense of alienation expressed a profound and even exhilarating response to the reality of industrial society. (An imagining of despair can be as bracing as a demand for joy can be ruthless.) And does not the sense of alienation, if treated not as a mere literary convenience but as a galling social fact—does this not continue to speak truthfully to significant conditions in our life?

I raise these matters because Bellow, as a serious writer, must want his readers to consider them not merely in but also beyond the setting of his novel. When, however, one does consider them strictly in the context of *Herzog*, certain critical issues present themselves. There is a discrepancy between what the book actually is—brilliant but narrow in situation and scope—and the sweeping intentions that lie behind it; or in other words, between the dramatic texture and the thematic purpose. In the end one feels that *Herzog* is too hermetic a work, the result of a technique which encloses us rigidly in the troubles of a man during his phase of withdrawal from the world. The material is absorbing in its own right; it is handled with great skill; but in relation to the intended theme, it all seems a little puny.

Bellow has conceived of the book as a stroke against the glorification of the sick self, but the novel we have—as picture, image, honest exposure—remains largely caught up with the thrashings of the sick self. One wants from Bellow a novel that will not be confined to a single besieged consciousness but instead will negotiate the kind of leap into the world which he proclaims, to savor the world's freshness and struggle against its recalcitrance, perhaps even to enter "politics in the Aristotelian sense."

GABRIEL JOSIPOVICI

Gabriel Josipovici is a literary critic who lives in England, where he also lectures in the School of European Studies at Sussex University. He has recently edited *The Portable Bellow*, a collection of Saul Bellow's writings. He has published two novels and has written extensively on modern fiction.

BELLOW AND HERZOG

There's a lot of movement in Saul Bellow's *Herzog*, but the only action is a botched action: Herzog's failure to carry out his plan and kill his former wife Madeleine and her lover, Valentine Gersbach. Anguished, Herzog rushes from New York to the peace of Vineyard Haven and his friend Libbie but he's no sooner there than he decides to fly back to New York. He spends the day in his apartment and the night with his current mistress; but the next day he's off again, to Chicago this time and his murderous mission. Instead of murder, however, he is involved in a minor traffic accident and hauled off to the police station for illegal possession of firearms. Bailed out by his brother, he ends up where we have first found him, in his vast decaying house in the middle of the Berkshires.

It is not, however, all this flurry of meaningless activity that gives the book its sense of continuous turmoil. That comes from the ceaseless inner activity which grips Herzog and of which the external movement is merely a symptom. The greater part of the novel is taken up with Herzog by himself, writing compulsive let-

From *The World and the Book: A Study of Modern Fiction* by Gabriel Josipovici. Copyright © 1971 by Gabriel Josipovici. Reprinted by permission of Stanford University Press and Macmillan London and Basingstoke.

ters to his friends, his enemies, the newspapers, politicians, "and at last to the dead, his own obscure dead and finally the famous dead." Sometimes the letters are only scribbled on odd bits of paper and promptly forgotten; most of the time they never get put onto paper at all. But though they seem to burst out of him wildly, spontaneously, and often peter out after no more than a sentence and nearly always before the end, a clear and consistent position does emerge from them, a position whose defining characteristic is that it cannot be reduced to any purely abstract statement, but which relates at almost every point to Herzog's own troubled life. To understand the novel we need to understand what this position is.

Like that of Swift in *A Tale of a Tub*, it can be expressed diagrammatically as the rejection of two false extremes. These Herzog calls "crisis ethics" and "potato love" respectively. Like Swift, too, Herzog goes behind the labels that people and movements give themselves and brings out the essential similarity between many apparently disparate phenomena. And like Swift he believes that extremes meet and that crisis ethics and potato love are only facets of one attitude to both man and history. What meaning then do the terms have for him?

"Dear Doktor Professor Heidegger," writes Herzog, "I should like to know what you mean by the expression 'the fall into the quotidian.' When did this fall occur? Where were we standing when it happened?" The question is of course rhetorical, but the ploy is the same as Swift's: By making concrete what his opponents keep at the level of metaphor he shocks us into an awareness of the implications of their position. He himself answers his questions later on when he writes:

> Very tired of the modern form of historicism which sees in this civilization the defeat of the best hopes of Western religion and thought, what Heidegger calls the second Fall of Man into the quotidian or ordinary. No philosopher knows what the ordinary is, has not fallen into it deeply enough.

Nor is it simply German existentialism which is dominated by this idea. Herzog sees in it a Christian, and especially a Protestant, view of history, one which regards "the present moment always as some crisis, some fall from classical greatness, some corruption or evil to be saved from." This idea has taken hold of modern man because it seems to be a way of saving him from himself and his daily responsibilities:

> Everybody was in the act. "History" gave everyone a free ride. The very Himmelsteins, who had never even read a book of metaphysics, were touting the void as if it were so much saleable real estate. This little demon was impregnated with modern ideas, and one in particular excited his terrible little heart: you must sacrifice your poor, squawking, niggardly individuality . . . to historical necessity. And to truth.

And what is truth? "Truth is true only as it brings down more disgrace and dreariness upon human beings, so that if it shows anything except evil it is illusion, and not truth." Facts are what's nasty, the rest is just idealism. The only way to get away from facts then is through ecstasy, through achieving an "inspired condition":

> This is thought to be attainable only in the negative and is so pursued in philosophy and literature as well as in sexual experience, or with the aid of narcotics, or in "philosophical," "gratuitous" crime and similar paths of horror. (It never seems to occur to such "criminals" that to behave with decency to another human being might also be "gratuitous.")

But all this, Herzog argues, all this talk of crisis and inspiration, is only a projection into history of private fantasies; they are ideas put out by intellectuals who long for the death of the intellect, something that will free them from the burden of daily living:

> Civilized individuals hate and resent the civilization that makes their lives possible. What they love is an imaginary human situation invented by their own genius and which they believe is the only true and the only human reality.

We must get it out of our heads that this is a doomed time; such talk is merely irresponsible, and is likely to lead to a loss of nerve which will bring about just such a doom:

Are all the traditions used up, the beliefs done for, the conscious-ness of the masses not yet ready for the next development? Is this the full crisis of dissolution? . . . Old Proudhon's visions of dark-ness and evil can't be passed over. But we mustn't forget how quickly the visions of genius become the canned goods of the in-tellectuals. The canned sauerkraut of Spengler's "Prussian Social-ism," the commonplaces of the Wasteland outlook, the cheap mental stimulants of Alienation, the cant and rant of pipsqueaks about Inauthenticity and Forlorness. I can't accept this foolish dreariness. We are talking about the whole life of mankind. The subject is too great, too deep for such weakness, cowardice. . . . A merely aesthetic critique of modern history! After the wars and mass killings!

It is time, argues Herzog, covering sheet after sheet with his des-perate letters, it is time we stopped talking about human nature being this or that or the other thing. Total explanations are a delusion, the desire to see everything in terms of simple antitheses a sign of paranoia.

But is it possible to see life in any other way? Herzog discovers that the people who talk most about the "hard facts" of life are really the most sentimental, the believers in what he calls, talking of Eisenhower, "potato love": "The general won because he ex-pressed low-grade universal potato love." But this too is a delusion, a form of self-pity, the wish to get rid of one's responsibilities by merging with the mass, the universal. Yet this merging is what Rousseau preached, and its appeal is enormous. Herzog is under no delusion about the power of words and ideas: "He took seriously Heinrich Heine's belief that the words of Rousseau had turned into the bloody machinery of Robespierre, that Kant and Fichte were deadlier than armies."

What is common to both the believers in crisis ethics and the believers in potato love is the notion that the world can be changed by a fiat, that if we will it hard enough we will find that our wishes and the reality of the world will coincide. It springs from the desperate need to shed the responsibility we are born with, a need which finds its ironic epigraph in what Tante Taube tells Herzog about making love with her first husband: "Kaplitzky-*alehoshalom* took care on everything. I didn't even looked." And yet the Romantics—for Herzog is in no doubt that if this is a Christian, and in particular a Protestant, movement, then it is with Romanticism that it gained its full momentum—the Romantics cannot so easily be refuted. For what model have we got to put in the place of the one they offer us? Herzog sympathizes with T. E. Hulme's rejection of Romanticism, but he cannot agree with his solution of the problem:

> He wanted things to be clear, dry, spare, pure, cool, and hard. With this I think we can all sympathize. I too am repelled by the "dampness," as he called it, and the swarming of Romantic feelings. I see what a villain Rousseau was, and how degenerate. . . . But I do not see what we can answer when he says: "Je sens mon coeur et je connais les hommes. . . ." Hulme's followers made sterility their truth, confession their impotence. This was their passion.

The men Herzog admires are not the conservatives, who want to preserve at all costs, for he sees that this too is a falsification of the reality of the world in the interests of a private wish. No. It is men like Montaigne and Pascal, politicians like Adlai Stevenson and Martin Luther King, who do not shy away from the complexity and uniqueness of every situation by opting for a single clear-cut solution, but on the contrary try to face and understand and control, knowing that their work will take a long time, that it will require patience above all things, and that it will constantly be undermined by extremists. They accept man as he is, try to keep close to the ins and outs of his thoughts and feelings. They accept a personal responsibility for history, a responsibility, notes Herzog, rooted in both Testaments. And they are always beaten by the idealists.

It is by such idealists, all talking the same language of "truth" and "hard facts," but all driven on only by the need to fulfil their private desires, that Herzog is surrounded. These people derive their power from the fact that for them life is simple. They know the score. And they know Herzog better than he knows himself. There is the psychiatrist, Dr. Edvig; and Sandor Himmelstein, the lawyer—"I know this isn't easy for you to hear, but I better say it. Guys at our time of life must face facts. . . . I know about suffering —we're on the same identical network." Above all, of course, there are Madeleine, Herzog's former wife, and her lover, Gersbach, his former friend. "She brought ideology into my life," Herzog recognizes, at the end of the book. "Something to do with catastrophe." For she and Gersbach never have enough of talking about Truth, though neither is very interested in the details of daily life:

> Dealing with Valentine was like dealing with a king. . . . He appropriated all the emotions about him, as if by divine or spiritual right. . . He was a big man, too big for anything but the truth.

What is important for Valentine Gersbach is the *intensity* of an experience, not its content. This intensity, this physical glow which seems to guarantee the genuineness of his emotion, goes into everything he does, whether it's talking about Buber on television or advising Herzog about the nature of life. And the same is true of Madeleine:

> Before Soloviëv, she had talked of no one but Joseph de Maistre. And before de Maistre—Herzog made up the list—the French Revolution, Eleanor of Aquitaine, Schliemann's excavations at Troy, extrasensory perception, then tarot cards, then Christian Science, before that, Mirabeau; or was it mystery novels (Josephine Tey), or science fiction (Isaac Asimov)? The intensity was always high.

Excessive rationality, the inability to bear criticism, to accept ambiguity, the desire to assert oneself continuously—all these are paranoiac traits, Herzog is convinced, and all can be found in Madeleine. How can he leave his children in the charge of people like her and Gersbach?

Yet are they unique? The whole of Western society seems to

have acquired these traits, and Herzog, in the course of his wild letters, finds their roots in such things as the notion of outward composure in Calvinist societies, where each man, fearful of damnation, has to *behave* as one of the elect in order to convince himself that he *is* one; in the fear of an increasingly mechanized world; in Rousseauistic notions of pity. There is no lack of evidence for the historically minded. But it is also there in the present, facing him, and Herzog doesn't know how to fight it. Even his current mistress, Ramona, beautiful, exciting Ramona, whom Herzog likes so much, is convinced that she understands Herzog's *real* needs better than he does himself:

> To listen to Ramona, it was all very simple. She said she understood his needs better than he, and she might well be right. . . . She told Herzog that he was a better man than he knew—a deep man, beautiful (he could not help wincing when she said this), but sad, unable to take what his heart really desired, a man tempted by God, longing for grace, but escaping headlong from his salvation. . . .

The difficulty with such arguments is that Herzog is perfectly well aware that they might all be true. Because he does not know what he *really* is, he cannot counter such assertions with any of his own, only with vague unease at such a formulation of the problem. Nor is it only Ramona who could be right. All of them—Madeleine, Gersbach, Edvig, Himmelstein—they might be right too, he might indeed be all that they say he is. Who is to say if they are wrong? Certainly not Herzog. And yet deep down inside him there remains the stubborn conviction that they *are* in some obscure way wrong, every one of them, including Ramona. The book, which charts his partial recovery from a mental breakdown, also shows his growing awareness of the nature of his own inarticulate attitudes and beliefs. He may not have the answers to the confident assertions of those who surround him, but that is perhaps a kind of strength, even if it makes him more vulnerable to their initial attacks. For one thing, he recognizes very well the propensity within himself to fall for this kind of argument:

It's about time I stopped laboring with this curse—I think, I figure things out. I see exactly what I should avoid. Then, all of a sudden, I'm in bed with that very thing, and making love to it. As with Madeleine. She seems to have filled a special need.

But even as he says this he knows he will labour under the curse all his life, that there will always be moments when he cries out under his breath, as he does earlier to Romona: "Marry me! Be my wife! End my troubles!"—only to be immediately "staggered by his rashness, his weakness, and by the characteristic nature of such an outburst, for he saw how very neurotic and typical it was." Knowing this, though, he is determined not to be a victim, not to indulge in bitter self-criticism. He is what he is—why always be looking for a motive? His duty is to live. To be sane and to live and to look after his children.

His self-awareness does not stop with the recognition of his own general desire to give up, be safe, not to have to make decisions. He realizes too that just at this time he is in the grip of a particular violence, that these letters, this way of talking are not the actions of a normal man. And, recognizing it, he can take steps to fight it, can even see that his own failure all along the line might not mean that his opponents are right but simply that he was confused and inadequate to the task. What he must avoid at all costs is imposing his own pattern on reality, trying to get at the essence of people and slotting them into pigeonholes in his mind. For man is always more complex than any of the models we create to explain him, be they Freudian, Jungian, Marxian, Thomist, or anything else. It may be, Herzog comes to see, that he cannot counter the image of himself that other people have, as being essentially this or that, simply because he has no essence, because he is not reducible in this way.

The episode of Lucas Asphalter and his monkey is an essential element in this self-discovery. Asphalter, Herzog's old friend with whom he goes to stay when he returns to Chicago with the object of killing Gersbach, recounts how, after the death of his pet monkey, he felt he had no more to live for, and, on the advice of a psychoanalyst, tried to follow the prescriptions of the Hungarian analyst Tina Zokóly. These consist of such spiritual exercises as imagining your own death: You pretend you are already dead and try to conjure up the coffin and attendant paraphernalia. Asphalter, however, finds that with him this doesn't work. His mind keeps shifting from the scene of his death to the image of his enormously fat old aunt being carried down a ladder from one of the top windows of the building in which she lived when it caught fire, or to that of the whores who used to play baseball in the street outside the flophouse where they worked. Asphalter recounts his failure to his friend in despair, but Herzog interrupts him excitedly:

"Don't feel so bad, Luke. Now listen to me. Maybe I can tell you something about this. At least I can tell you how I see it. A man may say, 'From now on I'm going to speak the truth.' But the truth hears him and runs away and hides before he's even done speaking. There is something funny about the human condition, and civilized intelligence makes fun of its own ideas. This Tina Zokóly has got to be kidding, too."

"I don't think so."

"Then it's the old *memento mori*, the monk's skull on the table, brought up to date. And what good is that? It all goes back to those German existentialists who tell you how good dread is for you, how it saves you from distraction and gives you your freedom and makes you authentic. God is no more. But Death is. That's their story. And we live in a hedonistic world in which happiness is set up on a mechanical model. All you have to do is open your fly and grasp happiness. And so these other theorists introduce the tension of guilt and dread as a corrective. But human life is far subtler than any of its models, even these ingenious German models. Do we need to study *theories* of fear and anguish? This Tina Zokóly is a nonsensical woman. She tells you to practice overkill on yourself, and your intelligence answers her with wit."

Wit is the element that won't be captured, the individual response of a man trying hard to lose his individuality. It is grotesque, but reminds him that man is always something else, over and above any description of him that we can give. It is consciousness of this that leads Herzog at last to say (in his mind) to Madeleine and Gersbach: "Excuse me, therefore, sir and madam, but I reject your definitions of me."

But it is this too that stops Herzog from murdering Gersbach. As he looks through his own bathroom window and watches the man bathing his little daughter he is forced to realize that Gersbach is decent after all, perhaps even kind, according to his lights. Herzog, aware how much his condemnation of his former wife and her lover may be the result of his own uncontrollable emotions, understands in that brief moment that he could never kill. Especially not this man. Killing him is one more role into which he has tried to slip—a role and not himself. Leave the roles to the movies, creators of myths. He steps down from the window and goes his way.

Something, however, must happen. All that pent-up emotion has to find an outlet. Typically, what happens is both farcical and banal, another victory of reality over any of its models. Herzog, taking out his little daughter for a drive the next day, is involved in an absurd car accident. No one is seriously hurt, but he is shaken by it, and especially by the confrontation at the police station with the furious Madeleine. How could he act like this, and show himself in this light to his daughter? Can she ever forgive him?

And yet the accident finally brings him down to earth "from his strange spiraling flight of the last few days." He can no longer run away from himself, he is, at last, up against the wall. Because, for all his talk of the ordinariness of life being the important thing and how one must be what one is and ask no questions, the whirlwind activity of those last few days did represent a flight from himself, from reality. Exactly like George Hoberly, Ramona's discarded lover, who tries to reawaken her sympathies by acts of deliberate self-destruction, Herzog has attempted to force from life an answer to the question: What am I? What am I really? The accident and its aftermath serve to free him from this compulsion. In a sense he bangs into reality. Not hard, but hard enough to remind him of what might have happened—like the blow the Green Knight delivers to Gawain, "nikking his neck." Herzog sees now how difficult it is to eradicate the notion of crisis from our minds, how we all unconsciously long for some one event that will change things irrevocably and tell us how from then on we are to lead our lives.

But now, back in his crumbling house in the heart of the countryside, he realizes that "I have wanted to be cared for. I devoutly hoped Emmerich would find me sick. But I have no intention of doing that—I am responsible, responsible to reason. . . . Responsible to the children." And, realizing this, he finds a kind of peace:

> Why must I be such a throb-hearted character? . . . But I am. I am, and you can't teach old dogs. Myself is thus and so, and will continue thus and so. And why fight it? . . . Must play the instrument I've got.

Now at last he can answer Rousseau. True, the only kind of knowledge we can have is what the heart feels, and yet "My face too blind, my mind too limited, my instincts too narrow." We must not generalize from our own heart, just learn to be content with it. And so, at the end, "I am pretty well satisfied to be, to be just as it is willed, and for as long as I may remain in occupancy."

Thus the letters come to an end. Herzog has no more messages for anyone. And the novel too ends, leaving him there in his decaying mansion, waiting for Ramona—another mistake?—to arrive. The letters were a symptom of his illness, but it is they who helped him through it. Like Hamlet he deliberately exaggerated his condition, "as if by staggering he could recover his balance . . . or by admitting a bit of madness could recover his senses." The others, Madeleine, Gersbach, Sandor Himmelstein, George Hoberly, are the really sick ones, because they do not know they are sick, imagine they are well: "It's possible to see that a man like Hoberly by falling apart intends to bear witness to the failure of individual existence. He proves it *can't work*."

Their madness lies in imagining that they are sane, reasonable, *animal rationalis* instead of only *animal rationis capax*. This is the other side to their insistence on Truth and their desperate desire to label, define, organize, their inability to live with paradox or ambiguity—with wit. Herzog, recognizing the infinite complexity of the human psyche, will not judge someone like Madeleine's mother, Tennie:

> Tennie took off her elaborate glasses, now making no effort to disguise her weeping. Her face, her nose reddened, and her eyes, shaped to make what seemed to Moses a crooked appeal, darkened blindly with tears. There was a measure of hypocrisy and calculation in Tennie's method, but behind this, again, was real feeling for her daughter and her husband; and behind this real feeling there was something still more meaningful and somber. Herzog was all too well aware of the layers upon layers of reality —loathsomeness, arrogance, deceit, and then—God help us all— truth, as well.

Nor, in the end, will he judge Madeleine. Judgment had best be left to God. He's got enough to do making sense of his own life without trying to make sense of those of other people too. Because Herzog is so aware of the infinite regress of consciousness, he remains far saner than all the people who surround him, with their constant search for the one essential truth, the one revealing motive.

Yet if his weakness is his strength, his strength is also his weakness. If he is open to details, careful not to force the multitude of facts into a private mould, the very profusion of these facts, details, overwhelms him. He looks at everything as if he was seeing it for the first time, but the very sharpness of his perceptions is a sign of his instability: "A rat chewed into a package of bread, leaving the shape of its body in the layers of slices. Herzog ate the other half of the loaf spread with jam. He could share with rats too." The childhood memories, the physical details he notes in everything, all threaten to submerge him—"at first there was no pattern to the notes he made." It is all very well saying "foo" to all categories, but if one has responsibilities there is an urgent need to organize one's life. Herzog's follies and errors come as much from his unwillingness or inability to categorize as from his wish to force matters to a head. Reading Geraldine Portnoy's letter, in which she tells him how Gersbach is treating his child, he finds the handwriting keeps getting in the way of the meaning. He can see so many sides to every question that in the end he is inhibited from acting at all. He is aware that all reasoning is rationalized instinct, that Shapiro's dribbling at the mouth as Madeleine serves up the food is as much a part of the picture as Shapiro's apocalyptic ideas. But it might be better for him to be a little less aware of such things. It is as though he is too close to the world to be able to make sense of it. Others are too far, but he is too close.

This being so, it is easy to see that the book, while charting his recovery from breakdown, simultaneously describes the final failure of his intellectual ambitions. It is clear by the end that Herzog will never write the sequel to his book, *Romanticism and Christianity*. The material is there, he's been lugging it around for years, but the will to put it together seems to be absent. No amount of letters is going to make up for that. Herzog knows—and it hurts him to acknowledge it—that to imagine he will write that book is to indulge in a Utopian dream.

But the reason for this failure is surely clear to us, if not to him. Were he to write the book he would himself be guilty of just the thing that he condemns in others: He would be setting up a model, albeit a highly sophisticated one, and saying: *This* is what man is like, this is what history *is*, this, ultimately, is what man is. As with the young Marcel Proust and his literary ambitions, it is more than a failure of the will which keeps him from his task. It is the unconscious recognition that to give shape to the feelings of the heart is to falsify the experience, that intellectual history, no matter how subtle, must always leave out more than it puts in. No volume in the history of ideas can do justice to Herzog's insight into the infinite regress of human self-awareness. If, as soon as I say "This is what I am," a part of me immediately dissociates itself from the definition, then what is required is a form that will convey the living person behind every speech and every gesture. What is required, in other words, is not history, but fiction, for only fiction can present the speaker as well as the words he speaks, can register the afterthought as well as the thought, and the afterthought to the afterthought, and the unspoken commentary on that.

Thus Saul Bellow's *Herzog* emerges as the work which Herzog, the fictional hero of that book, found it impossible to write.

All Herzog is able to do is battle with his demons and let the future look after itself. But Bellow, through his fiction, has been able to articulate the variety and richness of the world without being overwhelmed by it and without on the other hand imposing upon it the rigid categorization of the traditional novelist, who only includes as much of the world as is necessary for his plot. Bellow has in fact succeeded in constructing a work which is an attack on the structuring activity of the mind; in conveying a sense of the infinite mystery of human beings in a book which is a critique of the traditional link between motive and action; in keeping close to the twists and turns of a man's thoughts and feelings without either putting him in a straitjacket of theory or allowing the book to fall apart in chaos. He has done all this because his book is not called *Saul Bellow* but *Herzog*.

The name Moses Elkanah Herzog is to be found in James Joyce's own novel *Ulysses*. By making use of it Bellow makes it clear from the start that he is writing fiction, not fact, much as Defoe, by using ordinary English names, tried to persuade his readers that he was writing fact and not fiction. But what is fact? Who am I? Who is Bellow?

What is certain is that while writing *Herzog* he is Herzog and yet not Herzog, since he is always clear that he is the creator of Herzog. In his most recent novel, *Mr. Sammler's Planet* (1970), Bellow writes ironically of Marx's vision of the proletarian revolution needing no historical models and comments on the colourful variety of present-day Americans:

> They sought originality. They were obviously derivative. . . .
> Better . . . to accept the inevitability of imitation and then to imi-
> tate good things. The ancients had this right. Greatness without
> models? Inconceivable. One could not be the thing itself—Reality.
> One must be satisfied with the symbols.

414

Thus, had he written directly about himself, he would have fallen into the trap of either sentiment or prophecy, have been either a Gersbach or a Shapiro. Writing fiction, he frees himself from the dead weight of his own personality. "That suffering hero" Herzog writes of himself, and, having written it, knows that he is more than that since he has just formulated the description. And Bellow, formulating the formulator, creates himself as he writes. Creates us too if we follow Herzog and do not try to reduce the novel, as Madeleine and the others tried to reduce him, to a single meaning, an essence.

A piece of fiction is like a man: to ask what it means and expect an answer is to destroy it. But, unlike a man, it has the power to stay alive forever. Or as long, at least, as there are people to read it.

FORREST READ

Forrest Read is professor of English at the University of North Carolina and has written extensively on James Joyce and Ezra Pound.

HERZOG: A REVIEW

Perched on a cement block outside his former house, peering through the screen he left up last fall, looking for his ex-wife Madeleine's lover (his own former friend, adviser, and beneficiary), Moses Herzog has two bullets in Father Herzog's old nickel-plated gun and vengeance in his heart. But while he watches red-and-gold maned, gimp-legged Valentine Gersbach, "the poet of mass communications," giving his little daughter Junie Herzog a bath, the evil drains out of Herzog's heart with the bath water. "The human soul is an amphibian, and I have touched its sides," Herzog reflects as he steps down, reminding both himself and us that the soul may be a monster or a bird, or a computing machine with a taxicab's heart, or the buzz of a message on the telephone— or, maybe just darkness, or light, or silence. For the world has entered Herzog's soul, his heart, his nervous system, his cerebral cortex, and his digestive tract, and he spends his exuberance trying either to check the flood of, or throw his arms around, or press his own shape on (the mixed metaphors are an essence of Herzogism), what Yeats called "magnanimity of his own desire." And he does it with the absurd heroism of an absurd intellectual who can surprise us and himself by saying, "Much of my life has been spent in the effort to live by more coherent ideas. I even know which ones."

This article originally appeared in *Epoch*.

Herzogism (like quixotism) will probably become a catchword, but the book can bear even that, for *Herzog* is a great comic novel. Bellow has found a way of getting everything in—of including and making coherent the biggest chunk of reality since Joyce got his into *Ulysses*. Consider who Herzog is. He is a son, a father, an ex-husband (twice), a friend, a patient, a client, a "Reality instructor"; he is a consoler, a wanderer, a nature-lover, a Ph.D.; he interprets history, he knows he is responsible for the future, he writes letters: to the newspapers and to presidents, and to his own, the obscure, and the great dead, etc., etc. He lives in, and absorbs into himself, Chicago, New York, the Berkshires, subways, telephones, Western Union—in one of his rare triumphs, though maybe it's only an in-joke, he outwits Western Union by sneaking in a threat to Gersbach by cryptogram: *"Dirt Enters At The Heart"*—airplanes, trains, bedrooms, taxis, law courts, the police desk, a jail cell, washstands, toiletbowls, bathtubs—the list could go on and on. The point is that Herzog is (to adapt his own definition of Gersbach) "the poet of personal considerations" who takes into himself the X-ray particled reality which buzzes around and through us who live in the city. We feel the city of the past covering us as dust drifts down from buildings being demolished to move "metamorphic New York" toward the future; it beats from the garment district lofts, seeps up from the grotesque underground of bootlegging, from decaying neighborhoods. The city of the present assaults us in subways, in taxicabs, on streets, from skylines, and in Grand Central and Penn Stations; it spills over onto Belt parkways and into the Jersey Flats. Trains, planes, and buses are hustling the present out into a too predictable future. Herzog's "wild internal disorder" reflects it:

And why? Because he let the entire world press upon him. For instance? Well, for instance, what it means to be a man. In a city. In a century. In transition. In a mass. Transformed by science. Under organized power. Subject to tremendous controls. In a condition caused by mechanization. After the late failure of radical hopes. In a society that was no community and devalued the person. Owing to the multiplied power of numbers which made the self negligible. Which spent military billions against foreign enemies but would not pay for order at home. Which permitted savagery and barbarism in its own great cities. At the same time, the pressure of human millions who have discovered what concerted efforts and thoughts can do. As megatons of water shape organisms on the ocean floor. As tides polish stones. As winds hollow cliffs. The beautiful supermachinery opening a new life for innumerable mankind. Would you deny them the right to exist? Would you ask them to labor and go hungry while you enjoyed delicious old-fashioned Values? You—you yourself are a child of this mass and a brother to all the rest. Or else an ingrate, dilettante, idiot. There, Herzog, thought Herzog, since you ask for the instance, is the way it runs. On top of that, an injured heart, and raw gasoline poured on the nerves.

Herzog has the senses to respond, the emotions to care, and the mind to probe his surroundings, his people, and himself. He also has the conscience and the vision and the vitality to try to turn everything into a human reality—he is famished for the real, for everything, which is another way of saying that Bellow has been able to make a man and a novel which has room for and can pack in our statistical, fluctuating encyclopedia.

I use that notion with Flaubert and Joyce in mind, for Bellow has done for the 1964 "moving city" (New York–Chicago–Ludeyville) what Flaubert did for mid-nineteenth century Paris and what Joyce did for 1904 Dublin. Flaubert's Frederick Moreau receives the imprint of Paris in his heart, Bouvard and Pécuchet translate *idées reçues* into action with the enthusiasm of lovable but mindless automatons, Stephen Dedalus receives Dublin's material and moral atmosphere into his nerves and bloodstream before turning them off with his "patented refrigerating device," Bloom registers municipal Dublin in patience, meditation, dream, and regret. Herzog brings this history up to date. Herzog is not *l'homme moyen sensuel*, or the man in the street, or the artist, or the natural active man, though he includes these. He has, it seems to me, absorbed those ancestors (as Bellow has absorbed their authors) and found the best figure for the present American which we have had. Herzog's father was the perfect outsider (a European Jew who made his living in the Montreal slums as a bootlegger distilling fine Scotch whisky for the U.S. market), two of whose sons have become wealthy American businessmen and the third (Moses) a professor. Thus Herzog comes from the provinces (Moreau), grows up in and out of a suffocating tradition (Dedalus), and becomes a peddler of dreams (Bloom). But he does not sell ads; he is a Ph.D., and that is just right for the post-World War II "hero." Bellow does not use a professor because that is all he knows, but because he wants the kind of man who has one foot in the world of speculative intelligence and one in the active life.

Bellow has perfected "the academic novel" by *using* the academic hero: That is, he does not put Herzog *in* the settings and situations which are characteristic of such novels, but in the center around which whirl centrifugally the campus, the business world, the city of the mind, the sensual and emotional life, the family, personal values, and politics and history. Or, since he achieves a beautifully persuasive and moving proportion among these attractions, we can say with equal truth that they are rushing in upon Herzog centripetally and so give him his shape.

Herzog is heroically cosmopolite in women, ideas, and places. He has had affairs with women from Japan to Poland; he has a domestic ex-wife who is thought to be promiscuous but isn't, and a bluestocking ex-wife who is thought to be a model mother but wants to be promiscuous; as if that weren't enough he is taking on a woman who, by having combined the old Eve, the modern handbooks, and efficient business methods, has made Eros the perfect servant and all-purpose problem solver. Moreau and Bloom are brought up to date, for divorces and dream-girls hang over every middle-class marriage, stirred by romantic literature, by full-color ads, and by "the entertainment industry." The intellectual counterpart of these scramblings to resolve emotional conflicts is the compulsive letters Herzog writes to an expanding circle as his problems become increasingly metaphysical: to friends, to those who are giving him professional help, to fellow scholars who are interpreting life and history, to Adlai Stevenson, General Eisenhower, and Nietzsche, and finally to God.

An extraordinary wealth of what makes a man is brought to bear. But this is not "a novel about Man"; it is a man's novel, built up painstakingly and harmoniously from detail, character, and situation. Herzog is *engagé*, or to use his own term, "a relating animal." He doesn't like being "with it," "falling into the quotidian," but he can't exist otherwise, for he draws his exuberance from his reactions to people, places, things, and ideas, and his reactions make him real. The book exists in a moving present during which Herzog tries to come to terms with all of his experience and to shape his future. He confirms that he has a future, even if it is only to endure:

> *Survival!* he noted. *Till we figure out what's what. Till the chance comes to exert a positive influence.* (Personal responsibility for history, a trait of Western Culture, rooted in the Testaments, Old and New, the idea of the continual improvement of human life on this earth. What else explained Herzog's ridiculous intensity?) *Lord, I ran to fight in Thy holy cause, but kept tripping, never reached the scene of the struggle.*

But he can't get out of touch; when he does he has his one moment of panic and of incoherence. His exuberance ("scope" and "intensity," he calls it) is the true binding force of the novel and of his reality. His sympathy draws him toward everyone, uniting him with the human sufferer, and his intellect keeps him concerned with the secret cause, whatever it may be. The book thus has the tragic dimension which Joyce defined, but it is bathed in what Joyce called the perfect end of art, joy, which is most fully realized in comedy. What Bellow has achieved is the Shakespearean sense of variety which sees all around a situation and a passion, and realizes it in character, scene, and meditation. Herzog's obsessive "relating" makes all of his recollections and gestures dramatic. His exuberance is almost compulsive (a true condition of our time). In his passion to understand people and himself he rehearses them in retrospective narration and drama. These elicit his efforts to apprehend his experience in its connectedness, his stabs at intellectual and ideological resolutions, his letters to Anima Mundi. He makes us feel that we have experienced a contemporary anatomy of love, that (like Hamlet) he includes all of the others whether he is raging or meditating. His ecstatic amours, his imaginative flights, the theories spun from his spidery entrails, his "most" story to his daughter Junie in the police station, the cluttered pastoral at Ludeyville, are part of the same man and the same world. He is not a picaresque saint, for the network is too tightly woven; he exists *in* his world so that both he and it are simultaneously alive, and he is too much a man to be canonized.

What this means is that Bellow has written a novel with a great form. Driving, prowling, under arrest in plethoric Chicago, trying "out of its elements, by this peculiar art of his own organs," to create his version of it, and so to reshape his past and his present, Herzog feels at home: "He was perhaps as midwestern and unfocused as these same streets. (Not so much determinism, he thought, as a lack of determining elements—the absence of a formative power.)" (Cf. Dreiser, whose naturalism, whose Hurstwood and Clyde Griffiths light up in the background.) Bellow has mustered such a formative power; he forces, into a reality which can be lived, the American East and West, the city and the frontier. In artistic terms, Bellow has achieved a beautiful balance of personality and impersonality by making the novelist's voice sound through the whole and unify the whole ambience; he is sometimes with his character ("I"), sometimes around him ("He"). His voice moves in and out, creating the comic ether; it reflects the fluctuating border between involvement and detachment, color and line, tragedy and comedy. It has both the narrative drive of outer events and the meditative convolutions of the city-saturated modern soul. I am reminded that Pound called Henry James a "drinker of men, of things, of passions," whose voice could be overheard "weaving an endless sentence." *Herzog* is also what Pound called *Ulysses*, "a passionate meditation on life."

But Herzog is unmistakably modern: The vital interchange between the artist and his character is more nervous and compelling than that between Joyce and Bloom, and James's world of agreed-upon conventions and manners has properly given way to the fluid informality of a mass society. The artist is not paring his nails, nor can he have Olympian confidence in his milieu. Bellow's voice exploits his donnée fully, but it cannot be a calm voice, nor is Herzog drowned out by the garrulity of Molly Bloom. One might call it a combination of Cervantes's nostalgic voice and the agonized voice of Shakespeare's Hamlet, which is driving willy-nilly toward the future. I feel, as I read the book, that Bellow has opened up a new quixotism, a new hamletism, weighted with and weighted down by the very world which impinges upon us. Herzog is an American Josef K. with great powers of endurance, whose religious sense is freed from dogma, from the Freudian darkness, and from the terror of totalitarian inevitability. Bellow has included both the Idol of Refined Art and the Idol of Raw Life in a greater amalgam; he feels life, if not steadily (which surely it is not), at least whole. His voice is a great civilizing voice which picks up the challenge of D. H. Lawrence, for Bellow is willing to express "man alive" in his drive toward a transvaluation of values, a change of heart, a reinterpretation of the Holy Ghost (though none of these terms can define Bellow's voice or his tone precisely).

I have implied that Bellow's novel is something of a synthesis, one of those encyclopedic works which makes one feel that it has been built upon the work of the writer's predecessors, upon his own development as a writer and a man, and upon the work of his contemporaries. For instance, Bellow has reinvented the epistolary form to convey the sense of eighteenth-century urbanity and the sense of the present city-dweller who tries to get into events, and into *l'histoire morale contemporaine*, by writing letters to the editor. His use of the past, which today comes to us as fragments of racial consciousness, as theories, and as a fluid tradition, extends the Joycean use of literary and religious myth; it is more relevant to us, and it reflects the absence of any standard which would make the modern vision a satiric one. (Pound's insistence that Joyce used Homer primarily as scaffolding, and that *Ulysses* strikes more forcibly our sense of the relation between life and art, as we live them, than upon art as an end—a view which is reasserted by Robert M. Adams in his *Surface and Symbol*—adumbrates the perspective in which Herzog should be seen. Allegorizing is a clear and present danger; even Malamud's *The Natural* has been reduced to allegory.) Scenes recur: Herzog sitting on the toilet reading Pope measures exactly Bellow's sense of the difference between Herzog's reality and Bloom's: Flaubert's *encyclopédie d'idées reçues mise en farce* and Bloom's archetypal meditations have become creative ideas which measure and affect action. Frank Alpine braced in the dumbwaiter shaft to spy on Helen Bober while she takes a shower has been enriched by Herzog's balancing to watch Gersbach give Junie a bath. Herzog has rediscovered nature by extending and enriching S. Levin's adaptation from Thoreau. Again, his notes for a proposed "Insect Iliad" for Junie, inspired by tent caterpillars and containing ants, water-skaters, cicadas, a wasp, and a stag beetle, which he gives up, nods at but eschews the metaphysical overtones of Thoreau watching the war of the ants and of Lt. Frederick Henry playing God over the ants on the burning log. From his own work, Bellow has combined the man dangling in himself, the victim imposed upon by his own conjured municipal nightmare, the urge to seize the day, Augie March on the move. He has pulled the lines formed by the sequence of his previous novels into a single grand circle and filled it; the synthesis reflects not only his growth, but a new grasp on reality. Instead of constructing an abstract metaphysical and symbolic system, as Yeats did, to enable him "to hold in a single thought reality and justice," he has taken "the tradition" as a series of achieved realities. His intensity has "used" it, transformed, to make intelligible a present world.

Herzog is, among other things, a history and synthesis of "The Novel." It gathers in not only novels of the past and current novels, but part-novels and novels-manqué. It sweeps up the sociological scalpel-and-bludgeon novel, the bitch-goddess novel, the fairy-anddyke novel, the sex-machine novel, the howl novel, the addict novel. One goes on and on as new connections light up on Bellow's switchboard. To change media, which suggests not only Bellow's method but also the extent to which *Herzog* is alive to visions of the contemporary reality, we are reminded of Fellini's camera and his impervious surfaces, of Antonioni's sense of the haunt of places, of the tone qualities which give *Dr. Strangelove* its civilizing atmosphere. As a final illustration I am reminded of Ermanno Olmi's sense of the world as an organization, especially of that ominous breathing on the soundtrack of *Il Posto*, which seems to be the respiration and heartbeat of the actors, and of one's companions (?) in the audience of the dark theater, but at the end is shockingly revealed to be the regular beat of the mimeograph machine. Bellow is aware of the realities of the past and of the present, and he conveys them.

What I am being led to say is that Bellow's style is able to present this comprehensive reality on a scale ranging from the directness of presentation and statement to the obliqueness of the most subtle and revealing poetry. Take this description of Herzog coming up from the subway on his way to Ramona's perfect dinner table, perfect bathroom, and perfect bed:

This was his station, and he ran up the stairs. The revolving gates rattled their multiple bars and ratchets behind him. He hastened by the change booth where a man sat in a light the color of strong tea, and up the two flights of stairs. In the mouth of the exit he stopped to catch his breath. Above him the flowering glass, wired and gray, and Broadway heavy and blue in the dusk, almost tropical; at the foot of the downhill eighties lay the Hudson, as dense as mercury. On the points of radio towers in New Jersey red lights like small hearts beat or tingled. In midstreet, on the benches, old people: on faces, on heads, the strong marks of decay: the big legs of women and blotted eyes of men, sunken mouths and inky nostrils. It was the normal hour for bats swooping raggedly (Ludeyville), or pieces of paper (New York) to remind Herzog of bats. An escaped balloon was fleeing like a sperm, black and quick into the orange dust of the west. He crossed the street, making a detour to avoid a fog of grilled chicken and sausage. The crowd was traipsing over the broad sidewalk. Moses took a keen interest in the uptown public, its theatrical spirits, its performers— the transvestite homosexuals painted with great originality, the wigged women, the lesbians looking so male you had to wait for them to pass and see them from behind to determine their true sex, hair dyes of every shade. Signs in almost every passing face of a deeper comment or interpretation of destiny—eyes that held metaphysical statements. And even pious old women who trod the path of ancient duty, still, buying kosher meat.

The sense of his own bodily movements, the revolving and rattling of bars and ratchets, the grotesque human figures, the tendency of the city to turn into a lush jungle, a human womb, a sterile onanistic giant whose denizens have bettered nature by "creating" of themselves inverted biological mechanisms: These are indeed metaphysical statements in addition to being reflections of Herzog's own Ramona-dominated destination. But then, the beautiful ironic "And" of the concluding sentence!

The whole atmosphere has been ominously prepared by Ramona's siren-call over that emotional dentist's drill, the telephone, "drilling away at him," itself a primary instrument of metaphysical incitement and penetration. While he is taking to the lawyer Simkin about what justice he should invoke against Madeleine and Gersbach—the call which leads him to the law courts, to the vision of evil which drives him toward murder—the telephone appears to be communicating the decision of The Castle. But it is the ironic metropolitan version of the seashell, which gives us back the sound of our own bloodstream: "The telephone seemed to pick up the sound of his blood, rhythmic, thin, and quick, washing within his skull. Perhaps it was only a nervous reflex of his eardrums. The membranes seemed to shiver." Without knowing it, Herzog is drifting into the perilous solipsism which almost makes him assume that his desire for personal justice is the world's; he is on the verge of the horror which has resulted in our time when mechanisms have broken down our civilized sense, then have become in turn handmaids of a primitive brutality which can end in a Hitler.

Herzog's departure from Ramona before her flowershop (p. 206) evokes a similarly suffocating sense in which the mass and rhythms of body, sex, taxicab, city-become-hothouse-plants, plants-become-machines-and-exhaust gas, overwhelm Herzog and dull him into a thing.

This is the inescapable tendency in Bellow's book, and he handles it with beautiful modulation all the way from texture to situation to symbol. Everybody has become or is in danger of becoming a reflection of the machines of transportation, communication, and computation. Madeleine willfully drives herself not only into slacks, but into Catholicism, the Ph.D. mill, and cosmetics. (The fantastic scene in which, after she and Herzog have made love, she "labors to be beautiful" by encasquing herself in the cerements of an old woman to go to work is an appalling, grotesque, but true image of one face of the American woman; to put on lipstick after dinner in a restaurant she looks at her reflection in a knife blade!) Gersbach makes his gimpy leg an asset: It rouses him to sexual Adonism and enables him to find the right combination of egotism, sentimentality, opportunism, and adaptability to become "the poet of mass communications" and a lay analyst. The Herzog lawyer, Sandor Himmelstein, is a hunchback who compensates with a savage lust for power, becoming a sickly combination of brutality and maudlinity. Herzog has a biologist friend whose idealized love object is Rocco the monkey. The culminating figure in the horror scenes in the law court is an epileptic, orthopedic-booted young woman, sexually abused since childhood, who has refused to give up her illegitimate child, has moved into a cheap hotel with a lunchroom porter, and finally has beaten her three-year-old child to death in a rage because he has not been toilet-trained and perpetually cries. Bellow uses this method to link encroaching mechanism and emotional deformity; psychiatrists, lawyers, law courts, and marriage, which purportedly adjust or cure deformations and violence, merely manifest creeping mechanism or try to "adjust" men and women to it. All of the "Reality instructors" have, as it were, been operated on by Charles Bovary and have become Charles Bovarys themselves. Even physical nature is drifting from organism to mechanism, from matter to energy, as human instinct and creative power lose their sympathy and resiliency. Bellow shows the Daughters of Memory (and Herzog's own Muses, his mistresses) turning from women into systems; Thomas Pynchon's V. is hovering on the horizon.

That is not to say, however, that *Herzog* is an apocalypse or a diatribe. Both Herzog and his creator display the saving sympathy of broad vision; neither shrinks into self-justification and repudiation. The book has the vitality, spirit, and gaiety of genial comedy; it is full of great meditations, great conversations, dazzling turns of wit, and great lines that explode in the mind and into laughter. Marvelous characters are everywhere. Madeleine is an awesome creation in the line of Molly Bloom, who makes other efforts to write about "the modern woman" look puny; she is admirable in distortion, an Amazon, a Titanic bitch-goddess. Gersbach, a lovely parody of Herzog and almost his alter ego, is a compelling super-salesman of "potato love" who, because he lives it, rises to an heroic mission as a secular prophet of the sawdust trail. Ramona is perfect. Asphalter, Edvig the psychiatrist, the literary academician Shapiro, Himmelstein, Madeleine's father ("the American Stanislavsky"), Herzog's first wife Daisy, Nachman, Sono, Father Herzog and Moses's mother, Simkin, Tante Taube, Phoebe Gersbach, Herzog's brothers Shura and Will, the Yankee Tuttles, and an astonishing cast of New York cabbies, judges, cops, deadbeats, perverts: all of these come to life because they are all vivid and relevant inhabitants of the world of Herzog's actions, emotions, and imaginings (he was in the U.N. when Khrushchev pounded the desk with his shoe). He is intelligibly *related* to all of them, and they are all related in Bellow's version of this world. They come alive in surface and depth in exact proportion as they bear in upon Herzog, and we are convinced that that is just about the proportion which we ourselves feel. The powerful scenes in the book occur one after another, but always given the proper rhythm by the modulations from scene to flashback, from intense drama to Herzogian epistolary meditation (how perfectly Bellow uses the letter to give just that sense of the blurred line between public and private, between memory and event, between history and contemporaneity, in which we live).

I should end this review, but *Herzog* is an extraordinary book, and everyone will feel impelled to live with it, to come to terms with it, to discover its form. I'll make a stab at it. A critic or reviewer deserves his enthusiasms more than he does his antipathies (writers need such enthusiasms, I think). Having suggested how Herzog looks from without and how the book seems to grow from its historical context, I now want to look at Bellow's character from within, examine how his metaphysical odyssey unfolds, and try to define the impression it finally makes.[1] Above all, I want to suggest how *Herzog*'s form shapes itself to the touch of the mind. So here goes . . .

Herzog is an historian of our still- or post-romantic period who has gone to pieces and is testing fragments of reality to put himself back together. Immersed in the Berkshire summer at his sagging "estate," he tests in violent retrospect—observing, meditating, and writing—event after event, role after role, hypothesis after hy-

---

[1] While rereading *Ulysses* for another purpose, I discovered that Moses Herzog is a "hop of my thumb" tea-and-sugar merchant referred to by the garrulous Irish bill-collector at the beginning of "Cyclops"; the bill-collector has just been trying to get a plumber, Geraghty, to pay up on a transaction with Herzog. Herzog is also one of Bloom's pallbearers in "Circe," and joins the hue and cry after Bloom flees Bella's house. "Cyclops" is of course the great episode of aboriginal nationalism in which Joyce plays his Dubliners off against all the heroic ages (cf. Joyce's mythopoeic backgrounds and Bellow's letters; also Joyce's "hangmen's letters," by means of which he enters the dimension of metempsychosis, using Paddy Dignam's ghost as the medium). In "Cyclops" Bloom becomes "Herr Professor Luitpold Blumenduft," the "new Messiah for Ireland," and as "ben Bloom Elijah" ascends to heaven "like a shot off a shovel"; on everything, Bloom "had to have his say too about it," and his prescription for Ireland (which enrages the Citizen) is "Love." In *Herzog* we imagine a monolithic, municipal, monumental Paul Bunyan just out of perceptual range in the cosmic vestibule of symbol and myth. There are many other specific parallels to *Ulysses*; e.g. Bloom's potato and "potato love," "Vulcan" Gersbach, "bloody freemason" Herzog (cf. Don Giovanni, Papageno, and Sarastro). But much more striking is what Bellow has learned from Joyce's style; that will elicit the most extensive study by writers, critics, and scholars. It will be a long time before *Herzog* will be exhausted.

pothesis, to try to find out who and where he is. He may be a man who is keeping up a front, or a would-be do-gooder: "all the dead and the mad are in my custody, and I am the nemesis of the would-be forgotten. I bind others to my feelings, and oppress them." Maybe, like almost everyone else, he is one of the "Reality instructors" ("A very special sort of lunatic" who "expects to inculcate his principles"); or one of the listeners, psychiatrist, policeman, lawyer, judge. Ramona tells him he is "a man tempted by God, longing for grace, but escaping headlong from his salvation" (Ramona's version of salvation is for a world where "Now that it can't be political, it's sexual"). Thinking of his behavior while his mother was dying, he calls himself a "gesture-maker." He hits part of the truth when he considers himself a self-pitier who deliberately chose innocence and refused to know evil, so that "therefore others were appointed to do it to him, and then to be accused (by him) of wickedness." At any rate, he is lost in a welter of definitions of what he is to himself, of what others think of him, and of what he does to other people. Just out of jail, after his auto accident, and before his retreat to the Berkshires, he was

> A loving brute—a subtle, spoiled, loving man. Who can make use of him? He craves use. Where is he needed? Show him the way to make his sacrifice to truth, to order, peace. Oh, that mysterious creature, that Herzog! awkwardly taped, helped into his wrinkled shirt by brother Will.

That is Bellow speaking, questioning with his beautifully modulated point of view and tone, pushing Herzog toward us with an appeal so that for a moment he trembles on the edge of motion, delicately tipping toward symbol; then, unobtrusively, he is drawn back to where he belongs.

Whatever he is, the climax of his quest begins with his vision of evil in the great law-court scene, which makes him revert to primitive eye-for-an-eye justice, and ends when he reaps the consequences despite the change of heart he has outside the bathroom window. The law-court scene occupies the place of Ivan's stories, Dmitri's dream, The Grand Inquisitor fable; of Hans Castorp's snowstorm vision of the savagery underlying pagan beauty; of the Circe episode in *Ulysses* and of Kafka's world of endless guilt. Herzog's wandering from sordid case to sordid case brings up against the horrifying disparity between naked, degenerate brutality, and the forms and veils with which society must protect itself. Herzog's vision is neither Christian, nor pagan, nor psychological, nor is it a parable, or a dream, or an inner hell; but it subsumes all of those conditions and forces their Manhattan counterpart on the modern man who has an obscure sense of cosmic wrong and feels impelled to do something about it. The scene is overwhelmingly presented, and it elicits from Herzog the powerful ambiguities of anguish. His surprise and admiration at one judge's humane consideration makes all the more annihilating his sudden sense that the impeccably mannered witnesses, the tolerant, matter-of-fact lawyers, the clichés in which events are recounted, are hopelessly inadequate to the implications of the stolid, opaque mother and the screams of a child savagely beaten to death. The sense of gratuitous suffering overpowers Herzog, flooding the personal wrongs he feels and raising them in his heart beyond social to metaphysical crimes. Sickness or the terror of the child grips him; fighting to suppress his rising vomit, he leaves the courtroom. In the hall

. . . he concentrated. With all his might—mind and heart—he tried to obtain something for the murdered child. But what? How? He pressed himself with intensity, but "all his might" could get nothing for the buried boy. Herzog experienced nothing but his own *human feelings*, in which he found nothing of use. What if he felt moved to cry? Or pray? He pressed hand to hand. And what did he feel? Why he felt himself—his own trembling hands, and eyes that stung. And what was there in modern, post . . . post-Christian America to pray for? Justice—justice and mercy? And pray away the monstrousness of life, the wicked dream it was? He opened his mouth to relieve the pressure he felt. He was wrung, and wrung again, and wrung again, again.

The child screamed, clung, but with both arms the girl hurled it against the wall. On her legs was ruddy hair. And her lover, too, with long jaws and zooty sideburns, watching on the bed. Lying down to copulate, and standing up to kill. Some kill, then cry. Others, not even that.

His ecstatic love has turned to evil; he absorbs fully the lesson his mother taught him: that Adam is dust, which she had illustrated by rubbing her palm with a finger until the sweat and dirt produced a black particle (it does). But he has lost the spirit of wit which comes from resignation; the inner beating breaks down the boundaries of his life, "the force of balked longings coming back as stinging poison." Helpless against fact, reduced to wordlessness, his feelings swollen to meet the inrush of evil, he reverts to Chicago a man possessed. His journey by superjet and expressway, through side streets, in a rented Falcon, to his father's tomblike house, to get his father's gun, represents terrifyingly a retrogression into the primitive by modern methods: not under the psychiatrist's control, which leads to acceptance, but by instruments which drive to action.

Bellow has evolved this backfall in a brilliant series of bathroom scenes, evoking the specter of American and romantic infantilism in the comfort hall for which America is famous. Things had begun to go to pieces around Herzog while he was reading Pope in a cellar lavatory which had thick walls like a bunker. His psychological reversion began when he recalled how at the synagogue his only refuge from elders who kept telling him he would be a rabbi was the W.C. The most alluring of possible reliefs came as a bathroom meditation while he was cleaning up for Ramona's gourmet dinner and trimmings; he anticipated the luxury of self-justification, and recalled how Sono, his Japanese mistress, had soothed him by getting into the bathtub with him and washing him. In Ramona's bathroom he recalls adolescent sexual fantasies, luxuriates in her smooth tiles and medicine chest, and begins to write to the dead. After dinner and their upsetting discussion of his life, all is assuaged by Ramona's appearance, framed in the bathroom door, naked but for black lace panties and high heels: As whore-mother she fulfills his wishes. But at once, just before he

431

went to the law court and after the upsetting conversation with Simkin, Herzog had seen his brute self. Casually becoming aware that seeking comfort in the bathroom has become one of his habits, he remembers requiring Madeleine to make love on the cold tiles; that awakens sudden awareness of a moment, previously unperceived, when Madeleine's love for Gersbach had showed itself; the urge to punish them by holding a blowtorch to their feet rushes in on him. Though he ridicules such justice, his lathered face in the mirror shows him a creature "Not human of itself," only "longing to be human." It is this glimpse which thrusts Herzog toward prehistory.

But reimmersion is a way. Bellow evokes the double sense of childhood: savage in its first flood, but able to enlarge the over-civilized consciousness. When Herzog, gun in hand, views Gersbach and Junie through the bathroom window, he sees childhood in its shape of innocence, recognizing what it means to be a father. He understands that he himself has been one of the "bungling child-men, pure hearts in the burlap of innocence" (Bellow seems to be playing throughout on Huxley's Burlap and Beatrice, proponents of togetherness in the bathtub): "willingly accepting the necessary quota of consequent lies, he had set himself up with his emotional goodies—truth, friendship, devotion to children (the regular American worship of kids), and potato love." He realizes in the telegraph office, wiring Ramona, that "The necessary premise is that a man is more than . . . all the emotions, strivings, tastes, and constructions which it pleases him to call 'My Life.' " He has been driven by an "infantile terror of death"; but something incomprehensible, whatever it may be, includes both death and the self.

But Bellow does not stop with a change of heart. Herzog is still in Chicago, not Eden, and after his idyllic visit with Junie to the Museum of Science and the Aquarium he suffers the consequences of his homicidal intention: Edging too cautiously onto the boulevard, his Falcon is struck from behind by a speeding truck, and the police find in his pocket the fatal pistol, for which he has no permit. Yet though he is humiliated, the ride to the police station through his old neighborhood makes him face for the first time the

one incomprehensible evil of his childhood, an attack by a sex
pervert. This recognition accelerates his retreat from self-obses-
sion, so that at the police station he can face Madeleine without
losing his composure in either maudlinity or resentment.

What lies behind Herzog's ability to accommodate to himself
both himself and his tormentors is his saving sense of drama, for
adepts at self-dramatization have the knack of seeing life as scene
and as *dramatis personae*. Leaving the bathroom window, he had
become aware that Madeleine and Gersbach (like himself?) are
"grotesque love-actors": "his intended violence turned into theater, into something ludicrous." The upshot of his insight, and of
Phoebe Gersbach's refusal to help him expose her husband and
Madeleine, is an impersonal, historical definition of his "emotional
type":

> Herzog could not say what the significance of such generalities
> might be. He was only vastly excited—in a streaming state—and
> intended mostly to restore order by turning to his habit of thought-
> fulness. Blood had burst into his psyche, and for the time being he
> was either free or crazy. But then he realized that he did not need
> to perform elaborate abstract intellectual work—work he had al-
> ways thrown himself into as if it were the struggle for survival.
> But not thinking is not necessarily fatal. Did I really believe that
> I would die when thinking stopped? Now to fear such a thing—
> that's really crazy.

Moving thought replaces the bathroom as Herzog's psychological
comfort station; he gets motions and words meshed again, and is
once more in the state of mind to keep the creation of human
reality going. As he says to his fellow-estranged Asphalter, who is
trying to face life without his monkey Rocco by pretending that he
has already died:

> . . . it isn't a question of dread, or any such words at all. . . . Still,
> what can thoughtful people and humanists do but struggle toward
> suitable words? Take me, for instance. I've been writing letters
> helter-skelter in all directions. More words. I go after reality with
> language. Perhaps I'd like to change it all into language, to force
> Madeleine and Gersbach to have a *Conscience*. There's a word for

you. I must be trying to keep tight the tensions without which human beings can no longer be called human. If they don't suffer, they've gotten away from me. And I've filled the world with letters to prevent their escape. I want them in human form, and so I conjure up a whole environment and catch them in the middle. I put my whole heart into these constructions. But they are constructions.

The constructions at least give him "something great, something into which his being, and all beings, can go. He does not need meaning as long as such intensity has scope. Because then it is self-evident; it *is* meaning." And of course, for Bellow, and for us too, it is this novel.

But again, this is no final solution. The resolution, if the novel has one, is less a finality than a quality. One of the arguments about the book will be whether the conclusion brings us back to the beginning, so that Herzog pauses after full circle before another bout; or whether he gets himself and others sufficiently out from under his skin so that he can open himself to whatever will come and not be stampeded. He seems on the verge of some kind of new insight when he rejects the parlor romanticism of "safe, comfortable people playing at crisis, alienation, apocalypse, and desperation. We must get it out of our heads that this is a doomed time, that we are waiting for the end, and the rest of it, mere junk from fashionable magazines. Things are grim enough without these shivery games." Rejecting any "doctrine or theology of suffering," he sees his own suffering as merely "a more extended form of life, a striving for true wakefulness and an antidote to illusion" ("as people pinch themselves to feel awake"), and he takes no moral credit for it. He eschews metaphors (perhaps with Camus' Sisyphus in mind), and asks Nietzsche a friendly "question from the Floor" about the Dionysian spirit, especially its twentieth-century perversion, concluding with greetings "from this mere border of grassy temporal light." In his letters he now seems to slough off erotic, mystical, and psychiatric interpretations of life. His last letter, written from where he feels "easily contained by everything about him *Within the hollowness of God*, as he noted, *and deaf to the final multiplicity of facts,* as well as, *blind to ultimate distances. Two billion light-years out. Supernovae,"* is to God:

> *How my mind has struggled to make coherent sense. I have not been too good at it. But have desired to do your unknowable will, taking it, and you, without symbols. Everything of intensest significance. Especially if divested of me.*

This telegram modulates us imperceptibly out of the flashback; we, Herzog, discover that we are at a point just after the beginning of his metaphysical odyssey. Something has happened in the present. For a moment Herzog feels peace, "Confident, even happy in his excitement, stable. The bitter cup would come round again, by and by. This rest and well-being were only a momentary difference in the strange lining or variable silk between life and void." But for a moment he reaches *"out where it is incomprehensible. . . . So . . . Peace!"*

If the book is circular, it is a spiral, for in the last pages Herzog is either upon a new level, or down in the quotidian, or both: For him they have at last become one and the same. Herzog never stops living, and Bellow keeps it open; Clyde Griffiths's romantic, self-deceiving "And yet . . ." has become a simple, even gay, "Well, of course there is more to come." The book began with Herzog swamped in cluttered pastoral: Thoreau's nature, the scent of wild, and the wreckage of his "home." It is the detritus of a life, of a civilization, after the break. We have been through the retrospective journey, and we return to the clutter once more. But people are coming back, Herzog remembers, when peace has at last turned him inside out. He cleans himself up to greet his brother Will.

The conclusion is presented as a beautiful collection of images, gestures, and exchanges. Will almost persuades him to go to the Pittsfield hospital for a rest, but the specter of psychiatric treatment saves him. For a moment Herzog has misgivings. He thinks of the bird skeletons in his water closet, owls in the fixtures, a half-painted piano he has quixotically been refurbishing for Junie, the remains of meals, the wife-deserted atmosphere; but he fields these "bathroom" images carefully, realizing "My balance comes from instability." He fights off Will's remedy by feeling a "no" without words, merely gesturing, and finally resolving the crisis in gaiety when he compares his fantastic collection of wives, children, and a Berkshire estate to the picture of Father Herzog and his sons deciding whether White Horse, Johnnie Walker, or Haig & Haig should be the label of the day. In a funny way, the Yankee Tuttle ("the master spirit of Ludeyville"), who is summoned to turn on the electricity, and his frowzy wife, who comes to clean house, become for Herzog an image of placid, practical, easy domesticity, replacing for him psychiatrists or mother-and-father figures. Ramona's serious metaphysical eros gets reduced in marvelous comedy: As he invites her to dinner Herzog admires the courage and poise with which she overcomes the quiver caused by her efforts to be "a woman who took matters into her own hands," and her perfume stirs "the deep, the cosmic, the idiotic masculine response —*quack*. The progenitive, the lustful quacking in the depths. *Quack. Quack.*"

Finally, Will leaves. Herzog is left alone while Mrs. Tuttle finishes her cleaning, waiting for Ramona to come for dinner (and to help with the dishes—that's *all*!). The last, two-and-one-half page scene, dense and beautiful, leaves us with the sense that perhaps Herzog was right, that perhaps intensity, if it can find scope, is, in the end, meaning. The human "word-models" for life give way for a moment to a fleeting sense that "the model of natural creation seems to be the ocean." This model and the amphibian human soul seem to sustain the human dwelling: "What keeps these red brick houses from collapse on these billows is their inner staleness. I smell it yawning through the screens. The odor of souls is a brace to the walls. Otherwise the wrinkling of the hills would make them crumble." Herzog turns on the water pump, the hermit thrushes sing the water-dripping song, and he thinks of the blackbirds gathering in waves to fly to their waterside nests (the skeletons in the water closet have their counterparts in life; water is not only a cause of death but also the source of life; the bathroom is fitted into a whole house, and the house into the world). In a last meditation he sings inwardly along with the birds, ending one last aspiring meditation with delightfully cautious acquiescence and unpretentiousness: "I am pretty well satisfied to be, to be just as it is willed, and for as long as I may remain in occupancy." In the end, gestures only. Fetching the cold wine bottles from the spring, he takes pleasure in the vivid cold of the water. For the table he picks flowers, then wonders if he has—a corkscrew—or a nail—or he *could* break them. He fills his hat with roses from the rainpipe and lilies from the cistern. The lilies wilt instantly. Shall he look for peonies? He checks his impulse: "How would it be interpreted?" Yet he decides not to throw his flowers away. But how can he give further evidence of his sanity? He'll stop writing letters. With that thought he goes to his Recamier couch (this is Herzog's final place of reclining, replacing the bed, the psychiatrist's couch, even the grass):

> As he stretched out, he took a long breath, and then he lay, look-
> ing at the mesh of the screen, pulled loose by vines, and listening
> to the steady scratching of Mrs. Tuttle's broom. He wanted to tell
> her to sprinkle the floor. She was raising too much dust. In a few
> minutes he would call down to her, "Damp it down, Mrs. Tuttle.
> There's water in the sink." But not just yet. At this time he had no
> messages for anyone. Nothing. Not a single word.

The last dust-and-water image is a full, easy nod toward his mother's illustration that Adam is dust and sweat. Herzog is no longer in motion, he is not bathed in words; he chooses silence, "At this time." It is a great silence in a real place at a single moment. "Like a long-legged fly upon the stream His mind moves upon silence." We now wait for what Herzog and we will come up with.

But the question remains: Is the ending an oversimplification? Is it really adequate to the weight and density and violence of the world Herzog has come from? Is that world itself a genuine and inclusive representation of the incredible world around us? Does it aim too much at the past, giving insufficient weight to those awarenesses of the present which are pushing us toward the future? The novel may be beautiful; is it true? I myself, at this time, would answer those questions in favor of the novel. But do I know the reality? It might properly be asked, though, does anyone except Bellow know that reality? Or, can anyone better it? Until they can, it is Bellow's and Bellow's is it. Another thought occurs: Is the ending excessively pastoral? That is a harder question, one that has to be asked about the pastoral or near-pastoral endings of such city or "civilization" works as those of Lawrence (*The Rainbow, Women In Love, St. Mawr*), Joyce (*A Portrait, Ulysses*), Pound (*The Pisan Cantos*), and Hemingway. The question does not come up in the same way with such archetype novelists as Faulkner, but those who move their resolutions away from the city whose pressures form their central milieu have to face it. It probably resolves itself into the extent to which a work safeguards itself against making too great claims for life. *Herzog* seems to make great claims, but perhaps its comic tone musters sufficient ironies to enable us to feel that exuberance and catharsis can be real.

At any rate, I think that *Herzog* is a great American novel, whose vision will provide perpetual delight and whose techniques will repay other writers for their study. As I said, I think that it makes a near-epical synthesis. Hemingway said, "Every novel which is truly written contributes to the total knowledge which is there at the disposal of the next writer who comes"; Bellow's does that because he has been "able to understand and assimilate what is available as his birthright and what he must, in turn, take his departure from." *Herzog* has "the dignity of movement of an iceberg" whose bottom is in the tradition. We might ask, though, whether any book can really be a classic when it is centered too much in character, so that "action in character" replaces "character in action." Is there too little narrative? Is *Herzog* a *Sartor Resartus*? Again, Hemingway posed the problem aptly: "Prose is architecture, not interior decoration, and the Baroque is over. For a writer to put his own intellectual musings, which he might sell for a low price as essays, into the mouth of artificially constructed characters which are more remunerative when issued as people in a novel is good economics, perhaps, but does not make literature."

Yet Bellow has made the ideas fiction, because he has made what Hemingway called "people": "People in a novel, not skillfully constructed *characters*, must be projected from the writer's experience, from his knowledge, from his head, from his heart and from all there is of him. . . . a good writer should know as near everything as possible." Bellow has tried to know all that, and has taken the great risk of trying to give it fictional form.

What kind of novel is it? We can find there the elements of the historical, ideological, metaphysical, romantic, antiromantic, erotic, and picaresque novels; of the novel of manners, the antinovel, the romance, etc. But above all, it is a great comic novel. As an anthology of ideas and speculations it even has the quality of being an education. Even if you know all the antagonists, colleagues, and ideas that set Herzog off (I didn't), his angle gives you a fresh view of things you know. Further, Bellow relates ideas immediately to life (that is another sense in which *Herzog* is *really* an academic novel—or an intellectual novel—though we never get onto a campus). No novel I have read makes me keep saying "that is just what life is like." Yet, it is also magnificent art; Bellow continually gives one confidence that he is creating a great form, one which includes multiplicity with the shape and rhythm of beauty. It is astonishingly modulated in that space between life and art which it tries to express, so that I feel I am experiencing the novel with all of my faculties. I have not read a contemporary novel which comes as close to turning Hemingway's ingredients—the tradition, interior decoration, and experience—into a fictional form which can contain them and integrate them. But critics should keep in mind that *Herzog* is a great open form which is new (my interpretation is only provisional!—F.R.); that it calls for perspectives which can elucidate a form based upon our special "field" reality: the one which lies between—both separating and relating them, for it is their "stuff"—life and art, a man and the *res publica*, the infinite pulverizations of which we are made. Above all, there is Joyce's mild complaint about the critics of *Ulysses*, reported by Pound: "If only someone had said among all those critics, that the book is really damn *funny*!"

JOHN W. ALDRIDGE

John W. Aldridge, who teaches at the University of Michigan, is the author of several critical works, among them *After the Lost Generation* and *In Search of Heresy*. He has also published essays and reviews in *Commentary* and *The Saturday Review of Literature*.

THE COMPLACENCY OF HERZOG

For some years now our immediate age has been under the most fantastic pressure to produce a novel we could all accept in good conscience as major. Not only have we felt we deserved such a novel. We have *needed* it to vindicate our belief that this age, with its enormous awareness of literary values, should be as creatively vital as it is sophisticated about creativity, that our intense dedication to the life of the mind ought naturally to find its corollary in the production of major works of the imagination.

Bellow's *Herzog* has lately been acclaimed by the intellecutal community as such a work, and one of the chief reasons it has been is that it takes intellectual sophistication as its very subject and demonstrates that the life of the mind can in fact be as important and exciting a source of creative vitality as the life of the groin. It deals expertly with materials which most of our novelists have found immensely difficult to dramatize, the materials of consciousness itself, and it deals with them in such a way that we recognize them to be central to our experience, uniquely expressive of ourselves and our condition as intellectuals. Bellow of course sees the condition of intellectuality in *Herzog* as a mixed blessing, and it is proper that he should, since that is exactly what it is. It

Reprinted by permission of the author.

has given us our high cultural expertise, but it has also severely impeded us in the efficient pursuit of the practical and the amorous life. It has rendered large areas of experience unreal to us, and it has made almost impossible satisfactory relations with people who do not share our commitment to ideas. The character of Herzog embodies these contradictions and is even shown to be torn in two by them—until, that is, he achieves peace through positive thinking. Yet even as we perceive this and admire the honesty which prompted Bellow to lay before us both sides of the case, we also perceive that intellectuality, as he portrays it in *Herzog,* finally emerges as far more of a blessing than a blight. And it does so, interestingly enough, just because the blight has been *turned into* a blessing, just because Bellow makes it so clear that Herzog's suffering is right and admirable, and that suffering is not only the intellectual's occupational disease but his badge of honor, the very measure of his significance both as a person and as a dramatic figure. For it is ultimately his suffering that causes Herzog to seem worthy of major literary treatment and capable of achieving something of the largeness of reference of a major social and literary symbol.

Thus, Bellow has managed to make a virtue of what we had always supposed was our chief source of discomfort, and he has done this not only through his flattering treatment of Herzog's miseries but through his highly *un*flattering treatment of the people with whom Herzog is associated, and who are hell bent on causing him misery.

Bellow has always had the habit, which in his later work has tended to become a rather facile trick, of treating his secondary characters as if they were inmates of either a zoo or a madhouse. Augie March and Herzog in particular are depicted as quiet, deferential men set down among trolls in bedlam. Augie has to contend with the often antagonistic and at times downright berserk vitalism of Einhorn, Dingbat, the Magnuses, Mintouchian, Thea Fenchel, and Basteshaw, while Herzog is chronically badgered and exploited by Simkin, Gersbach, Shapiro, Himmelstein, Nachman, and the various other freaks and egomaniacs whom Herzog rather plaintively calls his "Reality instructors." Bellow's handling of these people constantly verges on caricature. In fact, there are moments when they seem to exist solely as verbal abstractions, creations of merely adjectival intensity. Yet their function is clearly not to suggest living people drawn from close observation of the real world. Rather, it is to provide a milieu of grotesque idiosyncrasy and self-preoccupation against which Herzog can be seen as saintly. To be sure, in comparison with them he is ineffectual, bumbling, and a fool—the very type of the silly intellectual helplessly adrift in the cutthroat world of practical affairs. But however ridiculous he may be, he is also so much more of a human being, so much more sensitive and responsible than they, that his ridiculousness becomes, like his suffering, a badge of honor, the mark of his moral superiority. For Herzog is selfless where they are selfish, loving where they are hateful, wryly comic where they are gruesomely grotesque, a wonderful, absurd, adorable Jewish Uncle Tom whose predicament is that he is finally too pure for this world. The intellectual is also too pure for this world, or so he has always secretly considered himself. But he has been obliged to assume that his purity was at best a negative virtue, one he had to settle for in place of the truly human virtues shared by those who are not intellectuals. Now, however, through the drama of Herzog, he is given abundant evidence that nonintellectuals are monsters, that if they are human, he is positively angelic, that, in fact, to be an intellectual among such people is perhaps to be the very best thing there is. For in Herzog human warmth and ideas, heart and high culture, are joined together to produce the most flattering image of the intellectual to be found in modern literature.

It would seem that Bellow could not possibly go beyond this in his effort to aggrandize Herzog and to persuade us to see him as a figure of transcendent meaning and saintliness. Yet this is actually only a modest rehearsal for the emergence of Herzog into the full glory of his ultimate incarnation in the role of the Jewish intellectual as symbol of contemporary Everyman. It would undoubtedly be even harder than it is to accept Herzog in this preposterous role if Bellow did not take care to create an atmosphere of such high fastidiousness about slick generalizations of just this kind that we almost became convinced that he hates them as much as we do and is standing guard for us against them. For example, he speaks with proper contempt of "the commonplaces of the Wasteland outlook, the cheap mental stimulants of Alienation," and that, along with his overall wariness of tone, his apparent abhorrence of obvious and easy answers, would seem to serve as effective insurance against any lapse into other commonplaces and cheap mental stimulants. But it turns out that our trust is grievously misplaced, for Bellow slyly slips Herzog into the breach left by the banished Wasteland cliché. Herzog emerges, in fact, as the Wasteland cliché irrigated and transformed into the Promised Land, while the platitude of Alienation is converted into the even hoarier platitude of Accommodation and Togetherness. For what he finally holds up for our inspection is a new hopeful doctrine of potato love not uncolored by righteous disdain. The trolls may be killing us, he seems to say. We may be exploited, cuckolded, hounded out of house and home, reviled, and spat upon. But we can afford to be compassionate and gracious in our torment, remembering, as Nick Carraway's father once said, that "all the people in this world haven't had the advantages" that we have had.

At the end the novel heaves a fatty sigh of middle-class intellectual contentment. "I am pretty well satisfied," muses Herzog in his lawn chair, "to be, to be just as it is willed, and for as long as I may remain in occupancy." And we sense that Herzog will be a long time in occupancy. For if it has been demonstrated that intellectuals have a corner on the world's love and compassion, it is probable that they also have a corner on the world's powers of survival. And of course Herzog is finally as arrogantly complacent in his new-found affirmative position, about being stuck with his loving and erudite self, as Bellow dares to allow him to be. In fact, it would appear that in Herzog the many intellectuals who have long felt guilty and defensive about their role in life have found their bromide, their hero, and the justification they have long been seeking for their secret sense of superiority. The novel, in short, is as wholesome and nutritious as a dish of cornflakes, a clearly "major" Establishment work in the sense that it dramatizes a theme of considerable size with complete honesty and without once expressing an idea that could possibly give offense to anyone. On the contrary, it has brought much good cheer and glad tidings to the intellectual community, and as is so often the case, such service has not gone unrewarded.

TONY TANNER

Tony Tanner, an English critic and teacher who has specialized in American literature, is the author of *The Reign of Wonder* and *City of Words*.

THE FLIGHT FROM MONOLOGUE

In the midst of the continual movement that agitates a democratic community, the tie that unites one generation to another is relaxed or broken. . . . It is not only confidence in this or that man which is destroyed, but the disposition to trust the authority of any man whatsoever. Everyone shuts himself tightly within himself and insists upon judging the world from there.

—De Tocqueville

Reviewing some of Gide's autobiographical work in 1951, Saul Bellow noted his predilection for monologue and commented:

The truth of monologue is exciting, but it is generally accidental in character; a man has only his own abilities to judge it with, and the assistance of other men, if he is a confirmed monologist, does not easily become available to him. . . . As human isolation increases while education and abilities multiply, the most vital questions and answers become the internal ones. Sadly enough, the number of intelligent people whose most vital conversation is with themselves is growing. . . .

Bellow knows that "dialogue, not monologue, is the foundation of a civilized life," yet his own work, from his earlier stories to his latest novel, has presented us with a series of monologists whose

This article originally appeared in *Encounter*.

most vital conversation is with themselves. They enact the plight which Bellow diagnosed—trapped, somehow, within their own heads, banished to lasting inwardness, mysteriously held *incommunicado* in the most crowded urban conglomerations in history. Bellow's work, as he said of Gide's, is full of "excellent monologists who want to advance to dialogue"—yet the advance is never fully made.

His first published piece of fiction was called, almost prophetically, *Two Morning Monologues*. It simply reveals the internal musings and agonizings of two characters: an unemployed man waiting to be called up and a small-time gambler. The first is nearly "sunk," the second is mainly a loser; both are unwilling to participate in the accredited routines of society, refusing any attachment to an environment they resent and people they despise. One is a passive resister, the other a pushing manipulator; one is immobile, suspended; the other slips through, finds a way round. Both attempt to preserve their identity; one by supine a-social negation, the other by energetic a-social assertion. The unemployed man is "driven" but refuses to comply with the forceful drift; the gambler sees all life as chance and accepts it, trying to twist it to his own ends. The latter is a dodging, weaving, risking man; the former is a withdrawing, denying, dangling man. These two types, "shut tightly within themselves," are almost archetypes in Bellow's work.

Joseph, in *Dangling Man*, is a relation of the narrator of Dostoevsky's *Notes from the Underground*. Bitterly at odds with society, he spends his time entering his thoughts in a diary which aches with compulsive self-communing and exacerbated self-probing. He holds himself in brooding apartness to preserve a sense of individual freedom; but, as he realizes, "goodness is achieved not in a vacuum, but in the company of other men, attended by love. I, in this room, separate, alienated, distrustful, find in my purpose not an open world, but a closed, hopeless jail. My perspectives end in the walls." His isolation is not a triumph, as he realizes at the end. "I had not done well alone." He is frightened of being trapped and coerced in society, yet by the end his "freedom" has become a morose and futile acedia. The monologist yearns to widen his perspectives, but every foray into the world around him sends him scuttling back into the burrow of the self. Thus a basic rhythm is set up, to be repeated by other characters in Bellow's work. Approach toward others and retreat from them; search for identity and fear of definition; involvement followed by disentanglement. The desire for community is counterbalanced by the instinct for flight. Plunges into what William James called "the rich thicket of reality" are offset by lonely flights of metaphysics. There is no true dialogue.

Bellow's second novel, *The Victim*, brilliantly explored the problem of man's relation to man in a society which is a turbulent sea of contesting greeds and fears. In the figure of Asa Leventhal, he has wonderfully caught the oppressed anxiety and sickly unease which modern man feels amidst the desperate, graceless motion and collision of this competitive, anomic age. Leventhal feels "that there was not a single part of him on which the whole world did not press with full weight," and indeed we see him forever knocking into things, banging himself against a packed and hampering environment. Bellow's great ability to evoke "the overwhelming human closeness and thickness" of the modern city is already in evidence (an ability which owes something to Dreiser, whose "carrying power" Bellow greatly admires). But the real focus is on the lonely Leventhal, stumbling through urban litter, racked by metaphysical questionings, trying to work out what are his true relations with Allbee, the anti-Semite with a grievance, who haunts him. He finally admits to some responsibility, but the end of the book scarcely presages a new sense of relationships and communication. There is, however, a hint that life might contain "a promise" which has not yet been properly explored.

Augie March undertakes that exploration. The riches of that book have been adequately acclaimed (in particular Bellow has something like a genius for evoking in heavy-pigmented prose the rich life of the Chicago ghetto). Augie is a much more energetic, mobile pursuer of destiny than his chair-rooted and heavy-footed predecessors. But though the tone is now more exuberant, open, life-welcoming—humorous rather than bilious—Augie does not establish any real relationships. The book is really the long monologue of a lonely man. Two quotations from Augie offer some light. "I touched all sides, and nobody knew where I belonged. I had no good idea of that myself." And: "I didn't want to be what they made of me but wanted to please them. Kindly explain! An independent fate, and love too—what confusion!" Augie indeed celebrates the self—but he can find nothing to do with it. He is a perennial American figure, rather like Henry James's American, who has "the look of being committed to nothing in particular, of standing in an attitude of general hospitality to the chances of life." He wants an identity and role, yet is wary of all social definitions. He allows himself to drift into all kinds of involving situations, but is always careful to elude the grip of society's many manipulating hands. He talks of "love" but ultimately cares little about the fate of other people. He resists all "determinisms" but the result is that his scattered adventures never add up to a destiny. Like Walt Whitman, he is "in and out of the game." He ends up a curiously light, even insubstantial figure.

It was Whitman who first defined this paradox which runs through much American writing. For Whitman asserted two contradictory values, two divergent dreams—the establishing of a new community ("ensemble") based on equality and love, *and* "individuality, the pride and centripetal isolation of a human being in himself—identity—personalism." A recent critic, A. N. Kaul, has pointed to this as a basic problem in American writing: "A common theme of the American imagination has been the problem of reconciling individual freedom with a mode of social life to which the individual can give his allegiance without danger of impairing his moral, spiritual, or psychological integrity." Many American characters yearn for a true "ensemble" (which would lead to dialogue), but they cling even more passionately to "individuality" (which condemns them to monologue). In one sense *Augie March* is rather like "Song of Myself" set in Dreiser's heavier, more impinging, more constricting urban world. Consider this definition of Whitman's poem by Richard Chase:

TONY TANNER

> The "self" who is the protagonist of Whitman's poem is a character portrayed in a recognizable American way; it illustrates the fluid, unformed personality exulting alternately in its provisional attempts to define itself and in its sense that it has no definition. . . . Of great importance is the fact that most of "Song of Myself" has to do not with the self searching for a final identity but with the self taking on a bewildering variety of identities and with a truly virtuoso agility extracting itself from each one.

That describes an important aspect of Augie very well. By the end of the book he has done dozens of jobs, met hundreds of people, screwed not a few, and even married one. But after all the collisions, the embraces, and the flights he remains at the end related to no one—unattached, uncommitted, undefined. Underneath his exhilarating rhetoric one sometimes hears a faint echo of that saddest of lines from that loneliest of characters, Melville's Bartleby, who could only say "I would prefer not to."

Where Augie March was slippery and adaptable, adroit and lucky in his evasion of the encroaching pressures of society, Tommy Wilhelm in *Seize the Day* is crushed, arrested, all but strangled by the unavoidable suffocating weight of the world around him. It is a world completely corrupted by "money," where "freedom" is meaningless without wealth, and "love" another word for cruel personal exploitation. The irony of the title refers to the persuasive advice given to Tommy by Dr. Tamkin, a brilliant pseudophilospher who bewilders Tommy with a farrago of confused but glamorous ideas. He tells Tommy "Only the present is real—the here-and-now. Seize the day!" (*Carpe diem*, perhaps; but also an echo from Emerson, that great apostle of self-reliance who never lived to see the difficulties involved in following his advice in modern America.) But all Tamkin does is trick Tommy out of his last seven hundred dollars. High ideas are debased to being part of a con man's patter.[1] In effect the day seizes Tommy. Passive, put-

---

[1] Bellow is clearly interested in masterful talkers, people who manipulate other people through words. He once interviewed the great con man, Yellow Kid Weil, whose self-justification was, "How was I to live? My power lay in words. In words I become a commander." In a world of semiliteracy, the

upon, spent, he is far from singing the self or breaking through to that more loving, constructive way of life which he feels ought to be possible. So far from attaining to dialogue, he ends by weeping over an unknown corpse.

In his next book Bellow created a character directly opposed to Wilhelm. Henderson in *Henderson the Rain King* is a giant character, liberated from the constraints of money problems and society, able to move outside the pressing determinisms which brought Tommy so low. He is big enough and free enough to confront man as pure spirit and evolutionary potential, instead of man as a victim of social forces. After realism, Bellow turned to romance. Yet Henderson is still a recognizable Bellow character. He has vague idealistic yearnings; he wants to fulfil the self in some genuine way and at the same time he wants to find a valid and rewarding role in society. He is protean, yet eager for a defining shape. His visit to Africa starts with a sudden revulsion from all the suffocating litter and rubble of contemporary civilized life. He makes a colossal effort of disburdenment because he feels his true self is lying "buried" within him under all the clutter and junk. He is the quintessence of ignorant, questing, well-intentioned individualism—"an exceptional amalgam of vehement forces." His prime need is to release that vehemence and awaken to reality and true selfhood. In his Africa, which is perhaps what the French call *l'Afrique de l'esprit* ("There is all Africa and her prodigies in us," as Sir Thomas Browne said—and Bellow has never been to Africa), Henderson undergoes the strange tutelage of Dahfu, who tells him that some new conception of the self is needed, something more "noble" with less "ego-emphasis." Henderson's initiation into the secrets of the deep, forgotten animal life in man (an initiation which was possibly influenced by the work of Wilhelm Reich) is all part of his quest to find some true way of realizing the self. Henderson, like other characters in Bellow's work, wants to

---

power to command through words becomes a terrible and easily abused power. Remember Hitler's voice? Bellow is very aware that words are now used more for exploitation than communication—deception rather than dialogue.

find out how a man can properly *submit* to reality (as Augie submitted to his "axial lines"), and at the same time *transcend* himself and slough off hampering limitations and encrustations. There are many Nietzschean echoes in the book, and indeed the motto of the prolonged metaphysical quest which occupies much of the book could be Zarathustra's contention that "Man is a thing to be surmounted." Henderson desperately wants to find a new hope, a new nobility in life—"Humankind has to sway itself more intentionally towards beauty"—but though he learns many new ideas it is hard to feel, at the end, as he returns to his wife with the intention of entering medical school, that his ebullient and tormenting individualism will ever be really surmounted or transformed. What he says at the start—"Society is what beats me. Alone I can be pretty good"—is scarcely modified at the end (like Augie, he talks of "love" but seldom manifests it). There seems to be no obvious way in which he can apply the lessons he learnt from his strange African quest (which is at times referred to as a "dream").

But perhaps this is Bellow's most interesting point. He once referred to the novel as being about "the comedy of self-concern" and in many essays he has explored the dangers of overvaluing, as well as undervaluing, the self. There is such a discrepancy between what the human imagination can conceive and yearn for, and what the physical individual can achieve, that the attempt to translate metaphysical aspirations into action may be comically foredoomed to failure. Henderson is a marvellous comic creation, trying anything and everything to "burst the spirit's sleep," bawling and tripping around on the edge of all sorts of new wisdom, but at the same time he is a tremendously egotistical and presumptuous buffoon. He can be almost ridiculous in his grandiloquence ("If I couldn't have my soul it would cost the earth a catastrophe") and like other Bellow figures he approaches solipsism ("Reality is *you*," he says to his face in a mirror). Is the book perhaps a critique of romantic individualism—showing intense subjectivity both in its high-flying grandeur and its stumbling futility? Is Henderson perhaps the funniest monologist of them all, escaping from the mess of his American life into the wonder of his African reverie? A man may throw off society to wander untrammelled through vistas of new possibilities and dreams of new definitions of man—but is this the best way to engage reality?

A man is sitting in a New York apartment waiting for a woman who is undressing in the next room. He has had a good meal; they will make love. But, characteristically, he starts "quivering" with his "wild internal disorder." An intense, questioning self-communing commences:

> And why? Because he let the entire world press upon him. For instance? Well, for instance, what it means to be a man. In a city. In transition. In a mass transformed by science. Under organized power. Subject to tremendous controls. In a condition caused by mechanization. After the late failure of radical hopes. In a society that was no community and devalued the person. Owing to the multiplied power of numbers which made the self negligible. . . . Which permitted savagery and barbarism in its own great cities. At the same time, the pressure of human millions who have discovered what concerted effort and thought can do. . . . You—you yourself are a child of this mass and a brother to all the rest. Or else an ingrate, dilettante, idiot. There, Herzog, thought Herzog, since you ask for the instance, is the way it runs. On top of that, an injured heart, and raw gasoline poured on the nerves. . . . Oh, for a change of heart, a change of heart—a true change of heart.

However, he does have an erection, and shortly he joins the woman in bed.

This is Moses E. Herzog, who gives his name to Bellow's new novel. This book—in many ways Bellow's most impressive to date—seems to summarize and contain all the questions, problems, feelings, plights, and aspirations worked over in the previous novels, and it follows them to their extreme conclusions. Herzog himself is clearly a descendant, if not a summation, of Bellow's other main characters—worried, harassed, brought down, messed up. His private life is at a point of chaos—for he is trying to recover from a disastrous second marriage which has just ended in divorce.

He is condemned to perpetual compulsive introspection, the victim of endless nagging cerebration. He seems terribly isolated and cut-off, wandering the congested city streets, brooding apart in lonely rooms. He is the silent monologist *par excellence*.

The book contains few actual incidents—an abortive trip to Vineyard Haven, a night with a girl friend, a visit to Chicago to see one of his children which ends in a car crash, his return to an old tumbledown house in the country which was where his second marriage reached its crisis. The significant action takes place mainly in his head. People and incidents teem through his memory, precipitating great bouts of agitated soul-searching and pounding speculation. More than that, his mind heaves under the pressure and weight of the modern city and the innumerable problems of the modern age. Ultimately he finds himself struggling with the deepest questions and mysteries of human existence. He constantly returns to that central problem in Bellow's work—what is it to be truly human? As a physical being, Herzog's relationships are fouled up, he is separated from his children, he is one of the struggling, sweating mass—powerless, something of a failure, not a little lost. Yet his circling mind will not be stilled. There is irony as well as urgency in his predicament, and Bellow excels himself in this book by presenting not only the importance but also the curse and the comedy of intense but "unemployed" consciousness. Herzog's is a representative modern intelligence—swamped with ideas, metaphysics, and values, and surrounded by messy facts. It labours to cope with them all. The book enacts that labour.

At first sight the meaning of the book might seem to be the sum of all the dozens of ideas that course through Herzog's head. Yet a more careful view reveals a deeper, subtler intent. The book moves from a corrosive internal restlessness to a point of temporary rest, and the most important meaning is in that actual movement: the interior tubulence finally giving way to a glimpse of peace. The important point to grasp is that Herzog is sick, in the throes of a riotous subjectivism. In his solitude he wants "to explain, to have it out, to justify, to put in perspective, to clarify." He is in the grip of a compulsion to understand, and this compulsion manifests itself in a habit of making endless, fragmentary jottings and writing letters—to friends, relations, dead ancestors, politicians, philosophers, finally to God. Many of them are unfinished, none of them, so far as we know, are ever sent. Perhaps they are all imaginary, part of his internal continuum, sudden moments of excited hyperconsciousness when the mind engages in silent partnerless dialogues—"having it out," trying to clarify. Meanwhile, Herzog is usually sitting or lying down, self-enwrapped, inert "in the coop of his privacy." For the bulk of the book we are in that coop with him—going over things, witnesses of his endless silent self-examination. It is as though he has been rendered immobile by his vulnerability to unrelated ideas. His mind is endlessly active, but it has no certainties, no fixed points, no sure focus. It is a mind on the rack. "He wrote to Spinoza. *Thoughts not causally connected were said by you to cause pain. I find that is indeed the case. Random association, when the intellect is passive, is a form of bondage.*" His thinking, like his life, is mismanaged and patternless. Unlike Proust he does not recapture the past: He is intermittently possessed by it. He is the victim of his own interior monologue.

He tries to "make steady progress from disorder to harmony," but as we follow the ramifications of his ungovernable memory and the fretful reachings of his mind we realize that this very compulsion to try to understand and explain everything mentally might be the most disabling sickness of all. While he writes his furious letters to the void, reality ebbs away from him.

One example. On a train journey he starts letters to people as various as Adlai Stevenson, his girl friend Ramona, Nehru, Commissioner Wilson, and himself. His mood is anything but stable:

> Quickly, quickly, more! . . . Herzog, now barely looking through the tinted, immovable, sealed window, felt his eager flying spirit streaming out, speaking, piercing, making clear judgments, uttering final explanations, necessary words only. He was in a whirling ecstasy. He felt at the same time that his judgments expressed the boundless, baseless bossiness and wilfulness, the nagging embodied in his mental constitution.

The sealed window—the soaring mind—the certainty as to the value of his thoughts—a suspicion that they are the symptoms of some personal feverish disequilibrium. This is typical Herzog. He cannot select or filter his thoughts. "I am a prisoner of perception." The prison he has to break out of is not so much society as his own head. The enemy is inside. As he says, he feels there is someone inside him "pounding for order," and he complains—"*I am in his grip . . . he will ruin me.*" The interior monologist is suffering from the disease of monologizing to himself.

In a sense the whole book takes place in Herzog's head; a reminiscence which ends where it began. At the beginning we encounter him in a state of "tranquillity" in his old country house, and at the end we return to that point, having seen all the turmoil which preceded that new tranquillity. True, the cityscapes through which our lonely metaphysician wanders are incomparably vivid, detailed, and pungent; essentially *there*, so that we can really feel the chaotic background against which the modern mind has to work. Herzog feels part of the urban mess, and indeed there seems to be at times an intimate connection between the city and his thoughts. Perhaps the teeming confusion of its tumult agitates his mind into a state of overexcited emulation—the city triggering off spasms of unrelated thoughts, just as the thoughts sometimes grind to an inconclusive halt in the congestion of the city streets.

But the actual incidents do not come to us direct: Rather, they are re-enacted and pondered over in Herzog's memory. For it is in his mind that Herzog is seeking some lost reality, some necessary key which will help him to return to the norms from which he has wandered and blundered into his personal chaos and separation. It is as though he is trying to extract some sense of significance and lineage from his random, disconnected past. Often he goes into a sort of catatonic trance, engulfed by the past and consequent reflections. "Engrossed, unmoving in his chair, Herzog listened to the dead at their dead quarrels." Some of the most moving scenes are of his youth, the sufferings of his "late unlucky family," all recreated with an astonishing wealth of compelling detail. More than that, he has to expose himself to everything—the incomprehensible evil he hears of in the courtroom, the sexual assault he suffered as a child—before he can learn true acceptance and a new orientation. Mental regurgitation is part of his therapy: The way back to a point from which his life can be resumed lies through memory. His achievement is to confront, and come to terms with, everything in his head. Not only does he recall all the many people he has met, people who have imposed on him and exploited him, people he has himself loved and let down; he also wrestles with many of the abstract issues which have vexed other protagonists in Bellow's work. What is the value of the self in an age of exploding population and mass-killings? What does "freedom" mean when even to step out into the street is to be buffeted by evidence of limitations? Despite all the black evidence, Herzog refuses pessimism. Spengler's theory of the decline of the West fills him with rage. When he reads that Heidegger talks about "the fall into the quotidian," he dashes off a letter asking, "When did this fall occur? Where were we standing when it happened?" The potentialities of human life must be perennial. Evil exists—but we must look away from it, beyond it. He feels our age is too fond of regarding itself as monstrous, that an insidious prestige is now attached to "the negative." We concentrate on Death and Cruelty and vengefully deny all possibilities of transcendence. The modern imagination feeds on horror as a pig at a trough. "Safe, comfortable people playing at crisis, alienation, apocalypse and desperation, make me sick." So he writes to a fellow professor:

> *Has the filthy moment come when moral feeling dies, conscience disintegrates, and respect for liberty, law, public decency, all the rest, collapses in cowardice, decadence, blood? . . . I can't accept this foolish dreariness. We are talking about the whole life of mankind!*

Herzog wants to get away from the dangerous attractions of nihilism. He is working for a change of heart.

Yet there is comedy in Herzog's inner gesturing—legislating for mankind while he is crammed helplessly in a subway car. Balance is restored by continual reminders of Herzog as a struggling, sweating, physical creature. He often breaks off a letter in a spirit of self-mockery, realizing how absurd he is being. We catch him at a transition point, coming awake to the ludicrous side of his conviction that "the progress of civilization—indeed, the survival of civilization—depended on the success of Moses E. Herzog." After all, his own life has been "a catalogue of errors"; he has been self-righteous, self-pitying, conceited in his suffering, egotistical (he is often caught looking at his own reflection—he is an unusually self-absorbed and self-important man). His thoughts are valuable, but in the end it is the comic futility of his thinking that strikes him. Throughout the book we are aware of a growing desire to pass beyond all ideas, all mental "explanations," all "abstract intellectual work," in an attempt to re-establish contact with ordinary reality. The letters Herzog writes merely serve to emphasize his indrawn-ness and apartness, but they are indications of an important aspiration. "I seem to have been stirred fiercely by a desire to communicate, or by the curious project of attempted communication." The monologist desperately wants to advance to dialogue. Too much solitary thinking has dislodged him from the world to a dangerous degree. To re-enter it he has to pass beyond thought altogether.

This provides the climax of the book. After the peak confusion of his Chicago venture—the car crash, the police interrogation—he starts to relax, to sink down into what James called "the lap of the actual."

Is this, by chance, the reality you have been looking for, Herzog, in your earnest Herzog way? Down in the ranks with other people—ordinary life? By yourself you can't determine which reality is real?

He starts to reacquaint himself with the ordinary world with deep gladness, learning new humility, new faith. Returning to the debris of his country house (which reflects perhaps the mess of his own life), he acquires a new calm as he ceases to strive for comprehension: "Go through what is comprehensible and you conclude that only the incomprehensible gives any light." The curse of pointless thought is lifting and he is on the verge of a new health, stirred by "indefinite music within." Instead of perverse self-communing, he now looks forward to "real, relevant work." He decides that he will "surrender the hyperactivity of this hyperactive face. But just to put it out instead to the radiance of the sun." He intends from now on "to share with other human beings"—in other words to move from monologue to dialogue.

The prose of the last chapter of the book is extremely specific and at the same time brimming with lyricism. It communicates Herzog's new delight in the simple objects around his house and the loveliness of the garden; his dawning reverence for the concrete, the rich plenitude of the seen world. At the same time it catches his inner trembling fervour as he moves beyond thought to a mood which is almost mystical. He is surcharged with a strange joy—mortal, but with transcendent intimations. In such a mood he can well drop a few lines to God: *How my mind has struggled to make coherent sense. I have not been too good at it. But have desired to do your unknowable will, taking it, and you, without symbols. Everything of intensest significance. Especially if divested of me.*

He seems to have broken out of the prison of the self. At the end we see him stretched out on a couch, for the first time experiencing a true pervading quiet after the remorseless inner clamouring which has racked him throughout the book. He stops writing letters.

At this time he had no messages for anyone. Nothing. Not a single word.

So the book ends. The resolution is completely internal. Externally there is still mess extending in all directions, but he has won through to a new attitude to it. We do not see his new good intentions in action. The book takes Herzog to the end of sickness and the beginning of a promise of cure. The inward work has been done. He has endured thought and memory to the point of madness; now he has passed beyond them to a state of calm, quiescent readiness. We feel a novel joyous sanity growing out of his harassed neurotic exhaustion. No new meanings, no solutions: rather, a change of heart, a turning to the sun. Not mere resignation, but a profound "let be," accompanied by peace and a prayer of praise such as can only be uttered on the other side of suffering.

A final word about the name Bellow chose for his most important protagonist to date. In 1950 Maurice Herzog, leading a French Himalayan expedition, conquered the first 8,000-metre peak, Annapurna. It was a climb of extraordinary difficulty, calling for phenomenal feats of endurance and bravery. In his own account of the climb Herzog wrote:

> In overstepping our limitations, in touching the extreme boundaries of man's world, we have come to know something of its true splendour. In my worst moments of anguish I seemed to discover the deep significance of existence of which till then I had been unaware. . . . The marks of my ordeal are apparent on my body. I was saved and I had won my freedom. This freedom, which I shall never lose, has given me the assurance and serenity of a man who has fulfilled himself. It has given me the rare joy of loving that which I used to despise. In this narrative . . . we bear witness.

"Maurice" is another form of "Moshe"—as is "Moses." My guess is that Bellow may have had Maurice, the great climber, in mind (and, of course, the original Moses climbed a mountain and came near to God). Moses Herzog could almost have written those words of Maurice Herzog, although his assault, ordeal, and newfound joy all take place inside him. In the figure of Moses Herzog, Bellow seems to have recorded the process and completion of some far-reaching inward exploration; a feat of internal "climbing," rewarded by a new sense of joy and freedom. In *Herzog* Saul Bellow himself seems to "bear witness." As Maurice Herzog wrote: "There are other Annapurnas in the lives of men."

In an article written in 1957, Bellow complained that "impotence has received more attention from modern writers than any other subject." He cited a variety of passive and alienated characters from Oblomov to Dostoevsky's underground man and commented: "They all tell the same story. The dread is great, the soul is small; man might be godlike but he is wretched; the heart should be open but it is sealed by fear." Yet consider Bellow's own characters—how lonely, insulated, and self-absorbed they are! That is why there is so little action in his novels. His characters seem to be in a state which external reality cannot penetrate for any length of time. Few of them actually *do* anything—a lot of Augie's adventures tend to be sexual in a not very profound way, while Henderson's puffings and blowings expend themselves in a land of romance. Bellow's characters want to understand the world, but they do not know how to act in it. As long as they are in a realistic setting they tend to be passive and immobile, neurotically lost in their own thoughts. They are as impotent and introspective as those lame, out-of-touch characters whose prevalence in modern fiction Bellow laments. Joseph is an underground man, and Herzog —so often prone and musing—is touched with Oblomovism. But they are not happy in this condition. Joseph yearned for some true community and Herzog really believes that "brotherhood is what makes a man human. . . . 'Man liveth not by Self alone but in his brother's face.' . . . The real and essential question is one of your employment by other human beings and their employment by us." Yet in none of the novels do we see the yearning fulfilled or the conviction put into practice. To revert to the terms we have been using, none of his characters really advance to dialogue. Norman Mailer made a valid comment on Bellow when he wrote: "He creates individuals but not relations between them, at least not yet." The fact remains that though his characters want to enter society, their notion of social fulfillment is often theoretic and ideal. Lionel Trilling, speaking of the political disenchantment felt by many Americans, once wrote: "Although we are willing, nay eager, to live in society, for we all piously know that man fulfils himself in society, yet we do not consent to live in a particular society of the present." He goes on to say that something in the American temperament dislikes the idea of being "conditioned" and adds, with words relevant for Bellow's characters, "somewhere in our mental constitution is the demand for life as pure spirit." Bellow's figures do seem to find the inner world of spirit more real than the outer conditioned public world, no matter how much they deplore the fact. It is not for nothing that the last book Herzog dips into is by a Russian who asserts "that private life is above everything. . . . It is a joy to be choked with thought." Herzog has come to find it a curse and is willing to move out of the private realm. But we do not see that willingness resulting in a new way of life.

Consider the endings of the novels. A man capitulating to the army; another sobbing in a funeral parlour; Augie standing in the cold French countryside; Henderson running round the Arctic wastes between plane stops. Herzog we leave on a couch in a disordered country house. All have tasks and journeys unfinished, problems unresolved, resolutions untested. These endings are vivid pictures—momentary gestures of hope, readiness, and reconciliation. They are often vibrantly, emotionally "right"; Yet from another point of view they could be called "conclusions in which nothing is concluded." Georg Lukács thinks that much modern literature, "by exalting man's subjectivity, at the expense of the objective reality of his environment," has in fact impoverished human life. He points to the "attenuation of actuality" in much modern work and relates it to the "surrender to subjectivity" so prevalent in our age. Instead of dialectic between man and environment we get interior monologue; the result is works which tend to be "static and sensational" rather than "dynamic and developmental." Now of course Bellow himself is supremely aware of this *malaise*, but the fact remains that he has yet to show the compulsive subjectivism of his characters actually transcended or left behind.

This, I think, explains certain characteristics of his work. Since his characters seldom initiate any action, his books lack the spine of plot. They have little dynamic dramatic necessity. This leads to a split: The internal emotional and intellectual development can be moving and convincing, the external chain of events is often rather random, meagre, and uncompelling (*The Victim* is an exception here). The result is that, at times, there is nothing to shape, organize, and discipline the endless flow of metaphysical garrulousness and wayward reminiscing. One sometimes longs for some significant interaction between the character and his environment. What carries the work is Bellow's own style. It can be exhilarating in its cascading vitality, breathtaking in its robust assimilatory zeal, very humane in the attention it loves to lavish on the humblest particulars of ordinary life. It can be comic and woeful, physical or metaphysical—whatever the mood of the character.[2]

Of course, his books show a marked progress. From a sulky, even churlish mood of passive nonparticipation, through a positive celebration of the self, thence to a quest into the complex meanings of selfhood, on to a genuine attempt to affirm positive values which transcend the self altogether. Herzog is wiser than Joseph, develops more of a conscience than Leventhal, is more weightily mature than Augie, more resilient than Tommy, more authentic than Henderson. Yet he does share one interesting trait with the other characters. At the end of his exhausting introspective journey he seems closer to "God" than he does to his relatives or to his girl friend Ramona. (Unlike some critics, I must confess that I find this last relationship pretty shallow.) Similarly Augie feels he gets in harmony with the "axial lines" of existence, but he is scarcely in harmony with any actual human beings. Tommy Wilhelm has a vision of universal brotherhood and weeps for all men who must die—but he is far from sorting things out with his wife and father. What I think happens is this. Failing to experience any specific sense of relationship with other people and contemporary society, Bellow's characters respond to a more mystical sense of oneness with some "larger body" which is transpersonal and relates them to the very currents of Being. Outcasts of society, they yet have

---

[2] This amazing and profuse verbal energy is perhaps a particularly Jewish aspect of his writing. He once wrote, of the ghetto, that "powerlessness appears to force people to have recourse to words"—an insight which extends far beyond the ghetto. Also of ordinary Yiddish conversation he said that it teems with historical and mythical allusions; metaphysical speculations and kitchen matters come bundled up together. Discussion of an egg may involve the Creation, The Fall, and the Flood. Clearly his own style has a debt to this habit. Because Bellow can handle ideas so vigorously and evoke scenes so vividly we tend to forget how little true human drama there is in his work.

moments when they feel at home in the universe. Again there are precedents in Whitman. A comment Bellow once made on contemporary American novelists is, in fact, self-applicable:

> American novelists are not ungenerous, far from it, but as their idea of society is fairly shallow, their moral indignation is non-specific. What seems to be lacking is a firm sense of a common world, a coherent community, a genuine purpose in life.

Those last three things are lacking in his own work, although the fact that Herzog genuinely reaches a stage where he seems on the point of acquiring that "firm sense" of ordinary reality and community seems to indicate that Bellow has completed a major phase in his evolution as a novelist. It remains to be seen whether Herzog's new-won attitudes towards reality will result in a new type of novel from Bellow.

There are several reasons for Bellow's emergence as the most important American post-war novelist—his sheer intelligence, his firm grasp of many of the central problems, concerns, and paradoxes of modern urban thinking man, his matchless feeling for cities—but perhaps one of the most important is his refusal to relinquish a sense of possible individual worth. He wrote once:

> We have so completely debunked the old idea of the Self that we can hardly continue in the same way. . . . Undeniably the human being is not what he commonly thought a century ago. The question nevertheless remains. He is something. What is he?

He has often taken issue with other writers who almost sadistically diminish the human image in their work, and he himself holds firmly to this tenet of faith—"I do not believe that human capacity to feel or do can really have dwindled or that the quality of humanity has degenerated." Agreed, the Self needs to be redefined— but not degraded. As he says, novelists "must value human existence or be unfaithful to their calling." Leslie Fiedler, to take a well-known example, asserts that "to fulfil its essential moral obligation (serious) fiction must be negative." Artists must say "No!

in thunder." Bellow has written well against the limitations of this doctrinaire negativism (though I think he underestimates the way in which a negative work may, in fact, affirm the superior power of human imagination and craft over hostile or recalcitrant matter). His own position is dignified—never didactic or glib. It is not folly to stress a need for new positive values—it may be dangerous to become too domiciled in the abyss. His own work is most honest and compelling when it points to that need. As we have seen, he cannot produce an authentic image of the desiderated new way of life. His work is full of would-be celebrants, moving slowly, heavily, out of some overlong and suffocating imprisonment in their own undirected, overactive consciousnesses.

Some critics find a positive affirmative joy, a mood of radiant reconciliation in his work (one critic thinks it is specifically "Hassidic"). I think there are a few such moments, but Bellow does hit some false notes where the euphoria is unconvincing and the joy too stridently asserted. He rightly condemns the "unearned" pessimism of many contemporary writers—but there is such a thing as unearned gladness as well. What he does show is the movement towards such a joy, the dawning recognition that such a reconciliation need not be an impossibility. He shows us contemporary man in all the comedy and anguish of trying to cope with the disorderly mess of modern life pouring in from all sides—haunted by failure, threatened by insanity, bedevilled by ideas he can never use, and occasionally lit up by intimations of irrational joy. Bellow knows the "thousand negatives" that can be uttered about "the individual life"; he knows, too, that "the sacred affirmative" will not easily be found (the terms are Emerson's). But he believes it must be a possibility and he is working to make sure that, should it be uttered, it will be understood. As he once wrote:

> If the human pride of artists has indeed exhausted the miracle of this world then nothing in art is necessary, all is superfluous. But here is the living man, and the last word concerning him cannot be imagined. We shall never know him in his entirety. Now, waiting in the darkness to be reanimated by a fresh impulse, we feel painfully the weight of everything superfluous. . . . But we

know that something necessary, something not to be evaded, is due and overdue.

It is no small praise to say that Bellow is one of the few writers likely to bring us news of the next "necessary thing," uttering words about the living man to which the living man will keenly listen.

FRANK KERMODE

Frank Kermode, a distinguished and wide-ranging literary critic, lives in England and is King Edward VII Professor of English Literature at Cambridge University. His many books include *The Sense of an Ending*, *Romantic Image*, *Shakespeare*, *Spenser*, *Donne*, and *Wallace Stevens*.

HERZOG

There is one famous compliment to a novelist that nobody is ever going to offer Saul Bellow, and that is to say that his books are the product of a sensibility so fine that no idea could violate it. It seems doubtful whether any interesting writer, even James, really fits that formula; in any case, if you think that is the condition the art should aspire to, Bellow is not your man. Yet for many people he is the man. In America, where more and more the hypotheses of literary historians tread the heels of literature, Bellow has already been snugly fitted into neat intelligible patterns. He is the big novelist who emerged at the precise conjunction of race, milieu, and moment—when, as Leslie Fiedler puts it, "the Jews for the first time move into the center of American culture" as the group best equipped to act as an urban, Europe-centred élite. Augie March is Huck Finn Chicago–Jewish-style, still, in Mr. Fiedler's dialect, in search of a primal innocence, but above all an urban Jew, with the appropriate worries, failures, and aspirations. Or, according to Norman Podhoretz, Bellow in 1953 came through with *Augie March* at just the right moment to encapsulate and

From the *New Statesman*, February 5, 1965. Reprinted by permission of the *New Statesman*.

typify the new revisionist liberalism, moving away from the Left at the same conscientious pace as *Partisan Review*.

Aside even from these professionally large and resonant explanations, much has been written about Bellow, and this is not surprising. When all the reservations have been made he is so good that anybody can see it with half an eye; only severe doctrinal adhesion prevents the recognition that he is a far more interesting writer than Mailer. One remarkable thing about him is that along the way he has conjured out of the air new talents, powers he apparently did not have, even *in posse*, when he started in the forties. With this bonus he is more gifted than the gifted young, including the handsomely endowed Philip Roth. Furthermore, he is, for all the glitter of ideas, accessible, easier to get to than John Hawkes, further out in the open than Malamud. Thus he made everybody flock to read him without sacrificing intellectual seriousness, and without growing plump enough to be caught in the meshes of the critics' hypotheses.

Bellow's career has some curious aspects. He has never lacked support. *Dangling Man* brought him respect, nearly twenty years ago, not only in America but here. Rereading it now, one finds it a little rigid, worthy but off-putting, a book one does not wish longer. I suppose that at the time, in a different and on the whole duller literary epoch, the intelligence with which the wretched but hard-thinking hero was placed, his eloquent and intellectually respectable introspection, were what won perceptive praise. Now the diagrams of alienation seem too square, the prose somewhat inelastic; it is hard to find in it the vivacity and inventive power one associates with Bellow. Perhaps it might be said that the austerity of the book gives it a kind of fidelity to its moment. Anyway, *The Victim*, though it had some of this rigour, and some of this period quality, was more various and flexible. But the big change, the *détente*, came only in the early fifties, with *The Adventures of Augie March*.

It would be easy to run through the rollcall of this book's deficiencies, but the point is that Bellow had found his new form. Perhaps it struck him that the tragic stance of classic alienation,

and even the existence of intellectuals, looked funny in this new world. They became a source of gags, and the hero turned picaro. Simultaneously with this new circumstance, Bellow became profusely inventive, exhibited a sense of the true comedy of intellect, which is painful as well as funny. There was some lamenting about what he gave up—the effects which arise from a firm management of structure, for example; it seemed that he thought these appropriate only to the short novel, and his guess was apparently confirmed when he next wrote a very good novella, *Seize the Day*, and went on to another inventive sprawl in *Henderson the Rain King*.

At least one ingredient is common to all the novels: The hero is, in Alfred Kazin's phrase, "burdened by a speculative quest." They all have the same humble need (however little this humility comes through in their conduct) to sort out human destiny by sorting out their own. In a world of chaotic particulars, where the only speculations which draw any support are bogus, vulgarized, or corrupt, the speculative quest turns into a sequence of extravagantly funny or pathetic gestures, and the happiest ending that can be hoped for is that of *Seize the Day*, when Tommy Wilhelm, a middle-aged flop, winds up weeping at the funeral of somebody he doesn't know.

The great merit, and at the same time the great difficulty, of such writing is that it does try to get into fiction the farcical excitements of thinking as distinct from behaving. To do this straight seems almost impossible, or, if you think it works in *La Nausée*, unrepeatable. Bellow gets round the problem in the same way every time. The speculative interest is never put straight in. In *Seize the Day* the wise sayings come from the fraudulent Tamkin; in *Henderson* fantasy bears the freight of speculation. The new book is full of furious thinking, and Herzog, the hero, does most of it, but not "straight." The first sentence of the book says: "If I am out of my mind, it's all right with me."

Herzog is in the line of the fat novels, but has more structure than the others. The hero is a very well-read Chicago Jew on the point of a breakdown. Most of his thinking is done in letters, the kind of letter you might frenetically compose, if you had enough in

your head, in the early stages of a sleepless night. "Dear Herr Nietzsche, May I ask you a question from the floor?" "Dear Doktor Professor Heidegger, I should like to know what you mean by the expression 'the fall into the quotidian.' When did this fall occur? Where were we standing when it happened?" "Dear General Eisenhower . . ." The letters, in a sense, do the work of Tamkin. As a way out of the difficulty, which was to show an intellectual operating in the world, they seem to me to have the exceptional merit of turning the technical trick and then, because sparingly used and full of wit, to become delightful in themselves.

Herzog is an authority on everything from romantic theology to fish scales, but all this equipment is of interest only as useful in the speculative quest. After all his adventures he may wind up where we find him at the start of the book, in his weird derelict Massachusetts country house in a state of peaceful choicelessness. But the main business of the novel is Herzog, under stress, trying to sort out Herzog. He can in various ways tell us all about himself: a genuine old Jewish type that digs emotion, but grown at this moment—his second marriage ludicrously broken—narcissistic, masochistic, anachronistic. His friends, a sort of traitors, a bunch of real grotesques (one of them gives the kiss of life to a monkey dying of tuberculosis), seem to be engaged in "a collective project" to destroy his vanity and push him "down in the mire of post-Renaissance, post-humanistic, post-Cartesian dissolution, next door to the Void."

Out of the goings-on that ensue there begins to emerge an interesting design. Herzog, forced into sacrifice anyway, sees that what he has to sacrifice himself to is the truth, and we watch him both consciously trying to do this and unconsciously doing it. Under the pressure of his "reality instructors" he moves hastily about, colliding with the world from which he is dissociated; in the subway he writes letters about negative entropy, and emerges to observe "an escaped balloon fleeing like a sperm, black and quick into the orange dust of the west . . ." (This is not only powerful and versatile, it concretely presents the dissociation between things as they are and Herzog's speculations.) He is on the way to see a splen-

didly undemanding sexpot, whom he enjoys with the same comic metaphysical detachment from sense. The truth about sacrifice can't be got to by that route, nor by fast useless journeys, made by Herzog with "all the dead and mad" in his company or custody, nor by surveying "the story of my life—how I rose from humble origins to complete disaster." When the answers eventually come, they come both from without and within.

This long climactic passage of this novel, which is about Herzog's trip to Chicago to see his daughter, is the first piece in which Bellow has improved on *Seize the Day*, a book it somewhat resembles. It has many layers, and a diagram would be misleading, especially if it sounded conventional or banal; but Herzog pays an important visit to an old, still Yiddish aunt, and carries off a gun he had once seen ineffectively flourished by his father. By this agency he gets his chance to come, though imperfectly, to terms with indignity and suffering, and that is a step in the necessary direction. As he had informed General Eisenhower in a particularly abstruse letter, the forces that make us human are history, memory, and a knowledge of death. A day in a New York courtroom had taught him more—for example, about how high he stood in the scale of affluent misery; and he feels this more keenly when in a prison cell himself, knowing that this is not the place for him to do time; he belongs to the privileged classes who do it on the street. Finally, as in *Seize the Day*, the decisive message comes from the wisdom of a crank: You can't live until you know death; practise lying in a coffin, know it while you still live; then live. So, as far as it can be done in a self-hating civilization, in an emotional language corrupted by all the fraudulent modern talk of crisis, apocalypse, desperation, Herzog touches bottom and finds health.

Bellow must be sick of hearing about his deficiencies, especially about his failure to invent women. There isn't a conventionally well-written woman in *Herzog*, though the hero's second wife is convincing as the inhabitant of a bad dream, a figure of fun who then bursts nightmarishly into the police station to press Herzog down to the bottom. The other girls, Herzog's mistresses, are about as real as Smollett's, but little more is needed. This is a

slightly caricatured world, male, Jewish, comic and pathetic, temporarily crazy too, so that the men friends are no less grotesque that the wife, and the remnants of Herzog's childhood are endearing emblems rather than original experiences profoundly evoked. This is the world refracted through the aging Bellow hero: bricks and mortar, cab-drivers, what might be seen from the corner of an abstracted eye, are idiomatic, accurate; dialogue also can have accuracy as well as comic energy. But the nearer the foreground, the nearer the main interest, they come, the more distorted the characters tend to look.

Still, it is plausibly the view from Herzog's disciplinary coffin. So although the book has clear limitations, they are a long way off. And why should we be surprised that Americans make much of such powers of invention and intellect, such comic energy, so genuine a speculative quest? Wouldn't we?

THEODORE SOLOTAROFF

Theodore Solotaroff, editor of the literary periodical, *New American Review*, has published a collection of his essays entitled *The Red Hot Vacuum*.

NAPOLEON STREET

Saul Bellow's *Herzog* is such a rich book, brimming with wit and thoughtfulness and feeling, that one can go on reading it over and over. So I have been doing, off and on, for the past three months. I am prepared to say that its interest is inexhaustible—one of the tests of literature. However, I also have to say that it is much easier and possibly more rewarding to reread passages than to try to hold them together in your mind. Its principle of composition is that of overflow: Bellow's consciousness of life, much of it no doubt his life, caught at the flood, with the form of the novel kept wide open to receive it. There is an action that develops briefly in the middle, but its purpose is mainly to effect a transition in thought and feeling, and the meaning of the book remains embedded for the most part in Herzog's memories, reveries, and especially in his letters to the world, which have only a fragmentary connection to one another. On the other hand, the writing is so clear, the sensibility of Herzog is so amazingly visible, the bearings of his situation are so graphically drawn that one should be able to say something more interesting than "Go read it."

From *The Red Hot Vacuum and Other Pieces on Writing in the Sixties*. Copyright © 1964 by Theodore Solotaroff. Reprinted by permission of Atheneum Publishers. This article appeared originally in *Commentary*.

The trouble, of course, is Herzog himself. He is one of those European-type intellectuals who teach at the New School in New York or the Committee on Social Thought at Chicago (where Bellow is currently employed), whose minds are like the Mafia—interests everywhere. Then, too, he is a cuckold, and there is nothing like that to make a man think strange obsessive thoughts. But even so, what do Herzog's grievances have to do with "the plebeian stage of evolutionary self-awareness," or with "the fact that so much of 'value' has been absorbed by technology itself," or with "what Heidegger calls the second Fall of Man into the quotidian or ordinary"?

Well, to make a start, Herzog can be viewed as a high-class version of Bellow's other recent heroes: Tommy Wilhelm of *Seize the Day*, Eugene Henderson of *Henderson the Rain King*, and Philip Bummidge of the play *The Last Analysis*. They are all trying to recover from a crisis of middle age in which a man is overwhelmed by a happening that makes a mockery of his settled contrivances and assurances and that testifies once and for all to the previous mismanagement of his life. Wilhelm, a salesman, loses his job; Henderson, whose vocation has been to exercise his powerful vitality, is seized by the dread of his imminent death; Bummidge, the TV comic, can no longer stand his own jokes; Herzog, student of romanticism and apostle of "heart," has been undone by his wife's love affair with his best friend. All four men are impulsive, self-dramatizing types who are impatient with their adversities. What King Dahfu says of Henderson is no less true of the others: "Everything about you . . . cries out 'Salvation, Salvation. What shall I do? What must I do? At once. What will become of me?' " Still, they *have* laid waste their powers and each is near the end of his emotional tether. The principal problem of Bellow's fiction, stated in *Dangling Man*, his first novel, as "How is a good man to live?" has thus come down to the more specific and desperate question stated in *The Last Analysis* as how is a middle-aged failure to be "reborn from an empty heart?"

Willy-nilly, then, all these later heroes of Bellow are gluttons for pain—for what hurts is still alive and still has the possibility of renewal. They are all also trying to reach the deeper sources of grief and impulse, to reconstitute the past in order to shed it, to clear away the cultural conditioning that has deflected them from a simple understanding of their desires. Herzog's case, however, is a much more complicated one. He has so many roles and self-images, is so divided among them, that simplicity is well-nigh impossible. A child of the immigrant Jewish ghetto, to which he remains so tied, he has written his first and only book on romanticism and Christianity. A bookish, urban type, he has tried to turn himself into a New England country squire. A scholar, a footloose intellectual, a lover of fancy women, he is also a dutiful man around the house and a patient caretaker of his wife's neurosis. No wonder he has problems of identity. He is a romantic who sets great store by "the heart"—a term that is constantly on his mind—but he is also a rationalist who has more principles of ethics than Spinoza. His innocence is no less phenomenal than his sophistication. How can a man who is an expert student of his own character turn over his wife's diaphragm to his best friend? How can he then bring the friend with them to Chicago and find him a job, consult him about his wife's moods, finally be booted out and supplanted, and still not seriously suspect? No wonder Herzog wishes to give up "the crushing burden of self-development." No wonder the time for a serious reckoning has come.

The problem, though, is not only that Herzog has to come to terms with his high-minded and tender-hearted childishness. He also conceives himself to be a representative contemporary individual as well as a serious humanist whose breakdown has a general significance. For Gersbach and Madeleine are not alone in cheating and degrading him, of robbing him of his belief in "faithfulness, generosity, sacred quality." There are his lawyer and his analyst, both of whom exploited him in bad faith and in their respective and typically modern styles of contempt for human nature. There are also his more impersonal enemies such as the politicians and nuclear gamesmen who hold his life in their callous hands and increase his private citizen's feeling of impotency and rage by building missile sites on public beaches and making plans to blow up the polar ice caps with hydrogen bombs to get at their oil deposits. There is the huge, amorphous, unreal public life itself that dispenses freedom without content, culture without nourishment, the cynicism of Madison Avenue and the "potato love" of Eisenhower. Herzog's angry sense of grievance from his cuckoldry rises and spreads in all directions as he busily scribbles his dispatches of protest to a society and an age that has less and less room, use, and respect for the traditions of humane and personal being, for true individuals like Herzog.

Though Herzog realizes that many of his ideas about the heart and its prerogatives are as hapless and mistaken as his life has been, he wants to continue to believe in something better than the grimy pseudorealism of the new "mass men"—people like his lawyer, Himmelstein, to whom all men are whores, all truth is facts, and all facts are dirty. Nor does he wish to fall back into the malarial pessimism of the Wasteland view, "the cheap mental stimulants of Alienation, the cant and rant of pipsqueaks about Inauthenticity and Forlornness," the "shivery games" people today play with themselves in advocating apocalyptic views, crisis ethics, the theology of dread. "I can't accept this foolish dreariness," writes Herzog to his friend Shapiro, who has apparently produced another fastidious treatise on the decline of the West, the nightmare of history, the death of God, the pathology of culture, etc. "We are talking about the whole life of mankind. The subject is too great, too deep for such weakness, cowardice."

However, the tone of Herzog's protest is unsteady; he lacks confidence. He recognizes that the facts of contemporary history and society are dead against the humanists. War and genocide have reduced the sacredness of the individual life, the significance of the civilizing virtues to a hideous mockery ("Limitless massacre!" Herzog reminds himself. "I never understood it, did I, because it was not compatible with my aims.") Then there is the other side of the coin: the revolutions of population growth and technology, the rapid transformations of culture and value that are necessary to help more people live a little better on this planet: "Would you deny them the right to exist? Would you ask them to labor and go hungry while you enjoyed delicious old-fashioned Values? You yourself are a child of this mass and a brother to all the rest. Or else an ingrate, dilettante, idiot." "A merely aesthetic critique of modern history?" he rages against Shapiro. "You are too intelligent for this. You inherited rich blood. Your father peddled apples."

However representative Herzog's crisis of belief may be, it takes on force only through being an expression of character and not merely a series of constructs to explain his failure as a man. Most of his ideas are too sketchy, in any event, to stand on their own. Herzog cannot write sustained discussions while he is supposed to be cracking up, though one wonders if Bellow himself doesn't want to have it both ways—to portray the "eager, grieving, fantastic, dangerous, crazed, and to the point of death, 'comical' " Herzog, who will eventually be rushing around Chicago with murder in his eye and a gun wrapped in old rubles, and at the same time to provide an important if fragmentary set of notes toward the definition of post-modern culture. He is indulgent toward Herzog's habit of broad speculation as he is toward nothing else about him, and the novel tends to become cluttered with "brilliant" thoughts at the general expense of narrative power and clarity. Be that as it may, one of Herzog's ideas is that "Romanticism is the form taken by plebeian envy in modern Europe." I don't think that this was true generally, but it is true of Herzog. He comes directly from the one segment of the formerly repressed masses who immediately set about to possess the wealth, manners, and cultural heritage of the elite. Bred in Herzog's bones is the romanticism of the Jewish Emancipation: It connects the deluded "Graf Pototsky of the Berkshires," as he calls himself, to the somewhat presumptuous scholar trying to crack and revise Hegel's "Law of the Heart." The ground of his complexity, Herzog's Jewishness, is also what finally connects the gifted analysand to the blind husband, and the comic victim with his "immoderate, heart-flooded way" to the gaunt and earnest seeker after Otherness. It enters into his grandiose conceptions of himself and into his stinging self-irony; it is the source of

476

his moral sentimentality, on the one side, and of his vestiges of sternness with himself, on the other.

Herzog's Jewishness is the one thing about him that goes deeper than his ideas about his life and so is seldom discussed as such. It emerges solidly, naturally, authentically, from the family experiences that he remembers so vividly and that function not as another construct but as the main province of his temperament. Herzog's prototype is his improvident father, the princely timid bootlegger, who rushed around town calculating "percentages at high speeds," much as Herzog rushes around in his "delirious" profession of intellectual history, making his quick, summary formulations and judgments, usually to much the same profit that his father earned. He is also the disciple of his tender, unworldly, and not very honest mother. In Montreal, he grew up on Napoleon Street—a name that evokes not only one of the archetypal figures of romantic individualism but also the Code that enabled the Jews to leave their ghettoes and enter the mainstream of Western culture and history on which Herzog feels himself being swept along. The ambience of Herzog's early life is beautifully encapsulated by the song the tragic family boarder sang when he returned from his nightly drunk, his wife and children having been swept away forever in the Russian Revolution:

> *Al tastir ponecho mimeni*
> I'm broke without a penny.
> Do not hide Thy countenance from us
> Vich nobody can deny.

In the humor of Ravitch's song, there is something not a little crazy, with its dizzying leap across the ages, the desperate irony of its transitions from the sacred to the profane, the old world to the new, its feeling of cosmic loss and social estrangement which is both acknowledged and spoofed in the last line. Remembering Napoleon Street, "the bootlegger's boys reciting ancient prayers," Herzog thinks: "Here was a wider range of human feelings than he had ever again been able to find." And one is tempted to add,

477

"Yes, and what gaps between them." Ravitch's profound division of consciousness bespeaks a culture in which all things are alienated from themselves and irony takes on the status of an ontological principle. This is the famous Jewish marginality that is currently being so much exploited and trivialized. However, it is the real thing in *Herzog* and he is its product.

The Herzogs have standards of "heart," and Moses has been one of those "young Jews brought up on moral principles as Victorian ladies were on pianoforte and needlepoint." All of which has helped him to know a great deal about life and to understand very little: The narcissism of his ambitiousness and the narcissism of his unworldliness are endlessly in conflict. Just as he is a natural for a profession in which "the main instrument is your opinion of yourself," so his inner life is regularly flooded by the self-enclosing emotional system of the ghetto, in which so much feeling circulates within the family, so little flows out to the bleak and hostile and corrupting world. Thus, though Herzog lives in the world, he has been able to spare himself real understanding of the vast range of human experience that exists outside his self-regarding categories. Similarly, his morality has remained one based on evasion and repression. It is only when he strays into a criminal courtroom and suddenly comes up against genuine sordidness and evil that he begins to realize how insulated he has been by his feelings, not only against the life of the drug addict or the child murderer that is revealed to him but also against his own balked desires that rise up in him as an evil taste in his mouth.

The jolt in the New York courtroom is followed by an automobile accident in Chicago in which Herzog almost kills himself and his little girl and is apprehended by the police for carrying his useless gun. These are the blows by which truth generally comes in Bellow's fiction. The first sharply teaches Herzog the limits and shallowness of his "essential humanity" in the face of what is merely another routine day for a criminal judge. The second brings him back from his dangerous preoccupations with his indignities, his rights, his need for justice. Returning to his abandoned country house and living amid the owls and butterflies and field mice, Herzog finally begins to move toward simplicity: a proper estimate of the interest of one small and ailing Self against the claims of all that there is in this world that is not Moses Elkanah Herzog; also a due respect for the mystery of experience that does not yield to explanations, much less to a "good five-cent synthesis." "Everything of intensest significance," he writes to God. "Especially if divested of me." Though Herzog ends the novel where he began it, flat on his back, he has come a distance in learning to keep still, to curb his vanity, and to let his heart fill of its own accord.

But the elegiac prose of the closing section is so gentle and moving that one tends to overlook the fact that it is quietly burying most of the issues that earlier had been raised in connection with Herzog's relations to society. At the end, he rests more firmly and spiritually in his passivity, but it is still passivity. He has taken Adlai Stevenson, among others, to task for being one of those "who think a good deal and effect nothing," but one wonders what Herzog is now able to effect besides another marriage to a woman lavish in all things, including advice on how he should live. True, he has begun to believe in the God of his friend Nachman and of his fathers, but isn't he merely availing himself of the solace of faith without committing himself to its substance? "I am pretty well satisfied to be, to be just as it is willed," says Herzog. One wonders what will happen when the trees of Ludeyville turn bare and Herzog's mind fills again with its dilemmas. God requires more desire than Herzog has to give; so far he hasn't abandoned the old Self but merely found a healing illusion of having done so.

I suspect that the same discursive looseness of structure that has allowed Bellow to indulge his flair for ideas has also ended by allowing him to indulge his flair for optimism. Like Herzog himself, the story of his recovery lacks the true opposition of Otherness, just as his protests remain too much the worldly discontents of an unworldly man. The finest thing about it is Bellow's incredible grasp of the individual intellectual plight—of the crisis of belief that lies beneath the complex surface of Herzog's behavior. As such, the novel is a great portrait of the contemporary humanist, Jewish-style, whose relations with the modern world are as increasingly hapless as Herzog demonstrates them to be. It's too bad that Bellow was driven to turn such a searching question of a book into a comfortable but evasive answer.

ALFRED KAZIN

Alfred Kazin is one of the leading literary critics in the United States. He teaches at Hunter College of the City University of New York and is the author of *On Native Grounds, A Walker in the City, Bright Book of Life*, and other works of literary criticism and autobiography.

THE EARTHLY CITY OF THE JEWS

When John Updike brilliantly conceived Henry Bech, who was in everything he did, and especially in what he couldn't do, "the Jew as contemporary American novelist," Updike was having his fun with that once unlikely but now well-known American product, Bellow-Malamud-Roth. Bellow said that the constant linking of these names reminded him of Hart, Schaffner, and Marx. But irritating as it might be to one proudly gifted and much-honored novelist to be linked with other *Jewish* names, Bellow more than any other American novelist of his ability used the modern Jewish experience in his work.

Most of Bellow's characters were Jews; his non-Jewish characters (rare enough) were, like Allbee in *The Victim*, obsessed with Jews or, like Henderson, clamorously produced wittily agonized definitions of human existence remarkably like those of the Jewish protagonists in Bellow's novels—Joseph in *Dangling Man*, Asa Leventhal in *The Victim*, Tommy Wilhelm in *Seize the Day*, Augie March, Herzog, Mr. Sammler. Over and again in Bellow's novels

From *Bright Book of Life: American Novelists and Storytellers from Hemingway to Mailer*. Copyright © 1971, 1973 by Alfred Kazin. Reprinted by permission of Little, Brown and Co. in association with The Atlantic Monthly Press and Secker & Warburg Limited.

there were the parents who to tyrants in eastern Europe had been nothing but Jews, and in the slums of Montreal and Chicago saw nothing but their own experience reflected back from the neighborhood. There was a natural, enchanted repetition of the Jewish neighborhood, the Jewish family circle, the Jew as college intellectual, radical, dreamer, explorer of lowlife—the Jew discovering worlds new to him. "Look at me going everywhere!" Augie March cries out after pages devoted principally to the emancipation and enlightenment of Augie's senses—"Why, I am a sort of Columbus of those near-at-hand!" More than anyone else, Bellow connected one novel after another with a representative Jew in order to represent Jewish experience itself.

This emphasis on one people's collective idiosyncratic experience, an emphasis so intense that it seems to follow from some deep cut in Bellow's mind, is nevertheless intense in attention rather than partisan. Bellow is positively hypnotized by the part of human life he knows best, as a novelist should be, and he sees everything else in this focus. But without being detached and "impartial" about the long Jewish struggle for survival, he is fascinated and held by the texture of Jewish experience as it becomes, as it can become, the day-to-day life of people one has created. This is very different from writing about people one names as Jews but who, no matter how one feels about them, are just names on the page. Texture is life relived, *life* on the page, beyond praise or blame. In Bellow's first novel, *Dangling Man* (1944), the hero writes of himself: ". . . To him judgment is second to wonder, to speculation on men, drugged and clear, jealous, ambitious, good, tempted, curious, each in his own time and with his customs and motives, and bearing the imprint of strangeness in the world." To Asa Leventhal in *The Victim*, crossing over to Staten Island,

> the towers on the shore rose up in huge blocks, scorched, smoky gray. . . . The notion brushed Leventhal's mind that the light over them and over the water was akin to the yellow revealed in the eye of a wild animal, say a lion, something inhuman that didn't care about anything human and yet was implanted in every human being too, one speck of it, and formed a part of him that responded

to the heat and the glare . . . even to freezing, salty things, harsh things, all things difficult to stand.

In *Seize the Day*, where the West Side of New York is the most living, throbbing character, Tommy Wilhelm, trying to make a confident appearance with a hat and a cigar, feels that the day is getting away from him: ". . . the cigar was out and the hat did not defend him . . . the peculiar burden of his existence lay upon him like an accretion . . . his entire chest ached . . . as though tightly tied with ropes. He smelled the salt odor of tears in his eyes. . . ." In the sunshine of upper Broadway there was "a false air of gas visible at eye-level as it spurted from the bursting buses."

This air of having lived, of experiencing the big city in every pore, of being on the spot, is the great thing about Bellow's fiction. It is this living acrid style—in the suddenly chastened, too glibly precise, peculiarly assertive bitterness of postwar American writing, with its hallucinated clarity about details, its oversized sense of our existence, of too many objects all around (what desolation amidst wonders!)—that made us realize Bellow as an original. He is a key to something that would emerge in all the American writing of this period about cities, the "mass," the common life. This was not the "minority" writing of the poignant, circumscribed novels of the 1930s. Even in the best of them, like Daniel Fuchs's *Low Company*, *Summer in Williamsburg*, *Homage to Blenholt*, one had been aware that "Jewish" equals ghetto. Bellow had come out of a ghetto in Montreal, the Napoleon Street that makes one of the deeper sections of *Herzog*. But what made him suddenly vivid, beginning with what was later to seem the put-on of *The Adventures of Augie March* (1953), was his command of a situation peculiarly American, founded on mass experience, that was as far from the metaphysical wit in Kafka as it was from the too conscious pathos of the Depression novels. With Bellow an American of any experience could feel that he was in the midst of the life he knew.

What was perhaps most "American" about it was the fact that despite all the crisis psychology in *The Victim, Seize the Day*,

Herzog there was a burning belief in commanding one's own experience, in putting it right by thought. Each of these narratives was a kind of survival kit for a period in which survival became all too real a question for many Americans. The Jewish experience on that subject—and what else had the experience been?—seemed exemplary to Americans, especially when it came armed with jokes. Good-bye to Henry Roth and how many other gifted, stunted, devastated Jewish novelists of the thirties. In book after book Bellow went about the business of ordering life, seeing it through, working it out. He was intimate with the heights-and-abyss experience of so many intellectual Jews, the alternating experience of humiliation and the paradise of intellectual illumination. And it was this depiction of life as incessant mental struggle, of heaven and hell in the same Jewish head,[1] that made Bellow's readers recognize a world the reverse of the provincial, a quality of thought somber, tonic, bracing, that was now actual to American experience yet lent itself to Bellow's fascinatedly personal sense of things.

In all of this Bellow became a style-setter for those many writers emerging in the fifties who found in him a kind of paradigm for taking hold, for getting in there, for being on top of the desperate situation. And indeed no one was more impressed by this angle on life, this sense of command, this ability to be *imaginatively* in charge, than Bellow himself, whose books, one after another, were usually founded on a protagonist who was the nearest possible spokesman for himself. Just as the success story of American Jews "making it" was represented by a bewildering succession of changes in their lives, so Bellow's novels, each registering a different state of awareness but all coming together as successive chapters of the same personal epic, made the nearest and best literary expression of the disbelief behind a Jewish ascent that was also haunted by the Holocaust. Bellow expressed both the American facts and the disbelief.

---

[1] "Up to their necks in dung," an old East European *rebbe* said of his seminarians, "they dream of ancient Assyria, Babylonia, Palestine."

Here was an American Jewish writer who had a powerful sense of his own experience as imaginative, yet could beat other Jewish intellectuals at putting the universe into a sentence. He was as clever as a businessman but racked by a sense of responsibility to his "soul." Bellow underwent all these phases in his fiction. But at the center of each narrative was always a hero, a single mind and conscience, adventurous but forever counting the cost of existence. Above all, the Bellow persona was an hallucinated observer of what Sartre called the "hell that is other people"—he brilliantly sized up the strength in other people's arms, lives, faces, seeing what they had to say to the predominating self's vision at the heart of each Bellow novel. The man had been an anthropologist, a traveler, a musician, an editor of the University of Chicago's "great books"; he was a teacher, a lover, a liberated Jewish male, and the most watchful of Jewish sons; he had found a way through the thickets of the big-city ghetto, the big-city university, the Depression, the merchant marine during the war; he had been a left radical, a welfare investigator; he was soon to become the sternest of Jewish moralists. And in all this Bellow influenced himself far more than others ever did, which is why book after book added up to what he had experienced and learned. The key belief was that right thinking is virtue and can leave you in charge of the life that is so outrageous to live.

The process of self-teaching thus becomes the heart of Bellow's novels, and the key to their instructiveness for others. One could compile from Bellow's novels a whole commonplace book of wisdom in the crisis era that has been Bellow's subject and opportunity. His novels are successively novels of instruction as well as existential adventure tales. The story as a whole tells, as the best Jewish stories always do, of the unreality of this world as opposed to God's. The hero struggles in a world not his own, a world run by strangers. The Jewish son has indeed lost the paradise that in childhood was within his grasp. In scripture this world is God's world; Jews must be grateful and obedient for being allowed to share it. In Jewish fiction this world is always someone else's world, though it is one in which Jews call themselves Jews and remain Jews. The so-called Jewish novel (there really is one, though only a few Jews have written it, and those who write it are not always Jews) takes place in a world that is unreal, never *our* world. The heart of the world is Jewish (said John Jay Chapman), but in Bellow's novels only one's mother and father have a heart. Bellow is in magnetized relation to the big-city environment, to the vertigo and clamor of New York, to the opulent yet sortable detail. But his is not a world in which a Jew feels at home. The Jew is always in some uneasy relation to "them"—he is a newcomer, parvenu, displaced person whose self-ordering becomes the issue in each book. In his humanist attack on anti-Semitism in France, *Jew and Anti-Semite*, Jean-Paul Sartre defined a Jew as someone whom others regard as a Jew. This understandably provoked Bellow by its lack of knowledge. When even "a prince of European philosophy" knows so little about them, Jews may wonder if this *is* their world. And so the Jew in Bellow's novels is a "stranger" because he really is one—not, like Camus's *"étranger,"* because he is free of other people's opinions to the point of total indifference. This representative Jew is involved in a catch-as-catch-can relationship to the world, that famous anchor of the old bourgeois novel, that keeps him lightly suspended just above the earth.[2]

But the vitality of Bellow's fiction comes from the importance of being a Jewish son, a figure of importance; this may be hidden from everyone but himself. The Bellow hero, though often distraught, has the powerful ego of Joseph relating his dreams to his jealous brothers. This hero is so all-dominating that other males tend to become distinct only if they are intellectuals who personify *wrong ideas*. Nonintellectuals, like the women in the later novels, tend to become "reality instructors," opaque emblems of the distrusted world. The central figure is the only pilgrim who makes any progress. From Joseph in *Dangling Man* to old Mr. Sammler, each of Bellow's heroes represents the same desperate struggle for life— by which he means a more refined consciousness. It is a concentrated example of the age-old Jewish belief that salvation is in

---

[2] An image in Kafka's parables.

thinking well—to go to the root of things, to become a kind of scientist of morals, to seek the ultimate forces that rule us.

Thinking is for Bellow the most accessible form of virtue. The "reality instructors" have become indistinguishable from the worldliness with which they are clotted. Bellow's recurrent hero, by contrast, is so concerned with thinking well that the imbalance between the hero and his fellows becomes an imbalance between the hero's thinking and the mere *activity* of others. Bellow is not a very dramatic novelist, and unexpected actions tend to be dragged into his novels—like Herzog's half-hearted attempt to kill his wife's lover—as a way of interrupting the hero's reflections. But evidently Bellow's personae attain their interest for *him* by their ability to express the right opinions. And not surprisingly, the protagonists of Bellow's novels are the voices of his intellectual evolution. A Bellow anthology would take the form of a breviary, an intellectual testament gathered from diaries, letters to public men and famous philosophers that were never mailed, arias to the reader à la Augie March, the thoughts of Artur Sammler that are neural events in the privacy of one's consciousness because they cannot be expressed to others—they are too severe, too disapproving.

Bellow has found fascinating narrative forms for the urgency of his many thoughts. He has been clever in finding a distinct *style* for so much silent thinking—from Joseph's diaries in *Dangling Man* to Herzog's equally incessant meditations and finally old Mr. Sammler's haughty soliloquies, where the style is one of the lightest, featheriest, mental penciling, an intellectual shorthand (here involving brusque images of the city) that answers to the traditional contractedness of Jewish thought. The favorite form for Jewish sages has always been the shortest, and Bellow's best fictions are his shortest. V. S. Pritchett, who admires Bellow for powerful descriptions of city life rare among "intellectual" novelists, thinks that in his long books Bellow "becomes too personal. There is a failure to cut the umbilical cord." Bellow's more lasting fictions will probably be those whose personae are not *exactly* as intelligent as he is—*The Victim* and *Seize the Day*.

In these books the weight of the world's irrationality, which is its injustice, falls heavily upon human beings who win us by their inability to understand all that is happening to them and why it is happening to *them*. Asa Leventhal at the end of *The Victim*, having been persecuted, exploited, terrified by a Gentile who accuses the Jew of having persecuted *him*, ends up innocently saying to his tormentor—"Wait a minute, what's your idea of who runs things?" Tommy Wilhelm in *Seize the Day*, who in one day realizes that he has lost wife, mistress, father, money, God, confronts the depths of his suffering only by identifying with a stranger into whose funeral he has stumbled by accident. These incomprehensions are truly evocative of the "existential situation" in contemporary fiction—that of individuals who are never up to their own suffering, who cannot fully take it in, who have learned only that their suffering has its reasons of which reason knows nothing.

ROBERT SHULMAN

Robert Shulman is professor of English at the University of Washington and has served as visiting professor at the University of Wisconsin and Fulbright lecturer at the Université de Besançon. He has published essays on such writers as Melville, Hawthorne, Poe, James, and Fitzgerald.

THE STYLE OF BELLOW'S COMEDY

Because of his exploratory range and vitality, Saul Bellow has had to be associated not only with American predecessors like Twain, Whitman, and the Chicago naturalists but also with the rhythms and turns of mind of Yiddish speech and humor, with English picaresque novelists like Fielding and Smollett, and with European existentialists from Dostoevsky and Nietzsche to Sartre and Camus. Bellow also and revealingly belongs to a line of descent (and dissent) characterized by the intellectual comedy and expansive prose of writers like Rabelais, Burton, Sterne, and Joyce, creators of a style that encourages a writer to draw vigorously on many genres and the range of the world's learning. In America this encyclopedic and often comic or satiric style is most fully developed by the Ishmael of *Moby-Dick*, and although I am not arguing for *Moby-Dick* as a basically comic book—the opening sections probably are—even central chapters like "Fast-Fish and Loose-Fish" do contain a significant charge of intellectual comedy and metaphoric probing. In his three open-form books—*The Adventures of Augie March, Henderson the Rain King*, and *Herzog*—

Bellow has unpredictably reanimated the possibilities of this expansive style of ideological, comic prose fiction. What makes his achievement all the more remarkable is that Bellow knows about those facts of the present hostile to the values of individuality, spontaneity, and exuberance, values he and his predecessors celebrate in the very rhythms, abrupt leaps, and resonant allusions of their style.[1]

Because writers like Rabelais, Sterne, and Melville are only occasionally mentioned in discussions of Bellow, and because Bellow himself does not mention them in his remarks about the authors who have meant most to him, we are in danger of overlooking their significance for an understanding of his three open-form novels. I suspect that the energies, organizing strategies, and speculative range of predecessors like Rabelais, Melville, and Joyce have stimulated Bellow to comparable achievements in his own comic prose fictions. But I am not arguing for a direct and conscious influence. I am interested in relating Bellow to a style and in discussing some of the concerns and formal qualities of his books relevant to that style.

Bellow's European predecessors are often called baroque, and some of them comprise a genre Northrop Frye calls "the anatomy."[2] From Rabelais to the present, the creators of these encyclopedic comedies of knowledge have been interested in the diverse and shifting implications of experiences on which they do not force a unitary interpretation. Writers in this metaphoric style of comedy have responded independently to the challenge of contriving fictional forms to do justice to an outlook not easily amenable to fictional forms. The formal traits of a style are of course meaningful: They almost always have significant substantive implications.

---

[1] In his essays as well as novels, Bellow articulately expresses his sense of the present and his unwillingness to submit to either wasteland clichés or Philistine affirmations of America. See particularly "The Sealed Treasure," *TLS*, 1 July 1960, p. 14.

[2] See, e.g., Morris Croll, "The Baroque Style in Prose," *Studies in English Philology: A Miscellany in Honor of Frederick Klaeber*, ed. Kemp Malone (Minneapolis, Minn., 1929), pp. 427–456, and Northrop Frye, *The Anatomy of Criticism* (Princeton, N.J., 1957), pp. 303–314.

Each in his own way, writers like Sterne and Bellow have taken the risks of an open style in order to render fully their commitment to metaphor and learning, to the individual and the free, probing intelligence of an "I"; to render fully their sense that process is more important than conclusion—and that fixed conclusions may be desperately hard to find in an often baffling and inhospitable universe. Although the authors of works like *Pride and Prejudice*, *The Scarlet Letter*, or *The Sun Also Rises* are not indifferent to one or another of these values, a writer's choosing to pattern his fictions and render his sense of things in the open, expansive, metaphoric, and encyclopedic style of *Augie March* or *Moby-Dick* —this choice does reveal the intensity and degree of his intellectual and emotional commitments. By viewing Bellow in the context of a style that includes *Gargantua* and *Pantagruel, Tristram Shandy, Moby-Dick*, and *Ulysses*, we are thus in a position to remove misconceptions about a novelist often called picaresque and, even more important, to clarify some of the inner workings and dominant concerns of Bellow's fictions as they reflect on an American present and a cultural past.

In the prose and patterning of *Augie March*, for example, Bellow has responded to the challenge, particularly of Melville's style; and in Bellow's development from the taut prose of *Dangling Man* and the restraints and tight plot of *The Victim*, Melville has perhaps helped him find a personal voice and rhythm adequate to express independently his sense of the openness, difficulty, joy, and darkness of contemporary life in the context of all of human existence. Integral to the voice and idiom of *Augie March* are the characteristic heightened metaphors and accumulation of unlikely learned allusions—to Napoleon and the Directory, to Anchises and Olympian Zeus, to the fissures of Eryx and "the clearnesses of torrid Messina."[3] One result is that, just as Melville elevates his

---

[3] *The Adventures of Augie March* (New York, 1953), p. 201, and hereafter cited in the text. As he was completing *The Adventures of Augie March*, Bellow wrote in a review of Sholem Aleichem's *The Adventures of Mottel the Cantor's Son*, "The most ordinary Yiddish conversation is full of the grandest historical, mythological, and religious allusions. The Creation, the

crew of meanest mariners and renegades, Bellow, answering to the impulses of his own imagination and sense of humanity, endows his immigrant Chicago Jews with an aura of epic dignity and imperial magnitude.[4]

American writers like Melville or Bellow must inevitably deal with common men—sometimes they are gifted common men like Ishmael or Augie or Ahab—and with the possibilities and impossibilities of a democratic society that, in affirming the value of the ordinary, also makes it difficult to write about the exceptional, the extraordinary, or the imperial. The expansive metaphors and resonant allusions of a baroque style are well suited to overcome this liability, so that American writers have understandably been attracted to the rhythms, allusions, and openness of an originally European style. One danger, of course, is that too much will be demanded of heightened rhetoric; that out of democratic and personal loyalty, more will be claimed for an Einhorn or a Grandma Lausch than is actually realized in the dramatized figure; that as the qualities of our American present harden and tighten, the novelist who would celebrate the old values of spontaneity, openness, and plurality may sometimes have to strain the resources of his language and imagination. But the risks are worth running; for Bellow the tension has been an animating one; and the comedy,

---

Fall, the Flood, Egypt, Alexander, Titus, Napoleon, the Rothschilds, the sages, and the Laws may get into the discussion of an egg, a clothes-line, or a pair of pants" (*SRL*, XXXVI, 30 May 1953, 15). Yiddish conversation is basic, but as it emerges in the prose of *Augie March*, I suggest that the energies and range of allusion of writers like Melville, Sterne, Burton, and Rabelais have also helped Bellow create his unique version of their style. As I indicated above, however, I am not trying to establish direct influences.

[4] In so doing, Bellow deliberately opposes T. S. Eliot's hostility towards democracy, the ordinary man in a democracy, and the Jew in the modern world. Where Eliot puts the resources of his learning and culture to the uses of denigration—we need go no further than Bleistein and Sweeney—Bellow accepts the challenge and uses the power of his learning and culture to criticize and celebrate what the early Eliot was able only to dismiss. The first third of *Augie March* is designed partly to reverse Eliot's images of Sweeney and Bleistein. To take only one example, the handling of classical allusions in the scene with Einhorn and Augie at the whorehouse should be related to the handling of similar allusions in "Sweeney among the Nightingales."

idiom, speculative range, and lyric resonance, as in the first half of *Augie March*, are all part of the gain.

Old Testament patriarchs and Greek heroes, Persian generals and Renaissance princes, classical myths and French history—the array of allusions is apparently inconsistent, but cumulatively the references argue for the dignity of the present and our continuity with the past. Bellow reanimates history and the old mythologies by showing this Augie or Einhorn or Joe Gorman acting out the old patterns—of Croesus or Anchises, of the Dutch painting or unfathered Moses—and, against the odds of our anti-intellectualism and complacency, he unsnobbishly shows the continued relevance of the cultural and learned tradition by seeing Augie's entrance into Erie, Pennsylvania, under the pressure of his sense that "there is a darkness for everyone"—for old Eastern monarchs and Napoleon alike, for "the liquid morn of Greek friendship" and "mud-sprung . . . mankind" in their "heaving Calcutta midnight." Both the present and the past, the commonplace and the exalted, are thus affirmed; and in the act of recording the universal darkness, Bellow's energy of style drains the insight of despair. The accumulation of words, details, and allusions; the leap from Augie on the lam in Erie to references to Greek serenity juxtaposed with an American "barbarshop 'September Morn' " and the allusions to imperial personages and exotic places—this procedure, achieved again and again in *Augie March*, is in part Bellow's implicit tribute to his stylistic predecessors.

Because Augie is convincingly open, intelligent, and exploratory, moreover, Bellow like Melville or Sterne can have his narrator suddenly seize on a metaphor or a learned reference, and through an imaginative leap or a process of reasoning and metaphoric extension, Bellow's Augie like Melville's Ishmael can at any time probe in his own way to the deepest implication of an issue. For all the free, unpatterned diversity of allusion, certain strains also recur in these flashes of advice and generalization—about the city and its role in human civilization, for example, and about reality and imagination, larkiness and death, passivity and resistance. Like its stylistic predecessors, *The Adventures of Augie*

March, open as it is, is also unified by the recurrence of underlying concerns. Critics typically emphasize the picaresque elements in *The Adventures of Augie March*, rather than the style of open, ideological comedy that allows Bellow to incorporate and flexibly unify elements from diverse genres: picaresque, essayistic, and autobiographical. Critics who stress the picaresque bring to the novel a set of expectations that leads them needlessly to undervalue the ideological play and linguistic exuberance and to miss the kind of unity *Augie March* shares with books like *Tristram Shandy* and *Moby-Dick*.[5]

This unity is also achieved through an idiomatic, speculating voice whose presence in episode after episode testifies for the continuity and unity of the novel. *Augie March* belongs to a style whose rhythms, asymmetries, and abrupt leaps present man thinking as he speaks, and it is appropriate for a style that also celebrates the first person, the "I" as value, that the voice of the protagonist should have a more central role in the formal economy of the book than it has in most fictions. The vigorous, lowermiddle-class Yiddish idiom of Augie's Chicago is incongruously fused or juxtaposed with a learned vocabulary and theoretical concerns to generate the novel's comedy, ideological range, and unifying resonance.[6]

Because that voice is compelling, affectionate, and intelligent, however, there is always a danger for Bellow that the solid realities

---

[5] See, e.g., Gerald Jay Goldberg, "Life's Customer, Augie March," *Crit.*, III (1960), 15–18; Robert Alter, *Rogue's Progress: Studies in the Picaresque Novel* (Cambridge, Mass., 1964), pp. 121–125; John W. Aldridge, *In Search of Heresy* (New York, 1956), pp. 136–139; and Ihab Hassan, *Radical Innocence: Studies in the Contemporary American Novel* (Princeton, 1961), pp. 309–311.

[6] Hassan locates the central failure of the novel in a distinction between Augie's voice and Bellow's style, between Augie's picaresque simplicity and enthusiasm and Bellow's sense of greater complexity (pp. 309–311). This distinction between voice and style is less convincing if we see *Augie* as more closely related to *Tristram Shandy* and *Moby-Dick* than to *Joseph Andrews*, and if we attend (as Hassan, in his perceptive account does not) to the complex unifying functions of that voice. J. C. Levenson, "Bellow's Dangling Men," *Crit.*, III (1960), 3–14, discusses Bellow's fusion of Yiddish and American language, as does Leslie Fiedler, "Saul Bellow," *PrS*, XXXI (1957), 108.

of the outside world will become less interesting than the rhythms and speculations of his first-person protagonist. Grandma Lausch, for example, is more interesting in Augie's mind, in his language and speculation about her, than in the passages where she is speaking and acting on her own. In *Augie March* the problem becomes acute only in relation to Thea (and sometimes Stella). In *Herzog*, the monologues of letter and meditation are again lyrical, perceptive, and idiomatically resonant, but now they tend to overshadow the sections of dialogue and objective action. The Himmelstein and particularly the magistrate's court episodes show that Bellow can still succeed in getting outside his narrator's mind to present others convincingly, their suffering, comedy, and complexities. The world of the self, moreover, is admirable, and because Herzog is immensely curious and responsive, the world of the self is also capacious. Nonetheless, the world a dialogue implies—an objective world filled with other selves rendered on their own terms—in his most recent book Bellow finds it harder to present the diversities and solidities of this world than he does the magnificent monologues of the self. Herzog knows he "must play the instrument I've got," and he plays it superbly. It is an instrument predecessors like Sterne and Melville had to master, and Bellow's difficulties as well as triumphs reflect not only on his personal problem with dialogue but also on the general problem, particularly acute in recent literature, of getting outside the mind and rendering a solid external world, a problem common to the creators of a shared style of speculative comedy.

More than ordinary prose fictions, this style is deeply rooted in the essayistic individuality of writers like Montaigne and Burton. But transferred to prose fiction, a compelling individual voice can make it difficult for a writer who wants to render an outside world. In *Augie March* and *Herzog* Bellow's failures and successes with dialogue, letters, and resonant monologues are a telling index of the formal possibilities and demands of an individualistic, comic style.

Whatever the liabilities, however, this open style is a perfect vehicle for the testing, exploring, and probing Bellow wants to subject his protagonists to. In *The Adventures of Augie March* (to concentrate on the earlier novel) Bellow, without coming to fixed conclusions, can have Augie try out different roles and put his easygoing nature and hopeful ideas to the test of different situations. Augie's accepting nature is both a formal necessity—it allows the diversity of episode Bellow wants—and also a theoretical concern.[7] All that Augie's reality instructors have to teach him is necessary, but through an act of faith on Bellow's part, Augie is also endowed with a core of integrity, opposition, and decency that will not allow him to be taken over or pushed beyond a certain point.

In the process of testing and affirming his protagonist, Bellow, like Rabelais and Sterne, both flexibly patterns his fiction and engages with issues ranging from the personal to the social (and beyond). Augie is thus made to try out different roles in a series of experiments which illuminate, particularize, celebrate, and criticize diverse strata of American society, and at the same time help to clarify Augie's identity. Augie, responsive and finally independent, pays a price for the way he is; and to find out fully who he is, he also pays a price. The society within which Augie functions is imagined as affluent and open: Because of the Renlings and Magnuses, even Bellow's 1930s, for example, reflect post-World War II prosperity, and the openness is a claim, an act of faith equivalent to the act of faith in Augie's nature. Within this imagined society and in the context of competing, deterministic, and unhopeful modern ideologies, Bellow imagines the difficulties and possibilities of creating an integral self, and in the process he shows what an American society might possibly offer in the way of challenge, beauty, plurality, and energy. He does not finally define a national identity any more than he does a personal identity, but Bellow does suggest valued characteristics.

He does it especially well in the costumes and liberated idiom he

---

[7] For a complementary view of the formal implications of Augie's nature, see Frederick Hoffman, "The Fool of Experience: Saul Bellow's Fiction," *Contemporary American Novelists*, ed. Harry T. Moore (Carbondale, Ill., 1964), p. 83.

imagines for Augie's roles, so that like his stylistic predecessors, Bellow not only fuses a concern for personal identity, social possibility, and philosophic theory but he also delights in showing his comic protagonist "in the shoeshine seat above the green tables, in a hat with diamond airholes cut in it and decorated with brass kiss-me pins and Al Smith buttons, in sneakers and Mohawk sweat-shirt," or, a little older, "in the perfect clothes we wore, of sporting hound's tooth or brown Harris tweed, carrying field glasses from the shop. . . . I was too much engaged with feeling this raiment on me, the closeness of good cloth to my body, or with thoughts of the clock-green Tyrolean brush in my hat and splendor of British shoes, to be able to see Renling as I did see him later." Because Augie can unsnobbishly respond to the appeal of American materialism, cash, and showiness, his criticisms—particularly by way of Simon and the crackup and coalyard of despair scenes—are all the more convincing.

Augie's later involvement on the peripheries of immense American prosperity is designed to show him related to but still detached from some of the dominant materialistic impulses of American culture (as part of the same pattern, he becomes engaged to but does not marry Lucy Magnus). Augie's costume at the end is his Citroën, sunglasses, and the dipping European landscape, emblem of distance from America but also a sign of Augie's American affluence that can afford it all. The image of the sea wastes beyond Normandy, however—"the ancient water," "wolf gray" and "savage," "this line of white which was like eternity opening up right beside destruction of the modern world"—this recreating of the vision of "The Whiteness of the Whale" complicates and universalizes the perspective, provides the counterpoint which makes fully meaningful the celebration of a difficult laughter, and gives the authority of a strong final passage to the consistently developed motif of wreck, destruction, and death. Bellow has an acute sense of trouble, pain, and difficulty that he does not want to give in to, that he does not want to become dominant. Opposed to his sense of darkness, nightmare, and breakdown is his commitment to the possibility of living vigorously, humorously, and sensually, fully aware of a range of intellectual and physical matters. The humor and the energy of style function to make the darkness bearable.

In his own version of a style that includes *Tristram Shandy* and *Moby-Dick*, Bellow thus acknowledges the claims of both the dark and the light, and he organizes his fiction around the tension between them. Like many of his stylistic predecessors, Bellow's apparently casual organization is deceptive, since he defines his central concerns and the very structure of his novels by means of unobtrusive and frequently convincing sequences and symbols.[8] *Augie March*, for example, is organized partly by the previously mentioned images of disaster. They provide the counterpoint to Augie's larkiness and his tendency to somehow hopeful views of man and history. Augie repeatedly hears "that I didn't have the profounder knowledge of life, that I didn't know its damage or its suffering or its stupendous ecstasies and glories." Just as he later does in *Herzog*, Bellow arranges *The Adventures of Augie March* so that his protagonist can find out. Augie is continually stripped down to his elements and reclothed in new guises; or from deaths and disasters—the death of Winnie and the exile and later death of Grandma Lausch; the Commissioner's death, Einhorn's failure, and the Crash; Mimi's choice-affirming abortion on New Year's Day; the car crashes, the failure in Mexico, and the final sea wreck—he either goes on to new births or learns to acknowledge and accept loss, death, and decay as the condition of growth, change, and hopefully development; or as the hard facts the imagination must acknowledge and triumph over. Against the episodes of danger, disaster, pain, rain, darkness, and death—those at the end of episodes help define the structure of *Augie March*—Bellow plays the scenes of joy or love: hence the importance of the initiation scene with Einhorn and the prostitute, or such lyric episodes as Augie's early fascination with Esther Fenchel at the resort.

Like other works in its style, from *Tristram Shandy* to the present, a central concern is understandably the process of creating

---

[8] See, e.g., Mark Schorer, "A Book of Yes and No," *HudR*, VII (1954), 137, and Robert Penn Warren, "Man with No Commitments," *New Republic*, CXXIX (2 Nov. 1953), 22.

the book and creating a self, a concern that indispensably speaks for life and freedom against the threat of death, wrecks, and determinisms. Like earlier "travelers," Augie, "by blow of a traveling man" and a "traveling man" himself, is busy "giving this account of myself that reality comes from and was not just at the mercy." The fused syntax emphasizes as the sources of "reality" both the self and the act of creating the book, "of giving an account" in prose as well as in the world. History, then, is inevitably one of Augie's major antagonists, particularly as it involves the "reality" of historical determinism. Bellow accepts the challenge of time and of his times by organizing his novel partly around a parallel between the stages in Augie's life and that of the nation—the twenties, the Crash, the politics of the thirties, World War II, post-War prosperity and problems—such that Augie's history becomes a representative history, and a testimony that the creating person is not "just at the mercy."[9] The fact that Bellow has more difficulty with the public episodes than with the speculative and ideological passages—Augie as a labor organizer, for example, is more melodramatic than socially revealing, and the Trotsky episode is more a tribute to Bellow's will than to his imagination—this weakness suggests the difficulty postwar writers have repeatedly faced in making the politics of the thirties come alive. Through the course of *Augie March*, the protagonist's impulse simultaneously to engage in history, to create a book, and to affirm the free individual is nonetheless cumulatively realized.

Augie's quest for a worthwhile fate thus helps to organize *The Adventures of Augie March*. Augie's quest, which in part governs the sequence of episodes, is another version of the grand old questions that have preoccupied Bellow from *Dangling Man* on: " 'How should a good man live; what ought he to do?' "[10] Augie's emphasis on fate raises the issues of responsibility and freedom in the face of the powerful, determining forces that try a man. In *The Adventures of Augie March*, this perennial sense of life, not un-

---

[9] Bellow perfects this parallel between the protagonist and his period in *Seize the Day*.

[10] *Dangling Man* (New York, 1944, 1965), p. 22.

known in the worlds of *Tristram Shandy* and *Moby-Dick*, is made integral to the twentieth century because the threat of historical determinism is one major antagonist. In the final third of the novel, the issue of psychological determinism is raised as another major antagonist, but it is not until *Herzog* that Bellow succeeds in making this issue come alive in the structure and substance of his fiction. Although it does not have the status of a theoretical determinism, it is an index of the American quality of *The Adventures of Augie March* that a third major antagonist is a free-swinging, acquisitive materialism. Bellow's ambivalence toward this pressure of American society is symbolized in the figure of Simon, another of the powerful, financially successful brothers or fathers in Bellow's fiction who testify that the protagonist is both related to and in tension with his society.

To return to our immediate concern, another of Bellow's most pronounced characteristics—his persistent interest in both the concretely real and the symbolically abstract—also connects him with earlier creators of an open style that allows a writer freely to express both impulses. Until the trip to Mexico, *The Adventures of Augie March*, for example, is a naturalistic-symbolic novel, and the weighting of the "realistic" and "symbolic" is similar to that in the opening twenty-two chapters in *Moby-Dick*. To effect the shift in emphasis Melville achieved gradually through the cetological chapters, Bellow creates a symbolic-naturalistic entry into a primitive and ritualistic world. Although the Mexican episode is generally acknowledged as a failure—Augie's talk about love, for example, is more convincing than anything in the dramatized relation with Thea—the attempt is necessary and valuable, and is fully validated by *Henderson the Rain King*. *Augie March*, however, never completely recovers its earlier sureness of focus.

Although the rhythm of the novel is slightly broken, the pace and patterning are not at all casual. We have seen that *The Adventures of Augie March* is organized partly around the tension between the sense of joy and freedom and that of death and determinism, partly around the parallels between Augie's history and identity and that of the nation, partly around the continuity of an idiomatic, speculating voice and the recurrence of generalizing theoretical concerns and passsages—on history and a creating self, reality and imagination, determinism and joy—and the novel is also organized partly around the shift from the more naturalistic to the more symbolic and, after the Mexican episode, the gradually accelerating increase in the abstractness of Augie's concerns and in the "symbolic" charge of nonetheless comic and "naturalistic" characters and episodes. To reinforce and be reinforced by the social and historical parallels, Augie moves from the mountains of Mexico to the cities of Chicago and New York (with a digression to Georgie's pastoral locale) to the elemental sea and a Jasperian shipwreck. Along the way Augie meets truth-tellers and ideologues —Kayo, Padilla, Mintouchian, and Basteshaw—and Bellow, in comic and existentialist forms, recreates the world-ranging and encyclopedic quest that has been the mark of a style from Rabelais through Melville to his own most recent achievements. Bellow's willingness to take scientific theory into account, to bring symbol and imagination to the test of science, makes for a particularly close bond with his predecessors, from Rabelais and Burton to the present, and so does his fusing of comedy and tragedy, idiom and speculation, social concerns and personal fates. Unlike Melville's Ishmael, at the end Bellow's Augie is not an orphan in the universe, but the *Les Orphelines* episode shows that he is not a father, either; and although he is married to his star and beauty, he is also likely to be betrayed. Until the very end, Bellow thus sustains the sense of comedy, affirmation, and openness—to desolation as well as to joy.

Herzog suggests how fully Bellow has mastered his own version of an open style of ideological comedy. Like his predecessors, he has always had an impulse toward the archaic literary forms this style both represents and allows a writer to assimilate. In *Augie March*, this open style accommodates picaresque, essayistic, autobiographical, and visionary elements; in *Henderson*, in addition to the visionary, the elements of folktale, anthropology, jokebook, and Rabelaisian philosophic quest. One of Bellow's remarkable achievements, and an index to his status as perhaps our finest living novelist, is that he has continued to imagine new ways of writing ideological novels, that he has successfully responded to the difficult challenge of inventing new ways of getting it said.

Bellow began his career with an independent version of the existentialist journal as novel, on the pattern of *Nausea, The Notebooks of Malte Laurids Brigge*, and *Notes from the Underground*. In *Herzog* he has gone beyond and behind the fiction of notes to the self merging with present and remembered action as the occasion for analysis and commentary. Although the fiction of the journal is in the background of *Herzog*, what is more to the point is that Bellow has reanimated the epistolary novel. Just as in *Augie March* he explored the twentieth-century possibilities of the picaresque, a form intimately associated with the eighteenth-century novel, so in *Herzog* he has made the eighteenth-century novelistic convention of letter writing the vehicle for a flexible, comic probing of an encyclopedic array of learned, personal, and social issues. The freely interpolated letters as a vehicle for comedy and ideas constitute one of the most brilliant technical inventions in postwar fiction. They allow Bellow the speculative freedom of Melville's cetological chapters and they also allow him simultaneously to characterize his intellectually powerful, unstable protagonist. The fact that the letters are not sent also contrasts significantly with the eighteenth-century epistolary novel and thus helps to characterize the twentieth century by way of the obsessive modern concern with a failure of communication, a strain *Herzog* both embodies and resists.

The satire that is one expression of *Herzog*'s power also relates the book to Bellow's stylistic predecessors. In a work as insistently twentieth century as *Herzog*, the vignettes of Valentine Gersbach, Madeleine and Shapiro are, unexpectedly, formalized satiric portraits which expose the pretensions, clichés, and fakery of the modern American literary intellectual in Bellow's version of *Mac Flecknoe* and *The Dunciad*.[11] Through his control of pace and

---

[11] Herzog reads Dryden and Pope in his bathroom, and Pope's line, "I am His Highness' dog at Kew" is one of the self-deprecatory refrains of this "broken-down monarch" (pp. 121, 311). The other half of the couplet—

climax, of moral standard and intellectual incongruity, of personal gesture and physical characteristic, Bellow, like Dryden and Pope before him, transforms personal animosity into satiric art. Because he is working in an open style which allows a writer to assimilate elements from many genres, Bellow, through his reanimating of eighteenth-century epistolary conventions and the strategies of seventeenth- and eighteenth-century satire, can embody his interest in the Enlightenment in the very texture of his work, as well as through the more obvious intellectual affinities: *The State of Nature in 17th and 18th Century English and French Political Philosophy* (the title of Herzog's doctoral dissertation) and the pervasive interest in the Enlightenment as the cornerstone of modern liberal, scientific, and democratic thought and the antagonist for those who oppose these tendencies in modern civilization.

In addition to the satire and the diverse formal elements, Bellow's comedy of knowledge is furthered by *Herzog*'s idiom, the resonance and humor of the letters and learning, and the affirmation of self and intellect, particularly in moments of exposure or wry self-deprecation. Herzog, "part-time visionary, cheerful, tragical mammal" (p. 258), earns his right to his qualified affirmations. Dressed in his blue blazer, Italian pants, and straw hat, the vaudeville costume of American affluence, Herzog suffers and speculates. Like Tristram Shandy pursued through France by death, Herzog ranges the timeless universe of the mind pursued by the disasters of his life and the threat of death. In one of Bellow's most deeply felt and recurring patterns, Moses, a patriarch deprived of his closest ties—wife, child, friend—is stripped of his protections and is made to confront the basic facts of his humanity and his existence under the pressure of threatening modern ideologies. The gradual and intricate process of confrontation and full acknowledgment to establish the possibility of renewal for the self and all

---

"Pray tell me, Sir, whose dog are you?"—suggests that Herzog is perfectly capable of using satire to fight back. Simkin, a name from *Mac Flecknoe* (1. 81), reappears as a character in *Herzog*; and the play on monarchy, which both elevates and satirizes Gersbach, perhaps echoes the opening of Dryden's poem.

of existence—this process helps to organize *Herzog*. The rhythms of depth psychology and therapy, a major twentieth-century contribution to the world of ideas, are thus basic to the organization of *Herzog*, so that the anticipations in *Augie March* are at last fulfilled.

Also integral to the structure of *Herzog* is the free-ranging theorizing of the letters and sketches of Herzog's projected books. The open form of the novel and the process of liberating confrontation are furthered by the periodic intrusions into the narrative present of episodes from Herzog's past; and the flexibly patterned speculation of the letters puts Herzog's wrecks and resonant endurance into a universal perspective. This "educated Jewish gentleman" becomes a sort of twentieth-century Everyman, and his mind becomes the focus for some of the major conflicts of modern thought. For the last decade and a half Bellow has been concerned about the life-denying dangers and resonant possibilities of what his Gooley MacDowell calls "the life of thought."[12] Bellow has accordingly developed strategies that express his commitment to both "the life of thought" and the life of common humanity. He subtly fuses Yiddish idiom and turns of speech with speculative concerns and a learned vocabulary, for example, and he creates protagonists like Herzog who are unpretentiously *schlemiels* and *schlimazls* and genuinely philosophical fools, protagonists related to Gimpel the fool as well as to Tristram Shandy.[13] Herzog as modern intellectual and representative of common humanity is particularly sensitive to those major strains in twentieth-century thought involving the abuses of a fashionable "Wasteland outlook" and the unearned *Angst* of literary existentialists, with their "cheap mental stimulants of Alienation, the cant and rant of pipsqueaks about Inauthenticity and Forlornness." To reinforce (and be reinforced by) the letters, he contrives sequences and recognitions—the suggestively juxtaposed scenes of intellectual comedy centering

---

[12] "Address by Gooley MacDowell to the Hasbeens Club of Chicago," *HudR*, IV (1951), 227.

[13] Goldberg, "Life's Customer, Augie March," twenty comments on the *schlemiel* and *schlimazl* in *Augie March*.

on Shapiro and Himmelstein, for example—so that he can both expose the clichés and acknowledge the grim truth as he sees it, even as he unobtrusively unifies his narrative, engages with everyday reality, and sustains the open form he values.

As in earlier versions of Bellow's style of ideological comedy, the patterning of scenes and letters, of past and present, of idea and action, of the personal and public—this patterning is meaningful, not simply arbitrary and chaotic. Take the strategy of rapidly juxtaposing fragments of letters on an unpredictable range of subjects and in a variety of tones. A few lines of personal reminiscence to and about Cousin Asher, in Beersheba, for example, are abruptly juxtaposed with an informed, impersonal fragment of a letter to the president on taxes, unemployment, and street gangs (p. 49). The implausibility of the scholarly tone Herzog takes with the president combines with the plausibility of the letter's content to generate an intellectual comedy that then unexpectedly leaps to a learned quip about Heidegger. Herzog repeatedly expresses his skepticism of fashionable existentialist abstractions, here by taking Heidegger's formula literally and asking of "the fall into the quotidian": "When did this fall occur? Where were we standing when it happened?" (p. 49).

Herzog, a vaudevillian of the mind, immediately experiments with a letter to a former classmate. The unexpected comic idiom—"Dear Emmett, I saw you on television making a damn fool of yourself"—then changes into the brilliant and revised letter to *The New York Times* on the "Philosophy of Risk with regard to radioactivity" (p. 50). Herzog interrupts the letter with apparently random thoughts of the innocence of remembered scenes with his children and the first of the nursery rhymes which gently come to symbolize his desire for innocence. When he abruptly returns to the letter and the general issue, "the power to tamper with the genetic foundations of life" (p. 52), the end of the letter has thus acquired a significant depth of meaning, because the abstract, public claims—they are strongly argued, sometimes with unpretentious comic incongruity—are now rooted also in Herzog's personal concern for his own children, whose immediate delight in life has

just been shown. The sheer variety and incongruity of such sequences—cousin Asher, the president, Heidegger, Strawforth,
radioactive poisoning, digressions on his children, De Toqueville,
and the non-Marxist connotation of "bourgeois"—all further the
openness and comedy of Bellow's style and flexibly contribute to
Herzog's involvement in personal and universal meanings. Any
sequence, it might be argued, can be made to sound meaningful—
and, in *Herzog*, many of them are in fact significant.

Like its stylistic predecessors, *Herzog* may nonetheless be mis-
understood and undervalued because of its open form. Although it
would be misleading to argue that it is a tightly organized book,
Herzog, like *Tristram Shandy, Moby-Dick*, and *Augie March*, does
have a unique and unexpected style of coherence and comedy. It is
helpful to see that the idiomatic comedy and speculation of Herzog's letters and theorizing are one major force of unity and generalization; that the total pattern of confrontation, acknowledgment, and potential liberation and renewal is another; and that the
Himmelstein and other sharply dramatized episodes from Herzog's
immediate and more remote past are a third. To further our understanding of *Herzog*'s open form, we must consider the role of the
magistrate's court scene, the central and most powerful of the
dramatized episodes.

In it all of the negations about human nature and modern existence, negations Herzog has resisted on principle, are driven into
the open and into the depths of his self. The cases become progres-
sively more intense and drive home the facts of human misery,
perversity, complexity, complicity, and brute cruelty. At the end,
the unintellectualized nausea and the frightening figure from the
mind—the accusing, maimed, cane-carrying woman—thus derive
not from books but from an immediately rendered experience of
common life, one of Bellow's major independent acknowledgments
of wasteland and existentialist insights.[14] Symbolically situated in
a police court to dramatize coldly the "justice" of modern civiliza-

---

[14] The magistrate's court scene is also particularly close to Whitman in its
accumulation of American faces and social classes and in its willingness to
deal with ordinarily suppressed horrors and sexual abuses.

tion and the real world, this urban scene is one source of the power and thus one center of the structure of *Herzog*.

The magistrate's court episode is vital to Bellow's most recent achievement of that flexible patterning characteristic of his style, since the narrative of Herzog's personal fate and particularly the generalizing letters illuminate and are illuminated by this scene and its revelations. Thereafter the concern with death and origins—personal and universal—has a solid grounding, and *Herzog* meaningfully progresses to the protagonist's encounter with his own past, his pursuit of personal, vengeful justice, and the continuing influence and death of his father. Juxtaposing these scenes from Herzog's distant past with his meeting with young June and the crash, far from being arbitrary, shows the continuity of determining characteristics, of the sins and traits of the father inevitably informing the acts of the son. But although Herzog must act out the old patterns, the action itself—and Herzog's insight and final acceptance even of Madeleine and Gersbach—helps to liberate him from bondage to his hatred, his compulsions, and his past.

True to the precarious affirmations and painful recognitions of the novel, the death of the father is juxtaposed with the recurring images of flowering roses and magnolias, the promise of June, and the symbol, reminiscent of Melville and Dreiser, of the hag fish, the sting ray, and the turtle, "the beaked head lazy, the eyes with aeons of indifference" (p. 281). This symbol generalizes the more powerful magistrate's court scene onto a cosmic scale and provides the impelling backdrop for Herzog's own crash and involvement with the law. Herzog has changed his clothes, but he is still driving his teal-blue Falcon, explicitly an embodiment of "his position in the scale of prerogatives—of affluence, of insolence, of untruth, if you like" (p. 243). The crash, then, also bears on the general issue of affluence. In this apparently random sequence, Bellow has thus meaningfully rendered the forces of reality and determinism —in the universe, in society, in human nature, and in Herzog's personal past. Although these sequences of reminiscence and immediate actuality do not have the lyric resonance of the early episodes in *Augie March*, as in *The Adventures of Augie March*, opposed to the energies of reality and determinism are the trans-forming powers of the imagination, speculation, acceptance, and—an advance beyond *Augie March*—humility. The contrast between the pastoral and the urban, anticipated in the earlier novels and carried much further in *Herzog*, develops this opposition and con-tributes to the organization of the novel.

Appropriately for a modern ideological comedy, the pastoral motif is handled with proper irony—the remains of father Her-zog's inheritance have gone into the broken-down house and over-grown land, and Ludeyville in the Berkshires is satirically named and is associated with the values of the WASP establishment. Al-though Herzog characteristically concludes the Himmelstein epi-sode, for example, with images of the pastoral, innocence, and God, expressive of his impulse toward purity and affirmation, in this scene and throughout the novel he also and characteristically opposes these images to his sense of a brutalized or decayed waste-land, a cruel reality, and the threat of death. Still, the flowers grow, the land is peaceful at the end, and Herzog has partially repaired his house. To ship the piano will be ridiculously expensive and perhaps like the letters it will not be sent. But the piano is now green, some harmony is possible, and the letters have been written. Bellow's imagination has long been impelled toward a concluding, universalizing landscape, away from the city: the eternity of white sea in *Augie*; the eternity of Arctic white and silence in *Henderson*. At the end of *Herzog* the silence is there again, again nothing is certain or finally resolved, but the pastoral landscape does contrast with the earlier vistas from "The Whiteness of the Whale."

In the concluding sequences of the novel, the letters to (and about) Kierkegaard, Nietzsche, and God are particularly signifi-cant. Supported and tested by his personal experience, Herzog is now able to move from the grim ideas of the courtroom scene—"not God is dead" but, in a turn characteristic of his ideological comedy, "Death is God" (p. 290)—to a rejection of the modern celebration of suffering juxtaposed with his own provisional ac-ceptance of Nietzsche on the ennobling power of pain (pp. 316–319). Herzog's crucial qualification is that we must survive.

In this concluding series of "weirdly tranquil," "radiant" (p. 2) insights, Bellow's style receives one of its most intricate, idiomatically comic, and finally affirmative embodiments. Herzog as survivor in the countryside opens himself to God, recognizes and does not suppress his doubts and failings, and momentarily accepts God, self, and humanity.

Because these limited affirmations are rooted in a fully developed experience and expression of pain and disbelief, *Herzog* is basically at odds with suburban complacencies and religiosity. Herzog's own suffering, for example, is convincing testimony for his reservations about the theoretical value of suffering. His repeated acknowledgments, moreover, through the final letter to Morgenfruh—"It sounds bad, Morgenfruh, for the optimists, for the lenient hopeful view of human nature" (p. 320)—help him say yes and—through the idiomatic, irreverent comedy—also no to the cruelty, lust, and destructiveness of human nature and the modern world.

Throughout the novel, in fact, Bellow has answered to the energies and openness of stylistic predecessors like Rabelais, Melville, and Joyce to help him once again do justice to his complex sense of modern existence, an awareness that has once again impelled him to risk difficult acknowledgments, affirmations, and combinations. What emerges in the course of *Herzog*—the comedy, suffering, and encyclopedic speculation; the concern for personal fates, social facts, and cosmic issues; the interest in observed actuality and abstract symbol; the tension between a cruel, deterministic reality and the impulse toward creative freedom and joy; the precarious reliance on metaphoric probing and an open form—all suggest that against great odds, both public and personal, Bellow has once again succeeded in reanimating a style of intellectual comedy that illuminates and celebrates the present even as it connects us and Bellow with some of the most powerful imaginations of the past.

EARL ROVIT

Earl Rovit, who is professor of English at the City College of New York, is both a novelist and critic. In addition to his three novels, he has published studies of Ernest Hemingway and Elizabeth Madox Roberts, and has edited the *Twentieth-Century Views* volume of critical essays on Saul Bellow.

JEWISH HUMOR AND AMERICAN LIFE

Quite clearly, the only observer who would be qualified to comment on the complicated relationship of Jewish humor to contemporary American life would be an American Jew with a superb sense of humor, a delicate comprehension of the American character in its variegated historical metamorphoses, and a profound intuition of those precipices of meaning where humor and faith shade off into the macabre, the pathological, the surreal, and the banal. Such a man would also have to possess in abundance that left-handed gift of the gods that is called in Yiddish *chutzpah*—a misfortune of temperament for which the Greek term *hubris* is, at best, a somewhat weak and mollycoddled approximation. I have waited in vain for such an observer to appear. Perhaps he became garroted on the Nietzschean tightrope that is supposed to span the primordial abyss. Or, more likely, he married the daughter of a wealthy businessman and put his childish toys away. At any rate, I can wait no longer for him. Pride forces me to offer myself in his place as a voluntary sacrifice of scholarly immolation. And if certain of my observations are in some ways faulty or excessively

Reprinted from *The American Scholar*, Volume 36, Number 2, Spring 1967. Copyright © 1967 by the United Chapters of Phi Beta Kappa. By permission of the publishers.

partial, I console myself with the wise aphorism of a learned Detroit rabbi: "A Cadillac has four wheels and it stumbles."

Nor will it be a digression to confess at the outset that my understanding of American-Jewish life has been constantly confused by a recurrent illusion that I keep shedding like a serpent's skin, only to regrow in a dark thoughtless time. As a young boy, cradled like a jellied egg in the security of my family, I knew that whatever unpleasantness might lurk in the external Gentile world, all Jews, at least, were good, intelligent, and humorous. My poor egg was cracked years and years ago, and I learned that like everyone else, Jews were all kinds of things—not necessarily good, intelligent, and humorous merely because they were born as Jews. And yet an early illusion refuses to die easily; it submerges itself to thrash around in the soup of one's emotions like a fish that is all energetic tail. It stirs the current on which our thoughts will flow and it provides the turbulence by which we measure our dissatisfactions with life and ourselves.

The good, the intelligent, and the humorous; a significant triad, no? Not, you will notice, the good, the true, and the beautiful, which is the average American's traditional birthright as a foundling of the Romantic Revolution. There is a subtle but far-reaching difference here between these triads. Keats's exhortation is the expression of a profoundly Gentile faith—Christian and Greek, Catholic and Protestant, certainly sublime, but patently unacceptable to Job or Spinoza, to Freud or Kafka. The good, the intelligent, and the humorous—this is something else, something more acerb, more rational, more profane, less democratic, but, I think, more grounded in what is humanly possible. What I think of as the Jewish triad swings away from an abstract transcendental system of values to those concrete qualities of personality that can be learned or painfully acquired. It shifts its locus from the divine realms of spirit to character, from implacable standards to human modes of behavior, from the resonances of spontaneous revelation where all men are potential saints to earthbound strategies of life survival. I cannot find truth in the twentieth century, but I can try to cultivate my intelligence in order to discern how little I know. I cannot fashion a beautiful life in a world that my reason insists is ugly, but I can learn to laugh. I can even learn that, under special circumstances, laughter may be a form of prayer, certainly no less efficacious than the humorless variety, and probably emanating from the same source. And, indeed, I doubt that my triad is peculiar to me. Whether it is a larger European inheritance (one thinks of Kierkegaard, of Dostoevsky) or a quasi-Jewish importation to American life, I believe that I am nowhere more a child of my time than in my adherence to this triangular faith.

Alas, all Jews are not, like myself, good, intelligent, and humorous, but in recent years there has been increasing comment on an emergent quality in American life that is purported to be a product of Jewishness—that is, that intangible pungency of atmosphere that is rather nebulously referred to as "Jewish humor." What a quixotic label that is! It pretends to describe in sober sociological tones, but it points nowhere and everywhere. Is there such a thing as The American Jew anyway? Some characterological amalgam of Williamsburg Hasidic and Shaker Heights Unitarian, Orthodox and atheist, passionate secularist of innumerable civic meetings and the assimilatedly indifferent? What monstrous portmanteau word could be fixed on such a creature? Only the Messiah could take such a form. And, despair added to despair, what is humor? (What is humor? Humor is when you laugh. And when do you laugh? You laugh when you don't cry. And what is Jewish humor? You laugh while you cry a little.) No, this is good enough for Sholem Aleichem or *The Fiddler on the Roof* perhaps, but too disingenuous for a people that must constantly remember six million of its slaughtered dead.

Jewish humor disembarked in America at Ellis Island with the immigrational waves of East European Jewry between 1880 and 1915. In its Ur-form it was a product of *shtetl*-life, intransigently Yiddish, severely defined by the accumulated defense mechanisms of survival in a tightly interlocked communal system where the family was not only the central unit, but the unit that was elastically expandable to encompass the entire community. "The Children of Israel" was more than a biblical epithet. It was a phrase of kinship (Israel's children) and a severe sociological definition. Outside the large family was an alien life—a shark-infested multi-Protestant and Catholic water inherently or potentially hostile to Jewish life. Alien food, alien women, alien customs, alien ideals. Outside the movable *shtetl* nothing was exactly kosher. One's neighbors, one's government, the very culture within which one breathed—these operated by motives that were different and hence dangerous. After all, the Jewish immigrants had been conditioned for centuries by pogrom and persecution to some form of ghetto life. Their relationship to the outside world had been constrained to a narrowly restricted buying-and-selling connection with their neighbors, and everyone knows that a customer is always a secret enemy who must be outwitted by cunning, flattery, and veiled intimidation—that is, by all the talents of the mind when the mind is unaccompanied by force. The initial Jewish adaptation to the American scene was a naïve attempt to re-create the old conditions of city life in this baffling New World. And Jewish humor remained defensive and private, a reserve for one's own bitter amusement in the homely curses muttered under the breath in Yiddish that the customer or employer couldn't possibly understand. "Of course, Mrs. Morgan—(You should bury your head in the earth like an onion.)—But naturally, you're absolutely right—(You should only swell up like a mountain.)"

But America is a vast country and even the newly landed immigrants found themselves possessed of the volatile mobility of the Russian boyars. The closed *shtetl*-system was doomed from the beginning by the awesome capacity of American life to absorb all of its citizens—at least, its white citizens—and to offer them undreamed-of prosperity. The religious training in Talmud Torah could not compete with a compulsory system of free mass education and open libraries. The synagogues and benevolent societies were unable to cope with a phenomenally rising standard of living and an equally phenomenal rise in religious indifference. The years preceding and immediately following World War I were years of great intellectual ferment. The slogans of emancipation were thick in the air and economic prosperity promised to translate the airy slogans into hard reality. Nor is it an insignificant fact that the most articulate American Jews of the first part of the twentieth century—the men who came to control the ideological policies of the major Yiddish newspapers and the burgeoning trade unions—tended to be Socialists and/or Zionists. Neither position gave more than short shrift to the orthodoxies of communal ritual life. Both positions labored for the establishment of a Promised Land and both insisted on political-empirical means in arriving at their goals. The age-old pieties of family worship had little place in the fiery dreams that exerted a tremendous weight of influence on the entire American Jewish community.

Hence, after World War I and the Russian Revolution, the typical American Jew was unwittingly caught up in a foredoomed struggle between his traditional communal insularity and the alluring fluidity of the outside world. Almost in spite of himself (and frequently burdened by a bad conscience), he became committed to seeking a better material life for himself and his children, doubtless without fully realizing that the price he would pay would be the virtual loss of his traditions and his religious identity. It is, after all, an old American story. While his Irish-American neighbors found a congenial strategy of upward movement in consolidating the political power of the urban communities in which they lived, the Jew resorted to his experience in merchandising (a term that can extend from door-to-door peddling to the amassing of great fortunes in retailing and wholesaling), as well as to the individual upward thrust of education. No, all Jews are not intelligent, but American Jews had both a heritage of adherence to the charisma of education and a fantastic internal pressure to take advantage of the free public school system that was miraculously open to them. If they were, as they had been called, "The People of the Book," they would use books to secure a good life for themselves. One by one the learned professions grudgingly opened their restricted quotas to the avalanche of pale-faced, worn-out at thirty, emancipated Jews who had qualified to become dentists, doctors, lawyers, university professors. "My son, the doctor," is not just a Jewish joke; it is close to being a Jewish disease, contagious like the measles, but not so easily quarantinable.

But there exists in all groups of people an urge not only to improve their material and individual conditions, but also to impress their indigenous stamp on the larger life that surrounds them. And this is especially true when that stamp of group identity is at the point of becoming a nostalgic reminiscence. At least this has usually been so in America. Politics was by and large a closed arena to the Jew—except in New York City and in such astonishing aridities as Arizona where a man of Jewish ancestry can be no more curious or Jewish than the ubiquitous cactus. The bastions of finance were securely closed to the Jew. From the professions of law and medicine, little direct influence could be exerted on the tempo and color of American life. But the entertainment industry was something else, and while there was spirited competition from the waggish Irish, the Jewish entertainer invaded vaudeville before World War I, and by 1950 had almost saturated radio, television, and the movies. From the old burlesque circuits, from Potash and Perlmutter and "Cohen on the Telephone," through the great Broadway age of Jolson, Cantor, Irving Berlin, Fannie Brice, and the Gershwins, through the thirties and forties of the Marx Brothers, Milton Berle, Danny Kaye, Jack Benny, et cetera, the American Jew came to possess a sizable leasehold on popular American comic entertainment.

The situations and characters they exploited were too richly idiosyncratic to be simply categorized, but distinct traces of the older Yiddish *shtetl*-sources can still be seen in some of the stock types that were seized upon and endlessly refurbished. The *schlemiel*, the *schnorrer*, infinite combinations of the two, and a type generally known in the old Catskill Borscht Belt as the *meshuggah*—the wild, irresponsible, disconnected buffoon who oscillates between the frenetic edges of obscenity and tearful sentimentality. The Jewish entertainer became master of a savage dialogue with his audience: "Go ahead, stupids, laugh! Go ahead, laugh! What you can't see is that I'm laughing my head off at *you* and you're paying me for the privilege!" Essentially, to become an entertainer, the Jew had merely to change his role as salesman a little bit. His new commodity was his own stage personality, and the old muttered curses and insults were now made audible and scarcely less direct. The customer remained the same—the great alien Protestant audience, guileless, easily gulled, of thickened wit, but always a potential danger in its resources of sluggish strength. There is inevitably a lubricant of hostility in all humor, I suppose. At least it is very difficult to imagine the sound of laughter without the surprise invitation to ridicule, but Jewish vaudeville humor has been markedly parsimonious in its compensating offerings of love. It has been profligate in assuming gestures of outrageous grotesquerie. It has delighted in playing the fool in order to make its audiences make fools of themselves. But its double-facings of absurd exposure and sly or open insult have rarely been mitigated by a passion to extol what is right, or a compassion to love what is incurably wrong.

The situation has not really changed very much since 1950. With the increasing sophistication of television, with the rebirth of vaudeville in the emergence of the "stand-up comedians" like Mort Sahl, Shelly Berman, or Lenny Bruce, with the massive circulation of quasi-humorous magazines like *Playboy* and *Mad*, the lines of influence have become slightly more complicated without substantially changing. The national advertising agencies and public relations firms have become an integral part of the entertainment industry, accepting without protest the well-worn comic types and situations. One can in America be exhorted to buy a beer, give up smoking, vote for a senator, drive safely, be mildly amused by a television clown, or be shocked by the verbal license of a nightclub comedian without much of an alteration in the accents and nuances of what was once the private property of a Yiddish wedding jester.

It is impossible to explain how this came about—why, that is, Yiddish humor (defensive-aggressive, earthy Yiddish humor) should have proved so successful in Protestant America. Doubtless there are many factors ranging from the economic ownership of the production and distribution of entertainment media to the peculiar need that Jews may have in being patrons of the entertainment arts. Among possible explanations might be suggested the very fact that America *is* a Protestant country. There is, of course, a vigorous theoretical ideal of *protest* running deep in the fabric of American history; and humor, by its very nature, is of the party of the opposition. It is also true that the Yiddish *schlemiel*-figure and the *schnorrer* have their native American counterparts in such eighteenth- and nineteenth-century folk creations as Brother Jonathan and Poor Richard, on the one hand, and the Confidence Man, on the other. Our psychoanalytical friends may also want to note that Yiddish humor, incontrovertibly involved with the physical—with the body and bodily functions—may at one time have provided a minor release of tensions for a society that had been trained either to ignore the body entirely or to improve it by an energetic course in hygiene. (The possible sadomasochistic elements, the latent homosexuality, and the rechanneling of sociological guilt are matters that I gladly leave to those scholars whose needs in these directions are more urgent than my own.)

But more than this, however, I wonder whether the defensive-aggressive dynamism of Jewish humor may not have fulfilled a more subtle function for a population that was historically lacking in the rigid structures of society and that, metaphysically, posited the lonely soul floating in isolation before the stark unregarding eye of God. Jewish humor automatically assumed a society—a human contact point between speaker and listener, between entertainer and spectator. Even an insult is a passable bridge between man and man. It is probably true that the central unit of the Jewish community, the family, has badly crumbled both sociologically and psychologically, but it is invoked nostalgically at the moment of the pratfall, in the riotous hysteria of the boffo punch line. At its best, humor is one of the ways in which human beings can attain a meager sense of their own brotherhood; and, at its best, the ironic insult of Jewish humor includes slightly more of humanity than it rejects.

But even this, I fear, is too optimistic a note to describe the contemporary condition. It certainly seems true that Yiddish humor has become a significant ingredient in American life, a natural resource for thousands who are unaware of the exotic sources of the commodity they so naturally embrace. Its bittersweet sentimentality and its delight in grotesque irony have been able to blend easily with the older tradition of American "frontier humor" (the tall tale, the inverted criticism) as well as with the "outsider's" humor that is found in Irish, Italian, and Negro comic strategies. (Jackie Gleason, Jimmy Durante, and Sammy Davis, Jr., are good examples of the extent to which Yiddish humor has been both an influence and a beneficiary in the creation of American comic types.) But for all the successful Jewish clowns from Mike Sachs to Mike Nichols, there is not one that can stand comparison to the lonely comic genius of a Chaplin. For all the shrewd irreverent commentators on the State of the Nation, the nearest Jewish replica that we can find to place against the giant shape of Mark Twain would be—you should pardon the expression—Harry Golden. And although the last twenty years have witnessed a magnificent florescence of genuinely comic Jewish writers—Bellow, Malamud, Roth, Salinger, Heller, et cetera—none of their books, insofar as they have aimed at satire, has had anything of the social power of Sinclair Lewis's novels. (George F. Babbitt quickly became a universal American type; Moses E. Herzog is inevitably a foreign curiosity.)

Perhaps Jewish humor has succeeded too easily in adapting itself to American life, and in its popular success in the mass media, it may have sacrificed its own fulfillment. Humor, after all, has to be against something—a concrete injustice, a specific affectation or hypocrisy. It is a strategy of intelligence moving into action, either to protect something of its own that it judges to be good, or to attack something that it deems to be bad. I wonder whether Jewish humor may not have allowed itself to accept without struggle the consensus of bourgeois ideals in Protestant America at the expense of its own intelligence. At any rate, merchandising has joined hands again and again with humor to denigrate intelligence and provide shallow, marketable entertainment. Individual Jews have made notable contributions in the causes of unpopular dissent in the twentieth century, but Jewish humor has been suspiciously silent on the major controversial issues that foster the dialectics for defining justice in practice. Jewish humor has lagged behind, waiting until it is fashionable to decry this evil, to expose that injustice.

The old show-business mottoes, "Give them what they want!" and "Leave them laughing!," seem to me to be merely theatrical equivalents of the equally false and hypocritical, "The customer is always right." Such a principle of salesmanship breaks my precious triad, separates intelligence from humor, and shamefully degrades the good. Perhaps the Jew must become more American before he can attain that security of citizenship that will enable him to afford the "insider's" disgust with the collective condition that sometimes results in great humane humor. But perhaps as he becomes more American, he will cease to be Jewish enough to maintain a balance between the gross realities he perceives and the ideals that convict his soul.

TOPICS FOR DISCUSSION AND PAPERS

The suggestions that follow have been kept deliberately plain and simple. They are meant to lead the student back to the text. They are meant to help, not to befuddle or impress. I haven't made any reference to the critical essays that appear in this book, though on certain matters, of course, you may find help in those essays. The main thing is for you to work by yourself, out of your own perceptions and understanding, and with as much honesty and clarity as possible.

1 HOW DO WE KNOW WHAT WE THINK WE KNOW?

Of all the terms used in literary discussion, "tone" is one of the trickiest. In ordinary conversation we can usually tell how someone wants his words to be taken. If I say to a young woman, "You're beautiful," she can usually tell whether I'm hopelessly love-stricken, nastily sarcastic, or objectively appraising (though she ought to be sharp-witted enough not to place too much confidence on her first impression). But if a writer puts the words "You're beautiful" on paper, then we have a problem in judging his intention. (Sometimes the writer may not even be sure himself.) An actor preparing a part faces the same problem: What emphasis, what coloring, what tone of voice shall he impart to a line or a speech?

The problem becomes more acute when the line or speech is spoken by a character in a novel. For then we have to make a judgment as to his attitudes, intentions, and feelings, and as a rule we can do this only if we see the character in the entire context of the book. That is, our understanding of how he speaks a particular line or speech will be conditioned by the sense of him that we have slowly built up in the course of our reading.

In a novel written in the first person singular ("I"), these difficulties are often aggravated, since all that we are given is the outlook and judgments of the speaker. He may be unreliable, he may be biased, he may be trying to twist our arm. But even in a novel like *Herzog*, written in the third person, such troubles prevail. For while Bellow writes about Herzog as "he" or "him," most of what we see in the book is through Herzog's eyes. Rarely, if ever, are we allowed to enter the consciousness of other characters as they make judgments about Herzog.

Precisely these difficulties form the substance of this book. For Bellow wants to show, among other things, the shifting nature of Herzog's feelings, the confusion and uncertainty that always bubble up to the surface of his behavior.

Take the opening sentence: "If I am out of my mind, it's all right with me, thought Moses Herzog." But *is* it? At first we just don't know, since we are only getting into the book. As it goes along, we may well suppose that for a time, as Herzog surrenders himself to self-pity, it really is "all right" with him to suppose he is going mad. But deep down, we soon discover, Herzog is convinced that he is not out of his mind—he is only into a lot of trouble. And furthermore, Herzog is the kind of man who thinks that being "out of my mind" is a kind of moral scandal, an indulgence such as no serious man ought to allow himself.

Finally, Herzog seems to believe that he has an obligation, a duty, to struggle for his sanity. On page 19 he says, "You have to fight for your life. That's the chief condition on which you hold it." In both tone and content, this sentence is very different from the opening one. Yet it's quite plausible that the same man should be saying both of these things at different moments, or even in quick succession.

The narrative method of the book—the fact that almost everything is funneled through Herzog's vision—creates the following problems:

- Herzog, by necessity, becomes an amorphous character, constantly changing and often very slippery. He can't easily be defined or pinned down in a few pat phrases.
- We're never entirely sure when he is speaking out of his

keen intelligence and when he is speaking out of his froth-ing sickness—or, more accurately, what the proportion of the two may be in anything he says at a given moment.

- Nor are we sure as to the amount of trust we can put in his views of the other characters. For remember: Almost all we know or see of Madeleine or Valentine Gersbach we know or see through Herzog's eyes. Bellow deliber-ately avoids entering the minds of these two characters to show us what they think of him. And he is not exactly a neutral or objective observer. Is it possible, then, that they are not quite as malicious or mean-spirited as he some-times makes them out to be?

- Least of all can we be certain about Bellow's own atti-tudes toward the characters and events of the story. How does he want us to respond to Herzog himself? Sometimes Herzog says things that Bellow surely accepts, as for ex-ample the passage that begins on the last line of page 74, "The canned sauerkraut . . ." and goes through the first paragraph on page 75. Here Herzog is saying something that Bellow has already said in print, which means that we're to take it seriously. But what Herzog says on page 188—"To look for fulfillment in another, in interper-sonal relationships, was a feminine game," etc.—may or may not be something that Bellow intends us to take at face value. Isn't it possible that in such a passage Bellow wants us to assume a certain ironic stance?

These are all familiar problems in the reading of fiction; they are exactly the kinds of problems we also encounter in our relation-ships with other people in actual life. But they become especially acute in the reading of *Herzog*. Consider, then, some papers or classroom discussions on the following:

1 Through a close examination of two or three crucial passages in *Herzog*, passages that you choose yourself, try to show at which points you believe Moses Herzog should be taken seriously as being (more or less) in accord with

the voice of the author and at which points he should be regarded as being merely a distraught character from whom the author has established an ironic distance.

2   Concentrate on the scene in which Herzog goes to Chicago and there, unobserved, watches Gersbach bathing Herzog's little girl, Junie. The action of this scene is very complicated and—clearly as the result of the author's intention—it upsets some of the impressions we have accumulated from our reading of the book. We can no longer be as sure as we may have been that Gersbach is quite what Herzog has told us he is. At least as important, Herzog himself must grudgingly admit that he too has to complicate his sense of his former friend: It's no longer quite so easy just to despise Gersbach. Through a close study of the language in this scene, show how Bellow provides correctives to Herzog's biases and brings us to a richer understanding of what is happening.

3   One of the usual ways in which an author keeps his central character from hogging the scene is to provide us with other characters who challenge his view of things, arguing with and contradicting him. At almost no point in the book do any of the other characters accept Herzog's view of himself or his problems, even though they may try to comfort him. Focusing on a few figures—especially, say, Ramona and Herzog's brother Will—show how their presence, their voices and opinions affect our grasp of what is going on.

4   A special aspect of this general problem—*how do we know what we think we know?*—concerns the letters Herzog writes, or imagines himself to be writing, to various famous people, alive and dead. I think it safe to say that, in general, these letters represent Herzog's effort to maintain significant contact with the outside world. They are a sort of lifeline that he is desperately throwing out. In these pained "messages" he argues, criticizes, and approves, as if to show the world that he, Herzog, still exists, still thinks

and responds. But these letters, like all the rest of the novel, are written in a great variety of tones of voice. Some are just intellectual vaudeville, hi-jinks and jokes; others are very serious. See if you can sort out the different kinds of letters and the voices in which they are composed.

5 What would be the story of Herzog if it were told by Madeleine and Valentine Gersbach? Do we know enough from the novel to be able to infer or imagine *their* version of things? It would be amusing, and instructive too, if someone wrote a paper in Madeleine's voice telling her side of the story, how she had to put up with Herzog's constant whining and self-pity, his intellectual vanity and jealousies, and so forth. The author of such a paper would, if shrewd enough, not only give what might be Madeleine's point of view, but would also try to show that Madeleine, finally, is not so different from what Herzog has said she is. Or am I wrong in thinking that?

2 "THE GREATEST SHOW ON EARTH"

Before everything else, Saul Bellow understands that the job of the novelist is to entice and lure us, to make us captive to his imagination. Primarily, the novelist must be a performer, able to create the illusion of a living world, one that "leaps off" the printed page and ignites our imaginations. If he is only a good performer, we don't believe he is finally an important writer. We hope that together with the bravura or virtuosity, there will be reflection, insight, sympathy, understanding, perhaps even wisdom. But in a novel these have to be worked into the grain of the action; they can't just stick out like lumps of unabsorbed thought.

Here are a few of the more brilliant incidents or episodes in *Herzog* that stay in memory. Consider them as examples of Bellow's powers as a literary virtuoso; also consider how they can be taken as miniatures of the book's larger intentions and meanings:

• The visit to Aunt Zelda, starting at the bottom of page 36, and ending at the top of page 42 with Herzog's bitter reflection on women, "*They eat green salad and drink human blood.*"

- Madeleine's announcement that she is leaving Herzog, starting in the middle of page 7 and ending on top of page 11.
- Gersbach giving advice to Herzog, starting at the bottom of page 58 and ending in the middle of page 62.
- Madeleine applying her make-up, getting ready to go to Fordham, and talking about marriage, starting on page 110 and ending about the middle of page 116.
- The flashback in which Herzog recalls his childhood, starting on page 138 and ending at the bottom of page 149.
- Herzog in Chicago, distraught, watching Gersbach bathe little Junie, starting on page 256 and ending in the middle of page 258.
- Herzog's visit to Ramona, starting on page 185 and ending on page 205.

3 A CIRCUS OF CHARACTERS

In most of Bellow's novels, and especially in *Herzog*, the minor characters are likely to be portrayed in extreme terms, what we call caricature—that is, with one or two traits wildly exaggerated. We can hardly suppose that such figures as Simkin, Shapiro, Himmelstein, and Nachman are meant to be rounded, three-dimensional portraits. Even Gersbach, who is a major character in the novel, tends to be a grotesque. Questions therefore arise: Is this the result of some deliberate idea that Bellow has in mind? Does this kind of characterization help or hinder the unfolding of the story? Is it interesting in its own right?

Here are a few possible speculations which you may want to discuss:

- In all novels, minor characters must be drawn quickly, with a few broad strokes. They just can't be given the same amount of attention that the major ones get; otherwise, they might get in the way and spoil the story. Necessarily, this means that authors are always tempted to treat minor characters as caricatures. Still, isn't there more at stake with Bellow?

- Bellow's world is composed of hyperactive figures, people who talk themselves wild, drive themselves crazy, burn themselves out with indulgence and grief. His vision of life in contemporary urban America is one of people crazily obsessed with money, ambition, power, yearnings, what he calls "distractions." It all seems a little like a movie that has been sped up, with people racing around as if they had gone berserk, out of control. Which is to suggest that Bellow knows what he is doing with his minor figures.

- All of them are meant to be seen, or refracted, through the eyes of Herzog. They come out as blurred or overfocused, sweet or sour, hateful or helpful—often enough, all of these together. They should be regarded not so much as people in their own right, but as the skewed *impressions* of what Herzog sees when he looks at or encounters them.

- Have you ever gone to an amusement park, Coney Island, for example, and looked into one of those distorting mirrors that makes your nose seem gargantuan, your chin disappear, your eyes bulge? That's not me, you want to shout, as you look into the mirror—but wait, look again, it *is* you, at least partly; it's a distorted view of you, and thereby it may make certain things about you stand out all the more clearly. In modern fiction, starting especially with the novels of Charles Dickens and Fyodor Dostoevsky, there are certain kinds of characters whom we call doubles, and they stand in the same relation to central characters that the distorting mirror of an amusement park stands toward you. The double is meant to bring out, accentuate, enlarge, and thereby clarify certain aspects of the central figure that otherwise might go insufficiently noticed. The intellectual pretentiousness of the young pedant, Shapiro, is like an intensification of Herzog's own pretentiousness—and thus, through his brief appearance, Shapiro helps to clarify the book. More important, Gersbach can also be seen as a double of Herzog: a freak impostor who mimics Herzog's views, even steals his wife. Does this idea of the double help us understand the ways in which Bellow treats his minor characters, and even some of his major ones?

4 WOMEN, WOMEN, WOMEN

Bellow wrote *Herzog* several years before the rise of the women's liberation movement, and his portraits of women, though extremely vivid, are by no means always flattering. But then, neither are the portraits of women in most of the novels recently written by women themselves, including the women who write under the influence of the liberation movement. (By the way, it seems a reasonable guess that some of the novels recently written by women—in their efforts to combine outcries of complaint with a comic perspective upon that complaint—have been influenced by *Herzog*.)

But what matters to us here is not Bellow's formal opinions about women's liberation, if he has any. What matters is the way he portrays women in his book.

Madeleine is given very rough treatment, though she seems quite capable of taking care of herself. She is beautiful, brilliant, overpowering, unnerving. She has, or has had, Herzog under her thumb. The scene on page 9, where she breaks with him, shows her at her most bitchily effective: "She had never looked more glorious. There was an element of theater in those looks, but much more of passion." Madeleine emerges as a mimic, hungry for the latest fashions in culture, intent upon taking the center of the stage, determined to subjugate whichever man she happens to be with. (Or is this a biased description, drawn mostly from Herzog's conscious or unconscious feelings of male supremacy?)

So the question needs confronting: Is Madeleine merely a well-endowed phony, a pseudointellectual who has mastered all sorts of high-powered maneuvers in order to beat men down? Or is this view of her itself a male counter-strategy devised in order to cope with the threat of her intellectual brilliance?

Take the scene that starts on page 297, where Madeleine makes a grand entrance into the police station in which Herzog and Junie are waiting. Is that an example of her tendency toward self-dramatization, or is she genuinely concerned about the child? For that matter, may it not be a mixture of both: self-dramatization and genuine concern? And may not the truth about her, supposing there is a single truth about her, be somewhere between what Herzog says and what we may suppose her reply to be?

By contrast, Ramona is drawn in a much more affectionate, if somewhat amused, tone. The first description of her, on page 16, is unforgettable: "She entered a room provocatively, swaggering slightly, one hand touching her thigh, as though she carried a knife in her garter belt." But it soon becomes clear that, likable and attractive as she is, Ramona has a head stuffed with preconceived notions: She honestly believes that sex is or can be a cure for just about everything that ails Herzog. Still, she is warm-hearted; she is generous; she is independent, earning her own living; and beneath all that sexual swagger, she is a little desperate too: The years are catching up. She can also talk sense, as when she tells Herzog, on page 157: "Poor Moses, unless you're having a bad time with a woman you can't believe you're being serious." (This seems one instance where we can largely trust a perception about Herzog advanced by another character.)

What are we to conclude, then, from Bellow's treatment of his women characters—bias? attachment? fascination? love-hatred? the usual run of human responses?

5 THE ULTIMATE VISION

Let me propose here a very sharp distinction between a writer's *opinions* and his *vision* (perhaps a little sharper than can be made in actuality). A writer may say that he is a Christian—that is his *opinion*. But what he writes may in fact be very far from anything that can be described as Christian in spirit or outlook. His book may reveal a deep cynicism and hatred of mankind—that would be his *vision*.

The opinions a writer holds are his conscious views or statements. The vision that emerges from his work consists of the complex of values and feelings, attitudes and biases that control the way he organizes his story, treats his characters, sees the world. A writer's opinions will often have rather little to do with what we actually find in his books, but if we can achieve a statement about his vision then we have penetrated deeply into his work. Often enough, the vision of a novel is something that, if made clear, might surprise the author himself, since the very process of writing the novel may have brought that vision into existence.

Shortly after publishing *Herzog*, Bellow said: "I consider *Herzog* a break from victim literature," that is, from the kind of novels that celebrated the helplessness and passivity of victims. Now, the question that needs to be considered is whether this opinion of Bellow squares, or to what extent it squares, with the vision that we actually find in the book.

Here are a few passages where Bellow—or Herzog—makes crucial statements. You will find others, but these should start you going:

- page 19—"You have to fight for your life," etc.
- page 24—"Live or die, but don't poison everything."
- pages 74–75—the letter to Shapiro.

From such passages, and from the thrust of the story as a whole, it ought to be possible to draw certain conclusions as to the underlying vision of the book. Describe it with as much care as you can, and then see how it relates to Bellow's own statements on pages 359–64 about his intentions as a writer.

6 A FEW OTHER MATTERS

A very important fact about Moses Herzog is that he is Jewish. One critic of *Herzog*, Theodore Solotaroff, has written interestingly on this aspect of the book:

Herzog's Jewishness is the one thing about him that goes deeper than his ideas about life. . . . It emerges solidly, naturally, au-

530

thentically, from the family experiences that he remembers so vividly. . . . The Herzogs have standards of "heart," and Moses has been one of those "young Jews [writes Bellow] brought up on moral principles as Victorian ladies were on pianoforte and needle-point." All of which has helped him to know a great deal about life and to understand very little: the narcissism of his ambitiousness and the narcissism of his unworldliness are endlessly in conflict. . . . The novel is a great portrait of the contemporary humanist, Jewish-style, whose relations with the modern world are as increasingly uncertain as Herzog demonstrates them to be.

What do you think about this?

Finally, there is the matter of Bellow's style, in *Herzog* seemingly a hodge-podge of fancy rhetoric, street vulgarisms, echoes of Yiddish, high intellectual talk, and so on. Here I'd suggest that as you discuss this question try not to be too "literary," try not to mimic the way literary critics write, but go at the question in your own way, using your own language, and taking a few examples from the text itself in order to make your points concrete and convincing.

BIBLIOGRAPHY

BOOKS: NOVELS, PLAYS, COLLECTED STORIES

The Adventures of Augie March (novel). New York: Viking, 1953.
Dangling Man (novel). New York: Vanguard, 1944.
Henderson the Rain King (novel). New York: Viking, 1959.
Herzog (novel). New York: Viking, 1964.
The Last Analysis (play). New York: Viking, 1965.
Mosby's Memoirs and Other Stories (collection of six stories). New York: Viking, 1968.
Mr. Sammler's Planet (novel). New York: Viking, 1970.
Seize the Day (novel). New York: Viking, 1956.*
The Victim (novel). New York: Vanguard, 1947.

STORIES, ONE-ACT PLAYS

"Address by Gooley MacDowell to the Hasbeens Club of Chicago," *Hudson Review*, Summer 1951. Reprinted in *Algren's Book of Lonesome Monsters*, Nelson Algren, editor. New York: Geis, 1963. Also in *The Writer's Signature: Idea in Story and Essay*, Elaine Gottlieb Hemley and Jack Matthews, editors. Glenview, Ill.: Scott, Foresman, 1972.
"By the Rock Wall," *Harper's Bazaar*, April 1951.
"Dora," *Harper's Bazaar*, November 1949.
"A Father-to-Be," *The New Yorker*, February 5, 1955.**
"The Gonzaga Manuscripts," *Discovery No. 4*, 1956.** Reprinted in *Prize Stories 1956: The O. Henry Awards*, P. Engle and H. Martin, editors. Garden City: Doubleday, 1956.
"Leaving the Yellow House," *Esquire*, January 1958.**
"Looking for Mr. Green," *Commentary*, March 1951.**
"The Mexican General," *Partisan Review*, May–June 1942. Reprinted in *More Stories in the Modern Manner*, from *Partisan Review*, Philip Rahv and William Phillips, editors. New York, Avon, 1955.

---

* The first edition (out-of-print) included three stories—"A Father-to-Be," "The Gonzaga Manuscripts," "Looking for Mr. Green"—and a one-act play, "The Wrecker." The 1961 Viking Compass paperback edition contains the novel alone.

** Included in the collection *Mosby's Memoirs and Other Stories*.

"Mosby's Memoirs," *The New Yorker*, July 20, 1968.*

"The Old System," *Playboy*, January 1967.*

"Orange Soufflé" (one-act play), *Esquire*, October 1965. Reprinted in *Traverse Plays*, Jim Haynes, editor. London: Penguin, 1966. Staged in 1965 and 1966 (see Chronology). Reprinted in *Best Short Plays of the World Theatre 1968–1973*, Stanley Richards, editor. New York: Crown, 1973.

"Out from Under" (unpublished one-act play). Staged in 1966 (see Chronology).

"Sermon by Doctor Pep," *Partisan Review*, May 1949. Reprinted in *Best American Short Stories, 1950*, Martha Foley, editor. Boston: Houghton Mifflin, 1950. Also in *The New Partisan Reader, 1945–1953*, William Phillips and Philip Rahv, editors. New York: Harcourt, Brace, 1953. Also in *Fiction of the Fifties*, Herbert Gold, editor. Garden City: Doubleday, 1959.

"Trip to Galena," *Partisan Review*, November–December 1950.

"Two Morning Monologues," *Partisan Review*, May–June 1941. Reprinted in *Partisan Reader*, William Phillips and Philip Rahv, editors. New York: Dial, 1946. Also in *The American Disinherited: A Profile in Fiction*, Abe C. Ravitz, editor. Encino, Calif.: Dickenson, 1970.

"A Wen" (one-act play), *Esquire*, January 1965. Reprinted in *Traverse Plays*, Jim Haynes, editor. London: Penguin, no date. Staged in 1965 and 1966 (see Chronology).

"The Wrecker" (one-act play), *New World Writing*, 6, 1954. (Included, as a separate work, in the first edition of *Seize the Day* [New York: Viking, 1956]; in later editions the novel appears alone.)

EARLY VERSIONS, EXCERPTS

These early versions of novels and excerpts from novels were published in magazine form. They underwent many changes.

The Adventures of Augie March (1953):

"From the Life of Augie March," *Partisan Review*, November 1949.

"The Coblins," *Sewanee Review*, Autumn 1951.

"The Einhorns," *Partisan Review*, November–December 1951. Reprinted in *Perspectives USA*, Winter 1953.

"Interval in a Lifeboat," *The New Yorker*, December 27, 1952.

"The Eagle," *Harper's Bazaar*, February 1953.

"Mintouchian," *Hudson Review*, Summer 1953.

---

* Included in the collection *Mosby's Memoirs and Other Stories*.

Dangling Man (1944):

    "Notes of a Dangling Man" (excerpt), *Partisan Review*, September–October 1943. Reprinted in *Best American Short Stories, 1944*, Martha Foley, editor. Boston: Houghton Mifflin, 1944.

Henderson the Rain King (1959):

    "Henderson in Africa," *Botteghe Oscure*, 1958.

    "Henderson the Rain King," *Hudson Review*, Spring 1958.

Herzog (1964):

    "Herzog," *Esquire*, July 1961.

    "Sono and Moso," *Location*, Spring 1963.

    "Letter to Doctor Edvig," *Esquire*, July 1963.

    "Napoleon Street," *Commentary*, July 1964.

    "Herzog Visits Chicago," *The Saturday Evening Post*, August 8, 1964.

The Last Analysis (play) (1965):

    "Scenes from Humanitis—A Farce" (play), *Partisan Review*, Summer 1962.

Mr. Sammler's Planet (1970):

    "Mr. Sammler's Planet" (early version of whole novel), *Atlantic Monthly*, November 1969, December 1969.

Seize the Day (1956):

    "Seize the Day" (early version of whole novel), *Partisan Review*, Summer 1956.

    An unpublished dramatization was read in New York, May 8, 1966, by the HB Playwrights Foundation at the Hagen-Berghoff Studio.

From two novels in progress:

    "Humboldt's Gift," *Playboy*, January 1974.

    "Zetland: By a Character Witness," in *Modern Occasions*, Philip Rahv, editor. Port Washington, N.Y.: Kennikat, 1974.

ESSAYS, REVIEWS, TRANSLATION

"Beatrice Webb's America," *The Nation*, September 7, 1963. (Review of *Beatrice Webb's American Diary* [1898], David A. Shannon, editor.)

"Broadway and the Book Shop," *The National Observer*, October 5, 1964.

"Cloister Culture," in *Page 2*, E. F. Brown, editor. New York: Holt, Rinehart & Winston, 1969.

"A Comment on 'Form and Despair,'" *Location*, Summer 1964.

"Culture Now: Some Animadversions, Some Laughs," *Modern Occasions*, Winter 1971. Reprinted in *Intellectual Digest*, September 1971. Also in *The Norton Reader*, 3rd edition, Arthur M. Eastman, *et al.*, editors. New York: Norton, 1973.

"Deep Readers of the World, Beware!" *The New York Times Book Review*, February 15, 1959. Reprinted in *The Plain Style*, Robert Hogan and Herbert Bogart, editors. New York: Van Nostrand, 1967.

"Distractions of a Fiction Writer," *New World Writing* 12, 1957. Reprinted in *The Living Novel*, Granville Hicks, editor. New York: Macmillan, 1957.

"Dreiser and the Triumph of Art," *Commentary*, May 1951. (Review of F. O. Matthiessen, *Theodore Dreiser*.) Reprinted in *The Stature of Theodore Dreiser: A Critical Survey of the Man and His Work*, Alfred Kazin and Carl Shapiro, editors. Bloomington: Indiana University Press, 1955.

"Facts That Put Fancy to Flight," *The New York Times Book Review*, February 15, 1962.

"Foreword" to Fyodor M. Dostoevsky, *Winter Notes on Summer Impressions*, Richard Lee Renfield, translator. New York: Criterion, 1955; paper, McGraw-Hill, 1965. (See: "The French as Dostoevsky Saw Them.")

"Foreword" to Isaac Rosenfeld, *An Age of Enormity*, Theodore Solotaroff, editor. Cleveland and New York: World, 1962.

"The French as Dostoevsky Saw Them," *The New Republic*, May 23, 1955. Reprinted as "Foreword" to F. M. Dostoevsky, *Winter Notes on Summer Impressions*. (See above.)

"Gide as Autobiographer," *The New Leader*, June 4, 1951. (Review of André Gide, *The Counterfeiters*.)

Great Jewish Short Stories, Saul Bellow, editor. New York: Dell, 1963.

"Hemingway and the Image of Man," *Partisan Review*, May–June 1953. (Review of Philip Young, *Ernest Hemingway*.)

"How I Wrote Augie March's Story," *The New York Times Book Review*, January 31, 1954.

"Illinois Journey," *Holiday*, September 1959.

"Introduction" to *Great Jewish Short Stories*, Saul Bellow, editor. (See above.)

"Isaac Rosenfeld," *Partisan Review*, Fall 1956. (Written on the occasion of the death of this young writer, Bellow's friend.)

"Israel Diary," *Jewish Heritage Quarterly*, Winter 1967–1968. Reprinted from *Newsday*. (Reportage from Israel on the Six-Day War.)

"Italian Fiction: Without Hope," *The New Leader*, December 11, 1950. (Review of *The New Italian Writers: An Anthology from Botteghe Oscure*, Marguerite Caetani, editor.)

"The Jewish Writer and the English Literary Tradition," *Commentary*, October 1949.

"John Berryman," foreword to John Berryman, *Recovery*. New York: Farrar, Straus & Giroux, 1973. Reprinted as "John Berryman, Friend," in *The New York Times Book Review*, March 27, 1973.

"Laughter in the Ghetto," *The Saturday Review of Literature*, May 30, 1953. (Review of Sholem Aleichem, *The Adventures of Mottel the Cantor's Son*.)

"Literary Notes on Khrushchev," *Esquire*, March 1961. Reprinted in *First Person Singular*, Herbert Gold, editor. New York: Dial, 1963. Reprinted in *Esquire*, October 1973 (40th anniversary issue). Also in *The Plain Style*, Robert Hogan and Herbert Bogart, editors. New York: Van Nostrand, 1967.

"Literature," *The Great Ideas Today*, Mortimer Adler and Robert M. Hutchins, editors. Chicago: Encyclopaedia Britannica, 1963.

"Literature in the Age of Technology," lecture presented at the Smithsonian Institution's National Museum of History and Technology, November 14, 1972. Printed in *Frank K. Nelson Doubleday Lecture Series/Technology and the Frontiers of Knowledge*, Introduction, Daniel J. Boorstin. Garden City, N.Y.: Doubleday, 1974.

"Man Underground," *Commentary*, June 1952. (Review of Ralph Ellison, *The Invisible Man*.) Reprinted in *Ralph Ellison: A Collection of Critical Essays*, John Hersey, editor. Englewood Cliffs, N.J.: Prentice-Hall, 1973.

"A Matter of the Soul," *Opera News*, January 11, 1975.

"Movies" (reviews and criticism), *Horizon, A Magazine of the Arts*; "Movies: The Art of Going It Alone" (on the films of Morris Engel and Ruth Orkin), September 1962; "Movies: Buñuel's Unsparing Vision," November 1962; "Movies: The Mass-Produced Insight" (on the state of Hollywood movies), January 1963; "Movies: Adrift on a Sea of Gore" (on *Barabbas*, producer, D. de Laurentiis; director, R. Fleischer; based on P. Lagerkvist's novel, adapted by C. Fry), March 1963.

"My Man Bummidge," *The New York Times*, September 27, 1964, Section Two.

The Noble Savage, periodical. Five issues (1960–1962). Co-editor, with Keith Botsford and Aaron Asher. Contributed some unsigned editorial comments.

"On Jewish Storytelling," *Jewish Heritage Quarterly*, Winter 1964–1965.

"A Personal Record," *The New Republic*, February 22, 1954. (Review of Joyce Cary, *Except the Lord*.)

"Pleasures and Pains of Playgoing," *Partisan Review*, May–June 1954. (Critique of four plays, including T. S. Eliot's *The Confidential Clerk*.)

"Rabbi's Boy in Edinburg," *The Saturday Review of Literature*, March 24, 1956. (Review of David Daiches, *Two Worlds*.)

"Recent American Fiction," Gertrude Clarke Whittal Poetry and Literature Fund Lecture. Washington: Library of Congress, 1963. Reprinted in *Encounter*, November 1963, entitled "Some Notes on Recent American Fiction." (See below.)

"The Riddle of Shakespeare's Sonnets," *The Griffin*, June 1962. (Review of book of same title, containing the sonnets, and essays by R. P. Blackmur, Leslie A. Fiedler, Edward Hubbler, Northrop Frye, and Stephen Spender.)

"The Sealed Treasure," *Times Literary Supplement*, London, July 1, 1960. Reprinted in *The Open Form*, Alfred Kazin, editor. New York: Harcourt, Brace & World, 1965, 2nd edition.

"Skepticism and the Depth of Life," *The Arts and the Public*, James E. Miller and Paul D. Herring, editors. Chicago: University of Chicago Press, 1967.

"Solzhenitsyn's Truth," *The New York Times*, January 15, 1974, p. 36.

"Some Notes on Recent American Fiction," *Encounter*, November 1963. (See: "Recent American Fiction.")

"Some Questions and Answers," *New Review*, London, October 1975; *Ontario Review*, Fall/Winter, 1975–76.

"Spanish Letter," *Partisan Review*, February 1948.

"Starting Out in Chicago," *American Scholar*, December 10, 1974.

"The Swamp of Prosperity," *Commentary*, July 1959. (Review of Philip Roth, *Goodbye, Columbus*.)

"A Talk with the Yellow Kid," *The Reporter*, September 6, 1956. Also in *The Writer's Signature: Idea in Story and Essay*, Elaine Gottlieb

Pierre Dommergues, *Saul Bellow*. Paris: Grasset, 1967.

Robert R. Dutton, *Saul Bellow*. New York: Twayne, 1971.

David D. Galloway, *The Absurd Hero in American Fiction: Updike, Styron, Bellow, Salinger*. Austin: University of Texas Press, 1966, revised edition 1970. Contains an extensive bibliography.

Irving Malin, *Saul Bellow's Fiction*. Carbondale: Southern Illinois University Press, 1969.

Irving Malin, editor, *Saul Bellow and the Critics*. New York: New York University Press, 1967.

Keith, Opdahl, *The Novels of Saul Bellow: An Introduction*. University Park: Pennsylvania State University Press, 1967. Contains an extensive bibliography.

Earl Rovit, *Saul Bellow*. Minneapolis: University of Minnesota Press, 1967.

Brigitte Scheer-Schaetzler, *Saul Bellow*. New York: Ungar, 1972.

B. A. Sokoloff, *Saul Bellow: A Comprehensive Bibliography*. Folcroft, Pennsylvania: Folcroft Library Editions, 1972.

Tony Tanner, *Saul Bellow*. Edinburgh and London: Oliver & Boyd, 1965; New York: Barnes & Noble, 1965.

Hemley and Jack Matthews, editors. Glenview, Ill: Scott, Foresman, 1972.

"The Thinking Man's Wasteland" (excerpt from acceptance speech for the National Book Award for *Herzog*), *The Saturday Review of Literature*, April 3, 1965.

Translation of Isaac Bashevis Singer's "Gimpel the Fool," *Partisan Review*, May–June 1953. Reprinted in *A Treasury of Yiddish Stories*, Irving Howe and Eliezer Greenberg, editors. New York: Viking, 1954. Also in Isaac Bashevis Singer, *Gimpel the Fool and Other Stories*. New York: Noonday, 1957.

"Two Faces of a Hostile World," *The New York Times Book Review*, August 26, 1956. (Review of Jean Dutourd, *5 A.M.*)

"The University as Villain," *The Nation*, November 16, 1957.

"The Uses of Adversity," *The Reporter*, October 1, 1959. (Review of Oscar Lewis, *Five Families*.)

"Where Do We Go from Here: The Future of Fiction," *Michigan Quarterly Review*, Winter 1962. Reprinted in *To the Young Writer*, Hopwood Lectures, 2nd Series, A. L. Bader, editor. Ann Arbor: University of Michigan Press, 1965. Reprinted in Irving Malin, editor, *Saul Bellow and the Critics*. New York: New York University Press, 1967.

"A Word from Writer Directly to Reader," *Fiction of the Fifties*, Herbert Gold, editor. Garden City: Doubleday, 1959.

"A World Too Much with Us," *Critical Inquiry*, September, 1975.

"The Writer and the Audience," *Perspectives USA*, Autumn 1954.

"The Writer as Moralist," *Atlantic Monthly*, March 1963.

SELECTED BOOKS ON SAUL BELLOW'S WORK

A great deal has been written about Bellow's work. Two of the books below contain extensive bibliographies, and one is a comprehensive bibliography, listing reviews and essays on Bellow's writings that have appeared over the years in various periodicals and the press, and/or in book collections.

John J. Clayton, *Saul Bellow: In Defense of Man*. Bloomington: Indiana University Press, 1968.

Robert Detweiler, *Saul Bellow: A Critical Essay*. Grand Rapids, Michigan: Eerdmans, 1967.